STEEL DRAGON 4

STEEL DRAGON 4
STEEL DRAGONS SERIES™ BOOK 4

KEVIN MCLAUGHLIN
MICHAEL ANDERLE

DISRUPTIVE IMAGINATION

Copyright © 2020 LMBPN Publishing
Cover Art by Jake @ J Caleb Design
http://jcalebdesign.com / jcalebdesign@gmail.com
Cover copyright © LMBPN Publishing
A Michael Anderle Production

LMBPN Publishing
PMB 196, 2540 South Maryland Pkwy
Las Vegas, NV 89109

First US Edition, May 2020
eBook ISBN: 978-1-64202-946-8
Print ISBN: 978-1-64202-947-5

THE STEEL DRAGON 4 TEAM

Thanks to the JIT Readers

Dave Hicks
Deb Mader
Diane L. Smith
Dorothy Lloyd
Jackey Hankard-Brodie
James Caplan
Jeff Eaton
Jeff Goode
Kathleen Fettig
Kelly O'Donnell
Kerry Mortimer
Paul Westman
Peter Manis
Veronica Stephan-Miller

If we've missed anyone, please let us know!

Editor
The Skyhunter Editing Team

PART I

CHAPTER ONE

Even though Kristen hadn't visited her parents in a while, it still felt like coming home.

The smell of her mom's lasagna from the front porch and the color of the maple tree in the front yard in early fall brought a wash of nostalgia. Her brother's face smirked at her through the windows, vanished, and reappeared as if to make her think he was a ghost like he had done when they were kids.

"Okay, so remember, let me do the talking. My parents have lived in this house for forty years," Kristen told Stonequest as they approached the front door. "They won't take this easily."

He smiled indulgently at her. "Well, I'll be...I've seen you face multiple dragons, mages armed with machine guns, and even the Dragon Council itself, but I don't think I've ever seen you scared. Are your parents so bad as to frighten the Steel Dragon herself?"

"Just...don't step on my mom's flowers, okay?"

"Noted."

"And wipe that stupid grin off your face."

Stonequest obliged and replaced his smile—that had steadily become goofier and goofier—with the face he used to interrogate hostile witnesses. "Better?" He grunted for effect.

"No! It's better if you merely smile normally—no, not like that! You know what? Do whatever you want with your face as long as you keep your mouth shut."

"Am I allowed to eat, Investigator?" he asked.

"I'll let you know if you earn the privilege," she retorted, not at all amused with him at the moment.

She rang the doorbell twice and opened the door before anyone could answer.

"Hey, Kristen!" Brian said from the living room.

Kristen was surprised to see that he wasn't burrowed into the couch. Instead of a fine dusting of cheese crumbs from a flavored chip product, her brother was coated in sweat. His face was red not from getting himself worked up defeating an opponent online but from doing…squat push-ups?

"Brian…are you all right?" she asked, beyond confused. Her brother normally complained about putting away the groceries but was now working out in the living room?

"I'm fine," he replied breathlessly.

"Good form, kid," Stonequest said and Brian beamed.

"I'll go hit the showers," he said a little too nonchalantly.

"Sounds good, Brian," their mom said and, unable to help herself, she added, "Seeing as how we have so many in our locker room, I hope you're able to find a stall."

"Ah, a pleasure to see you again Mrs. Hall," Stonequest said and bowed cordially before the woman like she was a member of the Dragon Council. "It is always a pleasure to be reminded where Kristen gets all her snark."

Marty smiled and extended her hand for him to take it and kiss it as he'd done before, but when he took it, she pinched his fingers and rapped his knuckles with her other hand. "I've told you before to call me Marty. Mrs. Hall was my mother-in-law."

"Yes, ma'am—I mean, yes, Marty," he said and looked embarrassed for either being admonished or for a woman at the high end of middle age being able to move quickly enough to slap his hand.

Before Kristen could think of something snarky to say to him that

4

wouldn't earn a tongue lashing for implying her mom was slow, Frank Hall appeared.

"Krissy, sweetie!" he exclaimed, a big grin on his round, red face.

"Dad!" She went to hug him, but he put his hands on her shoulders instead and studied her intently.

"Where is it?" he demanded.

"Where's what?"

"Oh, come on, Krissy! I've heard the rumors but I have to know if it's true. You know I've only ever seen one three times? Thirty years in the force and I barely ever meet a dragon. Now, my daughter is one of their highest-ranking officers."

"Right, sorry." She pulled her jacket back to show him her badge.

His eyes brimmed with tears when he saw the seven-pointed star with the stylized, slitted eye of a dragon in the middle. "Oh, Kristen," Frank said, choked up. "I…it's beautiful… It's truly beautiful. I know you don't need to hear it from the old man who changed your diapers and learned how to take care of your curly red hair but I'm so proud of you, sweetie."

He wrapped her in a hug and she let the world fall away so she could be held by her daddy. That he was her adopted dad and had taken the place of the dragon who had sired her meant the world to her. Frank Hall was her father. He was the reason she had become a police officer and the reason she thought one girl with curly red hair could make the world a better place. It felt better to be hugged by him and told he was proud of her than it had felt when Windlock had given her the badge.

Windlock.

Kristen still didn't know how to think about the old investigator without being overcome with emotion. He was dead and she couldn't help but think that if she'd only been a little quicker, a little more clever, or slightly more persuasive with Constance, he'd still be there.

"Kristen," Stonequest said simply when she pulled away from her dad. She nodded. It had only been a week since Windlock had died, but that was still more than enough time for Stonequest to be able to tell when her aura was focused on him. At first, it had been annoying but right now, she appreciated the reminder to not let herself sink into despair at the loss of a friend and mentor.

"You should be crying!" Marty snapped and ripped Kristen's thoughts away from two men she'd worked so hard to make proud.

"Mom?"

"Do you have any idea how much stress you've put us through? We follow the news, you know. We heard about your fight in Canada and some mess on a farm near here and now, the tabloids say you prevented a war from happening. Tell me they made that one up, young lady."

"No, ma'am," her companion said. "Your daughter is a hero."

"And I suppose you think that's a good thing?" The woman jabbed him in the chest with such force he looked as he'd been struck by a dragon bullet.

"Ma'am?"

"I spent my whole life worrying about Frank and she became a cop, but at least she had steel skin. Then, you dragons come along and whisk her off to the only job that could endanger her."

Stonequest was stunned into silence, but Kristen had far more experience with her mom.

"That's not the case anymore, mom," she said.

"Oh, here we go," Marty countered with a snort.

"Can we at least sit and eat before we get into all this?" Brian said. "Working out makes me even hungrier than videogames used to."

"I think that's a great plan, son. Marty?" Frank took his wife's arm, planted a massive wet kiss on her cheek, and escorted her into the kitchen.

Dinner was pleasant enough for about ten minutes. The lasagna was great, the garlic bread almost offensively garlicky—exactly as Kristen liked it—and the salad delicious.

Her parents carried the conversation as they ate, during which her dad asked her about work and her mom told them about her garden rather than asking more about her daughter's dangerous adventures. Brian made a few wisecracks, exactly like he always did, but there was something about him that was...different.

He was more quiet than usual and didn't snipe at her, which made her want to check his pulse and make sure he hadn't been replaced by a robot.

Stranger still, when he reached for seconds, it was only for more salad.

"So..." Frank said, having had his fill of updates. "What's next for the Steel Dragon?"

"Actually, that's why I'm here," Kristen said, straightened, and looked at each of her family members in turn. "We stopped the tech-nomages from starting a war, but that doesn't mean our fight is over."

"Well, uh-duh," Brian rolled his eyes. "You only took out *one cell.*"

"Exactly." She nodded despite the snark before she stared at her brother more closely. "How did you know that?"

"It's kind of obvious, right?" He shrugged. "They're terrorists and rely on small, dispersed, disconnected cells so they can appear to be a larger force than they really are. It doesn't make sense that she'd try to take on the whole world of dragons with only eight mages. I could do that kind of shit in World of Warcraft, but this isn't a videogame."

"That's...surprisingly perceptive of you," Stonequest said. "Although I have never heard of this Warcraft World. Is it on this continent?"

Brian laughed and seemed almost giddy under the dragon's praise. No one else shared his humor.

Kristen's father looked grim but resigned like a cop ordered to go into a hostile situation. Her mom looked downright ornery.

"What do you mean the fight's not over?" Marty asked after an awkward moment of silence. "How many times do you have to save the world?"

"As many times as it takes, Mom," she said and immediately wished she hadn't said a damn thing.

"Kristen has been tasked with a mission directly from the Full Dragon Council. It's an honor," Stonequest said before he added in a slightly more dour tone, "and a duty."

"What does that mean, Krissy?" Frank asked. "Will you be out of town for a while?"

"Yeah…but that's not quite why I'm here. We're building a fighting force to target the cells in their lairs, eliminate them, destroy the dragon bullets, and free my captive biological siblings."

"Your siblings?" Marty looked aghast.

"That's where they've obtained the materials for dragon bullets? They've taken dragon prisoners?" Brian nodded as if he had put the pieces together.

"Very perceptive," Stonequest all but purred again.

Kristen wanted to agree but was again confused with her brother's level of knowledge. They hadn't been able to keep it a secret that the lethal dragon bullets were made of dragon pieces. By this point, too many remnants had been found, primarily in the battlefield where she had engaged the mages in Canada and saved Amy, but the media had promoted the story that the mages had taken these bullets from the dragons they killed. For Brian to see through that was unexpected. But it was something to ask about later, not right now. Their lives were too important.

"These are lethal enemies. We're not talking robbers or crooks or whatever else, we're talking people who will not hesitate to use my family against me."

"They wouldn't be the first," Brian said and anger crept into his voice.

"I know, and I'm sorry. Both for the home invaders and for…for when you were abducted, Brian."

"It's fine," he said, his voice almost a shout. "I had to grow up sometime."

In any other context, she might have been proud of her brother, but the venom with which he said it made her fear she'd lost the care-free brother she'd fought so hard to protect.

"I can't let that happen again and if you stay here, it will happen," she finished.

"We don't think it's a question of *if* but of *when*," Stonequest added somberly.

Her parents shared a look.

"We're not leaving," Marty said. "Not after everything we've done to this house. This is our home, and I won't give my garden up for a group of terrorists."

"Dad, please, listen to reason," Kristen begged.

"Your mother's right, Krissy. This is our home and we've made a life here. We even have decent neighbors. We won't run away—not now and not ever."

"Dad, it's not safe."

"Kristen, I had a job that was not safe for thirty years. Do you think I forgot how to handle a gun when I retired?"

"Dad, these are *mages!*"

"Do you think I give a shit who these fuckers are?" Her dad's voice rose and his face reddened alarmingly. "I've lived in this house for forty-one years. *Forty. One. Years!* Do you think I'll let a robe-wearing terrorist come in here and take me quietly?" Frank thumped his fist on the table and all the dishes clinked. Still, he didn't stop. "They're only people, Krissy. They invade *my property* in *America?* I'll show them my favorite amendment."

"Frank! Frank, calm down."

"Damn it, Marty, I will not calm down," he said and stood abruptly. "These terrorist mage fuckers think they can remake the whole goddamn world and I won't have any part of it."

"Dad! Have some water," Brian said. He'd stood as well and now put a glass of water in front of his father, his expression imploring.

Frank looked at the water, seemed to notice how heavily he was breathing, and sat slowly.

"The water, Frank." Marty raised her eyebrows to emphasize her point.

"Right, sorry. Water." He reached for the cup but stopped to take a little vial out of his shirt pocket. "Brian, tell Kristen about your new workout regimen," he said as if that would distract her from what she'd seen.

"Dad, what are those?"

"What, these? These are nothing. Only a little nitroglycerin—good for the heart and all that. Didn't I tell you? It's not a big deal, honestly. A precaution like a vitamin."

"Dad, your water," Brian said.

Frank nodded and popped a pill under his tongue before he took a sip of water.

"How long has this been going on?" Kristen asked and tried not to make it sound like a demand.

Her father shrugged but Brian answered. "He's been on those since we were held at gunpoint in the house."

"Not right after."

"Frank, the doctor told you not to argue," Marty said and he nodded, took deep breaths, and let the red leech from his face.

"He began to have chest pain soon after, went to the doctor, and now, he's on a collection of pills," her brother said and looked at Kristen like it was her fault. Oddly, he also looked guilty for looking at her that way.

"Is this true?" she asked her parents.

Their silence told her everything she needed to know.

"This only proves my point even more. I want you guys safe, not having health issues from the stress because of me."

The idea of the stress of being her family making her dad physically ill struck her like a baseball to the chest. She felt guilt, terror, resentment, and rage all at once in a massive tangled knot in her gut. "I want you guys safe. Living in fear is not safe."

"And you think staying in a hotel and moving every few weeks is safe?" Marty demanded. She sounded much like Kristen when she demanded things, thus proving that many traits were taught, not inherited. "We tried that, Kristen. It was hell."

"It sounds like hell," Stonequest interjected.

All four pairs of Hall eyes settled on the dragon and he withered as if he were surrounded by a team of dragons and mages rather than humans and his dragon partner.

"I'm only saying I don't know why you would do that again." He raised his hands in surrender.

"Because your boss is demanding it of us!" Marty yelled.

"Mom, calm down. If you have to start taking pills too, I'll lose it," Brian said.

"Oh please, if your father had eaten half the salads I've put on this table for all these years, he wouldn't have any of these problems."

"Damn it, Marty, we are not going to talk about the food right now. You bake a good chicken and fry a good pork chop. How is it my fault I like your cooking?" Frank shouted and grew as red as a beet again. This time, he caught himself, though, sat again, and breathed deeply.

"I'm only saying it would make more sense for you all to leave the country. A hotel in Detroit is hardly a great way to keep you safe," Stonequest said placatingly.

"And where would we go?" Marty demanded, her words like knives.

"Well, why not go to Kristen's villa in the South of France?"

Again, all four Halls turned to him with some form of confusion in their expressions.

"Her villa? It's rather nice—at least it was the last time I visited." He shrugged.

"Stonequest…I don't have a villa. I've never even been to France," Kristen said.

"Oh? Pardon me, I assumed Windlock had taken you there. It's quite lovely."

"Kristen," Marty all but purred. "However did you fail to mention that you own a villa in the south of France? You know your father and I honeymooned in Europe. We never made it back."

"Well, why not go now?" Stonequest asked and beamed. Kristen could feel his aura working too but she didn't fault him for it. "It might make a wonderful place to 'vacation' for a while…only until all this is cleared up, anyway."

Her parents shared another look, their faces thoughtful rather than angry and obstinate.

"What do you say, Marty?"

"I've always wanted to visit the southern coast of France," she replied and batted her lashes. "Why didn't you tell us you had a house there, Krissy?"

"I didn't know." She smiled weakly. The depth and scope of the

11

wealth she'd inherited from Windlock was staggering to her. She had seen an estate outside Detroit and a vast trove of old treasures and assumed—like any sane human being—that had been the extent of his wealth.

"Oh, it's quite lovely," Stonequest said again. "And I know a few dragons in the area as well. I can arrange a security detail that won't even look out of place. What does everyone say?"

Marty and Frank beamed and relief washed over her.

At least until Brian stood and thumped his dishes into the sink. "I'm not running away." He looked as angry as Kristen had ever seen him and almost like he was ready to take a dragon on with his bare hands.

She wondered what he had in mind.

CHAPTER TWO

The rest of dinner passed amicably enough, if only because Stonequest continued to divulge more details of Windlock's—now Kristen's—villa in France. Marty seemed happy enough about it, although when she glanced at her, she could still see bitterness in her mother's eyes. She felt bad about making them go but at least they'd agreed to it.

That left her wondering what exactly Brian was thinking. He'd declined dessert, which made her think he must have cancer or was a robot or something, but her parents didn't react negatively. Frank even congratulated the boy on staying strong while he served himself a second portion of chocolate and peanut butter brownies with ice cream.

Kristen took her bowl and gestured for Brian to follow her into the back yard while Stonequest continued to woo her parents.

"Are you excited for France, Brian?" she asked and tried to sound as friendly as she could despite his earlier outburst. "You've lost weight. Keep it up and I'm sure some French girls will be quite interested."

"I've lost, like, twelve pounds. Nothing to be proud of...not yet." He paused, then looked her in the eye and squared his jaw. "I don't want to go to France with Mom and Dad."

Kristen nodded. He'd made that much clear. "Why not? I know I haven't been to this villa but Stonequest makes it sound great. Plus, if you stay here..." She swallowed and cleared her throat. "I can't let anything happen to you again. Can you please go so I'll know you're safe?"

Brian responded with a question of his own. "Will you be safe if I leave?"

She didn't mean to but she recoiled reflexively at the absurdity of the question. "Of course I won't be safe, Brian. No one will be safe until we root out all these technomage cells and make sure none of them do something that finally pisses the dragons off enough to start burning cities."

"So, you're saying I should simply sit on the sidelines, waiting for the world to burn, while my little sister does all the hard work and takes all the risks? What if the dragons decide to burn Detroit?"

"That's why I don't want you to stay here." Her frustration mounted but she tried to keep her tone level.

"So I should leave, while all our neighbors stay behind and risk being incinerated if all this blows up?"

"I know you're not asking me to send the neighborhood to France," Kristen replied and took a deep breath to help her stay calm, something she knew annoyed her brother. "But what are you proposing?"

"I want to help you. Not only you, but your army, or force, or whatever your guys are."

"Brian—I don't think that's a good idea."

"Please, hear me out," he replied and sounded eager for the first time since they'd come outside. "After what happened with Obscura—"

"I am still so sorry about that," she interjected.

"Would you please shut up and cool it with your aura for five minutes?" Brian snapped in response.

"Sure, right."

"Being abducted and almost killed by a dragon in a fucking LARP version of Pac-Man kind of put things in perspective for me," Brian said. "I used to think all this"—he gestured to the backyard, the trees, and the neighbor's boat—"didn't matter. I thought life was only about experiencing things, and I could experience almost anything in a videogame. Hell, I thought I could experience things *better* than real life in a videogame. I used to want to be a master of the digital world. That's where the most competitive people are these days, or at least that's what I thought until Obscura showed up."

Kristen tried to smile but she couldn't stop the tears from flowing down her cheeks. It was like watching her brother age ten years in a single conversation.

"None of it feels real anymore, I guess because none of it is," he continued. "I want more than I used to. I want to be a part of something that matters, and I can't think of anything more important than helping my sister stop a war and maybe end human and dragon segregation. I know I'm only a regular human but you have other regular humans on your new team too, right?"

"Yeah." She sniffed. "But they're cops. They've all trained for years. You've never even been to the shooting range with Dad. I hate to say it, but you'd be a liability. If you were killed, I'd never forgive myself. I can't let you throw your life away for nothing, and if you got in a firefight with these mages…that's all you'd be doing." She tried to wipe her eyes.

"Damn it, Kristen, why are you crying?"

"I'm sorry." She swiped furiously at her cheeks and grimaced. "I had really grown to appreciate you being a gamer."

"What? Why?"

"Because I knew you'd be safe as long as you had a high-speed connection. I thought Mom and Dad would fight me on getting them to leave but that you'd go for it as long as I could get you somewhere with an ethernet jack."

Brian laughed grimly at that as his eyes welled with tears. "You can't protect me forever, you know. Plus, I'm your older brother. I'm supposed to protect you."

"I'm a *dragon*, Brian!"

"It doesn't matter," he replied. "I bet the Internet in the south of France sucks."

"It might be good," she said, simply for the sake of arguing with her brother.

"It doesn't matter, Kristen. I don't care about that anymore. I want to help. And you're right, by the way. I'm not ready for fieldwork. Shit, compared to the rest of you guys, I don't know if I'll *ever* be ready for fieldwork." He laughed as he grasped his big round belly and jiggled it.

Kristen eyed it surreptitiously. He *had* lost weight and given the fact that she'd seen him both working out and eating healthier, it seemed like he'd lose much more. But he was right. He was in no shape for fieldwork. "What exactly were you thinking if it wasn't being shot at by a group of mages?"

Brian chuckled. "Something more on the intel side. I could help gather some of the information you'll need if you plan to strike the Texas cell first, although I'm sure you've considered the one in South America too."

She nodded. "We'll raid Texas first, I think, then Colombia because we think that might be the only cell in South America..." The words trailed off and she looked at him. She was so used to talking about operations with her people that she didn't notice that he had casually dropped a fair amount of confidential intelligence into the conversation. "Brian, how the fuck did you know about the mage cells in Texas and Colombia?"

"Internet," he retorted smartly with a dorky smile.

"That doesn't even begin to explain it," Kristen replied, concerned that her intelligence might be compromised. Had Brian found a back door into their computers or something? If he had, maybe others had. "Did you...did you hack us?"

He smiled. "Yeah, I'm sure hacking someone's new boss is a great way to get a job."

While she liked that he called her a boss and not his sister, she frowned at him saying he'd hacked her.

"No! I didn't hack you guys. I tried, though, and I probably could have but their whole server's not even connected to the Internet at large."

"That explains why the Wi-Fi at work sucks," Kristen mumbled quietly before she snapped her attention to her brother. "Seriously. How did you do it? If you want to work for me, I need to know your methods."

"Well, you've never really been that discreet. I read about what happened at Fort Drum—granted, it was in some of the darker corners of the Internet—and that farm with the super-obvious name? Deephealth Ranch was all over the news when they began to excavate to dig a dragon out, of all things. With those two as data points, I started looking for correlations.

"It seemed like checking industrial farms with a strong focus on meat was a good place to start. I ran searches on the shipping records of dozens of farms—like, seriously, *a ton.* I especially looked for shipments that went to military bases. There's a ranch in Texas, you see, that's sent shipments to Fort Hood. That by itself isn't crazy weird—soldiers gotta eat, and soldiers like bacon—but the ranch never sent anything until a couple of weeks ago and now, they're sending regular shipments—"

Kristen laughed. "Wow, Brian, I gotta say, I'm impressed. How did you know about Colombia?"

Brian's smile broadened. "I didn't. You told me."

"But you mentioned the South American base."

"I assumed they'd have cells on most continents and that South America would be the easiest for them to supply and for you to strike. I had thought Brazil, though."

Another laugh bubbled. It was a good thing he wanted to work for her and not a newspaper. "I'm impressed you found all that on the Internet."

"I've become good at ferreting out leads like that. It turns out being a gamer wasn't a total waste of time. Many of us found out how to find hidden content or download weird links from odd corners of the Internet. I agree with you that I'm not a good candidate for field ops, but do you have someone to manage the back end of things? I kind of envisioned myself being someone like 'Overwatch' from that show Arrow. I can help you find targets and during actual operations, I can provide up-to-the-minute intel. Also, I can help you with GPS tracking, cameras, and maybe hack a cellphone here and there or a CCTV system."

"You mean you want to be like Felicity?" Kristen grinned. The amount of time he had talked shit about that show must have numbered in the hundreds. Certainly, more times than there were episodes.

"Okay, I used her codename because I thought it was cooler, plus Overwatch is a videogame I totally kick ass at so..." He shrugged.

"Yeah. We won't call you Overwatch, that's for sure. But...well, I'm impressed. I think this could work. You could be like our Alexa or Siri."

"No, that is not what I had in mind." He held his hands up, but she could already see it had gotten under his skin.

"Yeah, we could use you. How about Jarvis?"

"No way!"

"Cortana?"

"That reference is, like, twenty years old."

"Zed?"

"You mean from Power Rangers? Isn't he bad?" Brian asked although he didn't sound like he hated it.

"Yeah...but didn't he stay out of the battles and send monsters in to fight? That's what you'll do."

"Zed...yeah, Agent Zed. It sounds good."

"It damn well better, Zed," Kristen snapped in her bossiest voice. "You work for me now."

He smiled at the harsh tone. "That's more like it."

"So...what do Mom and Dad think?" Kristen asked.

"Dad said, and I quote, 'about time,' and Mom..."

"Let me guess, she hates it?"

"Prize for the dragon," Brian agreed. "But she's been okay with it since I've been eating better and working out, plus...she never thought you'd agree."

"You mean she still thinks you'll go to France with them? Even after you yelled at the table?"

"Yes, boss, she does, and I'd appreciate it if you could do something about that for me."

She rolled her eyes but she agreed. It was like Stonequest had said. She'd faced dragons so she could face her mom.

The reminder didn't make her any less nervous, though.

CHAPTER THREE

Neal Havington had taken every precaution. Even though the exact details of what had happened to the mage cell in Detroit were unknown, their organization understood the general import of what had transpired.

Constance had been poised to destroy not only the North American Dragon Council but the Dragon Councils of the entire world.

She'd failed.

He knew this because the insufferable Shimmerclaw of the European Council had returned to the continent and not called for anything but forgiveness.

At least, that's what she said.

Havington wasn't naïve enough to think that just because a dragon said something, they meant it. He and his mages had spent the last week moving their entire base of operations. Constance wasn't supposed to know anything more about them than that they had been based in Pisa, Italy, but that didn't mean she hadn't. She was smart—is smart, he told himself because until he saw her body, he had to tell himself she was alive—but she was also wily. Her intention had been to lead the entire organization—scattered as they were—which meant she might have known exactly where his team had been.

Now that they had moved into a more secure location, he wanted to honor Constance's work by killing some goddamn dragons.

It was possible she had killed a few. Shimmerclaw hadn't made a statement about casualties. But it hadn't been enough to put a spark to the powder keg of human and dragon relations.

The cell leader couldn't wait for the dragons to decide to take action. He needed to light another spark. His plan was to inspire the European Council with a couple of surprises of his own.

His expression set and determined, Havington connected to the headset of the first mage.

The opera was perfect, absolutely perfect. There was no better way to celebrate than with street food.

Some dragons balked at Dentedoro's taste in food, but he found dragons to be fairly pretentious, by and large. To him, nothing was better than *arancini* with a little espresso to follow an opera.

He left the theater with the other attendees, regular people dressed in tuxedos and elegant ballgowns. They wore gold Rolexes like he did, had handmade shoes like his, and a chauffeur drove their mint-condition Lamborghini Miura exactly like his did. Well...maybe not that last one, the dragon mused. Even if one's human acquaintances were the Italian nobility, it still served him well to set himself apart. Thus, the sports car and the street food.

While most of the concert-goers made their way to fulfill their reservations or returned to their mansions to have their chefs prepare food for them, Dentedoro moved toward a string of booths above an entrance to the train station. He had his eye on the third cart from the left and the pyramid of *arancini* stacked inside the man's humble establishment.

Each ball of rice was filled with cheese, rolled in breadcrumbs, and baked...fried? He didn't know the first thing about food prep but he did know this man made the most delicious *arancini* in all of Italy.

"They're good, huh?" a man said to him in Italian from under a hood. He had a rice ball in one hand and his other hand in his pocket.

"The very best," Dentedoro replied. "I come here after every opera. This man is worth far more than he makes here. I have known kings with less skilled chefs."

"Why don't you hire him, then?" the man asked. There was something odd about him, something he seemed to sense was wrong, but he couldn't quite say what.

"Humans do their best work when under a little stress," he said with a shrug and a flash of his golden teeth. He'd had a mage gild his human teeth decades before. His dragon form always had them, but he had wanted the same effect when in this weaker body. "If I hired this man, he would become fat and lazy like a pig—good for nothing but slaughter."

The man nodded and adjusted his robe.

That was it! Dentedoro smiled at the realization. The man was dressed in a robe as if they were living centuries in the past. He hadn't noticed because he'd seen so many fashions come and go, but the robe had never really been a fashion. To see a man wearing it now could only mean—

"You're a mage."

"And you're a pig—good for nothing but slaughter," the stranger replied. He yanked his hand from his pocket, fired three shots from a gun into the dragon's chest, and spat on him when he crumpled to the paving.

The last thing Dentedoro saw before he died was the man remove his robe, throw it in a trash can, and give the man who made Italy's best *arancini* a fat stack of Euros.

Aya didn't love her job but she needed it. Her master wasn't cruel but she also wasn't patient. Frauenfeuer expected her to clean the entire castle while she slept, and if she so much as dropped a dish or knocked a broom over and woke the dragon, she would dock her pay by half. She had threatened to do far worse to her if she woke her more than once. As a result, she had learned to be very careful when she worked.

If she didn't make any mistakes, the money was good. When she messed up, at least she still had a job. Anything was better than the years she'd spent running from her home in war-torn Libya. Still, it was hard to feed her children when a simple mistake could cost her so much.

So when a man came and offered to pay her what she made in six months if she would merely leave a back door open to the Fraunfeuer's home, Aya hadn't asked many questions and said yes. After all, she'd never even seen two thousand Euros. This man had offered to give her half before she even did anything for him.

She was scrubbing the dishes when he came in through the backdoor. If she hadn't been expecting him, she might not have even noticed, but as things turned out, she did. She trailed him up the stairs and caught up to him before he entered the dragon's room.

"You will not do anything to make her angry?" she asked in her best English. Despite being in Germany, this man had always spoken to her in English and she was happy to have spent so much time watching TV and picking up the limited English she knew.

"She won't be angry at you ever again," the man said and stepped into the room.

When he drew a gun, Aya gasped and woke the dragon sleeping in her human body. That had been one of the only questions the man had asked Aya before he paid her—how the dragon slept.

"Aya, you little, Libyan whore!" Fraunfeuer shouted at her before the stranger shot her in the chest.

"Be sure to lock up here when you leave," he said and gave her another two thousand Euros—much more than he'd originally said —and left.

Although she knew she should take the money for her children, she let it fall and fled the castle.

It didn't matter that she left it behind though. As soon as she left, running as fast as she could to the bus stop, the man who'd paid her shot her in the back.

"You should have locked the door like I said."

Sir Silverscales hated the French but he loved France and Paris especially. He found it quite annoying that the humans had named it the city of lights even though they filled all their cursed cities with lights, but there was something *je ne sais quoi* about Paris. Something enchanting.

Despite the need to return to his estate in Wales, Sir Silverscales decided to make another loop around the city of lights, if only to tell Lady Coalclaw about how it had changed.

Perhaps he might have lived if he had flown directly across the channel to Wales.

As it was, as soon as he banked, he was shot in the heart by a high-powered rifle.

He plummeted to the city below, dead before he splashed into the River Seine.

"And you're sure Lady Coalclaw wants all this?" Dervin asked. He didn't know her personally, of course. Few did and besides, he was merely a sound guy from one of the more modern pubs in town. What would he have to do with a dragon who'd lived there for centuries?

"I assure you, she will not complain," the woman who paid the bills said.

He nodded and returned to work. While he didn't understand why anyone would want to have a concert on the hills when they had a mansion with a ballroom that was built for perfect acoustics, who was he to say anything?

When he finished, he showed the woman how to work the sound-board and turn the generator on for the speakers before he left.

Not long after, he reached the edge of the estate and stood on a high hill so he could see the gorgeous mansion in the center of it all when the woman played some kind of a test sound.

To Dervin, it sounded horrible—like trumpet mixed with the scream of a fish eagle, but Lady Coalclaw seemed to like it as she came out of her mansion all smiles and warmth.

That was when the woman who'd paid him shot her in the face.

For obvious reasons, he didn't stick around to see if she was okay. He wasn't a medic but he knew most people needed a head to live, so he wasn't particularly optimistic about her prognosis. More than a little panicked, he floored the gas pedal of his old truck in haste, which caused it to backfire.

The noise was louder than the literal gunshot to his terrified mind. He willed the truck to go faster, to get back to a town or a petrol station—*anything*—but he wasn't fast enough.

The woman caught up to him like some kind of pagan goddess carried by the winds themselves.

"You're a mage, you is," Dervin accused her before she shot him in his face, exactly like she had Lady Coalclaw.

Vertaile didn't need his band but they did make it more fun.

His voice was perfect, even when it wasn't. When he hit a wrong note, he simply flexed his dragon aura and made the crowd think he'd meant to. He wasn't French. While he was older than Napoleon and didn't consider himself French, he liked the French style. It was stripped down, elegant, and perfect in its simplicity.

His band emulated this.

He sang, a man named Dominic played a snare drum, a kick bass, and a high hat, and a woman named Adrienne played the bass. He didn't need the humans to draw the crowds he did but he liked the moody ambiance they provided. Plus, they were both great in bed, especially for humans.

Though Vert didn't need Dominic or Adrienne, he enjoyed it when the three of them made music together. It was heady, romantic stuff, not at all like the garbage the American dragons constantly pumped out. He was adored all over Europe and also here in Florence, Italy—a city never known for its music. Well, not for hundreds of years, anyway. Wherever he went, he always drew a large crowd.

They were into their third song and the audience had finally fallen into the melodic grooves Dominic and Adrienne so excelled at when it happened.

Gunshots rang out, exactly like in America.

Vert flung himself down with a burst of dragon speed, but it wasn't fast enough. His shoulder burned with pain unlike anything he'd ever experienced before.

He looked at his band members, who had both been shot—Adrienne in her beautiful breasts and Dominic in his face below his pierced eyebrow that Vert had tried to talk him out of. The man was dead already, but she still moved.

The dragon crawled to her, his shoulder burning with pain. He tried to stem the blood but there was nothing he could do. Her body was slick with blood and her last breaths came in ragged gasps. She even coughed flecks of blood in his face.

"Save yourself, my love." She wheezed and fell back, her eyes open but hollow and motionless.

The crowd screamed and he wanted to join them in their grief but he couldn't. He'd paid attention to the news and knew from the searing pain in his shoulder and the way his wound wasn't healing that he'd been shot by a dragon bullet. He also knew it had not hit him by accident.

He'd made sure there was a back exit from the venue before they'd begun, and he crawled there now, using every ounce of speed he still had available to him despite the pain that seemed to be growing worse.

Finally, he escaped into the night and vanished into the streets of

Florence before the gunman could catch him. It was the longest and most painful night Vert had ever lived.

———

Havington had poured himself a glass of red wine in anticipation of their victory. He'd told his last mage to wait for the third song to execute the green dragon singer, but he'd missed.

"Sorry, sir. I can't find him, sir," the mage said into his earpiece. He could have followed the target across the stage but had been given express orders not to. That kind of behavior might make people remember the assassin. It was better to run from violence, not toward it.

Obediently, the man had gone out onto the street and found that Vertaile had vanished.

"What should I do?" he asked, desperation in his voice.

"Make a few rounds to be sure you haven't been tailed, then come back to base."

He agreed and sounded relieved.

Although he'd failed, he'd still injured his target. With luck, he'd wounded him in an organ and given him a long painful death rather than a quick one. Either way, five dragons attacked in one night was good enough for Havington.

Let Shimmerclaw call for forgiveness and peace now, he thought as he sipped his wine. It tasted like victory.

CHAPTER FOUR

Stonequest and Kristen flew to her new base with Brian riding on her back and cheering like a little kid every time she so much as took a turn.

"That's it, huh? The Steel Trap?" he shouted.

"We don't have a name yet," she responded patiently.

"We do now," Stonequest replied, banked sharply, and began a spiraled descent to land outside the old industrial complex.

She had been shocked to inherit Windlock's vast fortune, but that didn't mean she wouldn't spend it. As convenient as the dragon's old office in the Detroit SWAT building was—although it was a tiny, cramped space overflowing with paperwork and wasn't nice at all— she needed something more. Detroit's Dragon SWAT team had a job to do, namely keeping the peace between dragons and preventing them from causing damage to humans or at least holding them accountable when they did. Her mission was different than that and she didn't want to be held back or slowed down by a bureaucracy that was already well-established, so she'd bought her own base.

The cluster of buildings had been erected on a paved parking area the size of a city block. It used to be a manufacturing center for car parts, electrical systems, lights, radios, and similar products. All the machinery had either been sold or stolen long before, so when she bought it, there hadn't been much to clean out except trash from some long-gone squatters.

Kristen had purchased it because the entire property was secured by an eight-foot fence and the buildings themselves all had fairly modern locking doors and no windows on the ground level. Apparently, the previous owners thought their failing business was due to corporate espionage and had hardened the perimeter of the complex as much as they could. It was as secure a location as she could find and could be used sooner than any of the other premises they'd scouted, even though it was a less than beautiful space in which to work.

It gave her peace of mind to know her people could work, train, and rest with some protection against attack. Yes, she knew the technomages could jump fences, disable cameras, and break locked doors, but at least the security measures would give her and her team time to react to attacks.

They landed and when Brian climbed from her back, his jaw almost met the ground before his feet did. "You bought all this?" He gestured at the buildings, the new cameras, and the motion sensors.

"Yeah, the previous owner cut us a good deal when I offered cash."

"I can't even imagine how rich you are," he muttered.

Before she could give her brother a tour, Emerald marched out of the main building toward them, his jaw locked in a grim expression.

Kristen transformed into her human form and moved to intercept him. Stonequest and Brian fell into step behind her.

"Is everything all right, Emerald? If you don't have our computers set up yet, I think I found the man for the job," she told him. When she'd left, he had been complaining that it didn't matter how state-of-the-art their tech was if they didn't have someone to operate it.

"Shit's going down in Europe. A heap of shit," he replied as he glanced at Brian and gave him a curt nod.

"Explain," Stonequest instructed reflexively and stepped over Kristen's authority as an investigator.

"That's the boss's line," Brian said to him.

Emerald answered the question as if she had asked it. "Five dragons were attacked, all of them in Europe but spread out. Four are dead. The survivor is under the protection of the Southern Europe Dragon SWAT."

"What else do we know?" Kristen demanded.

"Let's get you inside and secure, ma'am, and I'll brief you on everything we have." His green eyes scanned the perimeter as if the European strike meant that more mages might be waiting outside their gates.

"Lead the way," she agreed and strode to the main building. She looked up to where two of her team sat on the roof of the main building, Butters with his sniper rifle and Beanpole with a pair of binoculars. The sight didn't reassure the Steel Dragon as much as she would have liked it to.

They walked inside, and she finally let herself breathe a sigh of relief when the heavy steel door locked behind them with a click.

"This is fucking awesome!" Brian murmured, his mouth open.

She looked at him in bemusement.

The base was still very crude with concrete floors and brick walls built up about twenty feet before they gave way to old panes of glass that were mostly undamaged. A catwalk remained fairly intact and offices had been erected at the far side of the building. It was like any number of abandoned factories in Detroit, notable only for the lack of machinery inside and the recently swept floor. The first floor had an extremely tall ceiling—as tall as three stories in a regular home—which had been a necessity as they had to fit dragons inside. Above that—where the fourth floor of a normal building would be—was an entire level of office space. They hadn't moved anything there yet, though. The carpets had been moldy and had to be removed.

All Kristen had done thus far was set up a camera system, buy desks and computers, and purchase cots and mattresses to put on the second floor so her dragons and humans would have a place to sleep. They hadn't even set those up in the designated area yet. All of it was spread on the wide concrete slab that was the base of their main base.

The other two buildings in the complex were much the same as the first, although slightly smaller.

"Oh, my God. I've only ever seen computers like that while looking at computers on my computer," her brother gushed. He veered away from Kristen, Stonequest, and Emerald and headed toward a row of tables loaded with monitors and computers and connected to a distant wall by a thick group of cables duct-taped to the floor here and there so people wouldn't trip over them.

One of the screens was currently in operation and showed a map of what looked like a city to Kristen. Judging by the colors, the narrow streets, and the shit Emerald had alluded to, she assumed it was somewhere in Europe rather than the States. The other monitors were all dark. Keith was behind them and cursed as he tried to hook and unhook cables.

"What do you have for us, Keith?" she asked.

"A fair amount, actually, but these damn monitors aren't working..." His reply trailed into inaudible grumbling.

"Do you mind?" Brian grinned at Kristen and wiggled his eyebrows.

"It's about time you started pulling your weight," she quipped.

"Was that a fat joke?" he retorted but he didn't sound upset about it as he immediately began to undo everything Keith had done. In a few moments, all six monitors were working.

One of them showed the map of a city in Europe. The other five each showed a photo and profile of a dragon. Four of them had red X's across them. Only the fifth didn't.

"All right, it looks good," Kristen said to Brian. If he hoped for more praise than that, he wouldn't get it. "Report," she said to Emerald and Keith.

"Four dragons were shot and killed in the last twelve hours," the Rookie began. "One on the streets of Rome, one in Germany while asleep in her home, one shot out of the sky while flying over Paris, and one at her home in Wales."

"The one over Paris—Silverscales—and the one in Wales—Coalclaw—were lovers," Emerald said. "Other than that, there weren't any connections between them except that they all lived in Europe."

"Any witnesses?" Stonequest asked.

"None that are useful," Emerald said, perhaps a little too gruffly for Kristen's taste.

"A maid in Germany was found dead at the scene, and a sound guy at the estate in Wales was also deceased," Keith replied and also looked at the green dragon like he'd been a little callous. "We think they must have been used to help with the assassination."

"Are there any witnesses in Italy or Paris?"

The man shrugged and answered before Emerald could. "Dozens in Paris. It's not every day someone sees a dragon fall dead into the River Seine, but no one has come forward about the gunmen. I'd say that's a wild goose chase. There was a food vendor in Rome who said the gunmen came out of nowhere, shot the dragon, and ran off, but he won't say anything else. I've seen videos of the guy being questioned and I'd say he doesn't look like he'll give us anything more."

Kristen nodded. All that was bad news. "What about the survivor?"

Emerald answered. "His name is Vertaile but he goes by Vert and is the singer in a band. From what we found, he's not the most savory of characters and is well-documented for using his aura on crowds."

"That's not illegal," Stonequest interjected.

"Eh." Emerald shrugged. "If the King of rock and roll didn't have to do it, I don't see why dragons need to."

"He's all right?" she asked.

"We're fairly certain he was hit by dragon bullets. The Southern EU SWAT said he's not healing and is in considerable pain. They're trying to get the bullet out now and are supposed to let us know."

"I think we can assume they were all shot with dragon bullets," Stonequest said.

Kristen thought it was good her old boss could be the first to say that. He'd spent so long denying the danger of the bullets and they needed him to be willing to face them head-on.

"I guess Texas will have to wait, then," Brian said.

"You told him about Texas?" Emerald asked.

"He worked it out himself," Stonequest said and sounded impressed.

"This is the only activity we've seen anywhere since Constance was taken out of the equation," she said. "It looks like they're trying to heat things up over there, and it's up to us to stop them."

"It could be a trap or misdirection to try to get us out of here," Stonequest suggested.

"It could be, but they attempted to assassinate five targets. That's something we have to take seriously," she said.

He nodded and deferred to her judgment. Kristen wasn't sure she would ever get used to that.

"All right, I want the whole damn team ready to move in half an hour. Brian, my techie brother, it looks like you need to book us tickets. This will be a long flight, but I guess I can at least afford first-class."

Stonequest cleared his throat a little exaggeratedly and hid a smile behind his hand.

"What is it now?"

"Brian doesn't need to book those tickets. Windlock had a plane."

"So what? Windlock owned a—oh. Right." It was still beyond belief that everything the investigator had owned now belonged to her. He hadn't even left anything for Larry, the mage who'd served him for over a decade. Not that he minded—apparently, he'd been paid quite handsomely over the years.

"What kind of plane are we talking about?" Keith grinned.

"It's a decent-sized private jet. I'm sure it can easily make the trip faster than a regular airliner."

"I can't believe you own a plane. Do you own the People Mover too? What about Tiger Stadium?" Brian's grin was unrestrained. "I hope you at least put Mom and Dad in first-class on their flight."

"Good idea, Brian. See to that," Kristen said. "I want them on a plane when we leave. I don't want us gone with them still here."

He grumbled but turned to his bank of computers and let his fingers fly while she gave orders to gather the team and prepare everyone for an extended stay in Europe. By the time she'd tasked her team with their various responsibilities, Brian turned to her.

"All right. Anything else, Lady Steel? Do you want to take over the US economy with your gold or maybe buy furniture for this base?" Kristen wanted to wipe the grin off his face but it was good to see so she let it ride.

"Actually...yes. You've given me all this crap about being rich."

"Because you are rich."

"Right, but how rich am I?"

"Ah...a question for the ages," he replied pontifically.

"No, that's what I'm asking you. Find out everything I inherited from Windlock, and write a report up for me. I know he has a place outside Detroit, the villa in France, and now a plane. I'm sure you can find out the rest."

"I should have kept my fat mouth shut," he mumbled.

"No, Brian, you should know I always value the input from my team, especially when it comes to new ways they can help," she said sweetly.

He glared at her but focused on the computers without protest.

"Stonequest, tell me about this jet," Kristen said after she'd gathered a few changes of clothes and toiletries. She'd already moved out of her apartment and made this base home, and it now proved to be a wise decision. There was a shower in one of the upstairs rooms and she would simply eat out until they installed a kitchen.

"He called it Windchaser," the dragon replied and barely managed to not roll his eyes. "It's here in Detroit since Windlock had been stationed here. He had a pilot and staff who will probably work for you since you've been writing their checks for a week."

"Their checks?" she asked, wondering how many other people she currently employed. "You know what, never mind. Get everyone ready. I need to check on who is staying behind."

"Yes, ma'am."

Kristen went to Timeflash who was currently in one of the other buildings. "Are you all right staying behind, Erin?" she asked.

"Oh yeah, it only makes sense," Erin Timeflash replied. "My abilities let me sense these structures so I'm the only one who can make sure there's no sabotage or anything going on."

"And there hasn't been so far?"

"No." She shook her head. "Not really. I found a few guys slacking on day two and I fired them. That made everyone else very careful about their attention to detail. But other than that, we've been fine. I haven't felt any malicious auras, so I think Constance's cell really is done for."

"Well, that's some good news, I guess."

"It is," Erin reassured her. "So go. When you come back, it'll feel like you have a brand-new base. I trust the security team we hired and the contractors working on it are afraid of me, so we're good."

"Thanks, Erin," Kristen said, but she couldn't go quite yet.

Instead, she went into the third building of the complex.

Inside were two dragons—Lumos and Kristen's sister, the dragon Constance had trapped and used for parts for her entire life. The Council had recommended killing the dragon—putting her out of her pathetic existence had been the official language. Kristen, of course, hadn't allowed that.

"Hey, Lumos. How's she doing?"

"Better," he said. He was in his dragon form as it seemed to be the best way to show the other dragon that he wasn't a threat. "She's progressing remarkably quickly, but...well... There will be permanent damage, of course. She was held there for a long time."

Kristen peered around him to see her sister.

Despite the fact that she looked much better, it was still a little difficult to look at her. The terrible wounds were healing. Her claws were growing back, her teeth coming in, and her scales filling out. Her wings still looked mangled, but the webbing between the bones was at least solid now, although it still didn't look like it would be able to hold her weight.

"Hi, Stella, how are you?" she asked. They had named her Stella because she'd frozen in place when she'd first seen the stars after emerging from her underground prison.

"Good! I good!" the dragon said. Despite her being the same age as

Kristen, she was intellectually stunted after being in a tank her entire life. Still, she'd shown amazing improvement. It was incredible what a little love and care could do for a living creature.

She smiled. "That's good, Stella. I'll be gone for a while, but Grandpa Lumos will take care of you while I'm gone, okay?"

"You going to help more like Stella?"

"That's right, I am. More dragons are in trouble from the same people who hurt you. We're going to stop them."

Stella nodded and her jubilant smile twitched to something else. "Stop them," she growled.

"We will, Stella, I promise. We won't let anyone else hurt dragons like they hurt you."

CHAPTER FIVE

"Thanks for letting me come with you guys," Brian told Kristen once the pilot of the Windchaser said everyone could remove their seatbelts.

"You said you would throw a temper tantrum the likes of which the world had never seen if I made you stay behind," she replied drolly.

He shrugged. "I'm glad you didn't call my bluff."

"I still don't understand why you needed to come with us. You could have done all your fancy techie stuff over the phone."

Her brother recoiled visibly. "What if you get a data drive that needs decoding? Or what if there's a system not connected to the larger Internet that needs to be broken into? By the end of this, you'll be happy I came."

"I'll be much happier when you tell me the extent of my assets. Are you sure that laptop will be enough to get the job done?"

"It's slaved to the big computers in Detroit and linked by satellite, so it has more than enough power—not that I'll need it to do a little accounting. If there's a delay issue, maybe I can link with whatever system they have in Paris."

"I've been meaning to talk to you about that, actually," Drew said.

Kristen excused herself to her brother and walked up the length of the Windchaser from the back of the plane. It was a very nice jet, she decided. Apparently, Windlock had a penchant for white as the floor was all white carpet, the plush leather chairs and sofa were white leather, and the walls were all painted white. She would have felt like she was in a commercial if not for the undeniably utilitarian appearance of her crew.

She smiled at the thought—her crew. Until recently, the two teams on this plane had been separate but now, they all worked together, human, dragon, and mage united to stop a common threat. It was the start of her vision for a better world.

It was too bad that it happened with people who habitually wore bulletproof vests, tactical combat gear, and pistols at their hips. It wasn't exactly the kind of thing most people liked to see on TV, but a common understanding of what it took to defend a way of life was often where peace started.

"What's going on, Drew?"

"Well, I've thought about your decision to go to Paris."

"What about it?"

"The call is yours, of course, but I don't think that's where we'll find them."

"It makes sense," she replied. "Paris is centrally located and a dragon was shot out of the sky there. Plus, Vertaile is from there. It's the only place with two targets."

He didn't look convinced.

"Where would you have us start our search?"

"Honestly? I'd start with the survivor in Florence," Drew responded.

"Tell me why," she replied.

"I don't know why they would have targeted the dragon there unless they were stationed either in Florence or somewhere nearby. If they were from Paris, why not attack him in his home? They took a big risk when they exposed themselves to everyone at the concert, definitely the biggest risk of all their targets as far as witnesses are concerned. I don't think they would do that unless him being in

Florence was convenient for them and they knew the city well enough to know they could escape."

Kristen nodded. It made sense to her. They'd have to call the European SWAT team and redirect them to meet them at the airport in Florence, but if Drew's hunch was right, that would be well worth any potential friction it caused. "All right. We'll go to Florence."

"Do you want me to tell the pilot?" he asked.

She shook her head. "I haven't adjusted to having my own plane yet. I think I'll enjoy telling the pilot where we're going."

"No problem." He nodded and settled into a white leather chair next to Stonequest. The two leaders of their respective teams immediately began to talk shop. She smiled at their exchange of ideas and information.

The same tableau played out through the entire plane. After thwarting Constance and saving the Dragon Council, both teams were much more comfortable with each other and everyone seemed to try to pick up tips from their counterparts.

As she walked up through the body of the plane, she relished the exchange of information. Emerald was seated with Jim, Beanpole, and Butters. He was explaining to them everything he knew about mages —what they could do, what they couldn't, and what kind of powers they might encounter. The three men listened attentively and occasionally asked questions about detection abilities. The sniper obviously attempted to learn how to sneak up and take a shot at someone who could control magic as easily as a regular human could use a computer.

Heartsbane sat with Hernandez and Keith. The demolitions expert told the dragon all about different types of explosives, how to recognize them, and which ones might be most effective against dragons. Despite the fact that the dragon's wounds inflicted by a bomb filled with dragon shrapnel had already healed, she listened in rapt attention. Keith occasionally interjected something, but he mostly tried and failed to make the two volatile women laugh. *He must have a thing for dangerous women,* she thought and fought a grin.

A shout of surprise from the back of the plane was followed by laughter. Kristen turned to where Jim had drawn a gun on Emerald and the dragon had expanded his chest instead of dodging. Beanpole and Butters tried to tell him how to protect himself from a weapon that had only ever been a nuisance for the dragon's entire life between bouts of laughter.

In the front of the plane, closest to the cockpit, were the two mages. Sometimes, she wished Amy and Larry would spend more time with the other members of her team, but she understood that both had much to gain from spending time with each other.

"What are you two up to now?" she asked them.

"Larry's teaching me techniques for control." The girl levitated a pen and signed her name on a piece of paper—or tried to. It looked like a child's first attempts at scratching letters. Although it was legible—barely, but her effort deserved a generous response—it was nothing compared to the elegant flowing script that Larry was able to produce on his piece of paper.

Amy tried again with worse results than before and she cursed, frustrated, as the pen hurtled away and stabbed into a leather chair.

"You can't lose control like that," Larry chided her, although he was smiling. "You have to be the master of your powers. I know it can be difficult with all the raw power you have, but if you can learn finesse, you could be one of the greatest mages of all time."

She nodded, took a deep breath, and drew the pen back to her using only her telekinetic abilities.

He nodded in approval, looked at the chair she'd damaged, and wiggled his fingers, and the leather appeared to repair itself.

"It's fucking crazy you can do that." The girl shook her head in disbelief.

"I learned that from Timeflash." He grinned. "I'll show you how—once you can write a paragraph."

"It's so hard with all this power," she said. "Like trying to put a fire hose through a squirt gun."

"You can do it, though," Kristen assured her. "I'd much rather have you at full power than hindered, even though I know it's not the norm." She slid her hand into her pocket and withdrew a silver bracelet.

Amy gasped when she saw it. "No, Kristen, I don't need that, honestly. The feeling of being limited...it's terrible."

Larry eyed the bracelet and smiled. "I think you should try it on."

She looked from him to Kristen, crestfallen, but she allowed the Steel Dragon to shackle her again. "I guess if you think I need to limit my—wait a minute." She looked at the bracelet for a moment and narrowed her eyes in confusion. "I...I can feel an aura coming off this like the other one you first had me wear but...well, it must be broken. I don't feel like my power is limited at all."

"That's because I had Larry work this bracelet up especially for you." Kristen grinned.

"I put spells on it to make it seem like it's limiting your power without actually doing so," he said and sounded both proud and smug. "As long as you're wearing that, dragons shouldn't bug you."

"It's not spelled to me either," Kristen said. "So if you want to take it off to have a shower or whatever, you can."

"Oh, my God, you guys! This is so cool." Amy hopped up and hugged her.

"You're more than welcome," she said. "Although you should thank Larry. He did all the work."

"Thanks, Larry." The girl planted a kiss on his cheek.

"Ah, don't mention it. I only did what the boss-lady asked," Larry replied and blushed fiercely at the kiss from the younger woman.

"I have something for you too," Kristen said and retrieved a second bracelet from her pocket.

"Is that right?" His gaze settled on the bracelet and he paled.

"I had Atramento copy your work. At first, he didn't want to, but when he saw all the spells you worked into Amy's, he took it as a personal challenge. It works the same way as hers does. You'll still have full power without drawing attention."

"Yeah...thanks," he said, although his voice sounded hollow. His hand covered his wrist so she couldn't put the bracelet on him.

"Larry... I'm sorry, is something wrong?" she asked. "I wanted to show you the same trust I show Amy and the same trust that Windlock showed you. I know you'll only use your power to pursue justice and now that he's gone and you're with…well, you're stuck with me, I thought you'd be happy."

"No, no it's fine. It's nice of you, actually, but it's…" He raised his hand to reveal that he still wore the bracelet Windlock had given him, despite the fact that it had been crushed and mangled from when the investigator had destroyed it. "It's kind of all I have left of the old windbag, you know?"

"I miss him too," Kristen said, although she could see from the pain in the mage's eyes that she didn't miss him half as much as he did. And why should she? She'd known him for barely months and he had known him for years. "I know he didn't leave you anything in his will but if there's anything you wanted—"

"No, no, no," Larry said and cleared his throat and wiped his eyes before the tears could stream down his cheeks. "He already gave me more money than I would ever have had as a regular human working at a convenience store, and you're using his wealth better than I ever would have. It's only…he was always there, you know? Okay, I took a vacation now and then, but other than that, we were always together. It was the job and it was our lives. Mostly, it's all these little things like this plane. Do you have any idea how many times he had this cleaned? White is the dumbest color for a vehicle, let alone one that experiences turbulence. No matter how times I told him that, he never changed it." He smiled at the memory but winced when he once again remembered that Windlock was dead.

"I know I can't replace him—"

He shook his head sharply to cut her off. "You're wrong about that, Kristen. You have to replace him. Being an investigator's mage is all I have. It's all I know. If I can't be yours…" He shook his head and looked lost.

It was her turn to wince. While she liked Larry and wanted him to work with her, the idea of him being "hers" made her uncomfortable. She tried to say as much but he wouldn't have it.

"No matter what happens," he said and his voice hardened, "I'm sticking with you, Steel Dragon. Either we help both sides see a path forward or we die trying. That's what Windlock would have done. Hell—" Fresh tears welled in his eyes. "That's what the old windbag did."

"Everything I do is to honor him," Kristen said.

Larry laughed bitterly at that. "Don't you lie to me, Kristen Hall," he said and wiped his tears. "Windlock was part of your crusade. You weren't a part of his. He was a good dragon but you're a great one. Now, enough of all this blubbering. Put that bracelet on already so if the plane crashes and you die, at least I'll have something to remember you by." He removed the other bracelet as he said it, looked at it for a moment, then disassembled it without looking at either of the two women.

"Why did you do that?" Amy asked but he already had an answer. He used his powers to reform the links of the chain and stretched them into smaller and finer pieces of metal until he'd extended the crushed bracelet into a necklace. He put it on with magic as he extended his wrist for the new one.

"How did you do that?" the younger mage asked.

"I have full power now as well," he said as Kristen attached the decoy bracelet to his wrist. "I may not be quite as strong as you but I have a feeling we'll need everything I have in Paris."

"Florence," Kristen said and recalled that she had a pilot to boss around.

CHAPTER SIX

T hey arrived at the airport in Florence and the aircraft taxied to
a standstill near a small fleet of black SUVs. Kristen could feel
draconic auras emanating from inside the vehicles.

"I guess they're not taking any chances with shooters armed with
dragon bullets on the loose," Jim remarked as they walked down the
steps from their plane onto the tarmac. "That's bulletproof armor and
glass."

"Good," Kristen replied. "It's about time someone took these technomages seriously."

"I don't know," Keith said dubiously as they walked toward the
SUVs. "If the dragons are turning to bulletproof tech, the technomages will find a way to pierce it or use more bombs or something.
The dragons will adapt to the new weapons, so the mages will develop
more powerful ones and on and on and on."

She could see the implications of this better than anyone. There
was nothing to be done about it, though, other than what they were
doing—stopping the technomages from using dragon bodies like they
were resources to be mined.

"My name is Artigliorosso," a dragon dressed in an Italian black
suit said to Kristen as he extended his hand. "I am the leader of this

division of the European Dragon SWAT. You may call me Rosso." He spoke in an Italian accent and was essentially the epitome of a handsome Italian man—tall, dark, and with a wicked smile. "This is my partner La Flamme."

"Bonjour," La Flamme said. He also wore a dark suit, although his puckered expression made him much less handsome in Kristen's eyes.

"We barely made it here in time," Rosso said. "I assure you, there was no threat of being shot out of the air in Paris. The drive will now take us considerable time and is not any safer."

"We want to begin our investigation here in Florence," she said.

He bristled at either the way she said the name of the Italian city in English or for having the audacity to change their plans. "I assure you, the base of operations in Paris is better suited for this kind of...delegation."

"Rosso—I'm sorry, Officer Rosso," she said and not so subtly pointed out that as an investigator, she far outranked him. "But my team thinks the cell is here in Florence, so this is where we'll begin our work. I trust that won't be a problem?"

The two dragons argued with each other in a blend of French and Italian before Rosso finally deferred to La Flamme. "Very well. If you would come this way."

Kristen smiled and gestured for Stonequest to ride with her and the two European SWAT officers.

"I wish I knew what they were saying," she mumbled to him. She had taken Spanish in high school but had been terrible at it and had been far more into sports.

"Rosso is pissed we're here at all. He thinks they had everything under control and we won't help and will simply get in the way," he said quietly to her as they neared the cars. "La Flamme thinks they can solve all these murders as well but apparently, he also thought the technomages were here in Florence. I think that's why they agreed to stay here—because of La Flamme."

"You understood all that even though they're speaking in French and Italian?"

He shrugged. "I've been around a while, Kristen. You might want to start thinking about learning a few languages too."

They slid into the back of the car and blessedly, the two dragons reverted to English in the small space.

"We...I believe...they so close," La Flamme managed in English. He didn't seem to be as good at the language as Rosso.

"What La Flamme is trying to say is that we had it under control. This is the kind of thing Dragon SWAT is for," Rosso said and didn't sound pleased to have to drive them around.

"I assure you, this is not what Dragon SWAT normally does," Kristen replied. "This is not the work of a disgruntled dragon or a centuries-forgotten grudge. There are mages behind this."

La Flamme grew quite agitated at this and began to speak in French while he gestured dramatically. Apparently, he understood English fine.

Stonequest looked at her to see if she wanted him to translate but she shook her head. It was better to let Rosso do it.

"La Flamme remembers the last Mage War. He says he barely survived," the man translated. "He says we want to stop these mages more than you—after all, these were our dragons—but because of Shimmerclaw's insistence..." He trailed off and muttered in Italian.

Her companion leaned closer to her. "Rosso's pissed that Shimmerclaw told them to give us their full hospitality and to help us in every way possible. Neither of them is happy about it, but I wouldn't be either. I guess she didn't threaten them but it was implied."

Kristen nodded. It was too bad that these dragons weren't one hundred percent on board with her and her team being there, but there was good news too. It was certainly a good thing that Shimmerclaw entrusted an entire organization to Kristen. The dragon obviously wanted her to succeed. She'd count that as a good sign.

After another few miles—kilometers as they were called in Europe —of winding streets, they emerged from the maze of roadways that comprised Florence with what she would only be able to think of as a castle ahead of them.

"Welcome to Castillo Montalbano," Rosso said and gestured to the huge stone walls that served as a bulwark against the rest of the city.

She turned as mage servants opened the doors of a few of the SUVs behind them but strangely, not all.

"Why don't they open all the doors?" she asked.

"Oh," Rosso responded, seemingly surprised at the question. "The humans will stay at a local hotel. It's more than adequate and only a few minutes' walk down the road from here. Oh, I'm sorry. You must have thought the mages wouldn't be welcome but as you can see, we allow their kind in Montalbano."

"Yeah, that'll be a problem," Kristen said. She took her cellphone out and opened an app to find a local hotel.

The Italian didn't seem to understand what she was doing until she put the phone to her ear and made a request for rooms for her entire team—dragon and human.

"Forgive me if I was not clear, Lady Hall," he said and bowed slightly. "One of our agents called ahead. Despite the last-minute change of plans, we have accommodations inside that I trust you will find to be quite pleasant. The mages will be well-tended as well, and the hotel for the...other humans is a nicer one, by their standards."

"This will not happen," she replied firmly. "We won't start this whole endeavor by splitting my team up. I won't disrespect these men and women by putting them in second-class accommodations."

"I know the monkeys stink but sending them away is very stupid," Heartsbane said to Rosso as she stepped alongside.

"Stupid?" Rosso balked.

La Flamme laughed.

But Heartsbane wasn't done yet. "Splitting us up means having to secure two locations instead of one. Plus, it's inefficient. These humans may be weak little things but by the end of this, you'll owe them your lives."

"Well, I only hope they understand what a fortune that would be for them," Rosso muttered and hollered at a mage to approach.

He yelled at the woman for a moment in tones that needed no translation, slicked his hair back, and gestured for Kristen to enter. "It will take us a few minutes but we will prepare rooms for your entire team."

"Excellent!" She beamed as if they'd been in agreement the entire time. "And the rooms are all located in the same part of this castle, I assume?"

He ground his teeth, hollered something at the retreating mage, and turned to her with a smile. "Of course."

"Good." She nodded and put her phone away. "Let's begin, shall we?"

CHAPTER SEVEN

Neal Havington was from the United Kingdom and would thus always think that British ales were the best way to celebrate. French wine had never sat quite right with him, despite the years he and his team had spent in the city of lights. But there was something about Italian red that seemed perfect for the celebration of an enemy who no longer posed a threat.

He opened a second bottle and refilled the glasses of the five mages who'd carried out his carefully laid plans. Everyone was giddy with excitement over a job well done—after all, it had been years in the making. Everyone, except Ron.

"It's all right," Sarah assured him. "You hit him, didn't you? And you had the hardest target."

That was exactly like Sarah. Assassinating Coalclaw had easily been the hardest thing to do—what with needing to coordinate the sound equipment and get a recording of her mate's bugling call. Her comforting him was her way of bragging and Ron knew it.

He looked at his leader before he lowered his gaze to the floor and sipped his wine halfheartedly.

"She's right, Ron. You did well," Havington said, which was enough to at least encourage the mage to raise his head a little higher.

"Do you really think so, Boss?"

"I do, Ron, I do, and let me tell you why. For starters, we killed four out of five. I had hoped for three out of five, so that's great."

"But it could've been all five if not for me!" the mage protested.

"It could have, yes, but you also shot the bloke, right?"

Ron nodded.

"You had the hardest target and you still managed to hit him and make him bleed. I count that as a success."

"You're just saying that," he said, although he sounded like he wanted to believe it.

"Think about it, Ron. He was the only one of the five we chose who was a real celebrity in human culture. If you can believe the tabloids, that disgusting reptile even fornicated with humans—no doubt after casting his aura on them to make them unable to protest his disgusting advances. He was an abomination and a disgrace. Humans shouldn't treat those lizards as celebrities, and now they know not to. As soon as the other dragons let him resurface, he'll whine to the newspapers about how badly you hurt him. No human will want to get close to him or any other dragon. I'd say it's better than him dying, honestly."

"Do you really think so?"

Truthfully, Havington didn't. He would like all five dragons to be dead because it would have demonstrated the perfect orchestration and coordination of his team, but he wouldn't say that to Ron. It was far more important for his team to be confident, given the undeniable power of their prey. "You did well, Ron, honestly, now drink some wine and get proper drunk so we can wake up and lay our next plans in the morning."

"Right, sir. You got it, sir," Ron said, finally mollified.

The leader's phone rang and he straightened. "Pardon me," he said and stepped away from his team and into a different part of the crypt where they'd made their base. It was a large cavernous room where they'd planned to move the captive dragon they'd used to harvest materials from in Paris, but after what had happened in the States, Havington hadn't had the resources to move it.

Instead, he'd shot it in the brain with a bullet made from its own body.

The empty room was a reminder that the cursed Steel Dragon was already affecting his operations, despite her being on another continent.

He pushed all that from his mind and answered his phone. "Mr. Havington, I wished to call and congratulate you," said a smooth voice on the other end of the line.

"Who the fuck is this, then?" he demanded. "I've had this damn number for a week since I burned my last phone. How the fuck did you get this number and how do you know that name?"

Without fail, he switched phones weekly, and the only people who had his number were those in his cell and a few of the leaders of other cells. He didn't recognize the voice, which meant one of the other cell leaders must have given the number to a cell he didn't know. It was a damn breach of security measures if there ever was one.

"An ally, Havington—an ally who wishes to offer congratulations and my help."

The cell leader warred with himself for a moment and tried to decide if he wanted to hang up or keep talking. He didn't like that someone had given his number to the leader of another cell, but he was quite proud of his work and also concerned. Why would they need help after such a victory?

"Yeah, well, those lizards had it coming."

"Indeed. Cowards, every one of them, and I congratulate you on your efficiency."

"Yeah, well, thanks," he said, proud of himself despite not knowing exactly who this guy was.

"However, I want you to know that the Dragon Council has conspired against you."

"Shimmerclaw," Havington said.

"Indeed," the man replied. "The Steel Dragon has arrived in Florence with her team to help her. I have reason to believe Shimmerclaw herself has put her on your tail to hunt you and put an end to your group."

"There's no way she could already be here," he protested.

"I assure you, she is. Her resources are substantial but she is not all-knowing. She must have suspicions you are there, but she cannot yet know that you know."

"What are you thinking?" he asked, although plans had already begun to form in his mind.

"You know the terrain better than her, I hope? Perhaps you could turn the tables on the Steel Dragon and eliminate her instead. It would be a boon to the rest of us, especially after what she did to Constance."

"Yeah, pity that," Havington said. Constance had told him they had plans to assassinate the entire Council. Since then, although he hadn't heard any official reports, it wasn't exactly a stretch of the imagination to deduce who must have stopped her. The same steel bitch who had stopped her every damn action.

"Well?"

"We'll see what we can do. Where did you say you were stationed?" he asked, but the line was already dead.

"Who was that, boss?" Sarah asked.

"Someone with eyes in places I don't like," he said. That had to have been someone from another cell making the call, right? But how had another cell known something about Florence before he had? It was very troubling but a problem for a later date. "I'm turning in. You all enjoy that bottle, then go to bed. It looks like our next step starts tomorrow whether we're ready or not."

"Yes, sir," Sarah said and left Havington to his thoughts.

He wondered what cell had known about Constance—another one based in the States, perhaps—but once again, pushed it from his mind. The fact was, if the Steel Dragon really was there, this was a golden opportunity to remove a major problem for their cause. If he and his mages could eliminate the meddling Kristen Hall and her friends, the Dragon Council would have no choice but to declare war on humanity. At that point, he and the cells could openly retaliate and finally end the reign of dragons over humans and mages.

Havington knew Constance and knew she was driven by a desire to make humans and dragons equal. It was an admirable goal and certainly a good one for the media, but he had always considered the wider implications of having no dragons. With them gone, mages would be the most powerful group of beings on the planet. This applied especially if humans went all out for the war and really enraged the dragons. The damage to the infrastructure and social order of the world would be irreparable. In that future, he couldn't help but see himself as a future power player.

Lord Boneclaw put the phone down and picked up his most recently harvested mask. Like all the others, it was made of an actual human skull taken from one of the wretched creatures while their blood still pumped. He put it on, relished the smell of dead human, and embraced the persona he'd used for his own brand of diplomacy for so long—the Masked One.

He had never expected the Steel Dragon to outlive Shadowstorm or his mother Obscura, but there she was. After the unexpected first-hand view of what she was capable of, he had to admit that she was impressive in a flashy kind of way.

When he recalled that, he looked forward to ending her existence even more, but she was in no hurry and neither was he.

Dragons, after all, weren't afflicted by limited lifetimes. He had a position of comfort on the North American Dragon Council, he had wealth and riches beyond any human, and most of all, he had patience.

Part of his confidence came from the fact that he understood how the mages and, indeed, even Kristen Hall felt about the establishment of power. He had been deemed a bony runt thousands of years before and not been given much of a chance to live. With such an inauspicious beginning, he'd had to murder his creche mates and seize what was his. He'd taken much—as much as he could given the frustrating limits dragon society placed on him.

Now, he stood on the edge of a bonfire that was slowly being loaded with more fuel. The Masked One knew it would burn. Constance had failed to ignite it but she hadn't failed to add more fuel. Havington had contributed as well, but that obnoxious Shimmer-claw had doused it like she was always prone to do.

He wanted to see if Havington would have the cunning to kill Kristen Hall and her band of mongrels but if he didn't, there would be another opportunity. Every time she struggled, she pulled the webs he was weaving around her tighter and tighter. Eventually, she would be so tangled she wouldn't be able to move. The only question in his mind was whether the world would erupt in a war before or after she was removed.

It didn't matter, not to someone with the patience of the Masked One, but it was interesting. If all else failed, he could slaughter the whelp like he had so many others but in the meantime, watching this unfold would be more entertaining than his operas.

CHAPTER EIGHT

Kristen began her next morning by talking to Vertaile, the dragon survivor. They met in a dining hall inside the castle where she and her team were staying and spoke over a breakfast of poached eggs, wonderful rustic rolls, and espresso that was so strong even a dragon could feel it.

"How are you holding up, Sir Vertaile?" she asked like she had done with so many human victims of crimes.

"Holding up?" he responded in English heavily tinged with a French accent. "I was attacked at a show for doing nothing more than playing music and two of my friends—humans, I should tell you—are dead, and you ask how I'm holding up?"

"Sir Vertaile—"

"Vert is fine," he stated with a dismissive wave of his hand. Before she could go on, he gestured rudely for a mage to bring them more food. He'd already finished his meal and she noticed him eyeing hers and almost wanted him to attempt to snatch it. She was reasonably sure that not only could she stab his hand with her fork, but she wouldn't regret doing it.

Kristen cleared her throat to continue but again, Vert cut her off.

"You ask how I am holding up after being shot by one of these horrible American weapons? Not well. If they were only a few centimeters over, I'd be dead. As it is, I cannot fly and I can hardly use my arm."

Kristen nodded because she didn't think it was an act, not if his aura could be believed. "Did you get a look at the shooter?"

"Non," he responded. "The shot came from inside the venue, though, so it had to be someone there."

"Do you have any idea of who might want to hurt you?"

"One of these damn terrorists, perhaps? Other than that, I have no idea. I am loved by my fans. Adored! Who would want to hurt me?"

"Rumor is you use your aura to make crowds love your shows. If that's true, it could be the kind of thing that angered whoever did this. Many humans and mages don't like the power we dragons have."

Vert snorted contemptuously. "Next you will say women do not like it if I make them orgasm."

She reminded herself this guy was a wounded victim and that it was generally frowned upon to beat the shit out of them, even if they were arrogant dragons.

"Do you know if the event was recorded?" Kristen asked, ready to move on from witness testimony to hard evidence.

"Sure, of course," he said with another dismissive wave of his hands. "I am well-loved by fans, even when they are not in the presence of my aura. All my gigs are recorded."

"One camera or multiple?" she pressed.

"Multiple, of course. This is not a pedestrian recording but a video that hundreds of thousands of my fans will watch after I have released it."

"So you handle the footage yourself, then? Do you mind if we look at it?"

Vert shook his head as if she had asked him to clean a latrine. "I am the show. I do not handle the details. I have a human who handles all the tedious little details."

Kristen was quite done with him at this point so was incredibly thankful when she asked for the contact information of said human and he was able to produce the number from his cellphone.

"If you'll excuse me," she said, stood quickly, and dialed the number. It turned out she was not quite done with Vert, though. Despite the human on the other end of the line admitting that yes, he was still in town and yes, he had the footage of the night, he would not give it to her.

"I can't release it without Vert's say-so. How do I know you are who you say you are and not some tabloid?"

"What the hell would a tabloid do with concert footage?" she asked but bit her tongue. It didn't matter, nor did it matter that when she went to get the footage from the man, she could show him her badge and thus prove her identity. He had obviously spent too much time around Vert and thus thought his mix of dragon and celebrity trumped anything else, including the law.

She sat across from the victim again, put the phone on the table, and turned the speaker on.

"The manager won't release the tapes without your permission," she said and glared at the dragon as he chewed his roll and a third portion of eggs.

Finally, he swallowed and asked, "So?"

Kristen tried to wither him with a glare and eventually, it worked and he understood.

"Why must you be so dense, Williams? Give the woman what she asks for," he snapped into the phone once he'd identified the problem.

"Right, boss. Sorry, sir, I'll have it all ready soon. Send her over."

"There you go," Vert said as if he'd actually helped instead of mostly been a speed bump for her doing her job.

Her breakfast ruined, she left the dining hall and called Amy. She wanted to get the tapes as soon as possible but heading off without backup seemed like a terrible plan.

"Amy," she said once her mage had answered. "Get Larry, Drew, and Jim and meet me at the front. We have a lead."

"We'll be down in a minute," the girl said.

As Kristen waited at the entrance for her team, she pondered the luck of the whole show being recorded. Vert and his manager were both rather rude and annoying but hopefully, this would prove to be solid evidence. At the very least, it would give her team something they could chase down and help familiarize them with the narrow streets of Florence.

She dialed her brother and told him to start hunting through the web for anything that might lead them to the cell. He said he was on it although, from his voice, it sounded like he was mostly combatting jetlag.

Finally, she called Stonequest and made sure he and his team were ready. If something else happened, she wanted them on it as quickly as possible.

Amy emerged onto the street with the others behind her. "Ah, man, we're driving?" She sounded bummed. "I hoped to see this place from the air!"

"It sounds nice but we can't risk being seen," Kristen replied. She hoped they still had the element of surprise but couldn't help feeling like eyes watched them from behind every brick in this Renaissance city.

CHAPTER NINE

K risten was able to enjoy the first part of the drive. Florence was beautiful with its four and five-story buildings built over the centuries and capped with red tile roofs. Some part of her fantasized about perhaps seeing the Duomo when this was all over or getting away to another part of Tuscany, but that all evaporated when Drew announced that they were being followed.

"Damn it!" Larry said and jerked the wheel to turn the car down a narrow alley as he peered at the sky.

"By a car, not a dragon," the other man said. "Although I'm not sure yet."

"Oh, right, sorry about that," the mage said sheepishly. "With Windlock, we were mostly after dragons, not people in cars."

"It might be a false alarm," Drew said.

Jim shook his head. He was squashed in the back seat with Kristen and Amy. In all honesty, he was too big to fit in the back seat of anything and Larry was the only one of them with experience driving in Europe, so Kristen took the rear as well. "He's been back there a while. A black car?" Jim asked.

"Where is it?" Kristen asked.

"Behind us, I think," Larry answered and tried to crane his neck to peer behind them. Slightly panicked looks from everyone else in the car convinced him to rather watch the road.

"There it is," the Wonderkid said when the car turned down the alley they were already halfway down.

"What do you want us to do?" Amy asked. "I'm fairly sure I could flip it into the river if you'd like." She sounded eager.

"No, no. Larry, keep driving. Everyone, keep your eyes on the buildings on either side of us so we look like tourists."

Their heads snapped toward the windows, which had to be about the most suspicious way they could have all carried the order out.

Ah, well, there was nothing to be done about it now.

"Larry, turn right up here," Kristen instructed.

"It's one-way."

"Duh!" Jim and Drew said in unison.

"Oh, right, to test them!" the mage said and turned blithely into traffic.

Fortunately, it was early in the day in Florence and most of the traffic was tourists getting gelato or people hurrying to get a place in line at the big tourist sites. They drove down the alley without hindrance. She had begun to tell herself it was simply them overreacting when the black car also turned down the one-way street.

"Now can I flip them into the river?" Amy asked.

"No. Same plan. Larry, keep driving. Look for another wrong way to go down."

He complied and soon found one, this time on a street that bordered the river. The black car paused at the T before it turned in the other direction and went with the flow of traffic.

Everyone exhaled a sigh of relief.

"Larry, drive across that bridge there. That should put some distance between us."

Everyone else started throwing theories around.

"Secret police?" Drew asked.

"More like those European SWAT dragons," Jim countered. "They don't trust us at all. I bet they're trying to keep an eye on us."

"Did you sense anything from them?" Larry asked Amy.

"No…not really," Amy said. "But they were fairly far away."

He nodded. "They could have masked their magic too. It's not hard to do and a group of mage terrorists would no doubt practice the skill." He said it casually, but the words put tension in the air that lingered for a while after the unidentified vehicle had turned away.

Kristen didn't like it, but she had to consider the possibility that their cover was blown. But how could it be? It seemed like the only possibility was either Windlock's pilot—something she seriously doubted—or someone within the European force, an equally unpleasant prospect. Either way, it was better to let the rest of her team know. She took her cell out and called Stonequest.

"Kristen?" He answered briskly and using her name was his way to tell her he was in private. If he answered with "Investigator," she'd know there were people who were not part of their team nearby.

"I want you and the others ready and on your toes. It looks like we might have to go airborne sooner than I expected. Keep Butters on the roof."

It was always good to have a sniper keeping watch, she thought.

"Has something happened?" he asked. "We can send backup now if you need it."

"No, nothing yet, merely a feeling. I'll call you if anything happens."

Stonequest chuckled. "With you, I know better than to wait for a call. If anything happens, I'll follow the sirens and look for smoke."

"Yeah, well, make sure you're on the roof then," she replied. It might have sounded gruff, but he knew her so well that he only acknowledged the order and went to gather the team.

"We're getting close," Amy said as she checked the map app on her phone.

"Any sign of the black car?" Kristen asked.

"Nope, nothing," Jim and Drew said together. They had a broad view this close to the river and couldn't see the car anywhere. As the team drove into the winding streets of Florence again, one of the ubiquitous scooters pulled out behind them.

Havington had thought it a close thing when the Steel Dragon noticed their tail. He'd had no choice but to stop following them or at least to make it appear that way. The foolish girl didn't seem to have any idea that a mage had been on a boat in the river Arno and had sent a message to another mage on a scooter.

They might have identified that tail too, but they reached their destination quickly, exited their vehicle, and went inside the digital studio. His mage continued to drive past as the Steel Dragon and her team walked in, completely oblivious to how compromised their position had become.

CHAPTER TEN

"Watch the car, all right, Larry?" Kristen said and narrowly dodged a speeding scooter.

Drew, Jim, and Amy scrambled out of the vehicle and started toward the door. Before she could go inside, though, a woman wrapped in robes stepped up to her and held a burning candle.

"Bless this, will you, ma'am?" the woman said in English and pushed the candle toward her.

"Uh, no, no thank you," she said, thinking this was the first part of the woman's way to ask for money. She tried to step around her.

The stranger caught her wrist with surprising strength. "Please, miss. You are a dragon, are you not? A special dragon. Please, bless this candle...please?"

She honestly had no idea what to do and glanced at her team-mates. While she had never heard of such a thing, neither had any of the people with her judging by their expressions. Jim, Drew, and Amy had even less experience with the dragon world than she did.

"I'm sorry, but I'm really in a hurry," Kristen protested.

"Please, miss. It is for my mission to be successful—my mission to make the world a better place."

Kristen sighed as a man pushed past and hurried up the stairs into the building. "What can I do?"

Fortunately, it wasn't hard. She merely mumbled a prayer in Italian—repeating the words after the woman—and as if to confirm her earlier suspicions, the stranger asked for a couple of euros. She shook her head, annoyed she'd been duped into wasting time and money on the beggar, but she gave her a couple of euros all the same and sent her on her way.

They entered the building and the man who'd done so a few minutes earlier pushed past them. He practically bounced off Drew's chest as he went down the stairs.

"Italians are fucking rude," Drew said. Before she could point out that most of the Italians they had met had been fairly polite—or at least no ruder than a Detroiter—they were on the second floor. They stopped outside the door of the office Vert had directed them to.

She pushed it open and the manager—a man by the name of Williams who was obviously British—stood nervously in the tiny lobby.

"Here ya are, then," he said and held the hard drive up.

It didn't take a dragon investigator to see that something was up. The man's eyes were wide with real anxiety and his forehead was slick with sweat. His gaze darted constantly from Kristen to the door and to the hard drive in his hand and his aura was panicked. It was so strong, she could sense it like a rancid aroma.

"Are you all right there, buddy?" Drew asked. From his posture, Kristen could tell that he also suspected something was wrong with the guy.

"I'm fine, ya," Williams replied. Then, perhaps realizing that he was drenched in sweat and acting like the world was going to end added, "I have a big project due later and have to start work on it right away. So, if you don't mind, I'll head out." He stepped toward the door and tried to shove the hard drive in Kristen's hands at the same time.

"I thought you had important work to do. Isn't this your office?" Jim asked.

"Right. Sorry," the man responded, dabbed his brow with a handkerchief, and scurried away from them and deeper into the office space.

"This has all the angles?" Kristen asked as she held the hard drive up and used her aura to send a flush of fear through him. She wanted him to be afraid of the back of his office the same way he was afraid of her. It worked as it wasn't difficult to change the target of someone's fear. If the truth be told, it was much more challenging to make a fearful person calm.

"It has all the footage on it, ready for viewing. It's a lot of video," Williams said as if that was some kind of warning. "But it's all there. Tons of different angles. It'll probably take you all day to get through it, so I'd get a move on. Plus, like I said, I'm very busy," he added belatedly, perhaps realizing he'd ordered a dragon around.

Drew stepped forward and took the drive from Kristen. He turned it one way and then the other before he tapped the side of it. Despite the fact that the device looked new, he noticed scratches along one of the seams that kept it closed.

They didn't need a tech expert to know it had been tampered with, which made not an iota of sense. She didn't know computers, but her brother had almost ripped her head off when she'd once opened one of his solid-state drives.

Now, at least, she understood the source of the man's fear. It had very clearly been tampered with, probably by the same mages they were trying to stop. This meant, among other things, that they had been right about coming to Florence and that the technomages knew they were there.

It also meant that the hard drive was a liability. It had to have either a tracker, a bomb, or some kind of spell on it. There was no way to know without opening it, and she didn't want to do that without Hernandez on hand to check for explosives, Keith or Brian to check for a bug, and Larry to check for spells. But taking it to them seemed like exactly the intention of whoever had tampered with it.

"Would you mind if we took a quick look at the footage right here?" she asked and stepped in front of her team. If it was a bomb, at the very least she could turn her steel skin on and protect them.

"I really can't. Very busy. Quite busy." Williams began to sweat even more profusely now.

"The sooner you do it, the sooner we're gone," she said and nudged him with her aura to make him fear her. Maybe if she could make him scared of her, he'd acquiesce and send them on their way. She didn't push too hard, though. This man didn't seem to be guilty of anything other than being terrified, and she didn't want to harm his mind the way she had General Andrews'.

It wasn't much of a surprise when he accepted the drive, took two steps toward his computer, and stopped. "I can't." His voice was barely a whisper. "They'll know."

"Who will know?" Kristen asked and tried to make her aura show him that telling them would make him feel safer. It didn't quite work because she didn't have the kind of control of her aura she needed to make someone feel such a complex emotion.

Instead, he trembled visibly where he stood, frozen between wanting to get rid of her and the drive and his fear of whoever instigated this. "Them. You know—*them*," Williams finally managed to say, his tone low and rough.

"Tell us who, and we'll be on our way."

"I don't know their names!" His voice rose from a shrill whisper to a shriek. "But I know they're watching."

It could only be the mages then. Who else could it be? But if they had been there, it meant they knew about her presence in the city and what she was investigating. Were they scared of what the footage was or was this merely an attempt to harm her and her team? Logically, such an attempt would have been more easily accomplished with a roadside bomb or something like that. Why let them come all the way up there unless the footage itself was dangerous?

It might have been a bad decision, but she took the hard drive.

Williams's relief was palpable.

"Thank you, ma'am. Truly."

They stepped into the stairway that led to the office and she closed her hand around the device.

"It has to be a bomb," Drew said.

"Probably. Or something worse," Kristen muttered in response. "Amy. Can you make a shield to protect those offices? I don't want anyone to get hurt if this thing goes off."

"You got it, boss."

"Can you tell if it's magical at all?"

"No, I can't. I don't know much about detecting yet, but Larry could, I'm sure."

"We can't risk going out there. Detonating it when we get into the car would make the most sense."

"So you want to sit here?" Drew asked.

"No." She shook her head. "They must be nearby. If we take too long, I'll bet they activate whatever it is." Thinking quickly, she came up with as much of a plan as she could. "Drew and Jim, get to the car and call Stonequest. Tell him to bring Brian and Hernandez. I want this data and I don't want to be blown up to get it. Go down now. I want our enemies to see someone come out of the building."

"You know they might blow this—" he protested but she cut him short.

"I know. Just go. Amy, keep a shield on the door to that office. Can you do that while you go down the stairs?"

"Yes, but I won't leave you to be blown to pieces."

"I'll be fine, just go."

The girl started down the stairs behind everyone else. While she descended, Kristen looked for somewhere to stash the hard drive.

She finally settled on a location behind a large, potted ficus tree. If they were wrong about it being a bomb, no one was likely to notice the device there. But if they were right, she realized it wouldn't matter.

Kristen was about to head down the stairs when she realized that she couldn't simply leave it here. This building had businesses and apartments in it. If she left and the mages had indeed planted an explosive, people would die. She couldn't allow that.

But she couldn't be caught by the blast either. She'd learned the hard way that the technomages used pieces of dragon in some of their bombs. An incendiary device laden with dragon-scale shrapnel could kill her.

"Kristen, the guys are in the car. What are you doing?" Amy whispered from the stairwell.

"I'm making sure this doesn't hurt anyone. Can you keep it contained?"

The girl ground her teeth. "I can try,"

"Okay, keep trying." She removed her bulletproof vest and transformed to steel. If the device had dragon shards in it, her steel skin wouldn't protect her, but the bulletproof vest and Amy's shield might do the job.

Cautiously, she approached the hard drive still tucked behind the ficus and scooped it up to wrap it in the vest. Hopefully, that would contain any shrapnel. Now, if Amy could make sure the blast didn't blow up the offices, they could get whatever footage they needed after it exploded.

There were times when Kristen hated being right. As a girl, she had loved it when she'd outsmarted her older brother or demonstrated a tidbit of knowledge to her mom that she hadn't known. Now, though, she would have been more than okay about being wrong about the hard drive being a bomb.

Unfortunately for her, she was proven correct as the device detonated in her hand. Fortunately, she had also been correct that the vest would contain any shrapnel. Not only that, but Amy had been able to strengthen her shield on the side of the bomb closer to the offices.

Less fortunate was that the force of the explosion was still strong enough to hurl the Steel Dragon through a wall and out into the street below.

She pounded onto the cobblestones and her steel skin did more to damage the street than the landing had done to her. The target had been the information, then, and perhaps some of her human allies. She didn't think the hard drive had been loaded with dragon shrapnel because she found that the bulletproof vest had indeed been shredded by the explosive. Despite this, she felt none of the tell-tale pain that would accompany shards of dragon embedded in her body.

Kristen stood and noticed that she had barely managed to avoid impacting the roof of the armored car. Her friends were inside, still safe and unhurt as the vehicle had shielded them from any falling glass or brick from the explosion.

Now, all they had to do was go back into the office and demand the manager's computer to get the actual footage. She signaled for her team to get out of the car and they complied with stupid grins on their faces.

"That was crazy," Jim said and looked proud.

"And stupid," Larry protested. "You should've made Amy send it skyward. It would've blown up high enough not to hurt anyone."

"Yeah, but this way, the mages might think they got us—unless they're watching right now."

Of course, their enemies were watching. Kristen knew this because as soon as all her friends had stepped out of the easily defensible bulletproof car, it was dragged away from them as if some invisible claw had taken hold of it.

In the next moment, gunfire erupted.

CHAPTER ELEVEN

"What's the plan, boss?" Drew asked once he'd taken cover under the stone arch that framed the doorway to an apartment building.

Kristen had to wait for the gunshots to subside before she could answer.

"Let me try something," she shouted in response and sprinted to the door of the building she had been blown out of. As soon as she headed toward it, a barrage of gunshots let loose on the street and forced her to dive behind cover. It was exactly as she'd suspected then. "These assholes really don't want us to get that footage."

"Let me guess—your plan is to go get it?" Jim called. He'd managed to remain hunkered behind the car when the mages moved it and used its bulletproof armor to protect himself behind an open door.

"Larry, Amy, how are we doing?" Kristen yelled at the two mages.

"I'm fine," she replied from the stairwell.

"Me less so," Larry replied from the front seat of the car. How he'd managed to dive inside it was a mystery on top of a miracle, but at least he hadn't been shot.

"Amy, can you get a shield over Larry so he can join us here?"

Kristen asked. He could probably have done it himself, but he sounded a little shaken and she didn't want him to be distracted.

"Yes, ma'am!" Amy hurried down the steps and extended her hands once she was beside her, and a sphere of shimmering blue energy surrounded the other mage. He knew exactly what that meant and didn't waste any time. His head low, he flung himself out of the vehicle and raced toward them as the mages opened fire on him.

Kristen was able to count four of them—two on the ground and two on rooftops. "I have four hostiles."

"We see them," Drew responded from his alcove.

"I have a shot," Jim said and squeezed off a few rounds from his pistol. No one carried anything more than a handgun as they hadn't expected anyone to know they were there yet and walking around with two-handed weapons seemed a little extreme. Now, that felt like the epitome of naivete.

His shots prevented the two mages on the ground from approaching, but that was the limit of their effectiveness.

"Keep them occupied," she shouted as she pulled her phone out and dialed Stonequest.

Brian picked the phone up. "Hey, Krissy, Stone's driving—are those gunshots?" He went from sounding amused to terrified in the span of a single heartbeat.

"Yes."

"I think Kristen wants us to go to the headquarters!" Brian shouted to Stonequest.

"No! Tell Stonequest we're under fire and that when he gets here to go in the back with you and get the manager's computer. Take the whole damn thing if that's faster than simply getting the data."

"You want me to go in there?" he demanded, his voice an octave higher than usual. She could hear the echo of gunshots from his side of the connection, which meant they were close.

"I didn't want you to be here but you are, so now, I need you to go in. Stonequest doesn't know anything about computers. He might snag a microwave and think he has the data."

"I heard that!" the dragon said. "But she's not wrong." When car doors slammed, she knew they were at the back of the building.

"Make sure you get Brian back safely," Kristen shouted warningly.

"Kristen says to keep me safe or she'll rip you a new asshole."

"Protect yourself. I got the kid," Stonequest yelled so she could hear before the line went dead. He could no doubt hear the shots being fired and knew the conversation was over. It was time for her to escalate the distraction.

Now that she knew the mission was still on, she needed to direct all her focus to the task at hand. She poked her head out and used her dragon speed and senses to get a look at the four hostiles before they opened fire on her. About a third of a second passed before a volley of bullets was directed at her head. The attack answered one question anyway. Their primary target was the Steel Dragon, although that was hardly surprising.

Despite the fact that the mages had released their fusillade so quickly, she'd had enough time to see the four shooters. Unfortunately, she hadn't been able to see their faces as they all wore masks.

They had fired at her with pistols rather than rifles. It was a tiny comfort to not be outgunned, but given that they were all still alive, it wasn't a particularly surprising truth.

The two groups exchanged fire for perhaps thirty seconds before Kristen gestured for Drew and Larry to cover Jim so he could find a better position. They all opened fire—the two of them with bullets and the mage with glowing blasts of magic—while the Wonderkid scurried from the alcove he'd taken cover in to another one.

Kristen and Drew tucked into their shelter again, while the mages concentrated their attack on Larry. Apparently, they hadn't anticipated fighting a mage and he had drawn their ire at the fact that they had to face one. That anger proved to be a mistake, however. While they focused on their quarry, Jim made a lucky shot that eliminated one of the two on the ground whose ski mask had a skull on the face.

"Good shooting," she called as the wounded mage dragged himself to cover. He wasn't dead but appeared to be out of the fight.

She took a moment to assess their surroundings. While she had only hoped to hold the technomages in a standoff, now that they'd disabled one, she sensed victory. "Let's push this and make Brian and Stonequest feel like they missed out by getting the computer," she ordered.

It seemed they weren't the only ones interested in escalating the stakes of the conflict, though. From the end of the street, a cab careened toward them at breakneck speed.

"Amy! Now would be the time to flip something into the river," she shouted.

"What do you think I'm trying to do?" the girl said, her hands outstretched and teeth gritted. "It's like I can't get a hold of it!"

"Then get us out of here!" Kristen shouted and her companion obeyed without protest.

The young mage enveloped Kristen, Larry, and herself in an orb of energy and lifted them out of the entrance to the building as the taxi powered into it.

A small explosion followed when some of the gasoline inside the car reacted, but the force of the vehicle was still enough to crumble the face of the building.

Shots pursued them as Amy carried them across the street to land behind a delivery truck. It was from this new vantage point that Kristen saw who had sent the vehicle toward them.

That the masked figure was a mage was obvious. He floated above a bed of flame and wore a ski mask that completely covered his face with the image of a crown. When he landed in the middle of the street, the other mage at street level—this one with a bunny mask— came to stand beside him. Another mage who must have just arrived joined them.

The newcomer wore a long black coat like the rest of them and a ski mask with the image of a flower on the face. She was obviously a woman as she wore a black skirt under the coat.

"Traitors!" the man yelled before he scowled at his fire and extinguished it. Curls of smoke rose around him.

"It's great to have you admit to it," Jim retorted and the mage on the roof across the street opened fire at him as if to tell him to shut up.

"The Steel Dragon can't help but betray mankind. It's in her nature. But you mages should know better. Join us and help usher in a new era where mages rule instead of dragons."

In response, Larry threw a ball of energy at the man with the crown mask.

Rather than using a shield to block it, he batted it away with the back of his hand. It veered away and into a building with a bright explosion.

"The bastard's strong," Larry muttered. "I tried to make that blow up as soon as it touched him, but he was able to contain it."

"Do you think he's something like their Constance?" Kristen asked.

He shrugged. "It's too soon to tell and he seems to like fire while she liked wind, but he has to be their strongest one."

"I guess you've made your pathetic little decision," the mage said and released a great blast of flame from his hands.

Amy stepped out from cover and threw a wall up in front of them. The flames bulldozed into it and she had to take a step back, but her shield held. It helped that she had come into her magic by withstanding the fire breath of a dragon. Her powers were literally born in fire.

The blaze pushed against her wall and seemed to try to almost burrow inside the barrier, but the young mage remained strong. Kristen couldn't help but wonder what would have happened if she and Larry still wore their old bracelets. Bad things, most likely.

Apparently, their adversaries took her shield as a challenge as they opened fire as one. The two on the roof were each armed with a gun but the three on the road hurled blasts of magical energy.

"We need to move," Kristen said and her old combat skills clicked in. Remaining in one place in a gunfight was a great way to get shot.

Drew and Jim seemed to understand her and the mages' predicament and opened fire as well. Their volley prompted the one with the bunny mask to block their bullets with a magical shield.

Amy used the opportunity to levitate onto a roof, where she proceeded to lift stones from the wreckage the taxi had caused and hurl them at her enemies.

Larry focused on much flashier magic, but Kristen realized that it wasn't nearly as strong as either Amy's or the enemy leader's. It was bright, flashy, and distracting, but it didn't seem to pack much of a punch. She didn't know if that was simply the extent of his powers or if he had been handicapped for so long that he didn't know what else to do.

It didn't matter in their current situation, however. The two mages could block the bolts of energy easily enough. While they focused on that, she needed to protect her humans.

She raced forward with a burst of dragon speed and slid to a stop in the same alcove as Drew. She'd almost been struck multiple times and hadn't been able to fire a shot off. The logical assumption was that these were dragon bullets, so she had to play it safe.

"I feel useless out here," she told Drew in growing frustration. "If I took my dragon form, I could eliminate them all."

"You'd be a massive target. It's not worth the risk," he responded.

"But—"

"I spent hours of damned time training you how to be an expert as a human, even without your powers. If you start bitching about not being able to turn into a dragon, I'll tell Hernandez."

"Right, sorry," she replied hastily. "Do you have a plan?"

He darted out and took a few shots at the enemy leader, who hovered in a position where he could target Amy. She was able to deflect the balls of fire he launched at her either with stones or walls of force. The stones that were struck by fire, she hurled back at the mage.

"She has him covered. We need to get Jim to the high ground. Let's make a dash to the car and give him the time to get to a rooftop. We need to stop those two shooters up there."

It was crazy, but Kristen loved it.

They darted from cover as Larry delivered streaks of energy past them and Amy distracted the mage leader. They reached the vehicle and opened a door to use as cover but immediately, found the space to be woefully inadequate. The airborne leader merely had to land behind them to be able to take them out.

Fortunately, he didn't have time to do so as Jim had reached the roof. A string of gunshots rang out and a mage cried in pain as he tumbled from the roof and through the branches of a tree to fall heavily onto the street. He tried to push up but collapsed, although it wasn't clear if he was dead or badly wounded.

The mage with the bunny mask released a stream of sparks into the air that must have been some kind of code. As soon as she did so, the behavior of her team changed.

The second shooter who had been on the roof across the street jumped and slowed his fall with magic seconds before he made impact. His mask carried the face of a ram and together, he and his teammate with the floral mask lifted the mage who had been injured earlier and carried him away from the battlefield.

The bunny-masked individual ran to the mage who had fallen off the rooftop—who wore a ski mask with the screen-printed face of a gorilla—lifted him in her arms, and followed the other two.

That left only the leader. He continued to battle Amy but wasn't throwing as many fireballs at her. In fact, he only used one hand as his other held a ball of flame that glowed brighter and brighter with each second until soon, it looked like a miniature sun.

"Heads up!" the girl shouted as he lobbed the sphere. It didn't seek out a target as Kristen had expected. Instead, it careened above the rooftops and exploded in a blinding flash.

The Steel Dragon raised her hands faster than anyone else—it helped having dragon reflexes—so she wasn't blinded like the rest of her team was.

She prepared herself to fight the four uninjured mages alone, not a good prospect, but as it turned out, she didn't need to. They raced down an alley and vanished into the streets of Florence.

"Should we give chase?" Amy asked and sounded eager.

"Jim?" Drew called out.

"I'm hit," he responded. "Not bad, but...shit, I need a doctor."

They heard him sit heavily on top of the building he was on. Drew raced away to help him.

"No, no chase," she said to the young mage. "With any luck, the computer they tried to protect has information about one of them we can use."

"Okay," Amy said and joined the team.

Kristen took her phone out and called Stonequest. "We're coming up. I think the fight is over for now."

CHAPTER TWELVE

Kristen thought through the implications of what had happened as she worked to clear the rubble in the stairway to the manager's office. Between the explosion and the taxi, the building was a mess. Amy had said she could do it, but she had refused. She thought better when she was moving and besides, without Amy, Drew and Jim would likely have been cooked.

Hell, she might have been cooked too. Despite being a dragon, she didn't know much about mage fire. It didn't seem too far of a stretch to imagine that a mage with a grudge against dragons would develop the skill to the point where it would be able to hurt their sworn foes.

First, the good news, she thought as she moved brick and stone aside. She thought they were probably only facing a force of six, and two were injured. If the group was larger, they wouldn't have been so concerned when two of them were wounded. Plus, six fit with the murders. Constance had always acted alone, and Kristen thought it reasonable to assume that mages from the cells were trained that way. It meant five assassins plus one in charge, obviously the mage with the crown mask and the fire powers. Injuring two of six was good, she told herself, but she didn't feel it.

The bad news needed to be examined as well. The mages were

well-connected and well-organized. Somehow, they had known she and her team were here. They'd tailed her through the city—she now had no doubt that the car had belonged to them—and been able to maintain their surveillance even after they thought they'd ditched them. That meant they were an organized, efficient team. It also meant—little though she wanted to think about it—that they might have someone working for them on the inside of dragon society.

She had seen it before. In fact, Constance had been working with a dragon when Kristen had first battled her. Maybe another dragon played a similar role here. It would certainly explain how someone knew about them. But who? Rosso? He'd been gruff with them but she shook her head. She was jumping at shadows but how else could they have known they were there?

They'd entered immediately once they'd parked. Except...no, that wasn't entirely accurate.

"Has anyone seen the old woman who asked me to bless her candle?"

Everyone shook their heads.

That gave her pause. Maybe they'd somehow put her there as a distraction? If so, it meant the mages were incredibly well-organized. Still, it seemed like more jumping at shadows. She would have to ask Stonequest what he thought.

When she'd finally cleared the stairway, she proceeded to the second floor. The landing was a wreck—after all, a bomb had detonated there—but the wall with the door to the office was undamaged. Amy had protected it well.

Too bad Kristen simply kicked it in.

The door splintered in the middle and ripped the hinges off the wall as it catapulted inward. It might have knocked the manager over if Stonequest hadn't been in the way. He thrust it aside as if it were nothing but a fly buzzing near his head.

Brian, meanwhile, dove for cover behind the desk.

"Ah, Lady Hall." The dragon smiled malevolently at the manager. "I see you're finished downstairs."

"Indeed," she responded, caught the man by the lapels, and lifted him off his feet. In all honesty, she hadn't meant to lift him, but now that he was in the air...well, it wouldn't hurt to let him dangle a while to show him she was serious. It wasn't like he was choking or anything. "Who came in here before we did?"

"I d-d-d-don't know I s-s-s-swear!" Williams stammered.

"Tell her," Stonequest said and flexed his aura over the man. She might have balked at how quickly and almost casually he had done this—she still hated using those powers on a human mind, while he had no such compunctions—but the results were immediate. The dragon immediately relented and left the man scared but not broken.

"It was some asshole! That's all I know. A mage, definitely a mage. He said he'd set me on fire if I didn't do as he asked."

"What was that?"

"He said when you got here that I should hand over the hard drive I gave you."

Kristen nodded, although it wasn't terribly compelling evidence. It was obvious that if she went to the sound engineer's building after no doubt talking to the dragon performer, she'd want footage. All that proved was that the mages were smart.

"What else did they make you do?" she asked.

"He watched while I deleted all the footage from my computer. Speaking of which, Vert will be *pissed.*" There was despair in William's voice at the mention of the green dragon performer's displeasure.

"I think that's all he has," Stonequest said to her. She believed him. He was a better judge of auras than she was and had been interrogating witnesses—human, dragon, and mage—for a long time.

"I keep looking for a clue from them, but I feel like we always come up with nothing," she muttered.

"It doesn't seem like much of a trail to follow to me," he said. "And I bet if you had pursued them, you would have walked right into a trap."

"I can't help but feel like these guys are good. As good as Constance and much better at remaining hidden."

"Eh. Not that good," Brian said and sounded smug.

"What do you have, Zed?" she asked her brother.

He blushed at the use of the codename but hearing it did cause him to straighten his posture and pull his gut in.

"I got into this guy's computer. His password was Vertpaysthebill$? Really?" He looked at Williams in mock-disbelief. "You realize you said that to me and Stonequest, right?"

"I read an online article not to use pet names," the man muttered and sounded completely dejected.

"He deleted all the videos"—Brian gestured to Williams—"but he never reformatted the drive."

"English, please," Kristen replied. "Can you get them back or not?"

"Are you kidding? This is a piece of cake." He worked for a minute, retrieved his personal hard drive, and plugged it into the computer. "They're downloading as we speak. I need about...six minutes. Five and a half."

"Is there much there?" she asked.

"Oh yeah." He nodded.

She flashed him her most sisterly smile. "I am *so glad* we have such a great computer expert."

He had known her long enough for her words and tone to spark immediate suspicion. "Why are you complimenting me right now?"

"Because you'll be in charge of searching through all that video data for any sign of these assassins."

Brian groaned like she had managed to sneak her Brussel sprouts onto his plate without their parents noticing. "That's like..." He looked at his screen and clicked a few times, and his face fell. "That's like hundreds of hours of footage."

"And what's great is that I'm sure you understand that you don't have hundreds of hours to look at all of it. As soon as you have the data, we'll get you to Castillo Montalbano and you can get to work." She turned to the rest of her team. "Right now, this footage is our only lead. They all wore those weird masks, so unless anyone disagrees, I don't see much point in looking through any CCTV footage."

No one objected, another instance in which she wished she wasn't right.

After a few minutes, Brian had his data and it was time to return to base.

"Come on, kid, you can ride on my back while I fly to base," Stonequest said to him and moved toward the stairs to the roof.

"Hold up, Stonequest," Kristen said. "You came here in a car and you need to go back by car."

"What? Why?" The dragon sounded frustrated. He didn't often sound frustrated and that he did now sent a chill down her spine. "They know we're here now, obviously, because of this attack. What's the point in keeping a low profile?"

She clenched her jaw at this. It was another instance of the old dragon stereotypes toward humans coming out, and she reminded herself that change took time. He was so much better, but this wasn't the moment to entertain dangerous assumptions. "Because one of these mages presumably shot a dragon out of the air over Paris with a sniper rifle. If so, we have to assume they have an arsenal as extensive and dangerous as Constance's. Your dragon form is an easy target for them."

"Goddammit." He ground his teeth.

"Is that a problem?" Kristen asked.

"You're goddamn right it's a problem," Stonequest grumbled. "But that doesn't mean you're wrong. I guess if I get in a fight, I shouldn't transform into a dragon either."

"No, you shouldn't," she agreed. "I understand that you're more accustomed to your dragon form—I know all of Dragon SWAT is— but it will put you in grave danger. Remember that these mages have trained for years to face dragons. At the very least, we can assume our breath attacks won't do anything to them. On top of that, they're armed with dragon bullets, which—"

"I know all too well what it feels like to be hit by one of those damn things," he said and rubbed his shoulder.

"Will you be all right?"

He hesitated but nodded. "I guess I have to be. I've never been in a situation like this before—where my dragon form is weaker than my human one. It...it doesn't seem right."

"There's nothing right with these mages harvesting dragon bodies to use as bullets. But that doesn't mean we shouldn't be careful."

"Sure. Brian, do you want a ride?"

"Actually, I think we'll all take one," Kristen said. "Our car was badly damaged in the fight."

Stonequest nodded and no one complained until they all had to cram into one vehicle.

She hadn't been in a car this full of people since high school. Back then, she had found it hilarious and exhilarating—the press of bodies, the driver laughing, and everyone jostling and giggling as they drove home from school.

Now, it had none of that charm. As they drove, she couldn't help but feel that if they were attacked, no one would be able to reach their weapons in time. They would be roasted alive in this glorified can of sardines while their foe continued to outmaneuver them.

It was not a pleasant trip.

CHAPTER THIRTEEN

The journey was uncomfortable, but they arrived at Castillo Montalbano without another attack, which was a huge relief. Kristen would have suffered any amount of discomfort if it meant keeping her team safe. Sometimes, she found it cosmically ironic that the people she wanted to protect the most were people who made their living risking their lives for others. Until recently, she had at least been able to tell herself that her family could avoid danger, but with Brian now working for her, that was no longer true.

She only hoped her parents were enjoying their so-called vacation.

They scrambled out of the car and passed two dragon guards and two mages as they entered the building. It was a small comfort that at least this division of SWAT took their security seriously. They seemed to police their perimeter better than Detroit Dragon SWAT ever did.

"It'll take me a while to process all this on my laptop," Brian said to Kristen apologetically.

"I thought you said that you'd slaved it to the other computers back home?"

"I did, but that connection has to go through a satellite relay now, which causes a delay and will severely limit my processing power."

"Are you saying you need a local computer set up here?" Stonequest asked.

"Ideally, yes."

"Come with me. They have a great one here. At least I think they do. Computers aren't my thing." He gestured for the young man to follow and the two of them walked past the guards and deeper into the complex as if they belonged here. Too bad the European Dragon SWAT didn't treat the rest of her team as well.

Rosso and La Flamme strode toward them before they could leave the entryway and disperse through the building.

"What is the meaning of this?" the former demanded. He looked quite angry. La Flamme, on the other hand, didn't look angry, only profoundly uncomfortable. His gaze flicked continuously from Larry to Amy.

Kristen had a suspicion this wasn't about the mages who had attacked them. "I'm sorry about the collateral damage. We didn't think the mages knew we were here yet. I would have briefed my team on less damaging tactics if we had known. It won't happen again if we can help it."

As she had expected, that wasn't the focus of his fury. "And what tactics could you teach to these two?" He gestured at the two mages. "There were rumors that you have uncuffed mages on your team, but I never believed it."

"Yeah. Well, don't," Amy muttered and stuck her hand out with what appeared to be a magic-dampening bracelet on it.

La Flamme took her hand and examined the cuff. If it was a little rough for Amy's taste, she didn't say anything, which both made Kristen proud for her controlling her anger and pissed that the man was touching her mage.

"What exactly is the problem here?" she asked. It wasn't advisable for La Flamme to examine the counterfeit bracelets any longer than necessary.

"The problem is that these mages exhibited considerable power out there," Rosso said.

"And how exactly do you know this?" she demanded.

"Because we have back doors into almost every camera in this city. We saw the entire fight on camera. There is no sense denying it. You had power as strong or stronger than the leader of the enemy mages. What have you done to circumvent your bracelets?"

"We didn't do anything," Amy said quite petulantly.

Kristen appreciated the technically true argument but knew it wouldn't hold for long.

"Then who did? The mages we are trying to stop? A cuffed mage should not have that kind of power, period." Rosso's voice rose in pitch and filled with fury.

"If they hadn't been there to help us, we'd be dead," Drew said. "It was the mages who kept us alive."

"How do you know it was not the mages who told the enemy where you were?" La Flamme asked in heavily accented English.

"La Flamme is right," the Italian said quickly. "It seems we have a leak. How else could a mage get through their bracelets if they were not allied with the enemy?"

"I'm sure there's another explanation for this," Kristen said, a weak justification even to her. She had only now obtained the cuffs for her mages after a fairly long wait. While she had hoped the deception would last for some time—ideally until the technomages had been stopped—that seemed less and less likely.

"Another explanation for how these two circumvented dragon law?" Rosso asked and his smug expression confirmed her suspicion that he must have looked the English word up before talking to them. "Even if they are not in league with the enemy, this means they might as well be. It was unfettered mages who started the first age rebellion —and the second. It's unfettered mages who are attacking dragons across the world right now. Even if they found out a way around the bracelets on their own, it only shows contempt for dragon law. Sooner or later, they will turn against their master."

"No. I assure you, they won't." She knew this was not the time to try to argue that she didn't want to be their master at all and that she respected them as cool-headed individuals who were as committed to justice as she was. Those opinions might not go over too well with

Rosso's current line of reasoning. "I trust them both. Amy has shown no reason to not trust her, and Larry worked with Investigator Windlock for years. They're on our side."

"You can't know that!" he protested.

"You saw their power," Kristen said. "What they could do. If they wanted to kill me, they could have done so already a hundred times over. If they were against us, why would Amy have worked so hard to stop the one with the crown?"

"Crown?" Rosso asked skeptically.

"Their leader had a mask of a crown. It doesn't matter. The point is, they could have hurt me many times before and they haven't. I trust them completely and you can too."

The man shook his head. "It is impossible to understand the workings of a spy. Sometimes, they must fight against their loyalties—even kill—to prove themselves to their target. How else could the mages have known you were here?"

That was too much for Kristen. "If you think there's a spy, I suggest you start looking inside this castle, not on my goddamn team. There's no way any of my people are working against me. I would know."

"You couldn't possibly—"

"And you can?" she demanded.

"No one on our team circumvented the rules on controlling mages during a conflict with unfettered mages," Rosso said, his words like daggers.

Frustrated, she clenched her teeth. She'd tried to keep her little secret but could see now that she had been wrong to attempt to deceive anyone. Which suited her fine. The more she came to understand dragon culture and societal norms, the fewer shits she gave about respecting all their nonsense. There was so much good in them to be respected and sometimes, even admired, but they could infuriate her beyond belief with their obstinacy. Not, she reminded herself, unlike some humans she knew.

"Do you want to know how they circumvented the damn

bracelets? Fine." She snapped both Amy and Larry's bracelets with deft movements.

Rosso and La Flamme gasped but weren't so shocked as to drop them when she tossed them to them. "But…but they are fakes!" Rosso said.

"I know they are. I was the one who commissioned them to be crafted," she explained.

"Illegal!" the Frenchman objected.

"If I hadn't, half my team would have died out there on the street today. If we handicap our mages, it means losing a huge chunk of their effectiveness, don't you see? We have to trust our people. That's why I gave them the bracelets—to give you time to trust them."

La Flamme began to yell at her in French and she decided she was quite all right with Stonequest not being there and the words going untranslated.

"You can keep them, how about that?" Kristen snapped at the two dragons. "I won't make them wear fake cuffs. I can see it scrambled your reason—both of you—which I should have realized it would. It was a stupid idea to try to protect you from confronting your own misguided beliefs. Does that satisfy you?"

"Absolutely not!" Rosso shouted and stepped toward the mages, but she had heard quite enough.

"Then what should we do about it?" she demanded and stepped in front of him before he could get any closer to Amy.

"I… That is, she—"

"Is my mage, at least by your stupid rules, correct?"

"That is true, yes."

"Then come to me if you have a problem with the way I operate. But if you want us to stop these assholes from killing dragons on your continent, stay the fuck out of my way."

The two dragons bristled at that and looked like they both intended to respond vociferously. Heartsbane and Emerald came down the stairs before they could, however.

"Is everything all right boss?" Heartsbane asked. "From the auras, it seems like a few dragons here have their panties all knotted up."

Emerald nodded.

Rosso and La Flamme looked from Kristen's dragons to her mages, and finally, to Jim and Drew who—despite only being regular humans —looked like they were more than ready to start a fistfight with them. The two European dragons didn't look happy about it, but they did look intimidated enough to stop pestering them for now.

While she recognized their acquiescence, as reluctant as it was, she didn't want them to think she was some kind of upstart from another country there to lord it over them. She had orders from their boss and was more than willing to let them know it.

"If you have a problem with the way I do things, why not let Shimmerclaw know how things stand? I'm sure she'd love a report. Make sure you include all your complaints—and if you don't mind explaining how the hell these mages already knew we were here, that would be great too."

Invoking Shimmerclaw felt like calling the teacher in a playground scrap, but it worked. Rosso and La Flamme capitulated, although neither looked particularly happy.

CHAPTER FOURTEEN

Despite the two European dragons ostensibly standing down, Kristen had no intention to let them try to cuff her mages as soon as their argument was over. She escorted Larry and Amy to their level and told herself that spending a few minutes with them would help her nerves. But, if anything, the result was the opposite because although she had asked for everyone to be situated close together within the complex, the mages had yet to be moved closer to the dragons.

She hadn't protested this because of the sheer opulence of her room. Her somewhat naïve assumption had been that the reason the mages had yet to be moved was simply because it took time to prepare a room as perfectly as hers had been. It was decorated with art—originals dating from the renaissance by masters so famous even she had heard of them—and the comforts were beyond decadent. The bedding was hand-dyed silk. The chairs were gorgeous antiques that had once belonged to princes. Even the bowl of fruit contained delicacies from all over the continent. She understood that one couldn't exactly whip up another room like that, but after she saw where the mages were staying, she wished the dragons had at least tried.

It was like day and night. Where her room had a private bathroom and kitchenette, the mages shared one. While the television in her room was as modern as any she had ever seen, theirs had a corner of badly burned-out pixels. Amy led her to her room to show her rough cotton sheets, a poorly made chair that looked like it had been uncomfortable even when it had been new, and bland walls. It wasn't dirty, which was good, and didn't look dangerous or anything like that, but compared to what she'd been given, it was quite spartan. Her space was easily ten times bigger and she had a feeling that the dragons who stayed there permanently probably had even nicer rooms.

"This is where they have put you?" Kristen asked. She couldn't help the question any more than she could keep the disdain out of her voice and reminded herself of her mom when she'd first seen the dorm in college. The mages' situation was about on par with dorm living. "I can't believe they make you sleep here and have the audacity to treat you like they did down there."

"Aw, this ain't so bad," Larry said. "I've traveled with Windlock— well, I used to…" It took Larry the briefest moment to gather his feelings again, and she wondered how long he would have to do that when he spoke about his old boss. "Okay, I've seen better places, but I've seen worse as well. I'd say this is about on par and maybe a little nicer. The sheets are clean and they have the fridge stocked, which is a nice gesture."

"This is nice?" she asked.

"Well, sure," the mage replied and seemed to relish her discomfort. "Dragons make sure we mages are fairly well cared for. I think they see us like expensive cars. You gotta make sure to refuel us, keep us clean, and out of the rain." He chuckled. "But at the same time, you don't need to keep your Rolls Royce in the living room. Even the nicest cars get mud on the wheels. I don't think most dragons spend too much time thinking about our feelings and all that."

"They most certainly do care about our feelings," a woman wearing mage robes said as she approached. She spoke in a British accent and had face tattoos that hopefully augmented her power as they didn't do much for her look.

He shrugged, never one to shy away from conflict. "I guess. I saw the wine they have downstairs. It's a couple of decades older than what they have up here."

"At least they give us wine," the woman protested sharply. "They don't have to do anything but pay us a wage. We're lucky to stay here. We don't pay rent, you know. At least we didn't."

"Hi. I'm Amy, and what was that supposed to mean?" the girl said and extended her hand to the mage.

"Charm is my mage name," the newcomer said and took her hand. "But I suppose you can call me Priscilla, Amy. It's nice to meet you. Even if you are walking around here practically naked."

"What?" Amy asked, obviously confused until she saw that Priscilla quite pointedly looked at her wrist, sans bracelet.

"I heard what happened downstairs. You two had fake cuffs?"

"Yup." The young mage beamed and nodded at Kristen. "She gave them to us."

"Ah...pardon my interruption then." Priscilla visibly deflated when she saw that the Steel Dragon herself was responsible for the breach in protocol.

"Is there a problem?" Kristen asked. "I thought mages would be pleased to see a dragon trusting them to use their full powers."

"As you say, my lady." The woman bowed formally, her expression unreadable.

"No, no fuck that. Tell me what you're actually thinking. I don't do this deference to dragons bullshit."

Priscilla looked quite affronted when she dropped her F-bomb but uttered a guffaw when she said bullshit.

"Well, I can see I don't need to stand on formality with you."

"No, but I would appreciate it if you would tell me why showing respect to these people is a problem."

"Well...some of us... That is, I've heard—"

"Out with it!"

"Some of us are worried that now you have let your mages 'off the leash,' so to speak, the local dragons might watch their mages more carefully. Not that any of us are unfettered," she was quick to add. "I don't think anyone here would dream of such a thing. To break such tradition seems a very American thing indeed. It's simply…well…"

"You've said all that so say the rest," Kristen told her, both amused and annoyed with her hesitation. It was good the woman was saying something but a pity she was so frightened of her.

"It might make our lives a little harder is all." Priscilla avoided eye contact as she said this and fixed her gaze on the floor, no doubt as she had been trained.

"I'm sorry if I've already caused you problems and I don't see how I can promise to help you once we leave, but I don't have any other choice. I need my people at full strength so we can confront and hopefully defeat these technomages," she explained, feeling somewhat guilty but knowing she didn't have a choice. This was life and death. Period.

"It merely seems rather extreme," the woman managed.

"We live in extreme times," Kristen said. "These two saved lives today. Without their full power, some of my people would have died."

"Yes, well…I guess I hope you catch them, then. I want everything to go back to normal."

"I don't know how soon that'll happen," She saw that her words only made Priscilla feel worse, so she decided to change tactics. After all, they were stuck until Brian found something. "But surely it can't be that unusual to see a mage uncuffed. What happens when you retire?"

She wasn't proud of asking a question she thought she knew the answer to, but it seemed the gentlest way to go about learning more about mage culture.

"Retire?"

Her jaw tightened reflexively. That was about what she'd expected. "Do you mean you never retire?"

The mage tittered nervously as if she could laugh away the idea—or had been taught to try to do so, anyway. "Why would we ever stop serving in such an illustrious and honorable position?"

"Mages don't retire," Larry told her in low tones. "The term of service is for life. It's not a bad life, I'd say, especially if we're lucky enough to get a good dragon like Windlock or you. That's what we hope for as mages."

"So you've all accepted a life without freedom," Amy said bitterly. "And you merely hope to have a decent master?"

"I'd say Windlock was better than decent," he countered. "And Kristen is good other than the making us risk our lives every damn day thing."

"I never said you had to work for me," she reminded him.

Larry shrugged. "What could I do, go freelance? I'd have been executed within a week."

"But...but that's practically slavery!" Kristen was appalled. Of course, it wasn't a surprise and she'd had similar discussions with her mages and a few dragons. Mostly, she had learned to temper her reflexive judgment and reminded herself that change took time and that both humans and dragons needed to adjust their attitudes and perceptions. Still, at times like these, some of her instinctual protests against injustice pushed through her control and common sense.

"We get paid quite well," Priscilla said after another bout of her nervous laughter.

"But you can't spend it on whatever you want. You can't spend it on a retirement home," Kristen said.

"It's no wonder the mages form terrorist cells and try to rebel," Amy muttered.

"No kidding," she agreed. "I could possibly convince myself that dragons rule humanity with a relatively light claw—most of them, anyway—but it seems they have their tails wrapped around the throats of the mages of the world."

"That's not quite true," Priscilla said loudly as she looked around to see if such a seditious conversation was being overheard.

Larry looked glum but he nodded. "It kind of is, though. Free mages need to hide and flee. They live in fear, knowing that at any moment, a dragon could swoop down and kill them."

"Or they can dedicate themselves to a life of service to the noble dragons," the woman said, but even after talking to her for such a short amount of time, Kristen could hear the falseness in her voice. She didn't believe it any more than the rest of them did.

"And power blockage," Amy added and shook her head in disgust.

"It's a nightmare as far as I'm concerned," Kristen said. "I grew up human and abhor the idea of slavery."

"It's not slavery, not really," Priscilla said.

Perhaps she could admire the mage's dedication to her position in the world. She wasn't sure that if she had magic, she would have been able to stay so loyal to a power structure that so completely disenfranchised the mages.

It was a troublesome thought and one that should not be shared with Priscilla, but she couldn't shake it. She made sure Amy and Larry would be all right—the woman assured her that dragons rarely came into the mage quarters, so they'd be able to rest and recuperate their powers without being harassed—and wandered to the roof of the castle to see yet another city built on the backs of the powerless.

Yet, she reminded herself wearily, human beings weren't necessarily much better. History contained a long list of rulers who had abused their people, and she was honest enough to acknowledge that dragons couldn't be blamed for every dictator, genocide, or human rights atrocity. It was, she decided, a conundrum that might take her entire life to unravel.

CHAPTER FIFTEEN

The view from the roof of Castillo Montalbano was breathtakingly beautiful. Kristen could see over a gently descending hill planted with orchards of olives and grapes and beyond the farmland where pampered pigs ate acorns like princes until their inevitable slaughter. With her dragon eyes, she could see into Florence as well, the city filled with stone apartment buildings with their red-tiled roofs. Her gaze drifted to the Duomo itself, which dominated the city like a gorgeous gem on the twisted hand of the stony metropolis that seemed older than Detroit could ever be.

She wished her mood matched the view, but it didn't. If the truth be told, she felt terrible. A book her dad used to read to her as a kid summed her mood up perfectly. "It's a beautiful day to be grumpy." Though she might use a few other choice words than grumpy.

The problem was that she didn't know what the hell she was trying to save in Florence. She had left Detroit behind, sent her family scurrying away, and obeyed the Dragon Council's demands, and for what? So she could protect a society of slavers? Whenever Kristen thought she had made some kind of progress in understanding why the dragons did what they did, she found a new piece of the eternal puzzle that had previously been hidden in shadow. She shouldn't have been surprised that mages had no choice but to serve for their entire lives—because on some level, she already knew this and now that she thought about it, seemed to recall Larry mentioning it when he told her his story.

How could the dragons not see this as slavery? When the humans had changed their rules and fought their wars over this very practice, the dragons had thought to fix the entire problem of free will with a stipend? It was disgusting, made all the worse by the casual way the dragons didn't bother to even think about it. But, the voice of reason within reminded her, it was no different to human trafficking or forcing women into brothels and children into factories, except that it was on a larger and more widely accepted scale. Still, both were anathema to everything she believed in. They were un-American and guaranteed to stir her protective instincts.

She sighed and recognized that she stood on somewhat shaky ground. They weren't in America, but the freedom to decide what to do with your own life had to be a universal right, didn't it?

But maybe that was only an illusion. After all, mages didn't have any more choice about what to do with their lives in the States than they did in Europe. There was Canada, where at least some of the dwarves would hide mages, but a life spent in hiding was not a life of freedom.

Kristen had known there were problems when she arrived and she knew she would continue to fight to keep the peace. That was why the magic-wielding terrorists had to be stopped. Their plan of simply burning everything would hurt innocent lives. But again, she found herself looking at them from their perspective. So much of what they based their rebellion on was part of her personal struggle.

If she had known for her entire life that she could do nothing but serve a dragon, could she have accepted it like the mages she'd met had? If her home, her salary, and even her vacations would be determined not by her own will but by the will of her master, how readily would she have complied? If she had been forced to wear a cuff that hampered her natural abilities for her entire life, she might very well see violence as the only viable option.

After all, a war was fought in the United States to end slavery. No doubt innocent lives were lost and yet, it had to be done. Dragons might well have been involved somewhere in the background, but that had essentially been a human conflict, a war that resulted when neither side was willing to concede defeat.

Kristen didn't want a war, and that was a truth her conflicts always circled to. Wars between people were devastating enough, but a war between humans, dragons, and mages... She shook her head. Normally, she thought of it in brutal numbers. Millions, hundreds of millions, and even billions. But there, looking out over Tuscany, she couldn't help but see it played out before her.

How many of these fields would be burned?

How many centuries-old trees would be uprooted?

How many cathedrals and places of worship would be irreparably defaced?

How many buildings would be burned to the ground?

Too many. The answer to the question was always the same—too many.

And yet, what choice did the mages have? A claw at their throat or fight was hardly a choice, but they might believe it was the only choice they had been given.

Kristen sighed. She was tired and frustrated and felt like she didn't know enough about what was going on—a familiar feeling. Now, though, she also felt like she looked at it from too many sides. She could see how regular people would fare in a war, why the dragons were scared, why the mages were desperate, why the dwarves wanted no part of it... In that moment, it was too much to process.

She hadn't realized she was crying until Drew appeared on the roof beside her.

"I thought I'd find you here," he said but didn't elaborate on why he thought that.

With a deep breath, she wiped her tears. At least she didn't gasp or sound like she'd been crying or if she did, he didn't let on that he'd heard anything unusual.

They stood there for a while, looking at Florence sprawled below them. For a minute, it was pleasant. Drew being there took her mind away from the drain in which it had swirled, but before too long, it returned to the same old frustrating topics.

She waited for him to say something, offer some advice, or share an anecdote that might help her to see what to do, but he remained silent. He looked out at the city and leaned his body on the wall in front of him.

"Why did you come up?" she asked him finally, but before he could answer, she replied to her question. "Because right now, I can't seem to come up with a reason to come back down. It's insane—*insane* —that mages are treated like this and that the dragons act surprised when mages reject their rule and fight back.

"And it's not only mages, either. They've treated me horribly too. Their justice system is an absolute joke. I was falsely accused and spent a week in prison. Meanwhile, Obscura—an actual murderer— spent a few more weeks there than me and was granted leave, and why? Because a rich asshole agreed to pay her bills? That's what their justice system seems to think of human lives—that they're nothing but a few gold coins to be shelled out. I thought that was bad enough, but what they're doing to the mages is even worse."

Still, Drew focused on the city and stood in silence to simply let her speak until she'd offloaded it all.

"I'm tired of it all," Kristen continued. "I'm tired of finding a new low, a new level of corruption, a new group of people being stepped on. We came here to keep the peace, but that's merely another way to say we came to fight for the status quo. I can't support that, not anymore. The center cannot hold, not even if it's held for hundreds of years. It simply can't. Not anymore.

"And what's really crazy is that it's not like I can side with the mages either. Yes, they're fighting for their freedom and that of their brothers and sisters, and thus far, they've hurt far fewer people—a tiny fraction of a fraction's worth—compared to the dragons, but that doesn't mean they're right."

She drew a ragged breath and exhaled in a sharp burst. "Do you have any idea how many times Constance and I talked?"

"I don't," Drew said and didn't seem to mind her ranting at all.

"I don't either. That's how many times it was. Not two times, or five, but often. I understand why they're doing this and what they hope to accomplish, but not once—*not once*—did she talk about how to rebuild or how to bring the dragons to justice. And by that I mean actual justice as opposed to their vigilante terrorism.

"You say you thought you'd find me here, and I have to say I'm surprised to hear that because what I want to do is fly as far as I possibly can, find a tiny villa in a part of Europe no one goes to, and find a beach and a man who will accept gold to be my personal chef and forget about all this."

He nodded, took a moment to absorb it all, and cleared his throat. "So why haven't you?"

Her laugh was loud and bitter. "Don't dare me!"

Drew smiled. "I do. I dare you to run off. Right now. I'll cover for you, I promise."

She snorted another laugh but she shook her head. "You know I will never do that." Fucking Drew, calling her bluff like that.

"So, if you won't run away, what will we do about it?"

At first, the question only infuriated her because she didn't know. That was the problem and was why she was up there—to think. "I don't know the answer to that," she said, surprised at herself because admitting her shortcomings hadn't made her angrier but calmed her somewhat.

Drew only nodded and looked at her like he did during training sessions—like he waited for her to make the next move.

Kristen sighed. Despite being a dragon that might very well live for centuries if not millennia, she couldn't outwait him. "I know that leaving things as they are right now is totally unacceptable. Dragons want to continue to operate as they have, and they can't."

"Okay," he said.

"But the technomages' plan to burn the house down with everyone still inside is fucking crazy. That's how dictators are made and innocent people are killed."

"Okay."

"So…we need some kind of a third option. Another way to help shift the power between dragons, humans, and mages."

"Okay." Drew sounded like she had outlined a five-year plan despite her only having admitted that she didn't know what to do.

"So do you know how to do all that?" she asked. "Because I don't have a fucking clue."

He chuckled. "I don't have any idea of how to even begin with all that, but I'm sure you'll find the answer."

She shook her head and sighed. "How can you say that? I'm not infallible. I might fail."

"You might. But that's a risk I'm willing to take if we want you to succeed."

"But how can you be so sure?"

"I'm not," he said with a gentle shrug. "I wasn't sure you would stop those gangs that tried to start a civil war in Detroit. I wasn't sure you would beat Shadowstorm or Obscura. Hell, I wasn't sure you would get out of dragon prison." Drew smiled. "And I sure as shit wasn't sure that flying to a remote corner of Canada with you to stop a group of terrorists from detonating a bomb big enough to kill dragons would work, but I believed in you all the same."

Kristen rolled her eyes. She couldn't help it. "Gee, thanks, Drew. It's good to know I have my own mindless servant."

"I'm not mindless. I follow you because I choose to. You make good decisions. If you stop doing that, I'll let you know. We all feel that way about you. We know you'll work this out, and if you want help from any of us, ask."

"Okay. Okay, thanks, Drew," she said and realized that she could ask him what he would do right now but also that she didn't feel like she needed to. He merely smiled, nodded at her, and went downstairs.

Somehow, she felt better already, although she still wasn't sure how to fix anything. She wasn't sure if there was a way to simply fix it, but she knew that at the very least, she would take action. Not for the dragons, and definitely not for the mage cells, but for everyone. For herself, for her family, for the kids she grew up with in Detroit, for people fleeing their homelands—for everyone. She would find a way to right the wrongs that caused all this strife in the first place.

Somehow.

It wouldn't be easy, she knew that, but she'd never wanted an easy life anyway. There would be struggle ahead and sleepless nights, but she wouldn't quit, not until she saw a way through all this or until someone finally stopped her.

CHAPTER SIXTEEN

"Dammit, Havington, you said this would be routine!" Sarah shouted. She still wore her flower mask.

"Shut the fuck up, take that mask off, and get me some gauze."

She cursed him again but she did as he'd ordered. He would need her finesse if they wanted any chance to save Stephano's life. He'd been shot and then fell from the roof and seemed to have internal injuries.

Ron had been shot as well, but his wound didn't seem too severe. The cell leader had already had Beth patch him up, give him some meds, and put him to bed to rest.

He didn't think saving Stephano would be nearly as easy.

"Sarah, damn it—Sarah, I need you here!" he shouted.

"I'm doing what you asked," she called in response.

"Good, right. Gauze—there on the neck. Now, I need you to keep his lungs breathing okay?"

"What?"

"With your goddamn magic, Sarah. Will that be a damn problem?"

"No, sir. No, I can do that."

"Good, that's good," Havington said as he watched Stephano's chest start to rise and fall. "Be careful to not overfill his lungs or you'll cause them to burst."

"Damn it, Neal," she said and sounded like she had already fallen into the pit of despair. She never used his first name. That she did so now was not a good sign.

He didn't need his underlings to indicate that they were in bad shape. They might have done better if the damn Steel Dragon had given chase. She would have followed them through an alley and been wounded by all manner of dragon parts, but she hadn't.

They'd rushed to the base to try to save Stephano even though— those thoughts could come later. Right now, he needed to focus.

"Keep him still, okay, Mani?"

"I don't know, boss."

"I'll try to remove any shards of bullet I can find, but he cannot move. Do you understand me?"

"Sir, yes, sir," Mani said and held Stephano by the shoulders. The patient didn't even flinch. He was beyond unconscious.

Havington focused on the man's energy and found the shards quickly enough. The body did not want the pieces of bullet in there and fought against them with his help. He grasped the shards, pulled them out, and let them fall on the floor.

As soon as they emerged from the wound, blood started to flow.

"I think a vein's been cut," he said and looked at the swollen discoloration around the injury. "I'll try to suction it out."

"He'll need more blood," Sarah said through gritted teeth. She was still trying to maintain Stephano's breathing. Soon, she'd have to beat his heart for him as well.

"I fucking know he'll need more blood. Bunny! Damn it. Bunny, I know you have the same blood type. Get yourself hooked up to an IV."

Bunny—the only one of the team who always used her mask name —looked frightened but she did as she was told.

Havington focused on getting the blood out of Stephano's wound.

Moving blood was difficult. It was like water magic, kind of, except moving a swimming pool of water didn't have veins that might get sucked dry. He had to be very careful. If he drew the blood too quickly, he'd drain the man dry.

"Havington!" Sarah snapped. "He's losing his pulse."

"We do this now," he said and psyched himself for what he had to do. He reached out to Stephano's blood—feeling it all through his body confirmed that the internal bleeding was dire—and pulled. Gently at first, oh so gently, then harder and harder.

Blood began to pour from the wound—more and more blood and then too much blood.

"Bunny!"

"I'm ready."

He glanced at her to confirm that she had indeed inserted a needle into her vein and had a length of hose ready to go, but that proved to be Stephano's undoing. As soon as Havington looked away from his patient, he accidentally yanked on the blood in the man's veins.

"He's got no pulse," Beth said.

"I'm so sorry." Bunny spoke at the same time.

"It's over," he told them. When he'd yanked on the man's blood, it had sprayed out and soaked him.

But he knew whose hands this blood truly belonged on.

"The Steel Dragon did this," Havington said as he stepped away from Stephano's body.

"For fuck's sake!" Sarah shouted and stormed away, alternating between weeping and swearing. She and Stephano had been close.

"I'm so sorry," Bunny muttered again and again. "I'm so, so sorry."

Mani's eyes were wide. He shuffled to sit on a couch next to the unconscious Ron as if to make sure the other wounded man was still alive. In a daze, he pulled his ram mask down. Havington could tell from his shaking shoulders that the large man was weeping.

He knew they were at war. Inevitably, he knew they would lose people and yet, after all five attacks had gone so well, he hadn't thought it would happen so soon. He looked at his team. They were all taking it hard, worse than him. They looked like a pack of whipped dogs instead of the elite fighting force they had trained so hard to become. He couldn't let them sink into despair. While he was their leader, he was more than that. He was their friend—their family, exactly like Stephano.

"We can't let Stephano die for nothing," Havington said, his voice quiet and tight after working on the dead man's body for so long.

"Give it a rest, Havington," Sarah said. Her eyes were already swollen from her tears.

He shook his head. "We won't let Stephano die for nothing," he said with more strength.

His team turned to him and the attention swelled his confidence. It didn't feel earned, not after Stephano dying, but what choice did they have? They had to stop the Steel Dragon.

"If Stephano dies and we let it go, the dragons win," Havington said and tried to put conviction behind the words he didn't yet feel. "This is what they've done for millennia. They intimidate us, they roar and breathe their fire, and demand to have their way and we let them. It's us. We are the ones who emboldened these beasts. Our parents, our ancestors, mages we all know who we've lost to dragon servitude. And now, they send their little shiny lapdog here and expect us to blow away in the wind from her wings, but I say enough."

His team looked at him now with equal parts hope and fear. Sarah, though, was nodding. That subtle encouragement gave him what he needed to keep going.

"If we—that is, the five of us here in this room—can manage to take vengeance on the Steel Dragon, the world won't be able to turn away. We can do this. It's up to us and we have to because of Stephano. I want the streets to run red with the Steel Dragon's blood. And when she's dying in the gutter, we'll be there to tell her that enough is enough. She killed one mage too many and whatever comes next is her fault."

"You're damn right," Mani said. Bunny nodded and even Sarah agreed. Ron was still unconscious, but he had been closer to Stephano than any of them. He wouldn't back out, not until the Steel Dragon was eliminated.

"Do you have a plan, Havington?" Sarah asked, her tone careful and measured, a good sign from her.

"We had a good look at her team and I hate to say it, but we're outgunned," Havington said as he looked around. The others nodded. Good. They weren't idiots. "There were two mages, plus some of her old cop friends, and I bet there were more of her other allies from Detroit waiting to swoop in if needed. We can't beat them with only the...the five us." They had been six for so long, it felt like losing a part of their body.

"For now, I want everyone to get some rest. Bunny, you have first watch. Sarah, I need you asleep and ready for action. Mani, you too."

"What will you do, boss?" the man asked. "You threw magic around out there too."

"I'll get some rest too but first, I need to make a few calls. The Steel Dragon's not the only one with friends."

He stepped into a smaller room, shut the door behind him, and called one of the other cells in Europe. It wasn't easy to get through as they used burner phones too and he had to find a contact of a contact before he could speak to the boss. Finally, he connected to the person he wanted.

"Three minutes, King," the leader of the other cell said, a man who went by the codename Cobalt. Havington was King of course. He had been since he'd started wearing the mask with a crown.

"Cobalt, it's time. We need the Condor," he said and wasted no time with niceties. If the man said he had three minutes, that's what he meant and not a minute longer.

"Negative. The Condor stays in the nest until it's time to break bones."

"It's time to break bones," he insisted.

"We will not reveal the capabilities of the Condor until such a time as we deem it necessary."

"And when will that be, Cobalt? The Steel Dragon already destroyed our most powerful presence in the States and arguably, the world. We took action here and now, she's targeted us despite us moving to Florence." There were codes for major cities as well but given that the Steel Dragon already knew they were there, he didn't want to waste time going through the necessary clues to tell him where they were. "Did you simply want to wait for her to attack you? Let her destroy as many cells as she can while you keep the Condor all to yourself?"

"Once we reveal those capabilities, there's no going back," Cobalt whined.

"There's already no going back. Constance tried to kick this thing off and the Steel Dragon stopped her. We took action and she's trying to stop us. We have an opportunity here. She doesn't know the city like we do. Plus, we already engaged in a fight. She'll underestimate our next confrontation."

"Because you lost."

"And if we lose again, you'll be next—unless your plan is to keep the Condor safely tucked in its nest while you watch each and every cell get burned out."

"You should never have engaged with her," the other man insisted.

"It was that or let her find us. Will you help, or should we retreat and give this continent to the dragons as well?"

"Don't be so melodramatic," Cobalt replied.

"Is there a reason I shouldn't be?"

"The Condor takes flight," the man said but didn't sound happy about it. The line went dead.

Havington nodded with satisfaction and took a few deep breaths to bolster himself. The other cell leader hadn't been happy about it, but he had said he would send the weapon. Victory would be theirs.

He left the smaller room and returned to the larger area of the crypt that housed their base. While he'd been on the phone, his team had moved Stephano's body to one of the few tombs that didn't have some kind of carved statue on top of them. They'd covered him with a white sheet that was already stained with red spots here and there.

Obviously, moving the body had dampened the mood as everyone once again looked somber.

"The Condor is coming," he said.

That earned a gasp from Sarah and nods from Bunny and Mani.

"We fucked up that bad, huh?" Ron asked. Good, he was conscious again. It was time to fill him in on the details.

"We set things into motion," Havington said. "Once it arrives, this fight will be over and the foundations of dragon society will be shaken."

"So we sit tight until then?" Ron asked and tried to sound positive.

"I'm afraid not. You were burned, Ron. They defeated us and gained access to that footage. We need to operate under the assumption that they have your face."

"Are you fucking kidding me?" the man protested. "I knew I fucked up when I didn't kill that dragon."

He shook his head. "Expecting one hundred percent success in operations like this is unrealistic, but it's unfortunate all the same. Either way, you can't leave our crypt except on my orders and never without your mask. There are too many damn cameras in this city. The others will go to your apartment soon and scrub it."

Ron winced. "You don't have to scrub all of it, do you? I have a couple of signed comics there—"

"We can't make them sort through it before they burn the place. Sorry, Ron. It's already a huge risk sending them there at all. We can't waste time sifting through for one or two items."

"I told you those were a waste of money," Mani muttered.

The other man looked grumpy but he didn't protest. He understood how profoundly screwed they would be if the Steel Dragon found their base.

"Everything you need will be provided." Havington tried to sound cheerful. It wasn't Ron's fault that he was now trapped there. That blame lay firmly with the dragons. "And look on the bright side—no more shopping duties."

"Sorry, you guys," the man said as he grasped how much more dependent on all of them he had become. And after him making such a fuss about having his own apartment despite recently moving to Florence.

"It's unfortunate but not all is lost. If the dragons do get your face from the video feeds and we are able to prevent them from finding us here, we might be able to use that too."

Dragons were predators, first and foremost, and everyone knew how to catch a predator. All you needed was a little bait.

CHAPTER SEVENTEEN

When Kristen came inside from the roof she was almost run over by her brother. At any other time in their lives, this would have qualified as the first blow of a wrestling match. Now, however, in the middle of a dragon stronghold with deadly mages in the city, she controlled her impulse to try to perform a body slam on him.

"Kristen! I have big news! Come on." Brian strode away from her with as much as speed as he'd plowed into her with.

"What is this about?"

"I have a suspect!"

"What? How? I thought you said there were hundreds of hours to go through?"

"It'll be easier to show you." He didn't slow so she followed.

They reached the lab where a bank of computers was hooked up to multiple monitors. He sat in the middle of it all like this was the job he was created for and for the first time, she was pleased with her decision to allow him to come. Even though he'd gotten the data after the firefight, it hadn't felt like a success. It had felt like he might have died if they weren't careful. Him being inside a lab was a much better option as far as his sister was concerned.

"There are over two hundred hours of total footage of the several-hour concert, thanks to all the different views from various cameras placed around the venue. I was able to cut that down somewhat since I didn't watch the opening band or any of the footage between shows, but that still left me with close to a hundred hours to go through. Vert really likes his angles."

"It still doesn't explain how you did this in less than a day."

"I cheated." Brian grinned wickedly. "I wrote a search protocol that looked for facial expressions. Since most of the people at the concert were smiling, enjoying themselves, and dancing, I thought maybe someone contemplating the murder of the star of the show might look a little glum."

"And that worked?"

"Sure. Facial recognition has become quite good, and...well, you said Vert used his aura on the crowds and it showed. Almost everyone was smiling and moving, which narrowed it down to a few hundred hits. Out of tens of thousands of people, I think that's good. And that's our guy right there."

He played a few seconds of footage. Sure enough, smack dab in the middle of the crowd and fairly close to the stage was a man with a shaved head and a handlebar mustache. While everyone else danced, grinned, or bobbed their heads, this man stood completely motionless and glared at the performer.

"That doesn't necessarily mean it's him, though," Kristen pointed out. "He might have simply not liked Vert using his aura on his girl-friend or whatever."

"Oh, it's him," her brother insisted and his grin shifted to a grim expression. "Watch this." He scrolled through a few clips until the suspect reached into his jacket.

Brian pressed play and they watched in stunned silence as he drew a gun, aimed it at Vert, and opened fire. He targeted the members of the band methodically while the people around him first flinched from the noise, then plunged into full-scale panic.

Once the musicians fell, he joined the crowd and was instantly lost in the chaos.

"I'm impressed that you found him," Kristen said. "I'd say congratulations, but we still have to catch the asshole."

"I'm happy to do my part," he said, his smile wide.

"How far back did you track this guy through the footage?" she asked when she noticed multiple videos queued up. "Do you have any idea how he got in? I assumed this was a sniper job from outside and the reports of local gunfire were wrong. Shouldn't there have been metal detectors or something to identify the gun?"

"I tried but the cameras aren't really for security. There's nothing usable from his entrance, but…"

"What?" she asked, already positive that this would be one of his theories rather than hard facts.

"Well, I'm no expert, but these are mages, right?" He wiggled his fingers in a charade of a mage casting a spell.

"That's more than likely," she confirmed.

"So…magic? Maybe he could have…like, mind-wiped the security guy or…I don't know, floated the gun above the metal detectors? He could have been invisible or something and—"

"Magic, got it. Good idea," Kristen said and cut her brother off before he betrayed what corners of the Internet he liked to haunt. "Do you have any images of his face that are clearer? Mustache, I got that, but I'd like to ID him."

"Oh, I'm way ahead of you on that." Brian brought up several images of the man's face. "He'd spent most of the concert close to the stage, no doubt because he needed a close shot for his pistol, but that means there are a ton of shots of him."

"Can you—"

"Identify him based on his face? Of course." He brought up more windows of information. He showed her a driver's license, a French EU passport, and even an address of an apartment he'd bought in Florence. Apparently, Ronald Bisset—Ron, according to some of the documents he had found—had paid in cash and had been in the city for less than a week.

"Then we move," she said and flexed her aura to tell her team that it was time to get ready.

"All right!" Brian said and stood quickly.

"Not so fast, Zed."

"What? Why not?"

"Because you've just proven how useful you are working intel. If you think I'll take you into the field again, you're crazy."

"Oh, right—no, fuck that! I thought you would tell the team what's up over lunch. Solving your case for you made me hungry."

CHAPTER EIGHTEEN

Lunch was hasty and unceremonious. By the time they were finished, they were ready to move. Kristen headed toward the roof with the other dragons but Amy stopped her.

"You should take a car with us," the girl said.

"There's no point in keeping quiet anymore. They know we're here," she explained.

"So that means they can't shoot you out of the sky?" Drew interjected. "Take the car with us humans. You're too valuable to this operation to risk."

"Orders, Lady Hall?" Stonequest asked pointedly, thus reinforcing the hierarchy of command.

"I won't send the dragons in without me on point, but I see the danger. Amy, fly with me and give me a shield as we go. Everyone else, I want you in the car five minutes ago. Let's move!"

Everyone responded with a "Yes, ma'am," and they were on their way.

A few minutes later, they reached the apartment building. If not for Brian's detective work, she never would have expected it to house a cell of international magic terrorists. It looked much the same as many of the others around Florence, although the neighborhood was marginally quieter than some.

"Drones," Kristen said and Heartsbane and Emerald complied. They released drones from their talons that Brian took control of from the base.

"Zed has wings," her brother said.

"If you could not refer to yourself in the third person, that would be great," Kristen said over a headset that the EU team had designed. It fit inside her mouth and was thus close enough to her eardrum for her to be able to use it.

"Okay, sorry. I won't do it again." The briefest of pauses followed. "Naw, I can't help it. Zed out!"

The drones banked away as the dragons fell into formation and circled the building like hawks.

"I have eyes on the window. It looks normal. The dude has an impressive collection of comics, still mostly in boxes, but I don't see any scrolls or anything," Brian said.

"I still want in there," Kristen responded. "With Larry's experience using magic to track, we might be able to find something that leads us to them."

"We need to move fast," Drew said from below where their car had pulled up. "These guys will try to close this loop and prevent us from finding anything."

"Lock down the bottom. We'll go in from above," she instructed.

The apartment itself was on the top floor, so it was a shorter distance for the dragons.

"We're here," she told the ground team. "I don't want anyone going out of this building, even if they don't match our perp."

"Understood," Drew confirmed. He snapped orders to the others, the commands easily audible to her keen dragon ears, even from this high up.

"Brian, anything else?" Kristen asked.

"Zed sees nothing but the comics," he replied.

"What do you see?"

"One open blind to…like, his game room or whatever. The rest of the curtains are closed but if I had to guess, I would have to say I don't think anyone is home."

"Hernandez, how are you doing?" she asked over the radio.

"I'm one of two people who have to run up four flights of stairs and you ask how I am? I'm fucking tired," the woman replied between heaved breaths. "But I'm also in place," she said once she met Kristen at the front door to the apartment. "Larry will be here soon."

"Anything?" She asked as demotions expert began to poke and prod with her tools.

"No. I don't see any kind of trigger here. I don't think they left us a bomb. Well, not my kind of bomb anyway."

"Larry?" she shouted down the stairs.

"Just…a minute…" he wheezed.

"Larry," she urged him.

"I'm coming…I'm coming… Just let me…catch my breath." He stumbled toward them, beyond winded. A painfully long ten seconds followed as he waved his hands in front of the door "Okay, yeah. Don't go in there."

"Why not?" Kristen asked.

"This door is warded to hell and back. If we do anything other than open it with the key, this whole place will explode. I…I'm honestly impressed. I didn't know a piece of wood could take this much magic without going up in flames."

"Define hell and back," Hernandez said.

"Sure," Larry replied. "If we open this door, you, me, and the Steel Dragon are nothing but ash. I wouldn't give the entire floor much better odds than that either."

"Don't open that door," Kristen ordered.

"Thanks, boss, but we kind of realized that for ourselves," the other woman quipped.

What to do…what to do…what to do, Kristen thought before she had an idea.

"What about the ceiling?" she asked Larry.

"Good idea," the mage said, stretched, and sent blue tendrils of energy from his finger to the ceiling of the hallway. They penetrated the sheetrock as if it were water and vanished. A moment later, he smiled. "I don't think the wards extend that far. Too bad you can shift into a dragon and not into a little mouse."

"That's not quite what I had in mind," she said and spun to sprint toward the roof with her dragon speed.

She burst out onto the roof and immediately transformed into her dragon body.

"Are we under attack?" Stonequest asked as he shifted into his dragon form and hunkered close to the roof to make himself as small a target as possible.

"Nope, the roof is." She raised her tail as high as she could and pounded it into the roof. The ax blade on the tip penetrated the tile and most of the ceiling. "Anything, Larry?" she shouted.

"Nothing!"

That was good enough for her. She raised her tail again and repeated the blow twice more. Using the momentum of her tail to lift her, she transformed into her human form, fell into the hole, and shattered the occupant's coffee table.

"Are you all right in there?" Stonequest asked from above and extended his huge dragon head over the hole.

"I'm fine. Totally fine," she said and untangled herself from what was left of the coffee table. "Get everyone on the roof. I want more people in here."

"I don't think that's smart, Kristen!" Larry shouted. He had already reached the roof, so he spoke to her through the hole. "I feel a major build-up of magic in there. You must have tripped something. Get out! Now!"

His warning served no purpose. In the time it took for her to process what he had said, the temperature in the apartment soared to a hundred degrees. Her skin reddened like the world's worst sunburn and blisters formed on the exposed parts of her body—her face and hands—before she could turn to steel.

"Kristen!" Amy yelled from the roof.

"I'm okay," she responded, knowing full well that was an almost ridiculously optimistic assessment. Kristen had never quite understood spontaneous combustion, but she did now. The heat built rapidly until papers on the kitchen counter burst into flame as if they had been soaked in gasoline and touched with a spark and the furniture and carpet followed. A split-second later, the entire apartment erupted into flames as the heat continued to grow. Everything made of glass exploded like a horrible celebration of heat.

Kristen raised her arms—she was made of steel, so it was more reflex than actual self-defense—before the shards of glass from the TV struck her. By the time the slivers of glass had fallen, they'd already melted. The exploding cups in the kitchen had the same fate. No longer were they reduced to shards but instead, were now puddles.

The flames extinguished themselves as the furniture had already been reduced to ash. For a moment, she thought that signaled that the trap had completed, but it only meant that the flames had already used all the oxygen in the room. She knew this because she could no longer breathe.

A little dizzy, she crouched and tried to leap out of the hole in the ceiling but she was too heavy. She clutched the edge of the hole but it wasn't strong enough to support her in her steel form. While she could easily jump out if she assumed her human body, she would be roasted like a rotisserie chicken so that wasn't an option.

Frustrated, she looked around for a way out. Her vision had begun to close in—she was running out of oxygen in her blood—but she knew she couldn't panic.

She looked at the brick walls of the apartment and her semi-delirious mind used vital oxygen to wonder if her steel body would melt before the brick would. It decided that yes, indeed, she would become a puddle before the brick was destroyed. Could she break through it?

Thankfully, instinct clicked in with a possible solution. Her mind pointed out to her that the fire had shattered the windows to the apartment and she could escape without having to destroy the structural stability of the building.

Kristen stumbled toward the window and forced her oxygen-deprived muscles to go faster and faster. She needed to get out of the building and hopefully get clear of the sidewalk. It would be a disaster to save herself only to crush a resident of Florence below with her super-heated body.

She managed a decent jog—every muscle protesting as she did so —and flung herself at the window with her arms outstretched.

A flare of elation was short-lived and she sprained her wrist when she collided with the magical barrier that contained all the heat. Kristen fell heavily. She had barely enough strength left to punch uselessly at her prison before the still rising temperatures forced her brain from delirium to unconsciousness.

CHAPTER NINETEEN

It wasn't magic that told Amy her friend was in trouble. Larry might have called it the bond between a dragon and their mage and others would have called it friendship. The most prosaic might simply call it common sense. Whatever it was, it didn't take rocket science to realize that Kristen needed help.

"Kristen's in trouble," she shouted.

"I know!" Stonequest retorted. He was the only one who'd dared to approach the hole in the roof. At first, he'd tried to reach her with the tip of his tail to haul her out, but even with his stone-like scales, he hadn't been able to keep the appendage inside long enough to accomplish a rescue. The tip had already had its scales peeled away by the heat but he still looked like he intended to go in.

The simple truth was that it would only mean there would be two dead dragons at the end of this instead of one.

Drew—Kristen's old boss, apparently, although Amy was shocked to find out the two had never hooked up—yelled at Kristen over the radio. She didn't respond and it seemed fairly obvious that her radio must have long since melted. But what else could a regular human do?

For that matter, what could a dragon do?

This trap had been made for dragons. A mage had spun the web of spells that held it all together, and a mage would have to be the one to undo it.

"Can you see it, Amy?" Larry shouted.

She could. A magical sphere held the spell in place and trapped Kristen within. If it wasn't about to roast her friend, she might have found it appealing. It looked like the heat would be completely trapped inside the apartment, so at least the mage's neighbors weren't at risk of having their homes burned.

The Steel Dragon now shouldered that risk all alone.

But that wasn't all the young mage could sense with her magic abilities. She could also see there was a core to the web of magic in the middle of the apartment. She told Larry as much.

"Yeah!" he shouted in response. The heat was so intense that the aperture roared like a furnace. She knew she didn't have much time. "I call those knots. That's what is holding the spell together. If we could get to it, we could unravel it, but to get to it, you need to go inside the heatshield. I can't say I'm in a hurry to see how fast a non-steel-covered human cooks."

"I have to go in there," she snapped. The tar on the roof had begun to melt and turn to slag. Everyone took a few steps back. From her angle, she could see Kristen passed out in the charred apartment. Everything that could burn had already done so. They had to do something or the superheated air would burn the dragon's lungs if she didn't suffocate first.

"My stone skin is better in my human form," Stonequest yelled over the roaring sound. "There aren't chinks like in my dragon body. I'll go in and get her out."

"You won't be able to jump out of there in your stone skin any more than Hall could in her steel," Heartsbane said, her tone dire.

"What other choice do we have?" he countered, obviously pissed at the entire situation. And why shouldn't he be? This was the second trap they'd walked into. At this rate, the mages would trick them into killing their own team to start the war while they simply watched the chaos.

"My stone should be more heat retardant than steel. I might be able to outlast the spell." He sounded as if he tried to psych himself up. "Unless anyone has a better fucking idea?"

"I do," Amy replied and, before anyone could stop her, she rushed forward and drew her magic around her into a protective field. She had practiced making shields and right now, she poured everything she had into this one.

First, she formed a sphere around herself and fashioned the front of it into a point she hoped would be able to puncture the sphere that contained the heat. With that in place, she added more and more layers of shielding around her until she was wrapped like some kind of a magic onion.

She did this while she sprinted toward the hole. Before anyone could stop her, she took a deep breath—the air inside would probably be none too good to breathe—and dropped in.

The young mage landed on the floor of the apartment. Even with her shield, the room was fearfully hot. She could feel her skin start to burn like she'd been outside in the sun for hours. The soles of her shoes melted. In the time it took for that to happen, blisters began to form on her skin. All this happened while she tried to protect herself with everything she had. These mages were obviously skilled at what they did.

She held her breath as the air was painfully hot and probably devoid of oxygen anyway, but that didn't matter. While she wouldn't have time to waste, she didn't need too much of it. The core of the spell—the knot, as Larry had called it—was directly in front of her.

Focused on her task, she drew her shield tighter around her body —something she probably should have done, to begin with—and used a piece of it to strike the invisible swirling vortex of energy she could sense in front of her.

It didn't break.

More blisters began to form. If it weren't for the lack of air, her shirt would have already caught on fire. The thought was sobering but she couldn't quit, not yet.

Amy tried another blow on the vortex of energy. This time, it shook the spell and the entire apartment rattled. It didn't break but it told her she was on the right path.

She focused on a third blow and realized full well that she wouldn't have the power for a fourth. Again, she pulled her shield as close to her body as she could while her skin grew hotter and hotter as the energy of the spell got closer. While she retracted one spell, she expanded the other. It didn't take any corporeal form but she imagined it like a hammer. A massive sledgehammer with a spike at its tip that grew heavier and sharper while it begged to break free and crush the foe the mage had set it on.

When it was ready, she set it free.

It was like a dam breaking. At first, there was nothing as if the energy didn't want to move. In the next moment, more power and force than she had realized existed poured out of her and into the spell.

It pulled at her and demanded that she fuel it with more and more of her power. She gave it everything she could but still had to maintain two spells. If she dropped her shield, she'd be roasted, but if she failed to break the containment spell, she and Kristen would be cooked.

The hammer spell pushed aggressively against the knot in front of her. As it did so, it drained her strength. A headache blossomed viciously in her temples, her heart began to pound, and blood trickled from her nose. Her muscles seemed sapped of every ounce of energy they'd possessed. Amy let her body collapse purely by reflex. Who needed to stand, anyway? Still, the heat assaulted her and she curled, trembling from the loss of the energy she had spent. By sheer force of will, she kept her mind focused on the two spells. She couldn't let them slip. If either one did, it would be the end.

Blackness crept in from the sides of her vision. Her breathing slowed and her heartbeat grew so fast it didn't seem to be regular at all. Unless something changed, she would die of a heart attack.

She had almost reached the point where she could no longer sustain the effort when the spell shattered under the pressure.

It was as if every thread that held it together had been made of elastic. When Amy sliced one, they all simply unraveled. The core of heat she had faced dissipated to nothing at all. The sphere that contained the spell had shattered completely. She had done it.

But that didn't mean the superheated air or the brick walls of the apartment were suddenly cool. She realized she was waiting for a gust of fresh air that wouldn't come. Her initial belief had been that if she could only break the spell, she'd save Kristen. Somehow, physics had gotten in the way.

Amy tried to strengthen her shield to protect her already blistered skin but using the hammer spell had taken so much out her. She wouldn't be able to hold the shield for long but realized that she couldn't do this herself. There was simply no way she could manage alone. It was like Kristen always said. They had to work together.

So, with her last trace of strength, she took a breath—not so much for oxygen but to give her vocal cords something to use—and shouted for help.

The reply was instantaneous.

Stonequest pounded through the roof in dragon form. His massive wings flapped and created great gusts of air to dissipate the heat. He scooped Amy up in one claw, then snatched Kristen with the other and leapt upward.

The wind rushing over her skin was a blessing but it wasn't enough. Every inch of her body still hurt. She didn't understand why the dragon flew over a field of cool grass or why he'd cruised so casually over an ice cream parlor. Didn't he know those things were cold? Why was he flying so slowly anyway?

A part of her reasoned that it might be because her brain was shutting down. That would explain why she couldn't hear anything and why it felt like she was moving toward the middle of a traffic circle.

Amy heard the screech of car horns and the colorful Italian curses of a scooter driver and in the next moment, her skin felt blessedly cool.

She looked at a man who protected her from the heat with his umbrella. He had very dark skin, a broad-brimmed hat, and a long coat, both of which were the same color as his skin. His umbrella cast shade that was blessedly cool like drops of ice on her skin. Actually, like rain. It was like his umbrella was raining on her.

"Thank you." She gasped at him and tried to smile but he didn't respond. He merely stood above her and his umbrella—was it somehow made of water?—sprayed her with water. Was he a mage?

"If you're waiting for him to say you're welcome, it'll be a long wait."

Amy turned to where Stonequest, now in his human form, cradled Kristen in his arms. He stood in a pool of blue water. She realized she was in the water as well, which was why her skin didn't currently feel like death.

Kristen's body was still steel, and although Amy had seen her change her clothes to steel a few times, she hadn't done so this time or they had already melted away as she was stark naked in Stonequest's arms. She had never seen steel breasts before and might have been jealous of their shape and ample curves if her friend were breathing. But with her highly reflective steel skin and without her clothes, it was very easy to see that she was not breathing.

Stonequest's muscles bulged as he lowered her slowly into the shallow water. The young mage was suddenly reminded of Viking burials, of people being sent out to sea and set on fire. Was that what was happening? Had Kristen died and Stonequest was honoring her somehow, or—

Kristen gasped as soon as he submerged her body.

He sighed, made sure she was stable, and splashed through the water to the other woman.

"Are you all right?" he asked Amy.

"Yeah," she said and immediately realized it was a lie when she saw her blistered arms. "Thanks to that mage you found."

"You mean him?" Stonequest pointed at the man who still used his magic abilities to spray them with water.

"Who else?" she said and looked again at the man to thank him.

She frowned when she finally realized it wasn't a man at all but a statue. It held a pole in its hand that sprayed water into the air. That's what had looked like an umbrella.

"You should make a contribution to some of the art museums before you go," Stonequest said and shook his head.

Amy nodded, still shocked that she'd mistaken a statue for a man. Had she hallucinated that badly? How close had she come to dying? And that was with her using her magic to protect herself. Even though her control had increased significantly and she knew she had more natural strength than any mage she'd ever met or faced, it was a harsh realization that with the right spells, subtly cast, she could have her brain cooked.

A simple nod was enough to make her entire body shake convulsively. She had used everything she had on those two spells. Her body trembled like an out of shape athlete at the end of a marathon.

"That was a damned stupid thing to do," Stonequest muttered after he checked Kristen, who was breathing heavily but breathing.

Amy gave him a pained smile—she didn't want to think how much it trembled—and replied, "Well, it worked, didn't it?"

"You saved Hall, which of course I'm thankful for, but look at you. You're shaking like a leaf and you're covered in blisters," he told her as if this was somehow news to her.

"If I hadn't gone in there, you might have died," she replied. Even that sentence almost drained her of her ability to sit.

"I'm more expendable than you," he retorted. "Our team has dragons who can fight. You're our most powerful mage and our greatest asset besides the Steel Dragon herself. You need to be more careful. If you had made a shield for me to go in there, I might have been burned but I can heal much faster than you."

"Or you might have died."

"Like I said, I'm expendable. You're not."

She didn't know whether to be flattered or annoyed. Her body protested and reminded her she didn't have the strength for either.

"It's what she would have done for me," she said, which shut him up, most likely because it was true and also because they both knew Kristen would risk her life for even the least valuable asset.

Amy didn't know if Stonequest finally admitted she was right, nor did she find out the name of the fountain that had helped her. After saving her friend's life and having won this little verbal spat against a dragon, she passed out.

CHAPTER TWENTY

Kristen didn't exactly know how she'd gotten from the inferno of an apartment to a fountain in the middle of a traffic circle, but she knew Stonequest had something to do with it.

He had a stupid grin on his face as he moved to hold Amy's head out of the water.

"Is she—"

"She'll live," he replied. "And thanks to her, so will you."

She took a moment to study the young mage. Her breathing was regular, and her aura seemed strong enough. She wouldn't die, then, which meant she could focus on less immediate concerns—like the pang of guilt she felt looking at her injured friend.

"Do you mean her burns are my fault?"

"Don't be ridiculous. The mages did this to her, not you. I've never seen heat like that." Stonequest gestured to Kristen's body. "It completely burned your clothes away, even though they were steel at the time. That's never happened before."

"It completely what?" she asked, looked down, and realized that she was completely naked. Her skin was still steel but now, instead of her dragon SWAT uniform, she bared steel breasts and...everything else for all the world to see.

Which, currently, was a fair number of people.

She sat in a fountain in the center of a traffic circle. That alone would have drawn gawking but on top of that, she had been dropped there by a dragon, firetrucks and paramedics now raced toward her, and their approach made everyone pull over to gawk all the better. And, oh yeah, she was completely naked.

"Stop staring at me and do something," she yelped at Stonequest while she tried to simultaneously cover her boobs and crotch. At least no one could tell she had red hair down there when she was in steel mode. Currently, that didn't feel like much of a victory.

He laughed. "What? Do you want me to take my clothes off and give them to you?"

"No!" Kristen shouted. That would be far worse. This was Europe —Italy, no less. If they both got naked, everyone would think they something erotic in mind.

She transformed into her dragon body and almost toppled the statue that sprayed water on her as she did so.

"Kristen...take it easy. It's not like I've never seen a naked human body before. I'm hundreds of years old. I've been around."

"Yeah, well, I haven't. Don't tell me to take it easy."

"So, wait..." Stonequest grinned like an idiot. "You're okay with me seeing you completely naked in your dragon form but not your human one? What's the difference? I can tell you're a female in your dragon body as easily as when you are in your human form. I prefer your dragon body if I'm honest."

"That's not an opinion I asked for." She fumed and he simply laughed. "Right now, I need to know my team is okay."

He nodded, still chuckling, and pointed to the team a block away. It looked like Heartsbane and Emerald had evacuated everyone else. Kristen made a quick headcount, saw they were fine, and focused her attention on Amy.

"She suffered second-degree burns, at least," Stonequest said to two paramedics as they eased the girl onto a stretcher. "Plus, she might be suffering from hypoxia."

"We know, sir," the man said in an annoyed Italian accent. From his tone, he sounded like he rescued mages from fountains after a dragon rescued them from apartment buildings all the time.

Stonequest nodded, not bothered by the paramedics' self-confidence in their ability to do their job, then switched to Italian and said a few more things as he followed them toward the ambulance. He gestured to Kristen, who had difficulty keeping her dragon body contained inside the traffic circle, then crossed to her ahead of the stopped traffic.

"Are you all right?" he asked her. "You were quite badly burned as well."

She waved his concern off, an odd gesture when made by a giant talon. "Dragon healing powers. My skin itches—even in this body—but it'll be fine soon. That apartment is still on fire." She gestured toward the building. It looked like the fire had indeed spread outside the sphere of magic, which wasn't a surprise. It had been so hot in there, she wouldn't be surprised if the bricks had absorbed enough thermal energy to make items and furnishings in the neighboring apartments ignite.

"It looks like the Florence fire department has it covered," he replied.

Kristen was about to admonish him when she saw that indeed, three fire trucks sprayed water into the blaze while a fourth had a ladder extended to help people down. Already, the bottom floors of the building had been evacuated.

"What were you talking to the medics about?" she asked Stonequest. It seemed, for the moment, anyway, that the danger had passed.

"I told them she's a mage and that I wanted Larry to ride with her in the ambulance to Dragon SWAT HQ. He'll be able to provide some treatment before the healers the dragons employ attend to her properly."

She couldn't help but think about what would happen to anyone else who was hurt in the apartment. There'd be no magic to cure their wounds. Mages only helped dragons, not regular people.

"What happened? How did you get me out of there?" she asked as the two of them strode toward the rest of the team.

"Like I said, it wasn't me who saved you. It was Amy. She made some kind of shield and dove in there. Somehow, she was able to protect herself and destroy the spell. From the way Larry talked, she shouldn't have been able to do either. He said the spell must have taken considerable time to put together and probably multiple mages as well. She shouldn't have been able to break it."

"She jumped in?" Kristen was horrified that she almost caused her new friend's death but also damned impressed that she was able to do what she did.

"Yeah. It was a real Kristen Hall move, if I may say so. Once she deactivated the spell, I scooped you both up."

"I still can't believe she could do that. How powerful is she?" The last question was more for herself than Stonequest.

He shrugged, obviously as unsure as she was. "I don't think we've come up against her limits yet. I'm merely glad she's okay. She's a huge—"

"Asset to the team, yeah, yeah. You didn't chew her out for saving my ass, did you?"

It was his turn to look like he was wearing nothing at all. He blushed.

"I don't want anyone to get hurt on my behalf either," she said and spared him from having to reply. "But I won't lie, it means a lot to me that she risked her life to save mine. I expect that from you cops, but from a civilian who has done this for less than a month?"

"She's a real asset," Stonequest agreed as they stopped alongside their teammates.

"Did we get anything from that apartment?" she asked them.

Heartsbane shook her head. "I peeked in there once the heat started to dissipate. It's a wreck. And now, it's soaked. If there was anything, it's gone now."

"What's our next move?" Drew asked.

Behind them, wood cracked and bricks fell, followed by a dull explosion.

Kristen turned to see that the top floor of the apartment building had partially collapsed.

"That," she said and gestured at the structure, pumped her wings, and became airborne. "Stonequest, with me. It'll be hot and your stone skin might protect you to help save some people. It shouldn't be as hot as the magic was. Emerald, Heartsbane, I think there was a water tower two apartment buildings over. I want that dumped on this fire. *Now!*"

The dragons transformed and vaulted upward to swoop after her.

"What about us?" Drew yelled from below but she had no idea what to tell him. They couldn't rush into a fire and there were no signs of the mages. Then, an idea occurred to her. It was cruel, yes, but it made the most sense.

"I see a few news crews arriving. Make sure you tell them this was a trap set by the technomages and that they get footage of the dragons dropping water on the blaze."

Drew didn't look too happy about being put on PR duty but he snapped a "Yes, ma'am," all the same and led his team toward the news van.

Kristen flew over the building. About half of the top floor had collapsed and the other half was still standing but was filled with flames. She wouldn't be able to do anything about it in her dragon form.

"Stone, look for survivors in the rubble. I'll go into the fire." Without thinking, she transformed into her human body, only to remember that she still didn't have any clothes.

She landed amongst the wreckage, stark naked yet still protected by her steel skin. Ah, well, so much for modesty. Lives were at stake.

Kristen raced into the building. Compared to the magic-fueled fire from earlier, the heat was almost nonexistent, at least for her. For the humans she heard coughing and screaming for help, it would be more than enough to kill them.

When she kicked a door open, a little old woman stood holding a baby in her arms. She scooped her easily into her arms while she held the baby, then raced to the closest window. A firefighter met her at the top of the ladder and she put her down. If the man was shocked to see a naked woman with steel skin saving lives, he didn't show it. He merely gestured at the old lady to give him the baby and climb down the ladder before he shouted a question at the dragon.

She didn't need to speak Italian to know that he asked her to check for more survivors.

Kristen glanced at Stonequest, who dug through the brick as if it were nothing but a ball pit at a kid's playground. He dragged someone from the wreckage—a young man with badly mangled legs. Again, she thought about what a mage might be able to do for him but now wasn't the time. There were more people inside the burning section of the building.

Conscious of the fact that time was running out, she raced into the building again.

The fire had intensified, but she could still hear someone screaming for help. She kicked down door after door. Most apartments were empty—a good sign—but someone still called frantically. She had begun to wonder if it was a trap or something when she found a young woman holding two screeching cats.

"Can you walk?" she asked and cursed her lack of languages.

The woman nodded—she understood English, thank God—and put the two animals in Kristen's hands before she ran out of the apartment. She followed and yelled at her to come back. Not realizing that they were already filled with smoke, the occupant had headed instinctively toward the stairs. She had no way to know that the safest way out was through the wreckage.

Kristen led the way, a kitten in each arm—they conveniently covered her breasts—and the woman followed.

When they emerged from the blaze, a news helicopter filled with photographers hovered nearby.

"Is anyone else inside?" Stonequest shouted.

"No. All clear," she replied.

He gestured to the sky and Emerald and Heartsbane dumped the water tower onto the top of the burning building.

That, of course, was the moment the photographers had waited for. It was a rare sight for dragons to help people, unfortunately, and rarer still to see two dragons pour the entire contents of a water tower on top of a building. Better yet, in the foreground of a dramatic image of a dragon-spilled waterfall smothering a fire, the photographers caught a beautiful, steel-skinned woman, who was completely naked except for the pair of kittens she held in front of her breasts.

It didn't take a media expert to guess what the front page of every newspaper on the planet would be the next morning.

Their vehicle had been damaged so the flight to base was an awkward one for Kristen. For starters, none of the dragons understood why she now felt uncomfortable about giving the humans rides when she hadn't before.

"You're always naked in your dragon form," Emerald had said. "Why does it matter if your human form doesn't have any clothes when you're in your dragon form anyway?"

"Just...can you please give them a ride?" she had said through gritted dragon teeth.

"You can give me a ride, boss," Hernandez said with a wicked smile. "I'm not a dude."

"No, but you're still a perv."

The woman had only chuckled and seemed to enjoy seeing her nude steel body even more than Keith had. Finally, she persuaded Stonequest to take the two of them. He looked even more embarrassed than she did about the whole thing.

Butters and Drew got on Emerald's back. She couldn't tell who looked more uncomfortable. Butters' southern sensibilities apparently couldn't handle it. Every time he looked at her, his dark cheeks grew even darker or—worse—he giggled like a fool. Drew, meanwhile, looked like this would be the end of any respect police had ever been shown in history.

Kristen sighed. Maybe it would have been different if a naked male police officer had saved people, but a steel-skinned woman with a figure like hers? This would do nothing but help public perception of cops and dragons. She could see that. It was awkward for her but would be good, she kept telling herself. It would definitely be good.

She looked at Beanpole and gestured for him to climb on her back. She'd only agreed to take the quiet lookout because he seemed even more uncomfortable than she did about the arrangement. For some reason, that was okay. With the humans situated, they flew to the base.

"That was very slick, Steel Dragon," Emerald shouted en route. "I've never helped people like that before. Not that directly. It felt good."

"Aw, shut up, you big softy," Heartsbane said but her aura made it quite clear that she agreed.

"Did you find anything in the apartment, Stonequest?" Drew shouted over the wind.

"I'm afraid not. I got a few survivors out and had a minute to check where the apartment had been, but there was nothing. Between the blaze, the water, and the building collapsing, I think we're back to square one."

"Not quite," Butters interjected. "Yes, we've lost a lead, but I've never seen dragons save people like this before. Not in Detroit, not in the States, and not ever. If our goal—I mean our big, crazy ultimate goal—is to stop a war between humans and dragons, this kind of thing is really important. People need to see that we can all work together to solve problems better than humans or dragons could alone."

"Very true," Heartsbane said. "Plus, every teenage boy and most teenage girls will soon have a photo of Kristen saving kittens while dragons fly around in the background. If that doesn't do something for interspecies relationships, nothing will."

CHAPTER TWENTY-ONE

K risten and the other dragons landed at the Dragon SWAT castle a few minutes before the ambulance carrying Amy, but she couldn't do anything but wait for her friend to arrive. Although once she remembered she was still naked in her human form, she asked Heartsbane to get her some clothes.

Freshly dressed, she was on hand when the ambulance finally stopped close to the entrance.

"How is she?" she asked Larry, who hovered over the girl. Given how worried he looked and that he was a mage, she wouldn't have been surprised to see him literally hovering. But although his hands were extended over the patient, his butt was firmly anchored to one of the benches along the side of the ambulance.

"She's burned fairly badly—second-degree burns almost every-where. They put in an IV and I've been sensing for nerve damage. She has a few serious places, especially on her face and hands. Hopefully, the mages here can help her." He didn't take his eyes off the girl as he spoke.

In fact, the paramedics had to ask him to stand and step out of their way so they could unload the stretcher. He didn't understand at first—not being fluent in Italian—but soon realized the meaning behind their fussy pantomime and let them do what they needed to do.

Kristen had sent orders to fetch the healers, and the local dragons had listened.

A non-magical doctor, two nurses, and two magical healers were there to greet Amy.

The paramedics and the dragons' medical staff had a brief conversation in Italian that even without the language, she could tell was one team filling the other in on wounds and what they'd done for the victim. In minutes, they rushed the young mage down a hallway toward the infirmary.

"I think maybe I should stick with her. I have already identified much of that nerve damage so I could save them some time," Larry said, his gaze still locked on Amy. There was an intensity to his voice that Kristen took for something more than concern about a fallen sister-in-arms.

"Go ahead. I want her healed and if you can help, you should. I'll call you if I need you."

"Yes, ma'am." He hurried away without a backward glance.

She watched him go and wondered how the mage felt about Amy right now. He was older than the young woman by at least a decade, but it wasn't like someone could simply turn their feelings off. Plus, since she'd discovered she was a dragon, she had spent time with beings who were centuries old. A decade didn't seem like much anymore. And then there was all the time the two mages had spent together. She was bemused by this new possibility.

Could the two be falling for each other? It was an interesting idea to think there might a be romance blossoming in the middle of her little crew. Better them than her, she thought grimly. Romance wasn't something she'd even had time to even consider since becoming a cop.

Wearily, she shook her head to scatter thoughts of what could have been as she climbed the stairs and hurried to her room. When she'd first joined Detroit SWAT, she'd found Drew attractive—any heterosexual woman would, she thought. And Stonequest was also attractive with his carved-from-marble physique. There was also something about Jim, she decided. How nice it would be to pretend she could flirt and decide between the three rather than trying to stop dragons and mages from reducing their enemies to ash for the umpteenth time.

That she thought the idea of flirting sounded fun spoke volumes about how pathetic her love life truly was.

Still, dreams of her saving men with guns swirled in her mind as she sank into her bed for a precious time of sleep. Her burns were already in much better shape than Amy's, thanks to her dragon healing powers, but it was still exhausting to regrow a body's worth of skin. She realized how lucky she was to have two leaders working with her. Between Drew and Stonequest, her team could handle itself for a few minutes. If anything came up, they could call her.

A knock on her door demanded that she wake far sooner than she wanted to.

"Come back next year!" she called.

"I have pizza," Brian replied.

She groaned and pushed to a seated position. Her poor brother was probably scared shitless. He must have gotten pizza thinking that sharing it would make her hang out with him and thus assuage some of his fear.

"Come in," she said and glanced down to make sure she was dressed for once. Not that he would have been anything but disgusted to see his sister without clothes on.

He marched in, a pizza on a silver platter in one hand—the opulence of dragons never ended—and his laptop in the other. She snatched a slice of pizza and waited for him to do the same, but to her shock, he didn't even so much as sniff at it.

"All right...so the EU passed a law in 2019 that all new cars sold on the continent have to have eCall built into them," he began without preamble.

"I'm sorry, what are you talking about?"

"Ronald Bisset's new car. What did you think I've been working on?" he responded.

Kristen rubbed her eyes and willed herself to focus. "Ronald Bisset is the guy whose apartment almost roasted me and Amy alive."

"Yeah, that's the guy—wait, what? Are you okay?"

She shook her head and snorted a laugh. "I'm fine—fine enough, anyway. It's good to know my team is finally big enough that someone's always working."

"Amy's okay too?"

"Yes. Or she will be. Okay, so you were saying Ronald Bisset has a car. Tell me why I care? We found nothing at his home so why would his car be different?"

"Bisset used nothing but burner phones. Hell, for all I know, he might have not used a phone at all. The dude was careful, real careful, but it seems he bought a new car before he moved to Florence." Brian had focused immediately on his information.

"A new car with eCar?" she asked tiredly.

"E*Call*—come on, Kristen," he responded, obviously enjoying having an edge on her mental state at that moment.

"And that is?"

"ECall is an emergency system that automatically responds to a crash by signaling local EMS. Our mage has a unit in his car."

Kristen tapped her foot as she started on another slice. "I don't want to eat this entire pizza by myself but I will if you don't get to the point."

"Help yourself. I already ate and it's not as good as Buddy's anyway," he said with a shrug. She was impressed by how committed he was to trying to change. He continued, "It seems a key feature of eCall is that—in order to get help to people in crashes quickly—it has GPS built-in. I wouldn't be surprised if there's a way to turn it off. Europeans care way more about privacy than Americans do, but good old Ronald Bisset must have let it slip his mind because he never disabled it. It's tracked his location ever since he bought the car."

Brian grinned even wider as he popped open a window on his

screen that showed a red line superimposed over a map of Europe zoomed enough to include Paris and Florence.

"Do you think this guy will take us to his hideout here in Florence?" Kristen asked with the first glimmer of understanding.

"I can try that if you want, but I have something better."

Her ears perked up. "What could be better than knowing where their base in the city is?"

"I think I know where they make their bullets. He goes to a farm in the south of France."

"Because he went to a farm? I'll need more than that. Bisset might have family out there." She hoped he was right, but she'd do them both more good to play devil's advocate.

"This is not a family farm passed down over the years. It's not locally owned but is registered to a corporation."

"What corporation?"

"Franco Farms. It has existed for about six months and was set up by another corporation that was set up by a shell corporation, and so on and so forth. I can trace the money, but it will take me time to do it if you don't want anyone to notice."

"Don't do anything that will get you caught. No one knows we have a techie yet. I don't want them to know that given everything else they know," she muttered. "Is the car there now?"

Brian shook his head. "No, it's parked in the suburbs somewhere outside Florence right now. I have an address too, but it's at the home of someone who's owned it for eleven years. It seems fairly normal so far, not like the farm."

"From your tone, I can only guess that you have a plan?"

"Hell yeah! We know where the farm is. That must be where they have another dragon imprisoned. I say we swoop in, bust every damn mage in that place—Stonequest doesn't think there can be many more than we've already seen or else they would have used them—and save the dragon if it's still there. After that, we can drop in on Mom and Dad."

Kristen smiled limply at her brother. "Brian...dropping in on Mom and Dad won't be any part of any plan."

"But how stoked would they be if we simply showed up at your villa or whatever. Mom would lose it!"

"And say we miss one of these mages and they follow us there? What happens then?"

"We could be careful—"

"Brian, I know you're trying to help. You are helping. This is a great lead and we will use it, but we can't spring into action and then go visit our parents. If that's what you think you signed up for, it might be better if you went home now," she said but tried to keep her voice kind.

"Oh, come on, Kristen, that's bullshit. I knew this would be dangerous. I bet I understood better than you did when you became part of Dragon SWAT. I did some research."

"I don't think running searches on the Internet counts as research, I hate to say," she countered.

He flushed crimson at that but at least he didn't argue. "All right, so if you think this farm is so important, what do we do about it? I assume you don't want to leave it there."

"No… No, of course not. And I agree we need to move quickly. What else can we get on this farm? I'd like to know how many mages are there. If there are regular workers, that kind of thing."

"I can't simply show you whatever you want, Kristen. It's not like I have a satellite or a drone in the clouds."

"Why not?"

"Huh?" Brian startled and looked both confused and excited at what she was asking.

"Why don't you have a satellite and a drone to watch this place?" Kristen asked and tested the idea herself as she said it.

"We don't have a satellite or those kinds of drones," he replied and sounded much like a kid telling his mom that no, he did not have a bicycle and why was she making him leave his birthday party to go into the garage.

"These dragons probably have access to surveillance satellites," she added.

"Really?"

"It's never come up before, but yeah, I'm sure they do. Do you think fire-breathing dragons would let cameras they couldn't monitor into space? Without them interfering with the rocket launches? I'll put Stonequest on it but I'm sure we can get eyes on that place."

"Okay, sure, and then what?" He had opened a document on his computer and was taking notes.

"If we had eyes on this farm, could we trace every car that visited there in the last month or so?"

"Uh…I would probably need a drone to get license plates, but yeah, sure."

"And if you had the cars—"

He finished her thought for her. "We could track these assholes wherever they go and make sure that when we catch them—"

"We catch them all," she finished.

Brian nodded and typed furiously. "This might take a few days to set up."

"That's fine," Kristen said. "Now, go tell the team and leave me to finish this pizza and sleep off the repercussions."

"Sure." He scooped his laptop up and excused himself.

She thanked him as he left, not sure if he heard her and beyond caring either way. Her only focus now was pizza and a mattress—a blessed, blessed mattress. She would lay down for a moment and rest before she finished the pizza.

Seconds later, she was asleep.

CHAPTER TWENTY-TWO

I t took three days for Brian to acquire the necessary satellite footage. Three long days of waiting for another dragon to get shot, or another bomb to go off, or waiting for Castillo Montalbano itself to come under attack. The team encountered nothing besides frayed nerves. Even so, Kristen was relieved when they received their intel and were ready to spring into action.

For a time, she had thought it wouldn't happen. The European Dragon SWAT team had protested strongly against using a drone. Rosso, in particular, argued against the idea, which increased her suspicions regarding the Italian dragon until he explained that using a combination of satellite and traffic cameras was a better option because it would be more discreet.

She might have challenged him on the issue, but her brother had been quite pleased with the idea of surveying their enemies with traffic cameras, so she had relented. Fortunately, it had worked.

He followed four vehicles that regularly came and went from the farm. They now had four more probable terrorists—two women named Bethany Cruz and Sarah Mitchell and two men, Mani Espinoza and Neal Havington—plus Ronald Bisset. Based on the profiles, they were fairly certain Havington was the leader, as

Espinoza had a massive pair of shoulders and the mage who had thrown fireballs at them had been of a more slender build.

Two of the suspects, Havington and Mitchell, had not left the farm in the three days that they had been observing it, but the other two seemed to like to spend their time in Florence. They were the subject of Kristen's briefing.

"We'll strike them both as fast and as quietly as possible," she said to her assembled human and dragon force. "We'll split up because I think the two mages with the most power—our sources suggest those are Havington and Mitchell since she hasn't left the farm—are out of the city."

"Why don't we simply raid the farm?" Rosso asked. He and a group of his European dragons were in on the briefing too, apparently so he could play devil's advocate.

"These technomages already know we can locate and attack their bases," she explained. "I want them to know we can hunt them when they're in public too. They've had the advantage in intel over us for a long time. I hope this mission will send the message that those times are over."

"Plus," Stonequest added and stared sternly at the Italian, "if we raid the farm first, these two mages will go underground and we won't see them again until they join another cell and use whatever they've learned about us to hurt us. We must eliminate them first and then your team raids the farm. That way, we clean up this mess that's come to Florence."

Rosso nodded. "As long as we hit the farm as soon as this is over."

"We will, and I want your team ready, Rosso," Kristen assured him. "Because of that, I'll divide my people into two teams, one to target each of these mages."

Nods from her team confirmed their assent. The Italian's mages didn't look pleased to be left out of the operation, but they were all more interested in a strike on the nest rather than picking up the vermin that were hiding in the city.

"I'll lead a team to take Bethany Cruz at work. She's a security guard at the Uffizi. Apparently, she had waited to get the job for a long time before she moved here. I hope that if we apprehend her there in a public place she seems to care about, she won't put up much of a fight. Drew, Keith, Jim, you three will be with me, as well as Heartsbane."

"This kind of feels like bringing a paperclip to a knife fight," Keith said with a nervous laugh.

"Don't feel that way, rookie," Drew interjected. "These mages have trained to fight dragons while you've trained under me. We'll bring this Cruz in cleanly and quickly. With that done, we'll get a couple of bottles of wine and start aerating them for the other team."

The Rookie nodded but didn't seem convinced. "She'll have magic, though."

"And you'll have Tazers," Rosso said with a shrug. "I contacted the Uffizi. They agreed that you can have stun guns and projectile tasers as well."

"Guns might be better," Jim muttered.

"We'll be fine." Heartsbane snorted. "Two dragons and three cops against a mage? Like Drew said, we'll race the rest of you home."

"B Team will raid Espinoza's house," Kristen said to bring the meeting back on track.

"Can we stick with Mani?" Butters asked with a chuckle. "Espinoza is a mouthful."

"Sure. Mani, whatever. Stonequest, Emerald, Beanpole, Butters, and Hernandez will make up a team. I'll send Larry too because it's far more likely to be magically trapped like the other apartment was."

"How's Amy?" Keith asked.

"She's all right," Larry said and chewed his lip. "The mages are doing great for her, but Lady Steel and I agree that she should sit this one out. We'll need her if this goes south and maybe at the farm."

"It won't be a problem," Stonequest said. "We have the stronger dragons and the humans with the better eyes. I'd say we'd wait for you to start in on the wine, but we don't want to wait that long." A glimmer of a challenge was visible in his eyes.

"All right, enough chest-beating," Kristen said, inwardly relieved that her teams could still keep a light mood while preparing to face a possibly murderous mage. "We strike them clean and fast, get them back here, and raid the farm tomorrow before lunch. Brian's watching by satellite, but I can't see how they could get a dragon out of there in less time than that. We hope that none of them know we're coming, but we should all still assume that they are prepared for trouble, so be ready. Any questions?"

There weren't, so everyone got to work.

"Do we still have eyes on this asshole?" Stonequest asked over his radio. He, Heartsbane, Larry, and Hernandez were at the bottom floor of the apartment, ready to take the steps to the second story and capture Mani.

"Our target is still watching an Italian game show and laughing uproariously. I'm kind of jealous. I wish I could see the screen," Butters replied. He and his partner Beanpole were stationed across the street on top of another apartment building. When they'd all first started working together, Butters and Beanpole had seemed uncomfortable about using nicknames but honestly, Stonequest found them easier to remember than proper humans' names like Keith.

"Then we'll go in," he confirmed and led the ground team up the stairs.

They were in place in less than a minute. It could have been less, but Emerald and Stonequest didn't use their full speed to better accommodate the mage and the human cop.

They surrounded the door.

"Does he know we're coming?" Stonequest asked Butters.

"I don't think so. If he does, he must be a beast at poker. As far as we can tell, he's still enjoying the hell out of his show," the sniper replied.

"Check the door," he ordered Hernandez and Larry.

The woman went about her task with tools whose purpose Stonequest could only guess at and seemed satisfied after only a moment. A curt shake of her head told him there were no non-magical traps.

"Larry?"

"Don't make me rush this. I might set it off."

He nodded. They had expected the apartment to be trapped, of course, like the last one had been. At the same time, they had also hoped that since the mage was actually inside the apartment, the trap wouldn't be armed. It seemed logical because no matter how committed you were to a cause, it was still crazy to willingly roast yourself alive.

"This one's different, then? Hall's mage couldn't undo it from the outside," Emerald asked. Stonequest needed to remind him to stop calling Amy Hall's mage, but now wasn't the time to break down a lifetime of grammar habits.

"Yeah, this one's different. I'd have it done if you'd simply shut up and let me—"

A pop issued from inside the apartment and a flash of light from under the door.

"Brace yourselves!" Stonequest ordered his team. Everyone complied instantly. Emerald and their leader each stood to the right and left of the doorframe and Hernandez and Larry stood a step behind them.

Nothing else came from the apartment. Instead, Butters yelled into his radio. "Go, go, he knows you're here—go!"

The team surged into action. Stonequest kicked the door open. Emerald and Hernandez raced in with their weapons ready. It was kind of impressive to see the dragon with a gun. Dragon SWAT had never really bothered with petty firearms—why bother when one could simply take their true form and unleash fire upon one's foes?—but he had taken well to the weapon as well as the human tactic of fully securing a location.

"Living room's clear!" the woman shouted.

"The bedroom is too!" Butters shouted over the radio. "He went into a bathroom or something. Move now. He went straight there so he must have a tunnel or something. Damn it, Beanpole, where are you going? Beanpole!"

Stonequest used a burst of dragon speed to race through the living room, the bedroom, and into the master bathroom. Once inside, he found nothing at all—no mage and no secret door. Nothing but a faint trace of magic.

"The asshole's not here," he said.

"That's because he's outside," Larry shouted from the hall.

"Emerald, go!" he ordered, but it didn't need to be said as Emerald had already raced into action. He hurtled through the living room and sprinted down the hall. Gunshots came from the hallway—no doubt a pistol loaded with dragon bullets.

Stonequest raced into the hallway as well.

"He went down those stairs. I'd have pursued but standing orders—"

"It's all right, Emerald. I don't want you to get shot. Larry, do you think you can cover us? I don't want to take any of these bullets but I don't want him to get away either."

"I can try," the mage said, and the three of them ran down the hall, now shielded by a sphere of magic. They reached the top of the stairs and looked down to where Mani stood and aimed his pistol at them.

"You assholes will never take me alive!" he shouted vehemently, fired a few shots, and ran out into the afternoon sun.

"Shit. Butters, do you have eyes on him? Butters?" Stonequest yelled as he jumped down the entire flight of stairs and followed the mage outside.

The sniper didn't reply as he was too busy laughing.

The dragon thought it a bizarre time for gallows humor until he saw what had happened outside—and what Beanpole had accomplished.

The mage was crawling away from him, obviously delirious, with a tranquilizer dart protruding from his neck. Beanpole strolled along beside him. "It's good to know I'm not an asshole," he said a second or two before the tranquilizer worked its way into the mage's bloodstream and made the man pass out.

Stonequest strode toward them, both proud and impressed at how well the operation had gone despite the mage somehow leaving the apartment and almost escaping. He retrieved a pair of magic-blocking handcuffs and slipped them on the unconscious man.

"Let's hope Kristen's team is already done with their job," he said, but he knew that was too much to hope for.

CHAPTER TWENTY-THREE

The Uffizi was by no means a small museum. It was three stories tall and consisted of two long hallways lined by rooms filled with art and separated by a courtyard in the middle. Inside, they contained art more valuable than anything Kristen had imagined—priceless works by Michelangelo, Da Vinci, Caravaggio, Rembrandt, and even Botticelli, including The Birth of Venus. Her mom had a coffee mug printed with that painting so she recognized it immediately.

A replica of Michelangelo's David stood outside. Across from this, a covered walkway was filled with statues she couldn't even hope to name. They approached through a wide plaza surrounded by buildings made of sandy yellow brick.

On a clock tower above the Uffizi, Heartsbane was stationed in the bland coveralls of a maintenance worker. Keith and Jim were at the main entrance, ready to pop the mage with a tranquilizer and cuff her if she made it past their teammates.

Kristen and Drew would go in and it would be easy enough to play the part of American tourists. They weren't sure exactly where their mark—Bethany Cruz—would be, but she worked as a security guard so they at least knew she'd be in uniform and would pay attention to the patrons.

They reached the top floor—where the tour of the museum started —without locating Cruz. Kristen was no art buff, but it was hard to not be impressed with what she saw. The Uffizi boasted one of the most impressive collections of art from the Renaissance period in all of Europe. Everywhere she looked, she recognized images that had persisted in pop-culture even after hundreds of years. An angel played some kind of guitar—a lute, maybe, although she wasn't sure—that was way too big for it. Statues of people who'd lived centuries before included a marble torso of someone from ancient Greece. Pre-renaissance paintings were displayed as well. They seemed flat and somewhat lifeless compared to the works of the great masters, in her opinion, but they were still gorgeous. Most were images of how people represented the divine so long before.

"It's amazing what people have done, isn't it?" Drew said. "It's inspiring."

"It is," she agreed, although at that moment, her gaze settled on another of the great subjects of the Renaissance—a portrait of one of the dragons who had helped to stabilize the region and thus enabled the Renaissance to happen. The Occiodoro family of dragons was as important to the people of Florence as the Medici's had been, perhaps more so. If they had not made alliances with neighboring cities and put an end to the constant skirmishes that had marred the Dark Ages, who could say whether the Renaissance would ever have happened?

Primus Occiodoro stared out of his painting and looked like he understood all of this. He was in his human form but his eyes were still gold, and one of his hands had been painted as the claw of a dragon. In the background were the rolling hills of Tuscany and a dragon flew over them, incinerating cropland.

"That's Occiodoro's true form in the background," one of the staff said. The woman had mousy features and looked exactly like Bethany Cruz, their target. Her accent wasn't local either.

"Is that right?" Kristen said and looked away before the woman recognized her.

"It's said there would have been another three Italian masters of the Renaissance period, but in his rage at their failure to capture his benevolence, Occiodoro burned them all. This painting was done by Michelangelo, but there are no records of the two ever being together. It might be the reason Michelangelo was spared the same fate as the long-lost masters," Cruz explained. Kristen looked at her out of the corner of her eye while the woman fixed her gaze on the painting. There was a bitterness to her voice, one Kristen had heard before when talking to Constance.

"Do you think all dragons are like Occiodoro?" she asked and tried to sound polite.

The guard startled at the question and looked at her more intently. She immediately froze, recognition plain on her face.

"I believe some dragons believe in justice. Do you?" Kristen persisted.

"I...you're the Steel Dragon. I, uh...I saw your face in the newspaper." Cruz studied her and the scrutiny made it clear that she saw much more than only her face.

"I know who you are too. And I want you to know that we'll do everything we can to make sure you get a fair trial. If you're not your cell's leader and can help us get to him, we think that might help your sentence."

"I don't know what you're talking about," Cruz replied. "If you'll excuse me." She moved to walk past them, but Drew stepped in her path.

"Don't." He shook his head. "We have the exits guarded. There's no way out." He took out the pair of magic-dampening cuffs that Stonequest had given him.

"Come with us willingly, cooperate, and prove to the dragons that you got caught up in all this and that you mean to change," Kristen said.

"Dragons won't forgive," Cruz said and spat in her face. She didn't run and instead, raised her hands and let Drew cuff her as the Steel Dragon wiped the spit from her face.

"It's smart of you to come with us, ma'am," Drew said.

"I might not even make a note of your spit if you don't try anything funny," she added, happy that the woman was in cuffs.

"Excuse me." Someone tapped the Steel Dragon's shoulder. "Can one of you direct me to where I can see the Botticelli?" The woman's accent was slightly American and slightly Italian like someone who had grown up in different places.

"Sure." She pointed without turning fully away from Cruz.

"That room?" the woman asked again.

"Yes." Impatient now, she turned to see who this was and also to reveal the cuffed security guard. Handcuffs should be enough to turn off even the most persistent of tourists.

The error of that assumption was immediately apparent when she turned into an unexpected punch.

The blow was strong enough to hurl her into a statue of a woman looking at the sky—and reduce it to only a torso when her skull connected and shattered it.

Kristen pushed to her feet and grimaced. Her collision with the marble had inflicted a fair number of scratches. She was bleeding from her head and could feel a bruise bloom on her shoulder. It might have been enough to take a regular human out of a fight but of course, she wasn't any regular old human. She was the Steel Dragon, and her healing powers already began to shrink the bruise and seal the gash on her forehead before she had stood.

"Ma'am, I need you to back the hell away," Drew said as he released Cruz and reached for the taser at his belt.

"Yeah…that'll be a no," the woman replied.

"I warned you." He grasped his weapon but before he could draw it, the woman delivered a driving chest kick into him that catapulted him out of one of the windows and into the courtyard below.

Kristen ran to look out the window and saw that he had landed in a crumpled heap. There wasn't a pool of blood—thank God—but he wasn't moving either.

"If he's dead, I swear to God I will kill you," she said. "Try picking on someone your own strength, you coward." She walked toward the woman, who must be the mage who wore the flower mask—Sarah

Mitchell was her name. Their intel said she was still on the farm, though, and she hadn't displayed anything like this kind of strength in their last fight.

"I've looked forward to a challenge," her adversary said and advanced toward her with slow assurance like a parent who knew their child was about to come running toward them despite words that said the opposite. "But I should probably warn you. If you fighting your hardest depends on whether that traitorous rat outside is dead or not, you'll lose."

"I don't know who the fuck you think I am, but let me give you a clue," Kristen said and turned her skin to steel as the woman approached.

"I know who you are. You're a traitor to those who want equality in the world. You could have taken the chance to prove that dragons truly are better than the blood that courses through their veins, but you didn't. You're a disgrace, but I think I have you at a disadvantage. I am the Condor—but you can call me Katrina—and I'm here to kick your ass. I might not be as shiny as you but I am most certainly equally as strong."

As if to prove her point, Katrina's skin turned to iron.

Kristen froze when it happened. She had never seen anyone display an ability like her steel skin before. Stonequest's stone form was kind of close, but this woman was beyond mere marble. Plus, time and time again, dragons and mages had told her how unusual her powers were and how unique this ability was. And maybe it was, as this woman didn't look the same. Yes, she was covered in metal and yes, she could move as fluidly as she could, but while Kristen's steel skin gleamed like a new stainless steel blade, the iron form she faced was darkened like the spikes on the top of a cast-iron fence.

Katrina was fast too, and in the moment that Kristen hesitated, her opponent raced forward with a burst of speed and threw a shoulder into her chest that launched her through a wall.

It was like being a rookie in Dragon SWAT all over again. She didn't understand how this mage—was she a mage?—could be so fast.

Constance had been fast, yes, but she'd also avoided hand-to-hand combat unless forced into it. This woman seemed insistent on it.

Rather than attempt to rescue Cruz, she stepped through the hole in the wall to where the Steel Dragon untangled herself from a frame and a piece of painted canvas that was worth more than her parents' house a few times over.

"Everyone, get out of here!" Kristen shouted at the throngs of tourists. Some had snapped pictures of her, apparently thinking that a woman bulldozed through a painting would make a great story to tell once they'd returned home and changed into regular clothes to live their regular lives again.

No one listened to her, no doubt because she was dressed like a tourist herself and still struggled with the artwork.

As Katrina came closer, though, she stopped her attempt to minimize the damage and simply ripped the painting to free herself.

This drew more gasps from the tourists and a storm of camera clicks as people hurried to document the sacrilegious behavior.

"She's not wrong, you know," the attacker said as she released another burst of speed to reach her target. Before the Steel Dragon could block, an iron fist pounded into her gut. She doubled over and the woman grasped her by the throat and lifted her off the ground by her neck. "This exhibit hall is about to be closed for repairs."

That finally seemed to penetrate the tourists' complacency and they began to scream and run frantically to one of the two exits to the room.

Kristen saw all this but hardly processed it while she attempted to break the woman's hold on her throat. It was strong like the grasp of a dragon but impossible to break because her fingers were dark gray, almost black iron. She had broken dragon grips before by hammering on them with her steel fists, but that didn't work on her adversary.

"You're pathetic. You could have been so much more—like me, even. Alas. Instead, you're merely a glorified guard working for corrupt leaders."

She stared at Katrina while she choked her. It was almost like looking in a mirror. The skin was an obvious similarity but there was more to it—the way the woman's hair fell, her nose, the curve of her mouth, and hell, even her figure. It was all similar enough to her for the two to be sisters.

In silence, she processed all this while the other woman squatted and thrust up with enough force to hurl her into the ceiling. She careened into it, through the roof, and into the late afternoon sun of Italy.

"Heartsbane!" she shouted before gravity could drag her down again.

"Hall?" the dragon exclaimed. She stood barely a stone's throw away on the roof and watched the sides of the building instead of the middle because who in their right fucking mind would be able to throw someone through a roof?

"Get the team! I met our hostile!"

She let gravity take hold and fell into the museum through the hole in the roof Katrina had made using her body as a wrecking ball.

CHAPTER TWENTY-FOUR

K risten plummeted toward her opponent and grew ever closer, but Katrina saw her coming and stepped smartly aside.

As a result, it was the antique marble floor that she cracked rather than the woman's face.

Her adversary wasted no time and kicked her savagely in the gut. When the iron foot met her steel-covered ribcage, it sounded like the world's largest gong had been struck by the world's largest hammer.

It didn't hurt as much as being choked had. She was used to being pummeled and could knock bullets aside, so a punch from an iron fist wouldn't disable her. Not by itself, anyway.

Katrina seemed to realize this as well as she snaked her hand out to grasp her steel hair. Kristen recognized the danger of that, so she spun and knocked the other woman's legs out from under her—this time, it made the sound of massive wind chimes being struck twice—and she fell heavily to deliver a significant amount of damage to the flooring.

The woman crawled away and pushed to her feet before her opponent could scramble on top of her.

"What are you?" Kristen demanded and braced herself as her attacker ran toward her.

"Your worst enemy," Katrina replied before she lowered her head and drove into her. Again, their two metal bodies gonged when they struck but this time, the ringing was cut short as the force of the attack hurled the Steel Dragon through a wall and into the hallway.

She struggled to stay upright—being forced through a wall was not great for one's sense of balance—although the other woman seemed to have no such concerns. She strode through the hole to where the mage cowered, her hands cuffed together. With deft movements, she tore the bond apart like it was nothing more than a Christmas ribbon. The spell that had previously limited the mage's power dissipated like it was nothing but a small flurry of dust caught in the wind.

Katrina refocused on Kristen and each step of her iron body cracked the floor beneath her. If the fight continued like this much longer, it was almost a certainty that the entire Uffizi gallery might collapse from the extensive damage.

It seemed Jim had similar concerns about fine art as he shouted an insult when he reached the top of the stairs to the floor they were on. "That metal statue looks like a cheap knock-off of the Steel Dragon."

The woman smiled at the challenge. She surged at Kristen, kneed her in the gut, and raced toward the Wonderkid.

From her place of agony on the ground, Kristen saw that he didn't even try to run. Instead, he raised his weapon and fired three tranquilizer darts at his attacker's chest.

The iron-skinned woman didn't bother to deflect them. She simply let all three darts bounce off her chest like they were nothing more than ping pong balls. Jim had no time to run before she caught him by the throat and lifted him off the floor—her favorite form of intimidation, apparently.

Fortunately, it didn't work this time around. The rookie—showing some experience for once—had hidden on the other side of the doorway and directly beside Jim. "I guess tranquilizers don't work, huh?" he said and took a step toward Katrina.

"Not unless your intention was to prove your incompetence," she replied.

"No, not really." The Wonderkid gasped, his voice rough as his vocal cords were being crushed in the woman's iron hold.

"What about tasers?" Keith asked innocently.

"Wha—"

He fired a taser before she could finish and she fell forward and dropped her captive as she did so. Her muscles spasmed, useless to help her as she tumbled down the stairway and demolished a few of the stairs.

"What the fuck is she?" Jim wheezed as he tried to scramble away from the collapsing staircase.

Kristen scrambled to her feet and ran to her two friends. "I don't have a fucking clue. I've never seen metal skin on a mage before."

"Maybe that's because she's not a mage," Keith said as he stared down the stairway.

"What else could she—"

She wasn't able to finish her question as the Rookie shoved her back with enough force to make even her steel body move. "Run!" he bellowed.

Seconds later, the stairway exploded behind them.

Not like a bomb or a spell. It exploded like a massive dragon with iron scales destroyed it in search of its prey.

"She's a dragon!" Keith yelled repeatedly as he ran down the hallway.

Kristen braced herself, prepared to be struck by the dragon. She didn't want to transform inside the museum unless she had to, so it was with ease that the mage was able to run past her toward the dragon's claws.

Katrina, now in dragon form, roared as she caught the mage in one talon and lashed out with her tail to shatter the windows overlooking the courtyard in the center of the Uffizi. She took to the sky with the mage in her claw.

"Now!" she screamed at her partner. "Do it now!"

"We're not supposed to be seen," the mage shrieked and her terror betrayed the existence of the secret she was supposed to keep.

But whatever was at the heart of the argument would have to wait as Heartsbane had already transformed into her dragon form and taken flight. She divebombed Katrina and attempted to rake her claws across the dragon's iron hide, but her assault was ineffectual.

"You can't hurt me. You're nothing but flesh," her adversary roared as she pumped her wings and pushed the other dragon aside.

"Mind over matter, bitch," Heartsbane growled and her eyes flashed with temper.

A sudden and overwhelming urge to stay down overpowered Kristen. She felt like the sky was filled with death, dragons, bullets, fire, birds, needles, the dark—everything that had ever scared her. She wasn't alone in feeling this way as Jim and Keith both flung themselves prostrate and cowered with their hands over their heads. The few people still in the museum did the same and made no attempt to look at the unseen sky.

Even the people outside near the statue gallery and large courtyard in the front of the Uffizi reacted in terror despite all of them trying to flee the area only a moment before—a much more sensible choice when two dragons were in combat.

Even the mage yelled at Katrina to land, to go down, and to get out of the sky.

"It's her aura, you dolt," the dragon roared and blasted her adversary with fire.

Heartsbane pulled back and the aural power she'd exercised wavered. Kristen could see it fail in real-time when a group of people near the two combatants scrambled to their feet and resumed their frantic bid to escape.

Katrina saw this as well as anyone and pressed her advantage. She pumped her massive almost black wings and tried to gain height on Heartsbane.

It might have worked if Kristen had been content to sit and watch the battle, which she wasn't, of course. She launched out of the window and transformed into her dragon form in mid-air. Rather than donning her steel skin, she remained in regular flesh. She weighed less when she wasn't coated in steel and she was able to gain altitude and catch up to her quarry faster. As soon as she was within striking range, she turned her teeth to steel and bit the end of Katrina's tail.

The dragon yowled and almost dropped her mage. She remained airborne but only barely, and the Steel dragon released her tail as she dropped lower. Now, Kristen had the advantage of altitude.

The iron dragon understood that she was now trapped close to the ground—never a good position for a dragon—but she didn't accept it.

She tucked her wings and spread them moments before she made impact. Apparently, she could turn her iron skin off as well and she did so now. She still looked much the same—her scales were a dark-gray, almost black like the color of cast iron, but they didn't look as dense. With a single powerful thrust of her wings, she rocketed through the covered area of statues and swiped the head off one of them with the tip of her tail.

She turned into the plaza, no doubt with the intention to gain altitude.

Heartsbane was ready. While her teammate had latched onto the iron dragon's tail, she had gained altitude and moved to the end of the plaza. When Katrina tried to ascend, she blasted her in the face with fire.

Katrina brushed the flames off—her iron-colored scales didn't seem affected by the heat—and tried to leave down one of the streets.

Kristen was already there, blocked her path, and forced her to turn back into the plaza.

Again, the iron dragon tried to flee but Heartsbane clawed at her face. Apparently, her eyes were as vulnerable as anyone else's because when faced with a dragon hell-bent on scooping her eyeballs out with her talons, she turned away once more.

This time, Katrina turned her scales to normal and simply tried to fly over one of the apartment buildings, but the Steel Dragon had anticipated this. She slashed at her with the ax-blade tip on her tail. This didn't hurt her opponent, but it did force her to don her iron skin again. That made her lose a little height and she powered into the top floor of one of the buildings framing the plaza.

Kristen thought that might have been the end, but their adversary was a stalwart warrior. She wouldn't give in easily. The Steel Dragon pushed off the crumbling building and glided across the courtyard toward Katrina.

"You're pinned in. Give it up!" she shouted before she unleashed a stream of fire at her.

"Now, you fool—now!" the trapped dragon yelled at the mage in her talon. "Do it now or I'm captured and you're dead."

As if to prove her point, Katrina transformed into her human shape, despite still being airborne, and caught Cruz in her arms. The mage was crying as she took a scroll from her pocket and said a few words over it while the dragon held her cradled securely in her arms as if her strength wasn't lessened even an iota in her human form.

Still, impact with the asphalt at the speed she traveled at would hurt, even if she was made of iron.

It seemed, however, that Katrina had no intention of touching the ground at all.

Cruz continued to mumble the spell until a circle of swirling blue mist appeared below the two women. Katrina fell through it, as did Cruz, although they didn't come out the other side. Instead, they simply vanished into the ring of blue mist as if it were a door to somewhere else.

Kristen realized that it was exactly what must have happened. Somehow, this mage had a spell that could teleport not only herself but whoever went through it. She didn't know how it worked but she didn't think the mage would leave it open for the rest of the afternoon. She pumped her wings and tried to reach the portal.

Close...closer...*closer!* She transformed into her human form and shoved her feet forward, but the magical gateway closed and she plummeted into the plaza. She rolled for a short distance and ripped the surface like she was a piece of airline debris that had fallen from the sky.

She was all right, though. Steel skin had serious advantages.

Kristen pushed to her feet and looked around her. The entire plaza was empty except for her teammates, who raced toward her with their weapons aimed at the sky.

Kristen looked once more for Katrina and Cruz but saw nothing. She reached out for their auras and felt nothing.

They were gone.

"Dammit!"

CHAPTER TWENTY-FIVE

"What's the plan?" Heartsbane asked as she landed beside Kristen and took her human form. It was odd to see her in coveralls, but that was what she'd worn for the stakeout and despite all her bluster, it didn't seem like she wanted to get naked in the square any more than her boss had.

The Steel Dragon shook her head. She knew what she wanted to do, which was to hunt this...this dragon. Unfortunately, that would have to wait. "First, find Drew and make sure he's all right. Then, meet me, Keith, and Jim back here."

"Sure," the other woman said and didn't sound too pleased to be sent to carry a human. Then again, she seldom sounded pleased about anything.

While Kristen waited for her to return, the first responders began to arrive.

Dragon SWAT was the first on the scene. They'd been told about it, after all, and it didn't take a bright detective to realize that something had gone horribly wrong.

Human police made an appearance as well, much to her relief. While the dragons proceeded to sense for magic and appraise the damage to some of the art, the humans secured the museum, set up a perimeter, and checked on the few people who had managed to stay nearby during the brawl.

EMS arrived only moments later and rushed into the museum. She hoped their haste would prove to be unnecessary, but she had no idea if anyone had been hurt. The other woman—dragon?—had been so fast, she hadn't been able to focus on anything but her.

Keith and Jim exited the Uffizi but before she could go to them, her least favorite type of emergency responder blocked her path.

"Investigator Hall...Investigator Hall!" A man with an American accent cut through the din of the official interaction and the clamor of the other reporters to ask questions. "How much damage has been done to the Uffizi collection?"

"No comment," she replied.

"So, some damage has been done?"

She gestured toward the ruined staircase. "Obviously."

"And will you personally pay for the damages or will the Dragon Council?"

"I think the ones who should pay for this are the—" She caught herself before she voiced her thought. Obviously, the technomages knew they were there and what their intention was, but did the public as a whole know their purpose for being there? According to the papers, they had merely saved lives. "Those responsible, obviously," she finished lamely.

"Were any paintings damaged?" a female Italian reporter asked but before she could pretend to respond intelligently to the question, an officer from Dragon SWAT shooed her away and addressed the news crews.

"We do not know the full extent of the damage, but without the swift intervention of Investigator Hall, we believe the Uffizi itself could have been destroyed. While we are still assessing the damage, we are thankful for her assistance in this matter."

Ah, that was more like it. Nothing like a good PR guy to turn losses into a success. Yes, she had stopped the other woman from destroying the entire museum, but she might not have been there at all if she hadn't authorized the operation to catch Cruz at her place of work.

There would be time to play the blame game later, though. Heartsbane returned with a blessedly conscious Drew. Kristen pulled the two of them as well as Keith and Jim into a huddle among the statues that stood outside the Uffizi.

"What the fuck hit me?" Drew asked. He'd no doubt suffered a concussion as his speech was slightly slurred.

"I don't know for sure," Kristen replied and glanced at the other dragon for clues. "Could that have been a mage? I've never heard of them harnessing magic to change into a dragon. Is that possible?"

"It once was," Heartsbane replied. "But it has been ages since anyone has done such a thing. No mage has done that since the first Mage War, and as far as I know, the secrets of how to transform died with the last rebels in that conflict."

"So you don't think it could have been a mage?" she asked and didn't like the answer the evidence was already pointing to.

Her teammate laughed in her face as if to squash any hopes of her thoughts being wrong. "I'm sure that was a dragon. She had speed, strength, and reflexes in her human form, an aura, and—in case you didn't notice—she could turn into a fucking dragon. The evidence seems to point to one thing."

"But she looked so much like Kristen!" Keith said. He sounded too excited as if they hadn't faced a foe who had beaten her and made her look like a little girl on the playground.

"No," she protested and glanced at Jim and Drew to either confirm or deny what he had said. Kristen didn't want it to be true. It couldn't be true.

"Sorry, Red, but it's true," Drew said. "I had a decent look at her before she knocked me out. She was exactly like you."

"Except she fought for the wrong side," Heartsbane grumbled.

"Which means—"

Kristen finished Keith's sentence before he could. There was no point in denying it, not when everyone else had come to the same conclusion as she had. "That was my sister."

She didn't think she'd ever experienced a more awkward moment of silence. It was so bad that Heartsbane, of all people, was the one to break it.

"We don't think of siblings the same way as humans do, though, so don't beat yourself too much up about it. You're obviously from the same clutch of eggs but she was clearly raised somewhere other than the suburbs of Detroit."

"I don't understand," Drew said, his voice still a little rough from the blow to his head. "We found another of Kristen's siblings, but that one was chained and they used it for parts."

"Her name is Stella," Kristen snapped, perhaps a little too harshly given that he was still recovering from being hurled out of a building.

"I bet they raise most of them like they did Stella," Jim said and rubbed his chin thoughtfully. "That's the only way they could get all this ammunition, but maybe they had an extra or this one seemed healthier than the others or something."

Keith took up the hypothesis. "They must have trained her from a kid."

"But their goal is to kill all dragons," Heartsbane protested.

"Yes, but Constance also tried to get me to join their side every chance she had. From the way Katrina talked, she must have been indoctrinated since birth."

"Poor thing," the Wonderkid lamented and shook his head.

"How so?" Heartsbane asked. "She kicked the Steel Dragon's ass. It couldn't have been that bad."

He looked appalled at her callousness. "Kristen grew up in a normal human family with a focus on justice and honor. Her dad was a cop, for Christ's sake, and her mom thinks it's practically dishonorable to not offer people dessert. She had good, decent people for parents. This—"

"Katrina. She told me her name was Katrina," Kristen said.

"Right, Katrina must have grown up surrounded by people who were at war, fighting for their lives against an overwhelming enemy." Jim scowled as he considered that. "They were able to do quite a number on my brain in boot camp. I can't imagine what an entire life of that shit must be like."

Another moment of silence followed although this one was less awkward, maybe because they were all focused on the same tragic thing—Katrina's childhood.

Finally, Kristen cleared her throat. "Well, they're not here and we shouldn't be here either."

"What's the plan, boss?" Drew asked. That was quickly becoming both her favorite and least favorite question, if only because when she had the answer, it was never a good one.

"They will almost certainly move their base now. I had hoped to catch those two mages and take the base in the morning, but we can't wait. Heartsbane, what do you know about teleportation?" she asked.

"Not much. I've never seen it done but mages tend to specialize in a skill. If someone learned to write a scroll that enabled them to tele- port, I wouldn't be surprised if they had more like it," the other dragon replied.

"Which means they might be able to open a portal or gate or what- ever and simply teleport their whole damn base out of there." The Wonderkid sounded utterly dumbstruck by the idea.

"If they do that, we won't be able to find them again," Keith added. "Unless Larry knows a trick to follow them, they'll be gone."

"We wouldn't lose them forever," Kristen murmured. "They're murderers, after all. At some point, they'd try to kill again."

Everyone stared at her, and she realized what she might have inad- vertently made them all think. "But we won't let them, of course. We move, and we move now. Keith, contact B Team. Jim, liaise with Dragon SWAT. We'll want as much back up as possible. This is it."

A few minutes later, they were airborne and on the way to a base that no doubt expected some kind of attack. Her consolation was that she very much doubted that they were prepared to face her human team, her dragon allies, and two full wings of dragons from the European Dragon SWAT team.

She hoped that would be enough, but as she began to make her plans, she forced herself to assume it wouldn't be.

CHAPTER TWENTY-SIX

The flight out to the farm took a few hours. Unfortunately, it took the European Dragons slightly less time and they arrived first.

Kristen, Heartsbane, Jim, and Keith were about a mile behind them, far enough away to see them launch their assault. Drew had been left in the city. Although he'd steadily regained his mental faculties after suffering the concussion, Kristen didn't want to risk him in another offensive. If he was so much as bumped on the head, the injuries could compound and result in serious long-term brain damage.

"It looks like they've circled the location," Keith said from her back. Both men rode on the Steel Dragon as Heartsbane steadfastly refused to let a human treat her like a horse, as she continued to reiterate. Kristen couldn't catch the details quite as well as the Rookie could with his pair of binoculars, but she could see the ten huge dragons break their formation and start to form a line to surround the farm.

"So much for a sneak attack," Jim grumbled.

"I told them to wait. We should all attack together," she complained.

Heartsbane chuckled. "Did you think they would listen? These mages killed dragons in their territory. They'll rip them apart with claw and tooth. It'll be wicked."

"Going in together would have made too much sense?" she retorted. "Damn that dragon pride."

Kristen pumped her wings to increase her speed but the other Dragons were already in position and she knew there was no way she could close the gap before they obliterated the barn.

"This will be a slaughter," the other dragon said with glee.

And indeed, it was, only not the way she anticipated.

They were still too far out to see exactly the shape of whatever raised from the roof of the barn, but its effects were immediately obvious. It elevated and aimed at a dragon and the rapid-fire sound of automatic weapon fire followed before the target was obliterated.

"Down—get down!" she yelled as loudly as she could and sent a burst of her aura as well. Heartsbane obeyed and she and Kristen dove behind a line of pine trees.

The European dragons weren't so lucky.

The turret pivoted sharply to fire a burst of rounds at another dragon. Each volley seemed to have dozens if not hundreds of rounds in it and the target was simply savaged by the ordnance.

"Jesus Christ, that's a CIWS," Jim said, aghast.

"A what?" Keith asked, still on Kristen's back where she'd landed behind the tree line.

"A Close-In Weapon System. It looks very much like the Phalanx devices I saw on navy warships when I was in the marines. They use them to blow up incoming missiles."

"Except this one fires dragon bullets," Heartsbane growled. It was almost hard to remember how confident she had been only moments before.

"Get Stonequest on the radio," Kristen ordered. "They should be here soon and they need to know to stop outside that monster's range."

Jim took the device and went to comply, leaving Kristen, Heartsbane, and Keith to watch the carnage.

Although carnage seemed almost euphemistic.

The dragons were not used to dealing with a weapon like this.

The two who had been hit were obviously dead but rather than retreating, the other dragons tried to attack the turret. A third tried to divebomb it as if it could be intimidated. It was struck in the chest with what looked to Kristen to be over a hundred rounds. Its chest was turned to pulp and it fell to a bloody mess on top of the roof.

Another tried to use the third's attack as cover and managed to get damn close to it, but not close enough. The weapon pivoted and filled the dragon's wings and torso with dragon bullets. He screeched—Kristen could tell it was La Flamme from his cries—and tumbled from the roof before he crawled beside the barn, close enough that the weapon couldn't aim at him. He was badly hurt and she knew that with dragon bullets inside his body, he wouldn't heal.

The turret ignored him and targeted a fifth dragon, who managed to stay alive by tucking its wings and dodging the majority of the rounds. Unfortunately, it wasn't an entirely effective maneuver as it was struck and plummeted to mewl piteously as it writhed in pain.

The sixth dragon died instantaneously. A single dragon bullet could kill a dragon if it struck the brain. Fifty rounds delivered into the skull left little chance of survival.

The weapon targeted a seventh and again, its aim was true. This time, however, the dragon remained in flight. The tell-tale blueish flare of magic shielding explained its escape. Whoever it was, they didn't push the attack but called for a retreat. The other three dragons followed. The four of them barely managed to plunge into an orchard of olive trees before the weapon targeted them. It fired into the grove, shredding a tree as easily as a dog could shred a newspaper, but suddenly stopped firing despite the fact that the dragons were still in range and without much protection.

"It must be activated by motion," Keith said as they all watched it swivel repeatedly, looking for more prey to eviscerate. Now that the four dragons were hiding in the orchard, it didn't seem to know they were there.

This was a small win but had to be considered a temporary and probably short-lived one. "We have to assume there are mages in there and that it's only a matter of time before one of them manually targets those dragons. If that happens, we've already lost," she said.

"So, what do you want us to do, Steel, charge in there?" Heartsbane sneered. Kristen knew her well enough to see that she was terrified, although even in her terror, she didn't let her aura slip and influence the humans. Not that anyone needed much of a reason to be afraid of the automatic death-gun at the top of the barn.

"I don't know," she said. She was pissed with herself and more pissed with the European dragons. If they had only waited for her entire team to arrive, they would have had a mage with them. As it was, they were still waiting for Larry.

Thankfully, not for long as it turned out.

Stonequest and Emerald appeared over a grove of trees. She waved her tail at them and they banked slowly to land beside them. The turret didn't fire at them so at least they were outside its attack parameters if not its actual range.

"What's the problem?" Stonequest asked as Butters, Beanpole, Hernandez, and Larry climbed off the two dragons. Drew skulked behind his teammates and Kristen fixed him with a hard look. He merely shrugged, but his small smirk held a hint of a challenge. They both knew she would have refused to stay behind if the shoe was on the other foot.

Jim filled them in before she could remonstrate with Drew. The two dragons looked at the killing field with grim expressions.

"This is everything we've worried about," Stonequest said, his voice heavy. "This was why I didn't want to share any of the details about these dragon-killing weapons. Before, it was only handguns but now, we're facing military-caliber weapons armed with dragon bullets. The arms race has begun."

"Nah."

Everyone turned to look at Butters, who stared at the barn like a quarterback down by six with fifty yards to go and thirty seconds on the clock. "It's only a dumb robot. I can shoot better than it can."

For a moment, no one said anything, shocked that even in the wake of the carnage wreaked by this machine, someone was able to stay optimistic.

It was Heartsbane who broke the silence. "Then what the fuck are you waiting for?"

CHAPTER TWENTY-SEVEN

"I'm telling you I can make the shot," Butters reiterated.

"Is this like airsoft, when you say you'll win but you end up losing last?" Hernandez asked. "Because blowing that fucker up seems damn unlikely."

"My sniper rifle shoots fat, juicy rounds," the sniper explained while he patted his rifle affectionately. "All I need is to apply a couple of those rounds to the more delicate parts of the CIWS and it'll be a pile of junk."

"There's no way you can break that gun," Keith said and shook his head.

"No, not the gun, but the fancy little motors that enable it to point every which way. I can destroy those. Once I do that, we simply have to make sure we don't stand in front of the damn thing," he boasted.

"All right, then," Kristen agreed. "It's the best plan we have. Stop talking and start shooting."

"Well, sure," Butters said and suddenly sounded embarrassed. "The thing is, though, that I'll need a boost."

"A boost?" Hernandez laughed. "Ain't no one here who can lift your fat ass. What do you need a boost for?"

"I don't have the right angle from down here. And no, I agree, no one can lift a man of my stature in their human bodies, but I reckon a dragon could get me high enough."

"No problem," Kristen said but before she could transform, Stonequest put a hand on her shoulder.

"We can't risk you for something like this. One of us can do it."

"It's fine. We don't have time to—"

Emerald had already plucked three blades of grass and wrapped his fist around them. Without ceremony, Heartsbane and Stonequest each plucked one. Hers was noticeably shorter.

She grumbled about not being an elevator any more than she was a horse, but she transformed all the same and held her dragon claw out for Butters to stand on.

The sniper stepped gingerly onto her hand but apparently, not gingerly enough.

"What did you eat?" she snapped as his feet pressed onto her scaly palm.

"We are in Italy in case you have forgotten, and some of us don't have a dragon's metabolism. I have eaten a little of this and that."

"What he means is that he's eaten everything." Keith grinned.

Butters didn't deny it as Heartsbane lifted him above her head.

"Seriously, this is better training than the gym," she complained as his head poked above the treetops.

"Slowly now...go very slowly," Jim said from the ground. "That weapon is probably radar-guided. We can't make any sudden movements or it might go off."

"Make it snappy, then, Butterball. I don't want to have a claw shot off," Heartsbane snarked.

"I'll make it as snappy as I can," he retorted. "But you need to hold completely still for this to work. You're shaking."

"Yeah, well, you're too heavy. What can I say?"

He looked down at every inch of the huge dragon. "I would respond to that but I learned long ago never to talk to a lady about her weight."

"Just...take the shot." She grunted, then sucked in a breath and held it in an attempt to stop herself from shaking as much as she had been.

"Okay, here goes," He raised the rifle, aimed calmly, and squeezed the trigger.

A moment later, they heard the ping of the bullet as it struck the turret.

Kristen was extremely impressed, but the marksman cursed quietly.

"I missed the motors completely."

"You were three inches to the left," Beanpole said.

Kristen didn't know when he'd climbed one of the trees but climb one he had. His legs were clenched around the trunk, while one hand held the binoculars to his face.

"All right. That's my spotter!" Butters shouted from atop Heartsbane's claw. He aimed and fired again.

"There you go. You hit the vertical adjustment motor." The tall, skinny man sounded proud even though his teammate was the one who took the shot. "It won't be able to aim up or down anymore."

"Yeah, but it can still rotate," Jim shouted and pointed at the roof of the barn. The turret now swung slowly toward the source of the attack.

"Shit!" Butters cursed and raised his weapon again. "Steady, Heartsbane."

"What the hell do you think I'm trying to do?"

"Do you see your target?" Beanpole asked.

"I...I'm not sure. I thought that shot would disable the whole thing."

"There should be a track on the bottom—like a ring within a ring where it pivots. If you can put a dent in that, it might cause the motor to burn out," Jim shouted, his voice tense as the turret continued to pivot. It was not lost on anyone that the last thing it had aimed at was a group of dragons who had taken cover behind the trees. It was now locked at that angle and aimed slightly toward the ground. Kristen couldn't be sure if they were within the correct angle for the gun to obliterate them but she knew they were well within range.

"I have it!" Butters shouted.

"Wind from the west," Beanpole responded as a gust of wind blew across the field that separated them from the barn.

The sniper took a deep breath and squeezed the trigger.

It seemed the entire team held their breaths. The bullet hit the base of the machine and it stopped momentarily. Whatever targeting program controlled it wasn't the smartest as rather than stopping, it tried to push past the dent. A small puff of smoke a short while later told them that the turret had burned its motor out.

"Okay," Kristen said once the machine had failed to move for a good ten seconds. "We'll go wide, meet up with the other team and check for injuries, then reassess and strike from there. Any questions?"

Heartsbane cleared her throat. "Yeah, can I put this fatso down yet?"

"Just when I was starting to like the view." Butters smirked, although when the dragon transformed into her human form and rubbed her shoulder, the sniper was quick to help her work out the knot he had no doubt caused.

CHAPTER TWENTY-EIGHT

K risten led her human and dragon squad in a wide arc around the farm and closer to where the other dragons still hunkered in the trees. Nothing happened to hinder them, but by the time they finally reached the European dragons, Kristen half-wished the defenders had already attacked. Waiting for the mages inside the farm to launch an assault was agonizing and made all the worse by the dead and wounded dragons in the field.

"We disabled the turret. Is there anything we can do for those dragons out there?" she asked her team as they proceeded cautiously.

Emerald and Stonequest shared a look, and—without prompting—transformed and rushed into the field.

"Stop it, you morons!" she shouted, but her heart wasn't in it. Most of the dragons who had been shot were dead, but two of them might make it.

Emerald reached the one who had plummeted and who still writhed in pain. He managed to get him onto his back and dragged his body past the tree line toward where the dragons from European SWAT watched their efforts.

Stonequest wasn't so lucky. The dragon he attempted to save was the one who'd fallen beside the barn. As soon as he reached him, shots rang out.

Kristen's breath caught in her throat. Was this how he was going to die? Trying to save a dragon who had been too dumb to follow orders? It was a callous thought, but honestly, it would be a horrible way for him to go.

Fortunately, Larry was able to throw a shield up between the shooter and the rescuer to protect him from the dragon bullets. Butters joined the fight and laid down covering fire at the window where the shots had come from.

Using these advantages, Stonequest grasped the dragon with his front talons and pushed into the air with his back legs. A few more mages tried to take a few shots at him, but Larry maintained his shield.

"Nice work, Brockton," Kristen said.

"Thanks, but that wasn't me," he replied.

"But who else could—Amy?" She had finally reached the European dragons and frowned when she realized Amy was with them. She was sweating and had her hands up in obvious concentration as she tried to protect Stonequest until he reached cover.

He bulldozed into the orchard and dropped the wounded dragon, who whimpered in pain. She took that as a good sign, though. At least he could still whimper.

"Amy, you're supposed to be in recovery," she chided her although there wasn't much forcefulness behind the words.

"I hate sitting on the job," the mage replied and moved toward the injured dragon.

"How is he?" one of the European dragons asked. It was Rosso, Kristen realized, and the wounded one was La Flamme.

"Not good," Amy replied.

Kristen was surprised to see her, of all people, reply but she seemed to know what she was doing. She held her hands out and blue tendrils extended to the dragon's wounds.

"Can you help him?" the Italian demanded.

"I'm trying, but the wounds are a mess. There's a ton of damaged tissue. I learned a few things when I was in the medical wing but nothing like this."

La Flamme began to cough, a horrible hacking sound that wracked his body so hard, fresh blood began to weep from the wounds.

"Larry, you have to help the other one!" the girl shouted, still focused on the Frenchman.

"Sure," Larry said, although he looked out of his element. Fortunately, the dragon Emerald had brought back didn't look nearly as bad as the other one.

"I...I can't stop the bleeding," Amy muttered as she sent tendrils of magic to try to tend all the wounds. Kristen didn't fail to notice that every time she sent out a new tendril of energy, another one vanished. She had seen the young mage dismantle a truck and use all the individual pieces as weapons and stab a dragon's wing with a telephone pole. The fact that she couldn't do this was an indication to the Steel Dragon that her mage was still not fully healed.

"Please, you must," Rosso said. "You cannot let him die, not La Flamme."

"No, no, it's okay," La Flamme said in English. He still had a French accent but it was milder than it had been.

"Don't talk, La Flamme. Save your strength," his colleague demanded and waved his hands for emphasis.

"No, I must talk. I must tell you, Rosso, Lady Hall... It was me. It was me who was made to suffer."

"We know you were shot, La Flamme. Please, stop talking," Rosso pleaded. Kristen had never seen a dragon cry before, but he did now. Great, fat teardrops that looked like they were made of dirty motor oil fell from his dragon eyes.

"It is my fault that I was shot. All of this is my fault. I told him and he must have told them everything."

"What?" the Italian asked. "No—no, you couldn't have."

A fresh bout of bloody coughs stopped the instinctive protest. Rosso looked more than confused and more than betrayed. He looked like his heart was breaking as La Flamme talked.

Kristen gasped. She didn't know how she hadn't realized it before. The two were lovers.

"I did… I told him when she arrived. I told him we were following up with Vert's sound guy. I told him that we would raid the apartment. I…" More brutal coughs interrupted his confession.

She couldn't tell if Rosso was weeping because La Flamme was in such bad shape or because he was revealing that he had secrets when he thought he'd known them all. No one stopped his confession, though, not even his lover.

"I didn't think he would tell the mages… I thought I could trust him…at least that's what I told myself, but when we were attacked…I knew… I'm so sorry…I knew."

Rosso raced to the Frenchman as blood dripped from Amy's nose. The mage fell and her healing tendrils vanished in a puff of magic.

"Who? Who did you tell, you son of a bitch—who?" Rosso demanded, grasped La Flamme's wounded body, and shook him.

The wounded man took a deep breath, looked him in the eye, and wheezed, "The Masked One…" before his head lolled back and he died.

"The who? Who?" the Italian demanded and slapped his ex-lover across his face in fury and frustration.

"Who is he talking about?" Jim asked, but the distraught dragon ignored him.

He only wept as he hugged the body.

Kristen turned away. La Flamme was dead like the other four dragons in the field. Unfortunately, they didn't have time to mourn him yet. Not when his murderers were still waiting to kill the rest of them. This Masked One was an interesting idea. Could it have been Havington? After all, the mage had worn a mask when they'd faced him. Could La Flamme have been duped by a human mage?

Those were questions for another day, she thought as she surveyed the carnage in front of her.

"We need to end this now," she told everyone. They all looked at her—human, dragon, and mage and even Rosso, who seemed to want to do anything but continue to weep.

"This is what we've been afraid of. Not humans defending them-selves but them weaponizing this evil tech to do what they've done today. It will not be an easy fight, but it's a battle we have to go into all the same. I can't pretend that none of you will be hurt out there, but I will promise that if you are, I will take vengeance on these sick bastards."

"Fuck you," someone shouted from inside the farmhouse and a gunshot followed. It bored a hole in a tree branch not three feet from her head.

She didn't so much as flinch. "They know their only hope is to defend their base, and hope is the only thing we will let them keep. While I know they killed our people, we have to do what we can to bring them to justice. I want the world to see what a trial looks like—a trial for a crime committed by mages and one conducted by humans, dragons, and mages alike. I want everyone to know what happened here and to see the horrors that making weapons from dragons will cause. When this is done, those who fell here today will outlive us all, for they will be remembered as those who died for the cause of peace. But we will not lose anyone else. Are we ready?"

The others responded with a loud "Hoo-ah!"

Rosso snaked forward to stand near the front of the group. "You can all fight this battle for whatever reason you want. I'll do it for La Flamme."

Without warning, he charged.

She didn't even try to think of a battle cry. "For La Flamme!" she called and the battle began.

CHAPTER TWENTY-NINE

The mages weren't the only ones with a foolish hope. Kristen had harbored a secret dream that the reason the mages hadn't fired at them while they gathered in the olive orchard was because they didn't have many of the dragon bullets. She'd dared to hope that Stella was the only dragon the mages had captured and harvested from for ammunition.

It turned out that the enemy had more than enough ammunition. They merely waited for the dragons to commit themselves to the attack.

As soon as Rosso broke into the field, the mages opened fire on him. He hissed—still in dragon form—but didn't slow enough to take a breath for fire. Instead, he raced forward while he serpentined like the world's hungriest anaconda until he collided with a tractor that was parked outside the barn.

Kristen thought it was madness—or worse, suicide in memory of his lost lover—but there seemed to be a snippet of strategy left even his grief. Once he impacted with the tractor, he transformed into his human shape. Now the fact that he had drawn all the technomage's fire didn't seem quite so foolhardy, as dragon bullets could not punch through iron quite as easily as they could through a dragon's body.

"Go!" she shouted and led her team toward a truck with what looked like a larger rented trailer to use for cover. She reached it and thunked her shoulder against the vehicle before the mages in the barn shifted their aim. While she was significantly closer to the homestead, she could do nothing but clench her teeth and hope that no bullets hit Emerald, Heartsbane, Drew, Jim, or Amy as they sprinted to the trailer.

Beanpole and Butters laid down covering fire for the team as they ran to the vehicle and bullets blew field dirt past their legs as they ran. Twice, one of them would have been hit but both times, Amy was able to get a shield up and deflect the bullet. It was obvious, though, that after trying to save La Flamme and failing and barely managing to stabilize the other wounded dragon, the young mage now operated well below her optimal power of god-like magical abilities.

Her team thumped against the trailer one by one and drew the same echoed thunk Kristen had when she struck the truck itself, despite the fact that none of them were made of steel like she was.

She wondered how far they'd loaded it with the supplies of this base. How close had the mages been to leaving when the dragons had attacked? Not that it mattered at the moment. Whatever was inside the trailer wasn't valuable enough to the mages to make them stop their barrage of dragon bullets.

But that was okay in the present situation. The team all wore bulletproof vests—even her steel skin had a Kevlar vest over the top that she'd left in its normal state to better protect her from the bullets the mages now fired into the vehicle. And they'd drawn the techno-mages' fire exactly like Rosso had, which gave Stonequest the opening he needed.

While Emerald and Heartsbane had trained extensively with the human SWAT members and thus could help Kristen and her friends pinned behind the truck to lay down covering fire, Stonequest's experience made him better suited to fighting with the more old-school dragons.

Neither he nor any of the three European dragons who now advanced with him had taken their dragon form. They all understood the inherent risks in a body as large as a dragon's was. But they didn't attack armed only with their handguns either. These dragons had all seen action in the first Mage War, and it seemed they had previously faced mages armed with lethal projectiles as they had armed themselves with swords and shields.

She truly didn't know how effective the attack would be but damn, it was impressive.

He and the dragons sprinted forward in their human forms, stuck together, and used their plexiglass shields reinforced with steel mesh to form a wall in front of them as they moved. When the mages fired at their feet, they lowered the massive shields to the ground.

The swords the European dragons had brought seemed far more ancient than the modern-looking shields were, but they were no less massive. Each of them wielded a blade that was at least six feet long. The weapons were so large they almost seemed cartoon-like and she doubted that a human would ever be able to wield anything like these on a battlefield, let alone one-handed while using a shield. But dragon strength was far beyond that of humans, so after her time among her kind, it hardly surprised her.

That the four dragons were able to use the swords to deflect some of the bullets was quite impressive. They didn't redirect them back at the mages or anything like that—this wasn't a movie, after all—but now and then, one of them managed to catch one of the bullets with their sword and the ping was followed by the sound of a careening ricochet.

Whenever a stray bullet made it through their defense, Larry was ready with a shield of blue magic to deflect it.

He was impressive to watch, too. It was obvious that he had worked with dragons for years because he walked into the attack almost as courageously as they did. He didn't step out in front like them but he stayed close, behind their cover and out of their way, while he provided them with his magical blocks against the hail of bullets.

Stonequest's push forward seemed to be working, and Butters and

Beanpole continued to provide sufficient cover fire from the tree line. That meant it was Kristen's turn to move forward.

"To the tractor," she ordered. "Are we ready?"

"Are you sure about this?" Heartsbane asked although she sounded excited to try it.

"Hell no!" she responded. "But we'll never make it all across the field of fire without cover."

"Then let's not waste time." Emerald had already taken his position between the front of the trailer and the rear of the truck. Heartsbane moved beside him and grasped the other edge of the trailer.

Jim and Drew crouched behind the truck itself. Kristen looked around for the only two people she hadn't seen in the fight—the only two who hadn't followed their orders to stick with her—but she didn't locate Hernandez or Keith anywhere in the fraction of a second she had to look.

"On three!" she shouted and the two men took a deep breath and prepared to run.

"One..."

More gunfire was directed at the dragons.

"Two!"

A lucky shot from Butters struck home and a mage screamed from the hayloft of the barn. The torrent of gunfire slowed to a steady stream.

"Three!"

Heartsbane and Emerald tightened their hold on the front of the trailer and lifted with every ounce of strength they had.

The results were spectacular.

It flipped end over end two full times before it settled heavily between the truck that still sheltered Kristen and the tractor that kept Rosso alive.

The humans had already begun to run to where the trailer would land even before it ceased its tumble.

The remaining mages—obviously quite surprised by such a tactic —opened fire on the trailer itself, which gave the men and Kristen enough time to hunker behind it. As soon as it had settled securely, the three popped out and laid down covering fire.

Something pounded into the van and for a second, she thought the beast Katrina was somehow responsible. Except she wasn't a beast, she reminded herself. No matter how much she wanted to demonize her, she knew she was her sister. She grimaced, relieved to see it was Emerald, but her relief faded when he tensed in pain and held a wound on his bicep.

"Fucking bullet grazed me. Those dragon rounds..." He didn't finish, but she knew what he was going to say. She also agreed with the unspoken sentiment. The ammunition fucking hurt.

Heartsbane appeared with Amy in her arms. They'd talked about preserving the girl's power as much as possible, especially now that she knew a thing or two about healing after she'd spent so much time in the medical ward.

"Hey, Amy," Emerald said and gritted his teeth. "I've told you how I've been a shit before but that I respect you, right?" He laughed and chewed his lip.

"Shut up and hold still," the mage said as she leaned over the wounded arm and bullets streaked over their heads.

While she got to work extending tendrils of energy from her fingertips to pull out any of the shards from Emerald's arm, Kristen surveyed the battle scene once more.

Stonequest had reached the front of the barn. He and his team pounded at the wooden doors with their swords, but they constantly met resistance and generated showers of sparks. The mages had reinforced the entrance to their base with magic.

She took a few more shots at the mages, but her bullets met a shimmering wall of force. Now that their adversaries had suffered a casualty, they fought more defensively and used their magic to protect themselves as well as to attack.

One of them leaned out of the window at the top of the barn. It looked suicidal given how many people were shooting at him. His entire torso leaned out of the window, a big, broad target everyone immediately tried to shoot, but his allies had him well protected. He went to work and swirled his hands in complex motions until a cloud appeared between them.

Steaming green rain poured from it, which turned out to be acid. Where it touched the dragons' shields, the plexiglass melted and where it touched their skin, they screamed. Only the swords seemed capable of withstanding the magically conjured corrosive slime, but the dragons were in an awkward position. If they blocked the momentum of the goo, they inevitably splashed it on to each other.

Larry conjured a gust of wind, folded it into itself, and created a swirling vortex that grew in intensity until he launched it skyward toward the cloud of acid to dissipate it.

He wasn't the only one who thought Stonequest and the dragons were in need of assistance.

An old produce truck trundled toward the barn and backfired continuously. Kristen had never seen anything quite like it. It looked as Italian as the countryside—like it had been spawned there and used to carry bushels of olives since times of yore.

The only thing distinctly modern about it was the person driving.

Keith hooted and hollered at everyone, including the mages, and told them all to get out of the way.

She wondered briefly what had happened to Hernandez, but when she saw smoke pouring out of the back of the old delivery truck she had an inkling what the woman had been up to. Without questioning her teammates, she whirled to her human friends and wrapped them in her steel arms.

Kristen had to piece together what happened next after the battle. At that moment, all she experienced was an explosion powerful enough to destroy the tractor a few inches away from the truck.

She didn't see any of this, but after hooting and hollering, Keith flung himself out of the vehicle and into the dirt.

Stonequest, likely not wanting to earn her ire, raced to save the Rookie, and when he did so, the other dragons followed his lead. They scattered and cleared the way for the vehicle to bulldoze into the door.

Hernandez had gotten clear long before, and she laughed and laughed as the mages took a few potshots at it.

Then, it exploded.

When Kristen pulled her head up from behind the trailer, she was surprised to see the barn still standing. On closer inspection, she saw that standing was a generous term. The entire front of the structure was on fire, and the roof of the front third had been blown sky-high, only to be rained down as shrapnel in the form of broken shingle.

The barn itself only remained erect because the doors were reinforced with steel and those had needed a frame capable of holding them. That frame was now exposed and badly damaged.

Kristen was able to notice all these details because as soon as the mages had realized there wasn't anyone to hurt inside the truck, they had stopped firing. She wasn't naïve enough to think they would have let themselves get caught in the blast, but a girl could dream, couldn't she?

"Don't let them get away," she yelled and raced toward the door.

Even after being blasted by whatever the hell Hernandez had snuck in with her gear, the door was still strong enough to withstand a dragon's blow. It wasn't strong enough to withstand three, however.

"Let's go," Emerald said. His arm was bandaged but he looked much better. Amy must have removed the dragon scale from his arm already, a damn useful skill to have.

Heartsbane and Emerald raced forward and added their speed and momentum to their strike. Kristen took a step back before she kicked the doors again. She timed it so she connected at precisely the same moment as the other two dragons and between the three of them, the barrier didn't stand much chance.

It crumpled like a cardboard box karate-chopped by an eight-year-old.

"Where are they?" Rosso asked as he pushed past Kristen and Heartsbane into the interior of the barn.

Hay and pieces of wood burned everywhere, but Kristen only had eyes on the elevator shaft, which protruded through the farm implements and supplies like a steel tower.

The Italian hammered and pounded on it with his human fists but to no avail.

"Sometimes, it takes a woman's touch," she said, pushed him aside, and took each of the elevator doors in her steel fingers.

She was able to pry them open like a can of sardines without the delicious interior. It was simply an empty elevator shaft, exactly like they had at Constance's base.

"I'm going in," she shouted.

"Wait, damn it. Kristen, wait!" That was Drew, always the voice of caution.

If she hadn't listened to him when she was a fresh recruit, she didn't know why she'd listen to him now that she was his boss. She jumped down the shaft and turned her feet and knees to steel to brace herself better when she landed on the carriage.

From above, she could hear Drew's tireless encouragement and direction. "We trained for this, people. Drop the ropes and belay down. We won't wait for the investigator to send up a broken elevator."

Kristen landed with a heavy, solid thunk she had fully expected would crush the carriage. To her surprise, it resisted her mass driven by the velocity of her fall. It dented—how could it not?—but it didn't break or even crack.

A little disappointed, she began to destroy it. She stooped, transformed her hands into long-fingered, steel-tipped claws, and proceeded to rend the roof beneath her feet like a dog digging a hole. At first, she was only able to make a few full punctures, but once she had done that, her claws were able to find purchase and tear a hole large enough for her to get through.

She didn't jump in, though. While she might be anxious to win this battle, she wouldn't leave a gaping hole with jagged metal shards as an entrance for her team. She took hold of one of the sharpened edges and bent it back on itself so it wouldn't stab anyone.

In the next moment, an iron claw caught her wrist.

Before she could regain her balance and adjust herself to resist, she was yanked with sufficient force to pull her face-first into the reinforced top.

Kristen reacted with dragon speed, but her foe was equally as fast. She tried to pull back but another iron claw latched onto her Kevlar vest, dragged her through the hole, and drove her into the floor of the carriage.

An iron boot descended on her throat to crush the windpipe beneath her steel skin, deny her oxygen, and force her narrowing vision to focus on the person who tried to kill her.

Katrina loomed over her in her iron human form.

She smiled before she twisted the heel of her boot savagely into her neck. "It's time to die, sister."

CHAPTER THIRTY

S pots appeared in the tiny window of vision Kristen still had left. Already, her peripherals were gone. All she could see was Katrina's face, although her expression was almost impossible to discern because she was backlit by harsh lights and her iron features were already so dark.

"Why...kill?" she choked through the relentless pressure.

"To end the rule of the dragon oppressors," the woman answered casually as if she'd stepped away from a pleasant conversation with Constance.

"And...become them?" she asked with the last of her strength.

She wouldn't get her answer, however, because Drew dropped through the roof and opened fire at her attacker. Sparks flurried from Katrina's face as rounds impacted. The dragon flinched and took a step back.

Kristen only knew it was Drew when she sucked in a precious breath of air and her tunnel vision receded enough to see the other dragon race forward and backhand the man even more savagely than she had at the Uffizi. Again, he catapulted to sprawl in an unconscious pile outside the elevator doors.

Anger surged and she could only hope it was an unconscious pile and not something far more permanent. She couldn't check now, though. He had given her what she needed—enough time to take a breath of air. It meant she was still in this fight.

As her focus returned, she transformed her entire body to steel and drove into Katrina from behind. Her momentum was sufficient to bulldoze the woman's iron body into the wall. It was satisfying, although she had to admit she was a little disappointed that the stone wall broke and not her opponent's face.

The dragon threw her head back, but Kristen lowered her forehead in time for the back of her opponent's skull to smack her above the eyes instead of breaking her nose.

Despite her steel skin, it still hurt. Her pain was punctuated by another of the loud gongs that resonated every time they made impact with each other in their metal skin. This time—probably because the blow came directly to Kristen's forehead—her teeth rattled.

But she didn't release her opponent, however. She held her from behind and knew as well as anyone that simply because the dragon had iron skin didn't mean she could forego breathing. Her teeth gritted, she looped her arm around Katrina's neck and squeezed.

The iron dragon struggled. She kicked at Kristen's legs and threw an elbow into her gut, but all that did was cause blips of pain that she ignored. She felt her enemy weakening and her movements slow and realized she could win this.

Her confidence built until a boulder removed itself from the wall and pounded into her spine. The blow didn't break anything—although it damn well would have if she hadn't been steel—but it loosened her hold around Katrina's neck.

She glanced down the hall at a mage who wore a rose mask who stood with their hands up to lift more stones to hurl at her. The distraction was costly. She had foolishly assumed that after almost being choked unconscious, the dragon would need a minute, but she didn't.

Before Kristen's eyes had snapped to her foe again, Katrina dropped and spun to deliver the full force of a spinning kick into the back of her knee.

No matter how strong she was, her knee was still a knee. It buckled and she tumbled back as her adversary surged into the attack. Like a snake, she thrust from her coiled position and caught her. Rather than choking her, though, she held both her arms behind her back.

Kristen didn't understand it—if she hoped the Steel Dragon would tap out, fat chance—but all became clear when the mage hurled more stones toward her. They barreled into her chest, one after the other and shattered as they did so, sparking if iron were mixed in with the stone.

Now that her chest had been battered, the other dragon wrenched her arms even harder behind her back.

She screamed in pain as the flower-masked assailant took more stones from the wall itself. One of them was particularly large, and the mage hurled smaller stones against it to carve its tip into a shard small enough to pierce an eyeball.

The lethal stone rocketed toward her face as Katrina whispered in her ear, "Now you see me, now you—"

"Don't!" Drew and Jim said in unison. The former had not been too severely injured and the Wonderkid had made it down the elevator shaft and into the hallway.

As they stole Katrina's line, Jim aimed and unloaded his magazine at the mage. She was far too focused on impaling the Steel Dragon with a sharpened stone to be able to block the bullets. Her body jerked as the fusillade struck home and she fell.

It didn't take an emergency responder to see that she was dead.

Her rock, though, still hurtled toward her target, and Katrina still held her arms immobile. If seeing the mage killed bothered the dragon, she didn't show it. Rather than call out or gasp or show even an ounce of regret for her fallen ally, she simply kicked Kristen's legs out from under her to make her fall into the path of the stone spike that had been hurled at her.

It didn't catch her in the eye, but that didn't mean it didn't hurt when it rocketed into her shoulder. She tumbled a few times through a pile of gravel that had been rock only moments before.

"You won't stop them, you know," Katrina said to her as she approached. While she advanced relentlessly on the Steel Dragon, the two men fired round after round into her, but they didn't have dragon bullets. Their bullets struck her iron skin with dull plinks and bright sparks and nothing more.

Kristen scrambled to her feet and tackled her assailant.

Again, she was able to knock the woman down. As far as she could tell, they were almost identical in speed and strength. She hammered Katrina's head into the ground and could tell that it hurt, but she couldn't maintain her hold on her.

While she had trained for combat for barely a year, Katrina must have trained for her entire life. She wasn't faster overall but she was quicker to respond to attacks in the right way. While she wasn't stronger, she understood how to leverage her opponent's anatomy against her in a way that Kristen simply didn't.

Although she could acknowledge the truth of this, she continued to struggle to keep the woman pinned. Moments later, though, she slipped free and found her feet smoothly as she laughed.

"You should have killed Bunny. She's the only one of them proficient enough with her magic to make a spell sufficiently powerful to get our dumb and blind clone of a sister out of here."

"You know about that?" Kristen was aghast. How could Katrina condone such atrocities?

"My teammates respect me. A novel concept, I'm sure."

Kristen tried to race past her, but the dragon caught her across the ear with a karate chop. It was like she had been trained since she was a child. While she didn't know much about fighting beyond what Stonequest and Drew had taught her, the Iron Dragon seemed too well-versed in a variety of fighting styles.

"They're using your own family to make bullets and treat them like cattle!" she yelled as she tried to fend off a flurry of blows from her opponent. They came incredibly fast and while she had been beaten by dragons in her dragon body, she'd never met her match in her human form.

And calling Katrina her match was almost stupidly optimistic.

"Our family is making the world a better place for everyone. How is it different from the humans who break their backs picking apples and cabbages while billionaires rake in obscene profits? How is it different from a mother cat refusing to feed her runts?"

A vicious knee rocketed into Kristen's abdomen. She might have had the strength to stop it but hadn't been able to anticipate it. It struck and she doubled over. *I can't win,* she realized with growing dread.

"Jim, Drew, you have to get down there and stop them from running off."

"No problem," Drew responded, and the two raced away from the elevator.

Katrina glared at them as if the Steel Dragon was nothing but an afterthought, a lousy challenge to be defeated at her leisure.

"Don't you dare hurt them," Kristen growled at her adversary as she climbed to her feet again.

The dragon laughed. "We both know I've already won. The fight in the museum was more fun than this pathetic spectacle. What do you think you can possibly do against someone like me? I was made for this. I've trained every day of my life. You are merely one more dumb dragon."

A new voice rang out. "You're wrong about that."

She didn't look back this time because she didn't have to. Stonequest had arrived.

He sprinted down the hall and swung his ridiculously large sword at Katrina.

She stepped back and dodged the blow with a smile. "Now that's more like it."

"You talk too much," Heartsbane said as she joined the fray.

Together, the two dragons pressed Katrina. Heartsbane moved in to strike repeatedly. The iron dragon blocked each of her blows, but that was fine as she merely tried to create an opening for Stonequest. As Katrina pivoted and put her back toward him, she succeeded.

He swung the sword into the woman's back and the sound of impact was almost shrill. The dragon writhed in pain and a distinctive dent was visible in her back from where the blade had struck her. Kristen had never seen such a thing.

Katrina clenched her teeth and scooted away from him until she reached the wall. "That one was on me, dragon scum. You won't get to strike me again like that."

"That's fine with us," Heartsbane said.

"Yeah," Kristen nodded through the pain that Katrina had already inflicted on her body. "We wouldn't want Stonequest to have all the fun."

The two women raced forward in tandem and both attacked with everything they had. It was almost immediately clear that it wouldn't be enough. Heartsbane had less human to human combat experience under her belt than Kristen did. Katrina was able to prevent their blows from hitting her in any of her few vulnerable areas.

Stonequest took another swipe that his teammates both dodged, but the Iron Dragon saw their action and dodged as well. The momentum of the blow forced him to continue his turn and their adversary punched his face so hard that a chip of stone fell off his cheek.

Kristen tried for a headlock again as the woman had moved between her and Heartsbane, but Katrina anticipated it and thrust her fingers into her shoulder. She must have studied the nervous system in some depth as the pressure she applied was enough to release a jolt of pain down her arm.

Gunfire sounded beyond the end of the hallway, and she knew that Drew and Jim had successfully evaded the dragon, but had they made it past her in time? She didn't know and couldn't check as it took all her strength simply to hold her enemy at bay.

Apparently, their human teammates hadn't neutralized everyone, though, as what sounded like a controlled demolition came from the elevator shaft. Dirt and rock poured out the open doors, and she understood that no more reinforcements would be coming.

She rushed forward and again, she was thrust back. Heartsbane tried her aura but to no avail. Stonequest struck with his sword, but Katrina seemed always one step ahead of it.

Despite this, he remained calm and unruffled.

After a sequence of feints and attacks, he swung his sword and Katrina—rather than stepping back like she had done before—took the edge of the blade in her gut. It didn't cut through her iron skin but it did cause her to double over. Kristen took a deep breath and readied herself to vault forward, put her iron-skinned sister in a sleeper hold, and end this.

Before she could act, fortunately, she realized the Iron Dragon hadn't taken a blow at all. She'd only used the opportunity to take the blade from Stonequest. With a broad grin, she grasped it with her iron fingers and twisted with such force that he spun into a flip before he released it.

Astonished, Kristen only had the briefest of moments to remind herself once again of exactly how strong dragons truly were before Katrina laid into them with the blade.

In the instant since she had taken the weapon, she flipped it, caught it by the handle, and swung it into Heartsbane's chest.

Kristen's blood froze as her teammate pounded into the wall behind her. Her heart began to beat again when she realized that Katrina had used the broad side of the sword rather than the blade.

"It's unbelievable that your kind managed to stay in control for so long," the Iron Dragon snarled at Stonequest.

Not one to be intimidated, he engaged her in combat and dodged the sword almost as easily as she had. She jabbed at his abdomen and he stepped aside. When she made a horizontal slice, he ducked beneath it. She brought the sword down on his back and this time, delivered a powerful blow.

Stonequest landed with a thud. Katrina battered his back repeatedly as she smiled gleefully. "I told you! Did I not say that was the last time you'd land a blow on me? Did I not say that?"

The two teammates glanced at him, then at each other before they ran forward as one. The Iron Dragon knocked Heartsbane aside, but Kristen careened into her with enough force to dislodge the weapon from her hand.

They found their feet, both breathing heavily, and it was Kristen's turn to smile. Katrina was strong—much stronger than her—but she had difficulty with the three dragons. Given that Kristen had spent the last year of her life building the best team in the world, she thought that was good intel to have.

Then again, she wasn't the only one with a team.

Drew and Jim sprinted into the hallway, pursued by what looked like a living inferno. Flames in the shape of birds and horses raced into the narrow space after the two men until whoever was controlling the spell could no longer see them. The conjured fiery army collided haphazardly with the walls and the spell was broken.

"Do we have an exit strategy, Kristen?" the Wonderkid asked.

"We shot the skull and the ram, but the crown ain't so happy about it," Drew said. He sounded both proud and ashamed of how their operation had gone.

On cue, Neal Havington—wearing his skull cap with a crown printed on the front—entered the hallway. He held a pistol in one hand and a spell in the other. Kristen didn't know which she was more afraid of. The revolver was no doubt filled with dragon bullets, but the spheres of energy strained to escape the mage's hand.

Katrina dashed toward him with a burst of dragon speed and tucked into a roll before she reached him. He didn't give Kristen time to make her mind up about whether the spell or the gun was worse and fired his weapon at the dragons.

Weeks of training kicked in. Stonequest, Heartsbane, and Kristen flung themselves down. She grinned and decided they had proved the old adage false. These dragons had been around for centuries. They were the proverbial old dogs, self-assured in their ways, and yet she had taught them a new trick.

The mage didn't seem to mind missing, though. He bounced his hand and the spheres that had jostled each other for space vanished into the ceiling and walls. A deep rumbling followed as if the rocks were making themselves comfortable and the sound faded into nothing. Kristen had never seen a dud spell before but decided it was bound to happen sometimes.

The logic of the thought was contradicted when the roof caved in.

The destruction didn't happen all at once. First, a boulder fell from where the elevator shaft used to be, followed by another. By the time the roof itself began to disintegrate, Kristen had already surged forward, taken her dragon form, and spread her steel wings over Jim and Drew as the roof collapsed on them all.

The concrete of the hallway wasn't all that bad. She was able to knock some of it aside as the two men moved closer to huddle under her chest like baby chicks with their mother hen in a thunderstorm. But above that concrete was a vast amount of earth. Havington had prioritized the part of the passage farther from him, so her tail was pinned first, then her back legs and torso. Through the destruction, she stole a look and confirmed that Stonequest and Heartsbane were already buried in rubble. She doubted that the falling stone could kill them any more than it could kill her, but they were undoubtedly pinned and short of air.

The worst part was that she was in no place to lead the rescue.

Every part of her body was trapped beneath fallen concrete and earth, even her long, sinuous neck and her head. She fought the urge to struggle to free herself as she stared at Havington and Katrina from a tiny gap between the rubble. They stood barely out of reach.

"Let me make sure she's dead," Katrina said. "It will be cosmic justice to thrust one of the swords that were used in the first mage revolution through the head of the dragon who is trying to stop the third and final one."

"You had your chance," he said and studied the Steel Dragon where she continued to struggle against the rubble and debris. "Why you didn't finish them off when you could have is beyond me, but that opportunity is gone. The others have already left and we'll have to hope that killed her."

"I can dig her out in hardly any time." The woman sounded petulant and almost whiny like she was being denied dessert.

"Perhaps next time, you will not play when you should be working," Havington admonished her. "Now come. We have suffered too many casualties, but Bunny has kept the portal open long enough. She holds it open only for us now."

"But—"

"I said we leave now. When you were transferred to us, you were given orders to obey, correct?"

"Yes…sir," Katrina grumbled.

"Very well, then. Come along."

"Of course." The Iron Dragon moved in almost a blur and stood over Kristen's head. "This isn't over, Steel Dragon." She sneered and hurried to follow Havington out of the hallway to their waiting portal.

That left Kristen in a hallway completely buried in rubble with four of her friends lost somewhere beneath the debris. Despite that, she didn't feel as bad as she should have. They had lived and they'd forced the technomages to retreat. She had hoped to take prisoners but she didn't exactly feel terrible about her team ending some of their lives. After all, these people were murderers.

It was with quiet resignation that Kristen settled in to wait. She didn't know how long it would take, but she knew the rest of her team would get her out. They would stop at nothing to accomplish this, working together to use their formidable sets of skills to help rather than simply keep fighting.

Despite her aches and pains, she felt all right—until she started to feel an itch far away on the end of her tail.

"Jim? You're under my chest, right?"

"Yeah, Kristen," he replied. She could hardly hear his words through the debris and felt the vibrations more than she heard him.

"Is there any way you could reach my tail? It itches terribly."

"That's gonna be a negative boss," he replied and tried not to sound amused.

"Drew?"

"Gonna be a no-go for me too. Given how we're almost being crushed by your dragon boob, I think you'll simply have to deal with it."

She sighed. It would be a very long wait.

CHAPTER THIRTY-ONE

There was no way to know how long she was stuck inside the rubble, but given how loud her stomach was grumbling by the time the other dragons on her team dug her out, it had to be around dinner time.

No one had seen the mages escape, but Kristen still knew where they went.

"I haven't heard of a mage who can teleport in hundreds of years," one of the European dragons said.

"Well, believe it," Heartsbane replied. "We think it's only one of them, but she had to have learned it from somewhere. I think we've only seen the very tip of the iceberg of what these mages can do, both with magic and with weapons."

Kristen could see that was true. No one else had died in the attack —no one else had been able to make it down before the fight was over —but that still left the dragons who had been mowed down by the CIWS. She watched in dull horror as the European dragons moved the bodies of their fallen comrades into positions of repose and incin- erated them with their fire breath.

She couldn't help but count herself lucky. Her team—thanks to their training—hadn't suffered any losses. She wished she could have extended that same success to the fallen dragons, but that was beyond even the formidable powers of the Steel Dragon.

"I can't help but think we're racing toward a cliff and our wings have been clipped," Stonequest said somberly as he stared at the funeral pyres. "Now, after this turret, dragons will think more about how to defend themselves from human-style weapons while the mages will continue to find more powerful and more deadly applications of the technology. We have to stop them and stop them soon."

"We will stop them," she said, her voice a little louder than she'd intended because she was trying to keep it from trembling. When everyone—including the mourning European dragons—turned to look at her, she realized she had better keep talking.

"Today, we saw the effects of what happens when humans, mages, and dragons work together. Our enemies joined forces to manufacture these weapons and somehow convinced a dragon to join them. The only reason we stopped them is because we were working together too."

"But they got away," Keith said. He tried not to sound whiny and failed miserably.

"Yes. Havington, Katrina, and Bunny got away," she conceded, "but wishing for a victory when you got a stalemate is better than losing and being dead. Let's not mince words. This was a close call. If not for all of us working together, we would never have reached the barn. And, although we suffered losses, we have a victory, even though it's not the one we hoped for. We disbanded this cell and proved to any mages watching that—no matter where in the world they might be—we will stop them if they murder indiscriminately. All of you should be very proud of yourselves. I know I am proud of you."

Her team applauded but the European dragons hardly looked heartened. She couldn't blame them. This had probably caused more casualties than their team had ever suffered. And there would have been more if Kristen and her team of humans and mages had not come to help. Hopefully, the European team would see it in these terms—that by working across boundaries, they had been more successful.

But Kristen had lost people in the line of duty as well. She knew it was hard to look at the positive side of anything when someone you knew died.

With a sigh, she returned to work.

The dragons had dug the rubble and debris out above the hallway she had been trapped inside, which meant they now had a path deep into the earth that led to the heart of the technomage team's operation.

Kristen descended and looked around at the destroyed computers and maps. All that remained were the traces of clues their enemy hadn't been able to destroy in their haste to escape.

"I want all this bagged or photographed," she said to her team. "There has to be something in here that can tell us where they went."

"And no one touch the computers until Keith downloads everything he can off every drive," Brian said over the radio. He sounded excited about a new puzzle.

She walked through the wreckage and tried to make sense of it. At the center of it all was a collection of chains so large they could have only held one thing captive—another of her dragon sisters.

Her mind constantly wondered how Katrina could accept all this. She had made it clear that she understood what the technomages were doing to the dragons, and yet she'd seemed fine with it—even pleased. How could someone see such atrocities and let them slide? The fact that the Iron Dragon shared most of her DNA with Kristen also made her uneasy. Were the seeds for such callousness in her blood as well? If her parents hadn't taken her in, if she'd been left in whatever lab had grown her, would she have been convinced to become a killing machine who worked against her own kind?

Maybe she would have. It was something she had to face.

What continued to bother her the most was that other than the chained dragons—admittedly, it remained a large obstacle—she still couldn't help but see things from the mage side as well. Death or a life serving a dragon—a life with no chance of retirement, vacation, or privacy—didn't sound like much of a choice to her. Maybe a few hundred years before that would have counted for much more. But now, in an era of increasing freedom, it seemed downright barbaric. Maybe draconian was a better adjective, she mused.

Kristen shook the thoughts from her head as Larry approached.

"Do you have a plan for how to keep all this evidence properly stored?" Kristen asked.

"Honestly? Not yet," Larry gave her a half-grin. For him, that was practically an admission that he was beyond frustrated.

"What's up?"

"You were right about the teleportation spell," he said and didn't sound pleased about it.

"I know I am, Larry. I saw Bunny open a portal and take Katrina through it."

"Yeah, well, I won't lie, I didn't believe you. Teleportation is hard. It would have been way easier for her to create an illusion that they vanished than to actually vanish."

"What made you change your mind?" she asked.

He gestured toward the area of the room where the chains had been. "A spell was cast there. A big one. I've never sensed anything like it before either. I would have dismissed it as some kind of ward or perimeter defense but..." He chuckled darkly. "The Steel Dragon herself said she saw a dragon teleport, so that's what it has to be."

She nodded. "Can you tell where it leads?"

The mage shook his head. "I've already tried but I can't discover the destination. That's not too surprising, though, from what I recall of teleportation spells."

"I thought you said you've never done one."

"I haven't." He shrugged. "But when I first became a mage, I read about them. They are complex things and so much can go wrong. If you're off by a few inches, your feet end up in the ground or you're stuck in a wall. Most people use scrolls to get it all down, but because scroll magic is inherently more complex than simple casting, it's possible to write far more in there to make them hard to trace, that kind of thing. My guess is this Bunny has a couple of scrolls with destinations on them. If we had caught her..." He whistled wistfully.

"It's all right. We scared them off and proved that this world doesn't belong to them yet."

Larry nodded.

Kristen was about to dismiss him to get back to his work—she didn't want to be in this basement any longer than she had to be— when he cleared his throat and looked at her, his eyes even more pained than they had been before.

"What is it?" she asked warily.

"Well, I don't know if this is good news or bad."

"You look like it's bad."

That made him grin. "I don't think this was their permanent base. I've detected a number of magic signatures around here. I think another cell of mages worked out of here as well."

"Well, that's great! That merely means we scared off two groups."

"Yeah, I reckon it does."

They spent a few hours picking through the base in search of possible remnants of a trail. Kristen's feelings spiraled constantly toward despair. She might have sunken completely into it if not for Brian's pep talk over the radio. Despite the fact that she couldn't understand a word of what Keith was gathering for him, he was quite excited to get the stash, as he called it.

Finally, even he was done gathering intel and she told the group they would return to base.

"Can we stop on our way home?" Butters asked over the radio once they were airborne. "All that saving the world works wonders on the appetite."

"That is a negative, Butters. I repeat, a negative," Brian responded over the radio, his voice sharp with excitement.

"Brian, let's give the dragons' chefs a night off. We're in Italy. We can pick something up. It's fine."

"Are you saying you don't want meatloaf?" Kristen's brother asked before being shushed by someone in the same room as him.

"Brian? Who is there with you?"

"Just come home, yeah?" he responded.

"You mean back to base?"

"Sure."

By the time they reached Castillo, Kristen was exhausted. All she wanted was a shower and she was beyond hungry and tired. There couldn't be enough food or sleep in the world to make her feel right again and a shower seemed like the only thing that could immediately solve a problem.

Or so she thought until she walked through the front door. Brian was there, grinning like a fool.

"Brian, why does it smell like mom's meatloaf in here?"

Before he could answer, her parents appeared.

"I told you her dragon senses would smell it, didn't I, Marty?" her dad said as the woman rushed forward to wrap her daughter in a big hug.

"What are you two doing here?" she exclaimed, surprised at herself for how happy she was to see them.

"You show up naked on the front of a newspaper in Florence and you think we won't come? We were in the south of France so it was only two trains," Marty exclaimed as if it were ridiculously obvious.

"And they let you in?" she asked.

"Brian vouched for us," Frank said and beamed at this son.

"Plus, Mom is very persuasive. She started to flash baby pictures of the Steel Dragon and the mage let her right in." Her brother laughed.

Kristen rolled her eyes. Her mom had one baby picture of her she loved. "Not the one of me in the bath? You know I'm—"

"Naked? Yeah, I know," Marty snapped. "But now that everyone with a pair of eyeballs knows what that looks like, who cares about your cute little keister anymore?"

Stonequest sniggered at that, which only set the woman onto him. "And you look like you were buried under another stone dragon. Go wash up. Now. Dinner's almost ready and you're all filthy!"

No one—not Kristen, not the Detroit SWAT team, and not even the European dragons—had the courage to refuse Marty Hall. The next thirty minutes were a mad scramble through showers and into fresh clothes. Her mom seemed to have a nose for grime and any dragon that skipped a shower was promptly escorted to the facilities and given a bar of soap. She wondered if they would have tolerated her mother if not for their recent loss. As it was, the dragons seemed almost thankful for the distraction.

Finally, they all sat together in the main dining room. It was the first time she had seen it completely full. Usually, the dragons ate first, then their mages, and finally, the few human servants who did the work that was beneath even the mages.

Marty Hall hadn't allowed any of that. She had cajoled everyone in the castle into the dining room and she served them all dinner at once. The only consolation she made to magical capabilities was to let Amy serve everyone at the same moment. Plates filled with her specialty—meatloaf topped with ketchup, mashed potatoes seasoned with salt and pepper, and a salad of parmesan cheese, egg, and crouton with lettuce—all settled in front of everyone.

Those in the room—human, dragon, and mage—looked at each other and all waited for someone to dig in. She realized that as an investigator, manners probably dictated that she should eat first, which made her relish the moment all the more.

Kristen looked around at all the faces. Some of them were still heartbroken, others merely looked tired, and still others were optimistic about what the future might bring. But in that moment, they were all united around a plate of food and a hungry belly.

She cleared her throat in preparation for a speech as she recognized that this was another moment to bring everyone together. That impetus faded, however, when she realized that she was once again the focal point of this entire conflict which, in fact, was the problem. She shouldn't be given any special preference because she was a dragon, even if she was a shiny one. A little conflicted, she finally settled on, "What are you all waiting for? *Eat!*"

The dragons and mages were made uncomfortable by her words,

but the humans weren't. Her family and human friends dug in with gusto.

The dragons took that as a challenge and began to eat. The mages —despite Kristen's mom's protests—kept everyone's plates piled high with second and third helpings and by the time they were all done, the only faces that weren't smiling from sharing a meal were those of the dragons who had already fallen asleep.

If that didn't give Kristen hope for the future, nothing would.

PART II

CHAPTER THIRTY-TWO

The opera soprano wasn't bad, but she was exceptionally dull—boring enough that Lord Boneclaw couldn't even find pleasure in watching her beg for her life.

"Please...please, I didn't sing any wrong notes and my voice didn't crack. *Please*," she pleaded.

He sighed. Her response was so predictable. "It wasn't that you sang poorly, merely that it was boring."

"Please, I can do better—*please!*"

The dragon, in his human form, grimaced. It was pathetic to watch humans grovel for their lives like this. For all intents and purposes, she was already dead. Couldn't she see that? There was no point in prolonging it, he thought before he ripped the woman's skin from her face.

She screamed as she bled from the massive wound, a vibrant high note full of pain and the terror of losing her life.

"There! Why couldn't you sing like that?" he asked rhetorically.

The soprano didn't answer, of course. She had either died or passed out from the pain and crumpled into his arms. He removed her head from her body with one of his claws and skinned her skull deftly, separated the part that held her brain, and donned the front as a mask.

"Ah…" He sighed and relished the sense that he was once again like his true self, The Masked One. Truly, it wasn't the soprano's fault she had bored him. It was the cursed Steel Dragon who robbed him of his pleasure.

Once he'd left the opera house, he headed through the streets of Paris toward one of his many penthouses. All around him, the city of lights glowed and turned the night into an effervescent dreamscape. The Eiffel tower gleamed in the distance, a reminder of what humans could accomplish with time and a little steel.

Steel.

It seemed that everywhere he looked, he found reminders of the damn Steel Dragon.

He continued to his penthouse, a little petulant as he traversed the gleaming streets. He considered himself an American. America—and the United States in particular—did a wonderful job of shirking tradition. It was something the Masked One agreed with. In Paris, it seemed the continent of Europe couldn't do anything with their weighty past besides glam it up somewhat.

The mages there, at his instigation, had tried to eliminate the Steel Dragon and thus bring about their little revolution that much sooner, but they'd failed. Their lack of success had been because they hadn't been able to improvise the way she had.

Although there had been one member of the last battle he had not anticipated. He entered his penthouse and gestured for one of his servants to turn the television on.

As expected, footage of the other dragon no one had heard of until now—the iron one—was cued to play. He studied her and had to concede that despite all the centuries of tradition, it seemed some of the European mages could innovate.

"Where did they find her?" he mused. His servant had been with him long enough to know better than to answer.

The Masked One sank into his Italian leather sofa and re-watched the battle between The Steel Dragon and this new iron one, captured on the security footage from the Uffizi museum.

He had become quite familiar with Kristen's battle prowess and had watched her battle with the dragons while in dwarf-controlled Canada, although everyone had seen that. This had been as enlightening as the footage of her in combat with one of the technomages to save most of the Dragon Council high above the streets of Detroit. He'd been there when she'd stopped Constance and her technomages from blowing up the meeting venue of their Full Council Meeting.

These were the significant conflicts she'd been involved in but he had seen other battles as well, fights that hadn't been televised or recorded. He had only been able to see these because of his talents. No other dragon but him had seen the Steel Dragon defeat Shadowstorm in the bowels beneath the incinerator and the fuel tunnels of Detroit. He'd seen her face Shadowstorm's mother Obscura in the infantile maze she'd wasted time constructing.

In all those fights, Kristen had demonstrated an ability to control her human form that most dragons simply didn't possess. Yes, she was formidable in her dragon body, but the true threat of the Steel Dragon was that she didn't simply assume that one body was stronger than the other. She could—and did—use her human form to escape situations, minimize damage, and even deliver devastating blows against her opponents.

The Masked One had never seen anything like it until now.

While the Iron Dragon was every inch the steel one's equal in physical prowess, it was her combat abilities that made her excel.

He watched her—what was the human phrase for it? Ah, that's right...he watched the Iron Dragon pick Lady Steel apart. It was amazing to see this warrior battle her opponent and brutalize her so effectively. She used her iron body efficiently and showed an adeptness in martial arts so refined that even he—someone who had never bothered to learn the various forms of combat in his human body—could tell that she was a master of combat.

Intrigued by her, he had already sent operatives to ferret out the new hiding place of the European technomage cell the Steel Dragon and her mongrel horde of dragons, humans, and mages had disabled. He was rather annoyed that Havington hadn't told him about the Iron

Dragon, but it was also easy enough to see that she hadn't been his to begin with.

In truth, despite the obvious strategic value of the Iron Dragon, she simply didn't hold the Masked One's interest like the Steel Dragon did. There was something about Kristen, something indelible to his ancient mind. Maybe it was that she was raised by humans, perhaps it was that she was a law enforcer, or maybe it was her stubborn refusal to accept the world for how it was. Whatever it was, it drew him in a way that nothing else could. Not even the opera captivated him like it once did.

He knew, logically, it would make more sense to target the Iron Dragon. If he could convince her that he was like her—a dragon determined to destroy the dragon-controlled global culture—he might be able to make an ally out of her.

Of course, he also knew that simply would not happen. He wouldn't expend any of his personal energy to hunt the Iron Dragon. Yes, if his operatives brought her to him or gave him a location that proved to be convenient enough, he might follow up, but she didn't hold his interest.

The Steel Dragon did.

Part of him knew that despite the sway she held over his mind, he should eliminate her once and for all. She was an undeniable impediment, a thorn in the plans he had been laying for decades and might prove to become infected if he left it to fester.

And yet, her unraveling his plans—even the clumsy, boorish way she often went about it—provided the Masked One with something he desperately needed after living for thousands of years—entertainment.

To a dragon like him, there was only one constant threat and one existential drain on his mind that was constant and ever-present—boredom. For the first time in decades, he had found a cure to that in the Steel Dragon.

He finished watching the recording of the battle, his mind made up. Kristen would live for a while longer, but his time of watching from a distance was coming to an end. He wanted to be closer to the action and in the shadow she cast with her infernal light.

Better still, he wanted to watch her dance on a web while he pulled the strings. He'd snare her, of this he was certain, but how long would it take? How far could she be pushed? Questions swirled through his mind. If his servants could see past the skull mask he always wore, they would see a vast diversity of expressions on his face—delight, concern, worry, and intrigue all vied for dominance. Yes, he would enjoy these next few days and when he was done, he'd decide what to do with the Steel Dragon. If there was anything left to decide about, of course. Because, like the spider who sat at the center of its web, the delight of trapping one's prey wasn't truly over until they were dead, beaten, and being digested by their betters.

That would come, though. Oh yes, it would happen, and the Masked One would bring it about.

It was time to set in motion events that would create an opening for him. He would investigate the Steel Dragon's power up close, perhaps even with his own hands.

Yes, that had a certain justice to it. He had a brief but satisfying image of bone claws choking the life from a silver neck...yes, he could enjoy that.

He gestured to his servant, who brought him a phone. As the man turned, he caught his wrist and drew him close to the skull mask he wore. His retainer had good bone structure. Maybe he would honor the servant by wearing his skull when he went to face the Steel Dragon.

When he released the man, he noted how quickly he spun and hurried away. The Masked One only smiled—not that the servant could see past the skull he wore on his face—before he picked up the phone and made a few calls.

It was time to set his web a-twitching.

The time had come to watch the Steel Dragon dance.

CHAPTER THIRTY-THREE

K risten Hall wondered if most people felt the same sense of palpable relief upon returning to Detroit after spending a week in Italy. She reasoned that if they didn't, they were fools.

Although she and the rest of her team had only been home one night, she was already in love with the Motor City again. Her brother Brian still tried to determine exactly how deep her pockets were. She was well past millionaire and into the multi-category, but he thought that based on the real estate holdings Windlock had given her, she might even make it into the low billions. That made her more than comfortable enough to take her team out to a hip-hop show and let them enjoy her open tab, followed by Detroit-style pizza after the show at Buddy's. She hadn't even let them pay for the beer.

Which probably explained why every human in her employ currently held their heads and threw back cups of coffee.

"You poor humans and your hangunders," Emerald said and shook his head sadly at Butters.

"They're called hang*overs*, you big green dragon, and I hardly see how it's fair to complain about me having one when you were the one who continually brought whiskey from the bar at that concert," the sniper protested.

They were on the bottom floor of the largest of three warehouses she had purchased for her base of operations in Detroit. Despite Timeflash setting up the top level with office spaces, meeting rooms, and everything else an operation like the Steel Dragon's would need to run efficiently, everyone preferred to spend their time on the cavernous first level of the warehouse with its thirty-foot ceilings and windows high on every wall.

Not that she blamed them. Although they'd only been gone a week, Timeflash had made a ton of progress toward making the base seem more than a recycled auto parts factory. True, she'd spent considerable time and money on the second floor of the warehouse and filled it with necessary office essentials, but the first floor had been transformed as well.

The concrete floor was now stained a rich brown. The walls had been repaired and painted in reds and oranges—traditional dragon colors—although Kristen didn't fail to notice that much of the electrical and plumbing had been left bare and chromed. The bright silvery flashes throughout the area drew a smile from her. She was the Steel Dragon, after all. It wasn't too much to have a few touches here and there to remind visitors of such things.

Butters finished his cup of coffee and promptly proceeded to make another pot. He had converted a corner of the space into a kitchenette. The other former members of human SWAT crowded around him and watched the steaming black liquid drip into the coffee pot.

"You know I was waiting for coffee before all of you, right?" Emerald told the assembled crew.

"I heard you joking about not having a hangover. That's because you dragons can metabolize more quickly, right?" Hernandez asked. Kristen was impressed that no profanity had been included in that question.

"True, although we're not immune. We merely have a greater advantage."

"What about C4? If you steal my coffee and I jam a handful of C4 down your throat, can you burn that off too?" The woman smiled sweetly to accompany the threat.

It proved how far human and dragon relations had come that Emerald didn't transform into a dragon right then and there. Instead, he simply laughed. "You can go first if it's that important to you. Butters' coffee doesn't taste much better than C4 anyway."

"I think he's asking for you to feed him the C4," the sniper grumbled and earned another chuckle from his dragon teammate.

"Hey! Look who it is, the Steel Dragon herself!" Keith called from near the coffee station.

The assembled humans plus Emerald uttered a ragged cheer.

"Why are we celebrating?" Kristen asked.

"Forgive me if I missed part of the conversation, but didn't we break up a European cell of technomages?" Stonequest asked as he transformed from his dragon body to his human one and walked across the warehouse to the assembled coffee-drinkers.

"We might have pushed them underground and possibly derailed their plans for a while, but I don't think we broke them up. There's no indication where they might have gone or what other resources they could have to assist them to regroup. We failed to capture their leader, the Iron Dragon Katrina, or the captive dragon they presumably had," she pointed out.

No matter how her team tried to spin it, she couldn't see their last operation as anything more than a temporary stalemate. Yes, they'd driven the group out of Europe—presumably, as there had been no more attacks—but they hadn't taken any of the most important pieces off the board.

"You still did a good thing out there," Lumos said. Only he and Timeflash had stayed behind during the team's trip to Florence, Italy.

"I appreciate that, Lumos, but I'd feel much better if we had another of my siblings to take care of," she replied.

The old dragon nodded. He had been caring for Stella, whom they'd found imprisoned in a mage cell, her body continually harvested over decades by the technomages so they could make weapons to start the war that would initiate their new world order. "We won't stop until we free them all," he said, his voice like stone.

"That's what I tell Stella every day, and I only feel confident enough to say it because I know you won't stop until it's true."

He spoke with such conviction that Emerald and Stonequest, as well as Keith, Butters, Hernandez, Beanpole, and Drew all saluted her. Kristen shook her head at them and fought back a smile. Good gracious, it was hard to be down on yourself for failing as royally as she had when you had friends like these.

"Did the Steel Dragon fart or something? Why are you all saluting?" Heartsbane asked after she swooped in through the hangar door on one side of the warehouse and landed gracefully. "Ooh! Coffee. Yummy."

"Lives will be lost if you jump the line," Hernandez shouted at the dragon as she transformed into the woman with tightly braided blonde hair that she was in human form.

"Yeah, yours," the dragon retorted but she didn't jostle for a cup of coffee like the others did. "But seriously, why was everyone saluting? Did Lady Hall come up with a plan to beat the Iron Dragon or something?"

Kristen scowled. "I wish. I don't even know who she is, let alone why she's working with the mages."

"And you're sure she was working with the mages? It's not unheard of for one dragon to attack another. Yes, she helped the technomages, but maybe that was incidental. Are you certain she's not someone with a grudge to settle against you?" Stonequest asked, even though they'd been over this again and again on the flight from Europe.

Fortunately, she didn't have to answer for the hundred and first time because Heartsbane fielded it. "You're damn straight we know she was working with the mages. Kristen and I almost grounded her outside the Uffizi before the mage she was rescuing opened a damn teleportation gateway and got her out of there. If that's not collaboration, I don't know what is."

He nodded. "You're right, of course, although it's hard to comprehend. She held all three of us off in their base. She's one hell of a fighter. Too bad we can't locate her."

"Something tells me we won't need to. I don't think she was

Havington's to boss around. I think she came from another cell. My hunch is that as soon as we start knocking the other technomage cells around, she'll show up," Kristen said.

"Lucky us," Drew said mirthlessly. He had been hit hard by Katrina.

A moment of silence swallowed the previously happy moment. No one sipped their coffee. A blue jay screeched somewhere in the parking lot. Apparently, in the week they'd been away, Timeflash had some of the asphalt demolished and had planted a number of saplings. It wasn't like Kristen couldn't afford it.

Finally, her brother dared to break the silence that previously only a blue jay had been brave enough to intrude on.

"The mission to Florence wasn't a total bust, though," he said as he sauntered closer from his corner of the warehouse.

"Is that right?" she asked him and noticed that he wore slacks and a jacket over a shirt with actual buttons. No tie, but they were all cops and no one wore ties.

"As a matter of fact, it is." He beamed, obviously proud of himself.

"Show me," Kristen ordered with a grin that dared him to argue with his sister for the ten-thousandth time.

Brian only winked and said, "Right this way, Investigator."

Butters shoved a cup of coffee into her hands and she smiled her thanks and hurried after her brother. As she walked across the stained concrete floor of the warehouse, she once again admired the work Timeflash had orchestrated while the team was away.

They reached Brian's intelligence corner. Again, despite Timeflash providing generous office space on the top floor, he had chosen to house a large part of his intelligence operation on the main floor. Three huge monitors and a projector display took up a corner of the room. In front of them stood a table with a few smaller monitors and keyboards for workstations.

She noticed there weren't any fast food wrappers or remains of uneaten freezer meals. The only item that marked the area as anything other than professional was a small framed photograph of the two siblings and their parents at a Detroit Tigers baseball game.

Once, she might have remarked on how the photo could be used to link her and their family if the base were broken into but given that her family had already been attacked multiple times by dragons and technomages, there didn't seem much point.

Larry Brockton sat at one of the workstations in front of the monitors. He nodded at Kristen as she approached. "Investigator."

"What do we have?" she asked.

The keyboard in front of the mage began to type despite his arms being folded and one hand stroking his chin. She smiled at the subtle show of magic. Before, when she had met Windlock, the mage had worn a power-dampening cuff and didn't use magic as much as he did now. Although he still wore the broken cuff that Windlock had given him before his old boss died, now modified as a necklace and with no magic to hinder him, Larry seemed pleased with the freedom.

"We already found plans for further attacks on dragons in Europe," he said. "We had to uh…de-encrypt the erm…cache of bytes because those are always the first to um…" He frowned through a long pause as he searched his memory. "Malfunction."

"What are you talking about?" she asked and looked from him to her brother.

"Larry helped…some. Although he's still learning the ropes around computers," Brian confessed. "Keith helped more, though."

"Score one for the Rookie!" the man shouted out from across the warehouse.

"I thought you hated to be called that," Hernandez snapped at him.

Keith shrugged his most rookie-ish shrug.

"I identified the streets," Larry said as if that explained anything.

Brian nodded approvingly at the mage. He had grown up so much, she thought with a rush of emotion. His co-worker had served up a fantastic opportunity for shit-talking and he had simply left it on the platter.

"Larry did identify the streets, what with him and his rich-ass benefactor jet-setting all over the world on the dime of the Dragon Council." Brian grinned.

Kristen couldn't help but chuckle at the dig, even if Larry's benefactor had left her everything when he died and she had since used his private jet to do a little jet-setting of her own. "Streets for what?" she asked.

"At first, we didn't know," he replied and obviously relished his new role as their master of intel. "I thought bases, maybe. The thing is, there weren't numbers or much else to go on, so we were kind of guessing—looking for a pattern."

"But they weren't on any farms," the mage interjected, eager to explain how he had contributed. "I recognized some of the streets as sites of famous dragon landmarks. Windlock's hobbies included visiting historical dragon sites—*yawn*—but that's what some of these places were."

"Once we knew what to look for—places important to the dragons—we found a pattern. We think it's a list of all the possible targets the European dragons wanted to hit. There are a few private dragon residences but it's mostly public places. We think they will try to target events and assassinate multiple dragons like Constance did."

"You mean you thought they were target events," Kristen corrected. "We dealt that cell a fair amount of damage. Do you really think they're ready to strike again?"

Brian and Larry shared a look that said, "Yes, yes, we do think the fucking crazy-ass technomages might attack again." They didn't need to voice it. Instead, her brother cleared his throat and tried to steady his voice.

"Although we believe those plans might be foiled or at least on hold now that the cell is disrupted, we still advise forwarding the intel to the Dragon Council of Europe in the hopes that it will help them prevent further deaths. The targets are all well-considered, and if the Dragon Council hasn't thought about keeping a better watch on things over there, maybe this will serve as a reminder for them. I've put it all together in a briefing I can send as soon as you green-light it, Investigator."

Kristen smiled at him. She was so proud of him. At first, she had thought it a terrible idea to bring him on board. While she had been worried about him getting hurt, slowing her down, or any number of things, he'd proven to be extremely useful.

"Send the report, Brian."

"Zed's my name when we're on duty, Investigator," he said.

Kristen rolled her eyes. At least Brian was still Brian deep down. "Right, Zed. Send it— unless you need me to make you a letterman jacket to show you're part of the team first."

"Yes, ma'am," he responded. "That would be cool but it's not necessary, ma'am. Wait—do you guys have jackets? Because if you do, I totally want one but not until I lose enough weight to fit into an XL."

She knew her brother keeping it professional for more than a minute was too much to ask for, but she made a note to try to get something to make the team look more cohesive. Patches, maybe? She wasn't sure and made a note to have Timeflash look into it.

"What else do we have?" Kristen asked and scanned the room to see if anyone on her team had more leads for her. It was amazing to lead a force of people as large as this group. She had always been a follower—a cop and someone who understood the value of orders— but she didn't mind her leadership role at all. The trick was to make sure you trusted your people. If you did, anything was possible.

"The cell in Texas fell off the map," Keith said. "I think that's good because it means they're not killing people, but it's also a pain in the ass because now, we don't know how to find them." He sipped his coffee.

"About that," Stonequest interjected. "I think we might need to bring more people in."

"Just when I was finally coming to trust my whole team," she muttered in a tone low enough to not be audible to the others. Stonequest didn't hear her, but he felt her aura with his dragon abilities and gave her a small smile. He, more than anyone else in the room, knew what it was like to be in leadership and had extended his trust to her long before she'd done anything to earn it. It didn't surprise her that he now expected her to do the same with a fresh crop of recruits.

"It has to be people we trust, of course," Stonequest continued, "which might be a hard thing to vet given that we have humans, mages, and dragons and probably should have more of all three. But there is an advantage to having more numbers that can't be discounted."

Kristen nodded and rubbed her face at the prospect of even more people to command, but he had the right of it. When they'd gone to Florence, they'd left the base almost abandoned. Only two dragons had stayed behind, no one from Detroit SWAT, and no mages. That wasn't optimal, especially if they were successful in their missions and made themselves a larger target for the technomage cells.

"Stonequest, what if you look for volunteers among the dragons on this continent? I know it's considerable ground to cover, but I don't want you to take too many from Dragon SWAT and I don't want a language or cultural barrier. It's hard enough getting dragons to work with humans and mages. If we get someone hell-bent on shitting on America, I don't think I could stomach it."

"I think I know a few." He nodded, his response not surprising given that he had raised the idea of them bringing more people into the operation. "But I can't exactly call them and expect them to come to Detroit. It's been some time since I've had contact with them."

"If you need to make house calls, make them," she said. "If they play hardball, move on. We can send you on another attempt if we need to."

"Yes, ma'am, although I think we'll need more than only dragons—"

"I know. Jim! Is Jim here? Has anyone seen him?" Kristen asked her crew.

"I'm upstairs in the actual offices," Jim said, emerged from one of them, and hurried down the open staircase to join them. Despite the warehouse-turned-base having only two stories, the second was much higher than the first at more or less the same level as an apartment building's fourth floor.

"I hope your legs are rested," she quipped, "because I want you to make the rounds and maybe find some old military buddies to help. I know you guys saw action with dragons and that some of you took it harder than others, but that's the kind of experience we might damn well need."

"Yes, ma'am," the Wonderkid said. You'd never guess by his chipper tone and professional demeanor that when he'd first met her, he'd been involved with people trying to kill her.

"If anyone gives you anti-dragon attitude, let them know that won't work, but if you think they can be converted…well…" She looked at her hodge-podge group of dragons, mages, and regular humans. "I think this might be the place to do it."

"I can go to Detroit PD and get people," Drew volunteered. "Hansen has always worked well with dragons and now that one of her former cops is a dragon Investigator, I'm sure she wouldn't say no."

"I thought of that but I don't like it," she said. "Hansen would give us people and I'm sure we could trust them, but I don't want to weaken the police force of this city. I already took Detroit's best SWAT team away. I don't want to poach the talent from the rest of its teams. Us being here will turn this city into more of a target than it was before. We need to know that the local police will be able to handle themselves."

"Right," he said and remained professional despite having his idea shot down.

"What about the rest of us?" Heartsbane asked. "Something tells me you're not the let-them-come-to-us kind of boss."

"You're right about that. I think we head to Texas. They're our most solid lead and the biggest threat to us right now. I'll take a team down there—Emerald, Hernandez, Keith, and Butters."

"I can't go without Beanpole," the sniper protested.

"Fine, fine. Beanpole comes too, but then we'll need another dragon, so I guess Lumos can—"

The phone rang but she continued to detail the orders. She broke off, however, when Timeflash answered it and her face dropped.

"What is it?" Kristen asked.

"There's been another attack."

CHAPTER THIRTY-FOUR

Timeflash took the call in the middle of the room, while everyone crowded around and tried and failed to hear both sides of the conversation. As she spoke, she took notes on a tablet that was linked to Brian's station. While they'd been out of town, the dragon had apparently taken time to do the admin shit that no agency could exist without, like setting up a phone line.

"What's up?" Kristen demanded when the woman hung up.

The dragon gestured to her scribbled notes on the screen. "I put it there so you can all see."

"Erin, I think that's Latin," she said patiently. Sometimes, it could be odd working with beings who were centuries old.

"Oh, right. Everyone and their English." Timeflash shook her head. "There's been an attack at a manor outside Bogota, Columbia."

"What happened?"

"A dragon ball was bombed. They're not sure who did it but three dragons are dead and another four injured. They've taken shrapnel out of the wounds and it's made from dragon pieces, so the attack matches our technomages."

"You're damn straight it does." Heartsbane growled.

"Official paperwork just came in," Brian said. He typed faster on his keyboard and manipulated his computer with greater alacrity than Larry had been able to even with his telekinesis. A whirring noise issued from under one of the tables.

He leaned over, kicked something, cursed, and kicked it again. "Damn printers," he said finally as he straightened and put the official request for assistance in her hands.

She read it quickly. It was as Timeflash had said and it looked urgent.

"All right, we need a new plan," she told them.

"All hands on deck?" Jim asked and looked eager for more action.

"No, I don't think that's smart," she countered and took the wind from his sails. "Now, we have two targets. This demonstrates that we absolutely need more people. I still want you and Stonequest to follow up on any leads you have."

Kristen appraised the room. "Drew, Larry, and Lumos, I want you three in Texas. I want you to scout only. Do I make myself clear?"

The old dragon nodded eagerly, Larry grinned, and Drew looked disappointed.

She ignored the look the team leader darted at her. "We have no idea what's down there, and I don't want you in trouble without more of the team to back you up. Once you find something—and I am confident that you three will—contact us and we'll send in reinforcements. I'm sending you three because you are wise and experienced." She couldn't help but laugh, even if it was true. "And I don't want anyone shooting from the hip, am I clear?"

"As vodka," Larry said.

"Everyone else is with me. Timeflash, do you mind staying behind with Brian? You seem to have a vision for this base and...well, I want to see it finished."

"Yes, ma'am," the woman answered.

"What? Why do I have to stay? I did great in Florence if I may say so myself!" her brother whined.

"Because we'll have two active teams and you need to be here to support both. I won't jeopardize either group by sending them in without Zed's intel."

He nodded and blushed at the compliment.

"If there's nothing else—"

Kristen's cell phone rang.

She retrieved it out of reflex and was surprised to see the three-digit area code that indicated it was a dragon calling her. It seemed to her that kind of call should go to the building itself, not her cell. But even she hadn't known they had a building phone, so maybe it was too much to ask that every dragon on earth knew about it already.

She answered briskly.

"Lady Hall, this is Remus, one of the chief mages of the Dragon Council of North America. We're awaiting your report on your activities in Europe."

"Sure. Romulus, was it? I sent the report."

"Very funny, and if you sent it, we didn't get it."

"I'm sure we sent it—"

"Look, the Dragon Council doesn't exactly go in for the latest plugins, all right? It's possible they lost the report. There's no need to make a big deal about it. They'll straighten out whatever happened as soon as you report."

"Okay, well, we just received news of activity in Colombia. We were about to head out." She didn't mean to be rude but she had sent the report.

"Lady Hall, I am only the messenger and the Dragon Council wants to see you now, not at your earliest convenience. I was to deliver this message and the coordinates, that is all. I hope to see you in Kentucky."

"Kentucky?" Kristen asked, but the line had already gone dead. On the screen of her phone was a message with GPS coordinates that were, indeed, for somewhere in Kentucky.

Fuming, she glowered at the message. How like the Dragon Council to continue to pull at her strings and expect her to jump. She was about to give in to her internal prompting to fuck it when Lumos stepped up.

"Pardon me for being impertinent but I overheard your call," Lumos said.

"Damn dragon hearing," she muttered.

"I heard that too." He chuckled. "I'm sure you don't want to go—"

"You're damn straight I don't want to go. Hell, how do I even know it was really from the Dragon Council? It was a random phone call with a dragon area code. That doesn't prove anything."

"Was it Remus who called?" he asked.

"That's what he said," she confirmed.

"Then you ought to go," Lumos told her. "I know he's a sniveling little punk but they do expect him to handle anything that involves technology more modern than electricity."

"If they're so damn antiquated, you'd think they'd have better manners," she retorted.

"That"—the old dragon winked—"is an excellent point but it doesn't change my opinion of what you should do."

Kristen sighed. "I thought being an investigator would mean I could make all the decisions."

Lumos smiled warmly. "I'm afraid not. Being the leader merely means you have to say no to your team while saying yes to everyone else."

She nodded at the nugget of the wisdom, bitter though it was. "What do you advise?" she asked but she could already see where this would go.

"Take the meeting, enjoy the flight to Kentucky, and let us handle this. If you anger the council, they might decide to start their war anyway and not give us more time to resolve the situation. I know it's not the most glamorous option, but if you show them that you're still working with them, it will go a long way. Don't forget, it's been less than a month since Windlock made you an investigator."

Less than a month since Windlock died, she thought.

"The Dragon Council no doubt saw the headlines and the er... photographs. Now, they want your story. Oh, and probably to bill you for some of the damages."

"What? We were there protecting people."

He shrugged. "People's homes were destroyed and you can afford to fix them. If you want peace between our kinds, you'd better be willing to pay."

"Yeah, yeah, yeah." Kristen nodded reluctantly and gestured for her team to assemble. "All right, it looks like we'll have to change the marching orders. Amy, I want you with Drew and Lumos on the Texas investigation. Drew has final say down there. Amy, stay defensive and stay sharp. There's a good chance your ability to sense mages is what will give us our lead. Larry."

Larry hung his head like a dog that had torn through the trash. "I know, I know. I'll hold down the fort here while the rest of you head off to beautiful Bogota."

"No, Larry, I'm placing you in charge of the team going after the active cell. Emerald will be your second, then Butters."

"I'm sorry, but did I hear that right? You put me in charge?" He looked both extraordinarily proud and completely mortified. "Like, as in I'll boss everyone around? You know I talk too much, right?" He turned to Keith, who stood next to him. "She knows I talk too much, doesn't she? Are you sure—I mean, I'm honored, but, well…really?"

"I second his extreme doubt at this decision," Hernandez said.

"Are you sure you don't want a dragon on point?" Emerald all but hissed. He had made considerable progress but he still had anti-human prejudices behind those green eyes and dark skin.

"I'm sure," Kristen said matter of factly. "Larry has a cool head. He spent ages working with Windlock so he knows how to investigate. Besides, with his magic unlocked, he can probably keep you dragons in line better than anyone else until I get there."

"Windlock must be rolling in his grave right now." Heartsbane ground the words out.

"Larry has my confidence, so I trust he'll have yours, but don't worry about it too much. I need to meet the Dragon Council, but at least they're south of here, which is on the way to South America…kind of."

"We planned to take the jet," Larry said and stepped quite comfortably into his new role.

"That's fine. I'll fly to my meeting. It'll be quicker than booking a flight anyway. When I'm done, Brian will have a ticket ready for me to meet you guys in Bogota."

"I will?" her brother asked and didn't quite take the hint. In the next moment, his eyes widened at his obvious gaff. "I will."

"Then it's settled. Brian, tell our pilot they're on their way. I'll see you guys soon."

"Are you sure about this...leadership?" Emerald asked again.

"No, not completely," Kristen replied. "In fact, my gut tells me this Dragon Council meeting will be a waste of my fucking time and by the time I get to Colombia, you guys will already be in a world of hurt. But Lumos pointed out that I don't exactly have a good track record with the Dragon Council. If any of you dragons advise that I skip this meeting, please say so because I would be more than happy to oblige. Better yet, maybe one of you could go in my place."

"To speak to the Dragon Council?" He looked aghast.

"Precisely."

Emerald shook his head, walked to Larry, and threw his arm around him. "If it's all the same to you, I'd rather take orders from the blabbermouth, boss."

"That sounds good to me," she said and dismissed her team.

If she felt lonely with all of them going on missions while she had to turn in her homework, she didn't let it show.

CHAPTER THIRTY-FIVE

K risten thought the flight to Kentucky might be a lonely one, but it wasn't. It was a beautiful day—warm for fall and getting warmer as she pumped her wings and caught thermals that worked in her favor as she flew across the Midwest to Kentucky. The trees were already starting to turn below her. Most were green but here and there, vast swathes of forest were tinged with yellow or displayed hints of orange.

As she flew, she thought about the challenges they faced. At first, she tried to focus on the mission at hand—although mission was too strong a word. This felt like a glorified high school report, but she reminded herself that even senators and scientists made presentations. Maybe that was simply the way of the world. She had researched the location itself and found it odd that it wasn't in any of the major cities. While she could understand why it wasn't in Cincinnati or Louisville—dragons liked their privacy and could always fly into a major city for whatever entertainment they desired—that it didn't seem to be in Bowling Green or even Elizabethtown seemed weird to her.

Then again, the last time the Dragon Council had met, it had been in a remote northern region of Canada. Maybe they had finally taken the threat of the technomages seriously. Hopefully, the meeting would be at another old hotel built before cities were the true destinations, places where people would stay before the marvels of technology drew everyone to the city lights like moths to flames.

But the task at hand could keep her occupied for only a limited duration. Before too long—somewhere over Indiana that seemed little more than cornfields—she began to think about all she'd been through.

Becoming a police officer, discovering she was a dragon, and then defeating Shadowstorm and later, his mother Obscura, all seemed like a distant memory. Those were simpler times when all she had wanted to do was fit in.

Even in those days, though, there had been hints of the conflict to come. The most notable had been the dragon assassin Death, who had been armed with dragon bullets. She was dead now, killed by her hand, but she still wondered about her from time to time. Had she been the one to pioneer the bullets made of dragon scales? Or had that particular revolution in murder come from Constance, the former leader of the cell she had first gone up against, time and time again.

Kristen wondered about Constance, even after facing another cell with another group of arguably even more powerful mages, not to mention the Iron Dragon—and her sister—Katrina. What had the Dragon Council decided to do with the technomage leader after she had captured her? Had she been executed? That would be the logical thing to do with her, given all the dragons she'd killed. But she had a hunch that if anyone could talk their way out of an execution, it would be Constance.

She could imagine her, bruised and bloodied and beyond exhausted from whatever the callous dragons might have done to her to try to obtain information but still with her head high and her back straight. Despite the fact that she was Kristen's most dangerous foe, she was also the enemy she found she could relate to the most.

It was insane, honestly. The woman was a murderer, period, and yet her motivations were so close to hers. She wanted a better world, a world where everyone didn't have to ask, "How far?" when a dragon said, "Run!" She had gone about it the wrong way, of course. But even when she'd fought her and her team, even when her actions had killed Windlock, there had been something more to her. An inner compassion, maybe.

Kristen hadn't sensed any of that in Katrina. The Iron Dragon's heart had seemed as hard as her skin. The technomages she worked with might have been conflicted but she did not seem to be at all.

She paused her thoughts for a moment and vowed to ask the Dragon Council about what had happened to Constance. She knew that—at the very least—Decimus Aurelius would answer her. After all, she'd saved the dragon's life and he'd knelt before her in gratitude. She might not have risked the question in front of the Full Dragon Council but if it was only the seven from North America, she felt she could rely on him to shield her from any aggression the others felt.

Although there was one member of the North American Council that made her uneasy. She tried to tell herself not to judge the dragon because of the curious scars on his face or his name—Boneclaw—but there was something unsettling about him. It seemed to be in the way he looked at her and in how he'd fled from the threat of Constance's bomb while the other dragons had stayed.

The Steel Dragon took a deep breath and refocused on her flying. It would still be better to say something to the North American Council rather than all the councils. Not that they would all meet again anytime soon. Hell, given the remoteness of where the North American Dragon Council had asked her to meet, it seemed likely that council meetings would be rare indeed until she stopped the technomages for good.

She pushed on and drew closer to the destination the GPS coordinates pointed her to. Not that she could manipulate a cellphone in her dragon form, but she had an earpiece and Brian to redirect her if she veered off course.

He gave her the ten-minute warning and things began to make

sense. She now flew over a forest that was so thick and untouched that she knew it had to be a national park. Sure enough, she passed over a winding road with a billboard that said *Explore Mammoth Cave.*

That was obviously the meeting location. Caves had long held significance for dragons, and Mammoth Cave was the longest known cave system in the world. Kristen had been on enough road trips with her family to have visited it a few times. There were parts of it that were open for humans to go sight-seeing and spelunking, but there were huge areas of it that were cordoned off. As a kid, she had assumed it was as the tour guides had said—to protect the formation of rock structures—but after her time with dragons, she knew there was probably more to it.

It was more than likely that the sections that were off-limits to people were entirely available for dragons. As far as she knew, a dragon might even live there. For that matter, multiple dragons might call the cave system home on account of how large it was. Now that she was there, it made sense that it was the meeting place for the Dragon Council.

There were likely multiple entrances, she acknowledged. It was large enough to hide them, and—although it might have seemed strange at first—it being a tourist destination was probably an advantage. The technomages would no doubt look for isolated places coming online. Old hotels, long-abandoned buildings, or any building that came alive with electricity, Internet connections, and delivery vehicles would be obvious to anyone looking for them. If the other technomage cells were hunting dragons, they'd be on the lookout for isolated locations that suddenly became active.

Brian gave her final confirmation and she knew she was at the coordinates, only she didn't see anything. Well, nothing like a Dragon Council Meeting. Other things were visible like camping grounds, parking lots, a few buildings to house the staff, and gift shops and the like. Dozens, if not hundreds, of people walked the trails, meandered about the grounds, and waited for their turn to enter the cave or for someone to come out.

They saw her too. At first, it was merely the regular ripple of activity from people who saw what might be a huge predator over-head. Even though dragons hadn't hunted and eaten people for tens of thousands of years, how people first reacted to a dragon flying over-head was so deeply ingrained that it might have been called instinctual.

When her shadow passed over them, they glanced first at whoever was nearby as if to confirm there was a threat. After that, their reactions were different enough that she couldn't generalize their behavior, but she saw some of the more typical responses in the park below her.

A group of young men walked faster and their shoulders flexed involuntarily—not that fighting would accomplish anything against a dragon. A woman called her children to her and either intentionally or instinctively took shelter under a tree. Many simply froze, craned their heads, and watched the dragon soar above them. They seemed to try to assess if it was a threat to run from or whether it was better to stay still and not draw her ire.

A little girl cut through all that, though, and proved that humans had indeed come a fair way since their time in prehistory when some-how, they'd managed to claw a civilization out of the world they shared with dragons.

"That's Kristen Hall. The Steel Dragon. I saw her on TV," the girl shrieked in delight and began to run down the path after her, despite it being impossible for a human, let alone a child, to catch up to a dragon who was already airborne.

Kristen debated briefly whether she should land. This seemed to be her destination but she didn't see any dragons so she couldn't be sure. Part of her didn't want to land at all. She had already made enough of a scene to possibly give away the location of the council meeting, but she also reasoned that the Dragon Council had sent her there while the place was crawling with tourists. If they didn't want her to be seen, they should have said something about the cover of darkness or sent her to coordinates that weren't easily visible from the ranger station.

Not wanting to make the Council wait any longer and recognizing an opportunity for good public relations when she saw it, she landed near the welcome center.

It turned out that she had been wrong about the ground speed of a small yet motivated child. She had barely landed and was still in her dragon form when the girl emerged from the woods. "Oh, my God, *she's my hero*," she screamed at the top of her lungs as she sprinted toward her.

Despite all the practice Kristen had transforming to her human form as quickly as possible, she didn't think she would be able to do it in the amount of time it would take for the little girl to reach her.

As a result, the child leapt onto the chest of a massive steel-scaled dragon.

"Oh, my God. I have all your comic books and I always told my mom I would meet you one day and she said you'd never come to Florida—that's where we live, by the way, Florida—and I didn't believe her but I guess she was right because now we're in Kentucky and you're here." The sprinting plus the run-on sentence finally winded the girl and she took a breath and proved that the kid had typically human tendencies.

"Mom! Mom, can you take a picture? It's okay, she has her clothes on this time," she shouted at a woman who hurried across the field toward them using the undignified slow jog of a parent who didn't want to run but knew they couldn't saunter either.

Kristen was glad she was still a dragon because at least she couldn't blush. Truly, had everyone seen the picture of her in Italy? She sighed. Probably. Naked dragons holding kittens weren't exactly everyday occurrences.

While she waited for the mother to arrive to take the obligatory picture, she grilled the doting girl. "And what do you want to be when you grow up?"

"Are you kidding me? I want to be a cop." The girl said "cop" the way most kids would say Batman.

She couldn't help but smile and show some of her dragon teeth. At least she had made a positive impression on someone.

"You'd better be careful or that dragon will eat you," a skinny boy with dark kinky hair and thick glasses told the girl.

"Are you serious?" She made it sound like he had said ice was hot.

"She is a dragon," he pointed out smugly.

"She is not *a* dragon. She is *the* dragon! This is Kristen Hall. She's from Detroit and she's a hero. She would never eat a kid like me—or you, even though you're rude."

"I am not!" He looked like he wanted to protest further but then thought of something more important. "Wait, we can climb on you and you won't eat us?" he asked.

"I don't know about all that," Kristen mumbled. How funny, she thought. She had faced dragons and mages armed with bullets that could shred her flesh like paper, and two children seemed unstoppable.

It being funny didn't make her any more capable of stopping the two tyrants from climbing all over her. The boy had scrambled up her tail in mid-mumble and now scaled her back.

"Whoa, cool!" shouted a child with a pale face between his freckles and a body type she could only think of as beefy. He ran to her as well and without asking for permission or anything else, climbed on.

She doubted the wisdom of dragons going to a national park. Kids saw her in Detroit all the time. They asked her questions, demanded autographs, and a dozen other things but they did not climb on her. It seemed that kids who spent their time running around national parks and climbing trees rather than playing in the urban jungle that was any modern American city had a different sense of both propriety and safety when it came to dangerous things.

Soon, they grew bored with this adventure—all except Maria of course, who was from Florida even though her parents were from Cuba. Although she'd been on Kristen for hardly a minute, the dragon already knew her favorite food was fried yucca, and even though her mommy made very delicious Cuban sandwiches, she wouldn't eat them because she didn't like meat. She thought it was okay if Kristen ate meat because she was a dragon and besides, it was fine if people liked different things.

While the other children climbed down and Maria prattled on, the adults descended for their turn with a celebrity.

Kristen didn't think she'd ever heard the word "selfie" as many times as she did in the next five minutes. It made sense, though. People came to places like these to take pictures, but there were only so many trees and caves you could show people on social media before they grew bored. Meanwhile, an image of you near the Steel Dragon almost guaranteed that the likes would simply roll in. It was inevitable.

A park ranger approached and she had never been so thankful to see another member of law enforcement.

"Sorry about the crowd, sir. I was telling all these kind folks we should probably move on off the grass," she said.

"Are you kidding?" the man responded. His big bushy beard did nothing to hide the grin on his face. "The grass will grow again. Do you mind if I get in there? I bet my buddies in Pig that this job would be exciting and those fatsos didn't believe me."

She couldn't help but wonder at the size of the other men if this ranger—who was certainly not skinny—deemed them fatsos.

"I bet them assholes a meal at the Porky Pig Diner that working here would be better than moving to Louisville with a horde o' damn liberals. It looks like I'll eat pork sandwiches smothered in gravy for life after all this."

Kristen smiled for a photo with the man—not that most people could read dragon facial expressions any better than they could read the facial expressions of crocodiles.

"Do you get many dragons around here, then?" she asked the ranger.

"Are you kidding me or something?" He grinned. "I haven't seen a dragon 'round here ever. Some of the old-timers say dragons live deep in there. They have gold and stuff and that if you can go into some of the unused parts and fetch a piece, they'll buy you a beer, but no one ever done did that. It's only a passage like all the others."

"The caves are that deep?"

"Oh yeah. Longest caves in the world, but everyone knows that.

There are whole sections humans have never explored. It's too tight or too dangerous, or there's formations or rocks we don't want damaged. Damn liberals with their damn smartphones, always trying to take pictures with the rocks and getting their fingerprints all over them. Do you know how much damage the grease on your fingers can do to a crystal formation? It's a damn shame. God put these things here for us to enjoy and the least folks could do is conserve them."

She studied the man more closely. Conservation didn't seem to be part of most conservatives' agenda, but she began to see there might be more to him than he let on.

"Would you be able to give me a tour?"

"Well, hot damn, of course I can. The boys will never believe this. Name's Miller, by the way. Joshua Miller. You can call me Ranger Jay."

"Sure thing, Ranger Jay," she said and transformed into her human body once Maria had reluctantly abandoned her dragon perch.

"And you are?" he asked.

"I am an investigator for the Dragon Council here on a covert operation—" She began to build some semblance of confidentiality before Maria interjected.

"She's Kristen Hall, the Steel Dragon. She's the most famous dragon there ever was."

Ranger Jay looked more closely at her. She'd worn a designer suit to meet the Dragon Council—she could afford such things now, so why not?—plus heels because if she decided she didn't want them, she could always go barefoot and turn the soles of her feet into solid steel to protect herself.

It was her red hair that caught his attention, though.

"I...uh...you didn't happen to go to Italy, did ya? There's some...uh, websites I follow that have pictures of someone who looks like you..." He somehow managed to keep his gaze on her face rather than lowering it to her chest.

Not that there was much to see. Even in a designer suit, her body didn't look as good as it did when she wore nothing but a pair of kittens clutched in front of her breasts. It seemed the whole world had seen that damn photo.

"I can't say I have," Kristen said and gestured for Ranger Jay to take her on a tour of Mammoth Cave.

CHAPTER THIRTY-SIX

A few minutes later, they had blessedly moved away from the crowds. Ranger Jay paused every few minutes to snap pictures of him and Kristen—kind of odd given how much he'd railed on liberals for their cellphones, but she didn't mind the guy. He was outgoing and shockingly knowledgeable about the cave system.

"See, these stalactites form from water dissolving rock—calcium bicarbonate, specifically—and when it touches the air, the carbon is precipitated out and leaves a tiny ring. Over time—and I'm talking considerable time, longer than dragon lifetimes even—it makes these wild formations."

"And the colors?" she asked, although her real focus was on her attempt to find some sign of the Council. They had told her to come there, but where were they?

"Oh, that's merely impurities. It's all basically the same process, but once other minerals get in, it'll make crystals of different kinds and— you're not listening, are you?"

Honestly, she had tried but she wasn't paying him any attention. She'd stopped walking, even though she finally knew she should indeed go deeper. After searching and searching, her dragon aura had finally identified another draconic presence. The Council really was paranoid. True, it made sense to use their auras to guide her as humans and mages couldn't sense them, but it still seemed like a level of caution they had never previously imagined.

Their last meeting had involved feasting. Somehow, she didn't think they would manage to get a catering team down there. Had they changed so much? She thought it was possible. Humans were certainly capable of a paradigm shift after years and years of living by the same codes. She only had to think of World War II as an example.

Her father had told her again and again how Detroit had completely retooled itself to help fuel the war effort. Maybe dragons were more similar to people than she had realized. Despite being capable of living for millennia, they had undergone shifts in their culture's paradigm. She had hoped they would adjust their ways for something besides violence aimed at dragons, but she had already accepted that it was a dream from another era.

Kristen glanced at Ranger Jay. He'd stopped talking and looked back the way they came as if he'd remembered there was something very urgent he needed to attend to.

"Did you forget something, Ranger Jay?" she asked demurely. She knew he had not—or if he had, it wasn't what made him look toward the entrance right now. He did so because she had used her aura to make him feel like he'd forgotten something important.

"Yeah, that is... We might have another wave of visitors. I...I think... Maybe I should get going? I mean...you are a dragon and there ain't nothing down here can hurt you."

"If you insist," she said, proud of herself for finally being able to control her aura enough to make it do something besides what she outwardly felt. "Are you sure you've never seen dragons here or any evidence of them around Mammoth Cave?"

"I'm certain, ma'am. You'll be the talk of the—well, not the town as this is a national park, but you'll be the talk of it all the same. When you're done having a look around, follow the path out. It's lit and has guardrails so you can't miss it."

"Thanks, Ranger Jay."

"Oh, and...well, this is kind of embarrassing trying to give a dragon investigator rules, but…uh, don't touch the crystal formations. They really do take a long-ass time to form and when you touch them, the oils from your fingers interfere with the whole process and can even stop the entire—"

"Ranger Jay?"

"Uh…yeah?"

"You already told me all that. Twice." After another pulse of her aura, he looked like he was worried about missing the greatest tour this park had ever had. Kristen couldn't affect thoughts with her aura directly—not even Heartsbane could do that—but she could affect emotions, and the human brain wasn't so sophisticated a piece of machinery that it could always parse thoughts from emotions.

Ergo, he had thought about another wave of visitors and the aura she sent reminded him of his own thought. She hadn't put it there, only recognized the intellectual reaction his emotion had caused and stuck with that same tack— it seemed useful to get rid of the ranger— rather than switching to another one. After all her time working on her aura, it seemed elementary, but there had been a time when it would have been impossible.

She proceeded down the path alone. Mammoth Cave was beautiful. Amongst the stalagmites and stalactites were countless crystalline structures. Some looked like frost and others like chains of murky diamonds. Here and there, giant crystals protruded from the walls as if placed there by a Hollywood movie director. She moved past them all, noticed idly, but used her aura to sense the way ahead of her.

There was a dragon down there. She was sure of it. And the closer she got, the more certain she felt that this was where she was supposed to go. There weren't any people—not rangers or tour guides or anyone else. The only things her aura sensed were the occasional blips of insect life and once or twice, an essence she decided could only be a fish.

This suspicion was confirmed when she emerged into a room— she should have brought a map—in which a river or lake wound along the bottom. Stalactites hung from the ceiling and here and there, they poked from the hazy blue water. Fish swam in the lake, pale creatures with long whiskers and no eyes to speak of.

The dragon aura was still ahead and while it grew stronger, it remained out of reach. She followed the elevated path above the lake and wondered where the Dragon Council—or perhaps only a single Councilor?—planned to hold their meeting.

After a time, she sensed she was as close to the aura as she could be at this elevation. Before her was a gaping hole in the rocks that looked like melted snow with lights mounted around it that did nothing to illuminate its depths.

The aura emanated from below. Kristen smiled. This was beyond the pale. The hole was large enough to be intimidating, even to a woman with dragon powers, but not so big as to accommodate a dragon. She reasoned that it was a perfect choke point, especially if the Council was afraid of Katrina and what she could do to them. She and anyone else would have to jump down blind. They'd land—dead if they were a human and likely injured if they were a dragon—while whoever waited down there would be able to assess them and either finish them off or retreat further.

For the briefest of moments, she felt this was too much. There was no way someone from the Dragon Council could be this paranoid. The thought was pushed from her head as quickly as it had come. She wanted to go down there and meet the council member and wanted to report. That's why she'd come this far after all.

There was nothing else to do but jump into the pit.

Kristen looked around to check once more if there were any people, but she hadn't needed to. Her dragon aura made quite sure nothing else was around that was any larger than a cricket.

With a deep breath, she swung over the railing and into the pit. She let herself fall for a count of three before she turned her legs to steel and counted another two before she splashed into a pool of water and promptly transformed into a body that would not sink.

Quickly, she swam to the surface and emerged from the water to drag a breath of the warm, slightly stale cave air. Above her was only blackness with a few motes of light from the fixtures at the very top of the pit.

Seeing that distance made her doubt her decision to jump. Up there, she had been so certain that this was what she'd wanted to do but now, she was unsure. Even with her dragon strength and steel hands, it would take a long time to punch holes in the walls of the pit and climb out. Plus, Ranger Jay had made it very clear that destroying the crystals was not cool. If there wasn't another way out, she would be down there for a long time.

She swam to the edge of the pool and climbed out, then looked around the gloom. Already, her dragon eyes had begun to adjust to the extremely low light and located a few passages that led from this fairly large chamber. They all looked like they'd been carved by water over centuries. She didn't see any signs of paths, either human or dragon-made. Honestly, she didn't see much of anything. But when she looked down one passage, she felt the aura again. No doubt whoever's aura it was could sense her too, as it seemed directed at her like it wanted her to find them.

That made sense. She was there to find the Dragon Council, but it also made her nervous. Despite her growth, she was far from the most adept at controlling her dragon aura. She'd come a long way but compared to her combat abilities, her aura was fairly weak. Meeting Heartsbane had only further stunted her growth because she was so proficient with her powers that Kristen hadn't needed to use her aura much at all.

She knew enough about how it worked to know that it was difficult for a dragon to manipulate another dragon, although not impossible. Had someone convinced her to jump with their aura? She couldn't be sure.

But she did know that it ultimately didn't matter. If it was the Council...well, she had to meet with them. If it were some foe who wished to lure her to her doom...well, she'd meet them like she did every challenge with a pair of steel fists.

Cautiously, she started toward the aura, moving along a narrow rock shelf that hugged the edge of the small lake. Before long, the water formed a narrow lip that created a small waterfall completely made of crystal. It fell into the abyss and the lakebed dropped away, taking the water even deeper into the earth. The plunge was so deep that even with her dragon hearing, she couldn't hear the drops of water hit the bottom.

The aura was ahead, though, not down, so she clung to the lip and negotiated around a bulwark of stone.

She rounded a corner and stopped at a thin aperture. It was too narrow for her but it was also undoubtedly the way toward the aura. She sighed, knowing Ranger Jay would most definitely not approve, and turned her fists to steel to punch a hole in the limestone big enough for her to fit through.

Moments later, she stood in a room with a ceiling of hanging crystalline spikes. She imagined they might have been a shade of blue but she couldn't tell. Her dragon eyes could function in the almost nonexistent light, but there wasn't enough illumination for her to register color anymore.

More important than the color of the stalactites, though, were the pits beneath them. To her mind, it looked like someone had cranked the roof of the room off the ground and left the giant holes in the floor, but she was sure there was a more scientific and far less exciting answer.

Again, she made a silent apology to Ranger Jay and started through the room.

The first thing she discovered was that the floor was not sturdy. With one wrong step, the crumbly, porous limestone gave way to open air and her footing was gone, but she managed to leap forward and landed on another platform of stone.

This proved to be far sturdier than the last—it supported her for an entire three seconds instead of the scant moment the first had afforded her. That was more than enough time for her to tense her muscles and vault farther across the room.

The force of her leap was enough to jostle the stone and it tumbled away sooner than it would have otherwise. In turn, it ruined her trajectory.

Rather than career past one of the massive crystal stalactites, she was on a course to go through it.

No matter. Steel was harder than rock. She had proven that many times.

In the split second she had before she powered into the rock spike, she turned her fists to steel and struck the obstacle. It exploded in a shower of whitish powder and crystalline shards. Kristen would have liked to pause to take in the beautiful effect but the piece of stone she found herself on was no sturdier than any of the others.

She surged forward and no longer tried to avoid stalactites now that she knew how little force her steel fists needed to clear her path.

After a moment or two of what should have been almost impossible acrobatics and rock-destroying punches, she finally crossed the odd room and stood on more stable ground.

Regretfully, she looked at the damage she'd caused deep inside the earth. She knew Ranger Jay wouldn't like it but in a thousand years, this room might grow into something with an actual path through it now that she had cleared the stalactites. The future caretakers of the cave would have to build a bridge there after all Kristen had done, but they'd done that over the crystal lake so they could do it there too.

The next part of the cave wasn't so much a room as a hallway or tunnel. She followed it, broke entrances open when she needed to, and turned her body to steel and forced herself through tight passages whenever she could.

Once or twice, she stopped to look behind her. She swore she could feel something there—not the dragon presence she was pursuing but something else—but whenever she turned, the feeling dissipated. Still, she couldn't shake the feeling she was being tested.

Was a mage watching her traverse the route so they could report to the Dragon Council? Was there a dragon who could move through stone as easily as she'd seen some of them swim? She didn't know.

All she knew was that the path before her wasn't a true obstacle.

Where it was small, she broke it.

When it grew too steep, she changed to steel and simply slid down the ledge and broke rock formations with her feet as easily as a child might crush fresh snow.

After ten minutes of traversing the tunnel, she'd worked up a sweat and couldn't help but enjoy herself. She was deeper in the earth than a human could be without proper tools, and she hadn't even slowed. It made her realize how far she'd come and how much she'd grown both physically and in confidence.

If this was indeed the test she assumed it to be, she was knocking it out of the park.

Kristen stepped into a large chamber at the end of the tunnel and looked up. For the briefest of moments, she had a sense of déjà vu before she realized that she had seen something like this. When she'd jumped down the first pit, the view from the floor had been the same —inky blackness with a few artificial lights to stand in for stars.

Except this was a different pit obviously, as there was no pool beneath it.

Furthermore, across the passage, a low overhang opened into a cavern with a table placed in its center and orbs of lights floating about.

She shook her head at her foolishness.

In her impatience, she had jumped down the first pit she'd seen simply because the aura had been lower than her level had been. But she'd chosen the wrong one. If she had been a little more patient, she might have found this one and not had to cause so much damage to the environment.

With a deep breath, she shook her head at her foolishness and started across the room.

Without warning, the three lights far above her ignited and hurtled an avalanche of rock that crushed her before even her dragon reflexes could move her out of the way.

CHAPTER THIRTY-SEVEN

Drew, Amy, and Lumos boarded a flight to Dallas and disembarked two and a half hours later.

The SWAT leader was surprised at how much he already missed Kristen's private jet. He wasn't much of a flyer—he never had been and never saw the point of going somewhere he couldn't drive to where there were people who didn't speak his language—and yet he had already grown to appreciate the spaciousness of the private jet.

On her plane, they had been served hot meals and been given hot towels. There had even been a masseuse. On their flight down there, he'd had a TV screen in the back of the seat in front of him that didn't work. He was the only one of the three who hadn't sprung for first-class and now, reunited with Amy and Lumos, he could see that for the mistake it was.

While he was tired from the flight, his back sweaty, and his shoulders tight from hunching them so as to not spill into either of the seats beside him, his teammates seemed refreshed.

"Are you all right, Drew?" Amy asked almost dreamily.

"I've been better," he replied.

"Are you ready to fly?" Lumos asked as they retrieved their luggage and left the airport.

"I thought we did…" Drew said before he trailed off as he looked at the dragon in human form and the mage. The two of them grinned like fools.

He sighed. "We won't rent a car, will we?"

His teammates shook their heads and he rubbed his chin. At least he had extra motivation to catch the technomages, he decided

"So, do you want to ride with me or with Lumos?" Amy asked.

"How exactly do I ride…uh, with you?" Drew asked. She was at least fifteen years younger than him, and although he found her plain features pretty enough, he would in no way feel comfortable mounting her like a sea turtle as they flew across Texas.

In response, she opened her luggage and removed a huge beach towel.

"You know they usually have towels at hotels, right?" he snarked.

"This one's not to keep us dry." She spread it out on a patch of grass outside the airport. "So?" she asked as he realized exactly what she had in mind.

"You want me to ride on that?" Drew balked, his expression one of horror.

"What? I would have thought the whole magic carpet concept would work for you. Okay, no, this isn't a carpet, but it's as stable and easier to clean."

"I don't know…"

"You're always welcome here," Lumos said before he transformed into his true form—a resplendent golden dragon. He stretched his wings in the afternoon sun, yawned, and twitched his tail. "It looks like a beautiful day to do loops."

"I think I'll stick to the carpet," Drew said and studied the towel warily.

The dragon's tail twitched to his face. He had been with dragons long enough now to recognize that as embarrassment. Before he could ask what had upset him, Lumos flicked his suitcase open with the deft movement of a claw and tossed a small sack to Amy, who caught it gleefully in midair with her telekinesis.

"What the hell was that?" Drew asked and stepped onto the towel.

Despite her promise of it being a magic carpet ride, it didn't feel like magic. It felt like a towel spread on the grass.

"A bet I won," she said smugly.

"Yeah, yeah, I messed it up when I mentioned the loops." Lumos looked chagrined.

"I hardly find that—" He wasn't able to say appropriate because the carpet beneath his feet elevated sharply without warning.

Ten feet, twenty, thirty, fifty...a hundred feet in less than five seconds.

"Let me sit, at least," he sputtered when they leveled out and began to fly south.

"There's no need. I'm using my telekinesis to keep your boots stuck to the towel. You can't fall—well, not unless your shoes come off." To prove her point, she spun them in a barrel roll. Sure enough, although he felt his clothes pulled away from the towel, his feet both remained firmly in place as if they were stuck there with glue. It was extremely unsettling, to say the least.

Amy only laughed.

He gave her a grim smile. At the very least, he could respect someone who was willing to fuck around before they entered a potentially life-threatening mission. Then, he sat carefully and tied his boot laces tighter.

"Beautiful country," Lumos shouted to his teammates.

Drew realized he could only hear him because the young mage manipulated the air so there was a bubble of stillness around him. A strong gust broke through her subtle shield and became nothing but a swift breeze.

"I had no idea it was so green," she replied to the dragon. "I've never left the northeast as a kid. When I think Texas, I think cactus and oil wells."

"You're not wrong about that," Lumos said with a chuckle, "but that's the other half of the state."

"We're going to Elgin," Drew interjected. "It's between Austin and Houston. Zed traced it as the last location of what we think was a shipment of dragon scale munitions. After that, the trail went cold."

"No dragon killings? That's a relief," the dragon commented.

"No dragon killings yet," he replied. "But we know how these people work. They'll want to use the momentum they've been building."

"What do you think we should do first?" the mage asked. "I'll admit, I didn't exactly read the mission brief. Shouldn't we start with any big meat farming operations around here? It takes huge resources to feed a dragon, especially if they're actively using their abilities, and the one they probably have has been continually...harvested for pieces, right? That means they'll need hordes of cows or whatever. Let's follow the cows."

Lumos laughed so hard he snorted fire. "My dear, we are in Texas. The only thing they have more of in this state than cows are guns."

"Wait, seriously? I thought it was a desert. I thought cowboys drove cattle across Texas because it was as empty as shit," Amy said and stroked her chin while she guided the magic-powered towel forward.

"The briefing mentioned there are 4.95 million cattle," Drew said. "We can't follow the cows."

"We can have one or two, though." The golden dragon snickered and gestured toward a field filled with dark-red, heavy shouldered cows with short hair that looked as thick and as soft as moss. The SWAT leader knew nothing about cows, but even he could recognize that these were healthy.

That fact made it a little more distressing when Lumos tucked his wings and dove toward the herd. They immediately stampeded away from him and the ancient gold dragon only laughed as his long mustache flicked in the wind.

"Lumos, what are you doing?" Amy demanded and guided her towel toward the dragon without letting Drew know. His stomach lurched all the worse for not having warning.

"Having a snack," Lumos answered happily as if he didn't have a care in the world.

He flapped his great wings and banked into a glide above the cows. With the ease of centuries of practice, he followed them as they ran, slowed his speed, and used his wings to guide the herd around the huge grassy field they called home. With careful flicks of his tail, he separated a cow from the rest of the herd. To Drew, it looked like the fattest of them all.

Now that the golden dragon had his dinner in his sights, he opened his jaws and swooped at the creature—only to have a metal water trough careen into his mouth and wedge it open.

He sputtered as the trough dumped water down his throat, which unbalanced him and made him fall given his slow speed. His landing precipitated him into a tumble through the field and he gouged great swathes of grass and wildflowers with his huge wings and pointed tail. He came to a stop by powering into a massive pecan tree. It rattled when he struck it and since it was fall, hundreds of nuts rained on the disgraced dragon.

"Are we under attack?" Drew asked, although if they were, the technomage group responsible seemed closer to clowns than terrorists. How could anyone stop a dragon with a water trough?"

"No," Amy said, her voice tight as she guided them down and landed her towel in front of Lumos. "What the hell was that about?" she demanded.

"What? The cow? I didn't want to simply blast all of them. One is plenty," he explained as if it was obvious.

"Are you crazy? That's someone's livelihood. That cow is probably worth a hundred or a thousand or— I have no idea how much cows are worth but that was a big one so it must have been a lot," Amy sputtered, furious with him.

"I would've paid the man for his trouble. Better than whatever he gets from a cattle yard, I assure you," Lumos protested and sounded hurt. "I spent time in Texas when it was Spanish land. We've had a way to do things here for a long time. Beef for silver is—" He once again opened his suitcase deftly to fetch something but this time, found nothing.

Abruptly, he transformed into his human form, an older man with a brilliant mustache and pointed goatee. "Where is it?"

"You mean the sack of silver you gave me?" Amy said and held up the leather bag he had given her when Drew decided that a towel was safer than a dragon. He realized now after watching the hunt that it definitely was.

"Er...may I borrow a little?" Lumos asked, his human face a brilliant red.

Amy held the bag up and it levitated to his hand but didn't fall. "You can ask a farmer and offer to pay, and if he says yes, you can eat as many as you like."

The dragon frowned. "But there's no fun in that. They don't like it when we stalk the herd like that but they don't complain either as long as we pay well."

Drew was surprised. Lumos—despite his age—had seemed like one of the more progressively-minded when it came to human-dragon relations, yet this seemed like a cruel and arcane way of hunting to him.

"If they don't like it you should do as Amy says," he pointed out.

The mage nodded and dropped the bag of silver in his hand.

Lumos grumbled, but he followed his teammates to the farmhouse after which—after a few minutes of deliberation with the woman of the house—he left with a far skinnier cow. Part of their deal was that he'd kill it quickly rather than hunt it and scare it half to death, as Mrs. Mendez-Mangum didn't much like seeing the poor cows get scared.

The dragon obliged her sullenly and led his cow out behind the barn so the others wouldn't see.

Drew couldn't help but grin at his embarrassment. He knew they were fighting for huge stakes—the very world if one was being grandiose—but these were the things he sometimes reminded himself he was fighting for. Why should a dragon have the right to terrify a herd of cattle simply because they were a dragon? Why should a person have to live knowing that a dragon could destroy their house, their car, and even kill their wife while he was at work, but—not to worry—you would be given a sack of gold for your trouble. Dragon dominance was everywhere and in every part of culture. From cities like Detroit to the middle of nowhere, Texas.

Once Lumos emerged—in human form and still sullen—they thanked Mrs. Mendez-Mangum and continued their journey.

"There, that wasn't so bad, was it?" Amy gloated in as kind a voice as Drew had ever heard.

"I saved a little silver, yes, but it cheapens the whole experience. It's nice to hunt."

"Whatever," she replied with no trace of sympathy for the dragon.

"What do we do now?" she asked Drew.

He swallowed. "I think we should get dinner."

His companions laughed.

"There's a fast food place. I could eat a burger." The mage pointed at a parking lot with a glowing yellow and orange building in the middle.

Lumos clicked his tongue in disapproval. "My dear, as I said, we are in Texas. It will not do for us to not do as the locals do. And although, yes, burgers can be delightful, we're heading to Elgin. I know people there who have done the same thing for a very long time."

"And what's so great about that?" Drew asked.

"What they do is Texas Bar-B-Q."

He nodded toward a building that looked like a barn that had been repainted and set on fire. A steady plume of smoke billowed from it, and it took the man a second to realize that the smoke was being used.

They landed in the parking lot. Amy stowed her towel in the duffel bag she'd brought for herself. On the journey, Lumos had carried it but now, she levitated it off the ground and hurled it into the sky.

"What did you do that for?" Drew asked. It looked like she had thrown out all her clothes.

"Oh, it's for safekeeping. No one will take my things a hundred feet up. Do you want me to do yours?" Amy replied.

"You can do mine," Lumos said and nodded at his suitcase.

She obliged him and rocketed it up and out of sight. "Drew?"

"Are you sure you won't drop it?"

"Positive," Amy replied. "Larry's made me work on my control.

This is a great way to focus. As long as we don't come under attack in there."

Lumos chuckled but Drew only clenched his jaw. There was no better way to ensure you would get in trouble than to ask for it.

"It's not likely," the dragon elaborated as they walked toward the swinging doors at the front of the converted barn. "Smoked meat is like the sacrament in Texas. If whoever we're tracking is from here, they won't stir the pot. And if they're not local, we'll have the crowd on our side."

The SWAT leader didn't know about all that. Lumos made it sound like this was some kind of experience rather than merely dinner.

They walked inside and he quickly reassessed his original opinion. Rather than the clean tiled floor and bland paintings of a regular diner, this venue had a concrete floor sprinkled with sawdust and nothing on the walls but the heads of dead animals. Deer mostly, although he noticed a few people had been proud of the boars they had killed. He wondered if they were cooking one in front of him.

About a dozen people stood between him and the longest chain of sausages he'd ever seen. A cook—chef or grill master?—opened a metal box to release another great gust of smoke and reveal ribs large enough to either be from a cow or the aforementioned wild boar. Amy looked about as flabbergasted as he did. Lumos, though, looked positively delighted.

"Oh, I do like Texas Bar-B-Q!" He was more preaching than explaining. "You don't need sauce, you know. That's the secret. They smoke it to perfection after they rub it with all kinds of spices. You humans…" He shook his head in amazement. "For creatures who are supposed to mostly eat plants, you have a way with flesh."

"How can you even be hungry?" the mage demanded. "You ate an entire cow."

Lumos shrugged. "It wasn't a very big one."

Drew grinned and helped himself to a beer in one of the standing iceboxes that the line snaked past. He had begun to like Texas.

Faster than he had expected, they were at the front of the line and the dragon was ordering. "Five pounds brisket, six of those beef ribs I saw peeking out, and all your sausages. Oh, and a couple of chickens."

"Yes, sir. Do you want that whole sausage cut in half?"

"I'm sorry if I misspoke. I meant I want to eat all your sausages—as in every single one."

The woman gaped. "You want… Hold up." She turned to one of the pitmasters. "How much sausage do we have left for today?"

"Salchicha?" a man with a mustache asked. She nodded and he checked. "Twenty-five pounds."

The woman turned to Lumos and raised an eyebrow. "Do you really want all that?"

"Yes please." The dragon nodded happily. "Oh, and a half-gallon each of beans, slaw, and banana pudding." The assistant shrugged and tallied the bill.

"Are you gonna borrow silver for this one too?" Drew asked and elbowed Amy, who laughed.

"I intended to charge it. That usually works better in these kinds of places," Lumos said and took a credit card out. "Timeflash set me up with an expense account. There are advantages to missing out on the Europe trip."

His teammates nodded. He made a good point.

The woman accepted the card and gathered the food he had ordered. "It's gonna be a minute with the sausage," she said, retrieved a long stick with a piece of chalk on the end, and scratched out the line for sausage on the menu above the counter. A few people groaned.

The dragon took one of the trays of food. "Aren't you two going to order anything?" he asked.

"You're not planning on eating all that." Drew couldn't believe it. He'd shared meals with Butters, who could pack it away, but Lumos practically had an entire animal on the trays they all carried to the table.

"I guess I can share," the dragon said, although given the speed with which he dug in, those might have been false words.

Despite watching him inhale what appeared to be his body weight in smoked meat, the meal was exceptionally good. The brisket was insanely tender and beyond flavorful. Drew wasn't even tempted to add sauce. The chicken was perfect, although it paled in comparison to the beef ribs, which—while delicious—were a real treat because they made him feel like a caveman. Maybe there was something to hunting and eating your own meat, he thought as he attacked the rib with gusto.

The only sore point in the meal came toward the end when three young men approached the table. From their patchy facial hair and bratty expressions, boys might have been more accurate.

"Are you the high-falootin' out-of-towners who ate all our damn sausage?" one of them asked, a red-faced boy wearing a plaid shirt with the sleeves torn off.

"I'm afraid so," Lumos said and brandished his toothpick. Once they'd brought the chain of sausages, the dragon had not stopped eating until they were completely gone. "We still have chickens and ribs, though, if you boys are hungry. It appears I overestimated my appetite."

"Yeah, probably because you already ate a cow," Amy quipped, although Drew could tell she wasn't angry and merely teasing.

"I told you, Colt," the boy with the sleeveless plaid said.

"I guess you were right, Vince. Dinner's on me on account of the dinosaur." Colt wore a red baseball cap backward with something written on the front that Drew couldn't make out. His sideburns would look good on someone who might pride themselves in being a dumbass.

"Is that a reference to my species?" Lumos asked and dabbed his chin with a napkin.

"You're damn straight it is!" said the third man. He had no fear of denim, apparently, as he wore it from head to ankle and only chose a different material for his wide-brimmed, bleached white hat and his black leather boots.

"Easy, Dusty," Vince said, although he didn't sound like he meant it. "You wouldn't want to piss the great and powerful dragon off."

Lumos merely smiled as one might at a puzzle to be solved. "However did you know I was a dragon?" he inquired politely.

"It's fuckin' obvious," Dusty said. "You're the only asshole in here wearing a fucking gold suit. Are you his mage or something?"

Amy stood quickly, insulted. "I dress this way because I am a skater, not because I am a mage," she told the men, although from her tone, she also agreed they were little more than boys.

"Whatever. You three look like you're from the wrong end of a dog's dick," Vince said and laughed like that was supposed to have made sense.

"As opposed to the right one?" the girl asked coolly.

"What the fuck is that supposed to mean?" Vince demanded.

A moment later, three suitcases fell from the sky into the parking lot.

"Oops," Amy said, although the boys didn't notice.

"You three should move on, all right? We're from out of town, yes, but we're here on business. Do you know anything about dragon bullets?"

Colt and Dusty shared a meaningful look before Vince punched them both in the arm and replied for the group. "Fuck no! Come on, boys."

"Thanks for the food by the way," Colt said and picked up one of the trays of chicken and ribs.

Lumos stood at that, ready—by the looks of it—to eat them, but Drew put a hand on his chest quickly. "It's all right. We might have found ourselves a lead. Even money that they go to their car."

His instincts proved correct. Vince, Colt, and Dusty all piled into a massive truck on jacked-up suspension. The guard in the front looked like it had been added to and the entire vehicle was painted in camouflage, while two smokestacks protruded high above the cab. Two of them climbed into the front and the third went into the back and raised a Texas flag.

"Have a nice night, assholes!" he shouted, tossed an empty beer bottle in the air, and shot it before Drew even saw him draw a gun.

"Should we follow them?" Amy asked. "They reacted when you mentioned the munitions. Do you think they know about them?"

"I don't know. It's been big in the news recently. I could see many people flinching if they thought a fight might come to their town. I think I want to try to dig something up on them before we go further," he replied.

"You're not worried they'll get away?" Lumos asked.

"Nah. Those three don't exactly look like they know much about keeping a low profile."

"I still don't think you should have told them about our mission," the mage commented.

"Well, if those assholes are anything more than assholes, at least this way, they'll come to us." he countered.

They ate in silence for a minute before he wiped his face and stood. "Lumos, thanks for the meal. Amy, thanks for dropping our luggage. I'll have a talk to the local police and see what they know about our boys in the big truck or if there's anything else around here while I'm at it. Can I leave you two to get us a few rooms over there?" He pointed at a motel across the street.

They nodded. "That shouldn't be so hard," Amy said.

"You say that," Drew said, "but something tells me you two will find a way to make it difficult."

CHAPTER THIRTY-EIGHT

The flight over the Colombian countryside filled Larry with both hope and dread. Hope persisted because there was still so much green in the world. After they'd left the airspace over the Gulf of Mexico and passed Medellin, the landscape below was completely jungle with the occasional town or ranch carved out.

It was the ranches that made him uneasy. Last time he'd been down there five years before, there had been fewer of them. He had no doubt that the next time he came, there'd be far more. Part of him sometimes wondered if the dragons were right about people—that if left unchecked, they'd simply continue to spread like any other pest.

From his perspective, though, he didn't see why that same logic did not apply to dragons. After all, they were the ones who liked eating the cattle grown on those ranches of cleared rainforest.

But he'd have time enough for philosophy when this mission was over. One thing he certainly agreed with was the idea that the only way out of the mess the world had become was by working together with everyone. Step one of that process was to stop the mages from killing more dragons.

The pilot banked their private jet and descended to the airport, where they made a surprisingly gentle landing. It seemed it wasn't only the ranches that had been improved since he had last been here.

They disembarked from the plane to find no one waiting for them. He saw no sign of a welcome wagon filled with local fruit and coffee as had been typical when Larry had come with Windlock. Instead, they had to walk across the chilly tarmac through the gentle mist on their own.

"I thought it would be hot," Keith said. He wore a police uniform that had short shorts instead of pants. In the cool air, he looked profoundly out of place.

"Bogota is above twenty-five hundred meters," Larry said. "The weather here is like San Francisco, which makes us not having a ride all the more inconvenient."

"You don't suppose the local dragons are busy or something?" Butters ventured. "It is a city of millions, plus the report said the attack came from outside the city. Maybe they're stretched too thin."

The mage shook his head. "Maybe, but I don't think so. An airport is an ideal place for an ambush. They should have been here to clear the area, especially given that we're dealing with SWAT for this part of South America. They oversee not only Colombia but also Venezuela, Ecuador, Peru, and even Bolivia. They're a huge team."

"Still, it might be an all-hands-on-deck scenario," Beanpole pointed out.

Heartsbane shook her head. "Larry's right. This is a huge lapse in protocol. If they're stretched that thin, they should have called for help from law enforcement in other parts of the continent, not to mention moved the dragons to more secure areas. Them not being here is weird. Something is wrong."

"So what do we do about that? Fly home?" Hernandez asked in a huff.

"No, but we shouldn't go into the airport either." Larry took his cellphone out and called a private security firm for armored cars to escort them. "All right, they'll be here in ten minutes. Let's try to circle to the front of the airport. Everyone stay alert and watch the perimeter. I'll call Bogota SWAT."

He dialed the local number and a mage answered. It was easy to tell it was a mage and not a dragon because the man sounded nervous. Dragons rarely sounded anything but smug.

"This is Larry Brockton. I'm here in Bogota under orders of Investigator Steel."

"Oh! It's an honor to have you here, sir. What can we do for you?" the man responded.

"What can you—" He shook his head. "Your office said there was a dragon murder and requested that one of our teams respond."

"A murder?" The mage sounded genuinely surprised.

For a moment, his heart pounded and he considered sending everyone into the jet then and there. Before he could speak, a startled squeak suggested his contact had remembered what was happening in his city.

"Oh! You must be here about the dragon death. Lord Alanegra was caught in an avalanche. Do you think it was foul play?"

Before Larry could answer, the mage seemed to remember himself. "I'm sorry, sir. Where are my manners? If Investigator Steel is here, we can't have you all waiting while a couple of mages dither on the phone. I'll send a few cars and we'll talk about this somewhere more secure than a cellphone signal."

"There's no need for that. I already called a company—Seguridad. We've worked with them before." He saw no reason to tell him that Investigator Steel wasn't with them at the moment.

"They're a good one. You can trust them," the man responded cordially. "I do apologize for the inconvenience, sir. We simply didn't expect visitors. It makes sense, I suppose. The avalanche could have been foul play."

"That was what we thought," Larry lied.

This seemed too strange to him. How did the Bogota team not know about them? They had requested them to come. Was this mage merely incompetent and hadn't heard the orders? He didn't think so. It wasn't like the guy who answered the phones would be in charge of detailing a welcome committee, which made it seem like no one knew about them. If so, who had asked?

"Are you all right there, boss?" Emerald asked and used the word "boss" with a slight barb to it. At least he used it, though.

"Yeah. Yeah, it's fine. I'll have a long list of questions to be answered once we reach their local headquarters, but there's no point in getting all worked up when there's probably an explanation for all this."

"Sure," Emerald said, although he didn't sound mollified by the weak attempt to calm his nerves.

They walked around the airport, past palm trees and exotic birds, and through the smells of coffee and car exhaust until they reached the street and found three armored SUVs waiting for them with *Seguridad* signs.

Larry noted the bulletproof glass and ordered his team to get on board.

Everyone complied and they drove to the local SWAT office, hoping for more answers. He had a feeling in his gut that all they would get was more questions.

CHAPTER THIRTY-NINE

The chamber Kristen was in was wide enough that she couldn't escape it before the rocks struck her. As it was, she was barely able to get her steel skin into place. She felt a stone thunk onto her head and knew that without her steel skin—even with her dragon abilities—she would have been killed.

She tried to move out of the way of the falling boulders but there were too many. One landed on her leg to pin her in place—again, possibly breaking the bones if not for her steel skin. She held her hands up in a pathetic defensive gesture as more and more rocks rumbled into motion and pummeled her body.

Another deluge of boulders followed the first and soon, both her legs were trapped. She fought with her arms and struggled to thrust rocks away before they struck her head, reminding herself all the time about what she knew about her dragon healing ability.

Windlock had said—when they'd first found the wreckage Amy had caused with her mage powers—that dragons could only sustain a finite amount of damage. They could heal most injuries—other than those to their brain or heart—but if they suffered enough injury, their healing ability would be overwhelmed and they'd die. That was what had happened to the dragons who had been killed by Amy, and that might be about to happen to her.

The avalanche of rocks continued and she struggled to defend herself. If she processed at the speed of a regular human, she'd no doubt have already been crushed. But with her dragon speed to aid her, she was able to consider her arrogance and hubris. She'd run through this now obviously abandoned cave and disregarded the signs that this was a trap. When the corner of a rock finally caught her temple, she plunged into unconsciousness.

Kristen awoke sometime later and even that was a pleasant surprise. Her last thoughts had been of being overwhelmed by her injuries and rotting to nothing in the cave. Her dreams were of either being fossilized or rusted. She didn't know enough about geology to guess which would happen, so her subconscious had put Ranger Jay in charge of describing the process to a group of bored tourists while she watched, a rusted fossil from the past.

After a moment, she took a deep breath. That was also a surprise. Before she'd been knocked unconscious, the rock debris had been so thick that it made it difficult to fill her lungs. Now, she could breathe easily.

She pushed on the ground and registered the biggest surprise yet as she rose from the rocky surface. There was no rubble on top of her —as in none at all. Startled, she jerked her head from side to side to study her surroundings. Surely she was mistaken?

But no rubble was in evidence. In fact, she didn't think she was in the same part of the cave. From what she could see, she was in a fairly small chamber rather than the cavernous pit the rocks had come from.

That was bad—extremely bad. An explosion and being buried in an avalanche was one thing. Kristen knew she had enemies in both dragons and mages—hell, probably disgruntled humans as well because they could also be like that. But to have been buried beneath the rubble and then moved? What did that say about whoever set this up?

That they were confident in their abilities was the first thing she thought. The obvious culprits were the mages. She had actively thwarted them, after all. But this didn't seem like their work. If they had placed the boulders, why not use bombs with dragon shrapnel and simply kill her? Whoever had done this to her wanted her alive for some reason.

Plus, there was the dragon aura she'd sensed. As far as she knew, that could not be faked. She was sure that if it could, she would know already, what with the enemies she'd collected. The facts meant there had to be a dragon involved. But who? Could it be the Iron Dragon she'd met and battled in Florence?

Kristen didn't think so. Katrina had been a powerful warrior and ruthless in her efficiency. She didn't seem like the kind of woman to bury an enemy, dig them out, and move them. Her actions suggested she was more like the kind of person to find an enemy and slit their throat at the first chance she had. No, she didn't think it was her.

She realized with growing dread that it couldn't be. Whoever had set those charges to bury her had known she would be down there. It meant that the entire call to report to the Dragon Council had been a trick.

How could that be?

Lumos had recognized the mage who had called. It was one of the reasons she felt so compromised. Did that mean the council themselves had a mole among their advisors?

This train of thought didn't appeal to her at all, primarily because it made so much sense.

But how else could someone have convinced the mage to talk to her? And they led her on this merry chase through the caves with their aura. The more she thought about, the more she reasoned it had to be a dragon. It wasn't a pleasant thought, no matter which way she looked at it.

But damn, it made sense.

It should have dawned on Kristen far sooner, but it was entirely possible that there could be elements of dragon society who were as eager to start the war as the mages. She knew there were those who saw humanity as little more than cattle. While most didn't want to obliterate people, it seemed there was a fair share of them who thought "culling the herd" was an acceptable solution. Maybe her recent publicity had set her against one of these dragons.

Trying to play devil's advocate while she got her bearings—not an easy task given that she was in a tiny chamber with five more or less identical tunnels leading away from it—she forced herself to consider the possibility that it was mages.

There might be a spell they could have cast to trick her. Dragons didn't know everything about them, and Amy's formidable powers proved there was much mages could do when unbound—which all the technomages were. But again, the nagging question of why not simply kill her remained. Why would any of the mage cells leave her alive?

No, she didn't think mages had done this. The whole plan had the stench of dragon all over it. Whoever did this to her wanted her alive and trapped there for some reason.

Well, maybe not even for a reason, she realized. Maybe simply for their sick desire. Not long before, the dragon Obscura had captured her brother Brian and put him inside a "live" version of the old game Pac-Man. There had been no reason for that. Ostensibly, she wanted him to suffer and by extension, the Steel Dragon to be wracked with fear. But there were a thousand simpler, less elaborate ways to do that. She could have simply sent fingers or a video of her eating him, for Christ's sake, but she hadn't. Instead, the dragon had constructed an elaborate maze and dropped her brother into it so she would rescue him.

A maze exactly like the one she was in now.

Dumb realization dawned on her and Kristen reached instinctively for her cellphone, only to discover it was gone.

Seriously, this had become horribly creepy. It was supremely uncomfortable to think that someone had dug her out of the rubble, moved her there, and gone through her pockets, all while she was unconscious. Whoever it was could have easily killed her, even with her steel skin. She could have been drowned or crushed or any number of things, but she hadn't been.

Why not?

Kristen could already feel the walls closing in. What kind of a freak had done this to her?

Maybe someone who wants to see you crack, her mind answered.

Oh, shit. She was already talking to herself, which wasn't exactly a good sign. Her stomach grumbled and joined the conversation. Although it might have scared her a year before, her hunger grounded her.

She didn't know who had trapped her down there. Hell, she couldn't even be certain it wasn't some kind of demolition activity gone wrong—although they were in a national park so that seemed unlikely. All she knew was that she had sustained some injury in that avalanche. If she wanted food so she could better fuel her dragon healing abilities, she needed to get out of there as soon as possible.

With that decided, she looked at the tunnels and tried to determine the best choice.

Despite her feeling more and more confident that this was a trap, her first instinct was to search for the dragon aura. Whoever had done this to her had to be down there. Given that they had moved her, they were probably nearby. She didn't care if they were hunting her or testing her or whatever. If she could find them, she would turn the tables on them and make them rue the day they targeted the Steel Dragon.

She sensed nothing. No dragons, no humans, and not even any of the cave crickets that had been present in the upper level.

All the tunnels were the same uniform pitch black and gave off the stagnant smell of being buried deep under the earth. One of them appeared to slope up slightly, so she chose that one.

She walked for a few minutes and immediately began to feel better. Moving helped her think, helped her feel less trapped, and helped her feel less stupid for being tricked into being trapped down there.

All those warm and fuzzy feelings evaporated when the tunnel forked a little farther on. It was hard to see much as there was no light at all, but her dragon eyes could do things human eyes could not. They glowed ever so slightly—fueled by the same ability that let her breathe fire, possibly, but she didn't know—and that cast the faintest gleam that her vision could pick up the reflection from. It sounded cool in theory but in practice, it was about as useful as stumbling in your bedroom when the television was on in the living room. Still, it was enough to see that both tunnels were poor choices based on her criteria of wanting to return to the surface.

The tunnel on the left was little more than a sheer drop. The one on the right also slanted deeply into the earth. Kristen didn't want to go any deeper than she already had, so she retreated to the room where she'd woken.

She returned without incident, although her brain did try to tell her to panic. She wouldn't—she couldn't—and knew that if she let her fears take control, she'd starve down there. Which meant she had to keep moving, but which way?

Finally, she had an idea. Kristen turned to steel, earned another growl of hunger from her belly, and used her fingers to gouge an "X" above the tunnel she'd returned from. That done, she gouged an arrow into the wall of the next corridor. At least this way, she could tell which way she'd been and find her way back if she lost her bearings—something that was already beginning to feel inevitable in the darkness.

A heavy feeling had begun to grow in her gut that working her way free of this mess might take a while. That sense of forced patience argued with the other sensation that demanded food.

The trick would be to work to get out of there quickly and efficiently but not waste energy doing so. It wasn't impossible, merely difficult. Still, there was nothing to be gained by sitting there thinking. She had to get out and to do that, she had to keep moving. Accordingly, she set off down a corridor and marked her path as she strode ever deeper into the darkness below the surface of the earth.

CHAPTER FORTY

Though Drew felt a little uncomfortable leaving Lumos and Amy after the confrontation with the three boys in the barbeque joint, he wasn't exactly worried about their safety. Yes, they were looking for technomages armed with weapons that could kill dragons, but if those three boys were the best the technomage cell had to offer — He chuckled at the notion. Talk about a lucky break. It was far more likely they were simply unaccustomed to seeing dragons in their small town and weren't used to having a bigger fish in their pond.

He walked down the road and into the police station. Compared to the Detroit station, he found it delightfully small and simple. An officer manned the front desk instead of a designated receptionist. It looked like the little Elgin station might be able to hold two criminals but could surely process as many speeding tickets as they needed to in a day.

The police officer seated near the front of the station looked up from his newspaper. "What can I do for ya, partner?"

"Name's Drew—Officer Drew Manns from Detroit PD, SWAT division."

"Is that right?" The man put his newspaper down and replaced the expression of concerned curiosity he must normally have used on the little old ladies that came in asking for help with one that seemed less condescending. Drew appreciated it. "And what, may I ask, is an officer from Detroit PD's SWAT division doing all the way down here in Elgin, Texas? Did you get some brisket and come to ask if we could arrest someone for making something taste too damn good?"

He chuckled good-naturedly at the small-town pride as another officer walked up, his thumbs hitched on his belt. "Nothing like that, sir, nothing like that. Although I will say that spot you have over there is something special."

"Ain't it though?" the first cop said. *McMurtry*, his badge said.

"What can we do for you, sir?" the other man asked. His badge said *Ramos*, and although he seemed about as cool-headed and professional as his teammate, he lacked the small-town charm or maybe he simply didn't turn it on for a fellow officer of law enforcement. "Business or pleasure?"

"Business," he said firmly but pleasantly, "although I hope that if you boys can help me out, I can wrap it up quickly and move on to pleasure."

McMurtry chuckled at that.

Ramos obliged him with a tight smile and nothing more. "And what business would that be, Drew from Detroit PD?"

He didn't want to divulge the whole story quite yet. Although he'd told the boys in the restaurant, it was because they looked like hotheads who would drink away all the thoughts they'd had that day. There was something about Ramos, though, that didn't sit quite right with him. He couldn't say what, exactly, so it was probably nothing, merely a cop putting up a professional wall. Even so, he didn't want to tell them everything.

"I'm looking for illegal arms dealers, actually."

The two men shared a knowing glance that he didn't at all care for. "Illegal arms, huh? It doesn't sound like a Detroit PD kind of job to me," Ramos commented. "It sounds more like an FBI case. Is there a reason you're here instead of the Rangers?"

Drew shrugged. "I don't choose the assignments. My boss sent me here to ask questions and stir up clues and bring these boys back to Detroit. I don't want to horn in on anyone's turf."

McMurtry smiled broadly at that but again, the other man only managed a tight nod.

"But I can tell you guys don't know much about it, huh?" he said.

"Nope," Ramos said.

"I'm afraid not," his fellow officer agreed, all smiles. "But why don't you go ahead and tell us where you're staying and we'll let you know if anything comes up?"

"Wouldn't a cell phone be more useful for that?" he asked. "My partners were getting the accommodation so I don't know where it is yet."

"Sure, sure." McMurtry handed him a piece of paper to write his information down.

As he wrote, he could feel Ramos' eyes boring into him. "What kind of arms did you say those were? Not them dragon bullets?" the man asked.

Drew looked at him but if the cop had a tell, he wouldn't know it. He didn't look like the kind of man you'd want to play poker with if you liked to keep your money.

"I didn't say. Why do you ask about the dragon bullets? Do you know something about them?" he asked and hoped that such a pointed question didn't goad the man too much.

"Nothing. At. All," Ramos replied. "But seeing as how you're from Detroit and all and there's that dragon there who's on a crusade to stop them mages, I thought this might be about that."

"Speak of the devil," McMurtry said, picked up a remote control, and pointed it at a TV in the corner.

Drew turned to look and was surprised to see Kristen on the television. She was in her dragon form—he knew it so well at this point that he could recognize it as easily as he could her human body. He'd never seen children climbing on her before, though, nor so many people posing for selfies.

"I don't care who you are or where you're from, that's simply not right," McMurtry said, still smiling as he stared at the screen.

"How do you mean?" he asked.

"Parents letting their kids clamber all over that lizard. What next? They gonna let them swim with crocodiles too? It's crazy, I tell ya!" The officer laughed.

"Actually, I'm sure that's the Steel Dragon, Kristen Hall," he said casually so he didn't betray the fact that he knew beyond a doubt exactly who it was. "She wouldn't hurt those kids."

"Are you sure about that?" McMurtry asked. "Them dragons used to eat people. In fact, I have it on good authority some of them still do. You can't trust any of them."

"You can't believe everything you hear on talk radio," Ramos said to his colleague.

Drew merely nodded and watched the two officers.

After a moment, Ramos glanced at him with a forced expression of boredom on his face. "Say, that Steel Dragon—she was on Detroit PD, right? Did you ever meet her?" His tone said he barely cared and that he was only making small talk, but his eyes betrayed him. He was very interested in the Steel Dragon.

"Yeah, as a matter of fact, I did," Drew replied. He knew he couldn't lie about knowing her. Even the most cursory of Internet searches would bring up news articles about the two of them working together or photographs of them after busts. It was better to tweak the truth than to lie about it completely.

He assumed that was what these two cops were doing to him.

"Is she as bad as they say?" the officer asked, again as casually as possible.

"I worked with her on a couple of bad busts." He shrugged. "She was a little...arrogant. Hot-headed, I guess you could say, but she saved my ass more than once. In fact, I'd go so far as to say every cop in Detroit owes her something one way or the other. She uses that steel skin of hers to stop us from getting shot more than anything else."

"Is that right?" Ramos responded. Nothing about the police officer had outwardly changed. He still had his thumbs hitched on his belt and wore the same forced, polite expression. But at the same time, he'd changed completely. Drew recognized the shift in behavior as similar to a criminal finally deciding not to confess. It wasn't anything obvious unless you looked for it, but if you knew what to look for, it was plain as day.

"It is," he confirmed.

"I suppose I'd like a dragon to take a bullet for me too," McMurtry joked, and the three men laughed, although they also all knew they were all faking it.

"Yeah, I helped her bring in a technomage, actually—the leader of a cell. It was a crazy mission. Them mages think they're as smart as can be, but they make mistakes, exactly like everyone else." He watched the other two carefully, but they didn't give anything away. They were both frozen like deer in headlights.

"You did, did you?" Ramos asked. He still sounded friendly but no longer attempted to smile.

"Yeah, I did." Drew forced himself not to bristle.

"And you liked it?" McMurtry asked and made less effort than his fellow officer to hide his emotions. While Ramos seemed to hide some deep rage, his colleague seemed to be overcome by something more like gleeful, disbelieving curiosity.

"Yeah...it was all right. It didn't get boring, at least. I never had to bust dumb kids with her around. Oh, hey, speaking of kids. Do you fellas know three boys who go by Vince, Colt, and Dusty? They drive a big truck with a Texas flag."

"Yeah, what of them?" McMurtry asked and looked less than amused for the first time.

"You'll have to excuse my partner's temper," Ramos said coolly. "One of them is his nephew. We've talked to those three so many times. Did they give you trouble?" There was something in the way he asked the question that told him the answer had to be no.

He shook his head. "Nah. They talked some mess when we got here on account of one of the folks I'm with ordered the last of the sausage. I wanted to let you guys know in case they do that to regulars."

"Oh, we'll have a talk with them," McMurtry said. "Rest assured, they won't bother you at all while you're here."

"I wouldn't worry about all that." Drew waved away the empty promise. "We're leaving town tomorrow anyway." It was the truth, technically. They would go to see other towns the next day, which meant they had to leave this one. What he didn't say was that—after talking to these two—he had a feeling they would come back. There was no reason for them to know that.

"Well, make sure you get something for the family back home," Ramos said. "The antiques here are to *die* for."

"Is that right?" he asked and didn't miss the poorly veiled threat.

The officer nodded and he made his way out of the station.

Something wasn't right there. He didn't know much about mages, technomages, or dragons. In fact, everything he'd learned, he'd learned from Kristen, who was the first to admit she was far from an expert. But he didn't need to know mages to see suspicious behavior.

If he had to guess, he thought that maybe the two police officers did know a thing or two about the mages. Maybe it wasn't anything more than they knew where the shipment had been headed next, but maybe it was something much deeper. He couldn't be sure but given the way they'd been so quick to cover for the three rednecks in their truck, he didn't doubt for a second that these two knew a thing or two about keeping quiet when they were supposed to.

Still, Drew was a cop first, a police officer. He had nothing to work with except suspicion and an uneasy feeling in his stomach, and Hanson had told him a hundred times that wasn't enough—even if he ended up being right most of the time.

He glanced at his surroundings, not afraid to look like a sightseer. After all, the cops and the boys in the truck had known he was from out of town. They'd expect him to look about.

Which meant that when he noticed an unmarked car with Ramos behind the wheel, he was fairly certain the man only thought he was gawking at a display of antiques.

Shit. If they were following him, they were much more interested than they let on. But what did that mean? Could these two small-town police officers be involved in the mage cell? It was far more likely that they were merely paid off, but that spoke of a larger organization than their intel had led them to believe was down there.

None of it was good, but the worst was guesswork without intel and grasping at possibly baseless ideas.

He kept moving and noted that the car followed as well but hung back in parking lots. Ramos was doing a fairly good job of tailing him. Unfortunately for him, Drew was a cop and knew about tails.

When the man followed him all the way to the motel they were staying in, he also knew he was in trouble. He took a deep breath and prepared himself to fight or tell the cop off. It was either that or wait to be arrested later, but for some reason, the officer drove away without confronting him.

Which meant the horrible feeling growing in his gut didn't go away at all.

CHAPTER FORTY-ONE

K risten had lost count of how many dead ends she had found. Fortunately, she had continued to scratch marks into the stone so she could simply count them.

Six, dammit. She'd traveled down six tunnels—sometimes for up to a mile—before she reached a dead end and had to retrace her steps.

In doing so, she'd wasted precious time and energy and found no way out, no water, no food, and nothing to aid her.

Thankfully, she wasn't hurt. Even after being pummeled by an avalanche of boulders before being transported there, her dragon healing abilities had kicked in. But continually keeping her hands steel and having used those dragon abilities had severely drained her energy reserves. She found herself thinking about how many pizzas she could eat in her human form and what she would get on them. Sausage, definitely, plus peppers and onions and—

Now wasn't the time for that, she told herself forcefully and pushed the thoughts aside. She stood wearily, knowing she had to keep moving.

Her stomach grumbled as she looked into one of the passages that led down instead of up. She'd already explored one and hadn't found anything except a steep slope to climb on her way back.

Maybe I'll have better luck down there. She shrugged and started down the path while she tried to push hunger and thirst out of her mind.

After ten minutes and fifteen fantasy pizza toppings, she noticed something. It wasn't much or anything to celebrate, but she realized when she tried to gouge an arrow into the wall that this particular rock face was wet.

Moist was a better descriptor, as there wasn't enough water to drink. Still, she found it encouraging. The upper portions of the cave system had water everywhere. It was water, after all, that created all the crystal formations. Maybe this trace of moisture would lead up eventually.

Kristen proceeded down the path, her spirits raised slightly. After another few minutes, she began to doubt her sense of direction, though, as she began to see light.

"I can't be that close to the surface, can I?" she muttered. Logic told her she was still deep in the earth but she hoped she was about to find herself in a canyon or a hidden grotto somewhere in the backwoods of Kentucky.

She walked around a bend in the path and found that—unfortunately for her prospects of escape but fortunately for her sense of direction—she was right. It wasn't sunlight providing illumination in the tunnel but a kind of luminescent fungus that cast the faintest of glows.

To her dragon vision, after hours and hours of only the muted grays of pitch-black she could discern, it was like stepping into the sunshine.

The fungus grew along the walls and followed hairline seams in the porous limestone through which the water seeped. Here and there, tiny rivulets ran down the wall, enough water for her to drink if she was willing to lick the glowing slime.

As tempting as it was, the strange blue glow was enough to help her to resist. She reasoned there'd probably be more water nearby, as the ground in this tunnel was wet from the leaks in the walls. Plus, there was still the question of why she was there in the first place.

Someone had moved her to the room nearby, and while she still wondered why they hadn't killed her outright, she had assumed they would spring some kind of ambush after she'd expended so much time and energy walking the tunnels. Now, though, it seemed more likely that they simply wanted her to starve to death.

A third possibility entered the equation—death from poisonous mushrooms. She didn't know much about fungus or dragons, but maybe it was possible that the bioluminescent fungus had some kind of compound that would be deadly?

Kristen realized she might have to test that hypothesis, but she would have to test it much sooner if she stopped moving. With her gaze focused on the slick rock beneath her feet, she proceeded cautiously and watched the rivulets of water trickle into tiny streams that ran across the floor.

As she walked, the angle grew steeper while the floor grew more slippery with both the bioluminescent fungus and another variety that either helped the glowing one or consumed it.

Kristen knelt to look at this new organism and one of her feet slid out from under her. Her butt landed hard and before she could recover, she began to slide down the path, dislodging the two kinds of fungus with her feet and her hands as she tried to gain purchase on something.

Her efforts were futile. She tried to turn her hands to steel but that only made her heavier, which negated the additional grip strength it provided.

She gained speed at an alarming rate like she was riding the world's deepest and slimiest water slide. Finally, a stalagmite in the middle of the path offered her a way to stop.

Resolute, she gritted her teeth, turned her body, and careened into the rock spike. She refrained from turning to steel out of fear of breaking it, so her ribs and abs took most of the blunt force.

Still, she'd suffered far worse wounds in the line of duty. She unwound herself from the stalagmite and immediately thanked it for saving her life. A little beyond the piece of rock was a small, shallow pool. Hardly an inch deep and filled with all the fungus she had dislodged, it didn't offer much in the way of respite from thirst. Worse still was that beyond it was nothing but another plunging pit. If she hadn't caught herself, she'd have plunged...she could only guess how far.

Kristen looked at the pool of water collecting around her feet. It couldn't be that bad, right? Surely the fungus wouldn't be too dangerous, and she was so thirsty. Even the sound of the tiny pool of water dripping over the edge made her want to fill a glass and drink. She could almost imagine the drips falling and landing in a creek or a river.

Wait.

Was that her imagination?

Frozen, she listened intently.

She could hear water flowing below, not only a trickle but an actual sizeable body of water. Surely that couldn't be contaminated? She shrugged after a moment's thought. Soon, it wouldn't matter. She was getting thirstier and thirstier but she could make it farther.

Tentatively, she peered over the ledge and saw that the water fell maybe fifty feet into what looked like a choppy pool of water. It wasn't a straight fall but a series of tiny streams trickling down the rockface.

Kristen considered the odds. She could probably make the jump and reach the water. Months and months of flying as a dragon gave her a way better sense of her own aerodynamics than she once had, but she knew a jump would be too risky. Despite her keen dragon eyes, she still couldn't see below the surface. For all she knew, there could be a jagged crystal ready to gore her. Given her current condition and reserves of strength, it seemed unwise to push her dragon healing powers any more than she already had.

There was nothing to be done but climb down. She kicked her shoes off and turned her hands and feet to steel. Then, step by step, she descended the slick, slimy surface. Once, she lost her footing but she maintained her handholds and recovered. Another time, she misjudged the flow of water where she thrust her steel fingers into the stone and a trickle of water ran down her arm and into her face.

Despite her trepidation about the fungus, she swallowed a mouthful almost without thinking. It was blessedly cool and tasted more of minerals than mushrooms. If it planned to kill her, it seemed to want to taste good before it did so.

Finally, her forearms aching, she reached a rock shelf free of slime and fungus beside the pool.

The first thing Kristen realized was that it wasn't a pool at all but part of an underground river. In the low light, her dragon eyes could see that it was the rich blue of glaciers. She looked hastily around her, using both her eyes and aura sense to feel for someone or something that might be here. This was a great place for a trap. Watering holes had been used for ambushes since creatures had first lived on land, but she neither saw nor felt anyone. Unable to resist any longer, she dunked her head in the swift current and gulped the sweet, life-giving water.

She drank until she had to pee and damn, it was good.

With her thirst quenched, she studied her surroundings. Truly, there wasn't much to them. The slimy cliff wall she'd come down, a tiny chamber at its base, and the river. There might have been another exit, but the water blocked the way. It was simply another dead end.

Well, not dead as there was water, but it still didn't seem like a way to escape.

Disheartened, she plopped onto her butt and didn't mind that she got it soaked. She couldn't help but wonder about the rest of her team and hoped they were all doing better than she was.

CHAPTER FORTY-TWO

The drive to the local Dragon SWAT took longer than Larry would have liked. Traffic in Bogota was insane despite the fact that the entire city reversed the direction of many of its streets to better accommodate rush hour.

They drove past skyscrapers fighting tropical jungle trees for height and sunlight, cafes that filled the air with the heady aroma of coffee, and car dealerships that stacked their cars on the first three floors of their buildings because there simply wasn't enough area to build a parking lot.

After an hour that felt longer than their flight, the cars finally arrived at the headquarters. The offices were on the top floor of a building that overlooked much of the city, and as they stepped from the elevator, he caught a glimpse of the whole city laid out before him. It was amazing to see so many apartments, houses, shops, stores, and everything else jammed between two mountain ranges. It almost seemed that when it rained, the houses were washed out of the jungle to all grow in the valley between the two mountains.

Unfortunately, he didn't have time to gawk. He had a killer to catch.

They were greeted by a female dragon in a perfectly tailored black suit jacket, skirt, and heels. She looked elegant, gorgeous, and imperious as she ignored the mage and the other humans and welcomed Heartsbane and Emerald.

"Welcome, welcome!" she said in English with a touch of a Colombian accent. "I trust your trip was all right."

"It was long, actually," Larry replied.

The woman looked at him with sharp disdain before she turned to the dragons. "Please, come sit. I've had one of our mages prepare a *tinto* for you. It's the true way to enjoy coffee. None of that drip nonsense you Americans are so keen on."

"I don't mind if I do," Emerald said and followed the woman into a large conference room that had been transformed into a jungle at the top of the city. On a table made of a slab of wood that was probably worth more than everything in Larry's bank account sat a tiny pitcher of coffee, four cups, and a huge platter of perfectly ripe and beautifully sliced tropical fruit. A mage lifted one of the cups quickly and spirited it away to another room.

Emerald settled into a chair and reached for a cup of coffee as the pitcher lifted itself and poured it for him. Obviously, a mage hidden somewhere did the work but it was fairly impressive.

"This is great." He beamed. "Heartsbane, you have to try this."

"I would but it doesn't look like there are enough cups to go round," she responded.

"Oh, there are enough," their hostess said and pointed down the hall. "We always keep coffee for the mages, and there's fruit as well. Off you all go while the masters talk."

"Now, wait a minute," Larry protested. "I need to speak to someone in charge."

"I heard about you," the dragon replied. "One of the Steel Dragon's little pets, hmm? Well, I assure you, little mage, that your coffee will taste as good as ours. Now then, like I said, off you go."

That was quite enough for Heartsbane. She pulsed anger with her dragon aura so strongly that even Larry grew irate. "You do realize you are speaking to the personal envoy of Investigator Steel?"

"A pleasure to meet you, ma'am," the woman all but purred. "I am known as Muerte de Arbol, although you can simply call me Muerte."

"Not me, you moron. Him." Heartsbane shoved Larry forward and he managed to stay on his feet despite the enormous discomfort he now felt.

He had to admit, he'd never noticed how bad the anti-mage bias could be. He'd worked with Windlock for so long that he'd kind of grown accustomed to how things worked. The old investigator had always treated him with more than enough respect—and even tolerated his constant rambling jokes—that he had never noticed any negative attitudes. When they'd been in situations like this, his boss had always made it very clear that he wanted Larry to get as much information as he could from the mages while he worked the dragons. Had there been ulterior motives? Had part of Windlock's actions been designed to keep him out of the way?

No, he wouldn't entertain any notions that besmirched the memory of his old boss—or, rather, his old friend. Windlock had been special. He'd seen that Kristen Hall could change the world despite—no, because of—growing up as a human.

Larry needed to make this Muerte see the world in the same terms. He darted his teammate a look that he hoped expressed his cautious thanks.

To Muerte's credit, she didn't argue with Heartsbane. She was focused on the mage and her lips worked in confusion while her gaze tried to look directly at him rather than through him. Mostly, she failed.

I might as well make it easier on the poor dragon, he thought. "We'll need more coffee," he said, not to the dragon so much as to her hidden mage servants who no doubt waited in the wings of the jungled conference room to bring out whatever was demanded.

Their hostess nodded to add weight to his order, and he sat and used his telekinetic skills to pour himself a cup of coffee and lift it to his lips, all without touching it. He might as well show these dragons that they weren't the only special ones.

"This is good coffee—as strong as anything and as flavorful as hell.

You guys will love it," he said and turned to the members of the Detroit SWAT team who'd accompanied him.

Muerte didn't understand the significance of the look, but the team did. Butters took the lead and they all entered the conference room, ducked under the broad leaves of tropical plants, and sat around the massive boardroom table.

"This is nice," Keith said and drummed on it with his knuckles.

"It should be," Muerte said and made no effort to hide her annoyance. "It was taken from the largest tree this continent has ever seen."

"That's cool, I guess," Hernandez responded.

The Bolivian woman looked like she intended to say something, but Larry cut her off to guide the conversation back to the business at hand as a mage brought more coffee.

"Look, we don't mean to intrude here. I don't know what has you all so busy that you can't send us an envoy, but we're here to help. Do you want to show us the intel you've gathered on the assassination?"

"Assassination?" Previously, Muerte had looked uncomfortable when the humans pushed into her space but now, she looked downright confused. "What assassination?"

"Well, that's the big question, isn't it? The request we received stated that a dragon ball was bombed, killing three and wounding four others. That's why you called us in. The mage who answered my call knew nothing about that and mentioned that an avalanche not far from here killed a dragon.."

"An...avalanche?" she asked.

"Yes, apparently. So, if it's not too much to ask, I'd appreciate a full briefing on whatever the hell happened so we don't waste any more time."

At that moment, an overweight man in a stunningly tight blue suit rounded the corner and entered the conference room with a cup of coffee in his hand. Larry had spent enough time with dragons to recognize that he was one simply by his posture. He spoke without looking up. "Any marching orders today, Muerte, or is it another day of the usual—oh." He froze when he noticed a group of humans crowded around their table. "I see we have visitors."

"We're not visitors," Larry protested, now a little frustrated. "We were invited here—as in asked to come. We didn't simply decide to come all the way here when the world's on the precipice of a war. We're here to help, dammit!"

"I know this might seem unusual without Lady Steel herself here, but she reports to the Dragon Council and will be here to help soon. We want to be ready for her when she arrives," Emerald said from his place at the table.

Muerte and the newcomer shared a look.

"Well," the heavy dragon began, "My name is Hambre, by the way." He cleared his throat. "We didn't call for any assistance. We've heard of Lady Steel, of course—everyone has—but I certainly didn't know about this visit. Muerte?"

"The first I heard of it was when you called from the airport," she said. "Honestly, I thought this would be some kind of spot inspection. The Dragon Council used to do those kinds of things, although it's been ages."

"No, this isn't some kind of spot check," Larry said and tried to contain his temper. "We responded to the assassination of three dragons at a ball, only to discover that a dragon was buried alive."

"Yes, that's true," Hambre agreed. "But he dug himself out. Oro is obsessed with mining and always has been. He buries himself in an avalanche every few years. The last one had explosives involved, but that's hardly unusual."

The mage rubbed his eyes and tried to make sense of all this. "Look, I didn't want to do this, but I need to speak to Mr. Ham-ber. That's the man who sent the orders," he said and retrieved the printout Kristen had given him before they'd left.

Hambre smiled indulgently at him. "I am Mr. Ham-ber, as you say it. In Spanish, it sounds like ahm-bray."

"Ah, right. Well then, what's the damn problem? Your signature is right here on the order." He passed the printout across the wide table and the man took it.

"This certainly looks official," he began.

"I know it's official. That's why we're down here. We wouldn't have come all this way if we didn't get a request from you. So drop the crap and fill us in on what's going on. I understand that I'm not the Steel Dragon, but I know her damn well at this point and can assure you she'd be pissed at how much time we're wasting."

Larry could immediately tell from Hambre's posture that he had never been spoken to in this way before and especially never by a mage.

"I understand that it looks official and that my signature appears to be on the document, but I never gave these orders. What you have in your hands is a forgery, albeit a very convincing one."

He frowned at the document, then at the Bolivian. "Well, shit."

CHAPTER FORTY-THREE

Kristen looked at the underground river and wondered for not the first time where it went. It had carved a hole in the rock wall and vanished into it, and the aperture was large enough for her body. She hadn't yet made up her mind to go through it.

Her steel body could take a fair amount of battering. For that matter, so could her human form given her healing abilities. The larger concern was oxygen. How long could she hold her breath down there? It was a question she hadn't bothered to think about since she discovered that she was the Steel Dragon. After all, steel sank. Water was very much her weakness. Her plan to deal with it thus far had been to get out of it as quickly as possible. Even when she'd faced three dragons intent on killing her in the north of Canada, she'd focused on that strategy when she faced a water dragon. She was still alive so thus far, it had served her well.

The question was how quickly she would be able to get out of the river. Unfortunately, it was one she couldn't answer. Dragons had many powers that humans did not, but X-ray vision was still something relegated to comic books.

Or so she had thought. She still couldn't shake the thought that she was being watched down there. It was the only thing that made sense.

Why bring her down there if not to watch her? But if she was being watched, she had no idea by who or even what. She'd seen no footprints and no evidence of anyone but herself.

Going into the river wasn't following a path or fleeing an enemy but a chance to escape. She had to take it, she decided.

But could she?

She decided to test herself and hold her breath to give her an idea of how long she could hope to stay down there. On her first attempt, she managed to count to four hundred and seventy-two. That was almost eight minutes. Kristen was shocked. She had never been a swimmer and had never been able to hold her breath for anything close to eight minutes. While she had no idea how long divers could hold their breath, eight minutes seemed fairly good to her.

Encouraged by that, she decided she still wouldn't simply hop in without another test. This time, she counted past six hundred before she gasped for air. That was over ten minutes. Yes, her sides ached from the buildup of lactic acid and lack of oxygen, but she knew she could last a while down there.

But would it be enough?

There was no way to know. Based on the speed, she felt like she'd cover considerable distance quickly, but what if the river remained completely submerged for a half-hour? She'd be dead and no one would ever know how she'd gone.

But that was unlikely, wasn't it? The entire cave system had been anything but uniform. Every tunnel and cavern had heights of different levels and rooms of different sizes. The chances were the river would lead through a place with air. It flowed fairly quickly, which meant it had to go somewhere with room for it. Otherwise, it would merely sit there, right? She wished Ranger Jay, of all people, were with her. He'd probably know the answers to all her questions.

Without him, she had to simply take a chance.

The decision loomed before her but she knew what she would do. She couldn't wait down there, trying and failing to find a way out again and again and starving slowly while she lost her mind. She was a woman of action and would rather regret the decisions she made than the ones she didn't.

It was true that the outcome of this particular choice had higher stakes than most, but that didn't dissuade Kristen. She set a five-minute timer on her watch, thankful that whoever had taken her cellphone had left her with the device, and plunged in.

For a moment, she simply stood in the cold water, her steel hands digging into the rock of the shore while cold water rushed past her steel legs. Was this a good plan? Surely this water had to go somewhere, and wherever it was would have fresh water and maybe something better to eat than glowing fungus.

Procrastinating would serve no purpose, she reminded herself and released her hold on the rock.

She let the current take her and kept her hands, feet, knees, and elbows steel so she could protect herself without using any more energy than necessary. Very quickly—thirty seconds by her watch—she was sucked into a larger tube with even faster-moving water.

As best she could, she kept her feet close to the bottom as the water surged and carried her forward. She thought she could dig in and climb up if she needed to, but when the floor began to angle down, she realized that would be harder than she anticipated. One minute traveling downstream would not equate to one minute traveling upstream.

Kristen couldn't do the mental calculations to determine how long she could go before the point of no return. Her mind was fully occupied with the water that pushed her at what felt like breakneck speed and the jagged pieces of rocks that protruded and threatened to snag her and drown her.

All she could do was keep her head from impact with the ceiling and hold her breath.

After three minutes, the tunnel widened and seemed to stop. She bulldozed against a wall of porous limestone like a fish caught in a pump. The current pressed her against it and flowed through a multitude of cracks too small for her to get through.

This was it, her point of no return. She could try to climb up the tunnel again and still had seven minutes to do that. Surely she could travel half as fast as the current had pushed her.

She pushed off the limestone that blocked her path and launched herself as far as possible. Her effort didn't take her far but her pressure knocked a large chunk out of the dam. She took that as a sign that brute force was the way to go, let the current position her against the obstacle, and shattered it with rhythmic blows.

No sooner had she widened a large enough opening than the water behind her thanked her by surging even faster. Now, she moved so rapidly it was hard to keep herself oriented. She tried to dig into the sides of the tunnel and succeeded in jamming her fingers into the soft limestone but not halting her motion.

Every time she gouged a hole in the rock, it simply turned into a long gash as the water used her to erode the tunnel it had worked on for centuries.

Kristen checked her watch. Six minutes. Seven. Her lungs began to hurt.

The steep angle of the tunnel leveled out into a much wider pool of water. She turned her body parts to flesh and swam to the surface, only to find there wasn't one.

Well, that wasn't quite true. There was maybe an eighth of an inch of space in some of the more generous places of the cave. It made her wonder if this room would have been so flooded if she hadn't broken the obstruction.

She tried to gain air from the tiny layer at the top of the room but failed and only inhaled water and made her lungs scream at her to take in air. The current slowed, which was a bad thing as her lungs were burning and her vision began to close in as her brain protested the lack of oxygen.

Desperate, she checked her watch. Nine minutes. She would drown in a room with a breath of air at the surface that was too spread out for her to use.

When she reached ten minutes, her lungs burned far more than they had when she'd practiced and she knew the need for air was critical. She'd never needed anything so badly. Her brain either saw or hallucinated a fish and her delirious mind thought that if a fish could breathe underwater, why not her?

Oh no, you don't. She pushed the temptation aside and gritted her teeth.

Kristen continued to swim and tried to move with the current, although her arms screamed at her to stop and her legs tried to sink.

At eleven minutes, she began to black out. Her vision had almost gone and her muscles were essentially useless. Soon, breathing wouldn't be a problem as once the water filled her lungs, her death would follow quickly.

In the next moment, she realized she was in the air. Water droplets were all around her and below her was a huge pool of water.

She sucked the air in hungrily and managed to fill her lungs before she rocketed into the surface of the underground lake.

The pain made her turn to steel reflexively so she sank like a lead weight, ever deeper into this hell within the earth.

CHAPTER FORTY-FOUR

Drew's old cop instincts told him to move, to change places, and to get the hell out, but he didn't think it was wise. As a precaution, he went to the front desk of the hotel and gave the receptionist a couple of hundred bucks to tell anyone who came looking for him to go to a different room, but he didn't see the point of high-tailing it out of town simply because the cops seemed questionable.

It was encouraging rather than disheartening. They hadn't sniffed around for very long at all and had already found something that stank. It was time to follow the stench to the source.

Amy and Lumos were in a motel room playing cards. She was currently shuffling the entire deck with only her mind and was doing a good job until he said hello. Her concentration faltered and the cards were strewn everywhere.

"How'd the visit with local law go?" Lumos asked, stood, and—to Drew's absolute shock—went to serve himself some of the leftover banana pudding from the barbeque place.

"I don't know," he said. "Something's not right with them."

"Do you think they're mages?" Amy asked and scattered the cards she'd spent so much time reorganizing in her excitement.

"I don't know. Not really. But maybe? They didn't like that I worked with Kristen, that's for sure, and they seemed to know something about what's going on."

"Do you think we should go back and ask a bit more forcefully?" the dragon asked in an extremely polite tone.

"No, I don't," he said flatly. "I think if we show up there and start levitating their trucks and attacking them with a gold dragon, they'll either lay low or dig in. What I want is a way to lure them out or track them or something, but they know the area way better than we do, so that's a real risk."

"It kind of touches on an idea I've been working on," the mage said.

"Oh?" Lumos looked a little put out. "You didn't tell me you had any ideas."

"I wasn't sure you would like it."

"And you think I would?" Drew asked.

She grimaced. "Honestly? No. I thought you'd like it even less than him, but since you mentioned luring them…"

Her companions looked at her expectantly. "Go on," Lumos said when she wasn't immediately forthcoming.

"All right, well…here goes, then." The young mage grinned, which told Drew that whatever her plan was, even she knew it was a little crazy. "Mages can sense magic, right? So what if I fired a really big burst of magic—ideally at someplace outside of town we feel like we can lock down or whatever. They'd be sure to come looking."

Lumos nodded. "It's not…totally insane. I think that based on how Constance tried to track you and recruit you after your powers manifested, it's not unthinkable to imagine that this cell would also be interested in recruiting someone of your…shall we say power level."

Amy turned to Drew.

It was his turn to grimace. He didn't think it was quite as wise a plan as the dragon seemed to. "What happens after we lure them to this location of yours? Let's assume we actually can find a place where somehow, we're confident that no one can sneak up on us and have the advantage. What do we do once they arrive? It's not like we can simply roll out and arrest them."

"We could follow them to their base?" Lumos suggested.

"Hardly." He shook his head. "If they sense a magic blast and come to investigate—which I think they would—why would they simply leave when their search comes up empty? Even if they did leave, they won't go directly to their secret base. And let's say they did go back to there, then what? We can't tail them in a truck. They'd see us. A dragon or a woman on a magic towel will probably alert them too. We can't assume they're dense."

"If those rednecks are involved, dense looks like the name of the game," Amy snarked.

"We can't count on that, though," Drew insisted.

"He's right," the dragon agreed. "The wise warrior knows his strength comes from hiding it."

"Okay, well, those are good points," the young mage said, although her confidence didn't seem shaken. "So the next part of the plan was that maybe we can try the Chewbacca switch?"

Her teammates shared a long, confused look. Lumos didn't have a clue what she was talking about. Drew was only moderately more aware. "Is that like a skateboarding move or something?" he asked.

Her jaw all but hit the floor. "You two can't be serious? You don't know the Chewbacca switch?"

"Let's assume we don't," the old dragon said with a smile.

"I can't—you've never seen *Star Wars*?"

"Oh, sure. I saw *Star Wars*," the SWAT leader said. "Chewbacca, he's the uh...he's not the one with the laser sword...so he must be the, uh...the dog thing?"

"He's a Wookie," Amy said and almost fell out of her chair in shock. "He's Han Solo's—you know what, never mind. Lumos, tell me you've seen *Star Wars*?"

He smiled. "I'm afraid not. I'm more of a mystery man rather than war films."

"It's not a war—okay, seriously, when this is all over, I'll get pizza and you two will come over to watch the trilogy."

"A trilogy?" Drew started to complain but she silenced him with a look.

"Yes. A trilogy. The greatest trilogy ever made so—okay, moving on. The Chewbacca switch is—Jesus, I can't believe I'm worried about spoiling something from *Star Wars*, of all things. Anyway, so the Millennium Falcon is captured and storm troopers come on, right?"

"You understand we only know what half of those words mean, right?" Drew told her.

"Right. I'm working with a dinosaur and a caveman." The girl shook her head in disappointment. "We pretend we captured Lumos and sent the magic flare up to signal them. It could work because my bracelet looks like a power dampener to mages and dragons. If we put it on him, it would look like we caught him and blocked his powers. I thought Drew could play the part of my bodyguard or something."

He nodded. It wasn't necessarily a bad plan. If they could rough Lumos up a little, it might work.

"And then what?" the dragon asked and had clearly not grasped the full implication.

"I don't know." Amy grimaced and sank into her chair. "It was a dumb plan. I thought you guys might get it but since you don't even know who Chewie is... Never mind."

"Actually," Drew murmured, "I don't think it's the worst plan out there. Lumos, can you control your healing ability? Like, if I gave you a black eye, would you be able to keep it bruised so it looked like your healing powers were blocked?"

"Ugh, I suppose so," his teammate replied although he didn't sound pleased at the prospect. "I haven't had to walk around bruised in quite some time. Not since I lost a bet in the Dark Ages."

"Do you think it's a good idea?" Amy asked.

"I think that if we did it, we would certainly be able to get good intel on the cell. There's a real risk that we could be found out and we'll need a plan on what to say to those cops if they show up, but Detroit doesn't have the best reputation. I guess... I guess I could pretend to be a dirty cop." He couldn't help but shudder because he hated the stereotype of the corrupt police officer. But if he had to do it to help free another dragon, he could endure. "Do you think they'd be able to capture us if it went pear-shaped?"

"We'll have to assume they have dragon bullets," Lumos said slowly, although he looked at Amy.

"I've been learning how to sense magic and think I'll be able to tell if there's anyone as strong as me. If not...well, not to brag, but I can stop bullets," she replied.

"Okay." Drew nodded. "I think this could work. Our plan will be to spring this trap tomorrow, which means we have preparations to make."

"Like what?" Lumos asked.

"Well, I'll rent a truck and explore the land around here for somewhere to spring this trap."

"Wouldn't that work better if one of us did it since we can fly?" Amy asked.

"I don't think so. We need cover, which is not something either of you has ever had to think about. I want a location where we can get out without flying through a storm of bullets if possible, which means I need to find it, not either of you."

"What are we supposed to do while you're doing that?" the dragon asked.

"We need this cell to know there's a dragon in the area, so when they see you, they know what you are right away. That means you need to be seen."

"Can do." Lumos beamed. "I'd be more than happy to go out dancing tonight. I'll let myself glow a little."

"That'll do it," Drew agreed.

"And what if he is shot while he's out on the town?" the mage asked.

"That's where you come in," he said. "I want you to get into the character of a bounty hunter. Tail him and keep him in your sights and a glare on your face. If anyone is watching him and they see you, they'll simply think he's pissing you off. If anyone tries to intervene, stop them from shooting our golden dragon."

"What if it's those three boys we saw?" she asked. "They already saw us together."

He nodded. In all honesty, he'd forgotten about them.

"I could use my aura on them," Lumos suggested.

"That could work," he said. "Or, Amy, you could approach them and ask if the dragon was from around here? Make it seem like you just met him."

The others exchanged glances and nodded. This could work. It could go wrong but it could work.

"Hopefully, though, you won't see them tonight, and I kind of doubt that they're part of this cell anyway. Loose lips sink ships and all that," Drew said.

"So, we're doing this, then?" Amy retrieved her duffel.

"I think so," he confirmed. "I'll find somewhere for the trap and you two drop a few crumbs. We'll do this tomorrow, which means I'll simply camp when I'm done. I'll call you with coordinates and you can come out when you're ready."

"Do you think we should do it in town?" she asked.

Drew gave her a hard look. "I've seen what you can do. If this does take a turn, I have no doubt you'll be able to keep us alive but I'd like you to not destroy the town of Elgin to do it. I feel like the Texas scrubland will better be able to withstand your rage."

The mage smiled. "As long as you're doing it to protect everyone else and not me, it sounds good."

He nodded. That was why they were there, wasn't it? They needed to protect as many people as possible, even if it meant they had to walk themselves into a trap of their devising.

CHAPTER FORTY-FIVE

"I don't see how the hell this could be a forgery," Larry said and wished he could feel something besides the terror that threatened to overwhelm his disbelief.

"There's nothing else it could be," Hambre said. "I did not send these orders because we do not have a single murder, let alone three. We don't even have a dead dragon."

"But someone made it seem like you did. Someone on the inside," he persisted.

The Columbian stood from the giant wooden table, his hand to his chest in umbrage. "You dare accuse my mages of being traitorous? How dare you!"

The mage felt his year of conditioning snap when the dragon spoke to him like that. Yes, Windlock had always been kind to him, but Larry had spent considerable time amongst dragons. Most of them did not tolerate a mage speaking when not spoken to. Hambre, despite tolerating him thus far, did not seem inclined to do so any longer.

Fortunately, Larry had brought enough people who didn't have any compunction when it came to challenging dragons.

"Who said anything about mages?" Keith demanded. His tone was careful, controlled, and anything but accusatory, and yet Hambre reacted as if he'd been struck.

"How dare you!"

"Now, now," Butters said and tried to calm everyone with a placating gesture. "We've met a few lousy dragons over our time dealing with all this and one that was raised by mages. Is it so crazy to think that one of them might have somehow infiltrated the SWAT team here?"

"And why assume it was our team?" Muerte de Arbol asked as she reached for a piece of fruit and eviscerated it with a hand transformed into a claw. She barely contained her temper. Strangely, that put Larry slightly at ease. Dragons were masters of deception. They had to be, given their auras. He couldn't imagine either of these two tricking them into being there and then acting so affronted at the idea. If one of them did this, they'd have things to say to him—false reassurances, weird hypotheses, false leads, and certainly something more than anger and vitriol leveled with such indignation and conviction.

"I have to make a call," he said and pushed from the table. Despite him being the official envoy to Investigator Steel, they hardly noticed. They were too engaged in arguing with Emerald and Heartsbane, not to mention the uppity humans who didn't seem to mind responding vociferously to the dragons.

Still, to be cautious, he tapped Heartsbane's shoulder with an invisible telekinetic poke. She nodded. They'd worked out on the plane what to do if she needed his help—a way she could use her aura that wouldn't be misread as something else. If he suddenly felt like he was falling in love in the lobby, he'd return to the conference room with his powers ready to batter a few dragon heads.

But when he left, Heartsbane didn't immediately signal him, which again made him think that whoever had led them to Columbia wasn't necessarily from there. If the plan was to lure the team there and hurt them, it would make sense to strike when the mage was away. When no strike came, he leaned even more strongly toward the possibility that the Columbians had been used.

Larry didn't waste time, however. He dialed Drew and urged him to pick up his cellphone from thousands of miles away.

"Larry? How's it going down there in the jungle?" the man said and wasted no time, which was much appreciated.

"We're getting in too deep to see the whole thing. All I see is trees," he replied.

"That doesn't sound good. What's happening?"

"We're on a false lead down here. The Bogota office said the marching orders we responded to were fakes."

Drew didn't respond at first. Larry realized it was because he'd taken the phone away from his face and cursed up a storm away from the receiver. A few moments later, he came back on the line. "I don't quite know what to tell you, Larry."

"How's it going in Texas? I'm worried we were all sent off to split the team up. Are you guys all right?"

"Yeah... In fact, we've picked up some leads here and I think that if this is supposed to be a trap for us, we might as well spring it."

"How do you mean?" he asked.

"Well, I went to the local police who are obviously in on something that doesn't help dragons. They ain't exactly masters of discretion. I think since we're on the hunt and this intel is a little older, whatever took you down there doesn't have much to do with us."

"Have you talked to Kristen?" Larry asked.

"No. But I think you should call her. If someone tried to split us up, they did a good job of it and she's by herself." The statement immediately made his pulse pound a little faster.

"And you're sure your team is all right?"

"I am. I don't think they expected us here at all. We'll keep at it, but let me know the minute something changes and we can abandon ship. It's only...well, I'd rather not. I have a feeling we have them on the run here. I'd rather scare them into a fence than give them time to dig their way out."

"Fair enough," Larry agreed. "We'll be in touch." He hung up and immediately dialed Kristen.

It went to voicemail so he tried again with the same response. When he called a third time, there was no answer.

He knew some dragons would ignore a phone call from a mage if they were addressing the Dragon Council. Hell, most mages probably thought that was the right thing to do, but not Kristen. She always picked up when one of her team members called, especially if they called again in quick succession. Nothing could have induced her to simply let her phone go to voicemail. She knew they were heading into danger—or she thought they were heading into danger, as she didn't know that the whole thing had been a false lead—and would have made herself available in case they needed her.

The mage swallowed and felt both frustrated and helpless that he was in a different hemisphere than his boss.

Larry walked into the conference room to find that the argument between the dragons had escalated and little progress had been made.

"We all know there are dragons who don't have the interest of our society at heart," Emerald stated. "The whole damn reason we're on Dragon SWAT is because of dragons like them."

"But the dragons who are capable of sending you that message can be trusted," Hambre protested, his words like jagged stone. "It's far more likely that someone...what's the word for it—hacked into the system."

"I don't think so—" Keith, the closest thing they had to a tech guy, tried to say but the dragons ignored him.

"Kristen didn't answer," Larry said. The South American dragons paid no attention to him or his statement, but Heartsbane and Emerald immediately shifted their focus to the mage.

"What do you mean she didn't answer?" Emerald asked.

"Excuse me?" Hambre said as if he hadn't heard the lowly mage at all.

Heartsbane noticed the slight and proceeded to completely ignore the dragon.

"You tried her more than once?" she asked.

He nodded. "Three times."

She nodded grimly before she mustered enough bluster to say, "Maybe she's out of cell range."

"Or she could be somewhere indoors with bad reception," Emerald added, although he didn't sound like he believed his attempt at an excuse any more than she had believed hers.

"They could be in an area with cell-blockers," Keith added with a shrug.

"How in the cotton fields of Georgia is that supposed to make us feel better?" Butters demanded.

The Rookie smiled his goofy grin. "I mean that the Dragon Council might have cell phone blockers. If they are that paranoid, it means they're finally taking all this seriously. I don't think the mages would go through all the effort to block her cell when they could simply…" He swallowed, his discomfort obvious, and didn't need to finish the sentence for everyone to know exactly what he was talking about.

Muerte and Hambre's jaws hung wider in utter disbelief as the humans, mage, and dragons all ignored them. Larry couldn't help but smile at their discomfort. This was probably the first time in centuries —maybe ever—that they had received that kind of treatment. It was good to give them a taste of what the rest of the world felt like with dragons on the top rung.

But the feeling was short-lived. Kristen still hadn't answered, they were still there on false orders, and all of it still felt wrong.

"I hate to be the one to be a downer, but we can't make any of those assumptions given that we're here on false pretenses," he said.

That startled the table into silence. Even Muerte and Hambre looked like they weighed the implications of what their SWAT division had been roped into.

"I'll make another call." The mage retrieved his phone and dialed Brian. This time, he didn't bother to leave the conference room since everyone simply stared at him anyway.

"Zed speaking."

"Who?" Larry asked.

"Brian. Come on, man. You're supposed to use my codename."

"Whatever. I have bad news, Zed. Have you heard from Kristen?"

"Not since she left," he said and his voice dropped from know-it-all amusement to terror in the span of four words.

Larry filled him on what had happened, how they'd found nothing, how Drew was all right, and how Kristen was missing. As he spoke, something seemed to roar across the phone line. His imagination—filled as it was with a history of battling dragons and mages—conjured images of furious dragons and angry spellcasters, but it was something far more innocuous for the modern age—Brian typing.

"She's not responding but I'll get as much data from the cellphone as I possibly can," the techie said. His voice sounded both urgent and strangely vacant as his brain shifted into the ever-hungry mode of a man who devoured information from the Internet.

"Anything?" Larry asked after a moment.

"It'll take me more time than that," the young man mumbled. "I got a hit on a Facebook page for some guy named Ranger Jay. He took a photo with her. I'll see what else I can get. When I call you, pick up."

"Of course," he replied, but Brian had already hung up.

The mage had hoped that the conversation would help to calm him. He'd wanted Kristen's brother to tell him that she was sick of talking to him, that she was testing him, or that she did this kind of stuff all the time. What he hadn't expected was for him to devolve into panic-controlled research-mode so quickly.

"What's the plan?" Heartsbane asked.

"Thank you very much for having us here and for the, uh—"

"Fruit platter!" Butters interjected and saved Larry's ass from seeming rude.

"But we need to go. Did you send those armored cars away or are they still here?" he asked.

"They're still here," Muerte said.

"Dragon wings will be faster with the traffic here," Emerald said.

"We can't risk going airborne," Beanpole said.

"May I remind you that there was no murder here," their hostess said and sounded imperious.

"Our intel still says there was a cell here, though," Keith told her.

"They might be waiting to spook us into flight so they can pop off a couple of shots."

"Damn it," Larry cursed. "Keith's right. We take the cars, head home, and hope to hell that Brian can get us a location before we reach Detroit."

The team nodded, seemingly mollified by his orders and urgency. That was good. It meant he was at last being a somewhat competent leader. Windlock had always had that effect on him. They could face a team of murderous dragons and the investigator would talk about his coffee like there was nothing dangerous in the world.

The mage hadn't quite managed that level of control, but his team at least looked somewhat calmed. Lucky them. A tornado of panic swirled in his gut and he worried that it wouldn't go away until he found the Steel Dragon's body after she'd been murdered while she was all alone.

CHAPTER FORTY-SIX

K risten plunged into the frigid lake and sank like a stone. After being trapped alone and in the dark for so long, the embrace of the ice-cold water was immensely refreshing and the shock of the sudden contact made her gasp with a split-second of exhilaration.

She tried to change her steel skin but her strength was insufficient. Her body defaulted to her dragon form, expanding quickly in the subterranean lake, and filled it with glittery shards of silver that vanished once the transformation was complete.

Knowing she had only seconds before her weight became an issue, she pumped her wings and drove herself to the surface. Her stomach reminded her how hungry she was but she ignored it. She burst through the surface of the lake and into the largest room she'd been in yet, although it was still too small for her to stand as a dragon, let alone spread her wings. While the pool was deep enough to completely hold her form, the part where she could breathe was noticeably less spacious.

Her dragon eyes narrowed in the gloom, unable to make sense of the space. She knew it might not be the smartest idea, but she released a few tiny balls of flame so she could get her bearings in this odd cavern.

It was enormous. The size of a huge lake—being from Michigan, she was quick to tell herself not a great one—the room was mostly underwater. Only a handful of feet of air stretched from the surface to the ceiling. She would be able to stand if she reverted to human form but wouldn't be able to do so as a dragon, let alone fly.

As she changed into her human form once more, Kristen realized how tired she was. The ordeal through the tube had battered and bruised her body, and her healing powers had difficulty taking care of it. She swam to the shore and the effort left her almost winded.

Shore was a generous word for the edge of the underground lake. It was more like a stony shelf that ran up at a slight angle to the wall. Stalactites and stalagmites grew from the ceiling and the floor. Here and there, they joined into columns that were wide enough to hide a man's body behind them.

An unnecessarily paranoid thought, she tried to tell herself. If someone was following her—and she didn't see how they could, not after her little water slide adventure—why had they still not attacked? Theories began to swirl in her mind like eddies in the cold water. She shook them resolutely from her mind and the cold water from her skin as she scrambled out.

One of her school teachers had once told her that under the earth, the temperature was always the same, but she felt ice-cold. It was probably the water plus her lack of food and strength. She tried to remind herself that dragons rarely froze to death or died from hypothermia. They were hot-blooded, after all, with a much higher internal temperature than mammals, but she couldn't stop shivering.

So, as unwise as it might be, she transformed into her dragon form again and blasted one of the wider stalagmites with fire to heat it until it became cherry-red. Once it glowed like a stone in a sauna, she reverted to her human body and leaned against the heated stone. A normal human would have probably burned themselves but she was a dragon. Besides, she was cold.

It felt good to be warm, a human comfort in an inhuman place. Kristen realized that she was no longer thirsty either. She'd inadvertently swallowed water in the tube and drank some while paddling to shore. But she was still tired, bruised from the tube, and hungry—and getting hungrier.

The warmth helped, as did the warm light coming off the stalagmite and her lack of thirst, but her hunger would do her in. Using her dragon powers demanded energy, and her body would need to get it from somewhere. She would starve to death far sooner than a human would. A bitter, cynical part of her pointed out that she at least wouldn't be cold, but she couldn't chastise herself for trying to get warm. She had been so cold her chattering teeth had made it difficult to hold a thought in her head, let alone devise a rescue plan for herself.

But at least she was alive and in need of a rescue plan. If that tube had lasted any longer or if she hadn't been able to break through the dam, she'd be dead. Yes, she was trapped, alone, and hungry, but she was alive. She would get out of this because she had to.

Kristen pressed more firmly against the rock and tried to take stock of her situation. Moving back through the tunnel of water was out of the question. From there, it looked like little more than a hole in the ceiling with water gushing out of it. Her dragon powers were formidable but she was not a salmon.

There were undoubtedly dragons who could swim up waterfalls, but the Steel Dragon did not have that particular ability. Besides, even if she could manage it, what was waiting for her there? Dead ends and glowing fungus? That didn't exactly sound like the kind of environment she wanted to die trying to get to.

But she didn't see any other way out. She noticed a few dark holes in the ceiling but trying to climb up through one sounded daunting to her in her current condition. Plus, there was the threat of more dead ends. No, it was better to find another solution, but what?

Kristen looked at the water that gushed into the chamber. With a flow like that, she thought, the entire room she was in should be full.

She had gained a sense of the size of the room when she'd used her fire breath to illuminate the space, but she hadn't paid much attention to the actual details of the walls themselves. Could there be a hole in one of them that drew the excess water from the lake? If there was, she could use the path to escape this part of her subterranean prison.

There was always the possibility that the hole where the water drained was under the lake. For that matter, there could be a series of small holes similar to the dam of debris she had punched through. If that was her only way out of there... She didn't want to think about that.

With a heavy sigh, she studied the wide lake in front of her. How odd it was that less than an hour before, she'd been concerned about not having water and now that there was a lake of it, her brain had forgotten about how thirsty she was. She needed to escape, get out of there, and find out what the hell was happening with her team.

A splash in the water shattered the still surface and she launched to her feet, her fists raised, and turned into steel. Nothing confronted her immediately so she reached out with her dragon aura and sensed for the source of the disturbance. She almost wished it was whoever had trapped her down there so the suspense could at least be over and done with.

After another splash, she realized it wasn't a dragon, a mage, or even a resourceful regular human armed with explosives and night-vision goggles. It was something far better—a fish!

Kristen plunged into the water, heedless of her only recently dried clothes. She belly-flopped and scared her quarry away and out into deeper water.

She took a deep breath as she stood and focused on her dragon aura sense rather than her vision.

There were more of them out there. Her stomach grumbled at the thought. Most were fairly small but a few were a decent size. The larger specimens seemed to remain near the bottom of the lake, which —given her already empty stomach—seemed too far for comfort.

Rather than swimming after the larger ones she really wanted, she waited in the shallows and remained utterly motionless as only a woman who often turned to steel could.

Realistically, she expected to be there for an hour or more and glanced at her watch. She realized only a few minutes had passed before a fish came up to her from the depths. It was some kind of sightless catfish with pale skin that almost showed its muscles beneath and long, grasping white whiskers. It spoke volumes about her current condition that seeing it made her think of deep-fried fish sticks rather than trying to banish the creature to the depths from which it had come. While it wasn't a particularly large one—less than the length of her forearm—her current hunger decided it would be more than welcome.

It approached her and moved as directly as it could with its tail pumping its pale fleshy body through the water. Kristen realized it must be like her in that it had senses that most humans simply didn't. She recalled sharks having an electromagnetic sense that told them when fish were near, and from the way the catfish moved, she thought it must possess some way of sensing for sources of food. It certainly seemed unerring in its approach.

It required tremendous willpower to not tremble in anticipation as she waited until one of its long white whiskers brushed her ankle.

She lunged and tried to snatch it out of the water.

Unfortunately, she failed miserably. She had relied too much on her vision and with the refraction from the surface of the water and the low lighting had succeeded in doing little more than scaring the fish into deeper water.

Disgruntled, she took a deep breath and tried to comfort herself with the feeling that she could fill her lungs even more than usual given that there was no food inside her. Grimly determined, she settled in to wait again.

It didn't take long for another of the blind catfish—this one slightly longer—to approach the new obstacle that had suddenly taken up space in its pond.

Kristen stood still as it approached. The only movement she made was the slow elongation of the fingers of one hand into the steel claws of her dragon form.

She waited as the creature probed her with first one whisker, then another. It wouldn't do to spook this one—for all she knew, it might use some kind of undiscovered catfish communication to tell its friends to stay away. With a mental litany to remind herself to be patient, she let it probe her ankles with its whiskers. Finally, it swam under her legs and she snagged it out of the water with her claw.

Triumphant, she raised her prey aloft. It thrashed once or twice and died, dropping scales and fish blood into the water that then called the other catfish. That effectively disproved her vague theory about the catfish somehow being a community and replaced it with the more somber truth of cold, hard survival of the fittest.

Still, she thought, as she gutted it and left the offal on a rock near the lake, she could use the parts she didn't eat to catch more fish. She wouldn't starve, which was all that mattered.

Her mouth watered when she put her prize on the superheated rock and it sizzled. Once it had cooked through, she took a bite. It was rubbery, bland, and tasted far worse than the already less than appetizing taste of mud so common in many catfish, but to her, it was undoubtedly the most delicious piece of fish she had ever eaten in her entire life.

She soon finished the hopefully nutritious meal, having eaten it quickly both because she was hungry and out of fear of registering the flavor and realizing how disgusting it was. That aside, she'd managed to eat it all and wasn't grossed out about the idea of eating more of them if she needed to.

Kristen smiled as she leaned back against the warm rock that had doubled as her stove. She had water and food. All that was left to do was get out of there. She was confident that she would make it out because she was done doubting herself, done worrying, and done thinking about whoever had done this to her. This was about survival, nothing more, and she was a survivor. Period.

Nothing could stop her from finding a way out of this mess.

CHAPTER FORTY-SEVEN

The Masked One was there with Kristen from the moment she entered the cave with the laughable schoolboy of a ranger to the moment she dove into the stream and escaped his sights.

He had trapped her beneath a mountain of rubble and then dug her out and moved her to where he might better watch her. Often, he had been only paces away from her as she moved through the tunnels, talking to herself and wondering who had done such a thing to her.

The dragon relished her powerlessness. She was in his domain—the dark.

Lord Boneclaw's powers were not what one would think. His dragon form looked bony and wretched—even he could admit this—but his powers... Ah, his powers were a special thing.

Now, he used them to move through the passages and followed the stream she had dove into. In the tunnels, it had been easy to stay close to her. He could dissolve into shadow as easily as a cloud could dissolve into the air. In the darkness where he had put her, he could walk around as easily as a human in a market square. He never had to return to his corporeal form like some of the lesser dragons she had faced. With his abilities, he lived in the shadow, breathed in the shadow, and was the shadow.

Even when she had found the passage with glowing fungus, the Masked One had not been dissuaded. He had moved behind a stalactite and could have stayed there for days if he had wanted to, watching her from a place no one could see, not even a dragon—the heart of the dark.

Thus far, he had not been much impressed with this world-famous dragon who had survived on nothing but dumb luck. She had not thought of a way out of the maze he had devised for her, nor had she used her brute force to simply force a path up.

Diving into the water had shown some...courage...he supposed, but not much else and certainly not wisdom.

He didn't even know if she had survived. Although he had followed her closely thus far, he wasn't so curious as to risk his life by simply diving into an underground stream.

Besides, why would he dive in when he had more efficient methods.

His body shrank until it was nothing but a magical veneer in the darkness. In this state, stone was hardly a barrier for him. He found cracks in the weathered limestone and flowed through them, moving through tight spaces, reaching out with limbs of shadow, and finding dead ends only to redirect his search into more useful paths.

It didn't take him long to reach where the Steel Dragon was going. There were advantages to moving like a shadow—many, many advantages. One of which was that he could still feel surfaces, as that was the only place shadow existed if you could even say shadow existed at all. He could feel those surfaces and feel the water vibrating them as he crawled through the spaces between the stone. His seemingly endless descent ended when he emerged on the roof of a cavern that housed a huge underground lake.

And not a moment too soon, the Masked One thought gleefully as a hole in the roof that poured water briefly stopped its flow and vomited the Steel Dragon into the lake below.

She struck the water, made a tremendous splash, and proceeded to sink like an anchor.

He watched with bated breath. Would this be the end of the Steel

Dragon? He moved through the darkness and closer to the shore of the lake to watch her asphyxiate underwater.

When the Steel Dragon burst from the surface of the water, no longer in her human shape, he wasn't quite sure how to react.

Part of him was impressed. He had killed many foes over the millennia in his little tests. It was a rare thing that someone tried something so foolhardy as trying to traverse an underground river without the powerset for it and survived. But still, her success, at this point, was based on little more than luck.

If she had survived through nothing more than dumb luck—if, in fact, that was the secret to her success—the Masked One would be disappointed, but at least he wouldn't have an actual problem on his hands. Over the centuries, he had learned that luck only lasted for so long before it ran out. Only fools relied on luck.

What was better was understanding the odds and playing them again, and again, and again. He had not spun a web of connections that reached to every continent of this planet by luck. If anything, he planned for bad luck and that way, when things did work out better than expected, it was a true boon rather than one's only chance at survival. If luck was all she had...well, it was better to watch and study than speculate.

The Steel Dragon moved through the cave, swimming on her back as she tried to pierce the gloom and failed. He stood impassively on the shore. His arms were folded, but being a creature of shadow who existed in this state without corporeal form, the action was simply a figure of speech.

Still, his body—if it were solid—would be at the lake's edge, so it was there that he coalesced into his solid body when the Steel Dragon released a blast of fire to illuminate the cave.

The Masked One bit his tongue and scrambled away from the light. Being forced out of his shadow form never felt good. He could move in and out of it at will, of course, but when light shined on his form and he coalesced, it was painful.

Still, it had happened before so he didn't lose control. Instead, he scurried behind a stalagmite and caught his breath, hiding in the blessed shadow as the Steel Dragon moved to the shore.

He peeked at her again as she crawled out of the water, her human body shivering in the cold. Despite the pitch-black of the room, he could still see. She was bruised and tired, and although she'd survived this far, she was running out of energy and wouldn't last much longer.

It came as a surprise when she transformed into a dragon and exhaled a massive blast of fire in his direction.

The Masked One dove into the shadows and crawled across the ground like a rat behind a low stone to avoid being seen. What was she doing? Had she seen him? Had she somehow realized he was there and known what to do about his powers? He didn't know and all he could do was scurry away, farther and farther from the flames, while he cursed himself for letting her into a space where she could transform into her dragon form.

After a moment, the flames stopped. No footsteps came closer to him and he didn't sense her aura approaching.

In fact, careful prodding of her aura revealed that she wasn't hunting or ready to fight, merely cold and hungry. *So, she still doesn't know I'm here.* Ever cautious, he withdrew his aura sensing abilities. He was a master of his aura, unlike any other dragon. While there were those who could use their control to exert their will over others more authoritatively than him—he knew the Steel Dragon had one dragon on her team who could —no one could mask their aura quite like he could. Even when sensing other dragons, he was able to keep his out of their reach or, if the situation demanded, he could broadcast feelings different than his own. He did this when in Council Meetings because much of the debate was done via aura and it simply wouldn't do for him to turn his off.

As his aura sense recoiled, The Masked One noticed that the cavern didn't return to the wonderful embrace of pitch black. It seemed the Steel Dragon had used her heat breath not to attack but to blast a stone hot enough to warm herself.

It was clever and he'd never seen another dragon do it before, but it was also shortsighted because fire breath could be a real drain on a dragon's energy levels. It usually didn't matter much, what with dragon kind's unfettered access to whatever food they desired, but there, overusing one's fire breath was a truly foolish thing to do.

She had a place to warm her bones and a little light, which probably warmed her spirits as it seemed to do for so many humans. He knew the Steel Dragon still considered herself human, as disgusting a thought as it was, but she would inevitably starve to death. The eternal cold of death might even come sooner with the energy she'd expended.

The Masked One almost decided to end it then and there. *This little whelp has survived on nothing but luck. It's time to end her streak.* Before he could slink from his position behind the stone ridge, Kristen—still in human form—plunged into the water. She waded out into it and froze, waiting for something.

An unexpected splash startled him and he realized she was fishing like she was nothing more than a bird. He couldn't believe it. Of course, he had seen dragons fish in their dragon form over the ocean, where they could catch tuna or dolphins or something worth the effort, but he'd never seen one use their dragon claws to spear a fish the way the Steel Dragon did on her second attempt.

She took her meal to her hot stone and cooked it there. He wrinkled his nose at the stench of the white-fleshed fish cooked without salt or seasoning deep in the bowels of the earth, but he appraised the Steel Dragon more carefully.

This was something he had not expected—an enthusiasm for survival, one could say. A penchant for life that, in his twisted mind, most humans simply didn't have. There was something more than luck to the Steel Dragon, even if it was nothing more than the tenacity of the desperate. But he liked tenacity. In fact, it was through his tenacity that he expected to one day rule this world and all the species that called it home.

Not such a terrible performance, anyway, he thought. There was much more to a foe than an ability to survive, of course. She had not proven that she was any more formidable than the glowing fungus he'd seen in the other part of the cave, but he couldn't help but settle in and decide to watch her a while longer.

When she lost her entertainment value, he would kill her.

He would let her try to fill her belly with these sour cave fish and perhaps try to find a way out of there that didn't involve transforming her body into liquid shadow. It would be interesting to see how long she would last.

However long that might be, he would kill her.

It was the perfect finale and he would enjoy it very much.

CHAPTER FORTY-EIGHT

When her belly was full and no longer threatened to rebel against her, Kristen felt she could think again for the first time in a while. It was crazy how much hunger could affect one's mental state. Now that she was full, she felt much better. If she considered where she was now compared to where she had been an hour before, she was in a different world.

Yes, she was still trapped beneath the earth but she was no longer hungry or thirsty. She had managed to get out of the twisting tunnels leading from the room where she had been deposited by an unknown hand. Things had subtly changed and she was moving forward—if not literally, then at least figuratively, and that was more than enough for her.

A year ago—hell, even a month—she might have let this situation defeat her. Now, she wouldn't. Not because she had become stronger —although she was much stronger than she had been—but because she knew it wasn't her against the world. She had a team of people who cared for her. A team that was no doubt, at the very least, beginning to wonder where their leader had vanished to. She was certain that they would come looking for her. Until then, she merely had to stay warm, dry, hydrated, and fed.

Another part of her—a darker, niggling corner of her mind—told her otherwise. It insisted that her friends were already dead and she had been trapped there so an unseen enemy could eliminate the rest of the team in one fell swoop. She knew, though, that this was only fear trying to work its way into her brain. Her team had dragons and powerful mages. It included humans—regular humans—who had stood against dragons and mages and lived to tell the tale. They had each other and the knowledge of the truth of that was enough to enable her to push her fears from her mind.

Kristen knew they would come for her. That's what friends did and it was what teams did. Still, she couldn't help but want to be on the surface when they arrived.

She decided to explore. Her rock had lost enough energy to reduce its light and was now hardly warmer than the surrounding air. There was no reason to stay near it.

Filled with a new sense of purpose, she followed the shore and used her dragon vision to try to pierce the gloom and look for anything that might provide a way out. It wasn't easy. The shadows were thick and almost liquid, and although her eyes could make some sense of the darkness, there were still places she could not see. She avoided those edges and corners and had a sense from them that was deeply unsettling.

But there wasn't anything in them. She felt confident of that and used her dragon aura to try to feel for other dragons, sources of food, animals, or people who might lead her out of there and even for whoever had put her there.

She sensed nothing but the fish in the lake. They swam continuously, always in motion. Most were small, some were middling, and a few true behemoths called the depths home. She felt nothing besides them, though. No rabbits had found their way in and no bats, and nothing that might give her clues to a way out.

Kristen couldn't help but wonder about how she had gotten down there. Whoever had put her in this place had chosen the narrow tunnels they'd first put her in. Were they leading her somewhere or had they simply chosen a place where she couldn't use her dragon abilities? Either way, she felt confident that they could not have expected her to go through the water tunnel. Had she escaped them, or had they followed her through the passage? She didn't know.

"If you're watching me, show your face already, coward. If you hoped to starve me to death, you fucked that one up." Her words echoed off the rock ceiling and bounced between the stone structures, only to be swallowed by the placid surface of the lake.

After walking for perhaps half a kilometer—she had counted her paces—she paused to study her surroundings. There wasn't much to see. This part of the cave was identical in the way that different parts of the same forest felt the same. More stalactites, more rock shelves, and more water were the sum total of her landscape. She paused and scanned the gloom with both her eyes and her dragon aura sense.

Again, she felt nothing but fish. If someone was following her, they were damn good at hiding themselves. But surely she had ditched them, right?

Kristen shook her head, desperate to keep her mind from wool-gathering. But what choice did she have? This lake was huge and its shore was monotonous. If she walked around the entire body of water, she wouldn't be able to do a damn thing besides daydream or whatever you called it when it was a waking nightmare. That wouldn't do.

She took a deep breath and tried to calm herself. Her gaze settled on the lake and she wondered again about how the water was getting out. It obviously was but it didn't happen on the shore in any easily visible way. It had to take place at the water's edge or under the surface.

Although it might take more energy, Kristen considered using her dragon form in the water. She could swim although she was normally averse to it, but this might be the perfect place for a challenge. And after what she'd been through, it seemed a low-key one. She was alone with nothing to occupy herself—no challenge when that was what she thrived on.

The more she thought about it, the more it made sense. As a dragon, she could use her fire to better illuminate the area. Plus, she could cover ground more quickly. Yes, there was a risk of depleting her energy, but she could sense a substantial supply of fish in the lake. She knew there would be enough for a few days of survival, at least, and if she couldn't get out of here by then...

It was better not to think about it.

Her mind made up, she transformed and waded into the water. The chill of the lake was rather pleasant on her dragon skin. Heat constantly came from inside her dragon body, and although Kristen knew it meant she burned calories faster, it felt good against the water. She reasoned that a little pleasure wasn't so bad given how she'd struggled with despondency and depression since she'd been trapped.

She moved deeper into the water—her body flesh rather than steel, of course—and discovered that she floated quite easily. Of course, she could fly, so floating in the water shouldn't have come as too much of a surprise. Still, as nervous as she had been about being in water in her dragon body, this was a surprisingly pleasant revelation.

More confident now, she stretched her wings out—something that was impossible on the shore—and learned that she could use them and her tail to propel her through the water fairly efficiently. It would have been even more enjoyable if there was only a little light.

"Ah, to hell with it," she muttered quietly and launched a fireball at the ceiling. The shadows danced and moved as the ball of flame ascended until it met the roof and puffed into nothing.

She continued in this way for some time, moving through the water as she tried to find some clue of how the water flowed out of there and maybe where the fish would feed. The chill was much better at keeping her awake than walking along the shore had been, and after perhaps twenty minutes—she couldn't check her watch in dragon form—she rolled over, floated on her back, and released a fireball simply to watch the light.

It was pleasant to float and stare at the ceiling. Her gaze traced a black scorch mark directly above her.

Except, she realized after a moment, it wasn't a scorch mark or any other kind of stain.

Her brain told her the mark had moved. Common sense clicked in and told her unequivocally that of course it hadn't—she had. She fixed her gaze on the mark on the ceiling and held as still as she could. It was possible that she had moved and her motions had caused her to drift, and she wanted to make sure that it really was the current.

Kristen held still, breathed gently, and watched the ceiling as she floated slowly under it. After a few moments, she realized that she was definitely moving—very slowly but the water around her was flowing. The discovery meant she now knew which end of the lake the water exited from. She only had to swim in that direction and find out exactly where the place of egress was.

She knew that might be difficult but solutions already bubbled in her mind. Maybe she could spread something on the surface of the water—scraps of her clothes perhaps?—to see where they floated or better yet, she could kill another fish and use its blood in the water. Okay, perhaps that was a little morbid and hopefully unnecessary. With any luck, there would be an actual stream for her to leave through. Wasn't that what water did anyway? Erode paths in stone?

Kristen felt her confidence fill her chest as she took a deep breath and spun in the water so she was on her belly again.

She swished her tail and sculled her wings, moving toward the side of the lake that might very well be the last part of this trap she had to see.

In the next moment, something pounded into her spine and bolts of pain surged through her body as she was plunged underwater into the icy subterranean lake.

CHAPTER FORTY-NINE

"So, this is it, huh?" Amy asked, her thumbs hitched on her belt like she'd grown up in Texas rather than Maine.

Drew scanned the location he'd found once again. "Yeah. I think this is as good as we'll get."

Lumos nodded. "I think you could have done far worse. What is this place? An old gravel quarry?"

The man nodded. As close as he could determine, that was exactly what it was. "I think we wait in there—near the middle of that giant pit."

In all honesty, it was more like half a pit. It looked like a hill had been partially scraped away and a giant half-circle cut into the hill. A dirt road led out of the scooped-out area to the highway they had come from. The above-ground gravel quarry was in the middle of nowhere with nothing around except for mesquite trees and scrub.

"They could come up from that high ridge," he said and gestured to the top of the hill. "It all depends on what kind of mages they are. If they can fly or something, this whole thing could turn into a hot mess damn quickly."

"What other choice do we have?" she asked.

"None, as far as I can see. If they can fly, they can fly. We won't be able to choose a location that doesn't have the sky. At least here, if they come by truck, we'll know where to watch."

"I think that makes sense to me," Lumos agreed.

Amy nodded as well.

"So, are you two are okay with this?" Drew asked.

"Well…it was my idea," she reminded him. "I won't back out now."

"I'm comfortable enough with it," the dragon confirmed. "The idea of them thinking me captive and breaking free to their utter shock sounds wonderful. Kudos to this Chewie-barker for coming up with that one."

"Chewbacca," the girl corrected.

"Chewbatty?" Drew ventured.

"No, Chewbacca."

"Chewtada?" Lumos frowned.

"I don't understand how you two can face dragons and mages and you can't even say the name of one of the most famous Wookie's to ever come from Kashyyyk." She shook her head in disgust.

"Then it's settled. We do this," Drew said.

She nodded. "What, now?"

"If it's not too much trouble." He took a few steps back.

Lumos glanced at him. "You might want to take a few more steps," he said, grew dragon wings briefly out of his human body's back, and flapped them a few times so he was a good fifty yards away from Amy.

The man followed. "I hope we're doing the right thing," he muttered.

"I think the intelligence will prove useful. If we can get faces of these guys and a location for their base, Zed will be able to do a lot with it."

"You like his nickname, huh?" he said.

"I find it rather dapper, yes." The dragon grinned.

The ground began to shake and drew their attention to Amy. Drew didn't know there were earthquakes in Texas and hoped she was all right.

She was, fortunately. In fact, she seemed to be the cause of the earthquake.

The mage stood in the middle of the quarry, her knees bent like a sumo wrestler, her arms at her side, and her fists balled and held away from her body.

All around her, the wind blew to kick up dervishes of dust. That soon became gusts heavy with pebbles and stones. She screamed—a powerful, guttural sound—and when she did, a shockwave spread out from her. It shredded the surface of the quarry pit and hurled gravel everywhere with such force that her companions had to shield their faces for fear of losing an eye.

Still, she kept at it.

Amy took a breath and screamed louder. She raised her arms and released her fists as she brought them above her head. As she did so, the wind blew harder and another shockwave emanated from her body as if she couldn't control it and it was nothing more than a tremble, a footnote to what she would do, a mistake hardly worth her notice.

Her arms rose until they were only inches apart. She lowered them so they were level with her shoulders and slapped the palms of her hands together. Her fingers remained splayed as a blast of energy erupted through the ground, through her legs, her torso, and her shoulders, and finally blasted out of her hands.

At first, Drew wanted to compare it to a spotlight as he had never seen anything else paint the sky like that. But the colors were more like a firework show without the pops or the oohs and ahs of a crowd. Instead, a dull roar grew in pitch as she threw more and more energy into the sky.

All that energy—every ounce of the column of power—seemed to be focused on one place. Somehow, Amy was able to make it all coalesce on a point smaller than one of the pebbles she had so effortlessly hurled aside.

It exploded in a great, booming shower of sparks of every color of the rainbow.

Drew covered his eyes against the brilliant display, afraid of being blinded.

After a moment, the light no longer showed through his hands and he dared to open his eyes.

He fully expected to find the mage passed out or worse from such a display of power, but she wasn't. One of her nostrils was bleeding but she grinned like a fool and hopped up and down in a circle that was now devoid of pebbles, debris, and most of the topsoil.

The sight left him gaping in bemusement. How could this peppy little skater punk have used such power and simply dance about it?

"Do you think that'll attract the mages? I suppose almost everyone in Texas will have seen it, but the mages will know it was more than a bomb blowing up a plane filled with fireworks, right?"

Lumos didn't answer. Instead, he stared at Amy and the swath of land she'd cleared around her as nothing more than a side effect.

"Lumos...Lumos buddy? Do you think we're good?"

"I am stunned," the dragon said simply. "There is a spectrum to the abilities of mages, and yours are about as far along it as I have ever seen."

"So they'll come, then?"

"The amount of power released must have felt like a bucket of cold water dumped on every mage within a hundred miles of here. I wouldn't be surprised to find out that some of the more sensitive mages sensed it from even farther than that. I don't think Larry could, not being in South America but...well..." Lumos trailed off. He really did seem dumbstruck by the enormity of what she had done.

"Have you seen power like that before?" Drew asked, punched him in the arm, and gestured for him to move toward Amy. After all, they had a trap to set.

"Yes, I have, but not for centuries. Not since the Mage Wars."

He forced a laugh. "It's a good thing she's on our side then, yeah?"

That seemed to finally shake the dragon from his stupor. He laughed uproariously. "Indeed it is! To think, if she'd allied with these mages and they had trained her... Well, I don't know if we would still have a side left."

"Are you all right?" he asked as they neared her.

She nodded, although she sat and wiped the sweat from her brow.

"I probably should have done stretches or something beforehand. Did you see that? It was crazy."

"Indeed it was, young lady," Lumos agreed.

"Here," Drew said. He was about to toss her a bottle of Gatorade but thought better of it and placed it in her hand instead.

The girl opened the bottle and drank the entire contents in almost a single swallow.

Drew, his eyes wide, retrieved some jerky and trail mix he'd bought in town and gave those to her as well, which she devoured with relish.

"Whoa, hey, chew the jerky," he said.

"Yeah, sorry, but we have to be ready for the next step, right?" She scrambled to her feet. With food and drink in her belly, she looked better, but didn't everyone?

"That's right," he said and looked at Lumos.

"Time to pull the Tzu-zaca," the dragon said.

"You know, I realize you're doing that on purpose, but it simply makes you sound dumb. You know that, right?" The girl looked at her wrist and removed the bracelet that made her appear to be a shackled mage instead of the unfettered and powerful one she was.

She stepped forward and put it on Lumos.

"Funny," the dragon said and studied the bracelet. "I wonder if that's the first time anything like this has ever happened."

"Anything like what?" Amy asked.

"I bet a mage has never put one of these magic-suppressing bracelets on a dragon before."

"This one's a fake, remember," she said.

"Yes, of course, but still. It's a sign that times are changing, isn't it?"

Drew slapped handcuffs on him as well.

"What the hell are those for? Do you think because a mage shackles me, you will too?" Lumos asked, although his tone made it clear he was joking.

He smiled. "This has to look convincing. The bracelet should help with their...aura abilities or whatever, but the cuffs will make you look restrained." He couldn't believe he was seriously talking about someone's aura. A few short years before, auras had been something to talk about with women who were into yoga. Now, they were merely a part of life.

"What is the point when I can snap these off whenever I wish?" the dragon asked.

"That is exactly the point," Drew said. "You need to look powerless. Nothing makes someone look powerless like them being bruised and under restraint."

"Bruised?" Lumos scowled.

Drew nodded grimly. "We talked about this. You can suppress your healing ability, right?"

"Yes, I can, but I don't have any—"

He swung without warning and punched Lumos in the face.

Although he connected hard enough to make his knuckles ache and the joint in his wrist pop, the dragon barely flinched. He certainly didn't reciprocate. It was another reminder of the terrible power of dragons. He had punched with everything he had and his teammate seemed unperturbed.

His face, though, had begun to swell nicely.

Lumos sighed. "You might as well do my nose too. Don't break it, but if you can get some blood out of it—"

Drew obliged him. It didn't feel good to punch someone he so respected but there was also something unsettling about making a dragon bleed. It was something he had wondered about his entire life. Hell, maybe every normal kid wondered about it. Could a person do a damn thing to a dragon? Given the opportunity, could you even make one of the fire-breathing, winged demons notice you? *It looks like someone can,* he thought, but that didn't make him feel anything but uncomfortable.

The world was the way it was partly because the dragons had always been at the top. What would the world look like when those in power no longer held it? Would it be more egalitarian as the mages thought? Or would it be worse? Could a despot be replaced by anything but a despot? Certainly, a small group of people could change the world, but could they change it in any way besides lighting it on fire? He hoped so, but he didn't dare think he had the answer.

His job was to follow orders. It always had been and always would be. He was lucky enough to follow the orders of someone he truly respected. Kristen Hall had told them to find out about the mages there so that was what he would do, even if it meant punching one of his friends in the face.

"What do we do now?" Amy asked.

Drew smiled. This was part of the plan he knew better than any other. "Now, we wait."

The time passed slowly in the east Texas scrubland. They didn't dare do anything like converse. The mages could arrive at any time and it wouldn't do for them to see them chatting pleasantly with their phony captive.

Lumos sat in the dirt and let the blood from his nose harden into a respectable crust. Amy stood a few feet behind him and practiced with her magical abilities, focusing on control of individual pebbles. Somehow, after seeing such a show of power, even the mage manipulating these tiny pebbles was an ominous activity.

Drew reasoned that if she could make blasts of energy like she had and was able to lift an individual pebble, there was no reason that she couldn't use every one of these pebbles like a bullet. He shuddered at the thought and wondered about her powers and what kind of limits it had—if there even were limits.

Yes, he'd seen her tire, but he'd also seen her stamina increase. Would her powers grow to such a point that she would be unstoppable? He didn't know whether to hope for that or not. While it would be great to have a mage-goddess on their side, he was an American and thus believed in a separation of powers. Surely the world would be a better place if powers like hers were spread out rather than concentrated? He couldn't be sure.

All he could do was stand and wait with his hands clasped behind his back to play the part of the goon in their charade. He fixed his gaze mostly on the road but he made sure to check the ridge behind them as well.

After what had to be less than an hour but felt like a week, he noticed a trail of dust rise from the dirt road.

"Who is coming, servant?" Amy asked and deliberately sounded bossier than he thought she could.

"I can't tell," Drew said.

"You can't tell what?"

He rolled his eyes. "I can't tell, Lady Amy."

"Much better." She giggled. "That wasn't too much, was it? I don't want to seem too much."

"I think it was wonderful, Lady Amy," Lumos told her.

"Quiet!" she snapped and managed to restrain her laughter this time. "My servant can't see, so get on your feet, lizard, and see who is coming."

The dragon complied and staggered and swayed on his feet to make it look like he barely had the strength or coordination to manage it. Although their enemies were still far out, Drew was relieved that everyone was getting into character.

"Oh, shit," Lumos said and his dragon eyes narrowed to stare into the distance. "You guys won't believe this, but it's the boys from the barbeque place."

"Is that right?" Drew raised an eyebrow. "Those boys were all talk. Maybe we should change the plan and simply overpower them."

"I don't think so," the dragon commented wryly. "They brought friends."

"How many?" he asked.

"Enough to fill the back of a pickup and leave room for an arsenal of guns?"

"My lady?" Drew asked. "How do you feel?"

"Like these arrogant little pricks won't know what to do with us."

CHAPTER FIFTY

Larry had long since learned to appreciate the perks of a private jet. He loved the legroom, the full bar, and the real food, but he didn't think he'd ever appreciated how much easier it was to pace on a private jet than a commercial airliner.

"Are you trying to wear a hole in the carpet there, boss?" Butters asked, his tone light.

The mage swept a glare at him and was ready to snap something about the Steel Dragon's life being on the line. When he saw the man's eyes, though, he could see the rotund sniper was as concerned as he was.

"I have some gasoline so we might as well simply burn a hole," Hernandez quipped. Although she was joking, he could hear the concern in the normally blustery demolitions expert as well.

"Is this the gallows humor Lady Steel told us about?" Heartsbane asked. She did not seem even mildly amused. "Because it's not funny."

"Nah, that's not gallows humor," Keith said and a devilish grin crept across his face. "It would be like joking that she isn't picking up because she's probably already fought the North American Council to a standstill and is installing herself as god-empress."

"That's not gallows humor!" Hernandez protested. "That sounds like a good thing to me. Gallows humor would be to joke about how Kristen is probably dead and being melted into swords right now."

"Oh, come on!" Butters protested. "That's taking it too far. She's not dead. It's more like she's found another cell of technomages and has already recruited them to our side by eating their leader."

Larry was about ready to unload on the group of ingrates when his phone rang. He glanced at the screen and confirmed that Brian was calling. As he moved to the back of the plane to have privacy for the call, he wondered if this was how Windlock had felt when he talked so much. It was one thing he had not expected about being a leader. When he'd been the underling, it had seemed fine to say whatever he thought because, at the end of the day, Windlock would either tell him to shut up or take responsibility for whatever gaffes he made. Now that he was a leader—if only for this mission—he realized he had to be much more controlled about what he said.

He'd have to talk to the team later but right now, he hoped the techie had good news. Or, better yet, that Kristen was on the line so she could reprimand her old team for making the dragons uncomfortable.

He answered the call.

"About time! That was, like, nine rings. Why are you wasting my time?"

"Why are you wasting mine?" he retorted. "What's going on with the boss?"

"Well…I have okay news but it's also bad news."

"Just get to it!"

"All right, here's what I've found so far. There are all kinds of pictures up on social media of Kristen at the welcome building at Mammoth Cave National Park."

"That makes sense. It's where the Dragon Council told her to go. Where did she go next?" Larry asked.

"I don't know if she did. The last photo posted is of her and a weirdo who calls himself Ranger Jay. It was taken inside the caverns. After that, there's nothing else about the Steel Dragon on the web," Brian explained.

"Okay, but you're our intel guy. You can't base everything off social media."

"Honestly, social media is about the best we have right now," the other man said defensively. "I tracked her phone's GPS signal. It shows her leaving Detroit and heading to Mammoth Cave. She stays in that area during what I call selfie-o-clock. After that, she moves about a half-mile away. The signal gets kind of buggy at that point and fades in and out, so my thought is that she was underground at that point and her phone was looking for signal."

"And then what?" the mage demanded.

"That's exactly what I'm saying. After that, her phone simply goes dark."

"Do you think she turned it off?"

"It wouldn't matter. The GPS still runs even if the phone's off. Unless she ran out of charge, but she shouldn't for another day or two."

"So you think she's there? In the caves themselves?" Larry asked.

"I don't want to make a guess and be wrong, but I think that's where you guys should go. If she's not there, her trail will be."

"Okay…it makes sense, Zed. Thanks."

"Yeah, no problem. Zed out."

"Sure."

"Oh, and Larry, please don't let anything happen to my sister, okay?"

"That's the last thing I want, kid, believe me."

"All right, then."

"Thanks, Zed," he responded but Brian had already hung up.

The mage took a deep breath and tried to settle his nerves before he addressed everyone. It helped to think about how Windlock used to behave when they were in high-stakes situations. He'd always valued how calm the old investigator had been and how he had been able to choose the most salient information and share it in the right order. As soon as a question would arise in Larry's brain, his boss already had the answer. He tried to anticipate the questions everyone might have, took a deep breath, and straightened his spine.

"Ranger Jay is gonna die," Keith said.

"My money is he has nothing to do with this," Butters interjected.

When he turned, every single member of his team was crammed into the doorway at the rear of the plane. So much for carefully shared details. They had heard the entire conversation.

"If Ranger Jay does have something to do with this, I'll blow his damn mailbox up," Hernandez said.

"We need to go to Mammoth Cave National Park," Larry said and tried not to sound as dumb as he felt.

"Yeah, the pilot knows," Emerald told him from the back of the crowd near the door. The mage sighed and decided that at least it was some comfort that he had a competent team. "I already told him to head to the nearest airport."

"All right then, maybe we should contact—"

"Timeflash?" Heartsbane interjected.

He shook his head in both disbelief and amazement. Were they all really this tight? He pushed through them and returned to the more comfortable main cabin of the jet.

"It's standard protocol for national monuments like this," Heartsbane explained to the confused humans. "Her powers let her repair damage done to inorganic objects. If we fuck this place up badly, she can put it together again."

"She can do that to a cave?" Keith asked. "Okay, yeah, I saw her restore the incinerator that made the fuel for the steam pipes under Detroit after Kristen knocked it onto Shadowstorm's head, but I thought she could only do that because it was, uh…brick and shit," he finished with a shrug as if he wished it to be known that he was fully aware he didn't have any clue what he was talking about.

"Oh, yeah," Emerald said. "We trapped a dragon once in Carlsbad Caverns—those are in New Mexico—and damn near brought the entire place down on this guy. Timeflash put it all back together once we dragged his corpse out."

Everyone turned to look at him with awkward expressions on their faces. All seemed to try to fight despair at the potential loss of their boss and friend.

"What? You all get to do this gallows humor stuff and I don't?" he fumed before he flung himself into a plush sofa with his arms folded.

"From what I understand, gallows humor involves a joke. We really did kill that guy," Heartsbane said.

She grinned but no one laughed.

"Okay, let's try to come up with some theories of what we're up against before we get there," Larry said, desperate to guide the conversation away from jokes about death from two beings who were basically invulnerable and immortal compared to a human. "Our fearless leader has no shortage of enemies. Does anyone have any theories on this one?"

Glum looks all around followed the question. No one had liked being reminded that dragons, mages, and common thugs had all tried to kill Kristen in the past.

"I think dragon," Beanpole ventured after a long moment. "Mages have thus far operated from urban centers. This seems more... primordial. I...I don't like it."

The mage didn't like it either. In fact, a pit grew steadily in his stomach when he considered the situation.

"What freaks me out is that we were in South America when she went off the map," Keith said and swirled a glass of champagne that had loosened his tongue. "Think about it. What if whoever sent us on that wild goose chase did it to get to her? If we lose her—"

"We won't lose her!" Larry almost yelled the words. He'd bolted to his feet when he spoke and released a gust of magical wind through the interior of the plane that rustled everyone's hair and clothes. "I'm sorry, but we won't."

Truthfully, he was damn scared. They had been away for a long time. There was no telling how deep Kristen might be in the cave or if she was even there. He hated to admit the possibility, but he had to accept that it was very likely she was already dead. Why else would the team have been lured to South America without her if not to remove her from the gameboard? If someone went through all that effort, surely they'd have finished it by now.

But Larry couldn't share those feelings, not when he headed this team. A leader needed to inspire confidence, not beg it of others. He was supposed to be brave even in the face of impossible odds. In short, a leader needed to lead.

"I'm sorry, but we won't," he reiterated, his voice calm. "I haven't known Kristen as long as any of you have, but I know she's tougher than any of us."

"As tough as steel," Emerald muttered.

"You're damn straight she's tough as steel," he affirmed. "Not stone, not oak, but steel. And I'm not talking about her nifty little skin. We all know a dragon can get through it and that if she is fighting a dragon in her steel form, she might already be seriously hurt."

Everyone swallowed hard and didn't contradict him.

The mage realized that maybe it hadn't been the best place to pause dramatically and take a breath, but he had to soldier on. "I'm talking about her spine and her heart. And I'm talking about her goddamn resolve. Whether she's trapped underground, fighting somewhere nearby, captured, or worse," *Dead* his mind screamed at him. *She might be dead.* He ignored the voice and set his face into a resolute expression.

"Wherever she is," he continued, "she's fighting for the people who need her and that's what we need to do right now too. It's simply a dumb coincidence that the person who needs help the most happens to be Kristen."

"Goddammit, Larry," Heartsbane said, her jaw tight and her eyes moist. "That was fucking beautiful."

Everyone nodded and slapped him on the back, high-fived, or started to pump themselves up. They didn't have long before they landed and it seemed that no one wanted to simply enjoy the luxuries of the private jet when every second took them closer to their united purpose.

The regular humans checked their weapons. They disassembled and reassembled them with intense, almost uncomfortable focus.

The dragons were no better. Their warmups for the fight to come involved sparring with each other at speeds no one could track. They stopped their impromptu workout only long enough to eat meat, which they consumed in vast quantities even in their human form.

Larry closed his eyes, pleased that he'd helped the team into the right state of mind and acutely aware that all the pressure still might very well end up on his shoulders. He was the only mage there. That was a simple fact. He had grown to rely on Amy's insane power levels —they all had—but she wasn't there now. She was in Texas, hopefully on a real mission. He assumed that if her team was also on a wild goose chase, Kristen's entire operation might as well let the war between dragons and mages break out. It was a sobering thought and he prayed to whatever power had given him the gift of magic that it wasn't the case. That aside, he was all the team there had.

Yes, his power was much greater now than it had been when he was shackled. And yes, he had a level of control that far surpassed Amy's, but what if it wasn't enough? Or if they met a cabal of mages stronger than him? What if they met a dragon who simply shackled him to block his powers and devoured him whole?

He shook his head. It might all happen but it wasn't like he would face it alone. He was part of the team Kristen had built—hell, he could be considered a founding member of this iteration of the team—and together, they would save her.

Or avenge her if that was all they had left by the time they discovered the truth of her situation.

Whatever they found, he needed to be ready. He pushed all thoughts from his mind and focused his energy. While he knew he wasn't capable of blasting away with an insane amount of energy, he did have focus. What he tried to do now as the plane raced ever closer to their destination was to focus all the power he had into as fine a point as he could. A marble, the nib of a pen, a needle, a mote of dust. He didn't use his power—he had limits and he knew them well—but he did see exactly how dense he could get it.

His reasoning was simple. If he couldn't obliterate a dragon, he could at least blow a hole in one.

"Sir, I've taken the liberty of ordering cars for your team," the pilot said. "We're coming in for a landing."

"You can cancel them," Larry said. "It'll be faster to fly. That is unless it'll be a problem, Heartsbane."

"It's fine," the dragon said and her face lacked its characteristic scowl. "I'll take Hernandez and Beanpole, though."

"I have Butters and Keith, then," Emerald said. "Larry, are you gonna need a ride?"

"Nah. I've been practicing. But look, how good are y'all at changing shape? If we wait to land and all that, it's gonna burn twenty minutes we didn't have three hours ago."

Emerald grinned. "Are you saying what I think you're saying?"

He nodded. "Windlock called it 'riding with the wind'—or he did once, anyway." He punched a callbox and gave the order to the pilot.

The man sighed but acknowledged the command.

In the next moment, he opened the door to the plane.

The wind rushed through the cabin and made the gust Larry had produced earlier look mild by comparison. That had been a breeze. This was a hurricane.

"Are you serious?" Butters demanded as the mage approached the open door.

"Deadly," he said.

"Shouldn't we at least have parachutes or something?" Keith asked.

"Nah," Emerald said. "It makes you harder to track. This way, we all plummet at the same speed."

"Plummet? Did you have to say that word?" Keith demanded and sounded frantic.

"Oh, is the Rookie afraid of heights?" Hernandez purred, walked up to him, and put an arm against the wall to lock him in.

"Maybe," he conceded.

"Oh, honey." Hernandez made it obvious to Larry at least that the two must have been more than coworkers or maybe even still were. "Will this make it better?" She kissed him on the mouth.

He returned it but that was his downfall. Hernandez caught him round the waist and power-lifted him onto her shoulder. "Never kiss a pretty girl who you know wants to throw you out of a plaaaaaaane!"

she shouted as she shoved Keith out the door and launched out after him.

"Stupid bitch," Heartsbane growled. "Change of plans. I'll take those two." She surged through the door, transformed to her dragon shape, and used her improved aerodynamics to get beneath the couple. Hernandez, unbelievably, had resumed making out with Keith and the dragon caught them in her claws before she tossed them unceremoniously so they landed on her back.

"Boys?" Emerald said to Butters and Beanpole.

The sniper darted a warning glance at his spotter. "There's no need to kiss me." He jumped and the other man followed.

"See you in the air." Emerald leapt after them and managed to get below them before he assumed his dragon form. He broke his skydiver's position as he transformed and caught them on his back.

Larry stepped to the door. He'd never done this before but Amy had taught him. By using his telekinetic abilities on his clothes, he could fly. He knew it was true and had seen her do it multiple times.

Still, it was easier said than done.

He hurried to the door, extended his foot, and stepped out into nothing.

The wind whipped at his robes before he gained control and registered the fact that he'd done it. He was flying, but the moment of joy was short-lived. The reason he had attempted this was because time was of the essence. There'd be time enough for joyrides later.

The mage fell into formation behind Emerald and Heartsbane as the team flew toward Mammoth Cave. It was a comfort that he seemed to be leading his team capably. They worked well together, followed his lead, but still acted independently, all good things in his book.

He only hoped he didn't have to keep the position because Kristen was already dead.

The thought spurred him forward and he urged the dragons to hurry. Every second counted.

CHAPTER FIFTY-ONE

Kristen barely had time to suck in half a breath before whatever had bulldozed into her shoved her under the surface. It had hit her hard and forced the precious air from her lungs. She struggled to rise, pumped her wings, and discovered that they didn't work quite as well underwater as they did on the surface. Her tail did, however, and she drove it through the cold water to propel herself upward to breach the surface.

She gulped air, her dragon body far more reliant on it than her human one. No sooner had she inhaled when something once again pounded into her back. Jolts of pain raced through her body and made it hard to focus on what she needed to do to survive—push toward the air and breathe.

It took willpower to look around underwater because it burned her eyes but she didn't want to go to the surface until she had some clue about what had happened. The water was turbulent from her splashes, but no boulders were visible sinking toward the bottom of the lake, and no broken stalactites to spear her were in evidence. If this was whoever had attacked her earlier using bombs to release debris on her, they had changed tactics.

Carefully, she scanned the water with her human senses. She could see well enough—better than a human in a swimming pool but not by much—but saw nothing. No mages in scuba gear, no aquatic dragons, and no demons from the deep.

The response from her other senses was even worse. She felt nothing but the cold of the lake and heard nothing but the pounding of her dragon heart in her ears. Although some dragons could smell underwater through gills, she could not. Even her aura reported no sense from a new life form and no buzz from a dragon perched upside down on the ceiling.

But something had struck her—and it had done so twice. This wasn't simply a random coincidence. It meant an organism of some kind and if she couldn't read its aura, it meant it was blocking her. That, in turn, implied intelligence. Which meant Kristen had to outthink whoever—which seemed more logical than whatever—the hell was out there.

Her lungs reminded her that while she could hold her breath for over ten minutes in her human form, her dragon body demanded far more oxygen and would allow her less time beneath the surface of this frigid lake. She pumped her tail and moved horizontally through the water, hoping that whoever had attacked her perhaps couldn't see through the turbulence she'd stirred. As expected, she didn't make it far before her lungs demanded insistently that she breathe. She listened intently and rose slowly, careful not to make much of a wake with her massive dragon form.

When she reached the surface, she poked only the tip of her snout out so her nostrils were able to draw in another sweet breath of air.

But her lungs were still filled with her spent breath as she hadn't wanted to make bubbles and tip off whatever was hunting her. Rather than inhaling—much as she wanted to—she blasted fire from her nose high enough to strike the ceiling and spread but not so much as to heat the stone enough to glow as it had before.

Then—consequences be damned—she sucked in another precious breath of air and dove underwater.

Kristen prepared herself to once again be pummeled by whoever lurked above the lake, but the strike didn't come. Not immediately, she reasoned cautiously because it might still come, but the delay was something, at least. It wasn't a victory, obviously, but a respite, however temporary, that she would try to use.

Was it possible that she scared her attacker off? Or had they simply not followed her to the other side of the pool? Had her blasts of fire dissuaded them from further attempts to hurt her? Or had she simply alerted whoever the damn thing was to exactly where she had moved to?

The answers to these questions could save her life. It was frustrating to have none of them.

She didn't know what else she could do except try to get out of there. Obviously, she couldn't attack an invisible foe who trapped her underwater. She was completely out of her element and none of her abilities seemed of use. Out of options, she continued to swim an inch or two beneath the surface and released little balls of flame out of her nose when she needed to draw breath.

Her reasoning suggested that whoever had brought her down there liked the dark, or else they'd have taken her somewhere else. They'd used a surprise attack against her, which implied that they might not be able to beat her in an outright contest of strength—or so she hoped. It meant that if she could get out of the caves, maybe she could face this opponent on a level playing field. Thus far, the only clue to a way out was the flow of the water.

Even with this simple plan, the execution proved difficult. She had to constantly shift her gaze from the ceiling to below so she could see the lurking foe and also her escape path. Not only that, she had to both refill her lungs and exhale small balls of fire, as that seemed to keep the unknown enemy at bay. She had to move swiftly through the water and also pay attention to the current, lest she overlook an exit.

All these factors made her progress slow, and she felt more and more anxious as she proceeded. *Swim, fireball, breathe, look at the ceiling, look below the water. Swim, fireball, breathe, look at the ceiling, look below the water.* She repeated the mental guide until there was a rhythm to the manic survivalist behavior. It became her mantra as she drew closer to the shore the water appeared to be moving toward. She settled into the repetitive cycle and seemed to find encouragement in it until something plummeted from a pool of darkness on the roof of the cave and careened into her yet again.

This time, Kristen caught a glimpse of her attacker, although it answered none of her questions about their identity. It looked as if the shadows on the ceiling had coalesced into a massive blob—like one of the drips that formed the ubiquitous stalactites—only this one was ten thousand times their size. Rather than being filled with dissolved minerals, it looked like it was filled with nothing but the night itself.

As expected, when they made impact with her back, they thrust her deep beneath the water. Something sliced into her and the pain was intense and somehow even colder than the water through which she swam. The blob pushed off her and left her at the bottom of the lake to thrash in the darkness.

Although she couldn't see much of anything, she knew she was bleeding. She could sense it in the water through pits in the front of her snout she hadn't even known she possessed. The light was dim but her scales were pale in color so she could see the clean injuries on her flank that sliced through her scales like they were bologna.

Without a doubt, they had been inflicted by the claw of a dragon.

She searched the water for her dark attacker, convinced now that it was indeed a dragon.

Unfortunately, she felt much worse about her odds if that were the case.

Kristen had hoped mages were behind this and that they had attempted to lure her into the world's greatest trap. If that had been the case, she had already as good as thwarted them.

If it was a dragon down there—a dragon who had effectively hidden their aura—she might be in serious trouble. Her logic had previously assured her that the reason she hadn't been able to sense any auras was because the mages had developed some new kind of cloaking spell. It made sense. Constance had never been easy to track via aura. A dragon who could hide their aura so perfectly was a graver threat, if only because she couldn't guess at their motives.

Mages would have actively tried to kill her. A trap like this would have been meant as a funnel to draw her to where they could launch a concerted magic attack.

A dragon with the ability to become darkness could have killed her long before.

She returned to the surface but remained in the same place and alternated between breaths and fireballs released from her nostrils. That was the only thing that seemed to keep the dragon away. It had to be a dragon because nothing else made sense. A mage would have shot her by now. That was what this war of theirs was about—using dragon-based ammunition to kill dragons.

But what dragon wanted her dead now? She had killed Shadowstorm and his mother Obscura in brutal combat and had eliminated the dragon assassin Death as well. Later, she had saved the North American Council twice and the Full Dragon Council as well. What dragon was so determined to kill the woman who was intent on saving dragon kind?

Something clicked in her brain. Maybe it was the council member who had so unsettled her, she thought as she continued to breathe and launch fireballs toward the ceiling. That would explain how they'd directed her there and managed to separate her and her team. Hell, it might also explain how their technomage foes in Florence had always seemed to be one step ahead of them.

There were factions of dragon society that wanted a war. They believed that the herd of humanity had grown too numerous and must be culled. These factions would work with or against mages as long as it served their own ability to amass even more power.

It only made sense that one of these dragons was on a council. Their society was rife with the cruelty of inequality and the reductive logic of racism. Why wouldn't a council member on one continent not work to further those goals? It didn't even have to be a North American, she reasoned. Merely someone with an obscene amount of power who craved even more.

And whoever it was, they were toying with her. That, more than anything else—more than the frigid water or the wound that felt like a dagger of ice—made her blood run cold.

If it was a member of a Dragon Council, they had access to her reports and intel. They had known her team was looking at Texas but had also scanned the horizon for action in South America. Not only that, but they had also known how to get Kristen to Mammoth Cave. They were playing a game and she was merely a pawn. Logically, they could have killed her the second they trapped her beneath an avalanche and knocked her unconscious but instead, seemed to want to take her apart slowly.

But why? What kind of person did this?

Not a person, she reminded herself. People lived a century if they were lucky and achieved immortality only through their children. They had goals with timeframes established for lifetimes. People feared others, cared for others, and saw the world as something more than a source of entertainment.

It was not a person hunting her but a dragon of unknowable age. The being could have been planning her downfall since before she knew she was a dragon. They were a beast who cared only for their own aspirations and were willing to burn the world for a little more fresh meat.

In a word, she faced a monster and was trapped in there with them —a monster of fiendish intelligence with godlike powers. They not only used darkness to hunt but also to plan and plot and scheme. Without a doubt, they saw her as little more than an insect whose wings they could pluck at their leisure.

And she was trapped in their lair—or their playground, which was even more chilling.

She had to turn the odds against this dragon of the dark, but how was that even possible when she couldn't so much as take a breath deep enough to blast a plume of fire without being attacked?

How was she supposed to survive this?

CHAPTER FIFTY-TWO

The truck didn't slow until it was in the quarry itself. Even then, rather than stop conventionally, the driver threw it into a sideways skid. He only braked at the last possible moment so the wheels kicked up massive amounts of dust and pebbles as the vehicle careened toward the three team members.

Amy floated a foot above the ground, Drew stood three feet behind her, and Lumos sat in front of her. As the dust and pebbles rocketed toward her, she used her abilities to make the dust billow out of her way in dramatic spirals like waves trying to pound against a lighthouse but only breaking on the rocky shore at its base.

Although she felt bad about it, she didn't afford the dragon the same courtesy. She let the dirt coat him, which made his tattered suit look even worse. He flinched when the pebbles struck him and went so far as to whimper when one struck his face.

She hoped he was simply faking but reminded herself that she knew he was. He was a dragon, after all. As hard as it was to acknowledge, she knew what it took to kill one and it was about a hundred times more than a collision with a truck, let alone pebble.

Still, she wouldn't let Lumos get hurt, so when the camouflage-painted truck looked like it very well might bulldoze into the dragon who sat bound and cuffed in the dirt, she stopped it with her mind. The vehicle lurched on its jacked-up suspension and raised off its driver's side wheels before it settled again. The lone star on its red, white, and blue flag above the back flapped as if in protest.

That none of the people fell out of the back after being stopped so suddenly confirmed her suspicion that some of these men were mages.

It made things more difficult, although honestly, compared to the slew of shotguns, rifles, and AR-15s the men carried, having a few mages among them didn't exactly intimidate her much more.

If these guys wanted to kill her, she wouldn't let them, of course, but she didn't think the possible outcomes were worth betting on.

"What the fuck are you doing here? Did they cancel your fucking flight to California?" the driver of the truck demanded. It was Colt.

Amy swallowed. It was time to see if Drew's gamble about establishing an alibi checked out.

"I am here to find the mages I thought were in the area. What are a couple of dragon sympathizers like you doing here?" she said and tried to sound like one of the evil queens from a kid's movie. Her first choice was Ursula but she thought she'd come off more like the Wicked Witch of the West.

"Dragon lovers?" Vince demanded and sounded as if she had insinuated that he enjoyed performing sexual acts with farm animals. "You were the one eating brisket with that piece of shit." He spat at Lumos' prone form.

"Only to ascertain if he really was a dragon," she said and made her voice sound like she could barely control her fury. She tried to think about Dorothy and her stupid little dog too. "Something you should have known but did nothing about. I saw you at the dance hall. While this dragon used his aura to persuade your women into dancing, what did you do about it? Nothing. While he tricked your bartender into giving out free drinks, what did you do? Nothing. At. All."

"We saw you there too!" Colt said. "Why didn't you do anything about him then if you knew he was a dragon?"

Amy floated to Lumos and delivered a swift kick to his ribs. He responded to the phony blow, rolled over, and clutched his sides. "I delivered." She sneered. "I captured this beast in the hopes that the cell here would be more competent than the three stupid rednecks you three are turning out to be."

"Who the fuck are you to call us rednecks?" Vince demanded.

"I will be the world's foremost dragon hunter," she said. She'd thought about this and decided it was the best way to go about infiltration—with big, broad, bold lies—but wow, did it feel weird.

"The fuck you is!" Dusty seemed to agree with the alibi lacking credibility as he aimed a shotgun at her gut.

"I wouldn't do that if I were you," Drew said from behind her.

"Are you her bodyguard or some shit?" Colt demanded.

"Her cleaner. Do you know what a cleaner is?" he asked. He didn't wait long enough for anyone to reply before he answered his own question. "A cleaner picks your bodies up after you do something stupid like attack the world's most powerful mage."

"I know who you are," another man said from the back of the truck. "You're the mage who fought Constance in Canada. There's a whole fucking video of you fighting her. Give me one reason why I shouldn't fill your brain with lead right now."

"I'll give you five," Amy said smartly. "One. The bullet will never reach me. None of them will. If you saw the video, you know that. Two. I know Constance. She talked to me before the Steel Dragon bitch appeared. It was she who told me to come here if I needed help."

She took a breath and continued. "Three. I. Have. A. Fucking. Dragon. He can't transform into his other body right now because when he was transporting me under the Steel Dragon's orders, I broke free of my cuff and put it on him. Consider him a gift, a token of— well, let's not say goodwill but of my commitment to this cause."

"Four. Dragons killed my parents." She let her voice crack on that one. "I don't know how much of my story reached you here, but my powers were activated when I was attacked by two dragons. Not even attacked, honestly. My parents were merely collateral damage to them. I hate dragons. They're arrogant, entitled monsters—worse than the politicians in Washington." That statement drew a few nods.

She didn't know much about Texas, but she knew they didn't like the Feds. "And Five. I've met the biggest threat to your organization. I've spent the last few weeks with the Steel Dragon herself. If you want to know how to bring her down, I'm your girl."

One of the men in the back of the truck chuckled. "Well, shit," It sounded like shee-it with his accent. "That's one hell of a sales pitch. Even if we want it to be true, though, how can we be sure?"

"She's not lying about him being a dragon or his powers being dampened," said another man. Amy sensed him and could feel magic. Not all of them were mages, then, but this one was.

"So you really are that girl from the TV?" Colt asked and sounded a little awed.

"She is," Drew confirmed.

"Well…I don't know. That sounds like a damn good person to have on board," Colt responded.

"I guess you know our identities so it's not like we can let you go," Dusty said. She didn't know if the young boys merely talked too much or if there was a reason why they seemed to be in charge of this little squad of men.

A ripple of conversation passed through the group before Vince quieted them. "We'll take you to meet our cell leader," he said. Amy sensed something she hadn't noticed before. He seemed to have a touch of magic ability. That must be why he was in charge but it also meant his two friends were probably little more than thugs. "He can decide whether to kill you along with this dragon you captured or if we could use another pretty face."

"If that's what you're after, I'm sure they'll bring me on," Amy said. "From the looks of it, the only time pretty would be used to describe your moms would be if someone called them pretty damn ugly."

"What the fuck did you say?" Colt drew a handgun from his belt that she immediately yanked from his hand. She spun it in the air and clubbed him across the forehead with it.

"Any more takers?" she asked, looked around, and smiled.

A few disgruntled looks fixed on her and a couple of men spat, but no one drew a gun. Neither Vince nor the other mage attempted to use any of their abilities. All right, she decided. She had at least shown them she was powerful.

"Your…cleaner"—Vince sneered the word as if he didn't believe it—"can ride in the back with the dragon and the rest of the boys. You can come up front with me and help me work the stick."

"You can take the dragon," Amy said and lifted Lumos unceremoniously off the ground with her telekinesis to drop him roughly in the back of the truck. Truly, she caught him before he hit the bed and made the suspension rock so it looked like she'd let him land on his face. "But my cleaner stays with me."

"Ain't gonna be enough room for all us in the front seat." Vince smiled the cruel smile of a man with privilege over the law taking power over a woman who had nothing to do with it. It was a smile that had been used through the centuries, and she hated it. "What with the stick," he finished as if he tried to set a record for how sleazy a human being could truly be.

Amy had already demonstrated her power but apparently, it would take a little extra to get through the vacant spaces where synapses should have been in the young man's brain.

She reached out with her powers, located the largest, flattest rock in the area, and ripped it from the ground as easily as a ten-year-old could lift a stone to skip it across a pond.

The one she had selected wasn't flat and thin. The top was as flat as a driveway and big enough to fit two cars. The bottom of the huge boulder was rounded, which made it look like a giant had sliced the top fifth of the world's largest potato off with a massive knife and planted it in the ground for it to petrify. It levitated from beyond the ridge that framed the quarry pit and came to rest gently beside her. The rounded point on the bottom barely touched the ground. A thousand pebbles swirled to form a flowing staircase around it that she walked up.

Then, as her finishing touch, she scooped Drew up and deposited him on top of the stone like he was nothing but her pet.

It might have been too much—Amy knew it was too much—yet these men had come seeking power and she made sure that was what they found. She wasn't so naïve to think they had expected a girl. They'd doubtlessly expected a venerable old man with a long white beard or a muscle-bound beef-head. Instead, they'd found her with her recently pierced nose and pulled-down beanie. That she was different than their expectations was all the more reason to be sure they knew the extent of her power. Or, rather, what she was capable of accomplishing merely for her convenience.

The girl also knew that whatever she did now would only grow in the men's minds.

"Lead on," she said from the top of the half-ton boulder she now used as a flying carpet.

A few of the men nodded and most of them swallowed hard. The mage who'd spoken out earlier banged twice on the roof of the truck to signal the driver, and they drove away to take her, the dragon prisoner, and her cleaner to their secret lair.

CHAPTER FIFTY-THREE

Larry wasn't sure what he had expected to see at Mammoth Cave National Park. He'd prepared himself for the scorched earth often present in the aftermath of a dragon battle and thought maybe there would be bodies—dragon, mage, and human. In plain and simple terms, he had expected destruction of some kind.

It was a shock—although not necessarily an unpleasant one—to see people walking the trails above the park as if nothing was wrong.

"Are we sure this is the right location?" Heartsbane yelled over the wind before she banked to begin a slow circuit of the grounds. Down below, children and tourists gawked and screamed and pointed at the two dragons and a mage who glided so effortlessly above them.

The mage's flying skills were not quite to the level where he felt like he could retrieve his phone to check his GPS, so he landed like he had done a few times to check their position.

He looked at the dragons. "This is it."

Emerald and Heartsbane tucked their wings—and drew screams of terror and glee from the humans on their backs—and plummeted toward the earth. They extended their wings at the last minute to catch the air and land gently.

Hernandez and Keith cheered while Beanpole dismounted in a

huff and threw up the lunch he'd eaten on the jet. The mage moved toward a hill. According to the GPS on his phone, he wasn't far—maybe fifty meters? He saw nothing except rolling grass and the fading flowers of fall on the hillside. And, unfortunately, tourists armed with cameras.

Larry sighed. This was the last thing he needed right now.

"Butters, I want you and the rest of SWAT to maintain a perimeter. I don't want anyone on this hill at all. This is the last place Kristen was seen and she might, uh..." He wanted to inspire confidence in his team but he also didn't want to spark false hope or offer a hypothesis that might encourage them all to start to make false assumptions that could blunt their mystery-solving skills.

"Not a problem, sir. We'll maintain the perimeter and ask around. If any of these people have anything to offer, we'll find out."

"Good, thank you," he said as the humans departed and left him with only the dragons.

"Do either of you sense anything?" he asked. "The GPS sent us here but I don't see any signs. I guess we should assume she was standing on this hill when her phone broke."

"Or that she was under it," Emerald said.

Heartsbane nodded at the suggestion, although her eyes were closed and she was breathing deeply. Still in dragon form, she looked like she was meditating rather than searching for the body of their friend. She inhaled and released a slow breath, then shook her head in frustration. "I can't sense her aura at all. I don't think she's near here anymore."

This was exactly what he had been afraid of. He sighed heavily. If they lost Kristen, this whole mission—the whole organization she'd put together—would unravel. And if Heartsbane couldn't sense her, it was time for him to use the skills he had developed working as a forensics mage for Windlock.

He reminded himself that he had specialized in sensing the traces of auras of dead dragons.

Larry took a deep breath and reached out with his powers, desperate to find some clue of Kristen and simultaneously hoping he found nothing at all. The first thing he noticed was that she had indeed been there.

She was a powerful dragon, and while she lacked finesse with aura, he could sense it but not there. It seemed instead that the traces of her came from the visitor center.

"Anything yet?" Emerald asked.

"She…she didn't stand on this hill," Larry said. "She was here—or there, rather." He gestured at the visitor center and entrance to the cave.

"That has to mean she entered the cave," Heartsbane suggested.

The mage was inclined to agree. "I'll try once more," he said. "Now that I know she was here, I'll reach out farther. This might take me a few minutes. You two try to find clues."

"You got it," Emerald said and Larry couldn't help but smile. Thanks to Kristen, these dragons respected his orders and followed them. What would happen if she died? Would they all rally around their fallen leader or would they fracture, a sculpture portending equality shattered before it could be finished?

He emptied his mind of everything but his breathing. As he inhaled and exhaled, he expanded his tendrils of probing magic every time he blew air from his mouth and focused them like laser beams when he inhaled through his nose. No, Kristen had never stood on this hill, but she had been near there and with people. He could sense her presence on some of them. Campers mostly. Okay, that was good. It meant that when she had arrived, she'd been all right. He sensed one trail that seemed to snake under the earth, but he lost it before he could follow it to its end. It was too faint and too old to be of much use.

But it was also the last clue of her aura anywhere. Larry refocused his tendrils of energy into the subterranean space beneath his feet. He dug deeper and deeper and imagined his magic like drops of water that could find paths through the stone as they looked for some sense of her passage.

Despite his efforts, he found nothing. There was simply too much earth and stone between him and the faint aura that a dragon left behind. He inhaled sharply and tried finally to sense the terror one often felt before they were slain. If he could find that spike of negative energy, he could at least direct his team to find a body.

It almost surprised him that he didn't find a spike of pain. Instead, deep beneath the earth, he found the steely resolve of her tireless optimism and determination. Its presence confirmed what his heart and mind had desperately wanted to find.

"Kristen's alive!" he shouted. The cool, professional demeanor he'd struggled so hard to project shattered as he let tears of relief trickle down his cheeks.

Emerald, Heartsbane, and the humans working the perimeter cheered and ran toward him.

"She's way down there, but she's alive!" He was talking at a mile a minute but he didn't care. "I reckon she went through the entrance and encountered something down there—not the Dragon Council, obviously. Something must have trapped her. She's..." He reached out again and closed his eyes in concentration. "She's trying to do something. I can feel her focus. I don't sense anything else, though—not dragon, mage, or otherwise."

Larry looked at his team and schooled his face into a positive expression. Now they knew where she was, they had to determine how to reach her. He was about to broach this question to the team when a park ranger spoke.

"I told you she was down there, didn't I? I gave her a tour myself."

"May I introduce to you the one and only Ranger Jay?" Butters said to the mage.

"A pleasure, really," Ranger Jay said, extended a meaty hand, and grasped Larry's in a deathlike vice of a handshake.

"Larry Brockton," he said and nodded at the man to continue as he wondered if he should have introduced himself simply as Mage Larry.

"A real pleasure, sir, especially if you're a friend of the Steel Dragon's." The ranger had yet to stop pumping his hand. Larry extricated it and felt as if the bones within had been shattered. "Although I have to say," he continued, "that if you all want a tour, I'll have to insist on a few other rangers coming with us. We were about halfway through when she wandered off. It was weird. I didn't even notice until I was almost back at the entrance."

Heartsbane smiled. "That's good. It means she's been practicing her aura like I told her to."

Ranger Jay flushed crimson beneath his beard. "Are you telling me that dragon used her aura power on me? Well, hot damn. They'll never believe any of this in Pig."

Emerald shook his head, his arms folded. "If we're going through all this trouble because Red went and got herself lost in a cave, I'll laugh at her forever."

Larry wasn't able to joke about all this yet. They'd been sent on a fool's errand to South America and she was still beyond their reach. He saw the humans had the same concerns. They were used to thinking of their loved ones as mortal but dragons were not. The dragons had probably expected to find a blackened landscape there with a massive corpse still smoldering. Now that those expectations had not come to fruition, they were hardly concerned. The humans knew that death could come in many forms and that despite Kristen's steel skin, she was a human at her core.

He gasped when a change came to Kristen's aura. She went from stoic determination to the agony of sheer pain. He recoiled from the intensity of it like someone had stabbed him in the back with a dagger made of ice. It was far more intense than the remnants of aura left by a dead dragon and meant she was definitely alive but suffering. Was she fighting or being tortured?

"What the hell came over you?" Butters asked, his eyes narrowed.

"It's...Kristen's aura. She's badly hurt." He didn't want to let go of her aura but also wanted to distance himself from it. The pain was so intense, he could practically feel it himself.

"How long would it take us to get to where you last saw her?" Hernandez demanded of Ranger Jay.

"Moving at a good speed? Twenty minutes. But wait—can you tell where she is? She's below us?"

"Twenty minutes is too long," Larry said and pointed absentmindedly to where he felt Kristen was. Her pain had not abated and he didn't feel the surge of anger, confidence, and determination that often came from her aura when she was in a battle she thought she could win.

"Oh, shit," Ranger Jay said and didn't seem to have any problem with inserting himself into the team. "Well, there might be a shortcut or something. Can you tell where she is? I know these caves better than most folk."

The mage allowed himself a sigh of relief. This was the break they needed. If the man could get them to her quickly, they would have a chance to save her.

He gestured over the hill. "She's about a kilometer that way and down maybe three hundred meters. Something like that, anyway."

All gazes drifted to the ranger. Every single one of them let their hope shine through. This was it. If he could get them down there, they'd save the woman who had saved all of them too many times to count.

"Well, shit," the man said and looked crestfallen. "Are you sure?"

"I am." Larry tried not to let fear enter his voice and failed.

"That's where the water drains out. There ain't no way in there. The stone's too soft, not safe to walk on, and if you break it, the flow of water would change. That's how you drown—exploring that way."

"I thought you said she was alive?" Emerald said. Dragon ferocity bled into his voice and almost made Larry fear him as he had been taught to fear dragons for years.

But no longer, he reminded himself sternly. He was now a free mage and if Kristen was able to lead the world into a peaceful revolution, he might even be Emerald's equal one day. "She is alive but—" He winced. Something had struck Kristen again and he sensed the same icy pain, fear, and confusion from her rather than the confidence that would indicate she was fighting back. "But she won't be for much longer."

The team began to bicker about what to do next. The two dragons wanted Ranger Jay to show them the way in. Emerald said he'd carry the man and that they could use their dragon speed to drastically reduce the transit time.

Butters asked about ways in through the river and wondered if someone—his suggestions were Beanpole or Keith—could perhaps scuba up and find her from the water. Hernandez merely wanted to blow a hole into the cave system, an idea the ranger protested vociferously until Timeflash landed and transformed into her human form. He didn't know she could undo any damage that was done to the cave and was simply dumbstruck every time a new dragon arrived.

"Seriously, do y'all mind if I get a selfie? They never gonna believe me in Pig. Never."

Everyone ignored him.

Timeflash approached Larry. "Is she alive?"

He nodded.

"Do we have a plan to get her?"

When he nodded again, everyone stopped their bickering and turned to look at him.

The mage took a deep breath. He knew what he had to do. There was only one option when it came down to it, but it terrified him. He had been shackled by Windlock within weeks of becoming a mage and had never explored his full powers. As weak as it might sound to admit it, being limited had never bothered him.

Larry knew full well what happened to mages who overexerted themselves when they performed magic unbound. He had picked up the mess more than once, although blowing himself to pieces was one of his lesser concerns. Mages who did that to themselves usually died because they didn't know how to channel their magic effectively. He at least knew how to do that.

What he didn't know was exactly what he was capable of. He had seen what Amy could do and it terrified him. She could pick cars up like they were nothing but toys, move trees like they were twigs, and had killed two dragons without meaning to because of her formidable powers.

While he didn't think he had anything approaching the level she did, what if—in trying to do this—he made a mistake? Operating under Windlock had put hard limits on his powers. He had been able to work within those limits because he knew he wouldn't hurt anyone.

He no longer had that net to protect the world from his abilities. What if—in his effort to get to Kristen—he crushed someone with a misplaced boulder? What if he did some kind of structural damage to the cave itself and the whole area collapsed to kill Kristen and droves of tourists?

Larry realized everyone was still staring at him.

"Do you have a plan or should we start digging?" Keith asked.

The mage forced a smile. "Actually, that's what I'm going to do."

His human teammates looked confused and the dragons perplexed, although Timeflash seemed to have some sense of exactly what he would attempt and nodded encouragingly. Ranger Jay was oblivious but he was excited all the same.

"Hell yeah! Do you mind if I record this?"

"Go for it," he said, "but you'll need a zoom lens. I want all of you to stay here. I've never done anything like this before and honestly, so much could go wrong. I can't lose Kristen, not when I have the ability to save her, but I don't want any of you to be hurt either. This is new for me and I can't even begin to estimate the results."

"You've never tried anything like digging before?" Keith asked, still confused.

Larry tapped the side of his head, the source of his magic powers. "Like digging with a telekinetic shovel."

"Don't sell yourself short." Timeflash smiled. "It's more like an industrial drill."

"Right," he said and elevated himself with his magic powers.

His team looked at him with hard expressions. They supported him in this—what other choice did they have?—but they knew the risks.

The assembled crowd of tourists, though, had no idea what he was about to attempt. They cheered as this man in a robe levitated and flew a kilometer away from them. He glanced at his team again and shook his head when he realized they had joined the cheers.

He only hoped he could do something worth the applause.

The mage landed directly above where he could sense Kristen's aura. It felt much stronger there, which was good as it meant the lateral distance he'd covered across the surface put him almost in position. He reached out with his magic senses and tried to feel how far she was.

Another jolt of pain made him curse and he knew he had to hurry.

Still, the pain was an easy thing to sense and told him he was perhaps two hundred and fifty to three hundred feet above her. It was hard to be certain because the stone was porous and thus not a uniform density. He knew the direction, though, and it wasn't like he would be able to do it with one blow.

It would take a concerted effort and everything he had. "Be ready to move!" he shouted, confident that the dragons could hear him with their heightened auditory abilities. "I'll get through this but I don't know what I'll have left when I'm done."

Larry said that as much for his own confidence as to tell them his plan. It was only porous stone, limestone that had eroded. He could do this because he had to. The thought of expending so much magic terrified him but he had no choice. Kristen would do it for him if she could and he had to do it for her.

He reached deep and pulled all his power from every well of untapped potential he could find within him. With every drop, trace, and speck harnessed, he directed it into a spinning vortex of force in front of him. The whirlwind spun faster, tightened to amplify the force, and continued to increase in speed. When he sensed it was ready, he directed it into the ground but lowered it in rather than striking the surface.

Even with this gentle start to such a powerful force tool, the earth responded dramatically. The turf at the top of the hill shredded. The pieces of grass ignited as they were flung aside, fueled by an energy that might have looked like wind to the people filming it on a hill a kilometer away. He knew, though, that it was far closer to the raw energy of heat and pressure than it was wind.

The earth beneath the turf was ripped away next and geysered up and out, a gout of soil that he hardly even noticed. He was focused on the stone below and when he struck it with his vortex of force, it resisted him.

His teeth clenched, he dug deeper and spun the vortex faster, concentrating all the energy on the bottom of the spinning cone of energy and the point that touched the stone.

For a minute, he made no progress. His energy dislodged a few loose pieces of stone and grit but not much else.

Another stab of pain from Kristen overwhelmed his frustration and he refocused on his task with grim determination.

Larry thrust his energy into the stone and heated it until it glowed. After a few moments, it came loose and was hurled into his vortex and thrown skyward to rain down as molten stone. It didn't hit him—his magic instinctively protected him from its effects—but he was damn proud that he'd ordered everyone else to keep back.

It meant he could continue his attempt without having to worry about anyone. Now that he knew what to do, he increased the intensity of his power, heated the stone to loosen its molecular structure, and ripped it out before he cast it aside. Sweat broke out on his brow as he cut down two feet, then five, then ten. He gritted his teeth. This would be harder than he had anticipated—much harder—but that didn't matter.

He owed it to Kristen to not give up on her, not while he still drew breath, so he dragged even more deeply from the well of power within him and threw everything he had into digging the hole.

Even if it burnt his magic out, even if it ruptured his heart, and even if he had to die to succeed, he would break through so his team could rescue their leader.

CHAPTER FIFTY-FOUR

Kristen tread water and kept her nostrils positioned to pop fireballs at the ceiling while she attempted the impossible task of looking for the exit to this underground lake with her eyes. Not being a brachiosaurus, this was impossible. But even in the few glimpses she had, she wasn't able to make out any wide, yawning, dragon-sized tunnels for her to escape through. It wasn't surprising, of course. If there were any, there'd be much less water in there.

Ultimately, it meant escape would not be easy.

She had to face the fact that she would have to fight an opponent she could not even see let alone assess for strengths and weaknesses.

There was nothing she could do about that. Her hidden opponent intended to face her when she wasn't at her strongest. Yes, she had eaten and rebuilt some of her strength, but treading water in the cold while releasing fireballs slowly inevitably sapped her reserves.

Aside from anything else, she didn't want to simply wait for the unknown dragon who hid in the blob of darkness. It was better to face the bastard head-on.

Her mind made up, she changed direction and headed toward shore, keeping the balls of fire going until she was close enough to touch the ground under the water again. When her feet felt the silty lakebed, she couldn't help but draw a deep breath of air in satisfaction at having something solid beneath her feet.

It seemed that was exactly what the dragon had waited for. As soon as she breathed in, something bit her tail. She knew it was a bite because she could feel multiple teeth and knew it was a dragon because each tooth punctured her flesh. Her first instinct was to try to whip her tail free, but the dragon tightened his jaws and gave her no chance to try to break free before he hauled her under the water.

Kristen managed to suck in a precious breath of air before her back legs were yanked out from under her and her jaw struck the bottom of the lake. She was dragged into the depths before she could even try to find purchase and resist.

As the pressure of the water grew around her, her rage blossomed as well. She was tired of this shit. Whoever this dragon was, he had officially pissed her off. A real fight was one thing, but this cowardly, hide beneath the surface and never attack except from behind was pathetic.

It was time to see exactly how much this asshole really knew about the Steel Dragon.

She jerked her tail hard as if in an attempt to free it once more and the dragon responded as she expected. It pulled hard and used her effort to get away to exacerbate the wounds caused by its teeth.

Her purpose, this time, was not to escape from her attacker. She let the dragon yank on her tail—much as it hurt—so she was pulled deeper into the water. Once she achieved that painfully won burst of momentum, she changed into her human body but made sure to retain her steel skin.

Without a tail clamped between her adversary's jaws, she was free to use her dragon strength powered legs to propel herself toward her foe.

Kristen was at a loss as to how to describe him—except that some deep instinct insisted that her adversary was male rather than female. The beast existed within the darkness of the cave as an even deeper black—like the ink of a squid spilled in the darkest depths of the ocean. He billowed and filled the water, making no shapes and yet moving as if controlled by some hideous intelligence.

Although the suggestion of no shape wasn't quite accurate. Near the center of the cloud, the unmistakable jaws of a dragon were vaguely visible. They snapped at the water, trying to find the tail that had been snagged between them only a moment before. It was interesting that this dragon didn't rely on his human form any more than any of the others she'd fought did and hadn't expected her to transform into what it saw as a weaker shape. That weaker shape, fortunately, allowed her to rocket toward the still confused dragon and strike it with a steel fist.

She drove her steel knuckles into the tip of his snout near the nostrils and the pits she hadn't known could sense blood until recently. Exactly as she had expected, the blow inflicted significant pain.

Unfortunately, it only made the snout and jaws of the dragon dissipate into the inky blackness that seemed to make up the rest of his body. The entire mass moved away and made her think of a jellyfish or a squid moving through ink. That, more than anything else she had yet to learn about this dragon, terrified her.

The way he moved proved that he didn't need to keep his body in the form of a dragon or a human. He could take the amorphous shape of a cloud, both in air and underwater. She had battled a dragon with a power that was merely a fraction of this and it had been damn hard. Shadowstorm had been able to extend the period between his two forms so he could move through spaces that neither a dragon nor a human could fit through. It had been a tough fight, but she had won it because she had been able to overcome the limitations of his powers.

This foe didn't seem to have those same limitations.

Kristen had to get out of the water. If her enemy could stay down there and continue to drag her into depths time after time, she would never win. This was the only option she could see so she took her dragon shape, shed her steel skin, and propelled herself to the surface with every ounce of strength she had.

She burst through and this time, risked a full breath of air. Foregoing the balls of fire as she swam to the shore, she used her tail, her wings, and all four of her legs to drive herself forward. She reached the edge of the lake and heaved her dragon form out of the water without being attacked.

Had her blow stunned the dragon badly enough to slow him or had he simply decided to bide his time again?

There was no way to know, but either way, she didn't think her dragon form was the right choice for this fight. Although the subterranean room she stood in was massive, most of it was taken up by the lake itself. There wasn't enough room for her to fly. Hell, there wasn't enough for her to stretch her wings. Meanwhile, her enemy could become a literal cloud. A fight in tight quarters would only favor him, no matter how powerful she was in her steel dragon form. For whatever reason, her instincts still favored the presumption that her opponent was male, not female.

Quickly, she transformed into her human body and scanned the darkness for him. It was like looking for a blade of grass in a meadow or a tree in a forest. All she knew about this dragon was that he could take the form of a dark cloud, but the entire cavern was filled with darkness. He could be anywhere, she thought and tried not to panic as she backed away from the shore.

Her gaze moved constantly—up, down, anywhere, and everywhere in hopes of locating her foe. Despite her intense focus, she saw nothing. No shadows lurked within the shadows and no darkness surged toward her throat. She knew the dragon hadn't retreated. He was merely biding his time like the enormous catfish at the bottom of the lake, waiting for his prey to make a mistake, to lose her balance, or to stop focusing for a second. Then, he would strike and the hunt would be over.

Kristen's back struck the wall and she almost screamed. She was so desperate to locate her adversary that she had forgotten that her slow retreat took her somewhere.

If this was psychological warfare, the shadow dragon was winning. She looked left, then right, and searched for some kind of advantage or anything she could use to defend herself. Stalagmites and columns abounded where the dragon could hide in his inky state and pools of dark and rock shells were interspersed randomly between them. Her gaze traversed a crevasse that might be large enough for her body.

She knew an advantage when she saw one and darted toward the fissure in the cave wall. Her first hope was that the crack led somewhere and out of this damn place, but that hope was dashed as soon she squeezed into the space and almost immediately touched the back wall.

Still, although it didn't provide an escape, it might provide her with cover against the shadow. It provided sufficient space for her human body but there was no way a dragon could fit inside the tight nook.

Although an attack had yet to come, she turned her skin to steel and immediately felt a drain of her energy. Normally, she had more than sufficient and barely noticed the cost of changing forms. After so much time in this cave with minimal nutrition while her powers were constantly pushed and stretched, she felt the loss of energy like a punch to the gut. She might be able to change to her dragon form once or twice more and maybe use her fire breath a precious few times, but before long, she'd be out. Even using those tactics could prove to be fatal because if she depleted her resources too much, she wouldn't have the energy to use her dragon healing abilities.

Fortunately, her foe no longer seemed interested in a protracted war of attrition. The entrance to the crevasse she had squeezed into darkened and before she could so much as raise her hands to block, a dragon claw extended through the opening and raked across her shoulders.

Kristen kicked with—she knew from experience—enough force to knock down a three-inch wooden oak door, but the cursed dragon simply disincorporated his claw and she only kicked the air.

She kept her guard up now as her assailant beat savagely at her forearms and raked her again and again with cruel strikes of his talons. When she blocked those, he used his tail against her. The tip appeared from the inky cloud, as sharp as a spear and connected to what looked like black scaly skin stretched painfully tight over bone. He managed to deliver a strike to her face before she caught the tail and squeezed with her crushing steel grip.

The dragon yelped and turned to his inky black form of nothingness once more, and she had a moment to breathe.

A part of her began to think she could hold her enemy at bay long enough for—she didn't know what. Long enough for her friends to rescue her? That seemed less and less likely. Long enough to learn more about this mysterious dragon attacking her? Possibly, but what would be the point of that? As soon as he revealed more powers, he would doubtlessly use them to slaughter her which was hardly worth the increase in knowledge.

But then all thoughts of anything but survival were thrust from her mind as a vicious blow struck her in the middle of her back. She was hurled from her crevasse and to the floor of the cavern, where she writhed in pain. Her back was on fire. She had no doubt that if she had not been in her steel form, her spine would have been shattered. The most troubling thing about that thought was the idea that maybe it was exactly what her enemy was trying to discover about her.

Kristen tried to push to her feet but Jesus, her back all but screamed in pain. Still, she could do this. She had to do this.

Her teeth gritted in both pain and determination, she managed to get on her knees and finally to her feet before she peered at the crack she had been ousted from. Had there been another entrance she hadn't noticed? Perhaps there was a tiny fissure the dragon had moved through.

She understood that it was yet another question she would not get an answer to. A massive claw extended from the crevasse where she had been connected to what looked like a dragon arm, only with scales that frothed and bubbled like boiling ink.

Another claw emerged, followed by the massive head and neck of the dragon. It was extremely unnatural to see him unravel out of the slender fissure. How had he fit inside? Did the rules of physics even constrain him?

"Poor little dragon. Did you think you were safe, hiding in there?"

he said. His voice didn't come from a mouth but from the cloud of darkness that poured out of the tiny crack. "I am so very sorry to tell you that there is no place you can hide from my shadow."

"Who are you?" she demanded.

"I am what hides under mountains and behind the stars," the cloud of darkness said. "I topple kings and crumble crowns. I am nightmare incarnate and you, little dragon, have piqued my interest."

"Well, lucky me," she retorted and realized the dragon's true power wasn't his ability to become the dark but rather his ability to make her fear the dark.

The cloud of shadow continued to billow from the crack until his dragon form towered over her. He pumped his wings and when they stretched so high that they might touch the ceiling, he simply turned them into shadow.

"You have disrupted plans that were set in motion long before you were born," the dragon said as he glided toward her rather than walked. "For a time, you interested me but now, I see you for what you are—nothing but a human. A lucky one who masquerades as one of us but is nothing but a cheap copy."

"I'd rather be a human than hide from them in the shadows."

As quick as a snake, his tail struck, swept her legs out from under her, and toppled her with ease.

"You have a disrespectful little tongue on you," the dragon said, raised a claw, and swung it to crush her.

Kristen caught it seconds before it drove into her chest. The beast's fingers were like a cage all around her, one that increased in pressure and decreased in size. "Funny. Most dudes like my tongue."

He lifted her from the ground and hurled her with enough force to drive her through three stone columns before she struck a wall and landed with a clatter.

"I am not a dude," her shadowed opponent said as he slunk toward her. "I could have been your master—the one who gave you a path forward in this life—but I see now that the only thing I might still gift you with is a quick death."

She couldn't see him. Her head had struck the rock so hard that her vision spun, which made telling shadow from animated shadow extremely difficult. "If it's a quick death, does that mean you'll stop talking? I'm getting bored."

"Are you?" He was furious and his shape solidified as he lunged at her and delivered a vicious blow with bony spikes that jutted from his shoulder. They didn't penetrate fully although she knew a few more blows like that would wear her down enough that they became lethal.

Rather than simply wait for the next attack, she clenched her fists together and swung as hard as she could at the dragon's spine.

The blow was ineffectual as her adversary was gone.

Despite the fact that she'd been struck by the monster only a moment before, he had already changed his body into its incorporeal form. How was she supposed to battle something like this?

He laughed, caught her by the jaw with one of his massive talons, and threw her across the room. She struck a stalagmite with enough force to knock her out of her steel body and drive the point through her shoulder.

Kristen gasped in pain and forced her body to turn to steel, healing power be damned. She could not let him beat her, and if she remained pinned on the stone, she knew she couldn't win.

In her steel body, maybe she could get leverage to break it. She tried pushing on the ground but couldn't get a good foothold.

"Oh, this will be fun!" The dragon approached her from an angle she couldn't see. The worst thing about all this was that she still didn't even know what his true form looked like. She would die at the hands of a mystery, slaughtered by its shadow.

As if all that wasn't enough, the ceiling above her began to glow red like someone had detonated a bomb and it now tried to tunnel in. She knew that wasn't the case. Far more likely, the shadow dragon had called for reinforcements and this was one of their breath weapons, burning through the stone in an attempt to reach the Steel Dragon and kill her.

She laughed.

"Laughter in the face of your demise?" the shadow asked.

"It's a little something I learned from my human friends," she said and made no effort to quell her laughter.

"A waste," he stated as the ceiling above glowed even brighter. She waited for her death to come, either from claws made of darkness or from red-hot heat.

CHAPTER FIFTY-FIVE

They traveled for an hour behind the group in the truck. Drew rode atop the boulder and tried to look like he did this all the time when in reality, he was more comfortable on the back of a dragon. *How weird is that?* What seemed like only yesterday, dragons had been powerful, unapproachable creatures. He'd interacted with them only when they'd come to the precinct and demanded some kind of action. Now, he worked actively with a group of them with such a level of familiarity that one had let him bloody its nose.

Even after all that, flying on a boulder was crazy. The problem wasn't the big solid surface. It was that Amy thought she needed to impress the redneck mages by racing ahead and freezing in place, or by doing barrel rolls now and then. Whenever she did any of these maneuvers, he stuck firmly to the surface as if his rear had been glued to the rock. That she wouldn't let him go did nothing to settle the flips in his stomach.

Every time she raced ahead and stopped, he felt like he was going to puke. Each time she did a roll, his fingers dug involuntarily into the stone—not that they could, but they earned points for trying. He'd never envied Kristen's dragon strength but the idea of being able to cling tightly to the rock of his own volition instead of being stuck there by the whims of a mage—even a mage he trusted with his life—had a comforting appeal.

They followed the vehicle as it bounced along dusty back roads and he watched the occupants as best he could. The men in the back didn't seem to mind the rough ride. They held on tightly and managed to land where they had been seated whenever they encountered a particularly large bump.

Lumos didn't seem to be as comfortable, bound as he was with his hands behind his back and curled like a worm pecked by a bird in the bed of the truck. Whenever they hit a particularly large bump, he cried out in pain. It didn't seem too serious, but Drew had experienced many a bruised rib and he thought the dragon sounded like he was about on that level. A year before, he would have been amazed to see a dragon hurt by people at all. It had been simply unthinkable but now, he hoped his teammate was simply a better actor than he could be in that situation.

After maybe twenty minutes, they reached a dirt road with more traffic than the nonexistent cars on the last one. Amy used the opportunity to launch her boulder vertically—fifty feet, a hundred feet, two hundred, then five hundred.

Drew told himself he didn't have any fear of heights as his stomach tried to tell him he now did.

"I think this is going well," she said and sounded far too casual once they were so high that the truck below them was nothing but a pair of lights shining into the night. She stood tall, her arms folded and her feet planted on the stone as if it were a garden variety boulder rather than one airborne at high speed.

"Hopefully, we'll be there soon," he said, his voice shaky.

"I guess you were wrong about the cops, huh?"

"Sure, sure, whatever you say," he stammered.

"Oh no! Is the big bad boy from SWAT afraid of heights?" She laughed.

"Heights is flying on the back of a dragon or rappelling down the side of an apartment building. Being on a gyroscope masquerading as a boulder is a whole different level."

The mage threw her head back and laughed maniacally as she made the boulder plummet four hundred feet and follow the vehicle down a side street that crossed the road they had followed.

"I think you're maybe too committed to your role," Drew managed to say before he lost what brisket remains were still in his stomach over the edge of the boulder.

"Heh. Maybe I am enjoying this too much. Being an evil villain to the evil villains? What could be more fun than that?"

"I don't know. Flying completely level and at the same speed as the truck?"

"Oh, you're no fun!" Amy spun the boulder again.

This time, at least, nothing came up. He had already lost everything in his stomach.

They followed the vehicle onto another dirt road.

She was about to do another loop when Drew cleared his throat. "Amy, seriously, if you do any more of this, I'll be green when we get there. That might blow our cover since your cleaner or whatever the hell I'm supposed to be probably shouldn't get motion sickness from traveling with you."

The mage frowned. "It's a good point, I guess." She huffed petulantly and—thankfully—leveled out.

After about ten minutes on the dirt road, the truck reached an eight-foot fence topped with razor wire that seemed to separate a dead field from the rest of a dead field.

"That's weird," she murmured. "I assumed we'd go to a cattle ranch."

"This could be one, I guess," Drew said, but he doubted it.

One of the mages—or mage sympathizers, he wasn't quite sure yet —exited the truck, unlocked the padlock, let the truck drive past, and locked the gate once more. The process was almost bizarre as if there was something to steal on one side of the fence that wasn't on the other.

He saw nothing but mesquite, dried grasses blowing in the moonlight, a few wildflowers, and small patches of cactus here and there. He couldn't imagine why someone would want to hop a fence with razor wire when you could get the same poor assortment of plants on either side. Although it was curious that it was razor wire and not barbed.

They had passed quite a few ranches already and he had to admit, something was odd about this one. There was the fence with razor wire, for starters, a precaution far better suited for people intent on fence-hopping rather than cows who could knock the entire barrier down before they would even be able to touch the wire above it.

On top of that, Drew hadn't seen any cows as they glided above this fenced-off sprawling acreage. A few of the ranches they'd flown past hadn't had cows, but those had all been stocked with some kind of creature. Be it bison, sheep, goats, and even ostrich and zebras, it seemed that people in Texas liked their land to be involved in the production of meat. But there was nothing he could see on this land. He hadn't even seen any deer, which was odd because it was night and —being a city kid—he thought the countryside was basically taken over by deer at night time. Even if that was a little overblown, he should see something, right?

Strangest of all was the fact that he didn't see any actual structures —no barn, ranch house, or anything even remotely indicative of a human presence. All he could see was endless scrub and a dirt road that led through the center of it all, the literal middle of nowhere.

Well, Drew realized, that wasn't quite true. Up ahead, he noticed an old grain silo standing on a bluff that overlooked what appeared to be another abandoned quarry. Next to the silo was a shed that looked like it had seen better days—maybe in the last century. Despite how anticlimactic the base was, he still expected the technomages—or their henchmen as he had begun to think of the men in the truck—to take them to the silo. He frowned, puzzled when they didn't.

Instead, they skirted the base of the bluff on which the silo was built and continued toward what appeared to be the carved-out side of the hill.

"It's a good thing we tried to meet with them, huh?" Amy said. "We would never have been able to find this on our own."

"Yeah, I suppose not," he agreed. "But is this group really the threat? The only difference between this quarry and the last is that this one's even more desolate."

As they rounded the corner of the bluff, Drew realized he could not have been more wrong.

It wasn't a quarry at all but a place made to look like one. Someone had carved into a hill made of limestone and scattered pebbles all around in striking similarity to the location where they'd met these men. That, however, was where the comparison ended.

Under the ridge formed by the semi-excavated hill were a number of military-style trucks and jeeps. He counted seven, including two jeeps with mounted machine guns on the back.

"Fun," Amy said.

He couldn't help but disagree.

A massive camouflage tarp ran across the top of the hill so in the daytime, the vehicles could be hidden.

But Drew still couldn't understand the point. Yes, there was a garage and what appeared to be a termite-infested silo, but so what?

"Why do you think they have this out here, so far from any trappings of civilization, when they could have simply put it on ranch like the cell did outside Detroit?" he asked her.

"This might be the middle of nowhere," she replied, "but that doesn't mean nothing's here."

She brought her boulder closer to the earth as a huge, hangar style door opened and flooded the scene with light to temporarily blind them.

It was a stupid move in that the light could give away their position, but at the same time, it had disabled Drew's vision and put him and Amy off balance and at a momentary disadvantage. When your base was miles away from anyone and the closest thing nearby was a derelict silo, you could afford to flex a few power moves.

The young mage seemed to understand this theory well enough. Rather than set her boulder down gently as he knew she was able to, she let it drop the last few feet. It struck the ground hard enough to shake all the vehicles on their suspensions and rattle the men in the back of the pickup they had followed.

He was rattled too, but she didn't release the magical bond that glued him to the rock until he gave her the signal to let him go. As soon as he could, he scrambled to the blessedly sturdy soil.

The men from the back of the truck grumbled as they unloaded and tossed Lumos to the ground with less grace than he would have imagined a rancher would treat a bale of hay.

Fortunately, the dragon didn't land as everyone expected.

Amy caught him and lifted the human-shaped dragon, spun him slowly and languidly—upside down, then right side up, as if he were a forgotten doll floating in a pool.

It looked as creepy as hell to Drew, especially with the dried blood on Lumos' nose, but it had the added benefit of facing the dragon toward his teammates and away from everyone else.

He flashed them a smile and a wink.

The mage dropped him summarily in a pile in front of her. She stood with a bound dragon at her feet and the light from the secret base made her shadow into a much larger version of herself.

The men still at the truck recoiled. Only Vince managed to not look openly terrified, and he only succeeded in that by yelling at the rest of the men to start unrolling the huge camouflage tarp to hide their truck as well as the other vehicles.

That was a mistake. He might not have realized it, but it was. Given what she had proven she was capable of, he—at the very least—should have used his abilities to maneuver the tarp into place. It would have taken a fraction of the time these non-magical humans took and would have kept many more guns trained on the newcomers —including Lumos, although it seemed the men had bought the Chewbacca routine. That Vince hadn't done it was proof to Drew that he wasn't much of a mage at all. And if he was in charge of their recon team…well, for the first time since they'd met the group of redneck mage wannabes, he felt comfortable.

Although honestly, being on solid ground certainly helped.

"Are you all rats or is there a reason you all live beneath a derelict old grain silo under a hill?" Amy asked Vince as he stepped into the light that streamed from the interior of the hill with them.

He chuckled and looked smug and in control despite the fact that she scared the shit out of all his men. "I thought the silo would give it away, but I guess not. Right this way," he said and held a hand up in a gesture that looked far more friendly than he sounded.

The girl lifted Lumos with her telekinesis and made him follow as they walked inside to a room that had the cold, sterile atmosphere of a government building. The floors were off-white tile, the walls concrete, and the ceiling festooned with nothing but fluorescent lights.

At the end of the square room was an elevator.

Drew worked it out before Amy or Lumos did—which, given how outclassed he'd felt so far, was something of an accomplishment.

"Holy shit, this really is a silo, isn't it?"

Vince nodded.

"How the fuck did a cell of mages get to be in control of a goddamn nuclear missile?" he asked.

The man's expression soured.

"Oh… It's an abandoned silo, huh?" he surmised correctly.

"It's still a fucking great base," Vince said and sounded remarkably like a whiny teenager.

"Yeah. Wow. I'm sure the latent radiation isn't causing you guys any problems," Amy said with a smile as sweet as poison ivy.

"Get in the elevator," the young man said, but when she darted him a look, he corrected himself hastily. "Ma'am…uh, that is, if you please. My lady."

She nodded as if this stumbling attempt at manners counted for something and stepped inside. Drew followed and she brought Lumos in, swung him upright, and stood him on his feet. Not one to break character, the dragon sagged and leaned heavily against the wall. Vince entered and pressed the button to close the door, but not quickly enough.

Colt and Dusty raced through the entryway and the former barely managed to wedge his boot between the two closing doors with an, "Ow."

The doors opened and the two young men both stood awkwardly.

"What the hell?" Vince said and seemed embarrassed.

"The wait's real long for it to come back up," Dusty whined.

Their leader snorted in disbelief and this was followed by an uncomfortable pause. "Well, get in, then."

"Right, sorry!" Dusty said but he paused again. Apparently, his brain had fired at full speed and had gone through the necessary geospatial calculations to realize that he and Colt wouldn't fit very comfortably with everyone else.

"Dusty!" Vince snapped, and the young man sprang into action. Colt had already stepped forward, so both men crammed in together, which gave everyone barely enough room that they didn't have to touch.

The elevator started to descend.

"So, tell me about this base," Amy said and sounded like a villain shopping for real estate.

"It's kind of hard in the cramped space. I think it might be better if—"

"Tell me!" she commanded.

Drew was impressed that she'd managed to keep a straight face and not laugh at the ridiculous request.

"We...uh, bought it in an auction a few decades ago."

"You weren't doing shit a few decades ago but pooping diapers," Drew interjected.

Vince's dark skin flushed and he clenched his jaw. "Our people bought it and since then, have turned it into the pinnacle of technology."

"Why didn't they expand the elevator?" Lumos asked.

For show, Drew drew his hand back to strike the dragon and bumped into everyone else while doing so. Then, he pretended to punch the prisoner in the gut and stamped on the floor of the elevator for suitable effect. The sound was so loud that even Amy flinched.

"Fucking mages," Lumos wheezed.

"That's Mrs. Fucking Mage's assistant to you." He sneered.

"It seems kind of a mouthful to me," the prisoner muttered, so he once again bumped into everyone as he lunged at their captive.

"Enough! Enough!" Amy shouted, pushed Drew back with her magic, and shoved him into the other three men in the elevator with enough force to have knocked them over if there had been space for it.

By the time it finally dinged and opened, he was fairly certain that all three boys had a couple of bruises from him bumping into them so much.

It was a good thing they had managed to rough the boys up and steal some of their confidence, as when the doors opened to reveal the interior of the silo, all the three newcomers could do was gawk.

The interior of the space was vacant. Obviously, a missile had once stood in that position but was no longer there. Around this central cylindrical void were multiple levels—Drew counted five, although there could be more even farther down—all of them bustling with people. With a quick look, he was able to count more than thirty people. He had to assume there might be as many working in offices or rooms that weren't directly adjacent to the main chamber.

"What, no missile?" Lumos asked.

Dusty turned on the dragon, kicked him in the back of the knee, and made his leg buckle so he fell. The prisoner wheezed and Drew reminded himself for possibly the hundredth time that a physical blow from a regular human was harmless to a dragon. It was like a June bug bumping into a human, more of an inconvenience than anything else.

Lumos straightened, breathing heavily, which made the young man grin cruelly.

"I must say..." Amy looked around the space. "I'm impressed. Are all these men mages? If so, you've managed to build a substantial force."

"No, ma'am," Vince replied. "Most of them are freedom fighters. Texans and Americans who are sick and tired of the tyranny of dragons."

Colt cut in, "We're working to break the yoke and, uh...to get rid of these assholes."

Drew shook his head. The kid had started so strong. Whatever piece of propaganda he had repeated had sounded vaguely convincing, but then he'd gone and messed it up with schoolyard bad language. Still, he filed the information away for later. If these men could be swayed to fight for the mages, what would happen if they met a real leader like Kristen?

"And you have enough business to use this entire venue?" Amy asked as Vince began to lead them around one of the rings and toward a stairway to the next level.

"Sure, although it's all stairs from here on down."

"The basement is where we keep the lizards," Dusty said.

"We have multiple cells capable of holding dragons like this one. We would have caught him and brought him in ourselves if you hadn't, uh…"

"Stolen your fish?" she asked sweetly.

Drew didn't understand the expression any more than Vince seemed to. The young mage merely furrowed his eyebrows before he half-nodded and half-shrugged.

"Should we lock him up now or will he go on the tour?" Drew asked and tried to put as much venom in his voice as Amy had. They'd discussed this, and if there was any indication of a trapped dragon at this cell, they needed to know. Given that they were well past simple recon work at this point, he decided they might as well try to free it.

"We lock him up, of course," Vince said.

"Are you sure?" Dusty looked dubious. "The commander said we was always supposed to check in first."

"Well, sure, but—"

Vince tried to reply but Amy cut him off. "And there's a reason why you three can't split up?"

Their leader guided them from the level they were on and down through the complex. Each level comprised a ring of deck plates surrounding a circular open space, with rooms leading away from the open center where the missile had been stored.

Drew assumed Vince had been honest about the decades estimate. It looked like considerable time and money had been sunk into the base. It was almost a pity that Amy would undoubtedly try to fuck it up.

A spiral stair led down from where the elevator shaft ended to the very bottom of the complex. The lowest level was all flat and the apparatus that used to house the bottom of the missile had long since been removed. Four large rooms led off from the open space on that deck and all had large caged doors. One was filled with boxes and looked like every moderately organized storage space Drew had ever seen. Two of the cells had been refitted with tons and tons of little tanks of some kind, all of them filled with a writhing black substance.

He didn't know what the hell was in the tanks. His first guess was some kind of dark magic spell, but the smell was so unabashedly organic that he couldn't help but think it was something far more pedestrian and far more disgusting.

Amy froze, so he stopped as well. "What is that?" she asked, her words barbed.

"What, the bugs?" A guard who stood beside one of the cages chuckled. "It's weird the first time you see it, right?"

"What do you mean, bugs?" she asked him.

"They're crickets, actually," Vince interjected and relished the look of disgust on Amy's face.

"Crickets?" she asked, her voice so hard Drew was concerned she might blow their cover.

"Sure," the guard said cheerily, clearly not realizing that Vince was attempting to look tough and impress the visitors. "Crickets are cheap, easy to house and feed, reproduce like mad, and contain high levels of protein. They make perfect dragon fodder. The damn lizards don't even mind eating all the cricket shit and cardboard we mix in. Well, not after a while anyway," he said to Lumos as if that was supposed to make the prisoner feel better.

"You have a dragon, then?" Amy asked, her tone a little less edgy.

"Oh yes," Vince said, took her cautiously by the arm, and drew her toward the giant grate the guard stood in front of him until the two of them stood in the center of it.

Drew remained with Lumos so couldn't see inside quite as well, but in the dark, something moved.

"That's your dragon?" she asked.

"It is," the young man said and tried to sound tough.

"Sorry, the lazy bastard don't hardly move unless you put the floods on," the guard said and flicked a switch that bathed the dragon in light.

Drew didn't need Lumos's gasp of horror to know it was in a bad way. At least half of its scales were missing, no doubt ripped out to make bullets. Its claws were gone, as were chunks of its tail, for some reason. A dozen open wounds seeped but none of them seemed to bother it as much as the light did.

It writhed under the harsh glare and tried to escape but failed to even move. Its body was attached to the wall by multiple chains, so it could move only enough to reach the trough in front of it that was half-filled with grey goo.

"That's it right there," the guard said and pointed at the gross food. "They eat from that trough over a few days but this one's not finishing the batch. Eat up, buddy! That's the only way to get fresh food." He said the last words like he was talking to a customer about freshening a buffet instead of torturing the poor soul chained to the wall in there.

"That's why there's not a ranch above the site, then?" Drew asked, both dumbfounded and horrified.

The guard nodded. "That's right. Crickets breed fine in tanks. There's no need to waste perfectly good Texas beef on one of these damn lizards."

"That's disgusting," Amy said, her voice like hot oil waiting for a drop of water to fall in it and start a grease fire.

"I know, right?" the man said, which confused Drew until he realized that he had completely misunderstood Amy's objection. "To think they sometimes feed these dumb beasts actual meat when they could save a ton of resources by using crickets. It's not right."

The young mage began to float—not much, merely a few inches off the ground as if she couldn't control her magic in her fury. He could understand. This was even worse than what they had seen at the other mage bases. It was more grotesque like the dragon they were holding was simply livestock and nothing more.

"We heard there was some kind of tanks the dragons were kept in —some kind of substrate, I think. Does the dragon prefer the open air?" Drew asked.

The guard shrugged. "How the hell should I know what it prefers? We heard about those tanks. They are supposed to aid in healing or recovery or some shit. It sounds like a group of people getting concerned about shit that don't matter. When we rip off this fella's scales, they grow back. And when we rip off his, they'll grow back too." He gestured at Lumos and smiled as if he'd given them a guarantee on a used vehicle.

Then he went to the door to the cage to open it.

Drew took the opportunity to look at Amy, who was shaking with rage. Her hair had begun to whip in her unseen fury.

"I guess we finally found a place to lock this dragon up, ma'am," he said to her, his tone measured and calm.

She looked at him and anger and sorrow warred in her eyes. He met her gaze squarely. He had a handgun holstered that no one had been able to take because he'd been on the boulder with Amy. His mind calculated the odds and he decided he could probably take the assault-style rifle the guard carried before anyone else got down here. If he was armed with that, plus Amy's magic and Lumos's dragon abilities, they might get out of there alive.

Maybe.

He clenched his jaw and glanced at the guard's weapon. She nodded at that and in acknowledgment of his plan and her willingness to crack heads. They both looked at Lumos, who nodded at the cage in front of him and gave them both a flash of his dragon aura that felt like acceptance.

Drew was shocked. His teammate was all right with going inside that fetid hellhole? How on earth could he even consider such a thing? But then he understood. His gaze was locked on the whimpering dragon. He might be able to escape—although he didn't see how the hell he would be able to if they shackled him like they had the other dragon. But he was willing to sacrifice his freedom so he could offer comfort to this other dragon.

He looked at Amy to try to gauge what she thought. While he had taken point on this mission because he had the most experience in law enforcement—well, human law enforcement, given that Lumos was part of Dragon SWAT—if they had to fight their way out of there, he damn well knew they would need her to lead that fight.

She shook her head at Lumos to indicate that she was ready to attack, but before she could spring into action, Colt spoke from the top of the spiral staircase. "There they are." The relief in his voice was palpable.

Four men came down the stairway. At first, he felt only relief at seeing Dusty and Colt lead the way. The boys' barks were undoubtedly bigger than their bites. Having both of them there wouldn't change the nature of the fight much, especially since neither of them was a mage.

But then he recognized the other two men walking behind them and any relief he'd felt turned to dread.

It didn't surprise him that his instincts had been right about McMurtry and Ramos, the two cops from Elgin. The only surprise was that Ramos wasn't wearing his police uniform but a black robe.

"Commander!" Vince said, his voice heavy with forced tones of respect.

"Vince. Welcome. So, this is the mage you told me about on the radio," the man said as he descended the stairs to appraise Amy. "And this is the dragon she brought us to show her goodwill? Not bad, not bad at all. And you said something about her clean—"

He stopped talking when his gaze fell on Drew.

"What the fuck are you doing here?" McMurtry demanded. He still wore his police uniform but now had a massive assault rifle strapped to his back.

"I told you I was looking for a shipment of weapons," he said and tried to sound like he was astounded by the developments. "We came to sign up."

"The hell you did!" McMurtry shouted. "You told us straight, you worked with the damn Steel Dragon. And that mage is her personal puppet." The officer hauled the gun off his back in record speed.

But not faster than Drew, who had drawn his handgun and pointed it at Ramos.

"You damn fool. The commander can block bullets," the man said and made no effort to stand down, even under the threat of Drew's gun.

"So can I," Amy said as she rose even higher off the ground.

"Well then, we have ourselves a little stand-off then, don't we?" the cop said. "You have a gun pointed at our boss and we have one pointed at yours. She's a mage. So is he. It's about to get real fun when all the rest of our men get here and have their guns pointed at y'all too. Do you know how many bullets you can block, Ms. Mage? Or is that something we was gonna learn today?"

Drew glanced up as the barrels of weapons poked over the ledges of the missile silo to aim down the central chamber at them. Outnumbered didn't even begin to describe the situation.

"You're all forgetting something, though," Lumos said, turned to face Ramos, and snapped his cuffs. "I have the powers of Chumbaca!"

CHAPTER FIFTY-SIX

"Larry needs our help," Heartsbane said. She could feel his energy fading like he was falling asleep and losing blood all at once. "Get on," she shouted and turned into her dragon form.

"I must say this is quite the turn of events—" Butters protested before Heartsbane picked the rotund man up in one of her claws and glided from the hill to where Larry was, less than a kilometer away.

They barely made it in time. She dropped the sniper who—despite his girth—landed softly and used his forward momentum to carry him through a clean somersault that trimmed his speed. He found his feet, dove at the mage, and managed to catch him by his collar before he tumbled into the hole in front of him.

"Larry! Speak to me. What do we do?" Butters demanded.

"In...there..." he muttered before he passed out in the man's arms.

"Well, duh," the sniper said. "Why else would he be digging a hole to the center of the earth if we weren't going to use it to rescue Kristen? How thick does he think I am?"

"Too thick for the hole," Heartsbane said, still in dragon form. Before he could respond, she pumped her wings to hurtle skyward and into a back flip so her nose pointed at the hole. She was far too big in this form, obviously, so at the last moment, she transformed into her human body, tucked her arms in, and plunged through the aperture.

Heartsbane plummeted so fast that if she struck the wall with her head it might knock her out. It wasn't a good thing when one of the things she'd trained herself to do over the years was to revert to her dragon form if she was unconscious. Before the threat of dragon bullets, when the world had been a simpler place and the only thing dragons had had to fear was each other, it had made sense. Now, it was merely a bad habit she couldn't shake.

Rather than risk injury in the narrow tunnel, she kicked out with her feet, dug grooves into the stone all around her, and slowed her momentum.

The pit grew darker and she looked up quickly. Emerald had followed her example and taken his human form to plunge into the hole to save the woman who, until incredibly recently, had been the rookie on their force. She was now their boss and de-facto savior of the planet's stability and that was as good a reason as any for what others might consider suicidal.

Rocks crumbled and broke away as Heartsbane continued to fall. It was astounding how deep Larry had managed to dig, she thought before she approached the deepest layer. It still glowed faintly from the heat generated by the magical excavation.

Heartsbane dropped past it and powered into the rock.

She was on her feet in an instant. Her highly tuned aura senses told her Kristen was behind her. But they also told her that someone else—someone who was something like a dragon but different than what she was used to—was there as well.

"Red? Are you all right?"

"Oh—Heartsbane, thank God!" Kristen replied.

She tried not to roll her eyes.

As Emerald dropped from the tunnel, she took a hasty step back and he landed exactly where she had. He scanned the surroundings quickly before he stepped aside and Timeflash landed as well.

"I have nothing," he said and searched the darkness in front of them. They were in some kind of underground cavern—an enormous one from what Heartsbane could tell—that was mostly filled with water. "Tell me you have something, Heartsbane, because I have shit."

"I don't sense anything down here either," Timeflash said and moved toward the Steel Dragon. "Oh, Kristen, you're hurt."

"He's down here!" Kristen shouted. "He trapped me here and now, he's attacking me. He's a shadow. An inky shadow with dragon claws."

Heartsbane used her aura to calm their teammate, who was a mess. She could sense auras better than most other dragons could, and Kristen's was all over the place. She was hungry, tired, and also thankful that the dragons were there but worried for her team. Under it all, like a baseline carrying a song, was terror—unbridled terror that overwhelmed the rest of her thoughts and robbed her of any reason.

"Better, Red?" she asked.

Kristen took a few deep breaths and nodded. "Yes. Yes, thank you. I guess you all scared him away."

"Scared who away?" Emerald asked as he looked at the hole they'd come through. Even with dragon speed and strength, it would be a long climb out.

"There's some kind of dragon down here. He has a form like a pool of ink or liquid shadow or something. He... I can't beat him."

"That doesn't make sense, ma'am," Timeflash said, ever the professional. "The dragons who have shadow abilities can only use them when they change shape. There's never been a dragon who can stay between forms. That would be like you turning into a metal bird."

Kristen raised her middle finger at Erin. "How's that for turning into a bird?"

Heartsbane didn't understand the significance of the phrase but she sent another wave of calm over her. "Whoever he is, he's gone now. Let's get you out of here and back into the sunshine. You're probably going stir crazy down here."

"No, no, I'm telling you that—oh, my God. Heartsbane, he's behind you!"

She turned but could see nothing, merely shadow and dark and— Heartsbane gasped as something raked her across her belly.

The shock of the attack brought her senses to perfect clarity and she saw a pool of darkness that was somehow darker than the rest of the cave. She tried to swipe at it but her hands found nothing.

That didn't stop the shadow from wrapping a bony dragon tail around her neck and hurling her into a lake.

Heartsbane plunged into the water and fought to reach the surface as she sent out a message using her aura. *Danger! This dragon is gonna fuck you guys up!*

CHAPTER FIFTY-SEVEN

Amy was the only one who laughed at Lumos's butchering of the name of one of the most important Wookies in history. Everyone else was too busy turning their guns to aim at the suddenly liberated dragon.

Idiots, she thought and pushed all their guns—all twenty that she counted—harder than their operator had intended. She smirked when the armed men all smacked their guns against a wall like they were kids playing laser tag.

"You fools!" Ramos shouted. "Get the girl, not the dragon."

Some leaders didn't follow their own orders, but he did not seem to be one of this variety. He lashed out at the mage with a blast of energy. It was sharpened into a long point as if he intended to skewer her like a fish, but she brought up her magical abilities and stopped the point from stabbing her. Still, he was far stronger than she had expected. With the point of his attack blunted, he still shoved her back until her shoulders thunked into the bars of the cage behind her.

She grunted, impressed but also resolute in her desire to show this idiot exactly who he was messing with. Without hesitation, she raised her hands and launched a blast of her own.

Ramos was expecting it and made a shield to block her attack, but she wasn't an idiot. She had no intention to spear the idiot, not this early in the fight. All she wanted was to knock him back so he would collide with a wall and look like a buffoon.

He careened away and into a man carrying a crate of crickets who seemed blissfully unaware that all hell was breaking loose. The box shattered and the creatures scuttled everywhere.

The base commander struggled to pull something out of his robe while he yelled at his peons. "Kill them! Kill them dead!"

"Fat chance," Lumos said, floored the guard at the dragon cage with a roundhouse kick, and launched Colt at least twenty feet with a dragon-powered uppercut.

"You two are show-offs, you know that, right?" Drew took careful aim and squeezed rounds off at the men who still hadn't recovered from having their weapons almost yanked from their hands.

"You didn't hit anyone," Amy said.

"It's called covering fire! Use it!" he shouted as the enemy returned a volley of their own.

"Pah, these humans can't hurt me!" Lumos boomed, which immediately drew a fusillade in response. Drew flung himself across the space and tackled the dragon to thrust him beneath one of the rings.

"They have dragon bullets, you goon!" he snapped.

"I know that now," Lumos said and pointed to his forearm which had a tiny gash across it. Thankfully, he'd only been grazed.

"Come on out, you cowards!" McMurtry shouted from the stairwell to which he'd retreated.

"You first, asshole," Amy retorted, which earned her a barrage of gunfire even though none of the bullets even came close to hitting them.

"I think the only way out is the way we came in," Drew said, poked his head out, and fired three shots through the hollow center of the missile silo. Three bodies tumbled to the ground and he looked disappointed in his enemies. "That was only supposed to be covering fire, you idiots," he said to their fallen bodies.

"Who are the idiots, now, huh? You may have forced Ramos into a retreat, but you forgot about meeeeeee!" Vince yelled as Amy simply lifted him by the back of his shirt and rocketed him up through the central empty space of the missile silo. She heard a clang from somewhere high above her and knew he had made impact with something even harder than his head.

"I guess I could try to fly up there?" Lumos said and peeked up. Their adversaries responded with a hail of bullets and magical blasts of energy. "Or not. It might be better to keep my human form for a while. Dragons make a very easy target for cells of magical terrorists intent on killing dragons."

"Go figure," Drew said as he relieved dead guard of his assault rifle.

"What about her?" Amy said and gestured to the dragon in the cage behind them. "I don't want to leave her here. I know this was supposed to be reconnaissance, but if we leave her now, they'll take her and go even deeper underground."

"I see what you did there," he said.

"I'm not joking," she replied.

"The way I see it, we have two options." Lumos scanned the stairway with a small frown. "Either we rescue the dragon now and try to get the hell out of here with her, or we eliminate every single mage here."

"That's impossible," Drew said.

"I agree." Amy nodded. "She's not mentally stable. I don't think we can try to get her out of that cage, move her through a barrage of gunfire, and reach the surface. For all we know, she's never even been to the surface."

"That's not what I was saying was impossible!" he protested.

"Then we—what do you humans say?—bring the pain?" the dragon asked with a grin.

"I planned to go with fuck shit up, but a little pain might be in order, sure," the girl said. She turned to Drew. "You'll have a ton of cleaning up to do, cleaner."

"Better me than them," he replied a little grumpily, probably because she and Lumos were ignoring his battle experience.

"All right then. It's settled! We trash this place." The mage grinned.

"Now would be the time," he said. "They've assumed some kind of formation."

Indeed, even Amy with her woeful lack of combat experience could tell there was much less gunfire than there had been before.

"They probably think we'll try to escape through the elevator, which means they'll set up a barricade," he explained.

She smiled. "Well, let's go convince them we're not going anywhere."

CHAPTER FIFTY-EIGHT

Kristen's first reaction to seeing Heartsbane appear and be summarily hurled into the lake was that she was having a hallucination. She'd been down there long enough and with the stress of being attacked, she'd finally lost it.

As she considered this as if from a distance, Emerald rushed toward the water and slapped her on the arm as he yelled, "Let's do this, Steel!" He raced after Heartsbane and she decided that if this was a hallucination, she would simply go with it.

"Are you all right?" Timeflash asked.

She nodded and pushed the idea of shock-induced delirium from her mind. There were too many pieces that were too compelling and told her this was real. It had to be.

"I'm better now. Do you guys have a plan to get out?"

"Do you want to run before we defeat this asshole?" She smiled.

Just then, Emerald was plucked from the rock and tossed into the lake without warning. Kristen couldn't see what had picked him up and only knew that one minute, his feet were on the shore and the next, his voice echoed as he tumbled into the water. "Too late to run now!" he yelled before he splashed into the water.

The blob of shadow surged toward Kristen and Timeflash. The two women fought back to back and used fists and feet to defend against their amorphous foe. The Steel Dragon took deep breaths as she fell into the rhythm of combat. Truly, this was more like sparring as she couldn't land a punch. Every time a claw or tooth lashed at her, she tried to strike at it but she was too slow. The shadow dragon simply puffed into nothingness and her blows fell through empty air.

Timeflash fared no better. She wasn't much of a fighter given that her abilities lay elsewhere, and it showed. Her punches were slow and her kicks underpowered. While she still had enough strength to kick the ribcage out of a human, against this foe, she wasn't the partner Kristen needed.

The dragon had tossed those in the lake.

Fortunately, they both seemed more adept than she was at using their bodies underwater. Emerald burst from the surface in dragon form with Heartsbane on his back.

She vaulted off and spun in midair to accelerate her elbow to bone-crushing speed. Her perfect trajectory took her through the cloud of darkness but she hit nothing but the ground itself.

"Dammit!" she cursed, not because the blow that had cracked the earth had hurt her but because she didn't like to miss. She didn't dally, though. Instead, she lashed out at the cloud all around her. Unfortunately, she wasn't able to land a single blow.

Now that Kristen could see someone else fighting this beast of darkness, she began to understand his powers a little better. The dragon could keep as much of his body in shadow form as he wanted, which meant he could dodge any blow he anticipated. He could turn a claw or fang solid for long enough to hurt one of them, but as soon as they retaliated, he simply reverted to his inky darkness.

The realization gave her an idea. All she had to do was surprise it.

Emerald seemed to have the same thought. While Heartsbane battled the foe from the inside, the green dragon attacked. He leapt from his place beside the water, leading with both clawed forelimbs as well as a mouth filled with deadly dragon teeth.

The shadow dragon somehow saw him coming and vanished as the huge dragon barreled toward him, which forced Heartsbane to dodge at the last second lest she bear the brunt of the attack.

The three human-shaped dragons formed up around Emerald. Together, they scanned the darkness in search of their opponent but saw nothing.

"Do you think that scared him off?" he asked.

"Not even kind of," Kristen replied.

"I don't know. Whoever he was, he seemed like a chicken-shit coward to me," Heartsbane yelled and the words echoed through the cavern. "I learned that from your human friends—" Heartsbane's explanation was cut off when the shadow dragon returned.

"You cannot defeat me," he roared as a tail made of nothing coalesced into a whip of spines and bones that pounded into her. Both Timeflash and Kristen tried to grasp the tail but it was already gone.

Instead, each of them felt a claw thump into their back.

Emerald moved to defend them but in the next moment, the foe was gone, vanished to wherever he was hiding.

"You realize you cannot win, correct?" the disembodied voice gloated. Rather than speaking loudly enough to cause an echo, he delivered the words in a whisper as if he were right beside them.

Which he was, of course. A claw grasped Kristen's ankle and lifted her.

She thumped it with a steel fist but not before it had gained enough momentum to hurl her aside.

Helpless and horrified, she watched as the cloud of darkness seemed to bubble up from the rock itself and wreak havoc on her team.

He thrust Heartsbane and Timeflash away as if they were nothing but toys. Emerald tried to retaliate, but he unleashed plumes of jet-black smoke around his neck that solidified into his tail.

The green dragon began to choke.

"We can't let him separate us," Kristen shouted as she raced toward the fray.

Before she could get within ten feet of her teammate, a claw materialized and swiped her legs out from under her.

Timeflash fared no better and met a set of snapping jaws that made a gory mess of her arm. It began to heal immediately, but she would be at a disadvantage in this fight.

Emerald, gagging, transformed into his human form and slipped out of the shadow dragon's grip. His attacker roared in frustration before the cloud streaked to the ceiling and sank into nooks and crannies, no doubt preparing for another strike.

"That was brilliant!" Heartsbane said. She'd only reached Emerald when the dragon had taken a quick retreat. "Where did you learn to use your human form like that?"

"I picked it up from a coworker," Emerald said and nodded at Kristen.

"Soon to be former coworker," she quipped.

"Ah! The gallows humor," Heartsbane said. "Because he's going to kill you!"

"Hardly. More like I'll fire all of you if you let that dragon touch me again."

"Then fire them," the shadow dragon growled before he plunged from the ceiling and attacked the four of them at once.

Kristen fought with every ounce of strength she still had left after her ordeal. She tried to batter her opponent with fists made of steel and kicks that could crumple semi-trucks. Every time, she found nothing.

Worse, the dragon didn't seem to be contained by the exact shape of his dragon body at all. He could use all four of his claws more or less interchangeably and attack two members of the team in strikes that would have been impossible if he had a skeleton to worry about.

It took all they had simply to block its shadowy blows and stay together.

"You see how this will end, don't you?" the shadow dragon demanded, his mass nothing more than a cloud of darkness boiling furiously around the four of them as he struck again and again and again.

"You'll take us out for burgers?" Kristen asked.

She was answered with a claw raked across the face.

"You will all die and all this talk of peace and love between the species will die with you."

"Are you sure you don't simply want some love?" Heartsbane asked. "Turn solid for a second and you might feel better."

The dragon laughed and the sound seemed to come from all around them while the blows from his claws increased in speed. "I have not amassed this much power by falling for tricks as pedestrian as that."

"The way I see it," Emerald said as a tail swung into his gut and forced him to double over. "You haven't amassed anything. All you've done is hide in the dark."

"There is power in the dark!" the dragon replied. He adjusted his blows and forced them to move back to defend themselves or risk being truly savaged by his force that none of them had yet discovered how to stand against.

"For centuries, I have bided my time in the shadows, watching, learning, appraising, and acting when I must rather than when I wanted. And you think that you—a dragon raised by a human bitch—can unravel everything I've done in a year?"

"Honestly, at this point, I was only hoping for a sandwich," Kristen replied. Her reply earned her another hard strike, this one with enough force to knock her on her ass, which immediately got soaked as the shadow dragon had pushed them all to the water's edge.

"Such impetuousness from such a little runt. How dare you speak to me like that!"

"We don't even know who you are," Timeflash said. "Why the hell would we respect you if you're merely a mage doing this?"

Timeflash—of all dragons—knew what mages did for the world and respected them for their work. She had a team that helped her augment her power, so what she'd said had been nothing but a cheap jab intended to piss the dragon off.

It worked. "You think a mage is capable of the forethought and planning that I have worked at for the centuries? Do you think a mage could singlehandedly take on four dragons at once? No, it is not a mage you face, but a dragon. You brainless slugs will never earn the right to use the name my allies use to speak to me, but I will tell you my plans. Are you listening? When this battle is over, I will harvest the skulls of your human peons and wear them as masks. When I tire of their bone structure, I will toss them aside like the trash all humans are."

Kristen swallowed. Finally, she had a clue—an extremely weird, insanely creepy clue about this dragon who had toyed with her since before she'd even arrived at Mammoth Cave.

Now she could really piss him off. "Funny, I had planned to make a coat of your scales."

The dragon roared and hoisted her into the air and she pounded on the arm that was attached to the claw wrapped around her waist. She didn't have time to see if her blows caused any damage before her assailant hurled her into the lake.

She splashed into the cold water and pumped her arms and legs in an effort to swim to the surface. Before she could make it and suck in a precious breath of air, another splash was followed by two more and all three of her allies were beside her, swimming madly to the surface.

Kristen broke through first and sucked in a breath before she looked around to make sure everyone had made it.

They had, none of them being paranoid about water the way a person who could sink like steel was. Three dragon heads popped above the surface and the four of them all looked at each other.

Heartsbane grinned. "So now what? We play water polo or something? Did that dumbass not realize that there's much more room in the water for us to take our true forms?"

Emerald chuckled, as did Timeflash.

No, this is when he tries to drown us. Kristen wanted to say the words but something had already caught her by the ankle. "Take a breath!" she managed to blurt before she was once again pulled beneath the water.

She wanted to scream when she saw the other three—all still in their dragon bodies—all yanked beneath the surface as well. Thankfully, she resisted the urge as she knew from experience that in this place, every breath of air counted and that if she screamed, no one else would come.

CHAPTER FIFTY-NINE

Amy broke from cover and raced toward the spiral staircase that wound upward through the abandoned nuclear missile silo. Drew thought she was crazy, even though she kept her shield up as she ran. The magic barrier robbed bullets of their momentum and turned them into nothing but lumps of either lead or the harvested and processed pieces of dragon they were made of. He knew they had practiced this maneuver for some time and that she could keep the bullets at bay without much difficulty.

The blasts from the other mages appeared to be a more difficult challenge.

Bolts of lightning and fire streaked at the girl and battered through the shield she'd made for bullets. The attack forced her to dodge aside.

"I think we should stick together!" she yelled at her teammates, who both rushed forward to shelter with her under the dome of magic protection she now used to slow the bullets and the mage blasts.

"Are you all right?" Drew asked as he moved past her and fired at a mage at the top of the stairs who tumbled to finally sprawl motionless beside them.

"I can hold them for a while, but the mage blasts will drain me faster than only the bullets."

"It sounds like we should bring the fight to them, then," Lumos said and peered up the staircase with a grin.

"Careful, dragon," Drew reminded him. "You're not wearing bulletproof armor currently and these guys are armed with what can kill you."

"It looks like I need an escort then." The dragon smiled at him.

After a hasty scan of the enemy placements, he nodded. "Let's make for the next level."

He started up the steps with his assault rifle ready to provide cover and his teammates followed hard on his heels. Amy maintained her shield. It reacted as a kaleidoscope of colors above them when the bullets sparked and she somehow absorbed the energy from the mage blasts.

That was the impression, at least, when he glanced out of the corner of his eye. Much as he wished he could simply step back and rely on her to get them out of this, his experience told him that wasn't the case. Both resigned and determined, he pushed on with the task to clear the way for them to reach their chosen destination.

They hunkered close together on the landing and Lumos went to work.

Now that they were on the ring of plates around the center of the missile silo, the dragon could slip into the hallways and rooms carved into the earth that radiated out from the central chamber.

This ability wasn't a good turn of events for the mages and men who tried to kill the three of them.

Drew had seen enough dragon battles to know what to look for but still, he knew that if he so much as blinked, he'd miss much of the action.

Lumos moved through the men ranged against them like a hurricane sweeping through a beach town. He was incredibly fast and almost invisible, yet the devastation he wreaked was frightening.

A man fell and tried to breathe as he clutched his neck where the dragon had chopped him.

Another was hurled aside by a spinning kick that swept his legs out from under him.

A third defender's weapon was snatched from his hands to deliver a powerful blow to his face.

The fourth was simply tossed into the central chamber with enough force to career across and power into the fifth who had been focused on Amy rather than on his airborne teammate.

"Shoot the dragon, you idiots! The dragon!" McMurtry bellowed. He stood on the opposite side of the ring they were on with his assault rifle in hand. The man didn't seem to be a mage at all, which made him a perfect target for Drew.

"I'll deal with McMurtry. Are you all right?" he asked the girl.

"It's taking a ton of energy to stop these attacks, but if you guys can eliminate some of our enemies, I'll be fine."

"Roger," he said and raced into action.

He ran through the devastation that Lumos had caused, his gaze fixed on a level above and the men McMurtry ordered about from the alcove where he sheltered. The way the cop stilled was a clear indication that he'd locked onto Lumos and was about to pull the trigger when Drew flung himself in front of the barrel. The bullet struck his chest like a train, thrust the wind from his lungs, and forced him into a tangled pile on the floor.

"Got one!" his adversary shouted and sounded like a kid at a carnival instead of one of a town's chief law enforcement officers.

Drew's chest burned from the injury but he ignored it and pushed to his feet.

"You're supposed to be dead!" McMurtry said as he stood in front of him.

"Y'all small-town cops might not have heard of these things called bulletproof vests," he said and launched himself at the man despite his heart hammering in his ears. His lungs still felt tight from a lack of air and he dragged a breath reflexively as he closed the distance between them.

McMurtry snarled his fury as he began to pummel him.

Surprisingly, the older officer was able to hold his own against him, but only for about thirty seconds. He blocked the piston-like punches with his assault rifle and was able to dodge his knees, but when Drew managed to hammer the other man's fingers with a punch, the cop released his weapon reflexively from the pain.

Seizing the moment, he proceeded to deliver another unbridled attack.

He kicked the gun out of his hands and swung a fist into McMurtry's skull. The man sagged and fell.

"Goddamn, who the hell taught you Yankees to move like that?" he moaned.

"Your mom," he said, caught him by the collar, and lifted him bodily above his head. McMurtry struggled, but he was fortunately not strong enough. Drew took the smaller man and dangled him over the edge.

"You wouldn't!" his captive protested. "You're not supposed to kill —you're a cop!"

"So are you, you piece of shit," he retorted and released the man over the edge.

McMurtry screamed for far longer than he fell, but that was because he only dropped about two feet before he came to a stop, held in place by a piece of metal Drew had hooked the crooked cop's shirt on.

"Oh, God...please no. Oh, god," the man whimpered, his eyes still shut, and didn't realize what had happened and that he wasn't falling.

His closed eyes also meant he would never know who killed him.

"Take out that cop!" Ramos ordered from higher up the missile structure than Drew could see.

The volley of gunfire was immediate and bullets rocketed toward him as he scrambled to find cover. Fortunately, Lumos had already cleared the entire level, so no hostiles hid in the shadows. He made it to cover without getting hit but knew Amy had something to do with that, as a few bullets fell like they were nothing more than discarded coins.

Unfortunately for McMurtry, no one had provided him the same level of shielding from his own supposed allies. The people who had once obeyed him now cared only for Ramos' orders and fired indiscriminately at their former lieutenant. In an instant, the man was riddled with bullet holes.

Drew didn't want to imagine what the bottom of the silo would look like by the end of it. Already, bodies had fallen there, and McMurtry would now drip blood in a macabre shower of gore.

He focused his attention on the level where he stood. It looked like there were four floors in total, and they'd cleared the first two without sustaining injuries, which wasn't bad.

Unfortunately, most of the force looked like they were at the top.

"Maybe we should make a break for it," Drew said. "I bet we can reach the elevator and get out of here."

"No way!" Lumos protested. "We haven't eliminated the leader of this group yet."

"I'm with Lumos," Amy said. "We can do this. Let's not stop now."

He nodded. They had voiced his preference but he'd needed to make sure everyone was on board. "Does anyone have a plan for the next level?" he asked across the space in the middle of the compound.

"Oh, this is fun." Lumos peered at the next level and didn't sound at all like he was in the middle of a firefight. "From my angle, I see big yellow barrels with a flame symbol on them and the number four. Do you have any idea what that means, humans?"

"Not a clue," the mage responded.

Drew smiled. "Those barrels are flammable. I don't remember if number four or five is the highest, but I know they definitely mark anything that burns."

"Oh, this does sound fun," she agreed.

"All right," he said, checked his ammunition, and found it empty. He took an extra magazine from one of the men Lumos had knocked out. "I'll lead the way up the stairs, target those tanks, and land a few shots. They should go kaboom. You two follow once I have the area clear."

He darted forward and drew another spray of bullets that Amy blocked with a dome of magical power. In moments, he reached the steps and raced up them, taking them two at a time until he gained the landing and darted around a corner into cover.

As he'd been trained to do, he waited for the obligatory pot shots before he snapped his head out, sighted the barrels of explosive material, and fired.

Unfortunately, he hadn't noticed that Lumos had followed him to this level.

The bullet struck one of the barrels, punched through the outer casing, and burrowed inside. The explosion was immediate and released a shockwave that ripped through the other barrels beside it. Those detonations joined the first until it seemed like the entire earth would collapse on their heads.

The dragon didn't even flinch. He stood directly between Drew and the barrels while shrapnel seared into him and flames surged to engulf him. The ancient dragon stood strong and laughed as the deadly mixture ripped at his skin to cut him, burn him, and tear his clothes away until he only wore scraps and tatters.

It reminded Drew of when Kristen had first learned that she was something more than human. She had placed herself between a partner and a rocket and the weapon had lost.

Lumos seemed to be as strong. Before the blast was finished, he was already healing. "You gotta mix the dragon pieces with the gunpowder if you want to hurt me, you sons of bitches!" he shouted, apparently enjoying this.

Drew stood cautiously, tried to shake the ringing from his ears, and looked around the third level of the base.

It was a wreck, an example of what complete and utter devastation truly meant.

He approached Lumos and they looked at all the men who'd been caught in the carnage. The poor guys hadn't even had a chance to try to kill him. Well, technically they had, as they'd fired at him for a while now, but after they'd been wiped out so easily and completely, he couldn't help but pity their incompetence.

"I guess that's it, then, huh?" he said.

"Wrong."

Ramos floated from the top floor of the compound. He glowed, his skin like hot coals. His robes billowed around him and resembled smoke issuing from a smoldering fire. Each hand was wreathed in flames that twisted and curled like serpents. "You fucked with the wrong mage." He sneered.

In response, Amy floated up. While the energy that poured from the man seemed malevolent like red flames burning a house, the air around Amy held a cool blue sheen. Her hair blew gently in a breeze Drew knew she was creating. Her fingers were covered in energy as well. It was light-blue though, the color of a robin's eggs. Rather than writhing like snakes, it seemed to breathe like a snoozing animal.

"You tricked my men and you will pay for their loss!" Ramos screamed at her.

Before he could martial his energy, she delivered a massive blast into his chest.

It shredded whatever magical armor he had and flung him into a steel bulwark. He spun as he fell unhindered to the floor four stories below. He landed with a dull thud that made Drew cringe.

The girl floated closer and landed beside him. "Well, that was anti-climactic."

He chuckled. While he'd expected more of a grand showdown, Amy truly was in a class all her own. "I must say that was damn wicked."

"Thanks!" She beamed. "But did you see Lumos survive that blast? It was badass!"

"Why, thank you." The dragon tittered at the compliment. "Although in all honesty, that wasn't the wisest use of my resources. I was able to heal but barely. I'd love to stop and get more brisket before we head home."

"Are you feeling all right, Drew?" she asked.

"Yes, I'm fine." He tried not to sound annoyed. "I was the one who shot the tank if you don't remember. That means I killed more than both of you put together."

Amy indulged him with a smile before she said, "Yeah, but you're our cleaner, Drew. That means you have a ton of work to do."

He looked down four stories, past the moaning forms and unconscious bodies of many of the people in the cell, to some of the dead, including the leaders, at the bottom. She was joking, of course, but he also knew they weren't done there yet.

CHAPTER SIXTY

Kristen had believed there could be nothing worse than drowning alone and in the dark, but she found now that simply wasn't true. It was far worse to watch your friends drown.

Emerald burst above the surface and joined her briefly before he was yanked underwater again by the shadow dragon.

"Emerald!" she shrieked which was, of course, exactly what their opponent wanted. As soon as she emptied her lungs while she screamed for her friend, the shadow dragon attacked, dragged her down, and forced her to swallow a mouthful of water.

She changed to her dragon form—burning the last of her energy—as she tried to swim to the surface once more. A part of her had begun to wonder why she was still alive. Her enemy could have killed her any number of times already. He could have killed all of them. Why drag this out?

Heartsbane thrust through the surface of the water moments before her and sucked in a ragged breath. Kristen realized that maybe their enemy was finally finishing the job. Her teammate looked rough, worse than she had ever seen her. Before she could fully catch her breath, she was hauled under once more. This time, she blew fire at the ceiling in frustration.

Kristen thought maybe the tables would turn when the fire passed through a cloud of inky darkness, but it seemed the shadow dragon couldn't be hurt at all in his insubstantial form. She hadn't quite worked out whether he also managed to be in the water and on the ceiling at the same time or simply moved with incredible speed between the two.

Emerald and Timeflash bobbed to the surface in the wake of the blast. Both stayed up long enough to catch their breaths.

"What is this about?" Timeflash asked and craned her long dragon neck to look around in the low light.

"It was Heartsbane's fire," Emerald said.

"No, it wasn't," Kristen explained sadly. "It didn't hurt him at all."

"No, no, not the fire itself but the ligh—" He didn't manage to finish his thought because he was immediately submerged again.

"The light?" Timeflash asked before she was pulled under as well.

That was it, Kristen realized. When she had heated the stalagmite, she'd been fine, and when she'd blasted fireballs, she hadn't been attacked. The shadow dragon couldn't attack if he was in the light.

When Heartsbane surfaced, her boss was ready with battle orders. "Heartsbane, fireball—go!"

The dragon obeyed her without hesitation. She launched a fireball at the ceiling and again, the inky form retreated from the light. This time, he returned as soon as the light was gone to bite and slash at the two teammates before he dragged them down into a lake that was now red with their blood.

They couldn't beat him, her reason told her. He was simply too powerful and didn't need a dragon-sized shadow to hide his form. Any size seemed to work for his powers—which explained how he'd been able to follow her. Worse, he seemed to be able to send parts of him to attack in the spaces between blasts of fire. No matter what they did, they couldn't win this. They would be drowned, one by one, and she knew she would be last. The shadow dragon would kill her friends to make her suffer all the more.

She surged to the surface, sucked air, and waited to be struck yet again. It took a few moments for her to register that something had staved off the inevitable attack.

Emerald breathed fire at the ceiling again and again. When he stopped, the light remained.

"I thought we needed a lamp," he said and gestured at the stalactite above him that now glowed with heat.

"That's brilliant," she shouted. "Light this place up."

Timeflash surfaced, then Heartsbane. Kristen told them both to do as Emerald had and soon, the ceiling of the cave above the four dragons glowed with a rosy brightness.

The inky form of the dragon didn't enter the light. He pushed against the borders and each time he came too close, part of him would become solid to reveal his dragon shape.

"There's still darkness between us and the exit," Kristen said while she tried to marshal the strength she needed to make fire of her own and failed.

Their enemy saw this too and his dark, cloudy form swirled between them and the tunnel the dragons had entered through.

"It's time to shine a little light on the problem, then," Emerald responded and launched a streak of fire at a stalagmite near their exit. It began to glow and as it did so, the cloud of inky shadow retreated.

"Come on, people!" the green dragon shouted. Timeflash and Heartsbane swam forward, keeping Kristen between them. As they moved, they blasted more areas of the cave with fire until it soon seemed like every piece of stone or crystal she could see now sparkled with light.

None of this went unnoticed by the shadow dragon. He screamed in fury and hurtled forward in spears of dark energy that nevertheless coalesced into something more solid whenever he entered direct light. A spear became a claw and a cloud became a snout. Every time this happened, he retreated.

"What? Are you afraid of how you look in the light?" Kristen asked, knowing full well that what the dragon was truly afraid of was his identity being revealed.

"You will not get away, Steel Mongrel!" he roared, but she didn't feel the blow she knew he wanted to land on her. Now that they were bathed in light, the dragon couldn't use his abilities.

"Light up everything but our tunnel out of here. If this asshole wants to run, let him run into our friends," she proclaimed and the dragons needed no further urging to deliver fireballs that were dense with hot energy to every corner of the cave.

The enemy reacted like an animal. He shrieked and spun in circles like an angry flock of birds. His motion accelerated to the point where he was almost a blur until Kristen felt sure he would attack in his frenzy, using some other power.

Her instincts, fortunately, hadn't failed her. Like a cannonball fired from a ship moored in hell, the shadow dragon launched toward her, but she was ready. She lashed out with her steel tail and struck the dragon across the face with enough force to deflect the energy into a dark corner of the cave.

He mewled piteously, obviously in pain, but it faded into the sound of wind rushing over stone before the cave fell silent.

Nothing moved except the billowing lungs of her dragon friends who used their breath to protect her.

What had been a nightmare was now a dream. The crystals glittered like chandeliers, the stalagmites and stalactites glowed with rosy energy. Best of all, she wasn't alone. She was surrounded by people who cared about her—people who were willing to risk life and limb for their friend. She could joke and cry with them and simply be with them, even if they weren't people in the human definition of the word.

"Thanks for saving me, but one of you guys has really bad breath."

CHAPTER SIXTY-ONE

I t always felt good to come home, even if home was currently an old warehouse transformed into a base of operations.

Although Timeflash had been away for a day, it still looked great. The biggest difference was that it bustled with activity. People moved about, carried equipment, and set up more of the endless workstations it seemed they'd need. A few continued to work on landscaping while others—regular humans judging by the way they carried themselves—trained in hand-to-hand combat.

Kristen limped through the gate they'd installed in their secure perimeter and headed toward the main building. Despite the fact that she didn't know many of the faces, they obviously knew her. Most of them stopped and saluted, and those who didn't were chastised for missing their boss's entrance by their more observant coworkers.

Two dragons flew overhead as well, practicing dodges of rifle fire from humans who were being trained on how to shoot dragons from below. It was a tough world when your enemies could be anyone. Dragons had to train to fight humans and humans had to train to fight dragons, and everyone had to be ready to fight mages. Yet all she wanted was for them to work together.

It seemed Jim and Stonequest had been busy with recruitment.

The humans' obvious deference to Kristen made it clear these were Jim's people, and the auras of the dragons overhead held no hostility to her.

What a relief it was to feel dragons rather than guess where they were. She shook her head to clear the memory of facing the shadow dragon. It was a relief to bask in the warm sunshine, hopefully something he could never take away from her again.

They entered the base, where Stonequest, Jim, and Brian waited for them with a stack of pizzas higher than she had ever seen. Despite her bruises, she couldn't help but smile.

"You didn't get anything for anyone else?" she said by way of greeting and her brother rolled his eyes at her.

"She almost dies and is still bruised despite having dragon healing powers and all she cares about is pizza. That's my sister."

Everyone chuckled while he embraced her and hugged her tightly with muscles that had begun to emerge from beneath his once girthy body.

"I'm all right," she whispered to him but he held her for a second longer anyway.

"Hey, you're hogging the boss!" Jim joked. The young tech pulled away and everyone else teased him until he stepped aside and served a slice of pizza next to a massive salad on his plate.

"So..." Larry said once everyone had settled and he'd stacked his plate with more food than Kristen had ever seen him eat. "What the hell happened down there?"

Kristen didn't tell them right away. Instead, she introduced herself to the two new dragons and greeted a third she already knew—Amythist, whose garden she had destroyed while battling Constance, wanted to repay the favor of her life.

The other two dragons were much younger than her and both wanted to join the team because they agreed that the Dragon Council was mismanaging things in favor of those with vast powers. At the same time, they also wanted to make sure that the new world order the planet seemed to be marching toward still had dragons at the negotiating table. Neither had powers beyond the basics and both were concerned that this might make them a liability when fighting at the Steel Dragon's side. Kristen, having been through an ordeal where her steel skin had almost drowned her many times, assured them that their help would still be appreciated.

Finally, with everyone assembled, introduced, and offered food, she told them about what had happened beneath the earth.

It was odd to have to recount not only the dragon battle but the entire ordeal to her team. For so long, she'd worked closely with them. This was the first time in a while that she'd truly been afraid, and a big part of that had been because she'd been separated from the people who supported her. They had been right to bring more people on. Their only mistake had been to wait as long as they had. The other part of her fear was the bizarre powers of the dragon she'd fought.

Despite her personal discomfort, she told them of his powers, answered their questions as best she could, and tried to assuage their fear while also making it crystal clear that this was an extremely dangerous enemy—stronger than any of them had fought.

No one knew what to make of the dragon except Amythist.

Kristen also greeted the soldiers Jim had brought in and confirmed what he had promised. Yes, she would pay well.

Although she wasn't too worried about the money—it was hard to stress about that kind of thing when you had a private jet and a staff to fly it—Amythist was quick to offer her funds. Apparently, Windlock was considered working class by most dragons, and his holdings and fortune thus paled in comparison to hers. The old dragon pointed out that her funds might carry them into battle but she would most definitely not join them. Because of her generosity, Kristen couldn't help but listen respectfully to the wizened old crone.

"Tell me about his threats again," Amythist said when the large meeting finally finished and people broke into their working teams.

"That he would take the skulls of my human friends and use them as masks. Does that mean something? I thought it was only fear-tactics," she said.

"I can't say for certain, but I have heard rumors about such... fetishes. Tell me, did you get a look at either of his forms?"

She shook her head. "He knew how to use the shadows for more than only attacks. I never saw more than a tiny piece of him at any moment."

"Still, those details might prove helpful," the old dragon murmured.

In response, she reached into her memories. She'd found it so difficult to make anything out. It had been almost pitch-black in the cave and the inky form had stuck to the deepest of shadows as much as it could. What could she say? "He was vicious with his claws. Flexible, like he could use combinations of his claws and teeth that I've never encountered."

"Ugh, his bony tail, too." Heartsbane wrinkled her nose. "Instead of only having to worry about the bladed tip of this asshole's tail, we had to watch out for every piece. It was like a razor-tipped spine." She shuddered.

"Anything else?" Amythist persisted.

"He could mask his aura perfectly," Kristen said.

"You said the same thing, didn't you, Heartsbane?" Timeflash interjected.

Heartsbane confirmed that while the old dragon continued to nod with a thoughtful expression.

Kristen tried to think of more details but came up with nothing concrete. "He was toying with me, whoever he was. He seemed to think I was interrupting his plans."

Amythist chuckled and clucked like an old hen. "My dear, you interrupted the plans of every dragon on the planet when you burst into the scene as a police officer. That, at least, doesn't winnow the field. Still…I shall have to look into this. Those powers are certainly unusual and this individual sounds like he has gone to great care to conceal them for a very long time. I fear it will be difficult to shed light on this situation."

"If we're done using puns, I'd like to introduce my platoon—the Dragonbacks because we got your backs," the Wonderkid said with a wide grin.

"This young man is so delicate he wouldn't bruise a peach," the old dragon responded. He smiled at her and even winked while she undressed him with her eyes, apparently unconcerned that he was thousands of years younger than her.

Jim saluted. "We're glad to work with you, ma'am. These men and women are all ex-military and experienced warriors who have seen the true cost of war. None of them want to see the world embroiled in something like that."

"Yeah, and the paycheck ain't too shabby!" one of the soldiers interjected and drew a few chuckles from those standing in formation beside him.

"I'm happy to pay, my dears," Amythist said. "I love the look of men in uniform and dragons, of course, would never be caught dead wearing anything that wasn't couture. I'm invested in people sticking around."

"Thank you, ma'am," the Wonderkid said and dismissed his soldiers to their training exercises.

Kristen poured a cup of coffee and watched the base work. It was amazing that it wouldn't exist if not for her. Now, they were all there and operated more effectively and faster than she ever could have herself.

She was about to settle on a couch when the team she'd sent to Texas returned.

"Amy!" she said, managing to stay on her feet despite wanting to sit more than anything.

"What? No special greeting for the two of us?" Drew joked although she was quick to notice there was no laughter in his eyes.

"Is everything all right?" she asked.

"No, I'm afraid not." Lumos stepped forward, leading a fourth person she had never seen before. In seconds, she realized it was a dragon.

"This is... Well, she doesn't have a name—at least not one she knows." Amy's voice sounded hard and brittle.

"She's the lab-grown dragon from Texas?" Kristen asked. "But that's great. I thought you three were only going to gather intelligence."

"Once we found out what they were doing to this poor young lady, we couldn't even consider leaving her there any longer," Lumos said.

"It was worse than—"

"Stella?" the old dragon asked. "Oh yes, far worse. This one can't speak and is terrified of almost everyone except Amy and me."

"I...I don't think anyone has ever been kind to her—ever," the mage said, her voice hollow. "I was able to help her transform with magic. Once the spells keeping her in her dragon form were gone it wasn't that hard. I think that helped. I'm not sure when last she was able to be a human. Maybe never." While she spoke, her voice had grown tighter until it finally broke and she looked at her boss with rage in her eyes.

"She'll be all right," Kristen said.

"Will she?" Amy asked with true fury. "Because I don't know if I could be after the way they treated her. I've never seen cruelty like this, Kristen—*never*. What those two dragons did at my parents' house was callous, but it wasn't like this. She lived in filth and ate gruel made of insects. I...I want these bastards destroyed *now*!"

"We'll get them soon," Drew said. From his tone, Kristen had a hunch he'd had to talk Amy down a few times already. "We found good information in that base—maps, logs, and hard drives. Let Zed have a look at it and we'll decide on the next move."

"What about the Texas cell? How dangerous are they?" she asked.

For the first time since she'd seen them, the three shared a small grin.

"How dangerous *were* they? Not so tough, especially not when faced with little miss mage here. How are they now? Gone." Lumos smiled a smile that would have fit fine on his dragon body's face.

"Kristen, when I signed up to join you, you told me we would help people. That our mission would be to make the world a better place by making different sides see what we had in common." Amy took a deep breath. "I don't see how I can ever work with people who would do this kind of thing to an animal, let alone a thinking, feeling being like a dragon or a human. I want to stop them. More than anything."

She clenched her jaw. "I think in the days to come, we'll all come up against forces and foes we never expected. What I faced in that cave was terrifying, but it was cruel as well. So cruel that I can't imagine ever working with it so no, if it comes down to it, I won't stand in your way. As long as you continue to help me—to help all of us to right the wrongs in the world, regardless of who committed the crimes or who they were committed against— I'll have your back."

"How long of an R&R do we expect this time?" Butters asked.

Kristen shook her head and clenched her jaw. "I'm sorry, but I hope none of you were planning any vacations. The time to act is now. You eliminated a cell, plus the disruption to the one in Florence less than a month ago, which means we're on a streak. Every other technomage terrorist cell in the world is about to try to change hide-outs, dig in deeper, or attack outright. We have no time to wait and need to focus on an immediate assault to topple this organization before the cells can try to strike again. It's time for us to take the war to the enemy in a big way."

Everyone agreed. Working together was the way forward. This would be the body that would bring about a change in the world, and she would be the steel blade that would lead them all to victory.

PART III

CHAPTER SIXTY-TWO

A thousand shades of green raced below Kristen as she soared above the rainforests of South America. The beautiful scenery and calls of exotic birds almost made it possible to forget why they were there.

"You're two kilometers out, Steel. I'd descend to approach from the cover of the jungle."

"Thanks, Zed. We'll drop now." She signaled with her tail that it was time to land. Her people responded instantly and without question, something that had begun to mean more and more to her.

Heartsbane, Lumos, and Stonequest now each commanded a small wing of dragons. Drew and Jim commanded two small platoons of about twenty-five ex-soldiers turned dragon-human peacekeepers. Currently, each platoon was inside a converted shipping container and the two leaders waited for orders via radio.

They heard her give the order, and she knew that inside their somewhat creative airborne troop carriers, men pushed against their seats, tightened their seatbelts, and checked their ammunition.

Lumos's wing of dragons didn't carry a container because, during the battle, they would provide air support. Hopefully, the mages who rode with the old golden dragon—Amy, Larry, and a new recruit

Amythist brought in called Kristof—would be able to protect the dragons from any air defense.

Kristen was supposed to stay back—not an easy task given her history—but that was the way of things. Their intelligence said there shouldn't be any high-priority targets at this base, which meant she had to remain at a safe distance so she wasn't accidentally injured.

Heartsbane's wing moved to the right, while Stonequest went to the left. Drew led the forces that were carried by her dragons, while Jim led the ones with Stonequest. The Steel Dragon followed Lumos, who continued to fly forward and directly to the base they could now see occupied a clearing in the jungle.

Although the location didn't appear to be the most technologically advanced, it would still pose a substantial threat.

Its perimeter was a simple ten-foot fence created by wooden posts sharpened to points at the top. While a rudimentary defense, to be sure, it was an obstacle all the same. Inside the base—if Brian's satellite images could be trusted—barricades were spread across the landscape and four reinforced concrete bunkers, each of which was built like a three-stepped ziggurat—a stepped pyramid with a flat top and two levels people could patrol on the outside. It was odd architecture but not particularly intimidating.

All in all, it didn't look like much beyond a repurposed base that was probably once used to manufacture cocaine. The two massive cannons on its roof were the only exceptions and didn't look like the kind of weapons drug lords installed.

They looked like dragon killers.

"All right, first things first, you young pips. We need to find out what they're packing," Lumos shouted to the three dragons who flew in a V formation behind him. "I don't want anyone to get hit, but we do need to draw fire from that CIWS. It will tell us more about what kind of arsenal they have and how foolish the entire mission is."

He had argued long and hard against this operation. The last time they'd assaulted a base with a close-in weapons system, many dragons had died. He didn't want to risk such losses again, but the dragons from his wing had argued that they were determined to help the mission—their very first—even if it proved to be lethal. To their credit, they didn't seem frightened by the decision they'd made in the safety of their base. Their postures were solid, and their auras tasted of confidence with only a hint of fear, exactly what Kristen wanted her soldiers to feel in a situation like this.

Lumos pumped his wings and surged into a barrel roll as he and his wing moved into range of the two massive guns. One of them erupted almost instantly and fired what sounded like a hundred bullets in the blink of an eye with a buzz-saw sound. The team had expected this and they maneuvered in and out of the lines of bullets. Brian's research skills were proving to be a huge advantage as he had identified the particular make of the weapon there and had been able to define its range.

One of the younger dragons—a dark-scaled female with the ability to make tornados from the rapid beats of her wings—whooped with delight. "These dumbass mages are using regular bullets." Windspin whirled in her place in formation to display the holes the weapon had drilled in the membrane of her wings that were already healing.

The other young dragons smiled at each other and pumped their wings to propel them even faster towards the base.

Lumos, however, intervened before their enthusiasm could get the better of them. "We haven't seen the other gun fire yet. Stay in formation and follow my lead."

The old battle master's training showed when the young dragons fell into formation again and followed Lumos as he continued to approach the base. Despite his caution, his powers made his golden scales glow with excitement.

Only Windspin didn't obey her superior's orders. "I got this!" she shouted and began to beat her wings with such force that great gales of wind swept out from them and slammed against the wooden fence that surrounded the perimeter of the base. In moments, she had outpaced her allies.

Kristen had long since stopped being shocked by such displays of powers that seemingly broke the laws of physics. Dragons needed magic to function, period. This one could make wind without being blown back by it. That was simply the way of things. It made about as much sense as her being able to turn her body to steel and back. Or Heartsbane being able to control other people's emotions as easily as a professional pianist could play something by Scott Joplin.

But her assault did not go unnoticed. While she raced forward and the gusts of wind from her wings battered the crude fence erected by the technomages, the other massive gun that had yet to fire pivoted until it aimed directly at Windspin's chest. Without preamble or warning, it fired.

The young dragon's wind might have been able to demolish a fence made of hundreds of tree trunks if she'd had another minute to use it. Unfortunately, the ordinance launched at her seared a hole in her chest. She plummeted to land in a bloody pile with an aura no longer. It was shocking to see her struck down with such ruthless efficiency.

"The first gun's a decoy and second is loaded with dragon rounds!" Lumos boomed to his wing, who broke into two smaller groups and moved in slightly different directions. The gun followed one of them and fired, but they used every one of their formidable dragon talents to avoid flying in a straight line.

The shot missed, thank God.

"Everyone stay in formation!" their leader shouted, angry at the unnecessary loss of life so early in the fight. "We have mages on three of us. As long as we stay close, Larry, Amy, and Kris should be able to protect us!"

"Kristof!" the man shouted.

"Is now really the time for that?" he demanded as his wing reformed and made another pass at the two massive mounted machine guns.

"Are we a go?" Jim asked Kristen over the radio.

"Lumos is running interference. You have a green light to engage," Kristen told both her human team leaders.

Thirty people emerged from the forest on one side of the base and sprinted as one to close the distance between the walled base and the cover provided by the jungle. While the humans moved at what amounted to their full speed, five of them came nowhere close to their peak. Heartsbane and her wing had been ordered to embed themselves amongst the regular humans for this assault and to retain their human bodies rather than their dragons ones. They were smaller targets this way and—if Kristen's team failed—the enemy technomages wouldn't learn exactly how many dragons now worked with the Steel Dragon.

The thirty soldiers raced forward and fired constant volleys from their assault rifles at the mages atop a hidden walkway that ran along the interior of the wooden fence. It seemed they weren't all mages, though, or if they were, they didn't have any battle powers. The defenders returned fire with bullets rather than magic.

Drew's soldiers didn't flinch as they ran into battle or when a lucky bullet struck home in a man's chest and felled him instantly. Nor did they cower when another shot turned a man's head into nothing but red mist.

Kristen shook her head. She had known there would be casualties. All their information said this was a heavily fortified base that was a key distribution center for the technomage network of terrorist cells. It would be foolish and naïve to imagine anything less, but losing people this early still hurt.

Maybe the man who was shot in the chest is still alive, she told herself. She'd spared no expense on armor. Perhaps the end of the battle would reveal hidden surprises.

That battle itself was certainly supposed to if their plans played out as expected.

Jim's team approached from the other side of the base.

They consisted mostly of former Marines as well as Navy Seals and were the stealthier half of the pincer strike. As they had trained to do, they moved across the open space between the thick jungle and the wooden wall that surrounded the technomage base like jungle predators—silent, quick, and deadly.

They had almost made it halfway across the open space before they were noticed.

Blasts of fire, ice, and what appeared to be magical biting flies launched from the top of the wall and attacked the platoon.

Well, at least I know where the mages were hiding, Kristen told herself. But this confirmation of the intelligence her team had received didn't feel so great when she had to watch as a bolt of lightning seared through a soldier and sizzled his flesh before the man could so much as even raise his weapon.

"Lumos, we have mages," she told the older dragon.

"Yes, ma'am, we see them," the golden dragon confirmed. He and his wing swooped over Jim's platoons' heads to draw the magical attacks that human armor could do so little against. The mages on their backs were able to deflect the blasts of magic and buy Jim and his people a few more precious yards of advance.

"We have contact with the wall," Drew shouted from the other side and pulled Kristen's attention to that location.

Now was the time for the dragons to show their mettle. Humans could have demolished the wall made of dug-in trees, but it would have taken longer. The dragons hidden among Drew's platoon simply kicked it over, leveled a dozen tree trunks, and created a space large enough for them to enter the base. The invaders continued the assault on the concrete bunkers within. At the top of the wall, the men armed with assault rifles scattered before they were hurled from their perch.

"Dragons!" The word blared over a sound system and the mages attacking Jim traded places with those armed simply with assault rifles.

From her vantage point, Kristen could see that some of the men headed to one of the bunkers and exchanged their rifles for identical models. The difference could only be that the new ones were loaded with dragon bullets.

"Dragons, weapons will soon be hot. Continue to follow your human captains' leads," she called over their radio net.

Drew led his team through the gap in the fence. Rather than pushing forward, he led them to take cover at the nearest bunkers. Brian's intel had told them exactly which seemed to be the headquarters and which were little more than storage and sleeping areas.

Once again, the intel received proved its value.

No sooner had the platoon found cover than the freshly armed technomages opened fire. Kristen couldn't see the action in that corner of the base. All she could hear was gunfire and screams.

Her heart fell when a great blast of fire rocketed into the air and the rest of the fence that Drew had led his team through was leveled. Even though she knew what must have caused it, she couldn't help but look.

Sure enough, a dragon had been shot in human form with a dragon bullet. Death made them revert to their dragon body and it leveled the fence in its death throes.

"Damn it," she cursed. With two dragons down already, this was not going well.

"Orders?" Lumos asked.

She wanted to think about it and take the time to weigh every possible outcome, but it was a luxury she simply didn't have. They had to destroy the base and this was their only chance.

"Press on. Don't let them die for nothing."

"We'll target the big cannon, then," the old dragon said.

"Make it so," she agreed.

He and his team wheeled and launched a new assault at the mages who were now divided to be able to focus on both Jim and Drew's forces. Even though Kristen knew what was coming, she was impressed with the golden dragon's battle prowess. He was amazingly subtle, which made it easy to think he simply attacked the mages with his talons while his wing streaked past him and each blasted a ball of fire at the weapon that had fired dragon bullets at them.

Three of the fireballs struck its base, which—unfortunately—seemed to do no visible damage.

The gun pivoted towards Lumos, who systematically hurled mages from their positions on the walkway inside the wall. He watched the weapon more closely than he seemed to, though. As soon as its intended trajectory came too close to his position, he descended to the earth and used his tail to lash at the fence.

Whoever controlled the barrel seemed to think they still had a shot and fired.

Their assumption proved to be their great mistake, albeit perhaps unwittingly, as the fireballs had apparently weakened the apparatus that allowed the gun to pivot. When it fired, it was flung from its mooring and tumbled down the other side of the concrete bunker. It made impact with a boom so loud it rattled Kristen even at her fairly distant vantage point.

The person who piloted the other cannon seemed eager for vengeance, as he swung it toward Lumos and opened fire. The dragons, however, already knew it was loaded with nothing but good old-fashioned lead.

The golden dragon simply spread his wings and shielded the human soldiers from the ammunition that would have laughed at their armor if given the opportunity.

In truth, it wasn't his wings that blocked the bullets but Larry, the mage upon his back. As they didn't want the mages to know this, Lumos feigned pain and leapt skyward while Jim and his people raced through the gap he'd made in the wall.

"Kristen—" Brian said over her radio. He was back at their base and watched the battle unfold from cameras mounted on the captains and from satellite feeds of the area.

"Not now, Brian. This battle's about to change."

"You're right about that. She's here."

"Who?" she asked reflexively, but she knew exactly who her brother was talking about.

The Iron Dragon appeared as a shadow in front of the sun like she'd emerged from the burning pits of hell itself. She was already in an insanely fast dive by the time Kristen even saw her. By then, it was too late.

"Lumos!" she shouted when she realized he was the Iron Dragon's target.

"I have her!" Amy replied and launched a great blast of magic that made the cannon that had turned a dragon into mush seem like nothing but a firecracker.

She missed, however. The Iron Dragon tucked her wings and dodged the blast of raw magic as easily as Lumos had avoided the bullets a moment before.

Lumos was thankfully not taken completely by surprise. He rolled to put his claws between his vital organs and his assailant, who fell like a meteor from the sky.

The Iron Dragon made no effort to slow her assault.

She powered into her target, his claws be damned, like a freight train bulldozing through a shopping cart.

Still, he was able to dodge the brunt of her blow with only a few scratches on his chest from the encounter. Unfortunately, he wasn't able to block his adversary's tail that whipped behind him and knocked Larry from his back.

"Old fool. Dragons aren't supposed to work with mages and you failed to protect yours." She sneered as she continued to claw and scratch at Lumos to keep the dragon engaged and unable to help the mage, who now plummeted with no hope of aid.

"Come on, Larry. Come on," Kristen muttered, her eyes narrowed in focus on the falling figure. The mage seemed to gain momentum with each second and the wind of his rapid descent ripped at his robes as he fell end over end. "Why hasn't he caught himself with his magic?"

She answered her question because it was so obvious. He was unconscious and would be unable to either register his danger or slow his fall. The golden dragon still tried to keep his assailant at bay. His team attempted to destroy the other gun and save the lives of the rest of Kristen's soldiers.

Only one person present could save the mage.

"Fuck the battle plans," Kristen said, transformed into her dragon form, and swooped to catch her friend before he became nothing but another life lost in the jungle.

CHAPTER SIXTY-THREE

She flapped her wings faster and faster, focused on nothing but Larry's body as it plunged at a rapidly increasing pace. The only gun that could kill her with a single shot had been destroyed. The dragon who wanted to snap her neck was occupied. The mages were trying to kill her friends.

It was up to Kristen to save Larry.

Grimly determined, she pushed herself faster and closed the distance between them until finally, she extended a claw and caught the mage gently by his robes. She drew her friend to her chest and pulsed her aura with alertness, hoping to jolt him awake.

What she should have done was watch the Iron Dragon. At some point, the enemy had extricated herself from combat with Lumos and settled on her as a new target.

At the last moment, she saw the aggressor with seconds to spare but was still able to dodge. It seemed obvious that an attack would succeed on this pass.

Although Katrina barely skimmed her, she didn't seem frustrated by her failure. Instead, she shed her iron skin, banked into a tight loop that seemed impossible for a dragon, and transformed into her iron body in time to drive into Kristen's spine.

Despite the protective steel ridges that would have hindered lesser foe, the Iron Dragon was able to dig her claws into Kristen's back with such force that her wings spasmed in pain.

She clutched Larry against her chest as she pounded into the dirt in what she chose to count as a controlled landing. Her brother, though—who watched everything on the satellite footage—would no doubt say it needed work.

With her body positioned above the mage to keep him hidden, she pushed to her feet. Her instinct to protect him wasn't misplaced as it sounded like every gun and blast of magic was now aimed at the two of them.

Fortunately, the jolt she'd sent to him via her aura to wake him worked. Seconds before her steel skin was shredded by dragon bullets, he threw up a shield. Dozens of bullets dissipated into nothing but dust merely inches from her face.

"Kristen!" Larry shouted as if he hadn't saved her life and it was still in peril.

She understood his worry when the Iron Dragon bulldozed into her again. The two metal dragons tumbled in vicious combat and their strikes gouged the black earth beneath the carpet of tropical plants.

Her orders had been for dragons to transform into their human shape if they were grounded, but that strategy had assumed there wouldn't be any dragon support. No one had anticipated the Iron Dragon's arrival, Kristen least of all. It didn't seem wise to turn into her human form during a battle with this beast of a woman.

The time for what-ifs and strategic adjustment was over.

The aggressor extricated herself from Kristen's claws and lunged again to drive into her chest with horns made of iron. Sparks flew when iron struck steel, but the Steel Dragon was virtually unscathed. Yes, she felt the blow, but her steel skin blunted much of the force.

Before the Iron Dragon could withdraw, she sliced her across her body with her steel claws in the dragon version of a punch to the gut. The attack did even less to her opponent than the headbutt had done to her.

"Fool," her opponent hissed before she arced her tail to swipe the blade at the end into Kristen's neck a little below her jawline. Pain seared through her like lightning. "Oh, did I hit a nerve?"

"Why are you doing this, Katrina?" she demanded before she attacked again.

"Because meeting you only proved to me that I'm on the side that will win this war."

"We don't have to be at war," she protested before the other dragon barreled into her again and thrust her through one of the wooden walls that were still standing to bring the structure down on top of them.

None of that particularly hurt. Steel was much stronger than wood, after all, but she soon realized that the attack hadn't been anything but a means to conceal another strike.

As she tried to free herself from the tangle of fallen logs and wire, the Iron Dragon drove her claw into the joint at Kristen's armpit. Pain blossomed like wildflowers in springtime as she tried to get away and only entangled herself more in the wreckage of the wooden fence.

"Stupid dragon. You don't even know how to use your body."

Her attacker was goading her, but she was also right. She had tried to use her arms and legs to free herself and had ignored her wings and tail. When she flexed them quickly, wood catapulted in all directions. She hoped none of it crushed any of her teammates but she'd completely lost control of the battle and made no effort to command. All she wanted to do now was survive.

Katrina seemed hellbent on not letting that happen.

As soon as she extended her wings and tail to throw off the debris, the Iron Dragon's tail was there. It stabbed into the joint in the middle of her wing, cut through the steel skin, and reached the bone underneath. To Kristen, it felt like a red-hot poker.

She leapt away and tucked her wings, willing the wound to heal with her dragon powers.

Her enemy watched her and her long, forked dragon tongue slid from side to side in her mouth as if she were hungry.

Kristen decided she'd had quite enough of her adversary's arrogance.

She pressed an attack, lunged forward, and threw a shoulder into Katrina with enough force to propel her into one of the concrete bunkers behind her. Despite the power behind the blow being strong enough to make the Iron Dragon crack the surface of the structure, it hardly seemed to phase Katrina.

She merely used the wall at her back for support as she raised her dragon legs and used them to kick her opponent's knee savagely.

The first kick didn't hurt that much, but the second blow caught a better angle. The pain was so intense, she cried in her dragon form— something she'd never done or seen another dragon do. Tears welled and turned to steam as she stumbled back.

Her adversary laughed. "This is like fighting a child," she said.

The Steel Dragon pushed off the leg that didn't hurt, but before she launched a powerful kick, she whipped her tail around and managed to catch the dragon in her armpit.

Katrina winced and backed off a step. Then, she looked over Kristen's shoulder and grinned. "So much for your soldiers!"

Instinct made her turn to see who of her people were struggling.

It was purely a distraction and one which the Iron Dragon used to the fullest. She powered into her, delivered a blow on her turned neck, and launched her into another tumble. Kristen tried to stand but found she couldn't as her enemy was on her back.

"How is it that we can be the same age and yet you're so pathetic?" Katrina emphasized her point by using her tail to slash her other armpit. "You could be exactly like me. Hell, for all we know, you might even be stronger. But instead, you squandered your childhood among humans." She used a claw to gore a wound into Kristen's back. Her dragon powers should have blocked a blow like that but with all the wounds, her ability to heal used most of her energy. It seemed her assailant understood this very well.

"I thought you were fighting for people!" Kristen said.

Katrina's first answer was to simply punch her in the snout. The pain was as intense as getting hit in the nose in her human form.

"I am fighting because those in power do not wish to share. I am not fighting so a lazy human from the suburbs gets to sit on a throne when this is all done. There will be a new order to the world, and I will be one of its leaders."

"Is that why you obey the mages' commands? Because you're a leader?" She knew she shouldn't have asked such a question.

Her foe agreed and her response was immediate. She vaulted off and kicked her hard enough in the gut to make her roll from her stomach to her back. In that blurry instant while her head spun one hundred eighty degrees, she saw snippets of the battle raging all around her.

Drew hunkered behind a concrete bunker, yelling at Hernandez to blow something up.

Butters perched atop a wall, his sniper rifle to his eye and Beanpole at his side.

Keith was kicked mercilessly by two technomage lackeys.

A dragon set a mage on fire and simply blew away their puny shield of defense and turned them into nothing but ash.

That was all she saw before Katrina bit her chest above her heart repetitively.

Steel scales could only endure for a limited time, unfortunately. The Iron Dragon focused her attack on the one place and savaged it until a scale flecked away, followed by another. This enabled her to bite through the fleshy muscles below the scales and skin. She made it through those even faster than she had the scales and reached the bone. Iron claws grated horribly against Kristen's ribcage, but there was nothing she could do. The other dragon had her pinned with her legs on their side and her tail under her body. Her front arms were trapped by her adversary's front arms. Katrina somehow knew how to use her body against her.

The Iron Dragon laughed and both combatants understood that iron was about to beat steel. Even if Kristen could break free, her foe simply had to harry her with attacks until she died of blood loss. The wound on her chest bled freely, but if she couldn't escape, she knew Katrina would literally eat her heart out of her chest.

It was times like this when she wondered why she hadn't wanted to be a volleyball player or an accountant rather than a cop.

But she had to focus despite how much pain she was in. She had to stay in the moment and she forced herself to look at the other dragon's eyes. Her instincts rebelled but she focused her gaze on the pits of evil that looked so much like her own.

It provided a good view when Lumos bulldozed Katrina off her chest.

CHAPTER SIXTY-FOUR

"Excuse me, you were sitting on my boss," Lumos quipped as he soared past after Katrina sprawled away from him.

The Iron Dragon didn't take the insult lying down. She spun onto her feet and readied herself for him to circle and collide with her again. Despite Kristen having a clear view of the dragon and being fairly familiar with how she handled herself in combat, she realized she had no idea how she intended to attack Lumos. She looked equally ready to use her jaws, claws, tail, or even a blast of fire.

It made her think of herself and wonder if she was as difficult to read when she was in her dragon form. Was there something about her stance that caused problems in combat?

They were questions for later, she reminded herself as she watched the golden dragon rocket toward their enemy. He moved easily and dodged blasts of magic and volleys of bullets as he approached.

Katrina reared to fully engage with him, but the ancient dragon showed no interest in meeting her challenge.

He ignited his eyes with glowing golden energy. At first, his scales seemed to glow brighter, then his claws seemed to be made of white light, and finally, his eyes pulsed brighter than the sun.

The Iron Dragon stumbled backward, blinded by the unexpected power.

Lumos gave her no quarter. He powered into her and somersaulted moments before he made impact to drive his back claws into her chest and thrust the air from her lungs.

She wheezed as she tried to catch her breath, rubbed her eyes, and struggled to her feet all at the same time.

The golden dragon continued his attack, although his claws and tail were ineffectual against her iron scales. Still, Kristen saw the method in the way he fought. He started by striking at the easiest targets—his opponent's broad chest, her unguarded flank, and her back, but when those blows were rebuffed by the hard scales, he focused his attacks on some of the same regions where she had targeted Kristen like her armpits, her throat, and her groin.

It looked, for a moment, like Lumos might win, but his adversary shook her head and began to defend herself better against the strikes from the shining gold dragon.

It soon became clear that despite Lumos's excellent skill, Katrina was simply stronger. Whether it was because she was younger or because she had a power better suited for close combat was unclear.

The reasons, however, would make no difference to the outcome. He might be able to beat Katrina in a fair fight or maybe it would go the other way. What did matter was that Kristen wasn't about to sit back and watch. Her horrific chest wound had healed enough that she was able to stand. She joined the battle, followed Lumos' lead, and aimed her strikes at the Iron Dragon's weak points.

Their combined efforts seemed to have given them the advantage. Together, they were able to keep the Iron Dragon on the defensive. Kristen's raw strength and steel skin with Lumos' careful tactics and methodology proved to be a potent force against her. But as the tables started to turn, Katrina blasted them both with fire that forced them both to block and thus not pursue her as closely as they would have liked.

Still, Kristen gave chase, and when she did, Lumos followed. They dogged the dragon's tail until she drew them past one of the concrete bunkers and into the line of enemy fire.

Larry once more saved her life from a volley of dragon bullets with his magical shield powers.

"Let's finish this!" she yelled.

"I'm afraid the only way this will finish is with you having more holes than a pincushion," the mage said through gritted teeth.

She stole a glance and saw his nose was already bleeding, a sure sign that he was running low on power. They couldn't continue to rely on him to shield them, which meant they had to let their quarry retreat to her base. There was no time to lament the loss of this particular skirmish, however. Just because Kristen had been sucked into a duel with her counterpart didn't mean the battle had stopped.

"We need support, now!" Drew yelled into the radio. She realized that he'd done so for a while, but this was the first time her brain allowed her to process anything besides her personal admonition to not let the iron dragon rip her guts out in front of all her friends.

Kristen looked around the battlefield in search of Drew but saw only carnage and destruction. This was the first all-out invasion-style assault on a mage base they'd done with their new team. The results were staggering.

Bullets had predictably shredded anything that stood in their way, while the mage blasts added points of charred or blackened landscape to the devastation. Bodies had fallen from both these attacks. She was surprised that seeing a body turned to a skeleton from a magical blast was even more revolting to her than the gore of a gunshot wound. The smell too was a strange mix of gunpowder, blood, and the otherworldly aromas of magic manifesting.

Nowhere in any of it did she see Drew.

"He's behind you—your five o'clock. Getting ready to push toward the main bunker," Brian said in her ear. She wondered how much he'd been talking to her and how much she'd missed of his instruction during the fight.

Kristen turned and moved toward one of the bunkers. She hadn't realized the fight with Katrina had moved them well beyond the perimeter of the enemy base.

Gunshots rang out as she approached. She returned to her original orders and changed to her human form now that the Iron Dragon had retreated. Lumos followed suit and together, they raced forward. Lead bullets pinged against her steel skin and fell away. She dodged most of them, using her dragon senses and instincts to hear gunshots, identify a shooter, and move away from the path of the bullet, all in the blink of an eye. Of course, even a dragon couldn't dodge every shot fired at them, but those that struck couldn't hurt her. She experienced a slight sting, much like that inflicted by a paintball would hurt, but nothing severe, and none of them were enough to slow the Steel Dragon.

They reached their destination and threw themselves against the wall of the bunker Drew stood behind.

"Man, is it nice to see you!" He grinned. A bullet had grazed his forehead and blood trickled down his face but he didn't look frightened, only focused.

"Now is not the time to kiss up to your boss," Larry said once he'd joined them using his powers to fly there. "What's the plan?"

"I want to finish this," Kristen said. "These guys are not as well-armed as they could be. They don't use dragon bullets exclusively, which means resources are tight. If we let them go, it's worse than them escaping. They'll use this battle to study us and come prepared with more bullets next time."

"So we punch through those doors," Drew said and stuck his head out from the cover of the bunker they had gathered behind to point to another one. The mages and armed men supporting them took the opportunity to shoot at him, but he withdrew his head without earning another wound on his face.

"I think I can handle those," Kristen said.

"The problem isn't the doors themselves," Hernandez said. She gestured to a duffel bag that was no doubt filled with explosives that she had somehow managed to carry across a battlefield without dropping it or worse. "The problem is their defenders on the top of the bunker."

"Amy? Come in, Amy?" Larry said into a radio. "We need that other gun taken down."

"I hear you," the girl said from the back of a dragon as they flew overhead. One of them did a barrel roll and a blast of magic streaked to sever the automatic machine gun on one of the other bunkers. Kristen shook her head at the mage's power. The plan had been to keep the extent of her abilities as quiet as possible, but Amy didn't seem interested in sticking to that.

"Get ready," Lumos said, focused on the wing of dragons that glided over the jungle, banked sharply to turn in formation, and set a course toward the one bunker where the hostiles had dug in.

"And three… two… one… Let's go!" The golden dragon raced forward as the dragons flew overhead. Kristen sprinted close behind him. Her dragon powers fueled her muscles to enable her to increase her speed, dodge bullets and blasts, and finally vault up ten feet to land on the bunker itself.

It might have been more impressive if the other dragon hadn't done the same thing but with more grace. The two of them attacked the mages, who tried desperately to conjure magic blasts that could both overpower a dragon and be activated faster than a dragon could move.

There weren't many spells like that, though, so their efforts were futile.

The two dragons worked through their level of the outside of the bunker to thrust mages aside and hurl the people who fired the guns to the earth below. They weren't able to disable all of them, unfortunately, and some fled inside the structure itself and triggered explosives as they left. The blasts turned the interior of the ziggurat's upper level into nothing but impassible rubble.

On the level above them, Heartsbane and her dragons followed the same process to deal with the mages they could and force the others to flee.

The defenders at the very top simply jumped from their position as Amy and the dragons she flew with overwhelmed the magical shields with endless blasts of their fire breath. The outside of the bunker was finally clear and the battlefield fell eerily silent. The enemy had all fled inside, which meant they had reached the next stage of the battle.

"Can you get in up there?" Hernandez shouted from below.

"I think so, but they collapsed the entrances," Kristen answered.

"Don't go in! I'd bet a crate of C4 they put more explosives inside. Plus, it means they're probably not hiding in the top."

She nodded. The demolitions expert made sense, which meant their best option was to simply go through the front door. Kristen, Lumos, and the rest of Heartsbane's dragons all dropped to ground level.

"Do you think we should knock?" Kristen asked. "Or should we simply blow the fucking door down?"

CHAPTER SIXTY-FIVE

To Kristen's shock, Hernandez didn't want to blow the doors
down. Before she set explosives at the barrier, she made a
circuit around the building.

"What are you looking for?" she asked their demolitions expert.

"Nothing," the woman said. "Or I found nothing anyway. Despite
the way this building was pounded, I don't see any cracks in the
concrete. I guess our best bet is the front doors."

"Do I need to give you the order to blow them the fuck up or can
I trust you to do the right thing?" She hadn't intended to sound rude
but her blood was up and she didn't want this battle to end with
their enemies escaping. She knew they didn't have much time. The
technomages they'd faced in Florence had teleportation spells. Given
that these mages were supported by the Iron Dragon—exactly like
the cell in Florence had been—it stood to reason that they might
have the same kind of spells. With that in mind, every single second
counted.

"No, ma'am. Allow me," Hernandez said and began to place explosives strategically across the huge steel door. She didn't take long to
do it—less than a minute—yet it still felt like an eternity. Finally, the
charges were placed and the woman cheerfully told everyone to get

clear or risk being turned into mush. She didn't sound too worried about that happening to anyone, though.

Everyone took cover and Hernandez detonated her bomb with gleeful abandon.

Her laughter faded when she saw that her bomb didn't so much as scratch the doors. "How the hell is that even possible?" she fumed.

"Don't beat yourself up about it. They have magic," Heartsbane said.

The woman scowled at the kind words. "Jesus, you know you fucked up when the meanest dragon on the team is nice to you."

Everyone laughed at that except Kristen.

Neither she nor her team had time for this. For that matter, the world didn't have time for it either. If Hernandez couldn't gain access for them, she'd have to try instead. Kristen made sure her steel skin was as thick as she could make it before she applied her fists to the door.

She was immediately disappointed when her first blow only dented the surface an inch.

The demolitions expert, though, was much more impressed. "That shouldn't be...you shouldn't be able to do that."

It was unfortunately not enough damage and she punched, kicked, and screamed and made very little progress. While she would be able to get through, it would take too far too long.

"Do you mind if I take a stab at it?" Amy said and Kristen glanced at her in surprise. She hadn't seen her land.

"Be my guest." She reminded herself—although the dragon in her didn't want to admit it—that Amy's power surpassed her own.

"You'll need to step back," the mage warned.

She knew it was well-founded advice and complied without complaint.

The girl thrust her hands out like she was rolling on ecstasy at a rave and tried to cover the rest of the dancers in glitter. The doors lurched.

"That a girl!" Larry shouted.

Amy made no reply as she squared her feet and curled the fingers on her outstretched hands. In response, the edges of the door buckled like construction workers had loosened all the hinges at once and someone in a dump truck heaved on the massive pieces of metal that comprised the door.

"Is that all you have?" Heartsbane asked.

"Not even kind of." Amy grunted, braced her feet, and moved her hands in circles like she was wrapping a thick rope around each hand. Her hands were empty, of course, and the only thing she manipulated was the air and the invisible magic she'd cast between herself and the doors.

"Stand back!" she yelled and everyone retreated, thankful that they did not need to seek cover like when they faced armed hostiles and magic-hurling enemy mages.

The doors catapulted out of their place in the bunker and became airborne like a giant Olympian who had something to prove. They careened twenty feet, thirty, forty, and at least fifty feet before they plummeted. Both dug deep into the black earth and quivered while they emitted a low hum. Her teammates stared, everyone impressed with the evidence of the power she wielded.

"Jeeee-sus," Hernandez said, her mouth agape. "Remind me never to get on Amy's bad side."

"Lucky for us she doesn't have a bad side," Drew said.

The mage turned to them and smiled. "Unless you talk shit about my skateboarding. Do that and prepare to pay the price."

"Have you all finished joking? I have some mages whose ass I want to kick," Heartsbane said.

"Let the record show it was the grumpy dragon who crossed our mage, not any of us regular humans," Keith said.

They entered quickly with Kristen leading the way with her steel skin despite the protests of her team at risking her life over theirs. They finally agreed to it because Amy and Larry shrouded her in shields of magical energy.

The Iron Dragon wasn't waiting inside, nor did she find a team of mages or a battalion of men aiming their guns at the entrance. Instead, an empty room yawned to welcome them, strewn with rubble that had fallen from the upper levels of the concrete ziggurat when the mages had blocked their exit.

"It's clear," she said and signaled the other dragons to come in but to remain behind Amy and Larry's magic shield as they'd done a hundred times in training sessions.

"They couldn't have all simply disappeared," one of the new dragons said and surveyed the mess. Most of the chunks of concrete were small enough to be lifted by hand. A few were large enough to need a few people to move them. One piece was big enough that it would take nothing short of dragon strength or perhaps the magic of a particularly powerful mage to lift it. It was positioned in the center of the room which immediately made everyone suspicious.

"Give me a hand with this," Kristen said to Stonequest and Emerald. The three dragons grasped the huge piece of concrete and on three, lifted it and flipped it to the side of the room. Nothing exploded, fortunately, and no poison gas was released. It appeared that no hidden spells were activated either, but Kristen's stomach filled with dread.

Her instincts when she'd first seen the stone had been correct and she now stared at a staircase that led into the earth below the tropical jungle.

"What is with these assholes and being underground?" Emerald asked.

Stonequest shrugged. "They're like rats, I guess, and can't help but stick to the sewers."

"If they're like rats, they'll scatter now that we messed up their nest," Kristen said. "We need to move before they flee and destroy whatever intel we can gather."

She motioned for the rest of her team before she started down the steps. They were made of rebar and concrete and wound down in a tight spiral. Every step was blind and every move brought them closer to danger.

Despite her steel skin and the layers of magic protecting her, she was still nervous. They had been engaged in open conflict with these technomages for months. She told herself they had done an adequate job protecting knowledge of the extent of their defensive abilities from their enemy but was it something anyone could ever know?

For all she knew, the technomages could have pioneered a new kind of sniper rifle that could fire bullets faster than her mages could react to them, or perhaps a spell that rendered their magical defenses useless.

Despite her caution, no strike came and no enchanted sword severed her head from her neck. No bomb was waiting for her on the next step or the one after that.

Instead, she heard furtive footsteps and the labored breathing of people who tried to move quickly and not be heard. The rats were still on the ship, it seemed, and they weren't ready to flee yet.

That said, they certainly knew how to hide.

Kristen reached the bottom of the stairs and entered a room as large as the one at the top had been. Two doorways exited the room, one on the right and one on the left.

"Assholes," Drew said as he stepped off the last step and moved to stand next to Kristen. "I guess this is where we do the dumbass thing they always do in movies and split up?"

"I guess," she said. "But the mages are the foolish teenagers in this scenario. We're the ones hunting them."

She hoped that turned out to be true but she was no longer naïve enough to say such things for any reason other than a moment of confidence for her team. With luck, they wouldn't squander it.

CHAPTER SIXTY-SIX

Drew still felt weird giving orders to mages and dragons, but that didn't mean he wouldn't do it. "My team, left door. Heartsbane, back us up. Lumos, do you mind if we borrow Amy?"

The question was merely a formality. They had already planned on how to divide the teams if a situation like this occurred, but the new dragons responded better to orders framed as questions than direct orders.

The heat of the battle was still in everyone's veins, so no one complained too much. The dragons took point, the humans fell in behind them, and Amy fell in at the back of the formation. In that position, the humans could defend her while she provided magical shielding for the dragons at the front.

"Right, let's move," Drew said and took point despite not having a dragon's healing ability. He wore a bulletproof vest and carried a gun. That had always been enough for him and he didn't intend to start thinking otherwise now.

They moved through a narrow hallway with big windows on each side. He had seen enough of these despicable bases to recognize the equipment needed to turn the scales, claws, teeth, and even the bones of a dragon into bullets destined to be fired at their kin.

"I think I'll be sick," one of the dragons said, doubled over, and threw up way more half-digested meat than should have been possible for a human body.

"This is why we're fighting these technomage fucks," Heartsbane said, her voice cold. "I know that you all knew—at least intellectually —that our enemy is harvesting our kind and using our dragon bodies against us. But it's another thing entirely to see it."

"I can't believe they do this to dead dragons," the one who puked said and wiped the acrid bile from his stomach off his face.

"It's not only dead ones, honey," Hernandez said. "That might be kind of respectable at a stretch—like using every piece of the buffalo or making hotdogs. What they do is far worse."

"Did you compare dragons to livestock?" one of the other new recruits asked and bristled.

"You need to calm the fuck down before you get someone killed," Heartsbane said but her admonition was interrupted.

An offensive force of technomages and gunmen kicked open the door at the end of the hall. The dragon whose back was to them so he could face Hernandez as he responded to the particularly poor taste of her joke had no time to turn to face his attackers. Instead, his chest exploded from a gunshot wound and he fell, dead in an instant.

"Amy!" Drew shouted.

"There are too many," the mage responded, and he saw that she hadn't let the bullet through out of laziness but of necessity. Over a hundred bullets were frozen in the air, stopped by a veil of blue magic that churned more and more rapidly as the technomages tried to turn the hallway into a tunnel of death.

"Dragons, flank and close in! Humans, fire at will!"

Thank god for training, he thought as the dragons complied and moved to the walls of the hallway before they raced forward. Their human legs moved in a blur, fueled by the dragon powers they always had, even in this form.

While they got clear, the humans fired down the center of the hallway.

To Drew's surprise, their bullets found their targets easily.

The armed men who had burst into the hallway fell like grain before a reaper. There was no veil of magic to protect them and no defensive spells to extend their expendable lives.

"Go!" he said to the dragons who had already covered the distance of the hallway. "Remember our drills. Watch the corners and clear each room before you move on."

They vanished into the room and sounds of violence issued from it. The humans ran to join the combat as Amy levitated and flew down the hallway between the human soldiers.

Drew reached the room seconds after Amy, and thank God he did.

Six mages seemed to hold their own against the melee skills of the dragons and Amy's magic. They didn't have the upper hand against his team, but they weren't overwhelmed either. The room was an explosive, high octane stalemate in which the players continued to hurl balls of magic and dragon-powered punches at each other rather than hang back and wait for a power shift.

Unfortunately for the technomages, his human soldiers entered on his heels. The mages had been able to hold their own against the dragons and Amy but the concerted fusillade swept through their ranks and their defenses. Those who weren't killed in the first volley fell and covered the backs of their heads with their hands as if they were hostages rather than perpetrators of global violence.

What a difference perspective could make.

Once the gunfire ceased, Drew scanned their surroundings and realized that the room they were in was anything but normal.

The back was filled with a giant collection of crystals. Some of the larger ones were almost as tall as him. They were transparent or slightly milky. Now and then, they pulsed with a flash of yellow light.

He frowned as his mind registered a pattern. The flash wasn't now and then. It was regular like the pulses of a heartbeat.

"It's like something out of the original Superman movies," he said aloud.

"The what?" Amy asked.

"Oh, come on. You've seen *Star Wars* and quote Chew-dorka but you've never seen the cinematic masterpieces that are the Superman movies?" he asked her.

"Yeah, that's gonna be a no-go. *Star Wars* helped us with tactics. Will your dorky Superman movie tell us what the hell that collection of crystals is doing?"

"I don't think it's a collection," Hernandez said as she knelt and looked at the milky white shards as if they were a carburetor that could be conquered with a little help from an online tutorial. "I think they were grown here."

"Why? It's not like the technomages are competing in the science fair," Drew said, but he realized she might be right. When he'd entered, his attention had been on stopping the mages from hurting his people and he'd done that. Now that he had a moment to think, the mages who were still alive were a testimony to the fact that not all the people in this room had been intent on killing the intruders. Some of them had been doing something to the crystals.

"Whatever the hell it is, it reeks of magic," Amy said. "It's a much higher concentration than I've seen before. I'm not sure what it does, though."

Drew knelt beside one of the mages who lay face down on the ground. "What the fuck is this? Speak."

She rolled over and looked at him with a vicious grin. "*Mortalis totalis temtano,*" she said and spat in his face.

Amy used magic to catch it before her saliva collided.

That was Drew's first thought, but tendrils of what looked like black smoke issued from the mage's open mouth. It spread across the room but rather than targeting his team, it moved to the other two mages who cowered under the watchful eye of the human guards. It wound around their faces and within seconds, they convulsed and flailed before they lay still.

"What did you do?" he demanded of the woman he'd confronted, but the cloud must have been part of some kind of suicide pact, not a murder spell, as she was dead. Her teeth were already black with the substance and her body decayed at an unnaturally rapid pace.

"What the fuck," he said in disgust as he pushed a rising sense of terror aside. "I'll radio Larry to see if he has any idea what this is."

"Well, yeah…go ahead, but I can tell you exactly what these crystals are," Hernandez said as she straightened, her gaze fixed firmly on the odd formation.

Drew cursed under his breath. She was an expert in one thing and one thing only. The fact that she thought her knowledge extended to this bizarre device was not a good thing in his book.

"Do you think it's a bomb?" he asked.

"Oh yeah." Hernandez nodded and sounded cheerful. She was always excited when she faced explosive devices that might kill her and all her friends. "And that blinking light is a timer."

He flinched when the crystals flashed yellow again. "You can't know that."

"No, I don't know it. But I'm very sure that if someone could read these symbols over here, they'd confirm my hunch." She pointed to a cluster of rune-like symbols that seemingly floated inside the crystal. "I think this is the main circuit for it, and those yellow flashes are like a system status update or something."

"Okay." Drew nodded. "Right, this is good. If you know it's a bomb, I know you can do something about it. What else can you tell us?"

"That those yellow flashes are coming faster and faster and that they're shifting to orange too."

"Are you saying we don't have much time?" Amy asked.

Hernandez grinned. "I'm saying it looks like it'll blow us all to pieces and that it will do it sooner rather than later."

CHAPTER SIXTY-SEVEN

Drew and his team had been able to defeat the mages they'd encountered so easily because Kristen and her team had run into the more formidable fighting force.

The right exit from the entrance to this complex had also opened into a hallway with doors and large windows on each side, but these rooms weren't empty.

Mages were within and as soon as she poked her head into the seemingly abandoned hallway, bolts of fire, lightning, ice, and a dozen other far more alien and likely more deadly types of energy greeted her.

She wasn't a fool, though, and fell back immediately.

"What's the status, Lady Steel?" Larry asked.

"We have mages on both sides. They're in rooms off the hallway and have a nice little tunnel of death lined up for us."

Keith stepped forward and—despite being neither a dragon nor a mage—stuck his head into the hallway to assess the situation.

The same bursts of lethal energy that had greeted her streaked toward him and he wisely pulled his head out of the tunnel before he was either burned, electrocuted, frozen, or something far worse although far less describable.

"All right. I have a plan." He grinned.

"What is it, Rookie?" one of the dragons asked.

"Can you believe this?" he demanded. "I've been with the Steel Dragon far longer than you. How come all these guys get to call me Rookie?"

"Because they can eat you if you don't let them," Emerald said.

"Oh, right. Well I always was one to appreciate a little teasing," Keith said, chagrined.

"Your plan?" Kristen asked, impatient because they were wasting precious time.

"Right! Well, a few weeks ago, my party and I faced a room exactly like this in the Lich's lair."

"The Lich?" Emerald asked. "There hasn't been one of those for millennia."

"This was a tabletop role-playing game, so it doesn't matter who the opponent was. Also, I had no idea Liches were real. That is freaking radical," he said.

"Your plan!" the entire group yelled at him in frustration.

"Right!" Keith yanked a smoke grenade off his belt. "We cast a fog cloud." He pulled the pin on the grenade and rolled it into the hallway. Thick smoke billowed out of both ends, and the mages—not able to see the source of the cloud due to their positions in the rooms along the hallway—opened fire on it. They most likely thought it was a spell from a mage rather than the far more pedestrian alternative.

"Move! Jump through the windows or use the doorways if you can. Our goal is to draw their fire away from the hallway itself. If you can engage one on one, I know you can beat them," Kristen ordered and her team obeyed.

The dragons moved through the smoke as if it were nothing but a cool mist. She decided it made sense that it wouldn't bother them, what with the ability to breathe fire and release smoke from their nostrils.

She followed, took three steps into the hall, and vaulted through a window into one of the rooms. A blast of lightning struck her steel skin and traveled across the conductive surface. It hurt but it wasn't powerful enough to make her muscles seize, so she soldiered on.

Her initial surge placed her in front of one of the mages, but rather than moving into her first attack, she ducked and circled to get behind him. This wasn't because she was concerned about a sneak attack but because she didn't want his misses to launch bolts of energy into the hallway that was now filled with her human troops.

The mage spun as she'd expected and released a blast of fire that did absolutely nothing to her. It took considerable heat to melt steel, and this ball of fire was nowhere near the intensity needed. He made another attempt with much the same result, then tried to run. She caught him by the neck, lifted him by the throat, and flung him into a wall to knock him unconscious. After a hasty glance to confirm that he was out of the fight, she moved on to her next target.

Despite the man not being a mage, he was more formidable than the first. Rather than wielding magic, he carried an assault rifle loaded with bullets made of dragon pieces. She knew this because when he opened fire and she dodged instinctively, she wasn't quite quick enough to completely avoid a bullet and it gouged a white-hot wound in her upper arm.

Kristen flung herself prone. While a small injury normally didn't affect her, she landed on the gunshot wound and it screamed at her to be more careful as it struggled to heal. The draconic nature always demanded so much more from her healing power.

She knew she had to get back on her feet. These mages had to be brought to justice and she had to stop the violence and the endless cycles of kill and kill again. She couldn't do that if she was dead with a bullet through her forehead.

Unfortunately, the injury had slowed her far more than a non-dragon bullet would have. She struggled to get her hands under her and push her body from the floor despite the searing pain in her arm that seemed to be increasing. All the guy with the gun had to do was pull the trigger again. Hell, given the weapon he used, she doubted he even had to put any effort into it. With her essentially disabled, he simply needed to point the barrel slightly lower.

Unfortunately, he seemed to read her mind and did exactly that.

Gunfire erupted barely an arm's length from her, but the bullets never struck.

"Come on, boss. You didn't forget about old Larry, did ya?" The mage stood behind her, his arms extended and fingers spread, and his robe swirled in a wind of his creation.

Kristen made no reply. Instead, she lunged forward at the man who'd tried to shoot her with bullets made from the bodies of her siblings. She pushed through Larry's magical barrier as if it didn't exist at all. It swirled as she moved through and the bullets dropped now that they were no longer suspended by his powers.

"Oh fu—" the man tried to say before she careened into him, knocked the wind from his lungs, and cracked a couple of his ribs in the space of only a few seconds. She didn't slow to check that her attack had been effective. She was coated in steel, after all, and her mass and strength were considerably higher than the man she'd plowed through.

"This room's clear!" Larry said from behind her as she raced to help another dragon eliminate a mage. She hadn't needed to assist as once the dragons were close enough to engage in hand to hand combat with the mages, the fight was over.

"Back to the hallway!" Kristen ordered. Her people obeyed and hurried to the doorways on either side of the room or jumped through the windows on the wall between the doors. She reached the hallway first and could tell from her team's body language that the room on the other side of the corridor had been cleared as well. Her people now all fired toward the doorway at the end of the hall.

She couldn't see what they had targeted but knew it was a mage as great swirling clouds of purple smoke obfuscated the end of the passage. Although her team delivered enough lead to anchor a ship into the magical cloud, it didn't seem to have any effect. No shouts of pain came from behind the cloud, nor did the consistency or pattern of the defense spell change.

So they've finally discovered how to stop bullets. She grimaced at the realization.

Galvanized by the implications of this, she showed her team what she believed a leader should do.

Kristen lunged into the swirling cloud and lashed out with fist and elbow, swinging blindly but without hesitation. Her elbow clipped the doorframe and took the steel and cinderblock with her. She pressed forward, counting this as progress.

A moment before, it would have been impossible to hear anything. Now that her team had stopped shooting, however, voices were audible through the purple gloom.

"How much longer?" a female to her left asked.

"We need at least a few minutes each. You have to give us at least ten minutes if you want all of us to make it out of here alive." Kristen recognized the Iron Dragon and her mind once again struggled to process the impossibility of her involvement. Their intelligence endeavors had found no information on her. Even once they'd discovered her existence—discovery being a strong term when used about something that had punched her in the face—it had been hard to find anything more than rumors about her in the mages' files. Despite this, she was there and now issued orders to a group of people who had endeavored to end her species since before she was born. They needed to learn how Katrina fit into all this, but before that, she had to see what she was doing first.

"We can't give you ten minutes," a man said to her right. "They already stopped firing, which means they'll send a dragon—" She lurched from the mist into a flying kick aimed directly ahead at the third person near the door, whose voice indicated that he stood in front of her.

When she emerged from the cloud and attacked, her leg stopped short against a forcefield. The mage gaped at her and in his shock, let the spell drop.

Ah. It wasn't the purple smoke stopping the bullets after all but another mage. Her team didn't know that yet so she flipped toward the first voice she'd heard. Her elbow met a skull and the woman cried out with the last of her strength before she slumped unconscious.

"Greta!" the man across from her shouted and in seconds, the purple smoke dissipated.

"Dragons, advance!" Kristen shouted and swung back to engage with the mage who used his magic to create the bullet-stopping force shield.

She raced forward and thrust at the man's face, but her knuckles made impact with an invisible force that was nevertheless stronger than steel knuckles. Irritated, she attempted a kick to the man's ribs instead and—to her astonishment—connected. He gasped in pain as he careened across the room into a wall and plummeted into a pit below him. A roar of surprise issued from the cavity.

The sound—and the sudden defeat of her opponent—forced her to study the room she'd fought to gain entry to.

It was huge with a high ceiling and a wide cargo door on one side that led God knew where. The area felt even larger than its high ceiling because the four corners were dug out to create a huge pit. Each of these was larger than a living room, and she could only guess how deep—enough that they swallowed any light, certainly. She felt like she already knew what was in the bottom of each one.

Her suspicions were confirmed when she located Katrina off to the left in the far corner of the room.

Kristen had expected to see the Iron Dragon so that wasn't what surprised her. Nor was it the swirling mists around a glowing portal held open by two mages. Although the large size of this particular portal seemed excessive, it also did not surprise her.

What shocked and infuriated her was that the dragon and three mages all worked together to haul a fully grown, whimpering dragon up and out of the pit.

"Left corner of the room!" she shouted and honestly didn't care what else was in there at the moment because Katrina was there. Worse, wherever she attempted to take the captive dragon would almost inevitably be the place where the poor creature died. Compared to the life of this imprisoned soul, following proper procedures seemed unimportant.

She sprinted forward, her fists cocked and ready to crush the heads of these mages and the Iron Dragon herself if they took even one more scale from the suffering creature they'd hauled out of its prison. Katrina cursed as she approached and released the captive so she could engage her.

The two met each other with strikes strong enough to crack concrete. Each blow that landed on the other's metal skin sounded like a steel girder falling into another from a hundred feet up.

Katrina was a formidable warrior, but Kristen found that in her human form—and no doubt because of the fury she felt in her chest that powered her attack—she was able to hold her own against the woman who'd been raised since birth for a fight exactly like this.

Unfortunately, her attention wasn't on the combat itself.

The mages didn't use their physical muscles to hold the dragon up, but spells. Even so, they needed the Iron Dragon's assistance as the three of them grunted and strained. Their outstretched arms began to bulge with veins and tremble as if they lifted the captive with their bodies rather than their minds.

She didn't want the dragon to fall into the hole. Nor did she want the mages to force it through the portal. She tried to push past her adversary to reach the creature that even now had begun to slip into a pit of despair.

Katrina let her past and threw a wicked elbow into the back of her skull, and the blow made her sprawl forward. She still wasn't used to fighting someone who weighed as much as she did, so the force of the blow was enough to unbalance her and topple her into the pit.

Kristen screamed as she fell into the hole and tried to gain purchase on the walls but only gouged long, desperate gashes that matched those of the previous tenant.

She landed hard, the wind knocked from her, and immediately forced herself up and out of the mud that comprised the entire bottom of the prison. It stank horribly like rotten meat mixed with the sulfurous tinge of spent fireworks. She looked up the moist walls to the square of fluorescent light at the top. That was all the dragon who had lived there had been able to see for who knew how long. This was beyond anything she had yet seen.

It seemed every stronghold of the technomages revealed a new level of the depravity of the group. She had thought that Amy had truly seen the worst of it in the base in Texas. Surely nothing could be as bad as feeding dragons ground crickets and cardboard in troughs, but the raw filth of this situation was appalling.

Her gaze was distracted from the square of light above her when the dragon's hindquarters began to slip into the hole.

"Oh no," she said. "No. We will not let that happen."

Kristen knelt and sent every ounce of strength she had to her thighs and calves. She jumped and launched out of the pit like a character from a movie with too many people who wore capes.

Even with the superhuman leap, she wasn't able to get past the dragon. Instead, she changed her body to skin instead of steel and climbed it while it slid past her. She pushed aside the guilt she felt as she clambered past its tail and legs, up its back, and beyond its wings until she could see the surface. Quickly, she doubled back, grasped the dragon once she had transformed her arms into their dragon version, and slung them under the armpits of this pathetic beast.

She landed her feet on the edge of the pit and held strong.

The captive almost pulled her in but something lifted it and she noticed the telltale shimmer of Larry's magic aiding her. Additional hands appeared to assist with the dragon and Stonequest appeared to finally pull it to safety.

"Dragons, eliminate those mages," Kristen ordered.

The team Stonequest had recruited obeyed and raced towards the mages with their dragon speed. Before they could attack, the Iron Dragon moved into position to block their attacks.

"Go!" Katrina shouted, her expression furious as she looked at Kristen, Stonequest, the other dragons, and everyone else.

The mages obeyed without hesitation, which meant that whoever had created the portal operated it from the other side. Kristen knew that should mean something, but she didn't have time to consider it. Now that Stonequest was there, she released the dragon and launched herself at Katrina.

But the Iron Dragon chose not to continue the fight. She stepped through the portal and turned to face Kristen and her team, her fists raised and her face consumed with hatred. She both guarded their exit and dared the Steel Dragon to go through the portal and fight her in a place even better suited for her experience, no doubt.

Still, despite the obvious problems with simply racing through the portal, she would have. The mage who controlled it, however, didn't seem to agree with the need for more metal on metal combat.

The gateway closed and simply shrank until all Kristen could see was Katrina's face—so much like her own—staring at her through it. In seconds, their enemies were gone.

Her attention immediately returned to Stonequest and the dragon he attempted to keep from plummeting into its filth. He seemed to be managing fine. Once the mages had fled, the other dragons had gone to help him and together, they'd coaxed the dragon onto the floor of the room and away from the edge of the pit.

"We're all clear, by the way," Keith shouted. "Actually, we've been all clear since we came in. Us humans were, anyway, as the dragons and Larry handled the Iron Dragon and her henchmen. I do have bad news, though."

"What?" Kristen asked and her gaze darted to the captive they'd rescued as she felt her heart drop into her stomach.

"There's another of them in each of these holes," Keith said. "and they all smell about as bad as you do. I'm sorry, Kristen. This is totally fucked up."

She took a deep breath and tried to calm herself. "That's…that's good," she forced herself to say.

"Good?" Stonequest demanded and tried not to look furious as he attempted to calm the other dragon, but let his aura get away from him and make his emotional state quite clear. "What part of any of this could you possibly say is good?"

"These pits are hideously small, even for a single dragon. It would be impossible for them to hold two. If there's one in each one, it means we at least stopped their torture. There's nothing we can do for the pain they already caused you and your friends," she said to the dragon that still cowered against a wall, obviously unsure of what to do with its freedom. "But we'd be honored to help you however we can."

It didn't acknowledge her words or even that it understood them. The only response was to shake its head, its eyes wide like a cow on the way to the slaughterhouse instead of the sentient, thinking being she knew it to be.

"It'll be okay," she said and approached with her hands outstretched and palms up in the universal sign of peace. She made no progress with the dragon. The poor creature flapped its wings—to reveal that they were badly scarred and not healing properly—and whimpered as it tried to make itself into as small as a ball as it could against the wall.

Kristen sighed. This would not be easy, and they had three more dragons to rescue. At least this one wasn't trying to go back into the pit. That would have been a sign of a form of Stockholm syndrome and would have made their job of rehabilitating them far more difficult.

"All right," she said, turned to her team, and tried to stay calm despite the way her heart thumped in her chest. "The mages and the Iron Dragon retreated and left their prisoners behind, which is a huge success for us."

Everyone in the room responded with a ragged cheer.

"I'd like to celebrate too, but we all know there's still considerable hard work ahead of us. These dragons need to be helped out of the pits and cleaned and hopefully, they can be convinced to transform into their human forms."

"Yeah, maybe," Stonequest said. The dragon Amy had brought from Texas hadn't even known it had a human form, and these seemed to be in even rougher shape.

"Okay, people, let's get to our places," Larry ordered, cutting in to take control of the important task of delegating labor. "Humans, I want you to look for clues—maps, supply schedules, photos of loved ones, old post-it notes, receipts from convenience stores...nothing is too small. Dragons, work in groups of three to get these captives out."

"Yes, sir," everyone replied.

"But take your time with the dragons," Kristen said. "It'll take our human teammates time to gather intel, so there's no reason to traumatize them any more than they already have been. You can afford to spend a few minutes talking them through what we'll…"

She trailed off when Drew came through on her headset. "Kristen, we have a problem."

"Well, we have time to help. We sent the Iron Dragon and her mages into retreat."

"That's great, but, uh…I don't think you have much time."

Her hot dragon blood ran cold. "Why not?"

"Because we're in a room with the biggest goddamn bomb any of us have ever seen and we think it'll go off sooner rather than later."

CHAPTER SIXTY-EIGHT

Kristen looked into one of the pits at one of the dragons. It cowered even though she was in human form. Hell, she knew what the mages had done to their captives. It probably cowered because she was in human form. There was no way they could get them out of these pits, into human form, and up the spiral staircase to safety. At that point, she didn't even know what safety meant. If the bomb was big enough to blow up the entire base, she couldn't begin to guess how far they'd have to go to be out of the blast radius.

"Drew, I thought Hernandez was with you. Can't she disarm it?"

"That'll be a 'fuck no,' Red," the woman shouted over the radio. "This isn't made from TNT or C4 but some kind of crystals."

"But you recognized that it's a bomb? Can't you stop it?" she pressed.

"Do I look like a mage to you?" the demolitions expert snapped in response.

She knew she didn't have time to deal with Hernandez's tone and that in reality, she was only upset because she couldn't help.

"What about Amy? She's with you guys, right? Can she disarm it?"

Drew put Amy on the radio. "I hate to disappoint you, but I don't think that would be a good idea," she said. "This is pumped full of magic. I don't have any idea how I could stop it without destroying it, and that might unleash whatever the hell is inside. Maybe you guys can get clear and I can try that."

"Absolutely not. Drew, get your team clear of the bomb—now."

The briefest of moments of hesitation followed, which—for him, straight-laced as he was—felt like an entire minute. "Are you sure, ma'am?" he asked, his tone forcefully polite. Although they communicated over the radio, she could practically see his jaw clench she knew him so well.

"Yes. That is a direct order. All of you said you can't stop that thing from going off and I refuse to lose any of you to another of these mages' fucking explosives."

"But Lady Steel—the captives," Lumos said from her side of the radio connection. She knew that he and all the dragons had probably already heard every word of the conversation. Dragon hearing was a wonderful thing, although it was hell on one's privacy.

"Listen up, people," Kristen said, speaking to both inform the humans with their pedestrian senses and to calm the dragons. "There's a bomb—a big one. We have to get out of this place. Stonequest, I want you and those three to do your best to get that dragon out of here, but if you can't convince it to come in a minute... well, I won't lose you over a captive."

It almost broke her heart to say it, but there it was. She wouldn't lose her people. She couldn't. Not when they were the only souls on the face of the earth brave enough to stand up to both the Dragon Council and the technomage terrorists.

"My lady," Lumos said, his aura already pleading with her, "We can't simply leave the captives. They've had a horrible life, but we can't let it end like this."

"I know, Lumos," she responded. Tears filled her eyes and overflowed to run down her cheeks, even though she tried to make them stop. "I don't want to do this. They're my siblings—my blood. But what choice do we have? Can you save them? All of them?"

"I could..." He trailed off, obviously at a loss.

"You can what?"

"I can…"

"What?"

"Damn it, Kristen! I don't know," he snapped, then sagged. "You're right, of course. This is why I've never been a leader. It takes a real leader to make these kinds of decisions."

"I'll hate myself so the rest of you don't have to. Now, go! That's an order. The last one out will get their wages docked. Go, damn it, go!"

No one looked excited about abandoning the prisoners, but what could be done? Stonequest and his dragons tried to convince the one they'd already rescued to come with them, but they didn't seem to have any success. The creature whimpered and remained near its pit. It didn't try to go in but didn't attempt to flee either.

Everyone else obeyed. Heavy shoulders and heavier steps hurried out of the room and out of the base. Everyone except Larry.

"Larry, I know you have experience that the others don't, but I also know you can't lift those four dragons."

"I might not have to."

Hope fluttered to life in her chest.

"What do you mean?"

"Well, it's like you said. If that bomb detonates inside this base, it'll kill all those dragons if they're still inside."

"I'm waiting for the part where you have an idea instead of merely a prediction that we all know will come true."

He grinned. "Well, we can't move the dragons, so why not move the bomb?"

Kristen asked Drew the question. "Negative, Kristen. It's a huge crystal contraption. Even if a dragon was strong enough to carry it, the size makes it too bulky."

She was relieved to hear his heavy breathing. That meant he was leading Amy, Hernandez, and the rest of his team away from danger.

"Sorry, Larry," she said.

"No, no, no. I'm not thinking anything like that."

"Then what?" she demanded. The humans and dragons were already gone. It was only the two of them now. Yes, she knew she could pick him up, throw him over her shoulder, and overtake the humans even with their head start, but his delay in getting to the point had begun to frustrate her.

"I've been watching those mage portals. I've seen them used a few times now."

"And you can't track them, I know."

"Forget tracking, I want to open my own." To his credit, his grin didn't falter.

Kristen was impressed with both that and the sheer audacity of his plan. "You've never done anything like that before."

"I know, but magic has rules. It can't be cast however one wishes. I've seen them cast that spell and I've seen the remnants it leaves behind. I can do this!"

"Four times?"

"Oh no, not for the dragons. I think I know how to do this but for all I know, it might scramble everything inside out. I wouldn't want to do that. I only want to do it once."

Realization dawned on her like sunrise on a vampire. "You want to teleport the bomb?"

"Sure!" Larry said and his grin betrayed nothing but reckless optimism. "I drop a portal under the bomb, send it somewhere else—somewhere as far away as I can manage. It blows up—again, preferably as far away from us as possible. Then we'd have more than enough time to save the dragons."

She didn't give the plan the consideration it deserved. Instead, she weighed her options. Her life and Larry's versus these four prisoners who'd led lives little better than cattle. Worse than cattle. At least cows could graze on pasture before they were slaughtered.

These dragons deserved an opportunity for a real life. They deserved to see the sunshine, to taste fresh water, to stretch their wings, and feel the air lift their magical bodies. Everything in her said they deserved a chance, and she could give it to them. She grabbed Larry, tossed him over her shoulder, and sprinted toward the biggest bomb they'd faced yet.

CHAPTER SIXTY-NINE

They passed Drew, Amy, Hernandez, and the rest of the team that had been working on the bomb as they raced down the hallway.

"I need all of you out of here," she ordered.

Drew and Hernandez were obviously obeying. They sprinted away from the control room, out of the base, and to safety. The problem was that compared to her dragon speed, it looked like the two of them were swimming through molasses.

The demolitions expert began to shout as soon as she saw them. "That thing is bigger than a MOAB. It might damn well be a nuke for all I know."

"Do you have any tips?" she asked her.

"I think you gave the best advice," Hernandez replied. "Get the fuck out of here before it detonates."

Amy, fortunately, had more productive things to say as she glided down the hallway toward them. "It's like the big, big brother of the bomb we found in the base outside Detroit. A big magic charge is powering it up like an overblown circuit."

"I'm sure the flashing lights indicate the timer," Hernandez added and paused at the end of the hallway. "When it goes solid…ka-boom."

"What the hell will you do with it, Larry?" Amy asked.

"I'll show those mages that they're not the only ones who can open portals."

The girl froze in mid-air. "I thought you said you needed a scroll to cast a spell like that."

"I don't think so. Not after what I saw today. They're using the entanglement of magic—fusing locations using emotional resonance. At least that's my working theory. That's why they always use it to escape. They go from one safe place to another."

"And you think you can do it too?" Amy asked.

"I'm about to find out," he replied.

"I want to help you." She looked at Kristen when she said it, not Larry.

"No way, young lady," he answered, shook his head, and tried to look stern and fatherly even though he was literally on the Steel Dragon's shoulder like an uncooperative child.

"Kristen—" the young mage protested.

"No way in hell," Kristen replied. "I shouldn't even let Larry risk his life, but I sure as hell can't lose you. If this goes south, there's no way the team could survive without your powers. You have to get clear."

"And you don't?" Amy demanded.

She shrugged and jostled her passenger in the process. "Those dragons are my family, Amy. My flesh and blood. I can't simply leave them here, not if Larry might be able to save them."

The girl sagged. "Okay, I guess. What do you want me to do?"

"Get out of here and keep running until that bomb explodes. If they had it all the way down here and intended it to level this whole base, you guys will have to cover quite a fair distance."

"Yes ma'am." The girl saluted. "I'll use my magic powers to lift all the slow-poke humans and get them to safety."

"Perfect," she yelled over her shoulder as she left the hallway and entered the room with the bomb.

How Hernandez and Amy had identified it as a bomb eluded Kristen. It looked more like a science experiment left too long to its own devices or a rave held deep beneath the surface of the earth.

It was comprised entirely of crystals, some of which were larger than her. They seemed to grow from both the floor and the ceiling as well as from the walls. That they were fueled by some kind of energy wasn't much of a stretch of the imagination because light pulsed through them and they hummed at a low pitch that had grown higher while she surveyed the room.

She put Larry down and he darted forward to take a closer look.

"All right, time is of the essence and all that. Portal it up," she said to him.

"You got it," the mage responded, but he didn't open any portals.

Instead, he shambled around the room. First, he looked at one of the biggest crystals, then some of those on the ceiling and the walls. He half blinked and half flinched every time the light pulsed.

"Larry?"

"Sorry. This is more…elaborate than I realized."

"Elaborate as in we needed to get the fuck out of here a minute ago?" she asked.

"Elaborate as in I need to make sure that if I open a portal, this will fall through. I can't tell how securely these crystals are connected to the wall as opposed to each other."

He raised his hands and two tendrils of energy appeared. Guided by his fingertips, the appendages reached toward the bomb, probed it, and tested it for strengths or weaknesses—Kristen couldn't be sure but that seemed logical. Now and then, he seemed to find something he didn't like. He'd jerk one of the magical appendages away and suck in a breath.

"Are you all right?" she asked.

"What? Oh yeah, sorry. Amy wasn't kidding about this being filled with energy. I'm fairly sure if I so much as scratch any of these facets, this entire thing will go off."

"So maybe you should stop with the tentacle magic?" she suggested as he continued to poke, prod, and—worst of all—flinch at the pulsing crystals.

KEVIN MCLAUGHLIN & MICHAEL ANDERLE

"I have to find out where the core thing is. If I put the portal under it, hopefully, it'll drag the rest through with its weight."

"Hopefully? As in there's a chance that you'll simply blow it up?"

"If it was a hundred percent kind of deal I would have done it already," Larry said to her frustration. "This should work, though. Teleportation magic is rare. I'd only ever heard of it before this. There's no way they could have anticipated that we'd go this route. It's the only way."

"What about your shields?" she asked and already regretted not taking Amy up on her offer to stay and help. Her magic shields were far more powerful than Larry's were.

"Oh, they definitely anticipated those," he said and pointed to a few crystals that looked almost identical to all the others to her untrained eye. Maybe they were a little milkier but she couldn't say with any certainty.

He pointed out a few other crystals as he made his way to the center of the room. "Most of this isn't the explosive," he muttered. "It's merely wards against magic or tampering."

"But the lights—"

"Are a distraction," he told her.

Kristen exhaled the breath she'd held. "Oh, thank goodness. They're blinking faster and faster. I had assumed that meant it would explode." Already, the lights blinked every five seconds. When they had entered the room, it had been closer to eight.

"Oh, if I don't get this done before the lights stop blinking, we're definitely dead," Larry said.

"Then how the hell are they a distraction?"

"Because the actual timer is right here." He pointed to a line of runes that seemed to float inside one of the larger crystals like the magic equivalent of a hologram. Sure enough, when one of the symbols changed, the light that ran through all the crystals flashed. "The lights are there to make me scared to fuck with it."

"Well, I guess it worked," she said as the speed increased slightly to four seconds between the blinks.

"Not on old Larry Brockton, it didn't." He stuck his tongue out at the contraption. "That's the core of this, and that's what has to go." The mage pointed at a few crystals in the center of the structure. She couldn't see how they were different than any of the other crystals, but she didn't think this was the time to argue with him about how to best do his job.

Although it also didn't seem like the time to simply sit down on the job, although Larry disagreed. He sat, crossed his legs, and closed his eyes as if he'd completed a particularly demanding round of yoga and was now ready to spend quality time in meditation.

Kristen knew she could run and that if she left, he would continue to do his job as if she were still there. She also knew she wouldn't leave him there to die alone. After thirty seconds of him seated in silence while he did nothing at all, she couldn't help but wonder if maybe she should simply throw him over her shoulder again and run to the exit.

The truth, though, was that she couldn't, not after seeing the dragon so scared of open spaces and the people who wanted to help her. Even though she had never met these lab-grown dragons or clones or whatever the hell she and the others truly were, she felt a deep kinship with them. They didn't understand their past or their purpose any more than she did. They'd all been thrust into dangerous, painful roles in a society that demanded far too much from them. Her only consolation was that her job—a role she had at least thought she'd chosen—might free these dragons from theirs.

If, of course, Larry hurried the hell up.

She was about to say something to this effect when a change finally came over the mage. The floor of the entire room had begun to glow. It was faint—more subdued than the fluorescent lights above her—but it was something. Nothing else changed.

While she tried to be patient, it was damn hard to remain cool while waiting to be blown up. She checked her watch before she realized it wouldn't tell her a damn thing about the time left on the countdown sequence that used symbols she couldn't decipher. All she had to go on was the blinking lights of the crystals, which were faster than before. They had reached only a two-second gap between the flashes, and the light shifted in hue as well. The color had been yellow, then orange, but it now edged to red. It didn't take a wild imagination to realize that once the pulse was one solid red glow, the crystal conglomeration would go kablooey.

Larry still hadn't moved. The light on the floor continued to glow but hadn't changed as much as the light from the crystals had. She checked her watch again. It still didn't tell her when she was going to die.

The radio crackled to life.

"Everyone's out," Brian told her, "and they are almost two kilometers away from the bunker. It'd be more but our transport vessels are blown to shit. Stonequest contacted me and told me about how, since you went radio silent, you've encountered a bomb and are doing the stupid hero thing instead of running away."

"We have to save these dragons, Brian. They're like family—"

"Don't do that, Kristen."

"Do what? It's the truth. We share most of the same DNA. The lab results are always the same. It's my family that's suffering because of this."

"You're damn right if you mean Mom and Dad are probably crapping themselves with worry right now. Look, I get it. You should save these dragons and I'm not saying otherwise. I'm only saying don't ghost the dude on the radio because he's beaten you at every videogame on every system ever played."

"Noted."

"How's Larry doing?"

"I don't know. He hasn't moved."

"Okay, well tell me if—shit! Kristen! Something's creating interference with the..." He faded out and in. "...above the base! You have to..." He was lost, then returned. "Get the hell out! Get out now!"

CHAPTER SEVENTY

Brian's connection cut out and Kristen cursed. It was amazing how such a little, everyday thing like losing a connection could increase tension, even when already dealing with almost Herculean levels of stress.

Still, although she hadn't heard all of what he had said, what she had heard had been very clear. He'd told her to get out and do it now. Something was coming and it didn't look good.

She sighed. It was good advice but unfortunately, she already knew she wouldn't take it.

Still, they had to hurry. She didn't want to disturb Larry's concentration, but if he couldn't open this portal, Brian was right. They had to get the hell out of there. Already, the pulses of light were so close together that she wasn't sure if she could get them clear even with dragon speed.

"Larry, I hate to bug you, but how close are you to making this happen? I think the crystals are running out of patience."

"I'm close," the mage replied through gritted teeth. "But this is damn hard, and if you think you can do better, by all means do so."

"If there's anything I can do..." she offered.

"There is..." Larry said, his teeth gritted so tightly she was concerned he might crack a molar. "You can get the hell out of here. I think I can do this but if I can't, there's no point in us both losing our lives."

"I won't abandon you, Larry."

"You wouldn't be abandoning me. I'm doing my best to save those four dragons. If I die doing it, at least I know I tried. My worth is theirs, especially after everything Windlock did for me. You're worth more than an old mage who talks too much. Get out of here."

"Nonsense," Kristen replied. "I've trusted you with my life many times in the past and I'm not about to stop now. Plus, I'm the one in charge of your salary. If you want a raise, you'd better ace this performance assessment."

"Spoken like a true bureaucrat." Larry grunted but the words held a faint trace of humor. "The old windbag would be so proud."

A shout rose in the back of his throat and finally forced his jaws apart so the guttural scream could echo off the walls of the room. It had barely faded when the edges of the glowing floor turned dark and all that was left was a bright circle. Kristen held her breath as the circle slowly—painfully slowly—moved across the floor until it outlined the crystal bomb.

She recognized the glowing circle, having seen similar ones before. Larry's efforts mirrored the portals the technomages had before they opened. Somehow, he seemed to make this spell work, even though he'd never done it before. She didn't know much about how magic operated, but she hoped improvisation had a place in it.

"All right, here goes," he said, and the ring of light intensified. The color shifted from white to blue, and the ethereal glowing edge seemed to solidify. At the same time, the floor inside the ring faded as if someone had adjusted the opacity in photoshop.

"I'm getting close!" the mage grunted, but the words seemed to drain him of some of his concentration because the floor solidified again. The crystals continued to pulse and the flashes grew closer and closer together as the light edged toward solid red.

It was not a particularly pleasant atmosphere.

Larry grunted and squeezed his eyes shut as if watching the room whose physical properties he tried to circumvent distracted him from performing magic on it. He ground his teeth as sweat poured down his face. Again, the ring glowed brighter and the floor beneath the crystals seemed to lose some of its material substance.

Kristen braced herself. She didn't know what the hell would happen, but she knew that if the crystals exploded, her steel skin would be their only protection against being eviscerated by the bomb. She prepared herself to dive forward and put her body between her teammate and the bomb he was working so hard to get rid of.

Part of her wanted to take the position now and get between him and the bomb so at least she could feel like she was doing something. Anything would be better than standing there watching him sweat while she did nothing at all to help him.

Well, not anything. She knew that even now, she could sprint to safety. She might not make it—she probably would not make it—but it would be better than being at point-blank range, that was for sure. But the idea of abandoning him—even when she couldn't help him cast the spell—was anathema to her. She would not leave him to die alone. It would be even worse than leaving the four dragons to die.

"Here goes," Larry said again. The ring intensified in brightness. The floor flickered and became fainter and fainter until it seemed almost transparent.

The crystals—despite being inanimate—noticed as well. When the floor seemed to vanish, they shifted as if they attempted to settle onto a surface that was no longer solid.

Kristen noticed that a fair number of the crystals didn't move at all. Those on the ceiling and walls and possibly half of those on the floor didn't shift at all. But a central group, including the crystal with the runes counting down to destruction, all sank perhaps a centimeter. Even with this tiny shift, she could see the entire trap for what it was—an elaborate trick of the eye.

Most of the crystals weren't connected to the central cluster Larry had identified as the threat and source of most of the magic. They had a purpose as well, obviously, but it seemed it was largely to simply intimidate whoever wandered in there.

None of this made her think the level of destruction caused by the bomb would be less than apocalyptic.

"Here we fucking go!" Larry shouted and the floor beneath the crystal vanished completely.

The disk inside the ring of light transformed from concrete to the shining blue of the sky. Bright, unfiltered sunlight poured into the room as the bomb slid into the hole and vanished from the room.

He shouted again and the disk was replaced once more with concrete. It looked as if someone had performed surgery on the crystals and removed a tumor. She wondered if that maybe that was exactly the case, only it had been magic instead of a scalpel.

It was neither the time nor the place to waste time thinking about it, though. Kristen rushed to Larry and barely managed to catch him before he collapsed. He bled from both his nostrils at this point, was drenched in sweat, and every single muscle of his body trembled. Thankfully, the bomb was gone, although she had no clue where it might have vanished to. It wasn't there, thank God, so the two of them would live.

She'd no sooner thought that when an explosion delivered a shockwave so strong it threatened to collapse the bunker, even so far under the earth.

Drew was on the back of a dragon when the crystalline bomb he'd used every reserve of energy he'd possessed to escape appeared in the air above him.

"Lumos, get down!" he shouted as he gaped at something that should not have been possible. A circle appeared in the sky with glowing edges that were filled with what appeared to be the interior of the room he had recently left.

This was bizarre but not particularly troubling until the crystal bomb fell through the hole. It didn't take a senior mage to understand that the bright red color of it was a bad sign.

Lumos reacted only as a dragon could—instantly and with

inhuman speed. One moment, Drew was on the elder dragon's back, enjoying the cool but faintly humid air high above the tropical jungle despite the danger he knew Kristen was facing. In the next moment, Lumos plunged so quickly into a barrel roll that his rider was thrown from his back.

The golden dragon roared in a way that was entirely out of character. It was a high-pitched keening that Drew heard in his ears but felt in his toes and fingertips. A nightmare scenario of the crystal not being a bomb but some kind of mind control device raced through his head as he plummeted away from the dragon. Before he could begin to panic, Lumos extended his claws and caught him as if the battle-hardened officer of the Detroit SWAT was nothing but the delicate egg of a robin.

It was from inside this cage of golden scaled claws that he witnessed the enormous explosion.

The first thing to happen was that a sphere of transparent energy radiated from the crystals. He felt it on his face like a blast of hot air before he saw its effects as it pushed away every wisp and puff of the thick gray clouds that seemed to perennially hug this landscape.

Lumos spun to put his back to the blast and his body between Drew and the explosion.

Still, the man felt the blow like someone had dropped a bag of concrete on him. He gasped as the dragon cried out in pain and tried to flap wings that had been shredded by the explosion.

But Drew understood that he was one of the lucky ones.

The blast expanded in a sphere that first touched the tops of the massive jungle trees of the rainforest. Their leaves ignited, their branches were ripped off, and finally, the trunks were felled like they were nothing more than poorly stacked dominoes.

This happening to even a single tree represented a huge amount of energy. He had no idea if a dragon possessed the strength it would take to first fire-blast the foliage from a tree the size of one of these and then still be able to topple it. As extraordinary as it was, it didn't happen to one, but hundreds.

The massive trees surrounding the bunker were flattened. Seen from the air, it was a perfect blast radius and all the trunks pointed back to the bunker where the bomb had been positioned underground, waiting to inflict its destruction on the world. Drew had only seen something like this in photographs of a meteor strike in Siberia more than a century before.

He hadn't thought that humans were capable of such destruction. While he knew nuclear weapons possessed more power than this, a team of hundreds of scientists working together to devise a bomb was somehow easier for his mind to digest than a few mages growing crystals so that one day, they could fill them with destructive energy.

The shockwave struck the bunkers themselves and Lumos continued to fall, either unconscious or unable to use his mangled wings.

"Lumos!" he shouted and pounded in vain on the dragon's chest. He couldn't tear his gaze away from the destruction, though.

It savaged the concrete of all four of the bunkers and ripped a layer of the artificial stone off with as much ease as a gardener might till a patch of soil in his back yard with a hoe. This seemed to be the extent of the damage to three of the concrete structures.

The one they'd worked so hard to gain entrance to crumbled. It had been riddled with bullet holes and damaged by dragon bodies and the doors had been overcome by Amy, the most powerful mage he had ever met.

The blast ripped through it like it was made of puff pastry instead of concrete. He didn't know if the other bunkers had simply been built better or if the damage to this one had been far more than superficial, but speculation was pointless. The force chewed through it and left nothing but a pile of rubble.

And still, Lumos fell.

The ground raced closer at an alarming rate. The wind whipped past his face so hard that Drew was concerned he might get yanked free of the dragon's claw.

His mind raced to consider his options and finally, he drew his handgun.

He wondered about the dragon's strength and knew they could

feel bullets hit them even though they rarely caused more than super-ficial damage. Also, he knew that in certain situations, bullets could overcome a dragon's healing ability and kill them. Being struck by the biggest bomb imaginable seemed to qualify as an overwhelming amount of force, so rather than shoot Lumos in the shoulder and hope the pain would wake him and his healing powers would mend him, he fired every round into the air.

The old dragon's head had tucked in toward his chest as he fell, making it just close enough that Drew could get his hand near it. He stretched to the limit to hold the gun as close to the dragon's earhole as his understanding of the anatomy of dragons allowed.

Although he squeezed the trigger repeatedly and as fast as he could, his adrenaline-fueled brain could still parse the time between each shot.

The wind whipped at Lumos's long mustache along with the first.

With the second, the dragon began to shift and rolled so that instead of looking at the bunker below, Drew was looking out at the jungle.

As he fired the third, he saw Heartsbane—in dragon form—lift a tree branch in her teeth and check on the humans underneath.

He pulled the trigger again as Emerald burst from beneath the fallen, burned ash of the canopy, shockingly green amongst the black-ened trunks and branches of the decimated rainforest.

Somehow, his gaze settled on the shocking pink of an orchid as he fired the fifth shot. It must have grown fifty feet in the air before its host trunk was felled. He had no idea how it had survived while everything around it had died. He honestly didn't think he would be as lucky.

Lumos' massive chest muscles flexed like great cords of rope beneath scale mail wrought of pure gold.

Drew fired three more shots in quick succession.

The old dragon gasped for a breath of air, a wonderful sound to the man's ears despite it sounding much the same as the wind rushing past him.

"Oh dear," Lumos said as if he'd put milk in a cup of tea that demanded lemon. His dragon's wings spread and he twisted in midair. Drew's stomach dropped as their fall stopped and they leveled out over the burnt floor of the jungle.

Lumos managed to flap his wings three times before a sickening snap issued from one of the bones in the dragon's left wing.

"Bother. Hold tight!" he said and rolled onto his back to hold Drew up to the sky like he was a football that needed to make it into the endzone without touching the ground.

The dragon impacted hard and gouged a path through the charred undergrowth until his head thumped into the exposed root ball of one of the fallen trees. It was large enough to finally stop his momentum abruptly.

Drew tumbled out of his claw. He slid down the dragon's chest and landed beside him.

"Are you all right, big guy?"

"By most definitions of the phrase, no, but I have experienced far worse so yes, I will be all right."

"Good." He patted the dragon's golden scales, stood, and strode through the forest to where he had seen the other dragons. His radio had been lost during the crazy descent and he had to know if Kristen was okay. *She'll be fine. Right now, I need to find out how everyone else is and then find a radio.*

It was almost frightening how easy it was to move through the destroyed jungle. The approach to the base wasn't particularly long but it had been grueling when they'd first arrived. They'd had to hack through overgrown brush and vines as quietly as they could and remain under cover so as to not be seen by the mages. Now, there was nothing at all between him and his destination.

Nothing but death and destruction, he amended as he studied his surroundings. He didn't think of himself as an environmentalist—he'd been a cop for over a decade and his first priority was always to end human suffering as best as he could—but he couldn't help but feel appalled at the wanton devastation around him. He hoped death hadn't come to the people they had brought to this jungle as quickly as it had come to the landscape.

A little farther ahead, dragons, humans, and mages all worked together to free those who were still trapped. He wanted to demand a radio and almost did, but when he saw Butters' legs protruding from beneath a tree, his heart almost stopped.

No... No! Not like this. He'd known the sniper since he'd first become a police officer. The big guy was like a father to him. He couldn't bear to think that he'd died because he hadn't run far enough from a blast and had been caught up and become part of the collateral damage.

Drew lent a hand to wedge smaller trunks under the large one on top of his teammate—not corpse and not body, only Butters—and heaved with a strength he hadn't known he still had. He could have waited two minutes for a dragon to come and lift the tree trunk without so much as breaking a sweat, but that wasn't the kind of guy he was.

He heaved and grunted and prayed that none of the humans helping him slipped and dropped the tree again. They managed to raise and move it over before they let it settle on the ground again. He raced to Butters and felt for a pulse. His nerves and the man's girth made it harder than it should have been. At first, he felt certain his teammate was gone but the sniper finally opened his eyes.

"Gravy...I need...gravy." He wheezed and sat.

Drew finally let himself smile. Then he remembered he still hadn't spoken to Kristen and the brief moment of relief was gone.

"It's a good thing your big gut blocked that tree trunk," Beanpole said to Butters, and the larger man chuckled, although it was obvious that he only now processed how close he'd come to dying.

The SWAT leader looked around for someone with a radio. Finally, he saw Stonequest. He marched up to him, about to demand the one the dragon carried when he heard Kristen's voice issue from it.

He took the last few steps so rapidly that he almost fell. "Is she all right?" he asked as he fought to keep his balance. "Is Kristen alive?"

The dragon shot him a look that made him feel like a student asking a teacher if they had homework.

"What the hell do you think I'm asking her?" Stonequest asked.

"Right sorry. I only—"

"If you could give me a minute so I can hear her, that'd be great," the dragon drawled.

Drew smiled. He felt like a witness outside of every crime scene he'd ever had to lock down.

"Kristen, repeat that. There was an interruption," Stonequest said.

"We're okay," she replied over the radio, her voice barely comprehensible due to the static.

The dragon fiddled with the radio and her voice came in a little more clearly. "Larry did it. He disposed of the bomb. I have no idea where the hell he sent it, but he got it out of here."

"We have a location on that."

"Great!" She sounded excited and Drew understood the feeling. She was happy to be alive. "Is everything all right? We heard an earthquake or something."

"We're fine. Have you been back to the chamber with the dragons? The bomb...well, it detonated here. It collapsed most of the compound, including the building you're under."

Kristen laughed and it sounded sweeter than any music Drew had ever heard. "That's where I am right now. We're working on getting them out as we speak. Apparently, they'll come for food. It's not my proudest moment but we got them moving. We should be out soon."

"That's what I'm saying, Kristen. The compound collapsed. We can't get you out."

"That's okay," she responded cheerfully. "We opened the hangar door down here and it's a gentle slope all the way to the surface. We'll see you soon."

Drew couldn't believe it. They'd survived with minimal fatalities, driven out the mages, and even saved the hostages.

"Holy shit," he murmured. "We won."

CHAPTER SEVENTY-ONE

Rescuing people was one of Kristen's' favorite parts of her job. It had to be one of the main drivers for most police officers. What could be more rewarding than helping someone out of a situation in which they'd lost control and suffered? It certainly beat writing speeding tickets or processing paperwork, the two things her father always said took up most of his time as a beat cop in Detroit.

She had never had to do much of that. When she'd graduated from the academy, she'd been passed over for regular police work because dragons had taken an interest in her. They'd realized her abilities even before she did and because of that, a substantial part of her job had always been saving people.

The only problem with it was that she wished she was better at helping them recover from the trauma they experienced.

Four days had passed since their assault on the South American base in the jungles of Colombia. In that time, her wounds had healed, as had the wounds of every dragon due to their amazing powers. The bruises the humans had suffered blossomed to dark purples and now mostly faded to ugly yellows and oranges. Larry and Amy had both slept off their fatigue from their exertions. Everyone had attended a funeral service for the humans and dragons they'd lost. Those were the wounds that still hurt the most, or so she thought.

That was about to be sorely tested, though, as she tucked her wings and came in for a landing at Amythist's sprawling garden estate. The old dragon's home was truly a thing of beauty and a reasonably sized mansion stood at the center of the large grounds. She went so far as to call it a cottage-style home, but this was indicative of dragon wealth rather than that her home was anything a human would ever call humble.

All around the house, gardens stretched in every direction. Flowers in a hundred different shades of red, yellow, purple, and blue edged pathways of lush green grass. Often, dragons' homes were immaculately landscaped and not a weed or fading blossom could be seen. Amythist's estate was quite different, with flowers and herbs in all stages of growth and overgrown plants to provide habitat for the woodland creatures that visited her from the surrounding forest.

Although Kristen could see that even with the often-overgrown landscaping, her new guests were causing problems. Great swaths of flowers had been rolled in here and there. In other places, dragon-size holes had been dug and apparently used to wallow. A huge willow tree that bordered a pond had deep gashes in its bark as if the world's largest cat had decided to use it as a scratching post.

But she knew it wasn't cats who did this. It was the dragons they'd rescued from the base in Colombia. She hoped Amythist was coping well enough with the destruction and chaos her new house guests seemed to be causing.

Well, there's nothing left but to find out for myself, she thought as she settled on the brick pavilion in front of the world's largest cottage.

"Ah, Kristen," the elder dragon said, coming out of her house the moment Kristen landed as if she'd expected her. Which she had, given that she had been able to read her aura from a distance, which meant she also knew how she was feeling.

"You're worried about them, aren't you dear?" Amythist said and offered her a cup of tea.

She snorted in amusement, the closest thing she could bring to a smile right now. "It took Larry and I a fair amount of work simply to get them out of those pits. We had another fight to get them up the tunnel the mages had dug. They basically lost their mind when they saw the sunlight. The whole way out here, I kept thinking about how hard it must be for you to have to deal with them and of how much damage they're causing."

"Oh, pish-posh." The old dragon smiled and the wrinkles around her eyes deepened. Kristen wondered if she would be able to tell the dragon's advanced age as easily in the woman's true dragon form. "I don't mind them at all."

"It's kind of you to say that, especially given how much they mean to me and everyone who risked their lives to save them." *And those who lost their lives trying,* she thought but didn't say it aloud. "But you don't have to sugarcoat the situation for me. I saw how they were back there. Feral would be a kind way to put it. It was more like looking at animals that had somehow suffered PTSD."

"Oh, honestly, dear, it's nothing. I understand the situation you found them in was appalling and surely quite different from how you were raised in a human home, but they are adapting well here."

As if to prove her point, one of the dragons flew overhead and landed amongst a huge overgrown patch of wild roses.

"Scratch! Out of there. Get out, you big lummox," Amythist chided, took her dragon form, and pulsed her aura to let him know that he was doing wrong.

He snorted his acknowledgment and backed away until she stopped her approach. Once out of the flowers, he sprawled in a sunny spot, rested his head on his claws, and proceeded to stare at Kristen.

"Is he...okay?"

"Scratch is non-verbal," the old dragon explained. "We used to raise dragons this way, long before we spent so much time in our human forms. We have instincts, exactly like human babies do, and one of them is to obey the aura of older dragons."

"Are you telling me he can't speak?"

Amythist shook her head sadly. "I hope he's only adjusting. It's been less than a week, after all, but he's yet to say a word. The other male is the same. The two females have some language, but it's not as if they can hold anything like a conversation. They can ask for food and tell me when they're tired, that kind of thing."

Kristen's heart began to pound in her chest. How could the old dragon simply accept this? "Are you telling me dragons used to be raised this way? That the reason your culture is so horrible is because you cage your young? These dragons were chained to walls and trapped in their dragon bodies so they could be harvested for scales, teeth, and claws for their entire lives. Do you think they used painkillers or that they were given any consideration other than what was the most efficient way to get them to grow more scales? How can you be all right with dragons being raised this way? I don't care if it was a thousand years ago. This is horrible!"

The other male dragon bounded around the side of the mansion, his nostrils smoking and fire in its eyes. Scratch, who had been ready to take an afternoon nap, sat on his haunches and raised the spines on his back to prepare himself for a battle with this newly spotted rival.

"Kristen, my dear, you must calm yourself. Your aura is filled with anger and it'll make them fight!"

"How can you expect me to be calm when you can be so calm in the face of such abuse?" she demanded.

"Because I must be calm for these dragons to be able to learn humanity," Amythist said and her aura echoed her words and urged Kristen to shed her anger. "When I said this was the way things were done, I simply meant that language wasn't always such a priority. Never have dragons allowed our kind to be imprisoned, let alone used for parts."

"Do you swear it?"

"Yes! On my life and on the lives of every dragon I've ever helped raise. Dragons don't do this to our young. Now, calm down."

Kristen took a few deep breaths while Amythist flapped her wings and went to stand between the two young males. Scratch immediately lost interest in his prospective opponent and instead, preferred to watch the tip of her tail move through a particularly overgrown patch of wildflowers. The other dragon was more agitated and lunged at her, but Kristen had been in more than enough dragon battles to recognize that he wasn't attacking.

He collided with the old dragon without trying to strike her with his claws or teeth. She moved aside deftly and he toppled, and she put a claw on top of his chest and began to tickle it. He pretended to fight it for a minute before he snorted with laughter and exhaled a great cloud of gray smoke.

With both her wards calm once more, Amythist sent him off to swim in the pond. Once again, she did this primarily through her aura. While she said, "the pond," her aura reinforced the spoken command. Kristen felt like she wanted to get wet and play—like she was hot and wanted to cool her skin. Was this really how dragons spoke to each other before they'd adopted human language? It was fascinating and kind of amazing that they might have taken so much from human culture. It was also horrible, though, that they could turn their backs on humans after taking such an essential skill like language.

"I simply meant there was a time when we let young dragons behave in such a way. Although of course, these dragons are all fully grown and even by ancient standards should be able to speak by this point. I only wanted to assure you that I have experience dealing with dragons such as these, although admittedly none who were so large."

"But do you think you can help them?" Kristen asked and forced herself to remain calm for the dragons' benefit.

"I do," Amythist said, although she could have used a more confident tone of voice. "However, these dragons have suffered abuse beyond any I have ever seen. Dragons don't torture each other. It's simply not done. If there are grievances, we fight. If they are serious, it might even be to the death. Confinement and brutality for some unknowable purpose are human inventions. I do not know how they will recover after decades of such treatment. It is quite possible that they'll never be able to fully join society."

"I guess we have Constance to thank for that," she muttered.

"No, my dear, no. There is nothing constant about human cruelty.

Yes, your kind is capable of the most heinous acts of violence. There are times when I wonder what humans could accomplish if they would apply their most creative minds to something beyond violence, but that is not their only legacy. Humans are capable of great compassion as well. Few dragons would have risked their lives for the well-being of poorly bred, untitled runts such as these. It's remarkable that you got humans to do it and if Lumos wasn't simply being dramatic, some even laid their lives down to help these dragons."

"That's true," she confirmed. "We all understand that we're in this together. It's good to see you feel the same way as well. But I referred to Constance Vigil. As far as I can tell, it was she who first started working with my biological dragon father to harvest the genetic material needed to grow dragons and use them in this way."

"Ah, yes. The plain-faced little bitch who wore all black the last time she came here? She was the one who tried to put one of these poor fellow's scales through my skull, correct?"

"Yeah, her. She was the leader of the technomage cell near Detroit that was responsible for the deaths of so many dragons around here, and from what we've been able to tell, one of the true architects of this whole plan."

"A true monster, then," Amythist said and her aura shifted at the memory of being shot and made Scratch growl in his sleep.

"She was...is." Kristen corrected herself but was still unsure which tense was correct for the technomage leader. She had captured her and turned her over to the Dragon Council. All logic said that the mage must have been pumped for information and executed, but if that was the case, she didn't know it for certain. "But even she was motivated by good intentions."

"Impossible," the old dragon said but she didn't argue further.

"It's true. She told me many times that she was doing all this because she wanted to make the world a more just and equitable place."

"And she told you this when? In the middle of a fight in which she tried to put a bullet through your brain?" Amythist sneered.

She knew that in reality, Constance could have killed her a few times over but she'd never taken any of the opportunities she'd been presented with. Most of the time, she'd been too concerned with trying to recruit her. How ironic that she was now fighting for the same cause but with different means. "She fought for humans and mages to have rights in the eyes of dragons. I can understand those intentions."

"Maybe that's how she started, but she couldn't have fought for justice if this is how she treated her captives," Amythist argued. "How can you believe what she told you after this? The ends do not justify the means."

"I couldn't agree more. By treating their captives the way they did, they turned to ethical bankruptcy. That's why we're working so hard to root out the rest of these cells and end their obsession that war is the only way to make the world more equitable."

"Well, I wish you the best of luck in all your endeavors. I would like to see more of these dragons rescued. With a few more, I could form a proper classroom."

"Finally, something hopeful to work toward," Kristen agreed.

She spent some time after that walking the grounds with Amythist and meeting the two females. They were hardly more civilized than the males, their attempts at language barely more sophisticated than a parrot's. It was difficult for her to have to treat them as little more than domesticated animals, and even that was being generous. She had met dogs that had more social graces than they did but the healing process was beginning.

Kristen merely wanted to make sure no one else—not dragon, mage, or human—was forced to live lives of such horrid squalor while others had so much. That idea—and what to do about it—consumed her thoughts as she flew to her base in Detroit.

———

She arrived at the base to no fanfare. At this point, everyone had been on the team for almost a month and they'd all seen what combat with magic-slinging mages could look like. She could tell that Jim and

Stonequest had recruited professionals, as the base was alive with groups of humans and dragons running drills with more intensity and focus than they had before they'd battled the mages. Now that they had seen what they were up against, everyone knew that their already rigorous training methods simply weren't enough. She hoped they found something that was, impossible though it seemed.

When she walked inside the converted factory, Jim and her brother stood and stared at Brian's bank of monitors.

"Lady Steel!" The Wonderkid snapped a salute.

"At ease, Jim, and you don't have to use my dragon name." Kristen smiled at him. It never ceased to amaze her how much he'd grown and how much he'd changed. He'd once hated dragons with every core of his being because of what they'd done to some of his fellow men at arms. Now, he used their honorifics.

"We're talking shop, so I thought it'd be better than Kissy-Krissy," Jim said.

"You didn't!" She turned to Brian.

He grinned like a fool and thank goodness. She hardly recognized her brother. Since joining her team, he'd completely changed his diet and started working out every day. His slightly round middle and less than defined arms proved that he didn't push himself nearly as hard as the soldier beside him did, but he looked healthier than she had ever seen him in her entire life. Healthier than their parents, for sure. It was too bad she would have to kill him.

"Calm down, Kissy-Krissy. I give you smooch-smooch." Brian extended his arms, licked his lips so they dripped with saliva, and stumbled towards her like a toddler desperate for a big brother's love.

Jim almost died laughing at the impression. "And she did this until she was seven years old?"

"As a joke," Kristen said. "I did it because it made Brian laugh."

"You did it because you liked giving big wet kisses to your older brother. Don't deny it." Brian took another step forward, so she caught one of his arms and spun him into an armlock.

"Ow, ow, ow, ow, ow!"

"Did Brian also tell you how he used to give his little sister noogies?" She rolled her hand into a fist and rubbed her knuckle across his head until he stopped making kissy lips.

"Jeez, you didn't have to use your dragon speed to catch me," he muttered.

She rolled her eyes. He might be in better shape but she had always been far more athletic than him, even before she'd activated her dragon powers.

"Can you please tell me what the hell you've been working on so I can decide if I'll pay your lazy ass this month?"

"Yes, ma'am," he said and dropped the annoying sibling act, and his fingers danced over his keyboard.

"At the Colombian base, we turned up a good lead on what looks like it might be the main base for all the technomages," Jim narrated while Brian showed satellite images of a large farm complex. It contained multiple barns and rows and rows of huge hoop houses that she assumed were used to grow animals to feed to the dragons.

"Based on what we found in Colombia," the Wonderkid continued, "it seems like almost every order of dragon bullets traced back here. Even those that came from other locations had often ordered components from this location—hell, Colombia itself had four dragons they used for ammunition and they still got stuff from this location."

"It sounds like we hit the jackpot, then." She smiled. There was nothing like a lead to cheer her when faced with the obscure paths of the technomages.

"I'm afraid not," Brian said.

"What? Why not?" Jim said.

"As soon as we had a location, I positioned a satellite over this farm to start taking photographs."

"You can do that?" Kristen asked. She certainly hadn't given him the go-ahead to start hacking corporate and government satellites. Not only that, there was the point that she thought satellites had to be moving and couldn't stay in place anyway.

He grinned bashfully. "It's a figure of speech and it's more like I made every satellite that passed over that area take a photo. It took about twenty-two hours to get the first shot, but after that, I have an image from every couple of hours. Nighttime too."

Jim looked impressed. "How did you do that? Some of those must have been government satellites, and those that weren't don't simply let people take selfies with them."

"It might have taken some dragon access codes." He kept the grin plastered on his face.

"And you got those from?" She certainly hadn't given him any because she didn't know any codes, even if she had them.

"From you, dear sister!" Brian said. "Once you were promoted to investigator, you were given digital access to almost everything the Dragon Council of North America has. There are a few files that are encrypted enough that I can't get to them—"

"You shouldn't even try."

He shrugged like a basketball player who had forced a foul and caused two potential free shots instead of a slam dunk. "I didn't push against the secure stuff too hard. In fact, the toughest part was getting your credentials to mesh with the entire system. Apparently, mages usually oversee all this, but with the heightened security due to all the dragon killings, they were impossible to obtain."

"So you hacked in," Jim said.

Brian raised his hands from the keyboard in defense. "You say hacked, I say efficiently navigated a bureaucracy."

Kristen put her hands on her hips. "We'll come back to you stealing my identity later—"

"I didn't steal anything."

"Later," she said and used her aura on her brother because he had been affected by it enough to know that she was doing it. He felt it and smiled. It was time to listen to the boss. "Right now, I need to know what those satellites turned up."

"Nothing." He turned his hands as if he was pouring sand onto the floor. "And I don't mean nothing new, or nothing much, but *nothing*. If that was their base—and I think Jim's right, it probably was—it's not anymore. No goods have come in or out of there for a week and no lights have come on. No cars have driven off and no trucks have loaded a delivery. I did catch the motion sensor lights on one night."

"And?" Jim asked.

"Unless the technomages can transform into deer, I think it was exactly what I said—nothing."

"Well, shit," the Wonderkid said. "I suppose we could investigate it?"

She shook her head. "That's a negative. They're not stupid and won't leave a roadmap to their next location behind. If anything is left in the base, you can bet they want us to find it."

"And detonate it, you mean," Jim said glumly.

"Unfortunately, I think that's how we need to assume they will behave," she said and didn't like it any more than he did.

"Still, we're doing good, right? At this point, we've saved six dragons and stopped four cells. There can't be many more of them, can there?" Brian nodded as if he could will it to be true by positive thought alone.

"I don't think we can leave them alone now that they're only 'mostly defeated,'" Kristen said. "With one dragon, they can continue to make bullets. They won't be able to be as aggressive but it only takes one bullet to kill a dragon. As long as they're out there, the Dragon Council could still vote to go to war to try to root them out."

"Plus, they could capture more dragons or even grow fresh ones," Jim said. "I don't know much about dragon biology, but it seems that if they could get a couple of eggs, this whole process would simply start over."

"Come on, that would take years," the techie protested.

"Time is one thing they have demonstrated that they know how to use," Kristen explained sourly. "They must understand that their foes are immortal and that they can't rush anything. If we leave them alone now, they'll regrow into an even stronger organization. And in the meantime, we'd simply wait for them to strike. We still don't know how many bullets are out there or how many dragons they've used. But like I said, it only takes one dragon to make bullets and even a hundred of those bullets are enough to kill every member of every Dragon Council the world over. We can't let this go."

"I agree," the Wonderkid responded. "But how the hell do we do that if we don't know where to look?"

She sighed. "If I knew the answer to that, I wouldn't be here right now."

CHAPTER SEVENTY-TWO

Frustrated, Kristen headed to the training area between some of the old factory buildings that now made up the central complex of her base. It had been designed by Timeflash, as had most of the base, but Kristen could tell the dragon had consulted some of her old human teammates regarding what was essential for humans to work out.

She found the traditional equipment one needed for strength training—barbells, dumbbells, kettlebells, and more, all on racks under makeshift roofs to keep them out of the rain. Her first choice was to load a bench press bar with more weight than she had ever imagined she'd be able to lift before she'd discovered she was a dragon. She curled the bar as easily as a child might lift a pillow above her head. It was hard to get a burn from weights anymore, but by loading the bar, doing more repetitions than she could count, and alternating it with other high-intensity exercises, she could still make gains. These seemed to be getting to be incrementally less and less as time went on, though.

Still, it felt good to push herself to her limits. She put the weights down after doing a few lifts over her head and sprinted through the obstacle course.

This was obviously designed by a human, as a dragon's abilities made most of the obstacles that had to do with strength, grasp, or jumping irrelevant but it was still a challenge to break her own record. She jumped onto a crisscrossing path made of two-by-fours and moved from one to the other, landing carefully on each one and not letting herself jump too high. If she created too much momentum, it might snap the wood in half.

She reached the end of the elevated balance maze and leapt onto a hanging rope, shinnied up to the platform on top, and climbed down the cargo net on the other side. That, at least, was one thing her dragon powers didn't help with too much.

"Hey, boss, do you want to make this an actual challenge?" Hernandez shouted from the sidelines, an airsoft gun in each hand.

"I can't turn my skin to steel without breaking these platforms," Kristen said as she moved from the cargo net to the straight wall climb. Even without her steel skin, her fingers could punch grooves into the brick if she wanted to.

"Oh, boo-hoo, the Steel Dragon might have to feel pain," the woman jeered. "Should we tell the technomages to only attack when you feel up to it?"

She laughed, which counted as consent in Hernandez's book. The woman sprayed airsoft pellets at her, familiar enough with the Steel Dragon's abilities to know that she shouldn't aim where she was but where she would be.

Kristen ducked into the next part of the obstacle course, a number of pallets set up as a mini airsoft arena.

It quickly became obvious that the demolitions expert wasn't the only one who thought it might be good fun to shoot at their boss as pellets rocketed at her from all sides.

Normally, she would have ripped a piece of wood out of the scrap around her and used it for a shield, but that wouldn't achieve any gains in her speed or agility, the two things she knew she needed to build if she wanted to beat Katrina.

Truly, the Iron Dragon was why she was out there training. She dodged pellets, vaulted over them, slid under them, fell prone, and scrambled up in the cardio instructor's dream workout, and through-out, she kept her adversary in mind.

How did she beat her so consistently? She knew they had to be genetically similar because they were siblings. They looked the same, were the same height, and had the same powers in dragon form, and yet Katrina always seemed to have the edge.

A pellet popped her in the forehead and yanked her focus to the task at hand.

"Ha! You owe me a beer," Hernandez shouted.

She surged towards the demolitions expert and avoided every pellet the woman fired at her. No matter what Hernandez did, she could anticipate and protect herself from getting hit.

Why couldn't she do the same with the Iron Dragon?

Kristen pushed herself even faster and became a blur as people fired at her from all sides. In her desire to push her limits, she was able to dodge every shot aimed at her. She moved faster and faster until she became such a blur she could see the pellets flying past her and knock some of them out of the air.

Was this her limit? Did Katrina have the same limits? Why did she constantly lose to the other woman? Was it training or was it luck? Did her adversary have a genome she simply lacked?

A pellet hit her in the small of her back and she flinched, and a dozen more pellets struck her from all angles.

"Argh!" she shouted, more in frustration than pain, and punched the asphalt beneath her feet with enough force to crack it into chunks.

"Sorry, boss!" Hernandez waved. "But you now owe everyone on the team a beer. Even Lumos."

"Lumos?" Kristen asked and turned to see the ancient gold dragon lounging against the wall of one of the buildings that framed the training area. He radiated power even in his human form. It was odd to see him there. Most of the dragons rarely went to the human training area.

"Impressive." He nodded respectfully at her. "But it won't accom-plish what you hope it will."

She studied the dragon in silence for a moment. How much did he know? Was her frustration so obvious? Did the entire team know she was becoming more and more obsessed with her defeats at the hands of the Iron Dragon?

"That's a wrap, people," Hernandez shouted. "It looks like the big, tough dragons need to talk this one through. Good job, everyone, on shooting your boss. I'm proud of you today. Beers taste better when you've broken the chain of command. Believe me, I would know."

Apparently, her frustration was that obvious because everyone cleared the area and left the two dragons alone.

"What do you know about what I want to accomplish?" she demanded.

He favored her with another of his enigmatic smiles. "I haven't seen you push yourself like this since you first joined Dragon SWAT. But even if you can get faster and stronger this way, it won't be enough to defeat the Iron Dragon."

Kristen froze, unsure of what to say. She was surprised that Lumos was there at all. It was even more surprising that he seemed to know exactly what went through her mind.

"Do you have mind-reading powers you never told me about? Or am I that transparent?" she asked.

"The latter," he replied dryly. "You've fought against the enemy dragon three time now and came out worst both times. I know how frustrating that must be for you, particularly since this is a 'mirror match' of sorts."

She merely nodded because although she agreed, she didn't know what to say.

"I hate to tell you what to do because I do respect your leadership on this team, but you do realize that she's not the biggest threat, correct?"

"She's the biggest threat I've faced since Shadowstorm. She's beaten me consistently, and the second time she also outsmarted us and appeared when we didn't think she would."

"True enough, and I agree she is an obstacle and even a big one. But not your biggest one."

"Then what is?" she demanded and tried not to sound petulant, but her aura betrayed her.

"I know you didn't forget about the dragon you fought in the caves so quickly," Lumos said, his voice level.

Kristen shuddered. Of course, she hadn't forgotten that dragon. She still had nightmares about the inky black shapes it could take in the darkness. In those dreams, she'd be swimming across a pool or going to the lake with her family, when suddenly, the lights would go out or a cloud would blot out the sun. He would be there in the darkness to grasp her arms and legs and pull her underwater and she'd wake, drenched in sweat.

"That dragon hasn't appeared before or after that. The Iron Dragon is part of the organization I built this force to fight. She's a priority."

He shook his head. "Just because you haven't seen this dragon of shadow doesn't mean he hasn't been involved in all this."

"You can't know that, Lumos," she stated, her words like steel.

"No, but the evidence points to him being far more than some—what's the human expression?—lone wolf with a bone to pick."

"That's two expressions," she corrected him, not eager to talk about the source of her nightmares but not able to do anything but use humor to hide her fear.

"He—or someone working with him—sent most of your team to Colombia on a false alarm before we had located the technomage cell. He was also able to trick us into thinking that the Dragon Council wanted you to meet them alone. Both of those clues point to a dragon with connections—high level, powerful connections." Lumos paused, stroked his mustache, and let her put it all together herself, even though she sure as hell didn't want to think about any of this. She merely wanted to train and focus on the torturous technomages.

"What are you trying to say? That a member of the Dragon Council set me up?"

The golden dragon nodded. "Either that or someone who is very, very good friends with someone on the Council."

Kristen sighed. He was right, of course. She'd thought about all this before the mission to the base in Colombia. It was so frustrating, like hunting a whisper in the dark when another enemy stood in broad daylight and shouted profanities. "What do you recommend?"

"Focusing on that dragon, whoever he was. He was obviously an elder and a very powerful one at that. The way he used his powers indicates that he had a long time to perfect the subtleties of his abilities. You've made strong allies, but you've also managed to annoy an extremely powerful foe."

"I guess that means what we're doing is working," she muttered.

Lumos smirked. "Ah, I do so love human optimism. Yes, I agree that we have made progress. This dragon who attacked you wouldn't have made so bold a move and exposed his powers had he not felt it necessary. So yes, we are making our enemies uncomfortable."

"I want to do much more than make a group of bigots uncomfortable. That won't happen if I can't beat the Iron Dragon." She hated to admit it, but it was true.

"I agree. You're strong and you've grown much since I first met you, but you need to be better still." Lumos smiled enigmatically.

Kristen tried not to be annoyed. "Why do you think I'm out here training?"

"I understand your concerns and I understand that increasing your strength in your human form will make your dragon form stronger, in the same way that increasing your strength in your dragon form will increase the strength of your human body. Honestly, that might be enough to beat the Iron Dragon."

"Then why are you here interrupting me?" She didn't mean to be rude, but her frustration pushed through.

"I apologize. With your methods and the help of others, you could likely defeat the Iron Dragon, but that won't be enough. Not if—"

"Not if the shadow dragon attacks again," she finished for him.

"Precisely." He nodded. "You may very well need to face him again. In fact, if I am honest, I am certain you will face him again before this is over. He most likely interfered because you meddled with the technomages and probably has a stake in their success or, at the very least, some facet of their operation. If you wish to survive his next assault, you need to be a better warrior."

"But how?" Kristen asked and hoped she didn't sound desperate. "I've never been able to progress much in my dragon form, and if you think training in this body is a waste of my time, what the hell am I supposed to do?"

"It's true that there are limitations to the human form," Lumos agreed. "But worse, for all the strength you have amassed, you still fight like a human in both forms."

"I am a human."

He chuckled. "My dear, you are most definitely not a human. You fight well in this form but both the Iron Dragon and this unseen shadow dragon are more effective in their dragon bodies than you are. To say it plainly, you are unable to use your dragon body to maximum effectiveness."

"I've become stronger and faster as a dragon thanks to my training as a human," she countered.

"I'm sure you have," he conceded. "Human hand-to-hand combat and martial training are helpful for dragons and many train in those techniques. But for dragon versus dragon combat in our true bodies, the winner is often the one who understands that mode of combat best. I don't think the Iron Dragon is any stronger or faster than you but she's much better trained at fighting in dragon form."

"But how is that possible?" she demanded. "She was raised by mages. How can she be a better dragon than me? I trained with Dragon SWAT and I've trained with you. I even trained with Shadowstorm before I realized he was evil."

Her protest opened the door to understanding. The technomages had a dragon benefactor. It was the only way to explain how the Iron Dragon was such a good warrior in her dragon body. That meant Lumos' theory about the shadow dragon orchestrating at least some part of the technomage operation from the background suddenly made much more sense. He watched the realization come across her face as easily as a human could watch a sunset.

"I am not saying you are not a formidable warrior. The fact that you have fought so many dragons—including the Iron Dragon and this shadow one—prove that fact, but there is much you can learn. Also, you've never trained with me."

Kristen raised an eyebrow at that claim. "What are you talking about? We've sparred together plenty of times."

He chuckled. "That was not training. It was me working with a rookie because Stonequest told me to. You must remember that I am an old warrior with centuries of knowledge. I'm slower than I once was and not as strong, but I still have all the knowledge you need to succeed."

"And you're willing to share that knowledge with me?" she asked when she recognized this for the huge offer it was.

"I am," Lumos said. "although it won't be easy."

She nodded. "Can I ask one question that I promise I don't mean as rudeness?"

"By all means."

"Why now? If you're such a fantastic warrior, why not teach me all this sooner?"

"Honestly, I had hoped that it wouldn't be necessary. You are a formidable force. I had hoped your strength coupled with what we other dragons can do, plus the mages and humans you have recruited, would be enough. There are...methods of fighting as a dragon that can seem savage and barbaric and there are techniques I wish would be forgotten. I had hoped they might die with me, but I see now there is still much optimism leftover from my youth, as long ago as it was. I'll warn you again, this won't be easy, but I believe that if you commit to training with me, I might give you the edge you need against both these foes in the battles to come. Do you have any questions before you decide?"

Kristen thought for a moment. She was both frightened and honored. Frightened because she hadn't known about dragon techniques and she wondered how many battles she had survived simply by virtue of her steel skin. She felt honored because he trusted her enough to share these skills. While she had no doubt it would be hard, she still didn't understand how he could even frame this as a choice.

She had to defeat the technomages. Failure was not an option unless it meant that she was killed trying to make the world a better place. If all that was between her and victory were some tough stretches and a few extra pushups, how bad could it be?

"I guess I have only one question," Kristen said. "When can we start?"

Lumos transformed into his dragon body in a flash of golden light. One moment, an older gentleman with an impressive mustache and a gold suit stood before her and in the next, an enormous golden dragon with long tendrils in place of his mustache regarded her calmly.

"There's no time like the present."

CHAPTER SEVENTY-THREE

K risten and Lumos flew west from Detroit over highways, suburbs of the Motor City, and patches of trees heavy with the smell of pine. They soared above townships, farms, and the odd mixture of gas stations and fast food joints that made up much of the American countryside.

He didn't speak to her and instead, pumped his wings intermittently but mainly used the wind to speed their flight. Although the elder dragon didn't seem to work particularly hard at beating his wings, after ten minutes, Kristen found she was winded from the pace he set.

She wasn't quite sure how, but he seemed to fly faster than her with less effort. While she pumped and pumped and tried to force herself through the air like a fish through the sea, he glided more like a great bird of prey and somehow gained speed with the barest movements of his wings. She could fly like that too but not at such speed and not so low.

"How do you do that?" she asked after winding herself in her efforts to catch up with the golden dragon.

"It's not only wings that make a dragon fly but our body too," Lumos explained patiently. "If you hold your legs right, you won't feel any wind at all because they're providing lift. The same principle applies to your tail. Try to keep it rigid like one of your whirlybirds does."

"A what?"

"Oh, you know." He chuckled. "One of those great metal contraptions that are like planes but have propellers?"

"Ah. Helicopters," she said once she realized what he meant.

"Yes. Indeed. Helly-coppers. Keep your tail straight like one of those and focus on capturing the wind and riding it."

Kristen did so and found that her speed didn't exactly increase but the amount of work she did decreased. She counted that as an improvement. "Why didn't you tell me about this way of flying sooner?"

"For the same reason I did not bother to teach you how to fight. . Your methods are quite successful, and—given what the technomages are capable of—I think your unorthodox approaches to problem-solving are what will ultimately save this world from war. It is only because of the dragon of shadow—and to a lesser extent the Iron Dragon—that I feel it necessary to teach you more of dragon combat."

"I guess I'll take that as a compliment," she ventured.

"It was meant as one," he said fondly.

She didn't exactly beam at the praise. It was hard to get that kind of feeling from someone she regularly gave orders to but she also took his comments to heart. She had been successful in battles in the past and merely needed new methods for these new foes. It felt a little daunting, but she could do this. It was like learning anything else, after all.

They continued for a while longer before Lumos banked and glided over a huge wooded area that surrounded a few large lakes. "Half-moon Lake, right?" Kristen asked, pointing a claw at the lake on the horizon that they were already approaching as the earth seemed to spin beneath their great speed. When she held her claw out, it did indeed affect her aerodynamics and she slowed noticeably.

"Perhaps for a swim after we're done, but I was heading to that one." Lumos gestured towards a smaller lake that was already beneath them.

She felt like she should know the name of it because she'd been out there with her family a half dozen times and had driven past it at least that often. But flying and driving a car was totally different. On the wing, everything on the surface of the earth was laid bare for a dragon to see. She could read the land as easily as she could read a map on her phone. In a car, even a clump of forest that was only a few trees deep was more than enough to completely hide the rest of the landscape from view. She wondered how many places had already been transformed in her mind after becoming a dragon. Certainly, the city of Detroit felt like an entirely different place than the city she'd spent so much time in during her youth.

Lumos glanced at her and banked to spiral above the body of water below. She followed, but—unable to help herself—tucked her wings and plunged beneath him to drop into the water.

It was cold and refreshing—and if she was completely honest, a little terrifying. She'd never been the strongest of swimmers. Even as a young, extremely athletic girl, she had shied away from the water. She could swim—everyone in Michigan could swim. There were too many lakes to not learn how at some point in life, but she'd always been averse to spending her day in and under water. She wondered if that was because a part of her had always known about her ability to become steel and what a liability that was in a body of water.

The nightmares she still had about the shadow dragon who had attacked her in the subterranean lake were worse, but that fear was also why she forced herself to plunge in. If water was her weakness, her enemies would use it against her. It wasn't like drowning a metal dragon was terribly creative, after all. She'd have to assume that most of her foes might try to push the advantage by seeking to fight her somewhere she would sink.

She dove into the lake because Lumos was there and it was the middle of the day. There was nothing to fear and yet, as she pumped her wings and swished her tail to propel herself underwater, she couldn't shake a feeling of dread. It was truly exhilarating to burst from the surface and rise into the air again. It was something she hadn't done against the dragon in the cave. There had not been enough room, probably by her enemy's design.

Still, Kristen would be a fool to go that deep underground by herself again. It was far more likely that if she battled near water, it would be on the surface of the earth, not beneath it. She plunged into the water and burst out of it repeatedly, practicing the maneuver until it was comfortable for her.

Up ahead, Lumos had already landed on the far shore of the lake. Still in dragon form, he waited for her and tapped a claw like an impatient teacher.

She thrust from the water a final time, flipped, and landed on the narrow sandy bank that hugged the lake before giving way to grass.

"If you're quite done playing, I think it's time we began," he said, although his aura said that he was rather amused with her splashing.

"Sure. But why did we come all the way out here if we won't use the water?" Kristen asked.

"We may end up practicing an aquatic battle if you wish, although based on the powers of your foes, I don't think it's the most likely of arenas for your fights against them."

"Then why here?" she repeated.

Lumos raised a claw and pointed at the empty landscape around them. There were perhaps a hundred yards of grass between the water and a forest. No picnic tables, campsites, or roads marred the green of this particular location. "Because this part of the park is hardly used, and if we get a little...messy, no one will mind."

"All right, let's do this." She raised her tail to ready herself for a strike and pumped her wings so she could lift her front claws off the ground to strike.

He didn't fight back. Instead, he approached her and while she still flapped her wings, he touched the joint where her wing connected to her body with the tip of his tail. "You're leaving this joint open."

"But if I use my wings to flap up, I can get elevation and do more damage," she protested. She'd used the technique against more than a few mages.

"A fair consideration if you're a hawk hunting a squirrel, but you are not. We often use those kinds of techniques against humans as it makes us seem even larger than we are, but it's not wise against a dragon."

"Why not?" she asked.

"The most important part of fighting a dragon is understanding that it's an organism like any other. True, we have magic and healing abilities, but we are not invulnerable. The joints between our scales are a weak place on almost every body type out there. The most vulnerable of these are your wings. Observe." He tucked his wings tightly against the sides of his body and lunged at her. She tried to use her wings to help her evade him, but when she did, he put his claws to the membrane of her wing.

Kristen stopped immediately, not wanting to tear the membrane unnecessarily. "I don't understand. I've had that membrane torn more than once and I've ripped it on dragons. We can heal it almost instantly."

"Indeed," Lumos said and moved his long sinuous neck so his teeth hovered at the joint of her wings where all the bones radiated out. "But if I were to pin you and bite right here, you would be unable to fly for the rest of the fight. If you can bite this joint here or better yet, stab it with that ax-blade you have on the tip of your tail, you'll have an advantage over your foe. With practice, you should learn to snag the membrane, disable this joint, and strike at where the wing connects to the body."

He demonstrated by extending a long claw on one of his fingers to poke the joint at the place closest to her belly. It didn't particularly hurt until Lumos applied slightly more pressure.

"Ow, shit. Okay, you've made your point," she said and winced at the pain. It was deep and sharp and made her think of the time her brother had refused to clean his hands after getting cut while out fishing and how his hand had swelled. They'd had to lance it with a knife and squeeze the pus out. This felt like some horrible pressure was released.

"It's difficult to do much to that main joint of the wing from the outside," Lumos explained as he released her. "That's probably why you haven't suffered this particular injury. But if you can manage to force the dragon to open its wings or if you attack them from the front, it can be a much better target than going straight for the heart."

"So use pain as an advantage?" Kristen asked, surprised that the fighting method of this ancient race of beings who held themselves above humanity resorted to something as crude as pain-compliance strikes in their battles.

Lumos nodded. "It's the most natural thing in the world, especially considering that your opponent will be able to heal most wounds. It's damn hard to make a dragon bleed out or to even overwhelm their healing power, so it's best to disable a joint or two and go for a killing blow."

"And how would I make a killing blow if you think going for the heart isn't the best strategy?" She was strangely fascinated by the vicious savagery he explained so calmly.

"A blow to the heart is one of the best ways to kill a dragon," he confessed, "but it's a strike best saved for the end of a battle. It's the same with a shot to the brain or an attempt at decapitation. Any of those three will surely kill a dragon, but if you haven't weakened them and slowed their healing ability enough, they are all extremely risky things to do."

"Okay." She nodded and tried to internalize that it was good to use cheap shots when dragons were fighting. "It makes sense. Don't kill until you think it will stick."

"Sure." He chuckled. "I've never heard it said in those terms but yes, that is the short of it."

"Where else do I target besides the joints of the wings?" she asked.

"All the joints that connect a dragon's limbs to its body are good targets," he explained. "If you can knock a dragon on its back, do so, then bite at either a wing joint or where one of its legs connect to its body. The only exception to this is the neck."

"I would think the neck would be a particularly good place to attack," Kristen commented.

"It is if you can strike a dragon in the throat and as close to the base of the skull as possible without actually hitting the skull. If you can deliver a blow there, you'll likely stun a dragon if you hit it hard enough. The rest of the neck is well-armored. It's still worth it to try to bite through it but isn't something I'd recommend while your opponent is at full strength."

"Are there any more dirty little secrets you've kept from your boss?" Kristen teased.

"Only the eyes, although that won't help you as much as it does me," he said and stared directly into her.

"How do you mean?" she asked, a little confused.

"My light works so well as a weapon against dragons precisely because our eyesight is so keen. We can see in the dark quite easily, but that means a sudden flare of sunlight can overwhelm a dragon's eyes. It's odd but against dragons, my light is quite effective, while if a human simply blinks at the right moment, it's often enough to prevent disorientation. A dragon needs to turn its head or shield its eyes with something besides its eyelids."

"You're right. I don't see how that helps me," she said.

"Eyes aren't armored. If you can put a claw or the tip of your tail in an eye socket, your opponent will most assuredly be at a disadvantage for at least a few moments."

"Don't dragons disapprove of fighting like this?" she asked, still confused that the dragons—so often as prim and proper as any human she had ever met—would fight by trying to gouge each other's eyes out.

"Some do, yes, but not the ones you'll fight. Plus, we're surprisingly forgiving when it comes to wounds our healing abilities can mend. If you rip a dragon's wing off, it'll grow back most of the time and they will forget. But if you pull a single claw off badly enough to ensure it never returns, a dragon will haunt you for centuries, even over the smallest of claws."

"So are you saying I pissed these two off sometime?" she joked.

Lumos didn't laugh. "No, or I doubt it anyway. But if you do manage to seriously injure one, I'd recommend finishing the duel with lethal force. Dragons hold grudges and these already have issues with you."

"Okay, anything else?"

"Yes. Dragons don't give warning before they strike."

"You mean—"

He lunged forward at her chest.

Kristen fought her instinct to pump her wings and avoid him and instead, drew her wings close to her back, lowered herself to the ground, and protected her joints.

Her opponent still crashed into her, but he tumbled off her scales. "Good," he said and apparently didn't mind being thwarted by his student. "Your back is the most armored part of your body. As long as you don't let your opponent pull your wings away, you'll be all right."

Before she could respond, he lunged at her again. She tried the same maneuver but this time, he snagged his tail under her wing and made her tumble back.

Immediately, she tried to right herself to protect her belly and the joints that connected to it. He scratched and slashed at her armpits and seemed more like a feral badger than a man who could change to his dragon form and back, but she protected herself.

It was awkward to focus so much on defense, but she found that if she protected these areas, the rest of his blows didn't do much at all.

Lumos kicked off her, vaulted high, and spread his wings to surge into another attack. She dodged this one as she had before by ducking low rather than moving out of the way. He streaked overhead and she lashed out with the ax-blade on her tail and tried to land a solid chop on his wing joint.

He caught her tail in his teeth instead and bit hard, and pain erupted through her tail. It wasn't as bad as the weak places on her joints and wounding her wasn't his intention.

Rather than sinking his teeth deeper into the underside of her tail, he flew in a tight loop, lifted her off the ground, and hurled her into the dirt.

Her opponent pounded into her exposed stomach, pinned one of her wings that she hadn't meant to extend with a claw, and positioned his jaws around her neck.

Kristen froze, knowing full well that his teeth were sharp enough to cut her when she didn't have her steel scales engaged.

"Dead," he said and released her.

"Again," she demanded.

Lumos smiled long enough to put her off guard before he launched into another assault. He got under her defenses this time and lifted her off the ground, but as he slipped beneath her, she reached around his wing and landed a lucky jab of her claws into his armpit.

The dragon yelped in pain and knocked her off his back with his wings and tail.

"You said not to do that," she protested while she tried to right herself.

He spun and was above her before she could get her body back in action. This time, he put a claw at each of her armpits and forced her to open her guard so he could once again put his teeth to her throat. "Dead again."

"But you cheated!"

"I did no such thing. Based on your position, there was no way you would reach any of my vulnerable parts. Because of that, I risked using my wings and tail. Are you beginning to understand? A dragon battle is not a brawl but a game of chess, only faster and more vicious."

"You never played against my brother," she murmured. She'd never been one for chess and had preferred soccer, lacrosse, martial arts, basketball, tennis, and the more active sports. Having to outthink her opponent as they fought instead of simply overpower and outmaneuver them did not sound like it would come easily.

"Again," he said, ignorant of her ruminations.

This time, Kristen struck first and lunged at his chest as he had done to her in an effort to get under his guard so she could reach the tender places he'd shown her.

Lumos knocked her aside by simply dodging under her blow

before he stood and threw a shoulder into her chest that careened her away. She twisted in midair—careful to not fully extend her wings—and landed on her feet.

She was too slow, however. He had watched her like a dog watched a treat and as soon as she touched the dirt, he drove into her and forced her into a roll until he was on top of her and pinned her to the ground once more by her wings.

"I told you to guard these," he said and raised one of the bones of the wing with his claw. Before he could simulate a slice—or inflict a real gash, she thought, because she had learned dragons liked to go hard when training—she transformed her wing. It vanished as if she were turning to her human form but she left the rest of her body as a dragon.

Lumos lost his hold on her as soon as the wing vanished. He took a step back and focused on the space within her dragon body where he knew her human form would appear. Kristen had no intention to change into her human form, however. She had merely shed the wing to free herself.

She lunged forward, her head lowered and horns aimed at her opponent's neck.

In the time it took for her to attack, the gold dragon had recovered from his surprise. He parried her head butt with a slap of his tail, and when she stumbled, he grasped one of her back legs with a claw.

Kristen tumbled, opened her eyes, and found that Lumos had killed her again.

Frustrated, she sighed.

"Don't be too hard on yourself," he said to comfort her. "It takes most dragons a long time to master these techniques and you have already improved in this short session. Tell me, how much control do you have over your transformative ability?"

"Oh, not much," she said and assumed her human shape. She made her hands into human-sized versions of her dragon claws. "I can do my hands and feet, and that's about it. I've worked on the tail and wings, but it's slow going."

He nodded and his aura told her he was impressed. "It's interesting that you have so much control over that ability."

"You don't need to flatter me, Lumos. I've seen many dragons transform only part of their body. Hell, Shadowstorm could use his transformations to kind of teleport. He could move while he did it too. Beating him with that ability was a real bitch."

"And he no doubt practiced that particular tactic for centuries," he said ponderously. "You, on the other hand—pardon my pun—have only known how to do that for what—a year?"

"Less than that but yeah. It's not that hard, though. Changing my body to steel feels much the same as changing to my dragon body, and when I'm in my dragon form, I often activate only a small part of my body into its steel mode so I don't weigh too much. My steel skin was what I practiced the most early on."

"Hmm... Most dragons don't bother with that ability to the extent you have."

"Really?"

"Indeed," Lumos stated. "Perhaps because most dragons—myself included—think of our scaled form as our true self. You, obviously, do not."

"No...no, I suppose not."

He shrugged. "It's curious. However you've managed to do it, continue to push yourself. It could be a real asset in a fight. Some dragons turn to their human form to escape but even that is a rarely used tactic. Transforming only part of yourself to dodge a blow... yes...this opens up some possibilities."

"Should I practice that before our next session?"

"Next session? Why Lady Steel, we've only just begun."

Before she could blink, he had knocked her to the ground, forced her to roll over by stabbing her in the armpit with his tail, and killed her.

Kristen smiled despite being pretend-murdered by her teacher. "Again."

CHAPTER SEVENTY-FOUR

K risten wasn't entirely sure how she got back to base. She remembered leaving the training session with Lumos, beyond exhausted—dog tired and maybe more tired than an entire pack of dogs. Vaguely, she recalled trying to use the new method of flying he'd shown her that required her body to be more rigid to better use the wind instead of only her wings. Mostly, she remembered how much her aching muscles refused to obey.

The entire journey had been little more than a blur of almost delirious flying. If she had been driving, she would have pulled over and taken a nap. Being airborne, however, she simply made sure to not fly over any streets or people so if she fell asleep, she wouldn't crush anyone. She remembered telling herself this was smart of her when it had probably merely been reckless.

At some point—multiple points?—she had stopped to feast on fast food. It did nothing to sate her appetite and for the first time since she'd learned she was a dragon, she wondered in her delirium if she should have followed Lumos into the woods to eat a few fresh deer.

She'd apparently pondered her meal choices for most of the flight because when she arrived at the base, she couldn't recall any other thoughts, only fantasies of sleep—no, of a hot shower, then sleep. She could almost feel it now. Timeflash had installed a shower that had dragon-level water temperature and pressure, which was absolutely divine, even for someone who sometimes felt like she needed to scrub her steel skin. There were bunks, too. Delicious, communal, fairly uncomfortable bunks that right now, sounded like a personal paradise.

She walked through the front door and toward the stairs but didn't get halfway there before Brian intercepted her.

"Kristen! I've been looking for you," he said.

"What? No Kissy-Krissy this time? Did your check not clear or something?"

"Nah," he replied. "No one else is close enough to hear, so there's no point in irritating you."

"Did you have a point? Or did you decide to deny me a shower and sleep for fun?" she asked sharply.

"I was going to fix you a cup of coffee, but I thought this was too urgent."

Kristen sagged. She'd have loved a cup of coffee but he had piqued her curiosity. She tried to shake the need for sleep off and prepared herself to hear what he had to tell her.

"The Dragon Council called," he said and sucked in a breath of air as if to ready himself. Obviously, that wasn't the big piece of news.

She frowned. "Are you sure it's them? After that shit show with the wild goose chase in Colombia and me getting…" Lured? Tricked? What did you call it when an elder dragon tried to make you go insane before they attempted to murder you? "Misdirected?" she finished lamely.

"It was the real one this time. I spoke to them via video and connected via multiple lines. Apparently, they have a new protocol after that mess in the caves," Brian said.

"Well, it's good that they can at least adapt when needed," she snapped. She didn't mean to be so snippy but desperately wanted sleep. Instead, she had to listen to messages like her parents had once done on a machine. "Did you tell them about our mission to Colombia?"

"Yes. I updated them on our progress with the four dragons we rescued from there and confirmed that we haven't seen any further activity. They said they'd already read the report I initially sent in, but—"

"But what?" Again, Kristen hadn't meant to snap, but her fatigue plus speaking to someone she was familiar with like her brother took away most of her self-control.

"But dragons are hard to read. I can tell you're tired and annoyed right now, no problem, but this guy on the line...I don't know. I couldn't tell if he was pleased with our progress or not."

She sighed. The council was a constant worry for her. For now, she had managed to convince them to hold off on killing most of humanity, but she knew that decision hung by a thread connected to an ax that waited to drop and cleave the relative peace of the Earth in two. The dragons had only managed to hold onto their power via force. If their position as the preeminently powerful lifeform was taken from them, they would retaliate in the only way they knew how —with violence.

While she knew stopping cells was important and that the dragons probably understood this—at least intellectually—she also knew that the leaders of the technomages—like Havington, who they'd faced in Florence, and the Iron Dragon—were the real prizes. If she wanted to stop the dragons from slaughtering billions of humans, she needed to get them more results.

"I had hoped that they would be more pleased with Colombia. That was an entire cell," Kristen complained. Despair was able to worm its way into her mind quite easily given her exhausted state.

"Maybe they were pleased." Brian threw his hands up in a placating gesture that he'd used a thousand times on their mom. It was about as ineffective against his sister as it was on Marty.

"Yeah. Maybe not," she said. "But come on, what's the real news? You wouldn't have stopped me to say you filed a report."

"True," he said, his lips tight.

"And?"

"And they passed a message along as well," Brian stated.

"Will you tell me the contents of this message or should I assume that a force of dragons has already started burning Europe to the ground?"

"Honestly, I wish it were that straightforward." He shook his head.

"Brian." She used her most motherly tone.

He straightened. "The Dragon Council wants you to speak to Constance Vigil."

In an instant, every trace of sleepiness, exhaustion, and fatigue evaporated from her mind. "She's alive?"

"I had the same thought." He nodded grimly. "I assumed they would have pumped her for as much information as they could before..." He mimed dangling a tiny human above his mouth and pretended to drop it in and swallow it.

"Are you sure?"

"Of the message? Yes. They said she has information she will tell only to you, in person, and to no one else. They want that information badly, apparently, so want you at a location tomorrow morning."

Kristen wasn't sure what to do. She needed to appease the Dragon Council and knew that not only the lives of her team but the lives of millions of innocent people depended on her. But something about this seemed...off.

She told her brother as much.

"So...you want me to tell them to go fuck themselves? Or..."

She guffawed at the sheer absurdity of telling the most powerful group of beings on the planet such a thing. "No...tell them..." Something brilliant occurred to her. "Tell them you need to verify their credentials again and once that's all in order, I'll head out with a security force."

"I already verified it. I promise you, this message is legitimate."

"I know," she said. "But this will buy me time for a shower and a few precious hours of sleep."

"You got a message from the council and you intend to take a nap?" He looked both horrified and impressed.

"It's the middle of the night. That doesn't count as a nap."

He shrugged. "It depends on your sleep schedule, I guess, but yeah,

I can stall for you. I'm sure I won't be incinerated or anything because of it."

"Calm down. They won't do anything but ask again—and I do need a security team. While I turn my brain into a functioning body part again, do me a favor and assemble a few dragons to accompany me there in case."

"They said Constance wants to speak to you alone and were very clear on that," Brian said dubiously. He already knew she would not follow their orders.

"I won't be separated from my entire team again. If they can't see the wisdom of that after what happened, they don't deserve to be on the Council."

"Okay, okay," he agreed. "I'll tell them you're assembling a team, not that you're talking about a rebellion of your own."

"Good. See you in the morning. We'll try to leave before ten AM."

"Right."

Kristen didn't even hear him. She skipped the shower and hurried to the bunks. By the time her head hit a pillow, she was already blissfully unconscious.

CHAPTER SEVENTY-FIVE

What felt like moments later, Kristen woke with a jerk.

"What time is it?" she asked Brian, who stood over her armed with a cup of hot coffee in self-defense this time.

"Five in the morning," he said as quickly as humanly possible as if he didn't want her to realize she was up at such an ungodly hour after a day of heavy training.

"I told you I wanted to leave at ten. It won't take me five hours to shower and eat breakfast." She rubbed the sleep from her eyes but it didn't help.

"You try telling dragons to be patient and let your sister sleep in," he retorted.

"You didn't tell them it was an order?" She swung her legs over the edge of the bed and put her feet to the floor. Why wasn't she in her room? She thought hard until she remembered how tired she'd been and also that she lived there now. A moment later, she also recalled that she did have a private room but had been too tired to consider using it. She sipped the coffee and thanked it silently for the magic of caffeine.

"I told them you wanted a security force to escort you to a meeting with the Dragon Council and Constance Vigil, and they stopped

listening to me completely. When I told them you wanted to sleep in
—" He shuddered at the recent memory. "I thought you said they don't
eat people anymore."

"They don't."

"Well, they still threaten to."

She stood, drank more coffee, and headed to the showers.

"Kristen—"

"They can wait. They don't want to smell this."

Although she'd promised herself she would enjoy her scalding hot
shower, this did not turn out to be the case. Rather than letting the
hot water cleanse her body and mind, she was assaulted by the auras
of what felt like a dozen dragons who pestered her to hurry up, stop
dawdling, and remember that she had to meet the Dragon Council as
soon as possible.

Disgruntled, Kristen scrubbed without ceremony and rinsed her
hair until it was her natural flame-red instead of the dirty brown the
muck of Silver Lake had changed it to after she had trained with
Lumos. She toweled off quickly, dressed in her uniform, and went
downstairs to find the drove of dragons so impatient that they
couldn't even wait until dawn to start harassing their leader.

It turned out there weren't many dragons waiting for her but one
of them could make her aura seem like many.

"About damn time," Heartsbane said from the bottom of the stairs.

"Exactly what I thought," Hernandez said. She stood at the dragon's side and a duffel bag that was no doubt filled with explosives
rested near her feet.

Emerald was there too, his arms folded across his broad chest and
his eyes narrowed at her as she came down the stairs. Those were the
only two dragons, though. Hernandez, Larry, and Jim rounded the
team out.

"Has Brian filled you in all on what's going on?" she asked.

"Yes, ma'am," Jim said.

"And we won't let you anywhere near that bitch Constance
without backup," Hernandez added.

"She asked for a private meeting," Kristen protested.

"Yeah, and I request to stick a pipe bomb up her asshole. How will we both get what we want?" the woman asked.

Heartsbane chuckled at the vulgar humor. "I don't know how a bomb becomes a pipe bomb, but I support Hernandez's plan on what to do with it."

Kristen looked at the two women, one dragon and one human. She should have assumed that the two quick-tempered, foul-mouthed cops would get along, but she was still pleasantly surprised to see how much they seemed to have in common. A desire to blow Constance to smithereens, for starters.

"What about the rest of you?" she asked and looked at the others.

Emerald shrugged. "That was some bad shit that happened in Mammoth Caves. If we hadn't gotten there when we did..." The dragon shook the dreadlocked, dark-skinned head of his human form. "You taking forever to wash your hair would have been the least of our problems."

"Brian said he checked the intel," she explained.

"I know. And I recognized the location we're going to. It's a maximum-security dragon prison reserved for those the Dragon Council wants to kill but can't for some reason. I've taken a few prisoners there over the years."

"So you know it's not a trap," Kristen said.

He snorted in amusement. "I know that if it is a trap, it'll be a damn good one."

She nodded. While she didn't want to be paranoid, after what had happened the last time, it was probably better safe than sorry. "And what about you two?" she asked Larry and Jim.

"You should have a mage with you at all times if possible," Larry explained. "And this place will be filled with complex security spells. Amy's more powerful than I am, but if she got curious and poked at their systems..." He mimed an explosion with his fingers.

"And you, Jim?"

The Wonderkid half-smiled. "I know this might not make much sense on account of Constance saying she wants to speak to you and you alone, but I thought I should come in case I get a chance to talk to her."

"You want to talk to that bitch?" Heartsbane demanded and her aura made it clear what she wanted to do to him.

"I think I might be in a good position to understand where she's coming from. I used to hate dragons but I don't anymore. She needs to go on the same journey of understanding I went on. I might be able to remind her why she got into all this." He smiled his Wonderkid smile. "Plus, if shit goes south, I'm the best shot out of everyone here."

The group laughed at the tacit threat of violence, a pressure valve to release their tension.

"All right, then," Kristen said and acknowledged the team that would go with her. "I haven't checked where we're headed. Will we take the jet or go by dragon wing?"

"Jet," Brian said as he approached the group from his bank of computer monitors. "You'll take the jet to the Denver airport and from there, fly to the top of this mountain."

Her phone buzzed and she saw he had sent her a location.

"I've given you access codes and Larry knows a spell of identification that should get you in without too much trouble," her brother said.

"I thought they were expecting us?" She frowned. "When I was in dragon jail, I could still receive visitors."

"This facility is a couple of levels of security clearance beyond where you were locked up during that investigation," Emerald said. "They're extremely paranoid. There's never been a breakout but not for lack of trying. You have to remember that the only beings who might try to get someone out of this jail are either dragons, mages, or teams of both."

"Noted," she said.

"If you guys are all done chatting, I'd recommend getting your asses to the airport and on your way to Denver," Brian said.

Kristen couldn't help but smile at her brother's pushy language. "Did something happen that you now feel comfortable bossing around a couple of dragons, a mage, and cops who know how to apply lethal force?"

"Yeah. A group of dragons and mages have been on my ass all night for not accepting their credentials. I'll take my chances against you punks if it means they'll stop bugging me."

"It's not like they'd hurt you," Larry said sympathetically.

"Yeah, well, they certainly are more than willing to try to convince me otherwise," he grumbled.

"Brian's right," Kristen said. "I appreciate the sleep, as short as it was, and the shower. Now, let's go."

They hurried to the airport, boarded the private jet, and left without delay.

She focused on keeping her aura confident but in reality, she had no idea what to expect. Why on earth would Constance—the woman who had almost killed her half a dozen times and who had claimed to be like a mother to her—want to see her now? How was she even still alive?

While she needed the answers to these questions, she didn't know if she wanted them.

The flight to Denver was uneventful and the flight to the mountains only more remarkable in that she had to get used to flying in the thinner air. Her dragon healing powers made simple work of it, though, and pumped her body full of extra red blood cells to fuel her dragon form. Unfortunately, she didn't have the magic required to outsmart the wind.

It was a strange comfort that neither Heartsbane nor Emerald seemed better equipped for the thin air. All three dragons worked twice as hard to gain half as much altitude as they rose higher up the mountain to where the prison was located.

"Too bad Lumos didn't come," Emerald said when they were maybe halfway up. "I've seen that old dragon stay stable in hurricane winds. I bet he knows a trick or two about flying in thin air."

Heartsbane chuckled. "The old fart was too tired."

"From what?" Kristen asked. All he'd done the previous day was train with her, and from the way the session had gone—what with him killing her something like a hundred times—she'd come out of it worse than he had.

"From training with the Steel Dragon, no doubt," Larry said from her back.

"No way. He was fine the entire time and barely winded."

"I don't know." The mage sounded skeptical. "Windlock was like that, too. He'd be all claws and flames while we were on a case but when we had a day off, he would rest his old bones."

"Don't sell yourself short, Steel," Heartsbane said. "I've trained with you. It's not easy and Lumos is thousands of years old. It probably took him every ounce of strength he had to beat you."

She felt an immediate swell of pride at the praise of her team. It felt good to think that she'd done better with Lumos than she'd realized. But the emotional lift was short-lived. If he was already coming up against his limits while training her, what did that say about her chances of getting strong enough to face the Iron Dragon and the hidden dragon who had attacked her in the cave?

The thought left her uneasy but she'd have to consider it more later. Besides, holding back in a fight was sometimes more draining than going all out, so maybe he was suffering from something like that. In the next moment, her concerns were finally pushed from her mind when she saw the prison.

She had looked for it on the snowcapped peak of the mountain, thinking it would be tucked in on one side or the other or perhaps even nestled at the very top.

None of these proved adequate for the level of defense the dragons wanted.

The facility wasn't on any of the sides because it was built into the top of the mountain. As they approached, Kristen could see that four walls surrounded a sunken fortress. At the top of each of these walls was a dragon guard and a mass of explosives. She realized that the sides of the prison were rigged with bombs so they'd start an avalanche. Anyone who thought they could walk up the side of the mountain would simply be hurled to the bottom or worse, crushed to death by thousands of tons of snow, dirt, and stone.

At each of the four corners of the perimeter walls were massive crossbows—scorpions, she knew they were called from her time playing videogames with Brian. These were each manned by a dragon and they tracked her and her team as they approached the prison.

"Larry? Do you think you could block one of those bolts if they fired them at us?" Kristen asked.

He laughed. "Not a goddamn chance. Every one of them is enchanted to resist magic or anything that will slow them. I can feel the spells from here. Whoever cast them wasn't exactly subtle about it, but I guess that would defeat the point. I have to say, I don't think even Amy could block those."

"It's better not to cause them to launch," Emerald said. "Every one of them is tipped with a cut diamond bigger than any you humans have in your museums. It's sharp enough to even slice through dragon scale."

"At least they're taking something seriously," she muttered.

In the center of the recessed mountain top was a blocky structure of brick and concrete, completely lacking in windows. On its roof, seven dragons prowled in formation while an eighth signaled for the team to land.

Kristen nodded at Emerald and Heartsbane to get into formation, pointed her nose at the roof, and led them to the landing zone.

Simply stepping foot on the structure sent a tingle up her spine.

"I feel it too," Larry whispered as one of the seven dragons patrolling the roof changed to human form—albeit a human form that wore armor and was armed with a sword—and approached them.

"This feels as secure as dragons can make it. The same spell they use to rob mages of their powers with those bracelets and imprison dragons is woven into the very bricks here. I don't know if I could so much as conjure a spark."

"Now's not the time to try," she said as the dragon came to stand before them.

"Lady Steel," the woman with closely cropped hair in her human form said as she bowed. "We have expected your arrival and trust that your flight here was without turmoil."

"Thank you," she responded, not quite sure what to do with the woman's frigid tone. At least she welcomed them. She made an attempt at humor. "Are you sure you don't need to check our IDs?" She flashed the smile the media always played when they had footage of her.

The dragon appreciated neither the smile nor the joke. "Every dragon aura is unique. One of our people recognized you as soon as you came into range from a...celebration you both attended in Detroit. Most of us met Emerald when he came here in the past."

"What's wrong, Quickclaw? Don't you want to explain how you know my aura?" Heartsbane smiled at the leader of the guards.

The woman flashed the smallest, coldest smile that could still be counted as a smile before she simply answered, "No." She turned her attention to Kristen. "I recognize that you felt you needed an escort to come this far. I hope the rest of you can enjoy the spectacular views from the top of this mountain while I escort Lady Steel to see the technomage." She said "spectacular views" the way a doctor might describe an infected wound.

"Hell no!" Hernandez said as she clambered off Heartsbane's back.

"You must have lost your mind," Heartsbane said and transformed into her human form so she could approach Quickclaw until they stood face to face.

"I assure you, she'll be safe," the guard said, her sneer directed at Hernandez. She was evidently a dragon who didn't care for impertinent humans and wasn't concerned with hiding her bias.

"We're not worried about you." The woman sneered with equal disdain. "I have no doubt that the Steel Dragon could declaw you if she wished to."

"I see you finally found someone as skilled in social niceties as you are," Quickclaw said to Heartsbane.

"The human's right," Heartsbane said. "We won't let Lady Steel near that mage without backup."

"It's not an option," the guard said. "If I had my way, we wouldn't even let you in." Quickclaw nodded at Kristen.

"Why not?" she demanded.

"Because this is a maximum-security prison for dragons and mages. These people don't get visitors," one of the other guards snapped. They'd all listened to the exchange with their dragon hearing, of course.

"Besides that," Quickclaw continued, "we can't have random people in the prison as it would expose the layout and damage the security of the facility."

"I assure you that you can trust my people," Kristen told her.

"I have heard of you, Steel Dragon. Even up here on the edge of nowhere, we have heard the stories of how you work with human and mage and dragon. I have no doubt that you trust your people, but that does not change the nature of the world."

"They won't tell anyone."

"Not intentionally, no," Quickclaw admitted. "But what if they came under duress? What if a mage goes fishing in their mind and finds something of interest?"

"They wouldn't do anything to endanger our mission." She was adamant and aside from the fact that she believed it, she did not want to be separated from her team.

"And if someone could convince them that getting inside would help your mission? The person you are here to see fights for a new world order. What if someone can use magic and force to convince one of these people to divulge our secrets? What recourse do we have when the dragons and mages we have kept in here for centuries are released into the world?" Quickclaw looked at the team comprised of dragons, humans, and a mage. She seemed expectant rather than distrusting like she knew one of them would crumble as surely as a log would burn.

"Then why allow me inside at all?" Kristen asked. "I'm not particularly well learned in magic, and the entire world knows I don't like the way things are between humans, dragons, and mages. Why trust me and not them?"

"I don't trust you," Quickclaw said matter of factly. "In fact, I don't trust any of the guards on this roof with me, although some of them have worked with me here for decades. It is not in our job to trust or to be lenient or bend rules."

"Then why let me in?" she repeated.

"Because part of our job is also to obey the Dragon Council, and they ordered us to let you in." The guard ground the words out, obviously still aggrieved at being usurped of her power where she was master. "If it were up to me, I would let the magic bitch rot before she had any visitors, but the Council feels this is not wise. Thus, here we all are, arguing about things that none of us like and yet we will soon all agree to."

"Who says I'll agree?" Kristen asked.

That earned another tiny smile from Quickclaw that vanished as quickly as it appeared. "You didn't fly all this way to go home without coming inside. Come, I will take you to Constance's cell. If you still feel that she is a threat after you see what is in place to keep her secured then, by all means, come out here and fly home without speaking to the big bad scary mage. My orders were to let you in to speak to her, not to hold your hand while you two have teatime."

She looked at her team. Heartsbane and Hernandez shook their heads firmly but neither spoke out of turn, which she knew must have been a struggle for them both. She looked at Larry and was unsurprised to see him nod. His response made sense as he'd been a dragon investigator's mage for a long time. Of course he wanted the next clue. Emerald surprised her by nodding as well. She didn't know if that was because he thought she could beat Constance in a fight if it came down to it—a debatable hypothesis to be sure—or if he simply thought it would be worth talking to the mage. Finally, she turned to Jim, curious as to what he would do given that her team's opinion was tied.

To her surprise, he nodded. It was interesting that he now trusted dragons enough to trust her life to them. More interesting was that he seemed to trust Constance enough to want whatever information she had.

Kristen nodded as well.

"It's great to know the leader of the only group of people fighting to stop a war from breaking out relies on her escort to make her decisions," Quickclaw snipped.

"I know you lash out when you're stressed, Quickclaw," Heartsbane said. "But the freaking Dragon Council operates by working together to decide, so quite frankly, I don't know what the hell makes you think Kristen should be any different."

"Plus, a smart leader listens to the wisdom of her advisors, then does whatever the fuck she thinks is best," Hernandez said.

Neither of the two women made a move to follow Kristen, though, which proved that although they disagreed with their leader, they still respected her decisions.

Quickclaw didn't fail to notice this, either. She took it all in and frowned as she tried to parse the balance of power in evidence. Apparently, she found what she was looking for because she nodded at one of the guards on the roof to follow her and Kristen into the prison.

They walked to a padlocked iron trapdoor that was sunk into the concrete roof. Quickclaw stood upon it, and—to Kristen's shock—danced. It was an elaborate series of movements like something out of a Celtic festival that might look best if accompanied by bagpipes and a base drum. After a moment during which her legs moved incredibly fast and something pinged and clinked in a beautiful melody, the door clicked. The other guard—a gruff, bearded man who looked none too happy to see the visitors—opened the outside lock.

They descended a rickety ladder into a bright white room.

"Do you have any magic items?" Quickclaw asked. "Because if you do, they're about to be junk."

"Only one," Kristen said and took a magic dampening bracelet out.

"I thought you'd be above such things," the woman said.

In truth, the device was one of the special ones that appeared to block magic without actually inhibiting it. It was good—and slightly troubling—to see that it fooled even these security experts. "You never know," she said enigmatically, which seemed to be enough for their escort.

A dragon—they were all in human form now that they were inside the prison—took the bracelet upstairs and gave it to someone on her team before they returned.

"Are you ready? This will feel weird," Quickclaw said.

"I'm ready for whatever you have that—"

Before she could finish, a bright light flashed. She closed her eyes to protect herself from such a childish defense and wondered if this was all these dragons had when she realized that she could no longer feel her powers. She couldn't turn into a dragon or steel or use her dragon speed.

"It's a bitch, huh?" the guard asked.

"Do you do this every time?" she asked. She'd forgotten how much her body weighed when she didn't have magical energy to power her.

"It's the only way to be sure no magic artifacts or mages sneak inside. It hurts the mages worse than it does us. Your powers will be back in time for the other security measures...well, partially, anyway. I'll need you to stick close to me once we start moving, understand?"

"I thought we were only going to see a prisoner?" Kristen asked. Her brain had had difficulty functioning and her mind, like everything else, felt slower.

"This is the most secure building in the world," Quickclaw said. "One cannot simply saunter into this prison."

The woman pushed a door open at the far end of the white room to reveal a spiral staircase. They started down it. Every few feet, there was a hole in the wall. "Murder holes," the guard said proudly. "If you try something, my guards kill you. If I don't check in before I come out, they kill you when you try to leave."

"I thought I wasn't supposed to know your secrets."

Quickclaw chuckled. "Oh, child, the murder holes are no secret. There is a long way to go, yet."

Kristen nodded and followed while the other dragon guard brought up the rear. At the end of the spiral staircase, they reached a hallway carved out of the stone of the mountain itself. There were three paths, one to the front, and one to both the right and left.

"This one we show all the prisoners so we're all on the same page. Walk ahead and see what happens."

She took a tentative step forward, only for the floor to fall away as if it were nothing but sand. A few paces out—a jumpable distance— the effect seemed to stop. She was about to jump across the gap—she thought she could clear it even without her dragon powers—when a bolt of energy cracked where she had intended to land. Disconcerted, she swallowed and realized she could feel the spell across the distance. She didn't want to imagine what it would be like if she jumped.

"That is there because we know most people will reflexively jump past the crumbling floor. You need to understand that this entire prison is like that. It is a labyrinth made of traps created by guards with nothing better to do than find new and unexpected ways to kill those dumb enough to try to escape or break in here. Every time you think you can outsmart a trap, there is another one. When you think three steps ahead, we have thought ten. This facility is designed to kill you in as short a time as possible and drive you insane if you last more than a few minutes. You must stick close to me and step only where I step. If you dawdle, Oakfist will force you to go faster. If you dawdle again, we will simply let the prison swallow you."

"I thought the council wanted me to meet Constance," she said.

"They knew there were risks," Quickclaw responded.

Kristen nodded. "Is there a reason why we're waiting?" That earned her a tiny smile from her guide before they continued.

They proceeded down the right corridor, turned right, and after another few turns, she was well and truly lost. The problem wasn't only the twisting turns of the monotonous stone walls but that every few paces, Quickclaw would point out a tripwire, a pressure plate, or a dusty old rune etched into the stone itself.

Most of these allowed them to pass without incident but sometimes, that was simply impossible.

"Get ready to jump," Quickclaw said at one of them before she tripped a wire that delivered a barrage of spinning axes at their shins.

Kristen jumped and the weapons streaked on, only to vanish into the gloom behind them.

"Those get many of our visitors," Oakfist said as if having your legs chopped off at the knee was somehow funny.

They continued over pools filled with liquids far darker than water and past pits filled with creatures Kristen hadn't thought existed. Sometimes, they'd pause for Quickclaw to mutter spells under her breath that would set runes to glowing. This seemed to be the worst kind of trap as whenever she activated one of these, she and Oakfist would stop their banter—as infrequent as it was—and focus on escaping before whatever force they'd disabled came back to kill them.

"How can you do this every time there's a visitor?" she asked.

"I told you," Quickclaw said as she flung her arm into Kristen's chest and flattened her against a wall as a series of darts rocketed past. "We don't do visitors here. Our last one was…"

"Two years ago?" Oakfist volunteered.

"I was trying to think when the last one was who made it out alive."

He chuckled. "Oh. I think that was eight. One of the Dragon Council members wanted one of our captive dragons to know that they'd finally liquidated their entire estate. I lost a finger helping deliver that message, but the look on the dragon's face was worth it."

Great, Kristen thought as she dodged a swinging blade held up by a spell and nothing more. *I'm escorted to my death by a couple of suicidal masochists.*

"We're here," Quickclaw said after a particularly taxing set of jumps and flips they'd had to accomplish to avoid being caught on almost invisible strands of something both guards had assured her was far stronger than steel.

"Where?" she asked. It didn't look any different than the rest of the prison had. From what she could see, it was merely more endless twisting corridors that were riddled with traps.

"Her door," Quickclaw said, slid a key between two cracks in the stone, and opened a door Kristen was certain had not been there a moment before.

"Are all the prisoners down that hall?" she asked and peered down a long corridor that was lit with painfully bright lights. It was odd to see it after so much gloom.

The guard snorted a bitter laugh. "Prisoners are hidden throughout the maze. This might be the first cell we've passed or the fiftieth. That's the power of this prison. She's by herself, the only cell at the end of the hall. There are no traps in there. We keep a magic dampening field in place so they won't work."

"Now you suddenly want me to go alone?" she asked. "What happened to stick close to me or die?"

"Because that's the only way the technomage bitch would agree to speak at all," Oakfist growled.

"Do you mean she set the terms for this meeting?" For some reason, that deeply unsettled her.

"We haven't managed to get a damn thing out of her," Quickclaw said. "Not us, not the Council, no one. She told a councilor that she'd speak to you, and they're all desperate enough to prevent this war that they agreed to it."

"The idiots should have let her rot," Oakfist added.

Kristen nodded. She accepted what they said but didn't relax at all. She believed the guards were telling the truth, but something about all this felt wrong to her. Despite her reservations, she started down the hallway to speak to Constance Vigil, the woman who'd come closer to killing her more times than anyone else.

She only wished she didn't feel like she was walking into the biggest trap of the entire prison when the guards closed the door behind her.

CHAPTER SEVENTY-SIX

As Kristen walked down the long, stark, brightly lit hallway, she wondered why the hell the dragons would decide to illuminate the inside of their magic prison with the harsh light of fluorescent bulbs.

Perhaps the intention was to keep the prisoners on edge, but if Constance was any indication, it didn't seem to be working.

Her breath caught when she saw the technomage leader at the end of the hallway. She was seated behind a pane of glass reinforced with steel mesh—cross-legged and her eyes closed as she took deep, controlled breaths. Her posture suggested that she was meditating and was at peace with herself. It immediately stirred resentment and outrage. This woman—who had taken freedom from so many and the lives of even more—didn't deserve such solace.

She cleared her throat and drew the prisoner out of her meditative state. Still, the mage didn't look flustered. She opened her eyes slowly and a placid smile slid onto her face until she saw her visitor.

"Oh!" Constance said simply.

"Who the fuck did you expect? The Easter Bunny?" She was annoyed that she'd been summoned by this murderer and the woman had the audacity to act like she was surprised to see her.

"I wasn't sure you would come," the mage said.

"You told the Council you'd only speak to me. Some of us are willing to put our personal pleasure below a greater cause. I'd talk to far worse than you if it meant saving lives, although I guess that might not be possible," Kristen said.

"That's fair…" The woman still seemed shaken to see her and pushed to her feet. "I did ask for you to come but I never thought the Dragon Council would send the Steel Dragon to my cell to speak to me. I guess it's gotten worse out there?"

"Exactly like you planned. More people and dragons have died," she said.

"Then I owe you my gratitude." Constance bowed. "I know we've had our disagreements in the past. Honestly, I wasn't sure you would come at all."

"I didn't come for you, so don't act like I did."

The prisoner nodded. "You came because you want to know what I have to say."

"Don't flatter yourself." She retrieved her cellphone and showed the woman a picture of a dragon whose scales had been ripped from its body. "I came because I have a bone to pick with you—and I wanted to know if dragon security works to protect prisoners even when they don't deserve it."

She showed her another photo of a dragon, this one with her horns sawed off, followed by one of a dragon with no talons, a dragon's wings impaled with meat hooks to stop it from flying, and finally, of a dragon's eyes filled with terror. Her expression grim, she held up an image of a festering wound followed by numerous others, all similar.

"I'd ask what you have to say for yourself, but I realized a while ago that there's nothing you can say that can make any of this right." Kristen was shaking with rage.

"I know," Constance agreed. She hung her head as a tear slipped down her cheek to fall on the hard floor of her cell.

"It's good to know you haven't wasted your time here. Your acting practice is paying off," she said, determined not to let the technomage ruffle her. This was the woman who—as far as she knew—master-minded this entire operation and she now thought...what? That she could shed a few crocodile tears and her visitor would beg the guards to open her cell so she could give her a hug?

"I know you won't believe me, but I am sorry." Constance wiped her eyes and tried to meet her steely gaze.

"Sorry for not recruiting me? I had thought you wanted me to join your team and be a freedom fighter, but after seeing your...your assembly lines, I realized you merely wanted even stronger ingredients for your damn bullets."

"No!" the mage said and the fierceness in her tone surprised her. She sagged as if even that exertion tired her. "Not for you, Kristen—never for you. If you'd joined me, you would have been a prime ally and a powerful friend, hopefully one of our leaders like..." She trailed off.

Kristen knew exactly what had made her stop talking. "I've met your Iron Dragon. You would've turned me into a weapon like her instead of using my body to make weapons? Somehow, I'm not exactly flattered."

"No one could have made Katrina into a weapon without her wanting to become one," Constance countered with no effort to pretend she didn't know what she was talking about, a small triumph for Kristen. Maybe the bullshit the woman had spouted for so long had finally dried up.

"Oh, so she simply learned how to use her powers to fight and kill all by herself?"

"You have learned how to fight and kill and we never trained you," the technomage pointed out. "We should have...although then, perhaps you wouldn't have the moral resolve that so impresses me."

"Fuck your flattery," she said harshly. "You trained a child to be a warrior. Admit it."

Constance shrugged. "It's true. We did and would have done the same to you as well."

"Then why didn't you?" Kristen didn't see how this could be perti-nent to finding and stopping the other technomage cells. Still, ever since she'd known of the woman's role in her early life, she couldn't help her curiosity about how their pasts intertwined.

"Like fools, we didn't think you were a dragon." The prisoner laughed weakly as if it were all a cosmic joke played on her. "Most dragons respond to spells we have that can force you to change shape. You didn't. We thought that perhaps you were some kind of runt—a dragon stuck in its human form. It was an existence that Windfire couldn't allow. It pained him, but he ordered you disposed of and in those days, none of us mages were bold enough to talk back to a dragon."

"It's a good thing not everyone in your lab was so spineless," she stated.

"Indeed. If I had known the woman who stole you out from under our noses took you to a family before we ran her off the road, we might have a very different meeting right now."

"You're cheering that my father's sister was killed? How can you be so heartless?"

"I trained myself to be heartless," Constance said morosely. "I had to if I wanted to be able to fight dragons. I've lost so many people—friends, allies, lovers—all to the dragons." She shook her head.

"If you want me to pity you, forget it. That won't happen," Kristen said, although part of her had begun to wonder about why the woman had called her here. Had she finally been forced to come face to face with her regrets? Was this a changed woman? Or was it simply an act?

"I know," the technomage replied. "I don't deserve your pity. I should have fought harder for you like I did for Katrina."

"What do you mean?"

"The second batch of...you're not clones, not exactly. Each of you is genetically unique, but the methods we used were unusual and based on cloning methods devised by humans. There was considerable variation. Some of you and your siblings—like you and Katrina—are so incredibly strong, while others are...well, not like you."

"Those were the ones you used to create weapons from?"

Constance nodded. "I thought it would all be worth it in the end. Now...I don't know anymore."

She had known that the mage always believed the ends justified the means but did she still feel that way? There was something else she said that caught her attention. "What did you mean when you said you fought harder for Katrina?"

The prisoner looked at her as if it were her duty to answer these questions. "I fought to keep Katrina around, even when she didn't manifest an ability to transform into a dragon. She was such a happy baby, and once she started walking...well, it was clear she had dragon speed and strength. None of us had seen a toddler punch through a cabinet door until she discovered that was where we kept the animal crackers."

It was both horrifying and endearing to hear about this alternative childhood that she could have grown up with. "How long was it until she manifested her dragon form?"

"Not long. She was six years old. There was a raid—even then, some dragons knew of our activities—and she was almost incinerated in the attack. She turned to iron to protect herself. No one had seen anything like that before so of course, we devoted even more time to her. It didn't take long before Windfire got his precious little daughter to transform. Since then...well, if you have met, I'm sure you know she's a powerful ally and champion of our cause."

"And we'll stop her and throw her in this place with you, exactly like we will the rest of the technomages who come willingly."

Constance sagged. "Those photos you showed me...you took those yourself?"

"My team and I document the atrocities that have been committed in the name of the cause you champion. I don't take credit for having the stomach to be able to take all of those pictures."

"My mages are in trouble then. Our cause is hurting and maybe failing."

Kristen folded her arms. "It's my job to stop the fire you tried to start. I'm here because I was led to believe you could help me with this. Will that happen or should I leave you to rot like the guards seem so desperate to do?"

"I have information for you but first, answer me this." There was a tinge of desperation in the woman's eyes, so she let her speak. "Do you feel absolutely certain that the Council will follow through with not slaughtering humanity when you have removed the knife from their throat?" She let the question hang but before Kristen could answer she asked another. "Or will the Council go ahead anyway, once the risk of war is gone thanks to the Steel Dragon obliterating the mage cells, and remove the danger once and for all?"

"The Council won't kill all of humanity," she said. It was the only true statement she could make about the Dragon Council's motives.

"Of course not. They need their servants, don't they? But how many might they kill if they decide to? Have they promised you a number? A percentage?"

Kristen didn't know how to answer. The Council hadn't promised her anything. They merely held off on beginning a war to give her a chance. What the prisoner had said made a horrible kind of sense. Once the mages were out of the picture and the dragon bullets removed from play, the dragons would be free to decimate humanity without any risk to themselves. Was that their end game? She knew some dragons wanted to do exactly that. Others had more loyalty to the humans on which they so relied. She didn't know what most dragons thought about it, though, and worse, she didn't know the minds of the Council—the dragons who would ultimately decide the fate of the world.

"They've promised you nothing," Constance said and immediately saw through her indecision and doubt.

"And you have?" she shouted through the glass. "You asked me to join an organization that uses sentient beings for ammunition and you dare insult the credibility of others? You never told me the horrors you committed or what you were capable of."

"And they have?"

"This is not about them!" she shouted.

Constance recoiled visibly from the glass between them, but she didn't stop talking about the dragons. Then again, she never had stopped talking about them, even when the two of them had been in combat. "You're right, Kristen, about the way we treated the dragons.

There were dozens of them, you know, and many more besides who we lost to power outages or a bad pH in their tank or any other number of reasons that don't matter. Beyond that, we killed dragons. I admit it."

"And people. Don't act like humans weren't caught in some of your bombings."

"Of course humans were lost." The woman sneered and some of her old fury revealed itself. "Humans are lost every goddamn day on this planet, and do you know why? Because of them."

"That's why I joined Dragon SWAT—to stop dragons from hurting people. We could have used mages like you, you know."

"Oh, you poor, sweet thing." She shook her head as if she'd failed her. "Still? After all this? You still believe these things you say?"

"It's why I keep fighting," she said, the words like rock.

"Why exactly? To stop a few dragons from killing a few people? You're right in that dragons don't directly kill that many people. A few are incinerated every year and a few others crushed, but most people get to go about their business."

"Then why try to burn the world?" Kristen demanded.

"Because it was already on fire!" Constance raged. "Think about what most people's business was. You live in America so you should know better than most. When one of your fellow Americans was sick, who paid for it? If there was a car accident, who picked up the mess?"

"We did," she said. "Humans work for themselves."

"I know they do. Believe me, I know. I also know that when an insurance claim is denied, it's because a shareholder with a cave full of gold wants more profits. I know that when animals are killed and thrown to rot in the field, it's because it's more economical than butchering them and sending them to the places in the world with starving people. I know that so many Americans—thousands and thousands—don't have a roof over their heads, warm food in their bellies, or jackets to keep out the rain. Meanwhile, who sits atop their piles of gold, getting richer and fatter off the suffering of humans?"

"You don't get to preach after what you've done—"

"I know, Kristen, I know. I've made serious mistakes, one of the largest of which was letting you go and get brainwashed to believe that the status quo of the world you live in works for anyone but the very top."

Kristen shook her head. She didn't know about all that but she did know that Constance had done horrible things and hidden true atrocities from her simply so she could further her agenda. She wouldn't let the mage worm her way into her mind.

"What did you want to say to me? I hope it wasn't all this bullshit about a childhood you wished I had," she said and deliberately moved the subject away from conjecture and the political agenda the woman always agitated for—even there, apparently, in the depths of the bleakest prison ever built.

"You're right, of course, as you always seem to be," she said with a weak smile as she wiped the tears from her face. She'd lost control of herself and took a few deep breaths to try to regain composure. "I asked you to come because I know the name of the dragon who is behind the push to exterminate humanity."

CHAPTER SEVENTY-SEVEN

"You're lying," Kristen said to Constance. Maybe it wasn't the best tactic when interrogating someone for knowledge, but it was all she could manage and seemed to speak for itself. It was almost insane for her to think that a single dragon could be behind the entire technomage rebellion. She had come to understand that the prisoner was a huge player in all that had happened and even she wasn't fully in control of the technomages, as proved by their continued attacks even now that she was incarcerated.

"It's true," the woman said sagely. "All of this really does point to a single individual and what's more, it's a member of the Dragon Council."

She wanted to deny it. Her instinct pushed to scream in the technomage's face that she would remain locked in there forever with her bullshit. She wanted to walk away and leave and tell her team that this was all one huge waste of time but she couldn't. When she'd been attacked in the cave and her team sent on a false operation in South America, the orders had come from the North American Dragon Council. Larry and Lumos both agreed that all signs pointed to someone on the Council itself or someone powerful enough to influence its members. Now, the mage corroborated that.

"How can you possibly know this?" She tried to phrase it as a demand but her voice was too shaky.

"Remember," Constance told her, "a huge part of my role in the organization was intelligence gathering. We waited for over twenty years for the right moment to strike at dragon society. While we were doing that, we became quite good at gleaning information from patterns."

"You weren't that good," she retorted.

"Please," the prisoner said and raised an eyebrow at her. "We were always a step ahead of you. My teams were able to circumvent security systems in homes and at dragon events. We were able to track the motions of many of the world's most powerful dragons and strike with impunity."

"Until I came along."

Constance nodded. "Why do you think I asked for you?"

Kristen had no reply to that, so she simply said, "Go on," and folded her arms.

"There is a web of connected events out there, all of them pushing the world into a more chaotic state and bringing multiple factions to the brink of war."

"When did all this start?"

"Long ago—in our organization and probably before that—but the first event that directly crossed with your life was Shadowstorm's attempt to destroy Detroit."

"It wasn't a very successful attempt," she said.

"I know—because of you," the woman said. "You stopped it. You were a factor in this that no one expected, least of all him."

"Who? Shadowstorm?"

"No, Shadowstorm was only a pawn—a young dragon hungry for power like so many others. Who do you think told him to try to start a civil war using the gangs of Detroit in the first place?"

"The simplest answer is that he did it for personal gain," she said after a moment. "He wanted to control more land and wealth than he already did. I thought that was one of the reasons you and your terrorists were so opposed to dragons ruling the world."

Constance chuckled darkly. "Shadowstorm was wealthy enough that he could have purchased half of Detroit outright if he so desired. If he had only been more subtle, he could have had the entire city eating out of his hand. And you know—probably better than I—that subtlety was one of his strengths. Plus, dragons have thrived on the work of humans long enough to know that chaos isn't good for business. Why burn a city? No one will be left to cook your meals or clean your messes."

"Maybe he simply did it for the fun of it," Kristen said. "Shadowstorm was an asshole. Sometimes, assholes merely like to watch things burn."

The technomage nodded. "You're right of course. And Shadowstorm acted of his own volition much of the time. But I'm not asking you to trust me based on a single shred of evidence."

"Then what else do you have?" Kristen asked, not sure if she wanted more intel so she could disprove the woman or believe her.

"What about his mother? Who released her from prison early? That is not something that is done often for beings who live as long as the dragons do. A powerful player must have been involved to tip the scales of justice in her favor, especially after that mess with your brother. It was an embarrassment for dragons the world over. Those kinds of perversions are not the kind of thing they simply forget and yet they seemed to when they released her."

"At this point, you've only told me that a mother and son were working together. That hardly sounds like a grand conspiracy."

"What happened in Florence? Do you have all the answers to that?" Constance asked.

"How do you know about what happened in Europe? You were locked up here when all that went down," she replied flatly.

"This prison is powerful but these guards are weak. They're not used to dealing with matters this urgent. From what I can tell, they usually leave a dragon in here for years before they bother to ask them anything. They fear the rest of my organization and have been in here asking questions that are quite easy to glean information from. For example, they asked me how the technomages in Europe knew to blow up a certain sound studio before you even got there. Tell me, do you have an answer to that question?"

Kristen's blood ran cold. Florence had been a hot mess. Every step of the way, it had become more and more apparent that there had been a leak in European SWAT—something finally confirmed when one of the dragons had confessed. They had consistently been outmaneuvered by a small band of mages, and she had never fully known how...not until now when she recalled the fact that the betrayer must have reported to someone higher up the chain.

And there was the series of events that led to her being trapped in a cave, alone and at the mercy of the shadow dragon and his diabolical powers. That was the most compelling evidence of all that a powerful dragon was manipulating events to take her and her team out of the picture. Was it so farfetched to think that this wasn't all about her? That someone attempted to stop her because she was interfering with a larger plan? She didn't want to believe Constance at all. Everything in her wanted to dismiss the woman as a nut and a terrorist—as the murderer and the monster that she was.

But she couldn't.

There was something to what she was saying. Whether it could be proved or not was another thing, but she already knew she couldn't ignore it.

Still, she had to push. "You haven't told me anything but conspiracy theories yet. If you want me to believe you, I need to know the name of the dragon you say is behind all this."

Constance nodded fearfully, then leaned closer to the glass. She gestured for her to do the same.

She did, both curious and almost eager for the prisoner to try something. Her words were troubling but if she attacked, retribution would be automatic. That sounded far simpler than trying to untangle the web of deceit that seemed to stretch all around her.

Once she was sufficiently close to the glass, Constance whispered so quietly she almost had to read her lips to make the words out. "The Masked One."

Kristen wanted to dismiss the title as the stupid fake name it obviously was, but hadn't she heard that name once before? As La Flamme lay dying, he'd said something about a 'masked one,' hadn't he? It didn't make sense at the time and she'd almost forgotten it. Then she thought of her battle against the dragon of shadow deep under the earth. He had threatened to kill her friends and wear their skulls...was he this Masked One? Had she already fought against him and discovered how powerful he could be?

Her innate caution warned her not to reveal all that to Constance. She had more sense than whoever had let the woman learn too many of the details of what happened in Florence.

"That name means nothing to me," she said. That was true, at least. She didn't know why she didn't want to lie, but she didn't unless she had no choice.

"Ask some of your dragon friends about it, especially the older ones. They will have at least heard stories. I promise you that."

"And that's all you have for me? A code name? I can tell you right now that no one on the Dragon Council of North America is named 'the Masked One.' If this is it, I guess I should simply go." She was bluffing, but the technomage didn't seem to notice anything beyond the mention of the name.

"Don't say his name here. For all we know, he could be the one who got you access to me," she protested.

"Don't you think that's a little paranoid?" Kristen glanced over her shoulder and down the long white hallway, feeling paranoid herself.

"I have come to believe there is a player working behind the scenes to engineer much of what's going on," the woman confided. "Someone —a dragon—helped my cell get the initial DNA for our effort."

"That's bullshit," she said. "I met the dragon who provided the DNA. Windfire. He was nice until you shot him in the heart with a bullet made from one of his children—from my sibling. I guess I never got to tell you to go fuck yourself for killing my biological father."

Constance rubbed her face as if she could somehow wipe her past transgressions away. "Killing him was a huge mistake although not my biggest..." She looked at the Steel Dragon when she said that and her eyes were painfully mournful. "I thought—at the time—that him going public with what he knew was a huge threat to our organization. Now, I wish he had."

"Why?" she demanded.

"Because I thought I was a master of my fate but someone has pulled my strings for far longer than I realized. It was a dragon who set up the meeting between Windfire and myself."

"That doesn't mean it was this hidden actor," she said.

"No, not by itself it doesn't, but—"

"But what?" She thought she might as well get all the information she could. There would be time to parse the bullshit later, but she had begun to feel there was less and less of that.

"But when I first met with Windfire, he was extremely hesitant about agreeing to the entire project."

"Then why did he?"

"I never found out but I think he was blackmailed or threatened into the position. When he wanted to go public...well, it wasn't our idea to kill him. It was our dragon contact."

"That doesn't absolve you of his death," Kristen said.

"I know it doesn't," Constance agreed and took a deep breath. "If it did, maybe I wouldn't feel the guilt I do."

She ran a hand through her red hair as she considered this information. "But why not use his own DNA? Especially if he has these shadow powers?"

"I've thought about that as well and I have two theories. One, shadow powers aren't exactly conducive for bullet-making. Two, if he used his DNA to seed our project, genetic testing might have linked the dragons to him instead of you and Windfire. This way, he's still merely a rumor."

"But why?" she asked. "Why go to all that trouble? What could a dragon possibly gain from all that effort?"

The technomage clicked her tongue like a disapproving teacher. "Please, try not to be as dense as your steel skin. Human rights have improved steadily for over a hundred years. A good deal of that is based on the sheer number of humans, but the technology people have created is part of it too. Surely you can imagine the threat fighter jets with missiles represent for dragons?"

"Of course I can imagine weapons like that," Kristen said through clenched teeth. "I've worked to try to stop you and your mages from building weapons exactly like that. We've already seen machine guns and bombs made with dragon parts. The next step would be to try to get the military to take over the production and implementation of these weapons. If you recall, we stopped you from doing that too."

"I know. And thank God you did," Constance said quietly.

"Wait, what?" She was shocked. Had the woman admitted she was glad she had stopped her?

"A military—especially the United States military—gaining the production capabilities for those weapons would have been a disaster," the mage admitted. "I...I've had time to think in here, just sitting in this cell, and I've come to believe that much of what we were doing for our cause was wrong."

"No fucking shit."

The prisoner chuckled at her vulgarity. "When I think of all the times you told me to stop, I have to wish I had listened."

"Why didn't you?"

"Because I would talk to the leaders of other cells and we all spoke of how committed we were to the cause. But I see now there were patterns in the excuses my former allies gave. I now believe that me and my allies were manipulated and that the entire mage rebellion was engineered by a dragon who also wants this war and wants to win it before humans get so advanced that they cannot be beaten. He wants it to destroy any dragons or mages who could stand against him so he can rule what is rebuilt from the ashes."

"And you think this hidden foe—this Masked One— put all this into action?" Kristen asked.

Constance nodded and mouthed the word yes. "I only wish I had worked this all out sooner. So many lives were lost...or worse. I thought we were fighting for equality and justice. For goals as lofty as those, I was willing to let lives be lost, but to think that all that we did

—every bullet we built and every dragon we tortured—was all because a dragon wanted to burn it all down…"

The thought overwhelmed her and she began to cry. Big, heavy tears ran down her cheeks until they plopped onto the glass wall that separated the two women, where they trickled like streaks of rain.

Kristen sighed and tried to think about what her mom would do in this situation. "It's all right," she said. "We all make mistakes. I'm sorry for what happened to you. I'm sure you being duped makes it feel even harder to wash the blood from your hands."

"Yes!" The woman collapsed, weeping heavily with heaving sobs that she tried to hide behind her hands. The fluorescent lights of the hallway were merciless, however, and laid her pain bare.

"I only wish I would have stopped you sooner," she said.

"Me too…" Constance said between the tears. "Me too."

The mage clearly had nothing left to say, so she left her like that and told herself that the woman deserved to suffer for the atrocities committed against others. When she reached the end of the hallway, though, she couldn't help but look at the wreck of a human in the glass cell.

She found it wasn't fury that came into her heart but pity for a broken woman.

CHAPTER SEVENTY-EIGHT

Kristen opened the door from the bright, white hallway and entered the gloomy, twisting dungeon passage. She wasn't surprised to see a dragon in human form there—she knew she'd need an escort to leave the facility—but she was surprised to see that it was Shimmerclaw and not the two guards who had shown her inside.

It wasn't every day that one found a platinum dragon and head of the Dragon Council waiting for them outside a prison cell, although she supposed it made sense. The reason she was there was because Constance had said she had intelligence that she would only give to her. Of course, the Council leader wanted that intelligence. Hell, she probably already had it.

"Lady Steel, how are you?" Shimmerclaw asked and favored her with a slight nod of her head.

"We can skip the formalities since we're deep inside a torture maze and move directly to what you really want." She didn't mean to be rude to the most powerful dragon on the continent but damn, she had not expected to see her so soon after everything she'd heard from the prisoner. The fact was that she needed a minute or two to process it all and parse the truth from mistruth, but she wouldn't get it, unfortunately.

"Of course." The dragon nodded as if she had spoken with the utmost politeness. "So, what did the mage say?"

"Ma'am—or Your Ladyship, or whatever you wish to be called—"

"Shimmerclaw is my name."

"Fine, right. Of course, Shimmerclaw. We both know damn well that everything that was said in there was recorded, so you already know all the details of our conversation." She didn't want to be in the dungeon any longer and decided it was better to cut the crap and get to it. That's what she had done since becoming a dragon, and she saw no reason to stop now.

"You are right, of course. Everything was recorded. Humans are infinitely useful. The things they can do with electricity never cease to amaze me. I suppose what I really want is your take on everything the mage said."

That was something else she hadn't expected. "My take? Why on earth do you want to know what I think about it? You've been alive for longer than me. You're the leader of the Council."

"Yes, and you can rest assured that I won't ask you for any policy decisions any time soon." Shimmerclaw chuckled. It seemed like the platinum dragon's metaphorical feathers were impossible to ruffle. "But I am quite curious if anything Constance said was interesting to you. Or, perhaps more bluntly, does any of it ring true? Or is it a web of lies? I ask you because you know her better than any other dragon. You have fought against her multiple times, and she has tried to sway you to her cause. If anyone can provide insight into her mind, I would hope it would be you. So, what did you think—or do I have to threaten?" She smiled so sweetly that Kristen almost wanted to know what the threat was. Almost.

"Honestly?" she asked, perhaps a bit rhetorically.

"Lady Steel, there is no reason I would want lies," the Council leader said patiently.

"Well, if I'm honest, the whole thing sounds like a tinfoil hat conspiracy theory. If I were in her position, I would be desperate to lay the blame anywhere but on herself. She painted a picture using facts that fit it and only included examples that might bolster her case.

Plus, she has the whole 'master of deception' argument that can be used for everything from aliens to sasquatch. I don't think it holds much water…but…never mind."

"But what?" Shimmerclaw pressed.

She sighed, unable to dismiss the whole scenario as the fabrication she wanted to call it. For it to all be a lie, everything about Constance's actions had been a performance and she simply didn't think that was the case. The woman was too hurt and too regretful. It could be a lie, but her instincts said otherwise.

"Too many of the details match up," Kristen stated. "There have been too many weird little incidents that this explains far too well. If there is a big bad dragon out there making all this happen from behind the scenes, it's like the missing piece from a puzzle, at least to my mind."

"Do you have examples?"

She nodded. "We now know for certain there was a mole in Florence feeding the technomage cell information. We decided to follow a lead one morning, and they were able to plant a bomb before we even got there. I had assumed it was a low-level dragon, or maybe a disgruntled mage, and a member of European Dragon SWAT confessed. But someone at the top to whom he reported makes sense, especially when it comes to explaining how Shadowstorm's mother Obscura got out of prison."

"Yes, the paperwork on that case is…perplexing," Shimmerclaw admitted.

"Plus," she continued. "Constance is a bitch but she's never been a liar or crazy. In fact, that was one of the worst things about fighting her. She relied on facts so much that it was hard to argue with her."

The Council leader nodded and nothing about her aura changed. She still radiated placid, bemused calm, but there was the smallest twitch of concern across her eyebrows. Kristen had a feeling that the movement was so slight that a dragon raised by dragons wouldn't have even noticed. She, however, grew up in a human family, so she saw the twitch.

"So you believe there is something to her theory that a member of the Dragon Council is working hard against the rest of us?" Shimmer-claw asked.

God, it was awkward to answer a question about a corrupt official when the person asking was from the very group in question.

Kristen did her best. "I don't know about that. I've met the Council and it's not like I could tell you who is the bad apple."

The dragon raised an eyebrow at her unspoken "but."

"But there was the attack in the Mammoth Caves," she explained after a moment of silence. "I was tricked into thinking the Dragon Council had sent me there."

"Yes, I apologize for that. We've made our communications more secure since then," Shimmerclaw said.

"Thank you, I appreciate that, but there's more to it than only the message. The dragon I fought… I've never seen powers honed to that level of precision. When I fought Shadowstorm and Obscura, they could use their ability to transform from a human to dragon form to move without being able to be touched, but only to a certain degree. This was like that times a million. He could hide in any pool of shadow, no matter how small, for as long as he wanted. In fact, I think he could move through cracks so small that even a human couldn't fit through. And when my friends came and we fought him…" She shuddered. "It was a close call."

"And you believe this dragon is on the Dragon Council?" Shimmerclaw asked the question casually enough and her aura betrayed no indication that anything was out of the ordinary but again, a flicker of emotion crossed her face. This time, she thought it was recognition.

Had the platinum dragon recognized the power as belonging to someone who sat on the Council itself, or did she simply know a dragon with such abilities?

"Does that…mean anything to you?" Kristen asked. It was obvious that Shimmerclaw didn't want to say anything outright because her aura hadn't changed. She could understand. When conducting investigations, she often let her people take charge and not give them clues as a way to verify her assumptions. Maybe the Council leader was doing something similar. She only hoped that the platinum dragon keeping her cards close to her chest didn't cost Kristen her life.

Shimmerclaw shook her head sadly. "Not in particular." If it was a lie, it was a well-masked one. "It is clear, though, that an enormously powerful dragon is out there looking to do you harm." She sighed. "It's a pity…Lumos used to be one of the best fighters I knew. There was a time I would have entrusted such a foe to him, but he isn't the warrior he was in his youth."

"He has offered to train me," she admitted. "And he's able to hold his own fairly well."

The dragon brightened at that. "Lumos is an outstanding fighter and an excellent teacher. Many of our finest warriors were trained by the old Bright Knight. Him training you is an excellent idea that—hopefully—will give you a real edge."

Kristen nodded but still wondered what this dragon knew. She was experienced enough to know she couldn't simply demand that Shimmerclaw divulge all her secrets and theories, but she couldn't help wondering if the knowledge the dragon possessed would be what would truly give her the edge she needed so badly.

Before she could think of a polite way to press the dragon, Shimmerclaw nodded and said. "Thank you for coming all this way. I think it was worth getting the mage to speak and share her secrets but of course, it was no inconvenience for me like it was for you, so again, thank you. I hope you found it helpful in your hunt."

"Yes, ma'am, I did," she said and realized that the statement was true as she fell into step behind Shimmerclaw. The platinum dragon led her down one of the cut stone passageways, reached a wall, and muttered a spell that made the stone melt away like it was made of pudding.

"Through here, please, and step quickly. We wouldn't want you to be trapped in the rock. You'd think it would kill you quickly, but the dragons who have managed to make it this far always languish for a few days before they finally succumb."

A platform of stone waited inside the alcove. The two stepped onto it, and it lifted them with all the pomp and circumstance of a regular old elevator. Well, a regular old elevator that made the ceiling melt and reform into solid rock beneath them.

The ride stopped and they entered the blindingly white room that served as the entrance to the labyrinthine prison.

"Once more, I'd like to thank you for your time, Lady Steel," Shimmerclaw said with polished formality.

"Of course, Lady Shimmerclaw. I'm at the Council's disposal, as always. If you need anything, send it over an extremely well-secured channel."

If the dragon understood that she was joking, she gave no indication of it. Instead, she waved her hand at the words as if she could dismiss the sentiment. "You are already doing extremely important business for the Council. Please get back to it and forgive this interruption."

She nodded once more and chose not to take the last word from the Council member. Shimmerclaw transformed into her platinum dragon form, leapt skyward, and soared into the distance.

Kristen walked to her crew, who had not fraternized with the prison staff at all. The guardian dragons stood at attention as if her people might attack them at any moment. Hernandez made faces at them, but it didn't seem to have any effect on the stone-faced guards.

"What's going on?" Heartsbane asked.

"Did Constance have anything important to say?" Emerald demanded.

She looked around and wondered if ears were listening even now. Surely the guards could be trusted, right? But she decided the answer to that question was no. If she couldn't trust Council members, she certainly couldn't trust guards.

"I'll tell you on the wing," she said, paranoid that someone was listening. They took to the sky in silence, the mood heavy and the air pregnant with secrets.

CHAPTER SEVENTY-NINE

Kristen wanted to enjoy the flight down the mountainside and parts of it were pleasant. The air warmed from frigid cold to cool to pleasant and the smells changed from the painful cold of ice and snow to the aromas of pine and meadows blooming with wildflowers. All were appealing compared to the flight up.

The conversation was unfortunately much worse. She filled her team in on what had happened. Although she had briefly considered not telling them, she decided that if any of these people or dragons were against her, she was well and truly screwed. She told them what Constance had said about the mysterious dragon known as the Masked One, about how the technomage believed she'd been manipulated, and about how Katrina and Kristen truly were genetically sisters.

Her team took it all in stride. Yes, they grew glummer at the thought of facing an unknown and powerful foe, but Emerald was quick to point out that they'd already faced the asshole once and beaten him, so what was there to worry about?

She would have liked to enjoy his optimism but her phone rang.

"Telephone call," Larry said from her back. "It's your brother. Oh, wait. I should say it's our master of whispers, Zed."

"Answer it," she told him. "And tell him that if it's about pizza, I'll murder him."

The mage answered. "Uh-huh, uh-huh. Shit. You don't say? Holy hell, already? Okay. Yeah, I'll tell her." As he spoke, his tone grew darker and darker.

"What the hell is going on?" Heartsbane demanded and flew closer to Kristen and Larry.

He took a deep breath. "Detroit is under attack."

Everyone responded at once.

"What the fuck did you say?"

"We have to get back there."

"I knew we shouldn't have come and talked to that damn human."

"I need details," Kristen said and silenced her crew.

"Right," Larry replied. "Multiple mages are in different parts of the city, and all of them are using magic to toast things. Stonequest led a force to stop them but it didn't go so well. They've already killed one dragon who tried to intervene."

"Not Stone," Emerald said and terror crept into his voice.

"If it was, Zed didn't say so. He said they're doing their best to stop the mages, but if you could get back there at the soonest convenient time, that would be great."

"Now's not the time to try to lighten the mood with humor," Heartsbane growled.

"I'm only quoting what Zed said. He always talks bullshit like that," the mage protested.

"Shit," Kristen said.

Jim repeated the sentiment. "Shit, this is bad. We're not even near the airport yet. We won't be able to get there for hours. By that time…"

He didn't need to finish the statement for them all to know it was bad. Detroit had almost been lost to the chaos generated by a gang armed with regular guns and grenades when Kristen had first joined Detroit SWAT. She didn't want to think what a horde of zealous mages could do to the Motor City.

"Larry, talk to me about the portal spell. Can you do that to get us home?" she asked.

"Uh, well…hmm," he stammered. She had obviously caught him off guard.

"Damn it, Larry, I need a yes or a no. Lives are on the line."

"Right. Well, yes. I think I can. It would have to be much bigger to fit us all through and way farther."

"We could fly through it in single file," Heartsbane said.

"Sure, okay, that might help," the mage conceded. "But the distance will be the tough part. Last time, I merely focused on throwing the bomb straight up as high as I could. This time, I need to target a specific destination."

"I understand that we need to get there but Larry, you got that bomb what—a mile up in the sky last time? Maybe two or three? This is hundreds of times that," Jim said. "Can it be done?"

"I…I think so." They could tell from his voice that he had already closed his eyes and extended his magic to create a portal. "No. No, I can't. Not for all of us. I think I might be able to get me and Kristen there, but I can't keep something like this open for that long."

"That's fine," she said quickly.

"It is not!" Hernandez protested from Heartsbane's back. "What if some asshole needs to be blown the fuck to pieces? Who will do that for you if I'm stuck on the private jet?"

"We'll make do," she said. "But without Larry, Amy is the only mage."

"Plus, they'll need the Steel Dragon," Emerald added.

"There's still a chance I might open the other end of this under-ground or in a building or something and scramble our guts," Larry said.

"That's a risk we'll have to take," she responded briskly. "Plus, Shimmerclaw told me dragons can last a few days when that happens, so don't worry about me."

"Gee, thanks."

"I don't like this," Heartsbane said. "I don't like this at all."

"Is it your job to like orders or follow them?" she demanded.

"Right." Heartsbane ceased her protest. "Emerald, follow me! Hernandez, call the pilot and tell him to get airborne. We'll board on the wing. That'll save us a half an hour. Lady Steel, we'll see you in Detroit." She pumped her wings and put her body into the rigid position Lumos had shown Kristen. Emerald did the same, and the two raced down the mountainside.

"All right, Larry. It's you and me. Tell me what I can do to help," she said.

"Slow down and try to fly level," he responded, his voice already tight with exertion. "Do you see that big old pine tree over there? It's about a mile off."

"The one that looks like it was struck by lightning?"

"That's not what I had in mind but sure. Fly toward it and try to keep as even a pace as you can—and for the love of all that is holy, fly level. I have no idea what'll happen if your wings clip the edges of the portal. I don't think it would be good."

Kristen obeyed. "Anything else?"

"Yeah. Pray?"

She didn't respond but mumbled something to whatever power was out there that was greater than her, locked her wings into place, and focused on flying straight ahead towards their rendezvous with a pine tree.

Lightning cracked above it and struck the branches repeatedly, although she knew the effect was magical because no sound accompanied the flashes of energy, and there were no clouds in the sky.

As she approached—desperate to pump her wings and get there faster but terrified to do anything that might interfere with Larry's concentration—the sky above the tree began to fade from the crystalline blue of the Colorado mountains on a clear day to something drearier.

The mage uttered a grunt of frustration and suddenly, a disc of light appeared to perfectly frame the patch of gray clouds. Lightning cracked from the tree to the disc of energy but something was wrong. She couldn't see through the portal. It was like a veil hung in front of it or someone had put a filter in their path.

"Larry…"

"I know."

"Larry!"

"I know!" the mage shouted and a great blast of energy streaked from him on her back to the portal ahead. If he had been a second later she didn't want to even consider what would have happened, but he had done it. The portal solidified to create a window through time and space that she rocketed through as it began to close.

Kristen went from flying through the clear, thin air of the Rocky mountains to the slightly polluted, drizzling sky of Detroit in the blink of an eye.

The mage didn't make the transition with the same grace as the dragon he rode upon.

With a mumbled, "I did it," he fell unconscious and slipped from her back.

She immediately tucked her wings and dove after him. At least she had a little distance to travel. They were well above the Detroit skyline and directly over the old Dragon SWAT headquarters building in the middle of downtown. She pumped her wings, tucked her arms and legs in, and straightened her tail.

Although she had more than a few seconds to catch him, it only meant that if she failed, there was no way that he would survive.

As she raced towards the falling, unconscious mage, she saw that her city was burning.

Great plumes of smoke rose from Tiger Stadium. Fires burned on the roof of the opera house despite the steady drizzle. One of the stops for the people mover—the elevated train car that ran in a loop over downtown Detroit—had been completely obliterated, and the train had plummeted earthward.

Kristen was immediately filled with white-hot fury. She had to help her city and save the people who were no doubt already dying. Somehow, she had to stop the chaos these damn technomages were so determined to unleash.

But first, she had to save the man who had made all that possible. If not for Larry Brockton, she would be on her jet right now, tapping her toes with anxiety and waiting to be able to help. She couldn't let him suffer the same fate as the raindrops falling all around him.

She flew faster than gravity pulled her, so fast that the raindrops splashed against her face. A trail of dry air slipstreamed behind her as the raindrops that touched her dragon scales evaporated from the heat. Resolute, she increased her speed until the mage was directly in front of her, tumbling end over end in an undignified freefall that was defined by nothing more than the wind ripping at his robes.

As soon as she was within range, she extended a claw and caught him. He was unconscious so didn't say anything, but she thought she saw a smile creep across his face. Awake or not, the human body didn't want to die.

Kristen spread her wings to slow her descent and aimed for the roof of the Dragon SWAT headquarters building. It had been months since she'd worked there but the dragons and mages inside would still help Larry get back to good health and—hopefully—join this fight.

But it wasn't the mage she needed to worry about.

She spread her wings and caught the air to slow herself barely seconds before the Iron Dragon struck.

Pain lanced through her wing as her assailant's claw tried to rip it from her body.

Her reaction was instinctive. She lashed out with the ax-blade on the tip of her tail and forced her adversary to back away.

The motion almost knocked Larry from her claw.

Somehow, her flinch didn't dislodge him and she managed to curl her claw protectively around him. She went into a barrel roll as the Iron Dragon attempted another attack. Kristen parried this one with her one free front claw and her two back legs.

Her opponent laughed as if this were nothing but a sick, perverted game and pulled up as she placed Larry on the roof of the Dragon SWAT building.

She hadn't seen them from the air but now realized that mages stood on the roof, all of them with spells loaded into their fingertips and pointed at the sky. They worked together to keep the enemy dragon at bay, whose withdrawal had nothing to do with any sense of chivalry for the wounded and unconscious mage in Kristen's claw.

"Make her pay, Lady Steel," one the mages said. She nodded at Atramento, the head mage of the Paper Dungeon, whose swirling tattoos augmented his powers. Clouds of swirling ink floated in the air around him. Here and there, parts of the cloud focused into points finer than the tip of any pen. "And if she doesn't listen, tell her I'll be happy to write her a check."

"Jesus…even in the face of death…you're a true bureaucrat." Larry wheezed, apparently having regained consciousness to insult the other mage.

"I'll tell her that her credit line has been declined," she said to Atramento, who nodded, while Larry groaned either in pain or in response to the horrible pun.

Then Kristen launched herself into the air.

The Iron Dragon flew above the city and breathed fire indiscriminately at historical buildings and modern skyscrapers alike. When she saw that Kristen moved closer to fight, she turned to face her and pumped her wings so she hovered in place. Behind her, the storm grew in intensity. Lightning cracked and the wind began to truly rage, but it was the Iron Dragon's laugh—deeper and more ominous than any thunder—that sent a chill down her spine.

How did she know to attack my city when I wasn't here? she wondered as she gained speed and raced into battle. It was a question that—like so many others—would have to wait to be answered if she was still alive at the end of this fight.

CHAPTER EIGHTY

The battle was worse than any nightmare or dark fantasy that kept her from falling asleep in her bed.

From the very beginning, Kristen knew she was outmatched. Katrina—beneath all those scales and behind those claws and teeth and flaming breath, she was merely a girl like her—held the high ground in the sky. She let the Steel Dragon come to her and forced her to use the wing she hadn't thought had been injured but in reality, was quite damaged.

Before she could use her momentum to collide with her, the Iron Dragon tucked her wings and dropped on her like the massive weight of iron she was.

She tried to dodge but her wing prevented her from moving as quickly as she needed to. The impact didn't catch her head-on, but it did strike her hard enough to thrust her into a spin before she could get the wind beneath her wings again.

But catch it she did and she continued into a low swoop that took her between some of Detroit's taller buildings. As she traversed the space, she saw that she wasn't the only one engaged in combat.

A battle raged below. Stonequest, in dragon form and blessedly still alive, led a group of dragons to attack a formation of mages who hurled balls of ice at them. As soon as the airborne attackers came close enough to use their fire breath, the mages scattered into nearby buildings and left swaths of destruction in their wake.

As she crossed an intersection, she noticed Drew, who led a team of humans from the back of an armored vehicle. Mages harried them with both blasts of magic and dragon bullets. A man she didn't know who stood next to the human leader took a bullet in the shoulder and tumbled from the back of the vehicle. Drew shot the mage who killed his ally but the scene didn't fill her heart with anything but dread.

The battlefield was a mess. Buildings were being destroyed and both sides suffered brutal casualties, but that said nothing of the civilians who were no doubt hiding in the midst of all this violence and death.

She adjusted her course to rake the mages who'd shot at Drew with fire, but the Iron Dragon found her again.

"Does the steel bitch think she can hide from me?" her pursuer bellowed.

Kristen dodged and Katrina flew past her and careened into the street to create a massive crater, a pothole that even Detroiters would be forced to swerve to avoid. She didn't seem even slightly wounded from the massive collision and vaulted into the air to resume her pursuit.

The Steel Dragon tried to outfly her and gain altitude so their battle wouldn't take place within the actual city, but her wing was still injured. Her assailant caught up to her with little effort. She spun in midair and slashed at the dragon with her claws, hoping to injure her wing as Lumos had shown her.

Katrina parried her claws with her iron forearms and merely laughed. "Oh? So you won't try to go for my throat or heart with every damn strike? Someone's been taking lessons." She whipped at her with her tail. Kristen defended her neck, only to have the spiked ball at the end of the tail drive into her hip joint.

The pain was excruciating, and she instantly understood what Lumos had been talking about. Her entire body was steel but at that joint, her scales simply weren't as thick and her foe had capitalized on this. It was terrifying to think that this dragon—raised by mages to be a killer of her own kind—understood this better than she did.

But the wound wasn't lethal and her tail had an ax at its tip. She swung it at the Iron Dragon and forced her to retreat, if only momentarily.

"I spoke to our mother," she shouted into the storm.

"She was weak and a fool to be captured like she was," Katrina responded.

"She misses you," she said as she led the dragon through the streets. "She wishes she could have given me what she gave you so that we could be sisters instead of enemies."

"Then she's softer than I realized," the Iron Dragon said once she was close enough to bulldoze into her.

Kristen was so caught up in trying to protect her vulnerable areas —her joints, her wings, and her neck—that she let Katrina hit her directly in the chest.

The force was enough to catapult her away and through the glass wall of an office building. Her momentum drove her through cubicle after cubicle to destroy computers, copy machines, and coffee makers before she could even register what they were.

She managed to right herself before she plunged out the far side of the building. The Iron Dragon was already poised and ready to lunge at her through the mess of what had once been office space. She launched a blast of white-hot fire at her opponent, not because she thought it could hurt her scales but because she hoped to temporarily blind her like Lumos had taught her.

Katrina blocked this attack as she had all her other attempts. This time, she raised her wings to effortlessly bat away the ball of white flame. Her smirk seemed to say she was nothing but a child, a cub playing with an older sibling.

"We want the same thing!" Kristen shouted as her enemy continued to approach.

"Funny, I didn't know you wanted to die." The dragon sneered.

She cursed and jumped out of the building and into the rain.

Katrina followed her but had expected her to go down instead of up, so she was able to watch as the Iron Dragon cruised the streets below in search of her while she sprayed fire on the battle that continued to rage.

Kristen knew she couldn't defeat the Iron Dragon in a straight fight. She had to find an advantage and take it. Her gaze settled on the top of the building she'd jumped out of. Would the Iron Dragon think of using her environment? She only knew that her police training demanded it, so rather than flying after the dragon who now attempted to kill her friends, she clawed up the side of the building until she reached the roof.

"Katrina! Enough!" she shouted once she was at its pinnacle.

"There you are." Her enemy turned away from the humans she'd been about to incinerate and began to pump her wings to get up to her level.

"Work with me," she shouted from the spire she'd climbed. "Together, we can make the Dragon Council see there can be peace between us."

"Peace?" the dragon roared incredulously. "You want peace after what you've done to the mages who fight for freedom and equality? You want peace after I've seen you kill my friends and my family?"

"We're family," she shouted in response. "You, me, and the dragons those mages imprisoned are kin. Work with me to free them."

"They are nothing but failures doing their best to help a noble cause," Katrina said, surpassed Kristen's height, and circled her as the rain bucketed and lightning cracked. She dove at her and she readied her claws to parry but realized she might not need to when lightning struck the Iron Dragon.

Kristen smiled as electricity coursed through her attacker's scales. She had felt her form be electrocuted before. It was horribly painful and that had been from a source far less potent than a crack of lightning. There was no way—

The Iron Dragon barreled into her and transferred the power of the bolt of lightning through her claws and into her body.

She had no idea how Katrina had learned to do such a thing. Her body was overwhelmed with the energy and she was blown from the spire—a lightning rod, she now realized—and plunged earthward as her muscles twitched uncontrollably.

The other dragon joined her in her descent and fell at the same speed but a little above her. Her claws were outstretched and ready to strike while Kristen did nothing but twitch as she fell in the rain.

"You offer an alliance but have nothing to offer," Katrina goaded. "You are weak, a poor excuse for a dragon, and are driven by nonsense." She stopped speaking to bite savagely at the wing she'd already wounded.

Kristen writhed in pain as she fell. Her body still didn't respond to her commands but it was more than willing to show her opponent how much she suffered.

The Iron Dragon ceased her attack on her wing joint and instead, began to claw at her armpit while she struck her in the opposite back leg with the spiked ball at the end of her iron tail.

The pain was so extreme that she hardly noticed when she finally made impact with the road.

She blacked out for a second and woke with the Iron Dragon standing above the crater she had made with her dragon body. The storm raged behind her and lightning cracked at the tops of the skyscrapers and illuminated the teeth of the Iron Dragon that twisted in a cruel rictus.

"Please." Kristen gasped. She could hardly breathe and it felt like one of her lungs had collapsed. "You don't have to do this."

"Oh, but I do." Katrina all but purred and slunk into the crater like a stoat after a wounded mouse. "You see, although you are not a threat to me physically, you are something even worse."

"I'm not a threat because I want to work with you."

Her enemy ignored her as she continued to slide closer. She reached her tail and stepped on it to gore it savagely with her iron claws. "You have become a symbol and that is quite dangerous. Already, you have united a force of humans and mages in your directionless cause. The humans love you. The dragons respect you. Your dopey optimism must be removed from the equation."

"Please," she begged. "I only want a world where no one has to live in fear."

"I already live in that world," Katrina boasted. "The trick is to not be afraid to kill whoever stands in your—"

Something plinked off Katrina's back and the dragon straightened. She poked her head out of the crater and ducked inside quickly at a volley of gunfire. "Well, speak of the devil."

"Leave them alone," Kristen pleaded. Her body was too broken to move. She tried to push herself up so she could fight but her arm, leg, and wing had all been shattered by the relentless attacks. She was so wounded that she could hardly raise her head from the muddy water that pooled in the bottom of the crater.

"I don't think I will," her adversary said. "I think I'll see what happens to the Steel Dragon when she sees her little warriors slaughtered before her eyes."

"Don't do this!"

"Would you prefer I kill them where you can't see?" she asked. "Would you like to hear their screams and guess who they belong to? I suppose I can grant such a request." Katrina cackled in glee and leapt out of the hole.

Gunfire answered her attack and in the next moment—to Kristen's shock—the Iron Dragon slid into the crater with her and cowered beneath its lip.

"You crazy bitch!" Katrina spat and looked at a gunshot wound in her forearm. A bullet had punched straight through her iron scales. "You armed your team with our dragon bullets?"

Before she could answer, more gunshots rang out. The dragon flinched at the sound now that she knew the bullets could wound her.

"I can make them stop," Kristen said.

"Fuck you, you fucking hypocrite." Her adversary vaulted out of the hole to attack Kristen's friends, but she didn't have the chance.

As soon as the Iron Dragon emerged, a telephone pole swung and caught her in the chest to fling her aside, although the wooden pole cracked in half.

Kristen struggled to push out of the muddy water. She managed to twist her body around as Amy reached the edge of the crater.

"I found her!" the girl shouted as two dragons swooped overhead and human soldiers ran past on either side of the crater, their guns raised to release a sustained barrage at Katrina.

Amy enveloped her in a shield of protective blue energy and lifted her up and out of the hole. She placed her behind her allies, who continued to fire at the other dragon and her mages at the end of the street.

The enemy mages weren't throwing bolts of energy, though. Instead, they all concentrated with their arms raised and eyes closed until a portal opened. As the defending forces maintained their fire, the mages retreated into it.

Katrina, still unafraid of Kristen's forces, took to the air. She flew over their heads and unleashed fire on them that was so hot, it made all the rain washing over the street evaporate.

"No!" the Steel Dragon shouted through the steam but her people were still alive. Amy had diverted the flames away from the humans, so each of them now stood in a puddle although the rest of the street was dry.

"We can do this again any time you wish." Katrina sneered before she flew through the portal the mages had opened and vanished. The gateway closed and Kristen was alone with her people in the battle-ravaged streets of Detroit.

CHAPTER EIGHTY-ONE

Sometimes, it seemed like the world made the weather match events—like when it rained at funerals or the sun shined at a wedding. The thunderstorm during the battle had felt almost cosmic to Kristen, and when the fighting had ended, she had expected the sun to come out and perhaps grace her and the survivors of the bloody battle with a rainbow.

The weather did not oblige her, unfortunately.

It continued to rain in thick, gray, merciless sheets that hammered the roof of the warehouse and streamed off and down the windows so it seemed like the building itself mourned the losses they'd suffered in the battle.

They'd put out cots and makeshift beds all around the wide floor of the warehouse for the people who'd been injured in the fight. It was a bleak place with so many new faces suffering.

But it wasn't only new faces who had been injured. Butters had been shot in the leg—squarely in the thigh, in fact—so he couldn't walk. Keith was wounded as well. He'd insulted a mage and the woman had taken it personally and used some kind of spell to sever the trigger finger on his right hand.

Still, he was in high spirits. "It's a good thing I'm a decent shot with my left," he boasted.

"You are not, Rookie," Butters groused. He was coping far worse with his injury despite the fact that Amy thought she could heal it once she had some rest. She made no such promises about Keith's finger. "You're such a shitty shot with your right that your left seems decent by comparison."

"Whatever." His teammate was nonchalant about it. "Do you want to race to the shooting range?"

The sniper snorted in contempt but the comment also managed to draw a smile onto his broad cheeks. Kristen left the two of them with Beanpole fixing coffee and Hernandez fetching beers.

She wanted to stay at their side as well, but she knew they had no time. They couldn't afford to comfort the wounded, let alone mourn, not after a strike as aggressive as the one they'd barely survived. Regretfully, she left them and called a council of her team on the top floor of their base.

All her key leadership and most of her oldest friends were already there when she entered the boardroom. She stood at the head of the table and checked to make sure everyone she'd spoken to had come.

Both mages were there and looked equally exhausted, Larry from opening the portal that brought her to the battle, and Amy from her final efforts that saved her life.

Drew was there, as were Jim and Brian. She would have liked more regular humans to be present, but her other oldest friends were below. It wasn't a terrible situation, though, because she knew that of everyone on her force, she could trust them to follow orders the most.

Of the dragons, Stonequest was present—of course—as were Lumos and Heartsbane. Emerald and Timeflash were working security and fortunately, Amythist was at her estate with the rescued dragons. It had blessedly not been attacked during the strike on Detroit. She had expected some kind of feint given how quickly Katrina and her mages had retreated, but it seemed the technomages had no intention of recapturing the dragons who had been their sources of ammunition for so long.

As much as she wanted to sink into the chair at the head of the table, Kristen remained standing. Her arm and leg both ached but her dragon powers were working on the wounds. She was far luckier than the humans who'd have to suffer through the pain or endure the numbing fog of painkillers until Amy could heal them. If she could heal them. It seemed to be complex magic and despite her power, she couldn't perform too much of it. Larry didn't seem to be able to do it at all.

So—thinking of the people below as well as the civilians of Detroit who'd perished or lost a loved one in the attack—she stood as straight as she could and addressed her team. "We have to stop our enemy before they inflict any more damage."

Wide stares and dull nods answered her. Everyone had been as overwhelmed by the surprise attack as she felt.

"If we continue to fight defensively," she continued, "we can't win. I thought we could take the time to unravel their organization one cell at a time, but I don't think that's aggressive enough anymore. There's no reason to think the mages won't continue to strike and escape before help can arrive. They demonstrated that they can do it even in a city where help is right there. What would they be able to do in an area without any immediate backup available?"

"So you think this attack was simply a display of power?" Stonequest asked.

"I hope that's all it was," she said. "But the speed and efficiency with which they evacuated as soon as the battle turned against them make me think they'd already accomplished everything they wanted to. Maybe their goal was to damage the city, which they succeeded at. I think a big part of this attack was a demonstration against us, though."

"But why attack humans?" Drew asked. "They've always targeted dragons before. And not to be morose, but they could have gone to Amythist's and executed her and probably either killed or taken some of the dragons we rescued long before we got there."

"I'm not sure if this was an attack on people," Lumos interjected ponderously.

"People died," Jim said. "Some of ours, plus some civilians who weren't able to get out before we arrived. That makes it an attack on people."

"Yes, of course," the old dragon conceded. "They have proven time and time again that they see lives as little more than collateral damage. Even so, almost all the buildings that were damaged were real estate that is owned by dragons. The fighting caused some damage to human-owned businesses as well, but I don't think that was their original intention."

"Wait, are you saying dragons own a good chunk of Detroit?" Drew sounded surprised. "I didn't know they bought anything besides mansions in the countryside."

"Oh yes. Dragons collectively own a sizeable part of Detroit and most of the major cities in America. You should see New York and Chicago. All the rent checks flow to dragons there."

"But human-owned buildings were harmed," Brian said from behind his laptop. Kristen had no doubt that he'd run an analysis on what had been damaged and who it all belonged to. She was still surprised that all his time behind the computer continued to be so useful.

"Of course, once the fight started, some human-owned buildings were harmed," Lumos agreed. "And unfortunately, a few humans were killed when the dragon-owned buildings burned. But less than ten by my count. I know that even ten is too many, but I think it's worth pointing out that the mages kept human casualties to a minimum. They could have done far more to our community than they did."

"Did we kill any mages?" Kristen asked. "When I got here, I thought I saw some fall."

Heartsbane shook her head. "If any of them were killed, they took their dead with them. When it was all over, I checked for survivors so we could...interrogate them." She growled the last two words.

"We got in a couple of lucky shots that caused some injuries but nothing serious," Stonequest said. "They were in and out too quickly and fled as soon as opposition arrived. That portal of theirs makes it impossible to harry their exit."

"What about us?" Kristen asked.

"We lost a man," Drew said through teeth clenched. She had seen him die and he'd been right next to Drew. "But only one. We had a good handful of injuries but nothing too serious. I don't want to lose men in any confrontation, but with all the chaos of that fight, I think we can count this as a victory."

She knew the words pained him even as he said them because he was a cop, not a soldier. He wasn't trained to deal with casualties or collateral damage or whatever euphemism the dead were given in the bloody aftermath of battlefields.

"It sounds like we did well, given that we were completely blind-sided," she said. "But we all know it's not good enough."

Sullen nods around the room proved that she wasn't the only one to feel this way.

"The problem continues to be that they're a few steps ahead of us. We're playing defense and worse, catch-up defense. We barely held on in our hometown. If this attack had been even a hundred miles away, I don't want to think about what could have happened."

"It's a good thing Larry knows how to teleport." Heartsbane gestured at the sunken-eyed mage.

"Barely," he said. "But I had another look at how they did it. They all work together on that spell and there are many more of them than only two like me and Amy. I might be able to open a portal and follow them, but I reckon they could do that maneuver a couple of times in a row—in which case you could put a fork in me because I'd be done."

"And if we can't stop these attacks, I worry that Shimmerclaw and the rest of the Council will simply decide to go ahead with the war the mages want," Kristen said.

"After all they've done to slow this war?" Amy asked.

"I think so." She looked around the room at all the faces of these people she trusted with not only her life but the lives of everyone in the city she called home. The quiet voice of assurance within reminded her that she could trust them. She had to trust them. After a deep breath, she told them what Constance had said about a dragon operating behind the scenes to make all these events happen that she and her team had tried so hard to stop. She considered telling them that she knew an alias of the dragon and that he went by the Masked One but didn't want to give out the name yet. She'd had a sense from talking to Shimmerclaw that it could be dangerous to tell her people and decided she would approach some of the older dragons like Lumos about it quietly later.

Still, even without a name, Brian perked up. "That makes perfect sense," he said as calmly as if he'd discovered how to beat the final boss in a particularly vexing videogame.

Everyone turned to look at him, so he shrugged and smiled. "Think about it," he said. "That whole trap for Kristen in Mammoth Cave? The big bad dragon who almost beat four of you? It had to be a super-tough dragon, right?"

Everyone nodded because it was obvious.

"That has to be the dragon who wants this war. It's the only thing that makes sense."

Kristen sighed. "That means we have two foes to stop if we want to end this war before it begins." She could feel the weight of it all coming to rest on her shoulders. "We need to find and stop the mages and the Iron Dragon who is either their leader or high up in their chain of command, and we also need to identify and stop this enemy dragon—both before it's too late."

"So where do we start?" Stonequest asked. She knew the former leader of Dragon SWAT was eager to start chasing leads. There was nothing like a meeting to make someone feel like they weren't getting anything accomplished.

"I don't think we can ignore the mages," Kristen said and tried not to sound exasperated. "This...hidden dragon still seems to be content to attack from the shadows. As long as he doesn't operate publicly and hurt people, I don't think we can prioritize him."

"I don't know if that's wise—" Heartsbane interjected before she cut her off.

"I know it's not. But that dragon can turn into liquid shadow, and if we can believe Constance, he's done this for decades, if not longer. We won't find him unless he messes up and we simply don't have the resources to fight the mages with one hand and try to force a mistake from him with the other."

"Then we start with the mages?" Stonequest asked to confirm a way forward.

"Yes. Brian, I want you to collate all the data we have so far. Everyone else, Stonequest will divide you into teams of people to go to each of the hideouts we have already identified. I want our people at both those we raided and the couple that have been abandoned."

"It sounds like you have a hunch," Larry said.

"I do. If I were in Katrina's position, I'd gather all my forces in the most secure place I have, especially with their teleportation powers. It seems that if they were all stationed centrally, they could use their combined power to strike wherever they wanted. If we can find it, we can bring the fight to them. And if we can find even the smallest clue at one of those locations, maybe we can turn this war around."

Everyone nodded and went to Stonequest to be allocated their assignments.

She hoped it was the right decision but she didn't see what other choices she had.

CHAPTER EIGHTY-TWO

Although it pained her to send her teams out while she remained at the base, Kristen knew it was the smart decision. She kept Larry grounded as well so if anyone was attacked, she'd be able to get there in time—she hoped. Part of her hated that so many of her plans of late seemed to rely on hope.

It was better to rely on herself and her abilities, and that was why she had stayed behind. She'd suffered yet another brutal defeat at the hands of the Iron Dragon. The simple truth was that she needed to be able to defeat her or they'd never beat the technomages. With this in mind, she trained with Lumos—again, and again, and again.

"We've already been at it for four days. We should take a rest," he told her when she asked him to come to the training ground they had created in the parking lot of their base.

"It's fine. I've eaten well and used my dragon healing."

"You can't keep this up," he protested.

"Sure I can."

"Have it your way," the old dragon said and attacked.

Day after day, they continued the training. Kristen learned new definitions of pain as Lumos showed her how useless her steel scales were against a properly trained dragon. She made time for little else.

When she was hungry, she ate and when she was exhausted, she slept. She paid attention to the reports her teams gave her while she waited for her wounds to heal.

They were all much the same—nothing. No one had turned up any new clues and all they had found were the bare shells of bases with everything stripped away. It would have been discouraging if she hadn't had a master of combat like Lumos to show her the brutal strikes she would need to defeat the most powerful dragon she'd ever faced.

After a week of this endless and brutal regimen, Kristen was doing better. She learned the subtle movements a dragon needed to master to avoid being grievously wounded. The lessons included how to strike at the vulnerable places and—more importantly—how to mask those strikes within feints. She knew the Iron Dragon had a lifetime of training, but she was fighting for the living—for her friends and family—and for the people she'd already lost.

Grimly determined, she pushed herself until the old dragon was forced to admit that she had improved.

A week into this, he arrived for another early morning training session to find her already there, practicing with her pistol in their indoor range.

"Good morning, Lady Steel. Did you decide to finally take my advice and let your body rest for a moment before we resume our combat?"

"I suppose you could say that," she admitted.

"I must say, I am surprised," he confessed.

"About what?" she asked.

"Well, your marksmanship is excellent. The best I've ever seen in a dragon, in fact. What compels you to practice with a gun when you could be in bed and sleeping like a regular person?"

Kristen chuckled. "I gave up on being a regular person a long time ago. Plus, you're never so good at something that you don't need to practice."

He raised an eyebrow.

"There's also the fact that dragon bullets have different ballistics from regular bullets. I need to be as accurate with them as I am with the regular variety."

For the first time since they'd been training, he looked taken aback. She wasn't quite sure why. She'd ripped his wing from his body and savaged one of his shoulders so badly that he hadn't been able to use it the next day, but a little shooting practice upset the old dragon?

"Is everything okay?" she asked.

Lumos frowned. "You're using dragon bullets?"

She nodded. "We have to be pragmatic about it. I've had some of my old SWAT team practice with them since we faced the Iron Dragon, and I'm glad too. If not for those bullets, I don't think they would have been able to drive her off in the last fight."

"But...don't tell me you're making them?" Lumos tried to keep the horror out of his voice but it slipped into his aura.

"No! God, no!" It was her turn to be taken aback. "Lumos, I would never do anything like that."

"Then..."

"We've collected tens of thousands of rounds so far. I know that in the long run, they need to be destroyed but because they are dragon parts, that's easier said than done. It's not like I can simply douse them in gasoline and burn them."

"I suppose," he said, still on edge.

"The Dragon Council knows about this. In fact, it was they who left the bullets in my care. I had Timeflash set up an armored vault where we store them."

"Oh. Well, I guess it's all under control, then," Lumos said with forced cordiality.

"I'm sorry, Lumos. I didn't think to tell you because you never use a gun. Stonequest and Timeflash don't like it either, but with the Iron Dragon..." She shrugged. "We need to be able to maximize our abilities to fight our enemies. They have already proven to be a life-saver against the Iron Dragon, and we may very well need them against this elder dragon who wants me dead."

Lumos nodded. "Yes, I suppose that all makes sense."

"And yet your aura makes it very clear that you're repulsed."

He nodded again. "To me, it's rather vulgar—like using the femur of a dead human to carve into a knife or something. I can think of scenarios where humans might do such a thing but it's certainly rather macabre, isn't it?"

"Everything about this war is macabre," she agreed but didn't mean to sound as bitter as she did.

"Indeed." The golden dragon stood in silence while she unloaded a magazine into her target.

Satisfied with the tight cluster on the chest of her target, she turned to her companion. "What's the plan for training today?"

"Truly, I think you might be making the smartest choice of what to do," he said, his gaze fixed on her pistol as she returned it to the holster at her side.

"What is that supposed to mean?" Kristen asked, trying to decipher the meaning of the enigmatic smirk on his face.

"It means that I believe you are already close to the Iron Dragon's skill level. We've gone through much of what she did to you in her last attack and I think you're capable of defending yourself now."

"I don't want to only defend," she pointed out.

"And now you know how to attack. But remember, she's done this a long time. When you fight, she'll take advantage of any mistake you make. Your defense must be flawless so you can force her to make an error you can capitalize on. If you can make that happen, I would not bet against you in a battle."

"Thanks, I guess," she mumbled.

"Whatever did I say? I hoped you'd be cheered by the possibility of defeating your foe already. It's only been a week and you've progressed remarkably."

"I am," she said, "It's only...over this past week, you've done a good job of convincing me that the Iron Dragon isn't my biggest opponent."

Lumos let his smile fade. "Indeed, she is not."

"If you think I need to fight flawlessly against Katrina, where do you put my chances against the elder with shadow abilities?"

He took a deep breath and smiled warmly. "Even if you were to fight perfectly with your current skill set, it would not be enough to defeat the dragon who was able to escape you and three of our best fighters."

She wilted despite his obvious attempt to soften the blow.

"That should be expected, Lady Steel," Lumos said. "You are very young and your opponent must be very old. He's fought other dragons for many of your lifetimes. You should be quite proud of the progress you've already made. The fact that you're already so powerful is quite remarkable. Give it time. You have already grown so much. You will grow stronger yet."

"I don't know if I have time," Kristen said and tried not to sound depressed or let her aura show her anxiety. "I have a feeling that things will come to a head sooner rather than later. I can't think of another reason why the technomages would have attacked Detroit if they weren't ready to accelerate their plans to fruition."

"There is nothing to be done but continue to train. Until we know your foe, we cannot do anything else," he insisted.

"And if we do know the foe?" she inquired.

Lumos raised an eyebrow.

"Have you heard of a dragon called the Masked One?" she asked bluntly.

He inhaled sharply at the mention of the name. "Where have you heard of that dragon?"

"La Flamme mentioned it before he died, but most of what I heard came from Constance," she explained. "She told me she believes her entire organization of technomages may have worked to fulfill the Masked One's agenda without knowing that was what they did." She filled him in on everything the woman had told her—how there had been a dragon who had set up the first meeting between Constance and Windfire and how she believed there had to be someone in a high position within dragon culture who had been able to both track Kristen's work and guide the mages.

If he truly knew the Masked One, he didn't give away anything about what he thought of him. He listened intently as if any detail of what Constance told her might be the key to unraveling a weakness or failing of the elder dragon.

Finally, when she had finished, Lumos spoke. "Let me tell you what I know of him. It's not much, mind you—mostly secrets shared by various sources that have far too many details in common and rumors that have lasted for centuries. I've never seen the dragon, but I don't think anyone has seen anything but the mask he wears."

"And what mask is that?" she asked.

"It is said the Masked One takes the skulls of his human victims and wears them over his face."

"Why?" Kristen asked and recalled the threats the dragon she'd faced in Mammoth Cave had made. They'd been exactly that. He had said he'd kill her human friends and wear their skulls.

"Probably to appear as a bloodthirsty monster to both human and dragon kind."

"What else do you know about him?"

"Again, nothing concrete, but I'll tell you the details I feel the most confident about. For starters, the Masked One is incredibly old. Older than me, if you can believe that." He chuckled in an attempt to lighten the mood but his aura was wound so tightly that it did nothing to calm her. "There were rumors of him even when I was growing up."

"Rumors about what?"

"That there was a dragon who wished to operate outside the open and public setting of the Council. That he was incredibly powerful and valued secrecy as much as most dragons valued communication."

"So you don't know much?"

"As I said, nothing concrete." He frowned. "But the rumors have always had some element of a darkness-oriented ability."

"Like what?"

"I cannot say precisely. In fact, that is one of the reasons I've always been so interested in the Masked One. My powers derive from light and his from darkness. For centuries, I trained so I would be ready to fight him when the day came. I thought it was—and forgive me the arrogance of youth—but I thought it was my destiny, of sorts. However, I fear those days have passed. I am not as spry as I once was. If he were to attack us, I would fight, but I wonder if I could face him alone as I surely could have even a few centuries ago."

"So it makes sense that the dragon I fought in the caves was the Masked One. He could merge into shadows and lash out from the darkness. Who else could that have been?"

Lumos hesitated before he answered. "It's certainly possible. There are other dragons with powers that derive from darkness, however. Obscura had abilities like that and she was no Masked One."

"But you think the dragon I fought was?"

He nodded, although he looked like he didn't want to. "That might very well have been him but if it was, all of you were extremely fortunate to escape at all."

"How can you know that? If he works from the shadows, who is to say he has any power at all?" she asked. She knew it sounded falsely optimistic but was also unable to help herself.

"There are more to the rumors than only his powers," the old dragon said. "And I should also say that some of the details of these rumors only corroborate that your foe may indeed be him."

"Details like what?"

"Well—and again, this is not proven, because there is no one on the Dragon Council who openly wears a skull for a mask—but it is said that he ascended to the Council years ago and that every challenger for his position died. It is said that those who learn which Council member he is are found murdered and that no one has bothered to look into such a dangerous prospect for well over a century."

"What councilors have been on the Council for over a thousand years?"

Her companion smiled. "Did I not just say that he has killed those who ask such questions?"

She returned. "I heard you, and I also heard that it's time someone stopped this asshole."

"In North America, there are only three. Lady Shimmerclaw, Lord Boneclaw, and Lord Decimus Aurelius."

It was her turn to suck in a breath. Decimus had long been one of her only supporters on the Dragon Council. Could it all be an act? And to think that Shimmerclaw was against her and agitating for war was more frightening still, but she seemed the least likely suspect, at least on the surface. She was sure the dragon she'd battled under-ground was male. If that was the Masked One, it wasn't Shimmerclaw.

She didn't know much about the other dragon, Lord Boneclaw, but she hoped to find a ton of dirt on him so she could absolve the other two.

"Okay…well, maybe that gives us somewhere to start."

But Kristen wouldn't get to begin her investigation anytime soon as Brian burst out of their main building and ran to the shooting range. He wasn't breathless as he would have been months ago from a short run. Instead of red and splotchy, his face was pale, a visage of terror.

"What happened?" Kristen demanded.

"She's out," he stammered. "Somehow, they busted Constance out of prison."

CHAPTER EIGHTY-THREE

They came for her a week after the Steel Dragon paid her visit, exactly as Constance had known they would. In this twenty-first century world of satellite feeds, cell phone cameras, and big data, it was easy enough to keep tabs on Kristen. She had made her request to see the Steel Dragon and the technomages traced her movements as she went to visit her.

That alone would not have been enough, but she had practiced with the subtleties of the magic needed for secret observation for decades. She'd been drained of her power like everyone else when the dragons had taken her through the white room, but—exactly like the dragons—beyond that room, her powers had begun to regrow.

She wasn't foolish enough to think her abilities would help her escape the labyrinthine prison. There were too many traps designed to kill creatures far more powerful than her. No, her plan was far simpler—create a beacon where it was safe, a lighthouse spell that told the mages exactly where to open their portal outside her doorway.

Using a magic prison was the dragons' greatest mistake. If they had simply dropped her down a well and lashed it shut with anti-magic spells, she might have spent all her days dreaming of escape, but because they used spells to arm the traps of the prison, they needed magic to function. This meant her team could open their portal directly in front of the glass Kristen had stood behind a week before.

While the mages attacked Detroit—as Constance had planned—she had cast her spell that would tell them where to come.

This escape had all been planned and preordained, she would have once said, months earlier and long before she had been captured.

It was too bad she didn't feel the same about it as she once had.

When she had helped create the plans that caused the portal to now open outside her cell, she'd had only the faintest of hunches that a dragon was pulling her strings as well as the strings of everyone in her organization. Now, she believed that was the truth of her existence and the force behind her actions for decades.

So it was not pure relief that she felt when the portal opened and her adopted daughter—the Iron Dragon—stepped through and kicked down the bulletproof glass that had kept her imprisoned for so long.

It was not joy she felt as she stepped through the portal and out of the prison but trepidatious worry.

And it was not guilt she felt when she left the barest hint of magic behind to mark her time in this cell and her passing from it.

CHAPTER EIGHTY-FOUR

"**W**hat the hell do you mean Constance escaped?" Kristen demanded. "I've been to that prison. How far down the hallway did she make it before she was cut in half?"

"I don't know. The surveillance feeds were all cut so we don't have eyes on the location," Brian responded.

"What do you have?" She tried not to yell as they ran to his workstation monitors.

He fell into his chair and began to pound keys and bring up different items of interest on his screens. "The Council issued a full alert." He brought it up on the screen.

Somehow, the prison where the technomage had been held had been broken into. Only one prisoner had been freed—Constance. The rest of the notice was frustratingly vague.

"I need more."

"I'm working on it," he said. His fingers flew and in moments, they looked at a satellite feed of the prison as viewed from space. Even from this vantage point, she could see what had happened to the guards.

Their red blood shone quite plainly against the white stone and concrete that was the roof of the prison.

"Did they blow it up?" she asked.

"No one knows." He flipped through screen after screen of warnings and alerts and processed information far faster than she could. "From what I can tell, they did a hit and run, a smash and grab attack."

"Who?"

Brian showed her a frame that showed the silhouette of a dragon the color of cast iron. "Katrina was there with technomages to open a portal," he said and pointed at another frame that displayed the telltale glowing blue ring of a teleportation spell. "They were in and out before any help could arrive and their dragon bullets annihilated the guards."

"Goddammit."

"From what I can tell—and again, this is speculation based on satellite feeds and not much else—they teleported to the roof, killed the guards, busted in, killed more guards, and portaled to Constance's level. Once they freed her, they got the hell out."

"No one wore bulletproof armor?" Kristen asked.

He brought up another image. It looked like something from an old videogame and was grainy. He pointed to a spot on it that looked like nothing but a splotch of red pixels to her. "Armor doesn't do much when you are shot in the damn face."

"That prison was there for centuries." Lumos sounded stunned. "It was built before the United States was founded. It has never been seen except by a select few, let alone broken into. This is impossible."

"The impossible just happened," she said, none too pleased about it.

"But those were some of the greatest warriors who still walk this planet. Why, Quickclaw was the fastest swordswoman I had ever seen—"

"That's why the mages used bullets," Brian said. "Even if a dragon can beat one, you can't beat a hundred a second coming at you from different angles."

"Of course not..." The old dragon was shaken. "But they did this with the same cavalier recklessness with which humans rob banks. No one is even supposed to know about this prison and yet they were somehow able to penetrate its defenses effortlessly? How did they find it?"

Kristen wished she had an answer to that question, especially since she had a feeling she might be partly to blame.

But she didn't have any idea how Constance could have escaped. She knew they'd used their teleportation magic, but that only frustrated her more. How had these technomages unearthed a form of magic that the mages who worked for the dragons didn't seem to be familiar with? Were the dragons so assured in their control of the world that they didn't bother to push their mages to discover new forms of magic? Or was it simply that the technomages were all unbound by the dampening cuffs that mages who worked for dragons were required to wear?

She couldn't say. And the person who undoubtedly had the best understanding of how it was possible to get past all those defenses had used that knowledge to escape from prison.

With a heavy sigh, she acknowledged the feeling that nothing could go right. She'd been beaten by the Iron Dragon despite her commitment to training with Lumos. Now, one of her most dangerous adversaries was back on the street, an opponent she would need an entirely different skillset to beat.

Stopping the technomage cells had made her feel she was successful, but Constance escaping washed any feeling of success away. It felt as if for each step forward they made, they took two back.

"I want the jet ready to go in a half-hour and I want every person we can fit on it. We'll find out how Constance got out of there, and we'll help anyone who survived this."

She'd intended to say "this massacre" but chose not to. Someone had to be strong, and that responsibility had to fall on the Steel Dragon's shoulders, as always.

CHAPTER EIGHTY-FIVE

She had no idea how the hell Windlock had trained the pilot of his private jet to be so comfortable with people jumping out midway, but she was thankful all the same. Every time Kristen asked the man to crack the door so the dragons could launch, he responded with as much concern as if she'd asked the flight attendants to provide peanuts.

Now, she stood in front of the open door of the jet as the wind whipped her hair and stared at the mountain that housed the dragon prison below her.

"Does everyone know their assignments?" she asked.

Her team responded with a loud, "Yes ma'am!" She turned to check on them. Every single person on the jet—she had crammed the plane as full as any economy class airline—was suited up and ready to go. After fighting in Colombia, then defending Detroit against the Iron Dragon and the technomages, her team worked more tightly together than ever. Even the new troops Jim had brought in had meshed well with the old guard of the team. They wore parachutes, guns strapped to their chests, and grim looks on their faces.

Despite their resolution, she didn't envy them. It was scary enough to jump from a plane knowing full well that she could simply transform into a dragon and catch the wind with her wings. It was another thing entirely to rely on a dragon to catch you in mid-air.

"Remember, only open your parachute as a last resort. We'll use dragons to get there, so everyone on this plane has a ride. If we come under fire, your dragon might not catch you. In that case, deploy your parachute and rendezvous with us at the prison."

The dragons nodded to confirm this. She noted that they all watched the soldiers they were supposed to catch. The assignments had been made carefully. None of the dragons wanted to be the one who forgot which teammate they were responsible for.

"All right then, here we go," she said when no one posed a question.

She jumped from the plane and her stomach lurched into her throat as her body screamed at the sensation of falling. In seconds, she transformed into a dragon and her wings stabilized her. The other dragons followed suit and plummeted toward the mountains below in their human form for a few seconds before they transformed and caught the wind with their wings.

Larry and Amy followed as they could use their powers to fly but not carry others. The girl still used her magic to make objects besides herself fly. She was strapped onto a snowboard and cruised effortlessly as if she was on an obstacle course on the surface instead of falling through empty space. Larry was less graceful and used his abilities to tug on his robes to keep him from reaching terminal velocity.

Now that they were all airborne and the plane circled above the top of the mountain, the humans began to jump out.

Kristen swooped below some of her old SWAT teammates. She caught Drew, Jim, and Beanpole on her back and snatched Hernandez and Keith in her claws—although she let the woman fall for a longer period of time than the others because she screamed in delight throughout her freefall. Amy hadn't been able to regrow Keith's finger but she had healed the wound. The Rookie, to his credit, didn't seem to mind. The mage had better luck with Butters, but his wound still hadn't healed enough for him to walk on the leg so he'd stayed at the base with Brian.

With her team on her back and in her arms, Kristen glided towards the top of the prison, unsure if they would arrive to see nothing but a field of dead bodies, magical traps left by the mages, or something worse.

None of those things greeted them and instead, a dragon came up to meet them in midair.

"Southwest Dragon SWAT. You're speaking to Officer Heatburn. Can you please kindly tell me what the fuck you're doing here and why I shouldn't mobilize the other dragons to blast you out of the sky?" His scales looked dry and flaky like he needed to molt—not that dragons did that—and his aura was equal parts concern and bravado. It was clear he didn't want to fight this dragon with armed humans on her back but he would if he needed to.

"I'm Investigator Kristen Steel. We didn't report our movements because we weren't sure who would be here and didn't want to walk into a trap. It's good to see you made it here first," she replied.

Heatburn pulsed his aura in a wave of calm that was no doubt directed at his partners on the roof of the prison.

"I gotta say I'm glad to see you, Investigator Steel!" he admitted. "We mostly deal with dragons fighting out in the desert and legal disputes with the show business dragons in Hollywood. This is a little outside our wheelhouse." He guided them into a landing.

Two other dragons were on the roof in their dragon bodies and watched her approach in obviously aggressive stances. They weren't the guards she had seen when she'd last been there.

"Who the hell is this?" one of them demanded, a female whose scales were a richly patterned mix of browns, tans, and blacks. It looked like perfect camouflage for a dragon to hide in the desert. The idea struck her as odd as she'd never seen a dragon try to camouflage and hide.

"My name is Investigator Kristen Steel," she explained as the humans climbed off her back and stood at attention. She transformed into her human body and flashed her badge. When she did so, the desert dragon visibly calmed.

"Oh, thank God," the woman said. "My name is Sidewinder. Ma'am, are we happy to see you. This is…this is a mess."

"What have you done so far?" she asked.

Sidewinder straightened, although she didn't stand at attention as well as Kristen's humans did. "We set up a perimeter, ma'am, and investigated the guard station."

"That's good," she said. "Do we have survivors? We brought a mage who knows how to heal." Especially dragons, she thought a little bitterly. She'd like to have Butters there watching from behind a sniper scope. Somehow, the southerner's eyes seemed better than most dragons'.

The other dragon clenched her jaw. Kristen already knew what she would say. "No, ma'am. No survivors." She unintentionally looked around the rooftop at the bodies strewn there. "Most of the dead were up here. Our working theory is that whatever those technomage bastards did, the shooting started here. When they arrived, most of the guards came out to fight but they were mowed down as soon as they reached the roof." She gestured to the trapdoor that led into the magic dampening white room Kristen had passed through. "I don't think the poor bastards even thought about dragon bullets."

"Unfortunately, that makes sense," Emerald said as he landed and unloaded his group of human soldiers. "These guys were always aloof when it came to current events. They spent their days training in combat. I'm not surprised that they'd think their skills could have held strong against any attackers they might face. The crazy shit is that a year ago, they would have been right."

Kristen nodded. "What about the magic defenses?"

"They are still intact, thank God," Sidewinder said. "They trashed the roof but after that, it looks like they somehow skipped all the traps on the way to the leader of the technomages' cell." She shook her head. "It's like fighting demons. They don't follow the rules."

She realized that this dragon and her team didn't have access to the satellite feed Brian had shown them, nor did they know about the proficiency with teleportation that the mages had honed.

"No other prisoners escaped?" she asked as more of her dragons settled on the roof. Lumos and Timeflash immediately began to examine the dead for clues, but she knew damn well that every dragon had been shot and killed with dragon bullets. She'd seen enough of the brutal wounds—in both humans and dragons—to know that all the victims had died from that particular kind of gun violence.

"Not to our knowledge, ma'am," Sidewinder said. "But we haven't been here long. We left as soon as the Council sent the alert out, but we were only here maybe half an hour before you."

"What about Shimmerclaw?" she asked.

Sidewinder recoiled visibly. "You mean the leader of the Dragon Council? I haven't spoken to her. Oh, God—was I supposed to report in? We saw the carnage and tried to set up a perimeter—"

"No, no, I mean was she still here when the attack happened?"

The dragon looked confused. "No, ma'am... She wasn't among the dead, anyway. I had Heatburn check the visitor logs. You were the last person to come through and that was a week ago. There hasn't been anyone since then."

"And before?"

"No visitors, ma'am, and I would have noticed if the head of the Dragon Council had signed the log. Hers would have been the first body we looked for."

Kristen nodded. It was good that Shimmerclaw wasn't among the dead, obviously. She saw her as one of the more forward-thinking dragons on the Council and her strongest potential ally besides Decimus Aurelius. While she didn't want her dead, her not being on the visitor's log was also a concern.

Lumos said there were only three dragons who had been on the Council long enough to possibly be the Masked One and Shimmerclaw was one of them. She had reason to believe the Masked One was a male dragon but no proof of that yet.

While she wanted to trust the platinum dragon, she knew that professionally, she had to be careful. She wanted to believe that the Council leader had a perfectly sound reason for not signing the visitor's log, in light of the attack, it couldn't help but raise suspicion in her mind. Still, there was nothing to be done about it now. It certainly wouldn't help to tell Sidewinder, who seemed to be on the edge of paranoia already.

It was far better to focus on the task at hand.

"Dragons, I want you ready to go through the maze with me to get to Constance's cell. Mages too. Humans, you stay here and make damn sure no one else we don't want here comes to join this little party. There is no clue too small. Anything could give us a lead on their location or their next target. If there's something here, I want it."

While the humans went to work, she led the others into the maze. The white room that took their magic was the first stop but it wasn't white anymore. Apparently, the guard inside had failed to lock the door and paid for his unprofessionalism with his life. Now, the white walls had his blood and brains sprayed over one of them.

The maze wasn't easy to get through, but when tackled by a team of dragons, it was passable. They took turns to lead so those who sustained injuries were able to heal. Fortunately, they managed to dodge the obstacles that would have proven lethal and reached the hallway that housed Constance's cell without incident.

Kristen opened the door to the hallway to find it was the same as it had been the last time she'd been there. That was a shock to her as she'd expected destroyed walls, blood, and chaos, not the sterile white glow of fluorescent lights, broken glass, and an empty cell.

She and the dragons began to poke around, but none of them came up with anything of interest. There were no claw marks and no blasts from a mage's spell. Nothing indicated that anything was done in this hallway beyond something breaking the glass that had caged the technomage.

"Another dead end," Lumos said as he stood in the hallway near the cell and as close to a literal dead end as she had ever seen.

"Dammit," she cursed. "I thought there'd be something here. I can't believe we wasted all this time—" She noticed Larry and her outburst ended abruptly.

The mage stared at a space in the middle of the hallway, his head tilted to the left like a dog waiting for someone to reveal a treat he knew was hiding out of sight.

"Do you have something Larry?" Kristen asked.

"What?" He jumped at the question, shook his head, and turned to her as he pointed to a place in the air in front of him. "Yeah, actually. This is where the portal was."

"Of course that's where the portal was," Heartsbane grouched. "They got in here and took their precious mage leader out via portal."

She didn't want to be rude but she had to agree with the other dragon. "She's right, Larry. It's very obvious that they portaled Constance out from this hallway."

"No, I mean, the portal was right here." He pointed again as if he could touch something that none of them could see.

"And that's significant?" she asked.

He nodded. "It's not like the other closed portals. When we went to Colombia, the mages escaped via a portal and did the same in Detroit. Both times, I tried to focus on what they were doing."

"And both times, you had a ton of other shit going on," Emerald joked.

"True," the mage admitted. "But that doesn't mean the brilliance of Larry Brockton was in any way diminished." He smiled and gained steam. "Now that I've studied them, I've learned to understand the spell a little better. Not as well as the technomages understand it, but I have managed to cast it twice."

"Wow." Heartsbane's sarcasm was palpable. "Brilliant and humble. What a combination."

"The thing is, once the spell is finished, there aren't any traces left."

"And this is different?" Kristen asked.

"Yeah, it is." His gaze returned to the invisible point in the hallway. He stared at it so intently that she wondered why she couldn't see anything. "There's a faint touch of magic lingering in the air—almost like a loose thread from a spell. Some magic leaves those behind but not the portals."

"Does that help us or is this mage shit we don't need to care about?" Heartsbane asked.

"The thread starts in the cell and goes to this point, then it simply vanishes. It doesn't feel like a loose end, though—more like the middle of something. Also…I'm sure this will sound crazy, but I know who cast the spell, too."

"Constance," said Amy, who had stepped closer after she'd heard what he had to say.

"Do you feel it too?" he asked.

She nodded. "I spent time with Constance before I met Kristen. She was one of the first mages I saw do magic. I assumed this hallway felt like her because she'd been imprisoned here, but I now see that it must be this spell."

"Can you trace it somehow?" Kristen asked. "Like…can you sense the other part of the spell, wherever it is? I can't believe she messed up this badly but if we can leverage it to our advantage, we must."

"I'm sorry, but no," he said. "I can sense it but it's extremely weak. It's like trying to imagine what a sweater looks like after seeing a loose piece of yarn."

"What if I helped?" Amy asked.

Larry looked dubiously at her. "I don't know. We'd have to empower the spell, which is a tricky business. As soon as we get any sense of where it leads, one of us would have to stop and try to open a portal to that location. Then—depending on the distance to that portal—the first mage would need to drop the thread and switch to opening it. The process would take a ton of energy, plus there are no guarantees that it would turn up anything worthwhile. They could have portaled again."

"There are no guarantees in our line of work," Kristen said.

"I'm willing to try," Amy said. "I can pump energy into this one and when you open the portal—if it appears—I can try to help."

He shrugged. "Sure. Why not? The worst thing that could happen is the spell is some kind of trap and by adding our energy to it, we activate it and blow up our entire damn team."

All eyes—dragon and mage—turned to Kristen. It was her call, of course. That was the burden of being a leader.

"I think the alternative of a dragon versus mage versus human war is far worse," she said. What she didn't say was that after talking to Constance, she didn't believe this was a trap. She couldn't say that she trusted the woman but she didn't think the mage would kill her in cold blood. After she'd tried to convert her to her cause so many times, she couldn't imagine it all ending like that.

Of course, Constance could have had a change of heart, in which case she had no doubt that their death would be swift.

But it was her call to make, so she made it. "Amy, empower the spell. Larry open the portal. Dragons, race up top and get our human forces. If this thing is opened and we can't tell the location, we'll go through."

"Yes, ma'am," Stonequest said. "How long do you think that'll take?"

Amy looked at Larry, who only shrugged. "At least ten minutes, I'd say. Amy will have to discover how to augment the magic, and it'll take me a few minutes to open and stabilize the portal."

"We'll be back in five," the dragon said and raced out of the hallway with the others on his heels.

"Amy?" she asked.

The girl nodded and looked at her fellow mage, who reached out for the thread. Kristen frowned when she noticed a tiny filament of light begin to glow in the air. Although it wiggled and moved as Larry filled it with energy, as he'd said, one end of it simply vanished. It looked as if the thread had been nailed to a point that simply floated in mid-air.

"All right, Amy, if you would?" he said.

Amy joined her magic to his and the difference was immediate. If his was a babbling brook, hers was a raging river. The filament thickened and began to move even faster as it glowed brighter and brighter.

"Easy!" he shouted.

"I'm going as easy as I can. This spell is sucking my magic up," Amy yelled in response.

Larry released the spell and began to focus on the portal. To Kristen's shock, the ring of light that portended a portal appeared almost instantly. She looked down the hallway. This wouldn't take ten minutes.

She pulled her radio out. "I need everyone down here now!"

"Amy!" Larry shouted, caught in the spell and oblivious to how little time had passed. "Let the spell go and help me with this portal."

Again, the young mage's overwhelming magical powers became instantly apparent. As soon as she added her power to his, the disc in the middle of the ring of light filled with light before a window opened to somewhere very far and very different from the isolated mountain prison.

A beautiful beach was visible with sand only a few shades darker than white. Crystal-clear blue waters rolled gently inside what might have been a cove. The smells of hot air, salty sea, and a dense jungle wafted into the cold, sterile hallway. Kristen took a step closer and saw that the beach ran all the way to a tropical jungle that clung to a mountain that didn't rise high enough to be topped with snow. She saw no buildings, no distinctive landmarks, and nothing but trees, water, sand, and sky.

"I can't tell where it leads. It's a tropical island, but that's all I have," she said. Shit, she didn't even know if it was an island. It could simply be a tropical coast.

"Figure…it…out…please." Larry wheezed before he stumbled and fell to one knee. The energy he used to help fuel the portal flickered.

"Are you okay?" Kristen asked but tried to not look at him so she could spend every second she had trying to decipher where this beach was. Was the mountain a volcano? If it was, it was so covered by jungle that it wouldn't be much use. Could she identify any of the trees? Not even kind of.

"So…far…" Larry managed to splutter before he collapsed, drenched in sweat and bleeding from both nostrils.

Now, only Amy held the portal open.

"It's slipping," she said through clenched teeth and her skater hoodie flapped in the wind caused by opening the gateway.

"I'll contact you when I figure it out," Kristen said before she'd even consciously decided what she would do.

But there was no choice, really. This was their one chance to trace the technomages to their base and she knew what she had to do. She took a leap of faith and dove through the portal seconds before it slammed shut behind her.

CHAPTER EIGHTY-SIX

The portal snapped shut as Kristen fell onto the beach. It was hot and the warm breeze that had blown into the cold mountain prison now felt like a stifling wave of heat.

She looked around as she took her coat off and tried to find something—anything—that might give her a clue as to where she was. Despite her scrutiny, she found nothing except trees, sand, and water.

Not to be dissuaded, she took her phone out, hoping to use the magic of a satellite connection to find where she was.

The device displayed no bars, but maybe there was still the faintest signal she could use. She tried her maps app, which opened to show her downtown Detroit and a spinning loading circle, nothing else.

Still, she knew her phone was the key. She paced down the beach, hoping to pick up even the smallest signal. Staying on the move seemed like the smart course of action anyway.

There! She had...something showing on her connection icon. It sure wasn't 4G, but it would have to be enough. Kristen dialed Brian in the certainty that if she could get a connection, he could probably use his nerdy Internet skills to discover where she was. Honestly, she loved his nerdy Internet skills.

It didn't seem like he'd ever have a chance to use them for this, though. As soon as she dialed, a bolt of magic blasted the device from her hands.

Kristen reacted as any dragon who'd studied melee combat for the last week would—she transformed into her steel dragon form and raised her tail so she could throw the barbs near her ax-blade tip at whoever had attacked her before she incinerated them for good measure.

Unfortunately, it quickly became apparent that her dragon powers wouldn't be enough.

The mage who had attacked her stood near the shore, a swirling cloak of energy already up to shield her from whatever attacks she might attempt to launch at her. She knew she could probably overwhelm the mage if she was alone. But as soon as she transformed, she heard gunshots all around her.

There weren't that many and certainly not the barrage she knew the weapons most of the mages held were capable of unleashing. Still, it was enough for her to know that about ten mages surrounded her, all far enough away to be out of her range and all with weapons aimed at her except for the one who'd used the blast of energy.

"You don't all have dragon bullets," she said and used her aura to make them feel fear.

"You might be right," the mage on the shore said. "Would you like to find out?"

The others aimed at different parts of her body.

"You know I'm faster than any of you," she said. "Lower your weapons and I'll come quietly."

The mage shook her head and tsked at her. "You may be faster than any one of us. But you are not faster than all of us. If you think I'm wrong, attack me. We'll see what the rest of my patrol does."

Kristen didn't move. She knew exactly what they would do.

"Good!" The mage beamed. "It would be a shame to have to tell Constance that we used the Steel Dragon for target practice."

"She's here, then?" she asked.

"You don't seem as smart as Constance and Katrina say you are," the woman said. "You're still asking questions like you're in charge but you aren't. Change into your human shape and put your hands above your head. I'll come and cuff you. If you resist, you die. If you try to hurt me, you die. The rewards for the mage who kills the Steel Dragon are ample. My family would never want for anything."

She sighed, and—not seeing any other option that didn't end with her being filled with bullet holes—let the mage cuff her.

Immediately, she felt her powers drain from her like she was back in prison. She could not transform into a dragon or turn her skin to steel and wouldn't be able to access her dragon speed, strength, or healing abilities.

The mage knew this too. She shoved her forward and laughed as the once-mighty Steel Dragon stumbled and fell into the sand.

"You need to be better on your feet than that," she snapped. "We have a long walk and it's tougher going than sand."

Kristen prepared to take notes on how to get to the base, but one of the mages threw a sack over her head, and for the next thirty minutes, she was led on a march through the jungle.

When she stumbled, she was yanked to her feet and when she managed to stay balanced, she was shoved over. All the while, she listened for clues. Would that birdcall be what could tell her team where she was? Was the smell of a particular flower the clue they'd need?

It was hard not to lose hope given that her phone had already been shattered.

Finally, they took the bag off her head. She prepared herself for the bright light of a tropical sun but instead, found herself in a long tunnel. Perhaps a hundred yards behind them, the tunnel opened into the jungle from which she'd come. Even that wasn't much use, though, as it looked as if whoever had created this tunnel in the mountain had used a natural cave opening. She still wore layers of clothing for the cold so she hadn't noticed that the air temperature had dropped inside.

Is this a bunker from World War Two? she wondered. It seemed as a good a guess as any and might mean she was on an island in the

Pacific...which only narrowed it down to a needle hidden in the largest geographic feature on the entire Earth.

They pushed her through the concrete tunnels, took her to a cell, and thrust her unceremoniously inside before they locked the door.

Kristen sighed. This had not gone well. She hadn't expected such a distant location. While it probably was foolish of her, every other technomage base had been built somewhere with a supply of meat to feed captive dragons. There was no way this island could support even one dragon—not without a fleet of fishing boats, of which she had seen no sign.

But before she could sink too deeply into despair, Constance arrived.

"You were a damned fool to come here. Especially alone." The woman shook her head in disappointment.

She wondered if the technomage meant that she wanted her team to come. Was that why she'd left the spell in the prison? Or was she merely threatening her like any good prison guard would?

"What did you think you would accomplish?" Constance asked, unlocked the door to the cell, and stepped inside. "Now, you're our prisoner and better yet, a hostage. If your friends come for you and manage to penetrate our defenses, we threaten to kill you and it's over. One problem with the kind of fierce loyalty you inspire is that it can be exploited."

The woman punctuated this comment with a hard uppercut to her gut.

Kristen doubled over, not used to feeling pain without her dragon strength. Her assailant moved close to her ear and whispered. "If you're still in here when your friends show up, you lose."

Then, she rocketed her knee into her captive's face to break her nose and cover the concrete floor with blood.

"Your friends can't find you, can they?" she demanded.

Before she could answer, the mage stamped savagely on her arm and she gasped in pain.

Constance did it again and focused on her wrist. After another blow, she took a break to work her face into a bruised mess. "You dragons and your healing abilities. You have no control over those now. You have no choice but to keep these bruises. Do you hear me? No choice but to keep them."

There was concern in the woman's eyes. Kristen tried to decipher what that meant but her assailant stamped on her wrist again.

But this time, the blow—and a twinge of magic that burst from Constance's fingers—popped the cuff that had dampened her powers off her wrist.

"Pathetic," her attacker said and ignored what she'd done to free her. "You can't even heal. When your friends get here, you'd better hope you vanish. Otherwise, we'll slaughter every last one of you and end this stupid conflict once and for all."

In the next moment and with no warning, Constance left.

Kristen was left bruised and confused. Still, she knew enough to pocket the bracelet and listen to the cryptic command—don't let the bruises heal. While her dragon powers went to work to fix her nose and mend her wrist, she made sure the bruises remained on her face. She only wished she knew what the hell the mage was thinking and if this was simply another of her mind games or something entirely new.

CHAPTER EIGHTY-SEVEN

"Shit, shit, shit, shit, shit, shit, shit!" Brian cursed as his fingers clattered over his keyboard. He hoped he could somehow locate Kristen despite the call she'd made to his cell phone not connecting.

He knew that shit had gone wrong because the blip on his map that showed where she was, based on her cellphone's GPS tracking, had completely vanished from the prison complex. The young man had played numerous videogames in his day, so he made the leap of logic that others might not have. Kristen had vanished because she stepped through one of the portals the technomages had used.

Wherever the other end of the portal was, he assumed it wasn't near any city in North America. Otherwise, her blip would have registered as soon as her cellphone pinged a message off a cell tower. Without GPS, he had relied completely on her to call him, so it had been a huge relief when his phone rang and displayed his sister's face covered in whipped cream, a legendary prank he'd pulled on her.

He didn't find it funny when the line went dead before he even connected.

Damn it, he could do this. If the phone had been able to patch through, it meant Kristen had service. It might have been from a satellite, but he could work with even that.

Focused, he traced the message from his phone to the cell phone tower closest to them and from there to a satellite over the United States. He breached firewalls in the process, thwarted security protocols, and left a mess of open doors into computer systems as he forced his way through them. The signal led him from one satellite to another and he traced it from the middle of America to a satellite off the coast of California, another one over the Pacific, and finally, to a cell phone tower on an island in the middle of the ocean.

As his fingers moved of their own accord after years of playing games on every system known to man, Brian found images of the island as viewed from space.

"Shit," he said again for good measure. He didn't think this was the place. There was a mid-sized city on it with maybe ten thousand people, judging by the sprawl of houses. Most of the island was used for agriculture. He didn't see how a technomage base could operate there in secret. There were too many people and not enough cover. Plus, if she had made her call from this island, the connection would have been stronger. Despite the haste with which he'd raced through the connections, he hadn't failed to notice that Kristen had almost been unable to make her phone connect.

It took tremendous effort for him to not chuck both his cellphone and keyboard across the warehouse floor, but he managed to restrain himself. Instead, he zoomed out and looked for other nearby islands.

There were nine, so too many to search individually for clues. Plus, the technomages were smart. It wasn't like they would build a base with a sign on the roof that said *get your dragon bullets here*. He ran a search on the area, looking for signs of something that might bring him closer to the answers he needed.

Finally, he got a hit.

One of the islands had been used as a bunker during World War Two. Apparently, it had been used by the Japanese to house troops. There was a fairly large complex of tunnels built into the mountain that sprawled in the center of the island. Brian zoomed in on this location. He saw nothing of the base, only thick jungles and beautiful beaches, but he did see a couple of fishing ships docked in a harbor.

When he looked through the satellite footage of the last few days, he confirmed that the fishing ships were in operation. They went in and out of the harbor, which meant people were using them.

That was good enough for him.

He picked his cellphone up and called Stonequest.

"Brian, please tell me you have good news."

"I think I know where Kristen is," he said.

"Oh, thank the fire in us all," the dragon replied.

"I wouldn't celebrate yet," Brian said in a rush. "She's on an island in the middle of the Pacific Ocean. Most likely in an old Japanese bunker on a tropical island."

"You're kidding." Stonequest did not sound amused.

"If I was kidding, it would be funny," he said while he ran calculations on his computer during the conversation.

"Send us the coordinates and we'll take the jet there," the dragon said.

"No. I'm chartering a flight as we speak. We'll meet you in Colorado and we'll all head out together."

"Negative, Zed. That'll cost us hours your sister might not have if we want to find her alive."

"How can you say that?"

"It's the damn truth," Stonequest said, his voice stern. "Send the coordinates and we'll head out there. We have all our dragons, our mages, and a good force of human soldiers."

"You can't expect me to stay behind."

"That's exactly what I expect," the dragon confirmed. "She's in a bunker, you said?"

"Yes, I think so anyway."

"Then I want a map of it." Stonequest's tone brokered no argument but Brian couldn't help himself.

"I haven't found anything but references to it. How can you be sure there's a map?"

"I'm not!" the dragon shouted over the phone. "But if it exists, you're the only one who can find it. The best place for you to do that is in Detroit."

He nodded. As little as he liked it, even he had to acknowledge that it made sense. "What else do you need?" he asked as he sent orders to the captain of Kristen's private jet. It was a relief to see the captain's GPS beacon already at the airport closest to the prison.

"Shipping manifests to the island if possible. If they have non-magical defenses, I want to know about it. See if you can find out how much food they import as well. That might give us a clue about how many soldiers they have there."

"There'll be more than there were," he said. "If they captured Kristen, you can bet they'll be ready for us to attack."

"Still. If there's usually ten people at this base, that'll be a different fight than a hundred."

He nodded, relieved he was not on video with Stonequest so the dragon couldn't see the terror on his face.

It didn't take long for Stonequest to get everyone on the back of a dragon and headed to the airport. As soon as Kristen had gone through the portal and it had vanished, they'd all gone to the roof of the prison, knowing full well that they'd need to get somewhere else and get there fast.

They flew down the mountainside, reached their jet, loaded up, and were soon airborne.

He checked his phone constantly. While he knew Brian was digging up all the intelligence he could, did he damn well have to take so long? After about an hour—as they flew past the California coast and out over the Pacific—the techie called.

Stonequest answered and had to give the phone to one of the humans who seemed to have a better idea of how to accomplish what Brian wanted him to do.

An agonizing minute later, they had maps on the flat screen in the dining area of the jet. Everyone crowded closer while the young man talked to them from a tiny video feed in the corner of the screen and manipulated the rest of the display beside him from the base in Detroit.

"The bunker has a few entrances, all near beaches and all damn far from its center," he explained. "At first, I thought maybe we could punch into the center, as that's where I'm sure Kristen is, but it's not possible. This base was built during World War Two and it was designed to withstand serious damage. Plus, while I can't be sure, it looks like there's something built into the jungle."

"Turrets," Stonequest said.

Brian nodded. "That means approaching from the beach will be a shit show."

"Well, fuck," Heartsbane said. "We can't attack the center or the edges, so what the fuck are we supposed to do?"

Brian smiled. "I found an entrance near the fishing boats. I think it was added later after the base was abandoned but before the techno-mages started using it. There aren't any of the turret structures there. I think that's where you should land. I've sent the pilot a course that should be able to get you all damn close, keep you out of turret range, and get him out without landing."

"Excellent," Stonequest said, relieved that they had a plan. "I knew keeping you there was the right thing to do."

"And what about me?" It was Butters, the overweight sniper who Kristen had worked with for so long. He pushed into the tiny box that showed Brian's face. "How am I supposed to help?"

"Your leg still isn't healed," Amy said.

"I don't need a leg to shoot," he complained.

Stonequest cut the bickering off. "Any news from Kristen?"

"No." Brian shook his head. Even on the tiny, grainy video feed of his face, it was obvious his expression was grim. "The phone cut off almost as soon as she arrived. I haven't gotten anything else off it since then. I think it was destroyed when she was captured."

"How do you know she was captured?" Heartsbane asked. "It could be worse."

He clenched his jaw. "She was captured," he repeated. "She had to be." The young man stared out of the camera and somehow locked Heartsbane in his gaze until she looked away first.

Emerald cleared his throat. "We have to be prepared for all possible outcomes."

"We are not giving up on Kristen," he said and the crappy microphone he used distorted his voice as it rose in volume. "She's been through crazy shit before and come out in one piece. We have to believe in her ability to do it again."

Stonequest nodded. "He's right. We'll operate under the assumption that Kristen is alive, and we will continue to do so until we defeat every damn mage on that island and find her."

In his heart, though, the dragon was already preparing for the worst.

Hours later—far too many hours by Stonequest's reckoning—they could see their destination on the horizon. It was part of a cluster of islands, although none were so close to their target that a human would be able to swim between them easily. He could also see the other island with the cellphone tower Brian had mentioned.

Thank the flames for humans and their technology, he thought. Without that cell tower, he knew Kristen would be doomed.

As things stood, he still had hope.

"Everyone fasten seatbelts," the pilot said. "We're coming in hot, and the next ten minutes will be bumpy. When I give the order, unstrap and get ready to jump."

The dragon couldn't help but grin. There was something awesome about jumping from a moving plane as a human and changing into a dragon in midair. Cooler still was that they would use the method to surprise these mages and rescue the Steel Dragon.

Or so he thought until red lights started flashing.

"We have incoming," the pilot said.

"What the fuck does that mean?" Heartsbane demanded.

Brian answered from Detroit. His eyes in the sky could see a wealth of information invisible to everyone on the plane.

"I have good news and bad news," Kristen's brother said.

"Tell us!" Stonequest shouted.

"There's a heat-seeking missile headed directly toward you," he said in a rush.

"How is that good news?" Stonequest roared and his aura sent rage to everyone on the airplane.

"The good news is that there are no turrets on this side of the island."

"Dammit, Brian," the dragon said as the plane veered sharply.

Apparently, the techie had already told the pilot as the aircraft zigzagged in an effort to avoid the missile. But even Stonequest understood the difference between a passenger jet and a fighter, and this was no fighter.

Still, Windlock hadn't hired simply anyone to fly his private jet. The pilot did his job as well as he could and banked the plane at the last second. An explosion detonated outside but at least they were still relatively in one piece.

"We will go in with a barely controlled descent," the pilot said over the intercom. "That blast missed us but the shockwave destroyed most of our wing and fried the engine on that side. We won't make it to the island but I'll put us down as gently as I can."

Everyone braced themselves, but no one was prepared for what Brian said next.

"They've launched another missile. You guys need to get the hell off the plane!"

Stonequest knew there was no time to argue, not with as many squishy humans as they had aboard.

"Let's move, people! You heard Zed. Move your ass or you're all dead," he ordered. "Dragons, you know the humans you need to bring in. We've trained for this." They had not trained for a missile strike but they knew how to evacuate the plane in the air so that would have to be good enough.

"Dragons, I want you to stay as close to the aircraft as you can.

619

When that bomb hits, I want it to look like nothing fell from this plane but debris. Pilot, can you get us over that island?"

"I might make it to the bay but it'll be close."

"Do your best," Stonequest said and stepped forward for his turn to jump.

He leapt from the plane, transformed almost instantaneously, and scooped up Hernandez, Keith, Beanpole, Drew, and Jim.

Despite knowing it was being targeted by a heat-seeking missile, he flew closer to the aircraft.

The other dragons did the same, rescued the evacuees, and hugged the profile of the jet.

Finally, the pilot stepped out, and not a moment too soon. The missile struck and converted the jet to metal scrap. The dragons all took the blast and used its force to blow themselves and their human riders from their positions in the air.

They did so well that Stonequest was honestly afraid some of them were dead, but moments before they splashed into the water, they spread their wings and flew toward the beach. A minute later, he did a headcount as his team armed themselves with gear in the shadow of a few old fishing ships moored in the bay.

"Humans, how do we look?"

Drew answered for all of them. "We have most of our weapons—"

"I have my explosives!" Hernandez cut in enthusiastically.

The SWAT leader continued as if she hadn't spoken. "But our communications were fried. Does anyone have a cell phone?"

Those who did checked, but no one had service. Stonequest couldn't help but wonder if the technomages had disabled the nearby cell tower. He wouldn't put it past them. It was a novice mistake to underestimate a foe and it was far better to overestimate them. He had a feeling there was no way he could overestimate this particular band of opponents.

"Wasn't there supposed to be an entrance for the fishermen or something?" Larry asked.

Hernandez pointed to a pile of stones that protruded incongruously from the green jungle of the island. "That's a recent demolition.

I'd bet you a hundred to one they blew that when they saw we were getting close."

Stonequest shook his head at the savviness of their foe. They'd already enlisted deadly mages and a dragon even more fearsome than Kristen herself. Now, they'd somehow taken his team's element of surprise. Instead of coming undetected through a back door, it looked like they had a long slog through the jungle ahead of them.

"Mages, I want you ready to respond defensively. Everyone else, shoot anything that attacks. I don't give a shit if it's a monkey. If it moves, shoot. When we get inside, show caution so we don't hurt the boss, but there's no way they left her out here."

Stonequest only hoped they made it inside. It felt more and more like an "if" than a "when."

They set off with a team of humans in the lead to cut through the undergrowth and try to find the entrance they were looking for. The mages were in position to cover them, followed by dragons who both itched for a fight and were in danger of being shredded by bullets made of their own species.

He had seen numerous battles in his day, but none seemed stacked against them quite like this one.

Still, he wouldn't give up, not with Kristen in their clutches.

CHAPTER EIGHTY-EIGHT

Kristen's prison cell was a tiny part of a sprawling complex, of that she felt certain. But however large the base was, it wasn't so big that she couldn't hear the sounds of people springing into action.

She listened carefully as she lay on the stone floor of her cell and didn't so much as twitch. It seemed a logical assumption that she was being watched and she didn't want whoever was on the other side of the hidden cameras to know that she could hear what was going on.

If she was a regular human, she would not have been able to hear the echoing sounds of boots on stone, the telltale clunk of magazines loaded into guns, and the rough rips of Velcro used to tighten boots and vests, then torn loose to be tightened again. She shouldn't have been able to hear any of this because the scouting patrol that had caught her had put a magic dampening cuff on her wrist to strip her of her powers.

Inexplicably, Constance had taken that off.

Despite having full access to her dragon abilities, she had as yet done nothing with this secret advantage. She might have been able to escape—if she'd been lucky and missed any guards in the halls armed with dragon bullets—but that relied on too many mistakes on her captors' part and too much going right for her. She knew very well that it would only take one dragon bullet to stop any attempt at escape, so she bided her time and waited for the ideal moment. She hadn't let the bruises the technomage had given her heal, although she'd let her nose mend since she could leave the dried blood on her face to add to the illusion of injury.

But the time for action had come. The sounds she heard could only be explained by an invasion. If something else were the culprit—like a tsunami or a volcanic eruption—no one would have bothered with the guns. And if there were an invasion, she had a pretty damn good idea who was doing the invading.

She had no idea how the hell they'd found her as she still didn't know where she was. But she had given up on underestimating her team a long time before. If they could find a mage lost in the woods of Maine or locate her when she'd been hundreds of feet below the surface of the earth in a cave, finding an island that could be almost anywhere in the earth's tropics would be like child's play to them.

Whoever had solved the riddle had done so because they'd wanted to rescue her, but she couldn't help but want to throw an elaborate reward at whoever had cracked it. If it was Brian who had managed to trace her call, she'd dump a ton of cash in his account and tell him it was to buy more surveillance equipment. He'd probably say he needed drones or something and grin as he spent every penny.

If it was Amy who'd used her magic to trace her, she knew she'd start with a new skateboard deck and go from there.

But there would be no rewards if she didn't get out of there. It was a good thing she wasn't the helpless prisoner the technomages thought her to be.

The two guards who stood outside her cell hadn't shown any indication that something was going on, but the enemy had always demonstrated extreme competence. Even rookies in the Detroit police station knew better than to keep the prisoners informed of every detail of current events happening outside their cell.

Kristen coughed loudly enough to earn the attention of one of them. He looked at her with open contempt as if coughing were another sign of a dragon's superiority.

She coughed again—from the diaphragm this time and hard enough to sound like she'd hack up a lung.

"Do you need something, or what?" he asked. He had an American accent—New York, she thought—and although she didn't have any reservations about hurting technomages who had imprisoned and tortured so many dragons, his manners didn't earn the man much respect.

"Water? Please." She wheezed for added effect.

The man sighed, took a tin cup, filled it with water, and brought it to the cell. She limped to the bars and he rolled his eyes as he thrust the cup through. "I thought you dragons had healing powers or some shit. Can't you quench your own thirst?"

"Not without water." She wheezed again and grasped the man by the wrist. "But you're right about the healing powers," she said. "Did you know we can even turn them off if we wish?"

Before he could answer, she pulled him into the bars hard enough to make his skull clang against them. It didn't knock him out, unfortunately, and he reached for his gun with his other hand. She jerked his arm sideways and cracked the bone.

The man screamed for half a second before she thrust her other arm through the bars and across his mouth.

"You stupid bitch!" the woman guarding the cell said and aimed her gun at her. "We're packing dragon bullets. Let him go or you die."

"The problem with dragon bullets is that they don't have the greatest penetration," she said, holding the guard between them. "You might be able to shoot through your friend here, but your bullets might stop once they punch holes in his organs."

"Fucking bitch," the guard said and took a step to move around her teammate, who was used effectively as a shield.

Truthfully, this was what Kristen wanted. It was true that the dragon bullets probably couldn't drill through a human body to hurt another person, but the last thing she wanted right now was to have either of these guards pull the trigger. A gunshot from deep in the base would remind anyone who might be listening that the techno-mages still had an ace up their sleeve in the form of their dragon hostage.

Common sense said she needed to be out of this cell before anyone was smart enough to put a gun loaded with dragon bullets to her head.

Thinking quickly, she threw the guard she held at the woman. The female guard's reflexes proved to be better than her wits and rather than dodging the man's unconscious body, she instinctively tried to get her gun up.

She didn't manage it before the man careened into her. The two guards fell into an awkward pile but immediately, the woman attempted to untangle their limbs. It was lucky that she was short and slight while the New Yorker was tall and heavier. Still, that would buy only seconds, at best.

Wanting to stay quiet but left with no choice, Kristen donned her steel skin and yanked the door off the cell. The woman had raised her gun by then, but it was hard to keep one's aim when a door comprised of metal bars hurtled toward you.

Rather than taking the shot and being struck in the head by the iron bars, she moved her gun hand to protect her skull. That probably saved her life as the door bulldozed into her arms, which connected with her head and knocked her unconscious.

Kristen stepped from the cell as the clanging of the door being thrown off its hinges echoed down the hallways. The sound wasn't as problematic as a gunshot, but it still might bring technomages who weren't so keen on having the Steel Dragon loose inside their base. She stretched through the bars of the door she'd thrown on top of the guards, took the woman's assault rifle, and checked the magazine. As expected, it contained dragon bullets as the guard had claimed. They were good enough.

She started through the complex. Immediately, she encountered two more guards who moved toward her, probably responding to the sound of the door. With a burst of dragon speed, she disabled them both and moved on.

Her pace increased slightly. She needed to get her bearings, get out of there, and meet up with her team so they could finally defeat these technomages in the base where they had thought they'd always be safe. Grimly, she made her mind up that she wouldn't hesitate if anyone got in her path—anyone except one person.

Although she didn't know what she would do if she saw Constance, she was glad that she'd have a gun when they finally met.

CHAPTER EIGHTY-NINE

rew had never hated his job. He was one of those odd police officers who liked exchanging fire with criminals. It made him feel like a hero and like he drew their fire so normal people could get to safety. He'd loved his promotion to SWAT because it meant more opportunities to push himself to his limits.

His limits were being pushed right now and for the first time in a long time, he hated his job.

The jungle was thick—impossibly thick in his estimation. Huge leaves created far too much cover. Vines seemed to reach out and grab their feet as they marched. Tropical flowers pumped saccharine-sweet smells into the air that lulled him and the rest of the humans into a fuzzy daze. The heat didn't help with that either. He had already sweated through his bulletproof vest and protective gear. His mind wandered constantly to the beach and he dreamed of taking a dip in the crystal-clear water.

His daydreams ended abruptly when mages opened fire on them from deep in the jungle.

"Down!" he shouted as bullets ripped through a thicket of palm fronds and caught Beanpole squarely in his chest, thankfully in his bulletproof vest. The gangly lookout fell heavily, gasping in pain but alive.

Drew pushed to his feet and fired in the direction of the gunshots as he cursed volubly. Beanpole was the best damn lookout they had. The man could see a rat climbing a rain gutter from two blocks away, but he was as out of his element there as anyone else.

The technomages seemed to be the only ones with any kind of familiarity in the terrain. Despite the team always returning fire—it wasn't hard to ascertain where the shots came from when the leaves in one direction suddenly had bullet holes—they never found any bodies.

This time, they located a foxhole dug into the dark tropical soil. A few spent casings remained but nothing more. He cursed, growing more frustrated than ever.

"Down!" Keith shouted as he crashed into the SWAT leader.

A disc of energy rocketed overhead, cleared a path through the forest effortlessly, and severed trees, bushes, and branches indiscriminately. If a human had stood in the projectile's path, their legs would have been cut from their torso without even slowing the disc.

Drew scrambled forward to find the source of it, but nothing was left but a clay pot filled with some kind of acrid slime that poured smoke from the top. This was the third magical trap they'd found and none of them had been comprehensible to Larry or Amy.

"Damn it, no one's here," he said, but in the span of a heartbeat, that wasn't true anymore.

Gunshots erupted from the depths of the jungle all around him. Two men died before they could so much as return fire. The rest of his people retaliated with a concerted barrage aimed into the jungle. The thick leaves swallowed their bullets as if they were hungry for more.

"This isn't working!" he shouted into the chaos of it all.

Unfortunately, he was right. They would have been pinned down already if not for Larry and Amy, whose bulletproof shields swirled around them so no more people died after those first two soldiers.

"Where are we headed?" Emerald shouted over the din of the

gunfire. He and all the other dragons marched with them so as to not risk being shot out of the sky, but that only meant they didn't have eyes in the air.

Drew didn't know what to do. They needed to get somewhere with goddamn cover, which precluded all this damn brush.

"I can buy us a minute, maybe," Lumos shouted from somewhere near the back of the long procession through the jungle.

"We'll take it!" he yelled in response.

"Everyone, close your eyes," the old dragon ordered.

"Are you fucking crazy?" Hernandez demanded.

"That's an order, people. Close your eyes and squeeze 'em tight," Jim bellowed.

His soldiers listened but Drew kept his open a moment longer. Even though he knew the danger of seeing Lumos unleash the power for which he was named, he couldn't help but watch the old dragon crouch on one knee, look up, and leap forty feet into the sky.

The technomages did not fail to notice one of their targets break cover with superhuman strength. A hundred hidden guns tracked him skyward as the lean old man with a mustache blowing in the wind transformed into a giant golden dragon.

Drew shut his eyes but he still saw the outline of the dragon, his wings splayed and tail erect, as bright white light seeped through his eyelids.

"Uphill!" he shouted to his men when he opened his eyes. The flash of light had gone already, but its effects were everywhere in the forest. The mages had stopped firing their weapons. A few tentative spells issued from some of their hands in the form of clouds of mist or tendrils of electricity.

The dragons raced to each of these exposed mages but even blinded, their spells damaged the dragons who dared to approach.

Drew stumbled forward and led the human portion of their force up a hill. They pushed through a mass of vines and paused beneath a troop of monkeys that screamed in rage at their loss of sight. A mage stumbled beneath them, his weapon aimed at the monkeys but not keen to waste ammunition.

He shot him in the chest and took his weapon.

Forward, he reminded himself. He had to move forward and fast. As he pushed through the vegetation, blinded insects fell from the canopy and birds screeched to their fellows.

Through the rich greens and bursts of colorful flowers, he saw a patch of darkness. "There! That way...that way," he ordered and pushed toward the achromatic aberration.

They thrust through the thick undergrowth into a space that had been cleared of plants outside a cave. Two mages stood with their fists wreathed in flame. As soon as the team pushed through, they unleashed their magic blasts. One went wide, but the other caught a young man who Drew didn't know squarely in the chest.

Despite knowing they would lose people, the shock of someone dying so close to him still hurt. It took a moment for the surge of sadness to give way as the man who'd been struck raced forward and lifted the mage by the neck. He hurled him with superhuman strength that immediately made it obvious that he was a dragon in his human form and not one of the new recruits whose name he had simply failed to learn.

The dragon dispatched the other mage by pounding his head against the stone wall. For a moment, all was quiet. Drew peered into the cave. Mist poured from its interior to join the thick humid jungle air before it dissipated like the breath of a horrible beast waiting for a fresh meal to walk inside.

A rustling from the trees heralded a golden dragon who plowed through the canopy and into the underbrush. He transformed in midair and landed on his feet as gunshots were fired again in the jungle.

"What are we waiting for?" he asked, but Drew immediately noticed his voice was strained.

"You're hurt," he said to the ancient dragon. Lumos clutched one of his forearms to his body with the other.

"Not badly," he said. "I'll live."

"Not unless we get that bullet out," Heartsbane said. "As long as that is in there, your healing powers will be compromised. You know that."

"I know, I know," he said but held the wounded arm closer as if to hide his frailty from the younger dragons.

"That can happen inside," Drew said. "Humans, lead the way. I want that hallway cleared. Larry and Amy, you go with them and keep them covered."

"We have," Larry complained. One of his nostrils was bloody from his exertions.

"I know, and you've done a damn good job. Let's get inside. That way, they can only get us from two angles instead of three hundred and sixty."

The human soldiers entered the tunnel and the mages followed.

"Dragons next," Drew ordered and in moments, their entire team was out of the heat and into the technomages' nest.

Well, almost everyone. "Hernandez, I need you to wire this exit to explode."

"I thought you'd never ask," she said sweetly and whistled as she set her explosives.

"Are you ready, Lumos?" he asked and retrieved a pair of forceps from his belt.

"What on earth do you plan to do with that?"

"Get that bullet out."

"Amy can do that."

"I know, but we can't spare her right now. It'll only take a few seconds. I've had more than enough practice."

He didn't tell the old dragon that just because he had practice, it didn't mean it wouldn't hurt.

Lumos took in in stride, though, and clamped his teeth so hard on a branch he'd found that he cracked it in half.

That done, they proceeded into the tunnel to save their friend.

CHAPTER NINETY

Kristen's cell, unfortunately, had been located on the opposite side of the base from wherever the action was.

It meant that instead of breaking free to the outside and the faces of her friends, she now stood in a control room in the center of the base with two mages she'd met before—Constance and Neal Havington, the leader of the cell in Florence—plus one she hadn't who seemed to be particularly adept at shooting shards of metal. As if that wasn't enough, the Iron Dragon herself was present.

To call it an unpleasant surprise would be an understatement.

"The Steel Dragon!" Constance shouted when she threw the door open. Her mouth seemed to gape as wide Kristen's did.

"Kill her!" Katrina ordered and the other two mages hastened to do so.

Havington threw balls of fire at her. She could swat them away well enough with her steel skin, but if they got too close to her eyes, the brightness made it hard to see. The other mage launched a spray of needles at her.

At first, she had no idea where the shards of metal were coming from, but most of them bounced off her steel skin easily enough. The problem was that when they penetrated, they hurt, so it was quite troubling that she already had twenty or thirty of the damn things sticking out of the tender joints between her digits on her fingers. Not only that, but it also made her gun incredibly painful to fire.

She fired all the same, but Constance blocked her with a veil of magic.

Wisely, she dove for cover.

The metal-slinging mage didn't seem to have any issue delivering his swarms of needles around the bank of computers she had ducked behind. They continued to ping against her steel skin and occasionally stabbed where her armor was thinner. She poked her head out and fired as many dragon bullets as she could, but Constance blocked them again.

Shit, she cursed silently as she acknowledged that this wasn't going well.

Havington took the initiative to simply blow the bank of computers she was hiding behind into nothing but scrap. She raced to find somewhere else to hide, but there was nowhere. The mages cast spell after spell at her to harry her retreat and made it damn obvious that she was outmatched in a big way.

She threw herself behind a concrete pillar and tried to catch her breath and come up with some kind of plan, without much success.

"Surrender!" Havington said. "It's your only choice. Somehow, you used your dragon wiles to trick the guards. That's fine. It means they were weak. But you can't beat us. Put the gun down and come out and no harm will come to you. Persist, and Eric and I will be forced to kill you."

"How about you go screw yourself?" Kristen said and squeezed off another couple of rounds that Constance blocked.

"I'm afraid it really is over," Constance said, although she didn't sound pleased.

A team of troops rushed in. "The enemy forces have penetrated the base and are on their way through the tunnels to the inner sanctum," one reported.

"You moron!" Eric cursed. "We need all troops to engage. Now!"

He pressed a button on the console in front of him. Red lights began to blink and alarms blared throughout the complex.

"I won't lose this base because one of you idiots led the steel bitch here," the mage fumed and followed his troops into one of the tunnels, no doubt to try to kill Kristen's friends.

Unfortunately, she couldn't exactly follow him.

"Havington, are you coming?" Eric demanded.

"Of course." The man wreathed his hands in flames and followed him out. "Ladies, I trust you can put the steel bitch down?"

"With pleasure," Katrina replied.

The enemy dragon's heavy iron steps approached her pathetic hiding place.

Without much of an option, Kristen spun from behind the concrete pillar and emptied every round she had into Katrina's chest.

Once again, Constance blocked all the shots. "Not like that," she said and shook her head as she looked like her heart was being torn in half. Katrina couldn't see the mage's face because her back was to her. She wondered if the woman would have let such emotion show if the dragon could see.

"Thank you very much, Mother," Katrina said. "Now, you can leave the runt to me."

The technomage darted one last look at Kristen and ran from the room. There was nothing to be done now but fight.

She reloaded with a spare magazine she'd taken from a downed guard. Before she could so much as aim at the Iron Dragon, Katrina raced forward and knocked the weapon from her hand.

CHAPTER NINETY-ONE

Kristen didn't lament the loss of her firearm. Instead, she threw a knee into her opponent's ribs and shoved the iron-skinned woman back with a grunt.

"So you want to lose again, huh? How many times will this be?" Katrina asked and began her transformation into her Iron Dragon form.

She miscalculated, though, and the room they were in was barely big enough to house a dragon. While she was changing, Kristen simply left.

"Bitch!" the Iron Dragon roared down the hallway she had vanished into.

"It takes one to know one," she responded, which pissed the dragon off enough to compel her to change into her human form and follow her down the tunnel.

Of course, she hadn't fled and had stopped at the first intersection to wait. As soon as her adversary tried to pass, she struck out with a chop to the woman's windpipe. Steel clanged against iron and Katrina stumbled back and gasped.

Kristen pushed her attack. Every one of her blows sounded like a blacksmith beating an anvil with a hammer. She targeted her enemy's face, ribs, crotch, and the back of her neck with her elbow. Far more proficient as a human fighter, she knew where the weak areas were on a human and better yet, she knew where the weak points were on someone with metal skin.

Katrina tried to block, but she had an edge like the other woman had in dragon form. She pressed harder and moved faster and faster until she was a blur. Her adversary blocked most of her blows but finally, after a brutal combination of blows to her neck, she had an opening.

She vaulted and landed a dropkick on the woman's chest powered by every ounce of strength she had.

Her opponent catapulted away and bulldozed through tunnel after tunnel until she finally came to a stop when she impacted with a cave wall. Kristen raced through the human-sized hole she'd created and reached Katrina before she could pull herself out of the hole she found herself in.

She caught her adversary by her hair—knowing that iron hair wouldn't rip out any more than steel hair would—and hurled her through another couple of walls.

This time, Katrina was able to pull herself together before she reached her. She surged into her and their metal bodies clanged louder than any gong as Kristen now powered through the walls.

The woman tried to rush in and take advantage, but she was ready. She used her knees to drive into the Iron Dragon's gut, which made the woman double over.

Her follow-up kick was hard enough to launch her through the ceiling. Katrina plunged into a hard landing and a pile of rubble fell on top of her. When she made impact, the tunnel they were in sagged and a crack spread through the roof.

"We should get out of here," Kristen said. "We'll bring this whole place down."

"Our inner sanctum is fortified, you insipid bitch," Katrina snapped.

"It's your base, not mine," she said, caught the woman by the throat, and thrust her into the ceiling three times in quick succession.

She released her as the roof caved in.

Kristen raced back as part of the mountain collapsed onto the Iron Dragon and buried her in rubble. The dust hadn't even begun to settle when Katrina was already pushing herself out of the debris.

Before she made it clear, the Steel Dragon attacked again.

She launched a concerted assault, punching, kicking, headbutting, and doing anything and everything she could to prevent her adversary from realizing the collapse had given her enough space to transform into her Iron Dragon body.

When Katrina did realize that she had the room, Kristen simply vanished into another tunnel.

"Bitch!" she roared after transforming into her dragon body. She blew flames into the air, and—consumed by hatred as she was—made the mistake of changing into her human body to pursue her quarry through more tunnels.

Kristen was ready for her at another intersection. This time, when the woman tried to race past, she darted out behind her and locked an arm around the Iron Dragon's neck.

"Let...me...go..." Katrina wheezed as she squeezed her air pipe.

"You should try to save your air," she said sweetly.

"Don't...tell me...how to...fight..." The Iron Dragon was fading. It was damn hard to choke someone with metal skin—Kristen knew this from personal experience—but it wasn't impossible. The thing about steel or iron skin was that it could only be so deep. Muscles, veins and windpipes still needed to do their job, which meant they couldn't be solid metal.

Although Katrina's iron skin protected her from getting bruised, it also allowed her throat to be strangled. She fought back or at least tried to. Awkwardly, she elbowed Kristen in the ribs and stamped on her foot. She tried to gouge her eyes out but Kristen had a brother. She knew everything there was to know about headlocks, how to break them, and how to keep people locked.

She tightened her hold when Katrina fell to one knee and tightened it further when she pounded on her arm to release her. Her face resolute, she retained her stranglehold on Katrina's neck until the woman lost consciousness.

Even then, she didn't waste a moment. She knew that dragon healing powers worked fine when someone was unconscious. That was why she had to take them away from her adversary.

Fortunately, she had the perfect solution.

She took the cuff out of her pocket—the one Constance had taken off her, thus making her escape and this entire chain of events possible—and put it on Katrina's iron wrist.

The effect was immediate. Her adversary's iron skin vanished and she whimpered in her sleep, no doubt feeling her bruises more acutely. Kristen sighed and tried to accept the fact that it was over.

Or so she thought until an explosion collapsed the tunnel around her.

CHAPTER NINETY-TWO

L arry and Amy followed the regular human soldiers into the inner sanctum of the base. He couldn't believe that the mages had done it. They'd fucking hollowed out the center of the dormant volcano in the middle of the island and used it for their damn base of operations.

"At least now we know they're evil for sure," he said as he stared at the solidified lava formations all around the edges of the volcano. "Good guy bases are never in places like this."

"If you're done sightseeing, I'd appreciate backup," Amy replied.

"Sure," he said, although he didn't know why she even bothered to ask him for help. She was so much more powerful than him. Her powers coupled with the humans' weapons were more than enough to overwhelm these mages.

He'd almost convinced himself of that when two mages rushed into the heart of the volcano. Larry recognized one of them. Neal Havington, the leader of the European cell, was quite proficient in hurling balls of flame.

The other was a man he had never seen before who seemed to prefer throwing needles at his foes. He quickly decided he didn't like the asshole. While the rest of the troops focused on pushing deeper and deeper into the inner sanctum, Larry and Amy turned their attention to the two mages.

He would later wonder if this was how the ancient fights between mages had been, long before the rebellions when mages had ruled in their own right.

The man—Eric, he heard Havington call him—threw what must have been a thousand needles at Amy. She simply ripped a door off its hinges and spun it in a complex set of twists and spins that she'd no doubt picked up in her skateboarding days. Using it as a shield, she caught every one of the projectiles the mage hurled at her.

Havington joined the fight.

"Watch out for the European asshole!" Larry shouted and managed to throw up a defensive shield that slowed but did not block the man's ball of fire.

The girl reached out with her powers and somehow found the mages' source of water. She doused Havington's flame while Eric launched another attack.

What happened next was almost too fast for Larry to follow.

It seemed that Eric's powers were comparable to Amy's in that both mages were proficient in picking shit up and throwing it at each other.

In one minute, the battle inside the interior of the volcano progressed more or less like every battle sequence from every James Bond movie. The enemy fired and tried to move forward and the heroes shoot and try to move forward—classic and simple.

But in the next moment, it was like a Jedi battle.

Everything that wasn't part of the stone wall was lifted off the ground and hurled from one mage to the other.

Amy threw a desk and Eric caught it.

He threw a file cabinet and she deflected it.

Soon, a hurricane raged inside the volcano as furniture, rocks, and even bullets were snatched from their places and flung at each other.

Both mages, however, were too skilled to let the other break through their defenses.

"Damn it!" Havington cursed as he watched the epic battle with the same dumb amazement as Larry did. "We're losing ground."

Larry spared a quick glance and saw that he was right. The invading team had taken more than half of the floor of the cavernous room while the two mages battled above them.

"Open a portal!" Eric ordered as he directed a crate at Amy. It shattered on her defenses and dragon bullets spilled everywhere and were snatched up by the magic of both mages and used against each other.

A small group of mages broke away from the fight and began to work together to open an escape route.

"Larry!" Amy yelled, "You can't let them open that portal!"

He knew it was true and yet, try as he might, he couldn't stop them. When he tried to attack the mages, Havington launched fireballs at him to force him to play defense or be incinerated.

The girl couldn't extricate herself from her battle either.

The mages would escape again. Despite finally finding what had to be one of their best-guarded bases, it wouldn't be enough. This fight would continue forever and eventually bring the entire planet into it.

Larry had begun to feel a little desperate when a blast of flame exploded from above and raked the mage who had tried to open the portal. For a second, he thought the frenzied combat had somehow awakened the dormant volcano, but then he realized that what had happened was far better.

Kristen had come to their rescue through the top of the volcano. She'd blasted all the mages who had been leading the escape.

The remainder of the defenders scattered, no longer willing to fight now that they didn't have an escape plan.

"Destroy their boss!" Larry ordered, and every human troop began to fire at Eric.

It was a testimony to the mage's power that more than a dozen people firing hundreds of rounds at him wasn't enough to stop him, at least not immediately.

Finally, a round penetrated, caught him in the leg, and felled him with a scream of pain.

All the objects that had whirled around the room careened into the wall behind him, forced there by Amy's powers. In the chaos, Larry didn't see Kristen until she'd already transformed. She held a pistol pushed against Havington's temple.

"It's over!" she yelled to Eric, who still attempted to summon the energy to continue the battle despite his injury. He didn't look like he was the kind of man to go down without a fight, but before he could initiate anything, Constance stepped into the room.

Larry clenched his teeth, ready for the battle to start anew.

"She's right!" the woman shouted. "It's over. Everyone stop fighting. We don't want anyone else to die if they don't have to."

He was shocked that she agreed with Kristen. Eric, bleeding from his leg, looked from his former ally to Kristen's hard gaze. The Steel Dragon glared at him despite still holding a pistol against Havington's head. Finally, he glanced at Amy, who only tilted her head like she was ready to play another round.

"Fine," the man snapped.

"What was that? I don't think your troops heard you and they'll need to if you don't want them dead," Kristen said.

"Throw your weapons down," Eric shouted at his mages. "That's an order. I don't want anyone dying to these savages for no good reason."

Larry exhaled a breath he hadn't realized he'd been holding. Holy shit. It was done. It was finally done.

CHAPTER NINETY-THREE

A few hours later, Kristen was reasonably confident that they had dug through every inch of the enemy base.

Deep beneath the inner sanctum, they'd found a half-dozen captive dragons and more troubling, a lab where it looked like more could be made. There was also an enormous stockpile of dragon bullets, more than she had anticipated and certainly more than she'd seen in one place.

Constance admitted that the mages had been building and storing the ammunition in this location for well over a decade. It was a stockpile so big, the Steel Dragon wondered if it could be destroyed. She might have rested easier if the volcano in which the battle had been fought was still active. They could have dumped everything inside it, although she didn't know if even that would have the heat needed to melt refined dragon scales.

The surviving enemy mages were all cuffed to block their power and tossed into the cells where the captive dragons used to be. Despite her seeing the cosmic irony of imprisoning them in the same horrible place where dragons they'd tortured for so long had been, she didn't want to leave them there long. Her team worked on reestablishing communications with the outside world so she could obtain guidance on what to do with them from the Council. Katrina was there, too.

In the meantime, Kristen had questions and she thought she knew who had answers.

Heartsbane, Stonequest, Amy, and Drew all brought Constance to her. Drew kept a gun aimed at her head while the others stood tensely nearby, ready to use their powers if needed. Her other closest allies were in the room too—Larry, Lumos, Hernandez, Emerald, Keith, and Beanpole. Everyone had their weapon of choice trained on the mage. For once, she didn't feel it was naïve to think that Constance wouldn't be able to turn the tables on them.

"I need to know why you switched sides like you did," she said to the woman.

The technomage smiled. "I didn't switch sides."

"Can we kill her? Please?" Hernandez asked.

Constance obviously couldn't tell it was a joke—but, for that matter, Kristen wasn't entirely sure it was either. "No, please," the woman said as she glanced at the duffel bag near the foot of the demolitions expert and probably imagined tools of torture inside. "I've always been on the side of humanity surviving. I'm sure Kristen has told you what I told her." She sighed. "I realized that if a powerful elder dragon wanted war between dragons and humanity, it might not be in humanity's best interest to go ahead with that war."

Kristen nodded. She believed it. After Constance opened the cuff binding her powers and then called for an end to the fighting, she believed it.

"Wait, did you deliberately leave the trail for us to follow?" Larry asked.

The mage nodded. "I did. I felt certain that you or Amy would notice it and be able to trace it here. I'm glad I was right."

"You could've sent a text with a pin dropped on your location," Keith said.

"I could not have. If all of you had shown up, we would have blasted you out of the sky. I knew Kristen would come through, although I must admit, I did not think she would come alone."

"That's why you uncuffed me?" she asked. "You wanted me to defeat these mages because you thought their goals were fulfilling the plans of the Masked One?"

"Indeed, and I must say, I'm rather pleased that this all worked out with minimal losses. I was concerned the body count would be higher."

"I've always had a problem with your acceptance of human lives as collateral damage, Constance," she said. "Don't start saying stupid shit now and making me think that maybe your life could be collateral."

"I thought that by helping you—"

"We're grateful," she said. "But the actions of today don't erase the actions of yesterday. You've hurt dragons, humans, and mages. Many people won't be able to simply forget that."

Constance nodded and looked around the room, perhaps realizing for the first time how much pain she'd caused to the people gathered there before she even considered the others in the world.

"But you've done a real service by bringing this war with the tech-nomages to a close. With them finally gone, the Dragon Council should back away from the idea of war. If war is avoided between humans and dragons, I think I may be able to forgive you, although I'd never ask that of any of the people you hurt."

"If the prevention of war is what is needed to earn my forgiveness, I fear it will never come," the woman said.

"What in the hell is that supposed to mean?" Stonequest asked.

Constance sighed. "Although the stockpile here was large as you no doubt saw, the technomages at this facility have already shipped tons of dragon bullets around the globe."

"By tons, you don't literally mean—" Keith protested.

"Unfortunately, I do," the woman said. "Plus, we all know that human militaries everywhere now know how to kill dragons. The proverbial genie is out of the bottle."

"But none of that matters if the technomages stop their aggression," Kristen said, "There are still nuclear weapons, after all, but no one wants to use them, so we haven't had a nuclear war. The mere

645

existence of the weapons doesn't mean they have to be used. Reality doesn't need Chekhov's gun to be fired."

"But there is still a side agitating for war," Constance said. "The Masked One wanted a war long before we came on the scene, and he'll want one still. This might set him back but it will not stop him. The war may not take the form of a fight between dragons and revolutionary mages, but it will take place as long as he continues to operate on the Dragon Council. He will find a way to make it happen. That's what he does."

"And you're sure it's a dragon on the Council?" Stonequest asked. After the battle, she'd filled her closest advisors in on their next enemy, including the rumored name, and it was something Stonequest struggled with. Through all the twists and turns this war had taken, he had always wanted to trust the Council. Kristen couldn't blame him. He was a cop, after all, one who served on Dragon SWAT but a cop all the same. He needed to believe their leaders weren't violent or corrupt.

"It's what makes the most sense," Constance said matter of factly.

He looked at Kristen, his eyes hungry for her to deny the accusation, but she couldn't. Not after all that had happened, all the false leads, and all the strings they'd pulled at only to find themselves wrapped more tightly in a web that none of them could see the edges of.

"Everything I have ever heard of the Masked One indicates that he would indeed like to bring ruin to the world so he could remake it as he sees fit. A world of darkness instead of light, a world of shadow instead of sunshine." Lumos still cradled his wounded arm. Despite having the bullet removed, his dragon powers were taking time to kick in.

Kristen sighed and looked at the old dragon, who looked so frail with his injury. Somehow, he was supposed to give her the training she'd need to defeat the arch enemy. It was a frightening prospect.

"I'm not willing to say we're fighting a mythical legend," she told her team. "But we very well might be. Whoever is behind all this—if indeed there is a dragon agitating for war—I know that together, we'll be able to put an end to it. And when all this violence and bigotry and hatred is finally over, we can all sit down for some pizza."

The End

(for now)

Steel Dragon 5 is coming soon from Kevin and Michael.

If you loved Steel Dragon, you might also enjoy the Federal Histories series, from Michael Anderle. Book one is Witch Of The Federation and it's available from Amazon and through Kindle Unlimited.

The future has amazing technology. Our alien allies have magic. Together, we are building a training system to teach the best of humanity to go to the stars.

But the training is monumentally expensive.

Stephanie Morgana is a genius, she just doesn't *know* it.

The Artificial Intelligence which runs the Virtual World is charged with testing Stephanie, a task it has never performed before.

The Earth and their allies, may never be the same again.

Will Stephanie pass the test and be moved to the advanced preparatory schools, or will the system miss her? Will the AI be able to judge a human's potential in an area where it has no existing test data to compare?

Available now at Amazon and through Kindle Unlimited.

KEVIN'S AUTHOR NOTES

MAY 28, 2020

Hi there! Thanks for reading book four of the Steel Dragon series! These books have been a ton of fun to work on. Michael and I have really enjoyed the reader feedback as well.

In a lot of ways, this volume was the most challenging so far. After all, we're well past the initial introduction phase. In fact, we're gearing up for the finale. Bringing a series to a satisfying conclusion is always tough. As a reader, I usually want a story I'm enjoying to keep on going forever. But all good stories come to an ending eventually, even Kristen Hall's.

Book five will be the final one. It's the summary, the final chapter, the concluding package. Everything we've led up to and hinted at in all the previous books will be brought to a stunning conclusion when book five comes out later this summer. It should be one heck of a ride!

But that's not the end for this universe.

Michael and I have already been discussing ideas for a spin-off series, set immediately after this one finishes. While the main character will be new, we will see the return of some old favorites, and most important we'll get to see how the changes Kristen made in the world will impact life in the days to come. She's certainly been rocking society – dragon, human, and mage alike – to its core.

We all hear that phrase "be the change you want to see" a lot, but it's usually not so simple. I mean, it would be nice if we could wave our hands and make things around us better. That's just not how the world works. It's not how it worked for Kristen, either, if you think about it. Sure, she has magic powers that we all lack. But those have caused her almost as many problems as they solved.

What about the humans she's worked with? Each of them chose to make a difference in their own way. Captain Hansen chose to accept a novice cop as a SWAT member. (Well, she had her arm twisted a little, right? But when she made the decision, she went in full force.) Drew chose to follow the person he'd helped train. Jim chose to let go of his prejudices. These people all made a difference not just through grand gestures, but through simple changes and choices as well.

My gut says that most of us aren't ever going to be like Kristen. We're never going to be the pivot point around which the fate of the entire world revolves. Honestly, I'm sort of OK with that myself. That's a lot of pressure!

But even though our choices may never spell the difference between life and death for millions of people, we do change the world every day. We sometimes just miss the differences we make. The nurse taking care of sick people during a wave of illness; the police officer keeping people safe; the teacher helping kids to learn and grow; the person who gives a few bucks to a person in need; all of these folks have made impacts with their lives.

It's rare for one person to make such a huge difference that is rocks the world. What's far more common and ultimately much more useful are the billions of people making small differences every day. We can't choose to be a dragon with magical powers, but we can choose to act in kindness, compassion, justice, mercy, and integrity in our day to day. That has an impact. When it's compounded by huge numbers of people all striving together, it matters far more than the activities of any one person.

One personal change that's happened thanks to my work in this world is that coming back to writing fantasy again after a long break, I've remembered how much I enjoy it! I've been focused heavily on science fiction for the last couple of years, but spending a year in the clutches of the Steel Dragon has me thinking about stories set in fantasy worlds. I've got a ton of books coming out this year in the Blackwell Magic urban fantasy series; picture a cross between Buffy the Vampire Slayer and Harry Dresden from the Dresden Files, add in a touch of military academy for flavor, and you've got a good idea what these books are like. If you'd like to give one a shot, you can read a short prequel for free by clicking the link here: https://dl. bookfunnel.com/ae70xahfa3

So, thanks for that! I hadn't realized how much I missed writing this kind of story, so expect a whole bunch of these in the months to come, along with the fifth Steel Dragon book and a new trilogy (or more than a trilogy?) in the same world after Kristen's story is done.

I hope you've loved reading all these books as much as we've enjoyed spinning the stories. Don't worry – book five is coming down the pipe soon enough! In the meantime, I do love hearing from readers. While I can't always get back to everyone, I try to respond to as many emails as I can. You can always reach me at author@kevinomclaughlin.com

Thanks for reading!

Kevin McLaughlin

MICHAEL'S AUTHOR NOTES

MAY 25, 2020

Hello! It's another glorious day in Las Vegas and I understand that in two weeks or so a few casinos will open again.

I admit I am looking forward to that happening. Not for the reason that seems obvious (gambling), but the insides of the casinos have something I can't get to unless they open up.

THE RESTAURANTS!

Seriously, I'm hungry for some of the best Chinese food in America (and China, Hong Kong, Macau… I've tested them all, sacrificing my taste buds for you.) So, the best (in my opinion) is Ping Pang Pong inside the Gold Coast Hotel and Casino here in Vegas.

Yes, I have been to Chinatown in LA and tested a couple there. That info is for the two of you who might read the comment above and wonder.

I have tried to find other Chinese food restaurants here in Vegas, and so far, we are coming up with "Well, it's good…*ish.*"

Not exactly what I would like. I've had food from the Chinese motherland and other countries near China and thought, *Well, that's good, but I'd rather just eat at home.*

I'm presently on the dining part of the Gold Coast website looking at the Ping Pang Pong menu (I looked it up to provide the link below) and I see a Black Pepper Beef Medallions I have never tried.

I think I am missing out in life.

I've had the Orange Chicken, beef fried rice (no vegetables, extra rice—that is my go-to choice), and tried other recipes when I could. No one I know has ever been less than pleased with the food. Maybe not everyone is a Ponger fanatic as I am, but if you make it back to Vegas, give it a try and share the love if you enjoy it!

Here is the URL https://www.goldcoastcasino.com/dine/casual-dining/ping-pang-pong.

Update on what's happening next in the Steel Dragon Universe.
Kevin and I have had our first conversations about what's next, and we have the bones of another story in this world.

Surprisingly, it took very little time for us to agree on the premise and the protagonist's backstory. *Shocking, I know.* After giving Kevin so much grief over the last year and a half, I am now worried that this was so easy because of all of the comments I've made on podcasts, stage...pretty much wherever I had to provide an example of a challenging (but very successful) collaboration.

If that is the truth—that I mentioned it too often—then I'm sorry, Kevin. If that isn't true, then thank God we got through that so effortlessly. I raise my glass of root beer in your generally East Coast (he's in Boston) direction and salute!

BOOKS BY KEVIN MCLAUGHLIN

Adventures of the Starship Satori (Space Opera blended with military SF)

Finding Satori - prequel short story, available only to email list fans!

Book 1 - Ad Astra: Book 2 - Stellar Legacy

Book 3 - Deep Waters

Book 4 - No Plan Survives Contact

Book 5 - Liberty

Book 6 - Satori's Destiny

Book 7 - Ashes of War

Book 8 - Embers of War

Book 9 - Dust and Iron

Book 10 - Clad in Steel

Book 11 - Brave New Worlds (2019)

Book 12 - Warrior's Marque (2020)

The Ragnarok Saga (Military SF)

Accord of Fire - Free prequel short story, available only to email list fans!

Book 1 - Accord of Honor

Book 2 - Accord of Mars

Book 3 - Accord of Valor

Book 4 - Ghost Wing

Book 5 - Ghost Squadron

Book 6 - Ghost Fleet (2019)

Valhalla Online Series (A Ragnarok Saga Story)

Book 1 - Valhalla Online

Book 2 - Raiding Jotunheim

Book 3 - Vengeance Over Vanaheim

Book 4 - Hel Hath No Fury

Blackwell Magic Series (Urban Fantasy)

Book 1 - By Darkness Revealed

Book 2 - Ashes Ascendant

Book 3 - Dead In Winter

Book 4 - Claws That Catch

Book 5 - Darkness Awakes

Book 6 - Spellbinding Entanglements

By A Whisker (short story)

The Raven and the Rose - Free novelette for email list fans!

Dead Brittania Series:

Dead Brittania (short prequel story)

Book 1 - King of the Dead

Book 2 - Queen of Demons

Raven's Heart Series (Urban Fantasy)

Book 1 - Stolen Light

Book 2 - Webs in the Dark

Book 3 - Shades of Moonlight

Other Titles:

Over the Moon (SF romance)

Midnight Visitors (Steampunk Cat short story)

Demon Ex Machina (Steampunk Cat short story)

The Coffee Break Novelist (help for writers!)

You Must Write (Heinlein's rules for writers)

BOOKS BY MICHAEL ANDERLE

For a complete list of books by Michael Anderle, please visit:

www.lmbpn.com/ma-books/

All LMBPN Audiobooks are Available at Audible.com and iTunes

To see all LMBPN audiobooks, including those written by Michael Anderle
please visit:

www.lmbpn.com/audible

CONNECT WITH THE AUTHORS

Connect with Michael Anderle and sign up for his email list here:

Website: http://lmbpn.com

Email List: http://lmbpn.com/email/

Facebook:
www.facebook.com/TheKurtherianGambitBooks